PRAISE FOR

MORNING STAR

"You could call [Pierce] Brown science fiction's best-kept secret. In *Morning Star,* the trilogy's devastating and inspiring final chapter, . . . he flirts with volume, oscillating between thundering space escapes and hushed, tense parleys between rivals, where the cinematic dialogue oozes such specificity and suspense you could almost hear a pin drop between pages. His achievement is in creating an uncomfortably familiar world of flaw, fear, and promise."

—*Entertainment Weekly*

"Excellent . . . Brown's vivid, first-person prose puts the reader right at the forefront of impassioned speeches, broken families, and engaging battle scenes . . . as this intrastellar civil war comes to a most satisfying conclusion."

—*Publishers Weekly* (starred review)

"A page-turning epic filled with twists and turns . . . The conclusion to Brown's saga is simply stellar."

—*Booklist* (starred review)

"There is *no one* writing today who does shameless, Michael Bay–style action set pieces the way Brown does. The battle scenes are kinetic, bloody, breathless, crazy. Everything is on fire all the time."

—NPR

"*Morning Star* is this trilogy's *Return of the Jedi.* . . . The impactful battles that make up most of *Morning Star* are damn near operatic. . . . It absolutely satisfies."

—Tor.com

"Multilayered and seething with characters who exist in a shadow world between history and myth, much as in Frank Herbert's *Dune* . . . [*Morning Star* is] an ambitious and satisfying conclusion to a monumental saga."

—*Kirkus Reviews*

PRAISE FOR

GOLDEN SON

"Gripping . . . On virtually every level, this is a sequel that hates sequels—a perfect fit for a hero who already defies the tropes. [Grade:] A"

—*Entertainment Weekly*

"[Pierce] Brown writes layered, flawed characters . . . but plot is his most breathtaking strength. . . . Every action seems to flow into the next."

—NPR

"In a word, *Golden Son* is stunning. Among science-fiction fans, it should be a shoo-in for book of the year."

—Tor.com

"The stakes are even higher than they were in *Red Rising,* and the twists and turns of the story are every bit as exciting. The jaw-dropper of an ending will leave readers hungry for the conclusion to Brown's wholly original, completely thrilling saga."

—*Booklist* (starred review)

"Dramatic . . . the rare middle book that loses almost no momentum as it sets up the final installment."

—*Publishers Weekly*

"Stirring . . . Comparisons to *The Hunger Games* and *Game of Thrones* series are inevitable, for this tale has elements of both."

—*Kirkus Reviews*

PRAISE FOR

RED RISING

"[A] spectacular adventure . . . one heart-pounding ride . . . Pierce Brown's dizzyingly good debut novel evokes *The Hunger Games, Lord of the Flies,* and *Ender's Game.* . . . [*Red Rising*] has everything it needs to become meteoric."

—*Entertainment Weekly*

"[A] top-notch debut novel . . . *Red Rising* ascends above a crowded dystopian field."

—*USA Today*

"Reminiscent of . . . Suzanne Collins's *The Hunger Games* . . . [*Red Rising*] will captivate readers and leave them wanting more."

—*Library Journal* (starred review)

"A story of vengeance, warfare and the quest for power . . . reminiscent of *The Hunger Games* and *Game of Thrones.*"

—*Kirkus Reviews*

"Fast-paced, gripping, well-written—the sort of book you cannot put down. I am already on the lookout for the next one."

—TERRY BROOKS, *New York Times* bestselling author of *The Sword of Shannara*

"[A] great debut . . . The author gathers a spread of elements together in much the same way George R. R. Martin does."

—Tor.com

"Ender, Katniss, and now Darrow: Pierce Brown's empire-crushing debut is a sprawling vision."

—SCOTT SIGLER, *New York Times* bestselling author of *Pandemic*

MORNING STAR

Pierce Brown

DEL REY
NEW YORK

2016 Del Rey Trade Paperback Edition

Copyright © 2016 by Pierce Brown
Illustration copyright © 2016 by Joel Daniel Phillips

Published in the United States by Del Rey, an imprint of Random House, a division of Penguin Random House LLC, New York.

DEL REY and the HOUSE colophon are registered trademarks of Penguin Random House LLC.

Originally published in hardcover in the United States by Del Rey, an imprint of Random House, a division of Penguin Random House LLC, in 2016.

ISBN 978-0-345-53986-1
Ebook ISBN 978-0-345-53985-4

Printed in the United States of America on acid-free paper

randomhousebooks.com

8 9 7

Book design by Caroline Cunningham

To sister, who taught me to listen

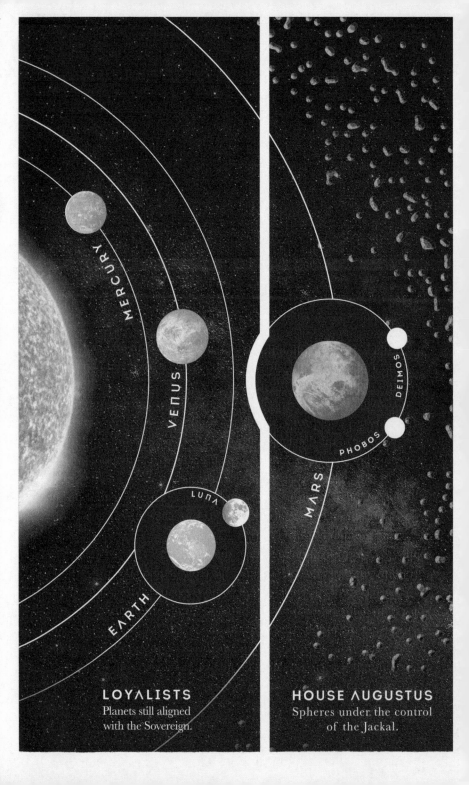

MERCURY

VENUS

LUNA

EARTH

MARS

PHOBOS

DEIMOS

LOYALISTS
Planets still aligned
with the Sovereign.

HOUSE AUGUSTUS
Spheres under the control
of the Jackal.

THE STORY SO FAR . . .

Red Rising

Darrow is a Red, a lowly miner slaving away below the surface of Mars. He toils to make the surface of his planet habitable for future generations, but he and his kind have been betrayed: the surface is livable and ruled by the unscrupulous Golds. When they hang his wife for voicing rebellious ideas, Darrow joins a revolutionary group known as the Sons of Ares. With the help of the Sons, Darrow is physically transformed into a Gold and sent to take the Society down from the inside.

He enters the Institute, a training school for the Gold elite that turns spoiled teenagers into the best warriors in Society. There Darrow learns the ways of warfare and how to navigate through the often treacherous—but sometimes genuine—friendships and complex political climate of the Golds. Only by changing the paradigm and relying on his new friends is Darrow able to best the Institute and all of its dangers.

Golden Son

From his victory at the Institute Darrow wins prestige and a position in the employ of the ArchGovernor of Mars, Nero au Augustus. However, he finds that it is difficult to live up to his own legend, as Darrow is unsuccessful at the Academy, where Golds train in ship-to-ship combat. Bested by a familial rival of his employer, Darrow's worth quickly declines in the eyes of the ArchGovernor, until that is, Darrow gives the power-hungry Gold what he wants: civil war.

Playing the Augustus clan against the Bellonas, Darrow throws

Society into disarray, sowing the seeds of chaos everywhere he goes. After amassing an impressive army and some dubious allies, Darrow leads a successful assault on Mars, ousting the Bellonas from control of the planet. But at the Triumph held to honor his military victory, betrayal once again rears its ugly head and all that he has worked for is undone. His friends and allies killed or missing, Darrow is captured and his secret identity is discovered; the fate of the rebellion balances on a razor's edge. . . .

DRAMATIS PERSONAE

Golds

OCTAVIA AU LUNE   Reigning Sovereign of the Society

LYSANDER AU LUNE   Grandson of Octavia, heir to House Lune

ADRIUS AU AUGUSTUS/JACKAL   ArchGovernor of Mars, twin brother to Virginia

VIRGINIA AU AUGUSTUS/MUSTANG   Twin sister to Adrius

MAGNUS AU GRIMMUS/THE ASH LORD   The Sovereign's Arch Imperator, father to Aja

AJA AU GRIMMUS   The Protean Knight, chief bodyguard to the Sovereign

CASSIUS AU BELLONA   The Morning Knight, the Sovereign's bodyguard

ROQUE AU FABII   Imperator of the Sword Armada

ANTONIA AU SEVERUS-JULII   Half sister to Victra, daughter of Agrippina

VICTRA AU JULII   Half sister to Antonia, daughter of Agrippina

KAVAX AU TELEMANUS   Head of House Telemanus, father to Daxo

DAXO AU TELEMANUS   Heir and son of Kavax, brother to Pax

ROMULUS AU RAA   Head of House Raa, ArchGovernor of Io

LILATH AU FARAN   Companion of the Jackal, leader of the Boneriders

CYRIANA AU TANUS/THISTLE   A former Howler, now a lieutenant of the Boneriders

VIXUS AU SARNA   Former House Mars, lieutenant of the Boneriders

Mid- and LowColors

TRIGG TI NAKAMURA   Legionnaire, brother to Holiday, a Gray

HOLIDAY TI NAKAMURA   Legionnaire, sister to Trigg, a Gray

REGULUS AG SUN/QUICKSILVER   Richest man in the Society, a Silver

ALIA SNOWSPARROW   Queen of the Valkyrie, mother to Ragnar and Sefi, an Obsidian

SEFI THE QUIET   Warlord of the Valkyrie, daughter to Alia, sister to Ragnar

ORION XE AQUARII   Ship captain, a Blue

Sons of Ares

DARROW OF LYKOS/REAPER   Former lancer of House Augustus, a Red

SEVRO AU BARCA/GOBLIN   Howler, a Gold

RAGNAR VOLARUS   New Howler, an Obsidian

DANCER   Ares lieutenant, a Red

MICKEY   Carver, a Violet

I rise into darkness, away from the garden they watered with the blood of my friends. The Golden man who killed my wife lies dead beside me on the cold metal deck, life snuffed out by his own son's hand.

Autumn wind whips my hair. The ship rumbles beneath. In the distance, friction flames shred the night with brilliant orange. The Telemanuses descending from orbit to rescue me. Better that they do not. Better to let the darkness have me and allow the vultures to squabble over my paralyzed body.

My enemy's voices echo behind me. Towering demons with the faces of angels. The smallest of them bends. Stroking my head as he looks down at his dead father.

"This is always how the story would end," he says to me. "Not with your screams. Not with your rage. But with your silence."

Roque, my betrayer, sits in the corner. He was my friend. Heart too kind for his Color. Now he turns his head and I see his tears. But they are not for me. They are for what he has lost. For the ones I have taken from him.

"No Ares to save you. No Mustang to love you. You are alone, Darrow." The Jackal's eyes are distant and quiet. "Like me." He lifts up a black eyeless mask with a muzzle on it and straps it to my face. Darkening my sight. "This is how it ends."

To break me, he has slain those I love.

But there is hope in those still living. In Sevro. In Ragnar and Dancer. I think of all my people bound in darkness. Of all the Colors on all the worlds, shackled and chained so that Gold might rule, and I feel the rage burn across the dark hollow he has carved in my soul. I am not alone. I am not his victim.

So let him do his worst. I am the Reaper.

I know how to suffer.

I know the darkness.

This is *not* how it ends.

PART I

||||||||||||||||||||||||||||||||||

THORNS

Per aspera ad astra

1

||||||||||||||||||||||

ONLY THE DARK

Deep in darkness, far from warmth and sun and moons, I lie, quiet as the stone that surrounds me, imprisoning my hunched body in a dreadful womb. I cannot stand. Cannot stretch. I can only curl in a ball, a withered fossil of the man that was. Hands cuffed behind my back. Naked on cold rock.

All alone with the dark.

It seems months, years, millennia since my knees have unbent, since my spine has straightened from its crooked pose. The ache is madness. My joints fuse like rusted iron. How much time has passed since I saw my Golden friends bleeding out into the grass? Since I felt gentle Roque kiss my cheek as he broke my heart?

Time is no river.

Not here.

In this tomb, time is the stone. It is the darkness, permanent and unyielding, its only measure the twin pendulums of life—breath and the beating of my heart.

In. *Buh . . . bump. Buh . . . bump.*

Out. *Buh . . . bump. Buh . . . bump.*

In. *Buh . . . bump. Buh . . . bump.*

And forever it repeats. Until . . . Until when? Until I die of old age? Until I crush my skull against the stone? Until I gnaw out the tubes the Yellows threaded into my lower gut to force nutrients in and wastes out?

Or until you go mad?

"No." I grind my teeth.

Yessssss.

"It's only the dark." I breathe in. Calm myself. Touch the walls in my soothing pattern. Back, fingers, tailbone, heels, toes, knees, head. Repeat. A dozen times. A hundred. Why not be sure? Make it a thousand.

Yes. I'm alone.

I would have thought there to be worse fates than this, but now I know there are none. Man is no island. We need those who love us. We need those who hate us. We need others to tether us to life, to give us a reason to live, to feel. All I have is the darkness. Sometimes I scream. Sometimes I laugh during the night, during the day. Who knows now? I laugh to pass the time, to exhaust the calories the Jackal gives me and make my body shiver into sleep.

I weep too. I hum. I whistle.

I listen to voices above. Coming to me from the endless sea of darkness. And attending them is the maddening clatter of chains and bones, vibrating through my prison walls. All so close, yet a thousand kilometers away, as if a whole world existed just beyond the darkness and I cannot see it, cannot touch it, taste it, feel it, or pierce that veil to belong to the world once again. I am imprisoned in solitude.

I hear the voices now. The chains and bones trickling through my prison.

Are the voices mine?

I laugh at the idea.

I curse.

I plot. *Kill.*

Slaughter. Gouge. Rip. Burn.

I beg. I hallucinate. I bargain.

I whimper prayers to Eo, happy she was spared a fate like this.

She's not listening.

I sing childhood ballads and recite *Dying Earth, The Lamplighter,* the *Ramayana, The Odyssey* in Greek and Latin, then in the lost languages of Arabic, English, Chinese, and German, pulling from memories of dataDrops Matteo gave me when I was barely more than a boy. Seeking strength from the wayward Argive who only wished to find his way home.

You forget what he did.

Odysseus was a hero. He broke the walls of Troy with his wooden horse. Like I broke the Bellona armies in the Iron Rain over Mars.

And then . . .

"No," I snap. "Quiet."

. . . men entered Troy. Found mothers. Found children. Guess what they did?

"Shut up!"

You know what they did. Bone. Sweat. Flesh. Ash. Weeping. Blood.

The darkness cackles with glee.

Reaper, Reaper, Reaper . . . All deeds that last are painted in blood.

Am I asleep? Am I awake? I've lost my way. Everything bleeding together, drowning me in visions and whispers and sounds. Again and again I jerk Eo's fragile little ankles. Break Julian's face. Hear Pax and Quinn and Tactus and Lorn and Victra sigh their last. So much pain. And for what? To fail my wife. To fail my people.

And fail Ares. Fail your friends.

How many are even left?

Sevro? Ragnar?

Mustang?

Mustang. What if she knows you're here . . . What if she doesn't care . . . And why would she? You who betrayed. You who lied. You who used her mind. Her body. Her blood. You showed her your true face and she ran. What if it was her? What if she betrayed you? Could you love her then?

"Shut up!" I scream at myself, at the darkness.

Don't think of her. Don't think of her.

Why ever not? You miss her.

A vision of her is spawned in the darkness like so many before it—a girl riding away from me across a field of green, twisting in her saddle and laughing for me to follow. Hair rippling as would summer hay fluttering from a farmer's wagon.

You crave her. You love her. The Golden girl. Forget that Red bitch.

"No." I slam my head against the wall. "It's only the dark," I whisper. Only the dark playing tricks on my mind. But still I try to forget Mustang, Eo. There is no world beyond this place. I cannot miss what does not exist.

Warm blood trickles down my forehead from old scabs, now freshly broken. It drips off my nose. I extend my tongue, probing the cold stone till I find the drops. Savor the salt, the Martian iron. Slowly. Slowly. Let the novelty of sensation last. Let the flavor linger and remind me I am a man. A Red of Lykos. A Helldiver.

No. You are not. You are nothing. Your wife abandoned you and stole your child. Your whore turned from you. You were not good enough. You were too proud. Too stupid. Too wicked. Now, you are forgotten.

Am I?

When last I saw the Golden girl, I was on my knees beside Ragnar in the tunnels of Lykos, asking Mustang to betray her own people and live for more. I knew that if she chose to join us, Eo's dream would blossom. A better world was at our fingertips. Instead, she left. Could she forget me? Has her love for me left her?

She only loved your mask.

"It's only the dark. Only the dark. Only the dark," I mumble faster and faster.

I should not be here.

I should be dead. After the death of Lorn, I was to be given to Octavia so her Carvers could dissect me to discover the secrets of how I became Gold. To see if there could be others like me. But the Jackal made a bargain. Kept me for his own. He tortured me in his Attica estate, asking about the Sons of Ares, about Lykos and my family.

Never telling me how he discovered my secret. I begged him to end my life.

In the end, he gave me stone.

"When all is lost, honor demands death," Roque once told me. "It is a noble end." But what would a rich poet know of death? The poor know death. Slaves know death. But even as I yearn for it, I fear it. Because the more I see of this cruel world, the less I believe it ends in some pleasant fiction.

The Vale is not real.

It's a lie told by mothers and fathers to give their starving children a reason for the horror. There is no reason. Eo is gone. She never watched me fight for her dream. She did not care what fate I made at the Institute or if I loved Mustang, because the day she died, she became nothing. There is nothing but this world. It is our beginning and our end. Our one chance at joy before the dark.

Yes. But you don't have to end. You can escape this place, the darkness whispers to me. *Say the words. Say them. You know the way.*

It is right. I do.

"All you must say is 'I am broken,' and this will all end," the Jackal said long ago, before he lowered me into this hell. "I will put you in a lovely estate for the rest of your days and send you warm, beautiful Pinks and food enough to make you fatter than the Ash Lord. But the words carry a price."

Worth it. Save yourself. No one else will.

"That price, dear Reaper, is your family."

The family he seized from Lykos with his lurchers and now keeps in his prison in the bowels of his Attica fortress. Never letting me see them. Never letting me tell them I love them, and that I'm sorry I was not strong enough to protect them.

"I will feed them to the prisoners of this fortress," he said. "These men and women you think should rule instead of Gold. Once you see the animal in man, you will know that I am right and you are wrong. Gold must rule."

Let them go, the darkness says. *The sacrifice is practical. It is wise.*

"No . . . I won't . . ."

Your mother would want you to live.

Not at that price.

What man could grasp a mother's love? Live. For her. For Eo.

Could she want that? Is the darkness right? After all, I'm important. Eo said so. Ares said so; he chose me. Me of all the Reds. I can
break the chains. I can live for more. It's not selfish for me to escape
this prison. In the grand scheme of things, it is selfless.

Yes. Selfless, really . . .

Mother would beg me to make this sacrifice. Kieran would understand. So would my sister. I can save our people. Eo's dream must be
made real, no matter the cost. It's my responsibility to persevere. It is
my right.

Say the words.

I slam my head into the stone and scream at the darkness to go
away. It cannot trick me. It cannot break me.

Didn't you know? All men break.

Its high cackle mocks me, stretching forever.

And I know it is right. All men break. I did already under his torture. I told him that I was from Lykos. Where he could find my family.
But there is a way out, to honor what I am. What Eo loved. To silence
the voices.

"Roque, you were right," I whisper. "You were right." I just want to
be home. To be gone from here. But I can't have that. All that's left,
the only honorable path for me, is death. Before I betray even more of
who I am.

Death is the way out.

Don't be a fool. Stop. Stop.

I lurch my head forward into the wall harder than before. Not to
punish, but to kill. To end myself. If there is no pleasant end to this
world, then nothingness will suffice. But if there is a Vale beyond this
plane, I will find it. I'm coming, Eo. At last, I am on my way. "I love
you."

No. No. No. No. No.

I crash my skull again into stone. Heat pours down my face. Sparks
of pain dance in the black. The darkness wails at me, but I do not
stop.

If this is the end, I will rage toward it.

But as I pull back my head to deliver one last great blow, existence groans. Rumbling like an earthquake. Not the darkness. Something beyond. Something in the stone itself, growing louder and deeper above me, till the darkness cracks and a blazing sword of light slashes down.

2

IIIIIIIIIIIIIIIIIIIIII

PRISONER L17L6363

The ceiling parts. Light burns my eyes. I clamp them shut as the floor of my cell rises upward till, with a click, it stops and I rest, exposed, on a flat stone surface. I push out my legs and gasp, nearly fainting from the pain. Joints crack. Knotted tendons unspool. I fight to reopen my eyes against the raging light. Tears fill them. It is so bright I can only catch bleached flashes of the world around.

Fragments of alien voices surround me. "Adrius, what is this?"

". . . has he been in there this whole time?"

"The stench . . ."

I lie upon stone. It stretches around me to either side. Black, rippling with blue and purple, like the shell of a Creonian beetle. A floor? No. I see cups. Saucers. A cart of coffee. It's a table. That was my prison. Not some hideous abyss. Just a meter-wide, twelve-meter-long slab of marble with a hollow center. They've eaten inches above me every night. Their voices the distant whispers I heard in the darkness. The clatter of their silverware and plates my only company.

"Barbaric . . ."

I remember now. This is the table the Jackal sat at when I visited him after recovering from the wounds incurred during the Iron Rain.

Did he plan my imprisonment even then? I wore a hood when they put me in here. I thought I was in the bowels of his fortress. But no. Thirty centimeters of stone separated their suppers from my hell.

I look up from the coffee tray by my head. Someone stares at me. Several someones. Can't see them through the tears and blood in my eyes. I twist away, coiling inward like a blind mole unearthed for the very first time. Too overwhelmed and terrified to remember pride or hate. But I know he stares at me. The Jackal. A childish face in a slender body, with sandy hair parted on the side. He clears his throat.

"My honored guests. May I present prisoner L17L6363."

His face is both heaven and hell.

To see another man . . .

To know I am not alone . . .

But then to remember what he's done to me . . . it rips my soul out.

Other voices slither and boom, deafening in their loudness. And, even curled as I am, I feel something beyond their noise. Something natural and gentle and kind. Something the darkness convinced me I would never feel again. It drifts softly through an open window, kissing my skin.

A late autumn breeze cuts through the meaty, humid stink of my filth and makes me think that somewhere a child is sprinting through snow and trees, running his hands along bark and pine needles and getting sap in his hair. It's a memory I know I've never had, but feel like I should. That's the life I would have wanted. The child I could have had.

I weep. Less for me than for that boy who thinks he lives in a kind world, where Mother and Father are as large and strong as mountains. If only I could be so innocent again. If only I knew this moment was not a trick. But it is. The Jackal does not give except to take away. Soon the light will be a memory and darkness will return. I keep my eyes clenched tight, listening to the blood from my face drip on the stone, and wait for the twist.

"Goryhell, Augustus. Was this really necessary?" a feline killer purrs. Husky accent smothered in that indolent Luna lilt learned in the courts of the Palatine Hill, where all are less impressed by everything than anyone else. "He smells like death."

"Fermented sweat and dead skin under the magnetic shackles. See the yellowish crust on his forearms, Aja?" the Jackal notes. "Still, he's very much healthy and ready for your Carvers. All things considered."

"You know the man better than I," Aja says to someone else. "Make sure it is him. Not an imposter."

"You doubt my word?" the Jackal asks. "You wound me."

I flinch, feeling someone approach.

"Please. You'd need a heart for that, ArchGovernor. And you've many gifts, but that organ, I'm afraid, is dearly absent."

"You compliment me too much."

Spoons clatter against porcelain. Throats are cleared. I long to cover my ears. So much sound. So much information.

"You really can see the Red in him now." It's a cold, cultured female voice from northern Mars. More brusque than the Luna accent.

"Exactly, Antonia!" the Jackal replies. "I've been curious to see how he turned out. A member of the Aureate genus could never be so debased as this creature here before us. You know, he asked me for death before I put him in there. Started weeping about it. The irony is he could have killed himself whenever he chose. But he didn't, because some part of him relished that hole. You see, Reds long ago adapted to darkness. Like worms. No pride to their rusty race. He was at home down there. More than he ever was with us."

Now I remember hate.

I open my eyes to let them know I see them. Hear them. Yet as my eyes open, they are drawn not to my enemy, but to the winter vista that sprawls out the windows behind the Golds. There, six of the seven mountain peaks of Attica glitter in the morning light. Metal and glass buildings crest stone and snow, and yawn upward toward the blue sky. Bridges suture the peaks together. A light snow falls. It's a blurred mirage to my nearsighted cave eyes.

"Darrow?" I know the voice. I turn my head slightly to see one of his callused hands on the edge of the table. I flinch away, thinking it will strike me. It doesn't. But the hand's middle finger bears the golden eagle of Bellona. The family I destroyed. The other hand belongs to the arm I cut off on Luna when we last dueled, the one that was re-made by Zanzibar the Carver. Two wolfshead rings of House Mars encircle those fingers. One is mine. One his. Each worth the price of a young Gold's life. "Do you recognize me?" he asks.

I crane my head to look up at his face. Broken I may be, but Cassius au Bellona is undimmed by war or time. More beautiful by far than memory could ever allow, he pulses with life. Over two meters tall. Cloaked in the white and gold of the Morning Knight, his coiled hair lustrous as the trail of a falling star. He's clean-shaven, and his nose is slightly crooked from a recent break. When I meet his eyes, I do all I can to not fall into sobs. The way he looks at me is sad, nearly tender. What a shadow of myself I must be to earn pity from a man I've hurt so deeply.

"*Cassius,*" I murmur with no agenda except to say the name. To speak to another human. To be heard.

"And?" Aja au Grimmus asks from behind Cassius. The most violent of the Sovereign's Furies wears the same armor I saw her in when first we met in the Citadel spire on Luna, the night Mustang rescued me and Aja beat Quinn to death. It's scuffed. Battle-worn. Fear overwhelms my hate, and I look away from the dark-skinned woman yet again.

"He's alive after all," Cassius says quietly. He turns on the Jackal. "What did you do to him? The scars . . ."

"I should think it obvious," the Jackal says. "I have unmade the Reaper."

I finally look down at my body past my ratty beard to see what he means. I am a corpse. Skeletal and pallid. Ribs erupt from skin thinner than the film atop heated milk. Knees jut from spindly legs. Toenails have grown long and grasping. Scars from the Jackal's torture mottle my flesh. Muscle has withered. And tubes that kept me alive in the darkness erupt from my belly, black and stringy umbilical cords still anchoring me to the floor of my cell.

"How long was he in there?" Cassius asks.

"Three months of interrogation, then nine months of solitary."

"Nine . . ."

"As is fitting. War shouldn't make us abandon metaphor. We're not savages after all, eh, Bellona?"

"Cassius's sensibilities are offended, Adrius," Antonia says from her place near the Jackal. She's a poisoned apple of a woman. Shiny and bright and promising, but rotten and cancerous to the core. She killed my friend Lea at the Institute. Put a bullet in her own mother's head, and then two more into her sister Victra's spine. Now she's allied with the Jackal, a man who crucified her at the Institute. What a world. Behind Antonia stands dark-faced Thistle, once a Howler, now a member of the Jackal's Boneriders by the looks of the jackal skull pennant on her chest. She looks at the floor instead of at me. Her captain is bald-headed Lilath, who sits at the Jackal's right hand. His favorite personal killer ever since the Institute.

"Pardon me if I fail to see the purpose of torturing a fallen enemy," Cassius answers. "Especially if he's given all the information he has to give."

"The purpose?" The Jackal stares at him, eyes quiet, as he explains. "The purpose is punishment, my goodman. This . . . *thing* presumed he belonged among us. Like he was an equal, Cassius. A superior, even. He mocked us. Bedded my *sister.* He laughed at us and played us for fools before we found him out. He must know it was not by chance that he lost, but inevitability. Reds have always been cunning little creatures. And he, my friends, is the personification of what they wish to be, what they will be if we let them. So I let time and darkness remake him into what he really is. A *Homo flammeus,* to use the new classification system I proposed to the Board. Barely different from *Homo sapiens* on the evolutionary timeline. The rest was just a mask."

"You mean he made a fool of *you,*" Cassius parses, "when your father preferred a carved-up Red to his blood heir? That's what this is, *Jackal.* The petulant shame of a boy unloved and unwanted."

The Jackal twitches at that. Aja's equally displeased by her young companion's tone.

"Darrow took Julian's life," Antonia says. "Then slaughtered your family. Cassius, he sent killers to butcher the children of your blood as they hid on Olympus Mons. One would wonder what your mother would think of your pity."

Cassius ignores them, jerking his head toward the Pinks at the edge of the room. "Fetch the prisoner a blanket."

They do not move.

"Such manners. Even from you, Thistle?" She gives no answer. With a snort of contempt, Cassius strips off his white cloak and drapes it over my shivering body. For a moment, no one speaks, as struck by the act as I.

"*Thank you,*" I croak. But he looks away from my hollow face. Pity is not forgiveness, nor is gratitude absolution.

Lilath snorts a laugh without looking up from her bowl of soft-boiled hummingbird eggs. She slurps at them like candy. "There *is* a point when honor becomes a flaw of character, Morning Knight." Sitting beside the Jackal, the bald woman peers up at Aja with eyes like those of the eels in Venus's cavern seas. Another egg goes down. "Old man Arcos learned the hard way."

Aja does not reply, her manners faultless. But a deathly silence lurks inside the woman, a silence I remember from the moments before she killed Quinn. Lorn taught her the blade. She will not like seeing his name mocked. Lilath greedily swallows another egg, sacrificing manners for insult.

There's animosity between these allies. As always with their kind. But this seems a stark new division between the old Golds and the Jackal's more modern breed.

"We're all friends here," the Jackal says playfully. "Mind your manners, Lilath. Lorn was an Iron Gold who simply chose the wrong side. So, Aja, I'm curious. Now that my lease on the Reaper is up, do you still plan to dissect him?"

"We do," Aja says. Shouldn't have thanked Cassius after all. His honor isn't true. It's just sanitary. "Zanzibar is curious to discover how he was made. He has his theories, but he's champing at the bit for the specimen. We were hoping to round up the Carver that did the deed, but we think he perished in a missile strike up in Kato, Alcidalia province."

"Or they want you to think that," Antonia says.

"You once had him here, didn't you?" Aja asks pointedly.

The Jackal nods. "Mickey's his name. Lost his license after he carved an unlicensed Aureate birth. Family tried sparing their child the Exposure. Anyway, he specialized in blackmarket aerial and aquatic pleasure mods afterward. Had a carveshop in Yorkton before the Sons recruited him for a special job. Darrow helped him escape my custody. If you want my opinion, he's still alive. My operatives place him in Tinos."

Aja and Cassius exchange a look.

"If you have a lead on Tinos, you need to share it with us now," Cassius says.

"I have nothing definitive yet. Tinos is well hidden. And we've yet to capture one of their ship captains . . . alive." The Jackal sips his coffee. "But irons are in the fire, and you'll be the first to know if anything comes of them. Though, I rather think my Boneriders would like the first crack at the Howlers. Wouldn't you, Lilath?"

I try not to stir at the mention of the name. But it's hard not to. They're alive. Some of them, at least. And they chose the Sons of Ares over Gold. . . .

"Yes, sir," Lilath says, studying me. "We'd relish a real hunt. Fighting the Red Legion and the other insurgents is a bore, even for Grays."

"The Sovereign needs us home anyway, Cassius," Aja says. Then, to the Jackal: "We'll be departing as soon as my Thirteenth has decamped from the Golan Basin. Likely by morning."

"You're taking your legions back to Luna?"

"Just the Thirteenth. The rest will remain under your supervision." The Jackal is surprised. "My supervision?"

"On loan till this . . . *Rising* is fully snuffed out." She practically spits the word. A new one to my ears. "It's a token of the Sovereign's trust. You know she is pleased with your progress here."

"Despite your methods," Cassius adds, drawing an annoyed look from Aja.

"Well, if you're leaving in the morning you should, of course, dine with me this evening. I've been wanting to discuss certain . . . policies regarding the Rebels in the Rim." The Jackal is vague because I'm listening. Information's his weapon. Suggesting my friends betrayed me. Never saying which. Dropping hints and clues during my torture, before I was sent into the dark. A Gray telling him that his sister is waiting in his salon. His fingers smelling like frothed chai tea, his sister's favorite drink. Does she know I am here? Has she sat at this table? The Jackal is still prattling on. Hard to track the voices. So much to decipher. Too much.

". . . I'll have my men clean Darrow up for his travels and we can throw a feast of Trimalchian proportions after our discussion. I know the Voloxes and the Corialuses would be delighted to see you again. It's been too long since I had such august company as two Olympic Knights. You're in the field so often, skirting around provinces, hunting through the tunnels and seas and ghettos. How long has it been since you had a fine meal without worry of a night raid or suicide bombers?"

"A spell," Aja admits. "We took the Brothers Rath up on their hospitality when we passed through Thessalonica. They were eager to show their loyalty after their . . . behavior during the Lion's Rain. It was . . . unsettling."

The Jackal laughs. "I fear my dinner will be tame by comparison. It's been all politicians and soldiers of late. This gorydamn war has so impeded my social calendar, as you can imagine."

"Sure it's not your reputation for hospitality?" Cassius asks. "Or your diet?"

Aja sighs, trying to hide her amusement. "Manners, Bellona."

"Not to fear . . . the enmity between our houses is hard to forget, Cassius. But we must find common ground in times like these. For the sake of Gold." The Jackal smiles, though inside I know he's imagining sawing off both their heads with a dull knife. "Anyway, we all have our schoolyard stories. I'm hardly ashamed."

"There *was* one other matter we wished to discuss," Aja says.

It's Antonia's turn to sigh. "I told you there would be. What does our Sovereign require now?"

"It pertains to what Cassius mentioned earlier."

"My methods," the Jackal confirms.

"Yes."

"I thought the Sovereign was pleased with the pacification effort."

"She is, but . . ."

"She asked for order. I have provided. Helium-3 continues to flow, with only a three point two percent decrease in production. The Rising is struggling for air; soon Ares will be found and Tinos and all this will be behind us. Fabii is the one who is taking his—"

Aja interrupts. "It's the kill squads."

"Ah."

"And the liquidation protocols you've instituted in rebellious mines. She's worried that the severity of your methods against the lowReds will create a backlash comparable to earlier propaganda setbacks. There have been bombings on the Palatine Hill. Strikes in latfundias on Earth. Even protests at the gate of the Citadel itself. The spirit of rebellion is alive. But it is fractured. It must remain so."

"I doubt we'll be seeing many more protests after the Obsidians are sent in," Antonia says smugly.

"Still . . ."

"There is no danger of my tactics reaching the public eye. The Sons' abilities to propagate their message has been neutered," the Jackal says. "I control the message now, Aja. The people know this war is already lost. They'll never see a picture of the bodies. Never glimpse a liquidated mine. What they will continue to see is Red attacks on civilian targets. MidColor and highColor children dead in schools. The public is with us. . . ."

"And if they do see what you're doing?" Cassius asks.

The Jackal does not immediately reply. Instead, he signals a barely dressed Pink over from the couches in the adjacent sitting room. The girl, hardly older than Eo was, comes to his side and stares meekly at the ground. Her eyes are rose quartz, her hair a silvery lilac that hangs in braids down to her bare lower back. She was raised to pleasure these monsters, and I fear knowing what those soft eyes of hers have seen. My pain seems suddenly so tiny. The madness in my mind so quiet. The Jackal strokes the girl's face and, still looking at me, shoves his fingers into her mouth, prying her teeth apart. He moves the girl's head with his stump so I can see, then so Aja and Cassius might.

She has no tongue.

"I did this myself after we took her eight months ago. She attempted to assassinate one of my Boneriders at an Agea Pearl club. She hates me. Wants nothing more in this world than to see me rotting in the ground." Letting go of her face, he pops his sidearm out of his holster and thrusts it into the girl's hands. "Shoot me in the head, Calliope. For all the indignities I have heaped upon you and your kind. Go on. I took your tongue. You remember what I did to you in the library. It will happen again and again and again." He returns his hand to her face, squeezing her fragile jaw. "And again. *Pull the trigger, you little tart*. Pull it!" The Pink shakes in fear and throws the gun on the floor, falling to her knees to clutch his feet. He stands benevolent and loving above her, touching her head with his hand.

"There, there, Calliope. You did well. You did well." The Jackal turns to Aja. "For the public, honey is always better than vinegar. But for those who war with wrenches, with poison, with sabotage in the sewers and terror in the streets, and nibble at us like cockroaches in the night, fear is the only method." His eyes find mine. "Fear and extermination."

3

||||||||||||||||||||||||

SNAKEBITE

Blood beads where buzzing metal pinches my scalp. Dirty blond hair puddles onto the concrete as the Gray finishes scalping me with an electric razor. His compatriots call him Danto. He rolls my head around to make sure he's got it all before clapping me hard on the top of it. "How 'bout a bath, *dominus*?" he asks. "Grimmus likes her prisoners to smell nice 'n civil, hear?" He taps the muzzle they strapped to my face after I tried to bite one of them. They moved me with an electric collar around my neck, arms bound still behind my back, a squad of twelve hardcore lurchers dragging me through the halls like a bag of trash.

Another Gray jerks me from my chair by my collar as Danto goes to pull a power hose from the wall. They're more than a head shorter than I am, but compact and rugged. The lives they live are hard—chasing Outriders in the belt, stalking Syndicate killers through the depths of Luna, hunting Sons of Ares in the mines . . .

I hate them touching me. All the sights and sounds they make. It's too much. Too gruff. Too hard. Everything they do hurts. Jerking me around. Slapping me casually. I try my best to keep the tears away, but I don't know how to compartmentalize it all.

The line of twelve soldiers crowds together, watching me as Danto aims the hose. They've got three Obsidian men with them. Most lurcher squads do. The water hits me like a horse kick in the chest. Tearing skin. I spin on the concrete floor, sliding across the room till I'm pinned in the corner. My skull slams against the wall. Stars swarm my sight. I swallow water. Choking, hunching to protect my face because my hands are still pinned behind my back.

When they've finished, I'm still gasping and coughing around the muzzle, trying to suck in air. They uncuff me and slip my arms and legs into a black prisoner's jumpsuit before binding me again. There's a hood too that they'll soon jerk over my head to rob me of what little humanity I have left. I'm thrown back into the chair. They click my restraints into the chair's receptacle so I'm locked down. Everything's redundant. Every move watched. They guard me like what I was, not what I am. I squint at them, vision bleary and nearsighted. Water drips from my eyelashes. I try to sniff, but my nose is clogged tight with congealed blood from nostril to nasal cavity. They broke it when they put the muzzle on.

We're in a processing room for the Board of Quality Control, which oversees the administrative functions of the prison beneath the Jackal's fortress. The building has the concrete box shape of every government facility. Poisonous lighting makes everyone here look like a walking corpse with pores the size of meteor craters. Aside from the Grays, the Obsidian, and a single Yellow doctor, there's a chair, an examination table, and a hose. But the fluid stains around the floor's metal drain and the nail scratches on the metal chair are the face and soul of this room. The ending of lives begins here.

Cassius would never come to this hole. Few Golds would ever need or want to unless they made the wrong enemies. It's the inside of the clock, where the gears whir and grind. How could anyone be brave in a place so inhuman as this?

"Crazy, ain't it?" Danto asks those behind him. He looks back at me. "All my life, never seen something so slaggin' odd."

"Carver musta put a hundred kilos on him," says another.

"More. Ever see him in his armor? He was a damned monster."

Danto flicks my muzzle with a tattooed finger. "Bet it hurt bein' born twice. Gotta respect that. Pain's the universal language. Ain't it, *Ruster*?" When I don't respond, he leans forward and stomps on my bare foot with his steel-heeled boot. The big toenail splits. Pain and blood rupture from the exposed nail bed. My head lolls sideways as I gasp. "Ain't it?" he asks again. Tears leak from my eyes, not from the pain, but from the casualness of his cruelty. It makes me feel so small. Why does it take so little for him to hurt me so much? It almost makes me miss the box.

"He's only a baboon in a suit," another says. "Leave off him. He don't know any better."

"Don't know any better?" Danto asks. "Bullshit. He liked the fit of master's clothes. Liked lording over us." Danto crouches so he's looking into my eyes. I try to look away, frightened he'll hurt me again, but he seizes my head and pulls open my eyelids with his thumbs so we're eye to eye. "Two of my sisters died in that Rain of yours, Ruster. Lost a lot of friends, ya hear?" He hits the side of my head with something metal. I see spots. Feel more blood leak from me. Behind him, their centurion checks his datapad. "You'd want the same for my kids, wouldn't you?" Danto searches my eyes for an answer. I have none he'd accept.

Like the rest, Danto's a veteran legionnaire, rough as a rusted sewer grate. Tech festoons his black combat gear, where scuffed purple dragons coil in faint filigree. Optic implants in the eyes for thermal vision and the reading of battlemaps. Under his skin he'll have more embedded tech to help him hunt Golds and Obsidians. The tattoo of an *XIII* clutched by a moving sea dragon stains all their necks, little heaps of ash at the base of the numeral. These are members of Legio XIII Dracones, the favored Praetorian legion of the Ash Lord and now his daughter, Aja. Civilians would just call them dragoons. Mustang hated the fanatics. It's a whole independent army of thirty thousand chosen by Aja to be the hand of the Sovereign away from Luna.

They hate me.

They hate lowColors with a marrow-deep racism even Golds can't match.

"Go for the ears, Danto, if you wanna make him yelp," one of the Grays suggests. The woman stands at the door, nutcracker jaw bobbing up and down as she gnaws on a gumbubble. Her ashen hair is shaved into a short Mohawk. Voice drawling in some Earthborn dialect. She leans against the metal beside a yawning male Gray with a delicate nose more like a Pink's than a soldier's. "You hit them with a cupped hand, you can pop the eardrum with the pressure."

"Thanks, Holi."

"Here to help."

Danto cups his hand. "Like this?" He hits my head.

"Little more curve to it."

The centurion snaps his fingers. "Danto. Grimmus wants him in one piece. Back up and let the doc take a look." I breathe a sigh of relief at the reprieve.

The fat Yellow doctor ambles forward to inspect me with beady ocher eyes. The pale lights above make the bald patch on his head shine like a pale, waxed apple. He runs his bioscope over my chest, watching the visual through little digital implants in his eyes. "Well, Doc?" the centurion asks.

"Remarkable," the Yellow whispers after a moment. "Bone density and organs are quite healthy despite the low-caloric diet. Muscles have atrophied, as we've observed in laboratory settings, but not as poorly as natural Aureate tissue."

"You're saying he's better than Gold?" the centurion asks.

"I did not say that," the doctor snaps.

"Relax. There's no cameras, Doc. This is a processing room. What's the verdict?"

"It can travel."

"It?" I manage in a low, unearthly growl from behind my muzzle. The doctor recoils, surprised I can speak.

"And long-term sedation? Got three weeks to Luna at this orbit."

"That will be fine." The doctor gives me a frightened look. "But I would up the dose by ten milligrams per day, Captain, just to be safe. *It* has an abnormally strong circulatory system."

"Right." The captain nods to the female Gray. "You're up, Holi. Put him to bed. Then let's get the cart and roll out. You're square, Doc. Head back to your safe little espresso-and-silk world now. We'll take care of—"

Pop. The front half of the centurion's forehead comes off. Something metal hits the wall. I stare at the centurion, mind not processing why his face is gone. *Pop. Pop. Pop. Pop.* Like knuckle joints. Red mist geysers into the air from the heads of the nearest dragoons. Spraying my face. I duck my head away. Behind them, the nutcracker-jawed woman walks casually through their ranks, shooting them point-blank in the backs of their heads. The rest pull their rifles up, scrambling, unable to even utter curses before a second Gray double-taps five of them from his place at the door with an old-fashioned gunpowder slug shooter. Silencer on the barrel so it's cool and quiet. Obsidians are the first to hit the floor, leaking red.

"Clear," the woman says.

"Plus two," the man replies. He shoots the Yellow doctor as he crawls to the door trying to escape, then puts a boot on Danto's chest. The Gray stares up at him, bleeding from under the jaw.

"Trigg . . ."

"Ares sends his regards, motherfucker." The Gray shoots Danto just under the brim of his tactical helmet, between the eyes, and spins the slug shooter in his hand, blowing smoke from the end before sheathing it in a leg holster. "Clear."

My lips work against my muzzle, struggling to form a coherent thought. "Who . . . are you . . ." The Gray woman nudges a body out of her way.

"Name's Holiday ti Nakamura. That's Trigg, my baby brother." She raises a scar-notched eyebrow. Her wide face is blasted by freckles. Nose smashed flat. Eyes dark gray and narrow. "Question is, who are you?"

"Who am I?" I mumble.

"We came for the Reaper. But if that's you, I think we should get our money back." She winks suddenly. "I'm joking, sir."

"Holiday, cut it." Trigg pushes her aside protectively. "Can't you see he's shell-shocked?" Trigg approaches carefully, hands out, voice soothing. "You're prime, sir. We're here to rescue you." His words are thicker, less polished than Holiday's. I flinch as he takes another step. Search his hands for a weapon. He's going to hurt me. "Just gonna unlock you. That's all. You want that, yeah?"

It's a lie. A Jackal trick. He's got the *XIII* tattoo. These are Praetorians, not Sons. Liars. Killers.

"I won't unlock you if you don't want me to."

No. No, he killed the guards. He's here to help. He has to be here to help. I give Trigg a wary nod and he slips behind me. I don't trust him. I half expect a needle. A twist. But all I feel is release as my risk is rewarded. The cuffs unlock. My shoulder joints crack and, moaning, I pull my hands in front of my body for the first time in nine months. The pain causes them to shake. The nails have grown long and vile. But these hands are mine again. I charge to my feet to escape, and collapse to the floor.

"Whoa . . . whoa," Holiday says, hefting me back into the chair. "Easy there, hero. You've got mad muscle atrophy. Gonna need an oil change."

Trigg comes back around to stand in front of me, smiling lopsided, face open and boyish, not nearly as intimidating as his sister, despite the two gold teardrop tattoos that leak from his right eye. He has the look of a loyal hound. Gently he removes the muzzle from my face, then remembers something with a start. "I've got something for you, sir."

"Not now, Trigg." Holiday eyes the door. "Ain't got the seconds."

"He needs it," Trigg says under his breath, but waits till Holiday gives him a nod before he pulls a leather bundle from his tortoise pack. He extends it to me. "It's yours, sir. Take it." He senses my apprehension. "Hey, I didn't lie about unlocking you, did I?"

"No . . ."

I put my hands out and he sets the leather bundle in them. Fingers trembling, I pull back the string holding the bundle together and feel the power before I even see the deadly shimmer. My hands almost drop the bundle, as frightened of it as my eyes were of the light.

It is my razor. The one given to me by Mustang. The one I've lost twice now. Once to Karnus, then again at my Triumph to the Jackal. It is white and smooth as a child's first tooth. My hands slide over the cold metal and its salt-stained calf-leather grip. Touch wakening melancholy memories of strength long faded and warmth long forgotten. The smell of hazelnut drifts back to me, transporting me to Lorn's practice rooms, where he would teach me as his favorite granddaughter learned to bake in the adjacent kitchen.

The razor slithers through the air, so beautiful, so deceitful in its promise of power. The blade would tell me I'm a god, as it has told generations of men who came before me, but I now know the lie in that. The terrible price it's made men pay for pride.

It scares me to hold it again.

And it rasps like a pitviper's mating call as it forms into a curved slingBlade. It was blank and smooth when last I saw it, but it ripples now with images etched into the white metal. I tilt the blade so I can better see the form etched just above the hilt. I stare dumbly. Eo looks back at me. An image of her etched into the metal. The artist caught her not on the scaffold, not in the moment that will forever define her to others, but intimately, as the girl I loved. She's crouched, hair messy about her shoulders, picking a haemanthus from the ground, looking up, just about to smile. And above Eo is my father kissing my mother at the door of our home. And toward the tip of the blade, Leanna, Loran, and I chasing Kieran down a tunnel, wearing Octobernacht masks. It is my childhood.

Whoever made this art knows me.

"The Golds carve their deeds into their swords. The *grand, violent* shit they've done. But Ares thought you'd prefer to see the people you love," Holiday says quietly from behind Trigg. She glances back to the door.

"Ares is dead." I search their faces, seeing the deceit there. Seeing the wickedness in their eyes. "The Jackal sent you. It's a trick. A trap. To lead you to the Sons' base." My hand tightens around the razor's grip. "To use me. You're lying."

Holiday steps back from me, wary of the blade in my hand. But Trigg is ripped apart by the accusation. "Lying? To *you*? We'd die for you, sir. We'd have died for Persephone . . . Eo." He struggles to find the words, and I get a sense he's used to letting his sister do the talking. "There's an army waiting for you outside these walls—does that register? An army waiting for its . . . its *soul* to come back to it." He leans forward imploringly as Holiday looks back to the door. "We're from South Pacifica, the ass end of Earth. I thought I'd die there guarding grain silos. But I'm here. On Mars. And our only job is to get you home. . . ."

"I've met better liars than you," I sneer.

"Screw this." Holiday reaches for her datapad.

Trigg tries to stop her. "Ares said it was only for emergencies. If they hack the signal . . ."

"Look at him. This is an emergency." Holiday strips her datapad and tosses it to me. A call is going through to another device. Blinking blue on the display, waiting for the other side to answer. As I turn it in my hand, a hologram of a spiked sunburst helmet suddenly blossoms into the air, small as my clenched fist. Red eyes glow out balefully from the helmet.

"Fitchner?"

"Guess again, shithead," the voice warbles.

It can't be.

"Sevro?" I almost whimper the word.

"Oy, boyo, you look like you slithered out of a skeleton's rickety cooch."

"You're alive . . . ," I say as the holographic helmet slithers away to reveal my hatchet-faced friend. He smiles with those hacksaw teeth. Image flickering.

"Ain't no Pixie in the worlds that can kill me." He cackles. *"Now it's time you come home, Reap. But I can't come to you. You gotta come to me. You register?"*

"How?" I wipe the tears from my eyes.

"Trust my Sons. Can you do that?"

I look at the brother and sister and nod. "The Jackal . . . he has my family."

"That cannibalistic bitch ain't got shit. I got your family. Grabbed them from Lykos after you got snagged. Your mother's waiting to see you." I start crying again. The relief too much to bear.

"But you gotta sack up, boyo. And you gotta move." He looks sideways at someone. *"Gimme back to Holiday."* I do. *"Make it clean if you can. Escalate if you can't. Register?"*

"Register."

"Break the chains."

"Break the chains," the Grays echo as his image flickers out.

"Look past our Color," Holiday says to me. She reaches a tattooed hand down. I stare at the Gray Sigils etched into her flesh, then look up to search her freckled, bluff face. One of her eyes is bionic, and does not blink like the other. Eo's words sound so different from her mouth. Yet I think it's the moment my soul comes back to me. Not my mind. I still feel the cracks in it. The slithering, doubting darkness. But my hope. I clutch her smaller hand desperately.

"Break the chains," I echo hoarsely. "You'll have to carry me." I look at my worthless legs. "Can't stand."

"That's why we brought you a little cocktail." Holiday pulls up a syringe.

"What is it?" I ask.

Trigg just laughs. "Your oil change. Seriously, friend, you really don't want to know." He grins. "Shit will animate a corpse."

"Give it to me," I say, holding out my wrist.

"It's gonna hurt," Trigg warns.

"He's a big boy." Holiday comes closer.

"Sir . . ." Trigg hands me one of his gloves. "Between your teeth."

A little less confident, I bite down on the salt-stained leather and nod to Holiday. She lunges past my wrist to jam the syringe straight into my heart. Metal punctures meat as the payload releases.

"Holy shit!" I try to scream, but it comes out as a gurgle. Fire cavorts through my veins, my heart a piston. I look down, expecting to see it galloping out of my bloodydamn chest. I feel every muscle. Every cell of my body exploding, pulsing with kinetic energy. I dry-heave. I fall, clawing at my chest. Panting. Spitting bile. Punching the floor. The Grays scramble back from my twisting body. I strike out at the chair, half ripping it from its bolted place in the floor. I let out a stream of curses that'd make Sevro blush. Then I tremble and look up at them. "What . . . was . . . *that*?"

Holiday tries not to laugh. "Mamma calls it snakebite. Only gonna last thirty minutes with your metabolism."

"Your mamma made that?"

Trigg shrugs. "We're from Earth."

4

||||||||||||||||||||||||

CELL 2187

They escort me like a prisoner through the halls. Hood on my head. Hands behind my back in unlocked manacles. Brother on my left, sister on my right, both supporting me. The snakebite lets me walk, but not well. My body, jacked with drugs as it is, still feels slack as wet clothes. I can barely feel my busted toe or feeble legs. My thin prisoner's shoes scrape the floor. My head swims, but there's a hyperspeed to my brain now. It's focused mania. I chew my tongue to keep from whispering, and to remind myself that I am not in the darkness like before. My body is shuffling down a concrete hall. It is walking toward freedom. Toward my family, toward Sevro.

No one here will stop two dragoons of the Thirteenth, not when they have clearance and Aja herself is here. I doubt many in the Jackal's army know I'm even alive. They'll see my size, my ghostly pallor, and think I'm some unlucky Obsidian prisoner. Still, I feel the eyes. Paranoia creeping through me. *They know. They know you've left bodies behind. How long till they open that door? How long till we are discovered?* My brain races through the possible ends. How it could all go wrong. The drugs. It's just the drugs.

"Shouldn't we be going up?" I ask as we descend on a gravLift deeper into the heart of the mountain citadel's prison. "Or is there a lower hangar bay?"

"Good guess, sir," Trigg says, impressed. "We've got a ship waiting."

Holiday pops her gum. "Trigg, you've got some brown on your nose. Just . . . there."

"Oh, shut your hole. I'm not the one who blushed when he was naked."

"Sure about that, kiddo? Quiet." The gravLift slows and the siblings tense. Hear their hands click the safeties off their weapons. The doors open and someone joins us.

"*Dominus,*" Holiday says smoothly to the new company, shoving me to the side to make room. The boots that enter are heavy enough for a Gold or Obsidian, but Grays would never call an Obsidian *dominus,* and an Obsidian would never smell like cloves and cinnamon.

"Sergeant." The voice scrapes through me. The man it belongs to once made necklaces of ears. Vixus. One of Titus's old band. He was part of the massacre at my Triumph. I shrink into the side of the grav-Lift as it descends again. Vixus will know me. He'll sniff me out. He's doing it now, looking our way. I can hear the rustle of his jacket collar. "Thirteenth legion?" Vixus asks after a moment. He must have noticed their neck tattoos. "You Aja's or her father's?"

"The Fury's, for this tour, *dominus,*" Holiday replies coolly. "But we've served under the Ash Lord."

"Ah, then you were at the Battle of Deimos last year?"

"Yes, *dominus.* We were with Grimmus in the leechCraft vanguard sent to kill the Telemanuses before Fabii routed them and Arcos's ships. My brother here put a round in old Kavax's shoulder. Almost took him down before Augustus and Kavax's wife broke our assault team."

"My, my." Vixus makes a sound of approval. "That would have been a gorydamn prize and a half. You could have added another tear to your face, legionnaire. I've been hunting that Obsidian dog with the Seventh. Ash Lord's offered quite the price for his slave's return."

He snorts something up his nose. Sounds like one of the stim canisters Tactus was so fond of. "Who's this, then?"

He means me.

I hear my heart in my ears.

"A gift from Praetor Grimmus in exchange for . . . *the package* she's taking home," Holiday says. "If you understand me, sir."

"Package. Half a package, more like." He chuckles at his own joke. "Anyone I know?" His hand touches the edge of my hood. I cower away. "A Howler would warm the heart. Pebble? Weed? No, much too tall."

"An Obsidian," Trigg says quickly. "Wish it was a Howler."

"Ugh." Vixus jerks his hand back as though contaminated. "Wait." He has an idea. "We'll put him in the cell with the Julii bitch. Let 'em fight for supper. What do you think, Thirteen? Up for some fun?"

"Trigg, kill the camera," I say sharply from beneath my hood.

"What?" Vixus asks, turning.

Pop. A jamfield goes up.

I move, clumsy but fast. Snapping my hands out of the shackles, I pull free my hidden razor with one hand and rip off my hood with the other. I stab Vixus through the shoulder. Pin him to the wall and head-butt him in the face. But I'm not what I was, even with the drugs. My vision swims. I stumble. He doesn't, and before I can react, before I can even focus my vision, Vixus pulls his own razor.

Holiday shields me with her body, shoving me away. I fall to the ground. Trigg's even faster on the take; he jams his slug shooter straight up into Vixus's open mouth. The Gold freezes, staring down the metal length of the barrel, tongue against the cold muzzle. His razor pauses centimeters from Holiday's head.

"Shhhhhh," Trigg whispers. "Drop the razor." Vixus does.

"The hell are you thinking?" Holiday asks me angrily. She's breathing heavily and helps me back up. My head's still spinning. I apologize. It was stupid of me. I steady myself and look over at Vixus, who stares at me in horror. My legs tremble, and I have to hold myself up by one of the gravLift's railings. My heart rattles from the strain of the drug in my system. Stupid to try to fight. Stupid to use a jammer.

The Greens watching will piece it together. They'll send Grays to investigate the prep room. Find the bodies.

I try to paste my splintering thoughts together. Focus. "Is Victra alive?" I manage. Trigg pulls the gun out just past the teeth so Vixus can answer. He doesn't. Not yet. "Do you know what he did to me?" I ask. After a stubborn moment, Vixus nods. "And . . ." I laugh. It stretches like a crack in ice, spreading, widening, about to shiver a thousand different ways, till I bite my tongue to cut it short. "And . . . and still you have the balls to make me ask you twice?"

"She's alive."

"Reaper . . . they'll be coming for us. They'll know it's jammed," Holiday says, looking at the tiny camera node in the elevator's ceiling. "We can't change the plan."

"Where is she?" I twist the razor. "Where is she?"

Vixus hisses in pain. "Level 23, cell 2187. It would be wise not to kill me. You might put me in her cell. Escape. I will tell you the proper path, Darrow." The muscles and veins under the skin of his neck slither and rise like snakes under sand. No body fat to him. "Two backstabbing Praetorians won't get you far. There's an army in this mountain. Legions in the city, in orbit. Thirty Peerless Scarred. Boneriders in southern Attica." He nods to the small jackal skull on the lapel of his uniform. "You remember them?"

"We don't need him," Trigg snaps, fingering his gun's trigger.

"Oh?" Vixus chuckles, confidence returning as he sees my weakness. "And what are *you* going to do against an Olympic Knight, tinpot? Oh, wait. There are two here, aren't there?"

Holiday just snorts. "Same thing you'd do, goldilocks. Run."

"Level 23," I tell Trigg.

Trigg punches the gravLift controls, diverting us from their escape route. He pulls up a map on his datapad and studies it briefly with Holiday. "Cell 2187 is . . . here. There will be a code. Cameras."

"Too far from evac." Holiday's mouth tightens. "If we go that way, we're cooked."

"Victra is my friend," I say. And I thought she was dead, but somehow she survived her sister's gunshots. "I won't leave her."

"There's not a choice," Holiday says.

"There's always a choice." The words sound feeble, even to me.

"Look at yourself, man. You're a husk!"

"Back off him, Holi," Trigg says.

"That Gold bitch isn't one of us! I won't die for her."

But Victra would have died for me. In the darkness, I thought of her. The childish joy in her eyes when I gave her the bottle of petrichor in the Jackal's study. "I didn't know. Darrow, I didn't know," was the last thing she said to me after Roque betrayed us. Death around, bullets in her back, and all she wanted was me to think well of her in the end.

"I won't leave my friend behind," I repeat dogmatically.

"I'll follow you," Trigg drawls. "Whatever you say, Reaper. I'm your man."

"Trigg," Holiday whispers. "Ares said—"

"Ares hasn't turned the tide." Trigg nods to me. "He can. We go where he goes."

"And if we miss our window?"

"Then we make a new one."

Holiday's eyes go glassy and she works her large jaw. I know that look. She doesn't see her brother as I do. He's no lurcher, no killer. To her he's the boy she grew with.

"All right. I'm in," she says reluctantly.

"What about the Peerless?" Trigg asks.

"He puts the code in and he lives," I say. "Shoot him if he tries anything."

We exit the elevator at level 23. I wear my hood again, having Holiday guide me along as Vixus walks ahead as if escorting us to a cell, Trigg ready with his gun close behind. The halls are quiet. Our footsteps echo. I can't see past the hood.

"This is it," Vixus says when we reach the door.

"Put in the code, asshole," Holiday orders.

He does and the door hisses open. Noise roars out around us. Horrible static from hidden speakers. The cell is freezing, everything bleached white. The ceiling flaring with light so bright I can't even look directly at it. The cell's emaciated occupant lies in the corner, legs curled up in a fetal position, spine to me. Back painted with old burns and striped with lash marks from beatings. The mess of white-blond hair over her eyes is all that shields the woman from the blazing light. I wouldn't know who she was except for the two bullet scars at the top of her spine between the shoulder blades.

"Victra!" I shout over the noise. She can't hear me. "Victra!" I shout again, just as the noise dies, replaced over the speakers by the sound of a heartbeat. They're torturing her with sound, light. Sensation. The exact opposite of my own abuse. Able to hear me now, she whips her head my direction. Gold eyes peering ferally out from the tangle of hair. I don't even know if she recognizes me. The boldness with which Victra wore her nakedness before is gone. She covers herself, vulnerable. Terrified.

"Get her on her feet," Holiday says, pushing Vixus to his belly. "We gotta go."

"She's paralyzed. . . ." Trigg says. "Isn't she?"

"Shit. We'll carry her, then."

Trigg moves quickly toward Victra. I slam a hand back into his chest, stopping him. Even like this, she could rip his arms from his body. Knowing the terror I felt when I was pulled from my hole, I move slowly toward her. My own fear retreating to the back of my mind, replaced by anger at what her own sister has done to her. At knowing this is my fault.

"Victra, it's me. It's Darrow." She makes no sign of having heard me. I crouch down beside her. "We're going to get you out of here. Can we lift—"

She lunges at me. Throwing herself forward with her arms. *"Take off your face,"* she screams, *"Take off your face."* She convulses as Holiday rushes forward and jams a thumper into the small of her back. The electricity isn't enough.

"Go down!" Holiday shouts. Victra hits her in the center of her duroplastic armor chest piece, launching the Gray meters back into the wall. Trigg fires two tranquilizers into her thigh from his ambi-rifle, a multipurpose carbine. They put her down quick. But still she pants on the ground, watching me through a slitted eye till she falls unconscious.

"Holiday . . ." I begin.

"I'm Golden." Holiday grunts, lifting herself up. The chest piece has a fist-sized dent in the center. "Pixie can hit," Holiday says, admiring the dent. "This armor is supposed to handle rail rounds."

"Julii genetics," Trigg mutters. He hoists Victra up on his shoulders and follows Holiday back out into the hall as she snaps at me to hurry after them. We leave Vixus belly-down in the cell. Alive, as I promised.

"We'll find you," he says, sitting up as I go to shut the door. "You know we will. Tell little Sevro we're coming. One Barca down. One to go."

"What did you say?" I ask.

I step suddenly back into the cell and his eyes light with fear. The same fear Lea must have felt those many years ago when I hid in the dark while Antonia and Vixus tortured her to lure me out. He laughed as her blood soaked into the moss. And as my friends died in the garden. He would have me spare him now so he could kill again later. Evil feeds on mercy.

My razor slithers into a slingBlade.

"Please," he begs now, thin lips trembling so that I see the boy in him too as he realizes he made a mistake. Someone somewhere still loves him. Remembers him as a mischievous child or asleep in a crib. If only he had stayed that child. If only we all had. "Have a heart. Darrow, you're no murderer. You're no Titus."

The heartbeat sound of the room deepens. White light silhouetting him.

He wants pity.

My pity was lost in the darkness.

The heroes of Red songs have mercy, honor. They let men live, as I let the Jackal live, so they can remain untarnished by sin. Let the villain be the evil one. Let him wear black and try to stab me as I turn my back, so I can wheel about and kill him, giving satisfaction without guilt. But this is no song. This is war.

"Darrow . . ."

"I need you to send a message to the Jackal."

I slash open Vixus's throat. And as he slumps to the ground pulsing out his life, I know he is afraid because nothing waits for him on the other side. He gurgles. Whimpers before he dies. And I feel nothing.

Beyond the heartbeat of the room, alarm sirens begin to wail.

5

||||||||||||||||||||||||

PLAN C

"Shit," Holiday says. "I told you we didn't have time."

"We're fine," Trigg says.

We're together in the elevator. Victra on the floor. Trigg, helping her into his black rain gear to give her a semblance of decency. My knuckles are white. Vixus's blood trickles over the inscribed image of children playing in the tunnels. It drips over my parents and stains Eo's hair red before I wipe it from the blade with my prisoner jumpsuit. I forgot how easy it is to take a life.

"Live for yourself, die alone," Trigg says quietly. "You think with all those brains, they'd have sense enough not to be such assholes." He looks over at me, brushing hair from flinty eyes. "Sorry to be a prick, sir. Y'know, if he was a friend . . ."

"Friend?" I shake my head. "He had no friends."

I bend down to brush Victra's hair from her face. She sleeps peacefully against the wall. Cheeks carved out from hunger. Lips thin and sad. There's a dramatic beauty to her features even now. I wonder what they did to her. The poor woman, always so strong, so brash, but always to cover the kindness inside. I wonder if any is left.

"Are you prime?" Trigg asks. I don't respond. "Was she your girl?"

"No," I say. I touch the beard that's grown on my face. I hate how it scratches and stinks. I wish Danto had shaved it off as well. "I'm not prime."

I don't feel hope. I don't feel love.

Not as I look at what they did to Victra, to me.

It's the hate that rides.

Hate too for what I've become. I feel Trigg's eyes. Know he's disappointed. He wanted the Reaper. And I'm just a withered husk of a man. I run my fingers against my cage of ribs. So many slender little things. I promised these Grays too much. I promised everyone too much, especially Victra. She was true to me. What was I to her but another person who wanted to use her? Another person her mother trained her to be prepared against.

"You know what we need?" Trigg asks.

I look up at him intensely. "Justice?"

"A cold beer."

A laugh explodes out of my mouth. Too loud. Scaring me.

"Shit," Holiday murmurs, hands flying over the controls. "Shit. Shit. Shit . . ."

"What?" I ask.

We're stuck between the 24th and 25th. She punches buttons but suddenly the lift jerks upward. "They've overridden the controls. We're not going to make it to the hangar. They're redirecting us. . . ." She lets out a long breath as she looks up at me. "To the first level. Shit. Shit. Shit. They'll be waiting with lurchers, maybe Obsidians . . . maybe Golds." She pauses. "They know you're in here."

I fight back the despair that rushes up from my belly. I won't go back. Whatever happens. I'll kill Victra, kill myself before I let them take us.

Trigg is hunched over his sister. "Can you hack the system?"

"When the hell do you think I learned how to do that?"

"I wish Ephraim was here. He could."

"Well, I'm not Ephraim."

"What about climbing out?"

"If you want to be a skid mark."

"Guess that leaves one option. Eh?" He reaches into his pocket. "Plan C."

"I hate Plan C."

"Yeah, well. Time to embrace the suck, babydoll. Unpack the heathen."

"What's Plan C?" I ask quietly.

"Escalation." Trigg activates his comlink. Codes flash over his screen as he connects to a secure frequency. "Outrider to Wrathbone, do you register? Outrider to—"

"*Wrathbone registers,*" a ghostly voice echoes. "*Request clearance code Echo. Over.*"

Trigg references his datapad. "13439283. Over."

"*Code is green.*"

"We need secondary extraction in five. Got the princess plus one at stage two."

There's a pause on the other line, the relief in the voice palpable even through the static. "*Late notice.*"

"Murder ain't exactly punctual."

"*Be there in ten. Keep him alive.*" The link goes dead.

"Goddamn amateurs," Trigg mutters.

"Ten minutes," Holiday repeats.

"We've been in worse shit."

"When?" He doesn't answer her. "Should have just gone to the goddamn hangar."

"What can I do?" I ask, sensing their fear. "Can I help?"

"Don't die," Holiday says as she slides off her backpack. "Then this is all for shit."

"You gotta drag your friend," Trigg says as he starts picking tech off his body except his armor. He pulls two more antique weapons from his pack—two pistols to complement the high-powered gas ambi-rifle. He hands me a pistol. My hand shakes. I haven't held a gunpowder weapon since I was sixteen training with the Sons. They're vastly inefficient and heavy, and their recoil makes them wildly inaccurate.

Holiday pulls a large plastic box from her pack. Her fingers pause over the latches.

She opens the plastic box to reveal a metal cylinder with a spinning ball of mercury at its center. I stare at the device. If the Society caught her carrying it, she'd never see daylight again. Vastly illegal. I eye the gravLift's display on the wall. Ten levels to go. Holiday grips a remote control for the cylinder. Eight levels.

Will Cassius be waiting? Aja? The Jackal? No. They would be on their ship, preparing for dinner. The Jackal would be living his life. They won't know the alarm is for me. And even when they do, they'll be delayed. But there's enough to fear even without one of them coming. An Obsidian could rip these two apart with his bare hands. Trigg knows. He closes his eyes, touching his chest at four points to make a cross. A wedding band glints softly in the low light. Holiday minds the gesture, but doesn't do the same.

"This is our profession," she says quietly to me. "So swallow your pride. Stay behind us and let Trigg and I work."

Trigg cracks his neck and kisses his gloved left ring finger. "Stay close. Nut to butt, sir. Don't be shy."

Three levels to go.

Holiday readies a gas rifle in her right hand and chews intensely on her gum, left thumb on the remote control. One level to go. We're slowing. Watching the double doors. I loop Victra's legs in my armpits.

"Love you, kiddo," Holiday says.

"Love you too, babydoll," Trigg murmurs back, voice tight and mechanical now.

I feel more afraid than I did when I lay encased in a starShell in the chamber of a spitTube before my rain. Not just afraid for me, but for Victra, for these two siblings. I want them to live. I want to know about South Pacifica. I want to know what pranks they pulled on their mother. If they had a dog, a home in the city, the country . . .

The gravLift wheezes to a halt.

The door light flashes. And the thick metal doors that separate us from a platoon of the Jackal's elite hiss open. Two glowing stunGrenades zip in and clamp to the walls. *Beep. Beep.* And Holiday pushes the device's button. A deep implosion of sound ruptures the elevator's quiet as an invisible electromagnetic pulse ripples out from the spherical EMP at our feet. The grenades fizzle dead. Lights go black in the elevator, outside it. And all the Grays waiting beyond the door with their hi-tech pulse weapons, and all the Obsidians in their heavy armor with their electronic joints and helmets and air filtration units, are slapped in the face with the Middle Ages.

But Holiday and Trigg's antiques still work. They stalk forward out of the elevator into the stone hall, hunched over their weapons like evil gargoyles. It's slaughter. Two expert marksmen firing short bursts of archaic slugs at point-blank range into squads of defenseless Grays in wide halls. There is no cover to take. Flashes in the corridor. Gigantic sounds of high-powered rifles. Rattling my teeth. I freeze in the elevator till Holiday shouts at me, and I rush after Trigg, hauling Victra behind me.

Three Obsidians go down as Holiday lobs an antique grenade. *Whooomph.* A hole opens in the ceiling. Plaster rains. Dust. Chairs and Coppers fall through the hole from the room above, crashing down into the fray. I hyperventilate. A man's head kicks back. Body spins to the ground. A Gray flees for cover down a stone hall. Holiday shoots her in the spine. She sprawls like a child slipping on ice. Movement everywhere. An Obsidian charges from the side.

I fire the pistol, aim horrible. The bullets skitter off his armor. Two hundred kilograms of man raises an ionAxe, its battery dead, but edge still keen. He ululates his kind's throaty war chant and red mist geysers from his helmet. Bullet through the skull-helm's eye socket. His body pitches forward, slides. Nearly knocks me off my feet. Trigg's already moving to the next target, driving metal into men as patiently as a craftsman driving nails into wood. No passion there. No art. Just training and physics.

"Reaper, move your ass!" Holiday shouts. She jerks me down a hall away from the chaos as Trigg follows, hurling a sticky grenade onto the thigh of an unarmored Gold who dodges four of his rifle shots. *Whoomph.* Bone and meat to mist.

The siblings reload on the run and I just try not to faint or fall. "Right in fifty paces, then up the stairs!" Holiday snaps. "We've got seven minutes."

The halls are eerily quiet. No sirens. No lights. No whir of heated air through the vents. Just the clunk of our boots and distant shouts and the cracking of my joints and the rasping of lungs. We pass a window. Ships, black and dead, fall through the sky. Small fires burn where others have landed. Trams grind to a halt on magnetic rails. The only lights that still run are from the two most distant peaks. Reinforcements with tech will soon respond, but they won't know what caused this. Where to look. With camera systems and biometric scanners dead, Cassius and Aja won't be able to find us. That might save our lives.

We run up the stairs. A cramp eats into my right calf and hamstring. I grunt and almost fall. Holiday takes most of my weight. Her powerful neck pressing up against my armpit. Three Grays spot us from behind at the bottom of the long marble stairs. Shoving me aside, she takes two down with her rifle, but the third fires back. Bullets chewing into marble.

"They've got gas backups," Holiday barks. "Gotta move. Gotta move."

Two more rights, past several lowColors, who stare at me, mouths agape, through marble halls with towering ceilings and Greek statues, past galleries where the Jackal keeps his stolen artifacts and once showed me Hancock's declaration and the preserved head of the last ruler of the American Empire.

Muscles burning. Side splitting.

"Here!" Holiday finally cries.

We reach a service door in a side hall and push through into cold daylight. The wind swallows me. Icy teeth ripping through my jumpsuit as the four of us stumble out onto a metal walkway along the side of the Jackal's fortress. To our right, the stone of the mountain surrenders to the modern metal-and-glass edifice above. It's a thousand-meter drop to our left. Snow swirls around the mountain's face. Wind howls. We push forward along the walkway till it circles part of the fortress and links with a paved bridge that extends from the mountain to an abandoned landing platform like a skeletal arm holding out a concrete dinner plate covered in snow.

"Four minutes," Holiday hollers as she helps me struggle across the bridge toward the landing pad. At the end, she dumps me onto the ground. I set Victra down beside me. A hard skin of ice makes the concrete slick and smoky gray. Snowdrifts gather around the waist-high concrete wall that fences in the circular landing pad from the thousand-meter drop.

"Got eighty in the long mag, six in the relic," he calls to his sister. "Then I'm out."

"Got twelve," she says, tossing down a small canister. It pops and green smoke swirls into the air. "Gotta hold the bridge."

"I've got six mines."

"Plant them."

He sprints back down the bridge. At the end of it is a set of closed blast doors, much larger than the maintenance path we took from the side. Shivering and snowblind, I pull Victra close to me against that wall to escape the wind. Snowflakes gather atop the black rain gear she wears. Fluttering down like the ash that fell when Cassius, Sevro, and I burned Minerva's citadel and stole their cook. "We'll be fine," I tell her. "We'll make it." I peer over the short concrete wall to the city beneath. It's oddly peaceful. All her sounds, all her troubles silenced by the EMP. I watch a flake of snow larger than the rest drift on the wind and come to rest on my knuckle.

How did I get here? A boy of the mines now a shivering fallen war-lord staring down at a darkened city, hoping against everything that he can go home. I close my eyes, wishing I was with my friends, my family.

"Three minutes," Holiday says behind me. Her gloved hand touches my shoulder protectively as she looks to the sky for our enemies. "Three minutes and we're out of here. Just three minutes."

I wish I could believe her, but the snow has stopped falling.

6

||||||||||||||||||||||||||

VICTIMS

I squint up past Holiday as an iridescent defensive shield ripples into place over the seven peaks of Attica, cutting us off from the clouds and the sky beyond. The shield generator must have been out of the EMP's blast range. No help will come to us from beyond it.

"Trigg! Get back here!" she shouts as he plants the last mine on the bridge.

A single gunshot shatters the winter morning. Echoing brittle and cold. More follow. *Crack. Crack. Crack.* Snow kicks around him. He sprints back as Holiday leans to cover for him, her rifle rocking her shoulder. Straining, I push myself up. My eyes ache as they try to focus in the sun's light. Concrete explodes in front of me. Shards rip into my face. I duck down, shivering in fear. The Jackal's men have found their backup weapons.

I peer out again. Through squinting lids, I see Trigg pinned down halfway to us, exchanging gunfire with a squad of Grays carrying gas-powered rifles. They pour out of the fortress's blast doors, now opened at the opposite end of the bridge. Two go down. Two more step near a proximity mine and disappear in a cloud of smoke as Trigg shoots it at their feet. Holiday picks another off just as Trigg staggers back into cover, hit with a round in the shoulder. He jams a stimshot into his thigh and pops back up. A bullet slaps into the concrete in front of me, kicks up into Holiday to impact her ribs just under the armpit of her body armor with a meaty thud.

She spins down. Bullets force me to crouch beside her. Concrete rains. She spits blood and there's a wet, phlegmy echoing to her breath.

"It's in my lung," she gasps as she fumbles with a stimshot from her leg pouch. Were the circuits of her armor not fried, meds would inject automatically. But she has to crack open the case and pull a dose manually. I help, pulling free one of the micro-syringes and injecting her in the neck. Her pupils dilate and her breath slows as the narcotic drifts through her blood. Beside me, Victra's eyes are closed.

The gunfire stops. Carefully, I peek out. The Jackal's Grays hide behind concrete walls and pylons across the bridge, some sixty meters away. Trigg reloads. The wind is the only sound. Something's wrong. I search the sky, fearing the quiet. A Gold is coming. I can feel it in the battle's pulse.

"Trigg!" I shout till my body shudders. "Run!"

Holiday sees the look on my face. She struggles up, wheezing in pain as Trigg abandons his cover, boots slipping on the ice-slicked bridge. He falls and gains his feet, scrambling toward us, terrified. Too late. Behind him, Aja au Grimmus rips out of the fortress's door, past the Grays, past the Obsidians who lurk in the shadows. She's in her black formal jacket. Her long legs reel Trigg in now. It's one of the saddest sights I've ever seen.

I fire my pistol. Holiday unloads her rifle. We hit nothing but air. Aja sidesteps, twists, and, when Trigg is ten paces from us, spears him through the torso with her razor. Metal glistens wetly from his sternum. Shock widens his eyes. His mouth makes a quiet gasp. And he screams as he's hauled into the air. Pried upward by Aja's razor like a twitching pond frog on the end of a makeshift spear.

"*Trigg* . . ." Holiday whispers.

I stumble forward, toward Aja, pulling my razor, but Holiday jerks me back behind the wall as bullets from the distant Grays rip into the concrete around us. Her blood melts the snow under her. "Don't be stupid," she snarls, dragging me to the ground with the last of her strength. "We can't help him."

"He's your brother!"

"He's not the mission. You are."

"Darrow!" Aja calls from the bridge. Holiday peers out where Aja stands with her brother, her face bloodless and quiet. The knight holds Trigg up on the end of her razor with one hand. Trigg wriggles on the blade. Sliding down it toward her grip. "My goodman, the time for hiding behind others is over. Come out."

"Don't," Holiday murmurs.

"Come out," Aja says. And she tosses Trigg off her blade over the side of the bridge. He falls two hundred meters before his body splits against a granite ledge below.

Holiday makes a sick choking sound. She brings up her empty rifle and pulls the trigger a dozen times in Aja's direction. Aja ducks before realizing Holiday's weapon is empty. I pull Holiday down as a sniper's bullet aimed at her chest slams into her gun, shattering it and kicking it from her grip, mangling a finger. We sit shivering, backs to concrete, Victra between us.

"I'm sorry," I manage. She doesn't hear me. Her hands shake worse than mine. No tears in her distant eyes. No color in her lined face.

"They'll come," she says after a hollow moment. Her eyes following the green smoke. "They have to." Blood leaks through her clothing and out the corner of her mouth before freezing halfway down her neck. She grips her boot knife and tries to rise, but her body is done. Breaths wet and thick, smelling like copper. "They'll come."

"What is the plan?" I ask her. Her eyes close. I shake her. "How will they come?"

She nods to the edge of the landing pad. "Listen."

"Darrow!" Cassius's voice calls over the wind. He's joined Aja. "Darrow of Lykos, come out!" His rich voice is unfit for this moment. Too regal and high and untouched by the sadness that swallows us. I wipe the tears from my eyes. "You must decide what you are in the end, Darrow. Will you come out like a man? Or must we dig you out like a rat from a cave?"

The anger tightens my chest, but I don't want to stand. Once I would have, when I wore the armor of Gold and thought I would tower over Eo's killer and reveal my true self as his cities burned and their Color fell. But that armor is gone. That mask of the Reaper gnawed away by doubt and darkness. I am just a boy, and I shiver and cower and hide from my enemy because I know the price of failure, and I am so very afraid.

But I will not let them take me. I will not be their victim, and I will not let Victra fall into their hands again.

"Slag this," I say. I grab Holiday's collar and Victra's hand and, eyes flashing with the strain, blinded by the sun on the snow, face numb, I drag them with all my strength from our hiding place across the landing pad to the far edge where the wind roars.

There's silence from my enemies.

The sight I must make—a tottering, withered form, dragging my friends, sunken eyes, face like that of a starving old demon, bearded and ridiculous—is pitiful. Twenty meters behind me, the two Olympic Knights stand imperious on the bridge where it meets the landing pad, flanked by more than fifty Grays and Obsidians who have come from the citadel doors behind him. Aja's silver razor drips blood. But it's not her weapon. It's Lorn's, the one she took from his corpse. My toes throb inside my wet slippers.

Their men seem so tiny against the face of the vast mountain fortress. Their metal guns so petty and simple. I look to the right, off the bridge. Kilometers away, a flight of soldiers rises from a distant mountain peak where the EMP did not reach. They bank toward us through a low cloud layer. A ripWing follows.

"Darrow," Cassius calls to me as he walks forward with Aja off the bridge onto the pad. "You cannot escape." He watches me, eyes unreadable. "The shield is up. Sky blocked. No ships can come from beyond to retrieve you." He looks to the green smoke swirling from the canister on the landing pad into the winter air. "Accept your fate."

The wind howls between us, carrying flakes of snow stripped from the mountain.

"Dissection?" I ask. "Is that what you think I deserve?"

"You're a terrorist. What rights you had, you've given up."

"Rights?" I snarl over Victra and Holiday. "To pull my wife's feet?

To watch my father die?" I try to spit, but it sticks to my lips. "What gives you the right to take them?"

"There's no debate here. You are a terrorist, and you must be brought to justice."

"Then why are you talking with me, you bloodydamn hypocrite?"

"Because honor still matters. *Honor is what echoes.*" His father's words. But they are as empty on his lips as they feel in my ears. This war has taken everything from him. I see in his eyes how broken he is. How terribly hard he is trying to be his father's son. If he could, he would choose to be back by the campfire we made in the highlands of the Institute. He would return to the days of glory when life was simple, when friends seemed true. But wishing for the past doesn't clean the blood from either of our hands.

I listen to the groaning wind from the valley. My heels reach the end of the landing pad. There's nothing but air behind me. Air and the shifting topography of a dark city on the valley floor two thousand meters below.

"He's going to jump," Aja says quietly to Cassius. "We need the body."

"Darrow . . . don't," Cassius says, but his eyes are telling me to jump, telling me to take this way out instead of surrendering, instead of going to Luna to be peeled apart. This is the noble way. He's putting his cape over me again.

I hate him for it.

"You think you're honorable?" I hiss. "You think you're good? Who is left that you love? Who do you fight for?" Anger creeps into my words. "You are *alone*, Cassius. But I am not. Not when I faced your brother in the Passage. Not when I hid among you. Not when I lay in darkness. Not even now." I grip Holiday's unconscious body as hard as I can, looping my fingers inside the straps of her body armor. Clutch Victra's hand. My heels scrape the concrete's edge. "Listen to the wind, Cassius. Listen to the bloodydamn wind."

The two knights tilt their heads. And still they do not understand the strange groaning sound that drifts up from the valley floor, because how would a son and daughter of Gold ever know the sound of a clawDrill gnawing through rock? How would they guess that my people would come not from the sky, but from the heart of our planet?

"Goodbye, Cassius," I say. "Expect me." And I push off the ledge with both legs, flinging myself backward into open air, dragging Holiday and Victra into thin air.

7

||||||||||||||||||||||||

BUMBLEBEES

We fall toward a molten eye in the center of the snow-covered city. There, among rows of manufacturing plants, buildings shiver and tip as the ground swells upward. Pipes crack and spin into the air. Steam hisses through ruptured asphalt. Gas explosions ripple out in a corona, threading lines of fire through streets that buckle and heave, as if Mars itself were stretching six stories high to give birth to some ancient leviathan. And then, when the ground and city can stretch no more, a clawDrill erupts out into the winter air—a titanic metal hand with molten fingers that steam and grasp and then vanish as the clawDrill sinks back into Mars, pulling half a city block with it.

We're falling too fast.

Jumped too soon. I lose my grip on Victra.

Ground rushing up to us.

Then the air cracks with a sonic boom.

Then another. And another, till a whole chorus resounds out from the darkness of the clawDrill-carved tunnel as it gives birth to a small army. Two, twenty, fifty armored shapes in gravBoots scream up out of the tunnel toward us. To my left, my right. Painted blood-red, pouring pulsefire skyward behind us. My hair stands on end and I smell ozone. Superheated munitions ripple blue from friction as they tear through air molecules. Miniguns mounted on shoulders vomit death.

Amidst the rising Sons of Ares, a crimson, armored man with the spiked helmet of his father zips forward and catches Victra seconds before she impacts on the roof of a skyscraper. The howling of wolves babbles from his helmet's speakers. It's Ares himself. My best friend in all the worlds has not forgotten me. He has come with his legion of empire breakers and terrorists and renegades: the Howlers. A dozen metal men and women with black wolfcloaks kicking in the wind fly behind him. The largest of them in pure white armor with blue hand-prints covering the chest and arms. His black cloak is stained with a red stripe down the middle. For a moment I think it's Pax come back from the dead for me. But when the man catches me and Holiday, I see the glyphs drawn in the blue paint of the handprints. Glyphs from the south pole of Mars. It is Ragnar Volarus, prince of the Valkyrie Spires. He tosses Holiday to another Howler and pushes me behind him so I can wrap my arms around his neck, digging my fingers into the rivets of his armor. Then he banks through the smoking valley city toward the tunnel, shouting to me: *"Hold fast, little brother."*

And he dives. Sevro to the left, clutching Victra, Howlers all around, their gravBoots screaming as we plummet into the darkness of the tunnel's mouth. The enemy pursues. The sounds are horrible. Screaming of wind. Rupture of rock as pulsefire rips into the walls behind us and weapons warble. My jaw rattles against Ragnar's metal shoulder. His gravBoots vibrate at full burn. Bolts from the armor dig into my ribs. The battery pack above his tailbone slams into my groin as we weave and dart through pitch black. I'm riding a metal shark deeper and deeper into the belly of an angry sea. My ears pop. Wind whistles. A pebble slams into my forehead. Blood streams down my face, stinging my eyes. The only light the glowing of boots and the flash of weapons.

The skin of my right shoulder flares with pain. Pulsefire from our pursuers misses me by inches. Still, my skin bubbles and smokes, lighting my jumpsuit's sleeve on fire. The wind kills the flames. But the pulsefire rips past again and boils into the Son's gravBoots just ahead of me, melting the man's legs into a single chunk of molten metal. He jerks in the air, slamming into the ceiling, where his body crumples. Helmet ripping off and spinning straight toward me.

Red light throbs through my eyelids. There's smoke in the air. Meaty. Stings the back of the throat. Fat tissue charred and crispy. Chest hot with pain. A swamp of screams and howls and cries for mother all around. And something else. The sound of bumblebees in my ears. Someone's above me. See them in the red light as I open my eyes. Screaming into my face. Pressing a mask to my mouth. A damp wolf-cloak dangles from a metal shoulder, tickling my neck. Other hands touch mine. The world vibrates, tilts.

"Starboard! Starboard!" someone screams in the distance, as if underwater.

We're on a ship. I'm surrounded by dying men. Burned, twisted husks of armor. Smaller men atop them, bent like vultures, saws glowing in their hands as they peel the armor away, trying to free those dying of their burns inside. But the armor's melted tight. A hand touches mine. A boy lying beside me. Eyes wide. Armor blackened. The skin of his cheeks is young and smooth beneath the soot and blood. His mouth not yet creased by smiles. His breaths come shorter, quicker. He mouths my name.

And he's gone.

8

||||||||||||||||||||||

HOME

I'm alone, far away from the horror, standing weightless and clean on a road that smells of moss and earth. My feet touch the ground, but I cannot feel it underfoot. To either side stretches the grass of wind-beaten moors. The sky flashes with lightning. My hands are without Sigils and drift along the cobbled wall that meanders on ahead to either side. When did I start walking? Somewhere in the distance, wood smoke rises. I follow the road, but I feel I have no choice. A voice calls to me from beyond a hill.

> *Oh tomb, O marriage chamber, hollowed out*
> *house that will watch forever, where I go.*
> *To my own people, who are mostly there;*
> *Persephone has taken them to her.*
> *Last of them all, ill-fated past the rest,*
> *shall I descend, before my course is run.*
> *Still when I get there I may hope to find*
> *I come as a dear friend to my dear father*
> *To you, my mother, and my brother too.*

All three of you have known my hand in death
I wash your bodies . . .

It is my uncle's voice. Is this the Vale? Is this the road I walk before death? It can't be. In the Vale there is no pain, but my body aches. My legs sting. Still I hear his voice ahead of me, drawing me through the mist. The man who taught me to dance after my father died, who guarded me and sent me to Ares. Who died himself in a mineshaft and dwells now in the Vale.

I thought it would be Eo who greeted me. Or my father. Not Narol.

"Keep reading," another voice whispers. "Dr. Virany said he can hear us. He just has to find his way back." Even as I walk, I feel a bed under me. The air around cold and crisp in my lungs. The sheets soft and clean. The muscles in my legs twitch. Feels like little bees are stinging them. And with each sting, the dream world fades and I slide back into my body.

"Well, if we're gonna read to the squabber, might as well be something Red. Not this poncy Violet shit."

"Dancer said this was one of his favorites."

My eyes open. I'm in a bed. White sheets, IVs going into my arms. Under the sheets, I touch the ant-sized nodes that have been stuck to my legs to channel electrical current through my muscles to combat atrophy. The room's a cave. Scientific equipment, machines, and terraria litter it.

It was Uncle Narol I heard in the dream after all. But he's not in the Vale. He's alive. He sits at my bedside, squinting down at one of Mickey's old books. He's grizzled and wiry, even for a Red. Callused hands trying to be gentle with the frail paper pages. He's bald now, and deeply sunburned on his forearms and the back of his neck. Still looks like he was cobbled together out of cracked old leather. He'll be forty-one now. Looks older. More savage. A brooding danger to him, lent teeth by the railgun in his thigh holster. A slingBlade has been sewn onto his black military jacket above a Society logo that's been peeled off and inverted. Red at the top. Gold the foundation.

The man's been at war.

Beside him sits my mother. A bent, fragile woman since her stroke.

How many times did I imagine the Jackal standing over her, pliers in hand? She's been safe the whole time. Her crooked fingers weave needle and thread through tattered socks, patching the holes. They don't move like they used to. Age and infirmity have slowed her. Her broken body is not what she is on the inside. There she stands tall as any Gold, broad as any Obsidian.

Watching her sit there breathing quietly, intent on her task, I want to protect her more than anything else in the world. I want to heal her. Give her all she never had. I love her so much, I don't know what to say. What to do that can ever show her how much she means to me. "Mother . . ." I whisper.

They look up. Narol frozen in his chair. My mother setting a hand on his and rising slowly to my bedside. Her steps slow, wary. "Hello, child."

She stands above me, overwhelming me with the love in her eyes. My hand is almost larger than her head, but I gently touch her face as if to prove to myself she is real. I trace the crow's-feet from her eyes to the gray hair at her temples. As a boy, I did not like her as much as I liked father. She would hit me at times. She would weep alone and pretend nothing was wrong. And now all I want is to listen to her hum as she cooks. All I want are those still nights where we had peace and I was a child.

I want the time back.

"I'm sorry . . . ," I find myself saying. "I'm so sorry . . ."

She kisses my forehead and rocks her head against mine. She smells like rust and sweat and oil. Like home. She tells me I am her son. There is nothing to apologize for. I am safe. I am loved. The family is here. Kieran, Leanna, their children. Waiting to see me. I sob uncontrollably, sharing all the pain my solitude forced me to hoard. The tears a deeper language than my tongue can afford. I'm exhausted by the time she kisses me again on the head and pulls back. Narol comes to her side and puts a hand on my arm. "Narol . . ."

"Hello, you little bastard," he says roughly. "Still your father's son, eh?"

"I thought you were dead," I say.

"Nah. Death chewed on me a bit. Then spat my bloody ass back out. Said there was killing that needed doin' and some wild blood of mine that needed savin'." He grins down at me. That old scar on his lips joined by two new ones.

"We've been waiting for you to wake up," Mother says. "It's been two days since they brought you back in the shuttle."

I can still taste the smoke from burned flesh in the back of my throat.

"Where are we?" I ask.

"Tinos. The city of Ares."

"Tinos . . . ," I whisper. I sit up quickly. "Sevro . . . Ragnar . . ."

"They're alive," Narol grunts, pushing me back down. "Don't rip out your tubes and resFlesh. Took Dr. Virany hours to thread you up after that bloody mess of an escape. Boneriders were supposed to be in EMP radius. They weren't. They ripped us to pieces in the tunnels. Ragnar's the only reason you're living."

"You were there?"

"Who do you think lead the drillteam that punched up into Attica? It was Lykos blood, Lambda and Omicron."

"And what about Victra?"

"Easy, boy." He sets his hand on my chest to stop me from trying to get up again. "She's with the doc. Same for the Gray. They're alive. Getting patched."

"You need to check me, Narol. Tell the doctors to check me for radiation trackers. For implants. They might have let me go on purpose, to find Tinos. . . . I need to see Sevro."

"Oy! I said easy," Narol says sharply. "We checked you. Two implants were in you. But both fried in the EMP. You weren't tracked. And Ares ain't here. He's still out with the Howlers. Came back just to deliver the wounded and scarf down grub." There were almost a dozen wolfcloaks. So he's recruited. Thistle betrayed us, but Vixus mentioned Pebble and Clown. Wonder if Screwface is with them too.

"Ares is always on the move," mother says.

"Lots to do. Only one Ares," Narol replies defensively. "They're still out looking for survivors. They'll be back soon. By morning, luck holds." My mother shoots him a harsh look and he shuts up.

I lean back in the bed, overwhelmed by speaking to them. By seeing them. I can barely form sentences. So much to say. So much unfamiliar emotion running through me. All I end up doing is sitting there, breathing fast. My mother's love fills the room, but still I feel the darkness moving beyond this moment. Pressing in on this family I thought I lost and now fear I cannot protect. My enemies are too great. Too many. And I too weak. I shake my head, running my thumb over her knuckles.

"I thought I would never see you again."

"Yet here you are." Somehow she makes it sound cold. So like my mother to be the one with dry eyes when both the men can barely speak. I always wondered how I survived the Institute. It damn well wasn't because of my father. He was a gentle man. Mother is the spine in me. The iron. And I clutch her hand as if such a simple gesture could say all that.

A light knock comes at the door. Dancer pokes his head in. Devilishly handsome as ever, he's one of the only Reds alive who makes old age look good. I can hear his foot dragging slightly behind him in the hall. Both my mother and uncle nod to him in deference. Narol steps aside respectfully as he approaches my bedside, but my mother stays put. "This Helldiver's not done yet, it would seem." Dancer grips my hand. "But you gave us a hell of a scare."

"It's bloodydamn good to see you, Dancer."

"And you, boy. And you."

"Thank you. For taking care of them." I nod to my mother and uncle. "For helping Sevro . . ."

"It's what family is for," he says. "How are you?"

"My chest hurts. And everything else."

He laughs lightly. "It should. Virany says that crank the Nakamuras gave you almost killed you. You had a heart attack."

"Dancer, how did the Jackal know? Every day I've wondered. Picked it apart. The clues I left him. Did I give myself up?"

"It wasn't you," Dancer says. "It was Harmony."

"Harmony . . ." I whisper. "She wouldn't . . . she hates Gold." But even as I say it, I know how reckless her hate is. How vengeful she must have felt after I did not detonate the bomb she gave me to kill the Sovereign and the others on Luna.

"She thinks we've sold out the rebellion," Dancer says. "That we're compromising too much. She told the Jackal who you were."

"He knew when I was in his office. When I gave him the gift . . ."

He nods tiredly. "Your presence proved her claims. So the Jackal let us rescue her and the others. We brought her back to base, and an hour before his kill squads came, she disappeared."

"Fitchner is dead because of her. He gave her a purpose . . . I understand how she could betray me, but him? Ares?"

"She found out he was a Gold. Then she gave him up. Must have given the Jackal the base's coordinates." Ares was her hero. Her god. After her children died in the mines he gave her a reason to live, a reason to fight. And then she discovered he was the enemy, and she got him killed. It crushes me to think that's why he died.

Dancer surveys me quietly. It's clear I'm not what he expected. Mother and Narol watch him almost as carefully as they watch me, deducing the same.

"I know I'm not what I was," I say slowly.

"No, boy. You've been through hell. It's not that."

"Then what is it?"

He exchanges a look with my mother. "You're sure?"

"He needs to know. Tell him," she says. Narol nods too.

Dancer hesitates still. He looks for a chair. Narol rushes to pull one out for him and set it near the bed. Dancer nods his thanks and then leans over me, making a steeple of his fingers. "Darrow, you've gone too long with people hiding things from you. So I want to be very transparent from here forward. Until five days ago, we thought you were dead."

"I was close enough."

"No. No, I mean we stopped looking for you nine months ago."

My mother's hand tightens on mine.

"Three months after you were captured, the Golds executed you on the HC for treason. They dragged a boy identical to you out to the steps of the citadel in Agea and read off your crimes. Pretending you were still a Gold. We tried to free you. But it was a trap. We lost thousands of men." His eyes drift over my lips, my hair. "He had your eyes, your scars, your bloodydamn face. And we had to watch as the Jackal cut off your head and destroyed your obelisk on Mars Field."

I stare at them, not fully comprehending.

"We grieved for you, child," Mother says, voice thin. "The whole clan, city. I led the Fading Dirge myself and we buried your boots in the deeptunnels beyond Tinos."

Narol crosses his arms, trying to seal himself off from the memory. "He was just like you. Same walk. Same face. Thought I had watched you die again."

"It was likely a fleshMask or they Carved someone, or digital effects," Dancer explains. "Doesn't matter now. The Jackal killed you as an Aureate. Not as a Red. Would have been foolish for them to reveal your identity. Would have handed us a tool. So instead you died just another Gold who thought he could be king. A warning."

The Jackal promised he would hurt those I love. And now I see how deeply he has. My mother's façade has broken. All the grief she's kept inside thickens behind her eyes as she stares down at me. Guilt straining her face.

"I gave up on you," she says softly, voice cracking. "I gave up."

"It's not your fault," I say. "You couldn't have known."

"Sevro did," she says.

"He never stopped looking for you," Dancer explains. "I thought he was mad. He said you weren't dead. That he could feel it. That he would know. I even asked him to give up the helm to someone else. He was too reckless searching for you."

"But the bastard found you," Narol says.

"Aye," Dancer replies. "He did. I was wrong in it. I should have believed in you. Believed in him."

"How *did* you find me?"

"Theodora designed an operation."

"She's here?"

"Working for us in intelligence. Woman's got contacts. Some of her informants in a Pearl Club caught word that the Olympic Knights were taking a package from Attica back to Luna for the Sovereign. Sevro believed *you* were that package, and he put a huge portion of our reserve resources behind this attack, burned two of our deep assets . . ."

As he speaks, I watch my mother stare distantly at a crackling lightbulb in the ceiling. What is this like for her? For a mother to see her child broken by other men? To see the pain written in scars on his skin, spoken in silences, in far-off looks. How many mothers have prayed to see their sons, their daughters return from war only to realize the war has kept them, the world has poisoned them, and they'll never be the same?

For nine months, Mother has grieved for me. Now she's drowning in guilt for giving up and desperation in hearing the war swallow me again, knowing she's helpless to stop it. In the past years, I've trampled over so many to get what I think I want. If this is my last chance at life, I want to do it right. I need to.

". . . But now the real problem isn't materiel, it's manpower we need. . . ."

"Dancer . . . stop," I say.

"Stop?" He frowns in confusion, glancing at Narol. "What's wrong?"

"Nothing's wrong. But I'll talk with you in the morning about this."

"The morning? Darrow, the world is shifting under your feet. We've lost control over the other Red factions. The Sons will not last the year. I have to give you a debriefing. We need you back. . . ."

"Dancer, I am alive," I say, thinking of all the questions I want to ask, about the war, my friends, how I was undone, about Mustang. But that can wait. "Do you even know how lucky I am? To be able to see you all again in this world? I haven't seen my brother or my sister in years. So tomorrow I'll listen to your debriefing. Tomorrow the war can have me again. But tonight I belong to my family."

I hear the children before we reach the door. I feel a guest in someone else's dream. Unfit for the world of children. But I've little say in the matter as Mother pushes my wheelchair forward into a cramped dormitory cluttered with metal bunks, children, the smell of shampoo, and noise. Five of the children of my blood, fresh from the showers by the looks of their hair and the little sandals on the floor, are scrumming on one of the bunks, two taller nine-year-olds holding an alliance against two six-year-olds and a tiny little cherub of a girl who keeps head-butting the biggest boy in the leg. He hasn't yet noticed her. The sixth child in the room I remember from when I visited Mother in Lykos. The little girl who couldn't sleep. One of Kieran's. She watches the other children over her glossy book of fables from another bunk and is the first to notice me.

"Pa," she calls back, eyes wide. "Pa . . ."

Kieran bursts up from his game of dice with Leanna when he sees me. Leanna's slower behind him. "Darrow," he says, rushing to me and stopping just before my wheelchair. He's bearded now too. In his midtwenties. No slump to his shoulders like there used to be. His eyes radiate a goodness that I used to think made him a little foolish, now it just seems wildly brave. Remembering himself, he waves his children forward. "Reagan, Iro, children. Come meet my little brother. Come meet your uncle."

The children line up awkwardly around him. A baby laughs from the back of the room and a young mother rises from her bunk where she was breastfeeding the child. "Eo?" I whisper. The woman's a vision of the past. Small, face the shape of a heart. Her hair a thick, tangled mess. The sort that frizzes on humid days, like Eo's did. But this is not Eo. Her eyes are smaller, her nose elfin. More delicacy here than fire. And this is a woman, not a girl like my wife was. Twenty years old now, by my count.

They all stare at me strangely.

Wondering if I am mad.

Except Dio, Eo's sister, whose face splits with a smile.

"I'm sorry, Dio," I say quickly. "You look . . . just like her."

She doesn't allow it to be awkward, hushing my apologies. Saying it's the kindest thing I could have said. "And who's that, then?" I ask of the baby she holds. The little girl's hair is absurd. Rust red and bound together by a hair tie so it sticks straight up on top of her head in a little antenna. She watches me excitedly with her dark red eyes.

"This little thing?" Dio asks, coming closer to my chair. "Oh, this is someone I've been wanting to introduce to you since Deanna told us you were alive." She looks lovingly to my brother. I feel a pang of jealousy. "This is our first. Would you like to hold her?"

"Hold her?" I say. "No . . . I'm . . ."

The girl's pudgy little hands reach for me, and Dio pushes the girl into my lap before I can recoil. The girl clings to my sweater, grunting as she turns and wriggles around till she's seated according to her liking on my leg. She claps her hands together and laughs. Completely unaware of what I am. Of why my hands are so scarred. Delighted by the size of them and the Gold Sigils, she grabs my thumb and tries to bite it with her gums.

Her world is alien to the horrors I know. All the child sees is love. Her skin is pale and soft against mine. She's made of clouds and I of stone. Her eyes large and bright like her mother's. Her demeanor and thin lips like Kieran's. Were this another life, she might have been my child with Eo. My wife would have laughed to think it would be my brother and her sister together in the end and not us. We were a little storm that couldn't last. But maybe Dio and Kieran will.

Long after the lights have dimmed throughout the complex to ease the burdens on the generators, I sit with my uncle and brother around the table in the back of the room, listening to Kieran tell me his new duties learning from Oranges how to service ripWings and shuttles. Dio went to bed long ago, but she left me the baby, who now sleeps in my arms, shifting here and there as her dreams take her wherever they may.

"It's really not that wretched here," Kieran is saying. "Better than the stacks below. We have food. Water showers. No more flushes! There's a lake above us, they say. Bloodydamn dazzling stuff, the showers. Children love it." He watches his children in the low light. Two to a bed, shifting quietly as they sleep. "What's hard is not knowing what'll be for them. Will they ever mine? Work in the webbery? I always thought they would. That I was passing something down, a mission, a craft. You hear?" I nod. "I guess I wanted my sons to be helldivers. Like you. Like Pa. But . . ." He shrugs.

"There's nothin' to that now that you got eyes," Uncle Narol says. "It's a hollow life when you know you're being stepped on."

"Aye," Kieran replies. "Die by thirty, so those folk can live to a hundred. It ain't bloodydamn right. I just want my children to have more than this, brother." He stares at me intensely and I remember how my mother asked me what comes after revolution. What world are we making? It was what Mustang asked. Something Eo never considered. "They have to have more than this. And I love Ares as much as anyone. I owe him my life. The lives of my children. But . . ." He shakes his head, wanting to say more but feeling the weight of Narol's eyes on him.

"Go on," I say.

"I don't know if he knows what comes next. That's why I'm glad you're back, little brother. I know you've got a plan. I know you can save us."

He says it with so much faith, so much trust.

"Of course I've a plan," I say, because I know it's what he needs to hear. But as my brother contentedly refills his mug, my uncle catches my eye and I know he sees through the lie and we both feel the darkness pressing in.

9

||||||||||||||||||||||||

THE CITY OF ARES

I t's early morning as I sip coffee and eat a bowl of grain cereal my mother fetched me from the commissary. I'm not yet ready for crowds. Kieran and Leanna have already gone to work, so I sit with Dio and Mother as the children dress for school. It's a good sign. You know a people have given up when they stop teaching their children. I finish my coffee. Mother pours me more.

"You took an entire pot?" I ask.

"The chef insisted. Tried to give me two."

I sip from the cup. "It's almost like the real thing."

"It is the real thing," Dio says. "There's this pirate who sends us hijacked goods. Coffee's from Earth, I think. Jamaca, they said."

I don't correct her.

"Oy!" a voice screams in the hallways. My mother jumps at the sound. "Reaper! Reaper! Come out and play-e-ay!" There's a crash in the hall and the sound of stomping boots.

"Remember, Deanna told us to knock," says a thunderous voice.

"You are so annoying. Fine." A polite knock comes at the door. "Tidings! It's Uncle Sevro and the Moderately Friendly Giant."

My mother motions to one of my excited nieces. "Ella, do us kind." Ella darts forward to open the door for Sevro. He bursts through, scooping her up. She shrieks with joy. He's in his undersuit, a black sweat-wicking fabric that soldiers wear under pulse armor. Sweat rings stain the armpits. His eyes dance as he sees me, and he tosses Ella roughly onto a bed and charges toward me, arms outstretched. A weird laugh escapes his chest, hatchet face split with a jagged grin. His hair a dirty, sweat-soaked Mohawk.

"Sevro, careful!" my mother says.

"Reap!" He slams into me, spinning my chair sideways, clacking my teeth together, as he half lifts me out of the chair, stronger than he was, smelling of tobacco and engine fuel and sweat. He half laughs, half cries like an excited dog into my chest. "I knew you were alive. I bloodydamn knew it. Pixie bitches can't fool me." Pulling back, he looks down at me with a rickshaw grin. "You bloodydamn bastard."

"Language!" my mother snaps.

I wince. "My ribs."

"Oh, shit, sorry brotherman." He lets me sink back into the chair, and kneels so we're eye to eye. "I said it once. Now I'll say it twice. If there's two things in this world that can't be killed, it's the fungus under my sack and the Reaper of bloodydamn Mars. Haha!"

"Sevro!"

"Sorry, Deanna. Sorry."

I pull back from him. "Sevro. You smell . . . terrible."

"I haven't showered in five days," he brags, grabbing his groin. "It's a Sevro soup in here, boyo." He puts his hands on his hips. "You know, you look . . . erm . . ." He glances at my mother and tames his tongue. "Bloody terrible."

A shadow falls over the room as a man enters and blocks the overhead light near the door. The children cluster joyously around Ragnar so he can barely walk.

"Hello, Reaper," he says over their shouts.

I greet Ragnar with a smile. His face is as impassive as ever. Tattooed and pale, callused from the wind of his arctic home, like the hide of a rhinoceros. His white beard is braided into four strands, and the hair on his head shaved except for a tail of white that is braided with red ribbons. The children are asking him if he's brought them presents.

"Sevro." I lean forward. "Your eyes . . ."

He leans in close. "Do you like 'em?" Buried in that squinting, sharp-angled face, his eyes are no longer that dirty shade of Gold, but are now as red as Martian soil. He pulls back his lids so I can better see. They're not contacts. And the right is no longer bionic.

"Bloodydamn. Did you get Carved?"

"By the best in the business. Do you like 'em?"

"They're bloodydamn marvelous. Fit you like a glove."

He punches his hands together. "Glad you said that. Cuz they're yours."

I blanch. "What?"

"They're yours."

"My what?"

"Your eyes!"

"My eyes . . ."

"Did yon Friendly Giant drop you on your head in the rescue? Mickey had your eyes in a cryobox at his joint in Yorkton—creepy place, by the by—when we raided it for supplies to bring back to Tinos to help the Rising. I figured you weren't usin' 'em, so . . ." He shrugs awkwardly. "So I asked if he'd put 'em in. You know. Bring us closer together. Something to remember you by. That's not so weird, right?"

"I told him it was odd," Ragnar says. One of the girls is climbing his leg.

"Do you want the eyes back?" Sevro asks, suddenly worried. "I can give them back."

"No!" I say. "It's just I forgot how crazy you are."

"Oh." He laughs and slaps my shoulder. "Good. I thought it was something serious. So I'm prime keeping them?"

"Finders keepers," I say with a shrug.

"Deanna of Lykos, may we borrow your son for martial matters?" Ragnar asks my mother. "He has much to do. Many things to know."

"Only if you return him in one piece. And you take some coffee with you. And bring these socks to the laundry." My mother pushes a bag of freshly patched socks into Ragnar's arms.

"**As you wish.**"

"What about the presents?" one of my nephews asks. "Didn't you bring any?"

"I've got a present for you . . ." Sevro says.

"Sevro, no!" Dio and my mother shout.

"What?" He pulls out a bag. "It's just candy this time."

". . . and that's when Ragnar tripped over Pebble and fell out the back of the transport," Sevro cackles. "Like a dumbass." He's eating a candy bar over my head as he pushes my wheelchair recklessly through the stone corridor. He sprints fast again and hops on the back to coast till we swerve into the wall. I wince in pain. "So Ragnar falls straight into the sea. Thing was at full chop, man. Waves the size of torch-ships. So I dive in too, thinking he needs my help, just in time for this huge . . . I dunno what the hell you'd call it. Some Carved beasty . . ."

"**Demon,**" Ragnar says from behind. I hadn't noticed him following. "**It was a sea demon from the third level of Hel.**"

"Sure." Sevro guides me around a corner, clipping the wall hard enough to make me bite my tongue, and sending a cluster of Sons pilots scattering. They stare after me as we trundle on. "This sea"—he looks back at Ragnar—"demon apparently thinks Ragnar is a tasty-looking morsel, so he gobbles him up almost as soon as he hits the water. So I see this, and I'm laughing my ass off with Screwface, as one would because it's bloodydamn hilarious, and you know how Screwface loves a good joke. But then the beasty dives. So I follow. And I'm chasing it, shooting my pulseFist at a bloodydamn sea"—he looks at Ragnar again—"*demon* as it swims to the bottom of the damn Thermic Sea. Pressure's building. My suit's wheezing. And I think I'm about to die, when suddenly Ragnar cuts his way out of the scaly bitch." He leans close. "But guess where he came out? Come on. Guess. Guess!"

"Sevro, did he come out the sea demon's rectum?" I ask.

Sevro squeals with laughter. "He did! Right out the ass. Shot like a turd—" My chair rolls to a stop. His voice cut short, followed by a thump and sliding sound. My wheelchair rolls forward again. I look back and see Ragnar pushing it innocently along. Sevro isn't in the hallway behind us. I frown, wondering where he went, till he bursts out of a side passage.

"You! Troll!" Sevro shouts. "I'm a terrorist warlord! Stop throwing me. You made me drop my candy!" Sevro looks at the floor of the hallway. "Wait. Where is it? Dammit, Ragnar. Where is my peanut bar? You know how many people I had to kill to get that. Six! Six!" Ragnar chews quietly above me, and though I'm probably mistaken, I think I see him smile.

"Ragnar, have you been brushing your teeth? They look splendid."

"Thank you," he preens as much as a man eight feet tall can preen past a mouthful of peanut butter bar. "The wizard removed my old ones. They pained me greatly. These are new. Are they not fine?"

"Mickey, the wizard," I confirm.

"Indeed. He also taught me to read before he left Tinos." Ragnar proves this by reading every single sign and warning we pass in the hall till we enter the hangar bay some ten minutes later. Sevro follows behind, still complaining about his lost candy. The hangar is cramped by Society standards, but is still nearly thirty meters high and sixty wide. It's been cut into the rock by laser drills. The floor is stone, blasted black from engines. Several dilapidated shuttles sit in berths beside three shining new ripWings. Reds directed by two Oranges service the ships and stare at me as we wheel past. I feel an outsider here.

A motley group of soldiers ambles away from a battered shuttle. Some are still in armor with their wolfcloaks hanging from their shoulders. Others are stripped down to their undersuits or go bare-chested.

"Boss!" Pebble cries from under Clown's arm. She's as plump as ever, and she grins at me, hauling Clown along to move faster. His puffy hair is matted with sweat, and he leans on the shorter girl. Both their faces are bright when they approach, as if I were exactly as they remembered. Pebble shoves Clown off her shoulder to give me a hug. Clown, for his part, gives a ludicrous bow.

"Howlers reporting for duty, Primus," he says. "Sorry about the kerfuffle."

"Shit got prickly," Pebble explains before I can speak.

"Exceedingly prickly. Something different about you, Reaper." Clown puts his hands on his hips. "You look . . . slender. Did you trim your hair? Don't tell me. It's the beard . . . terribly slimming."

"Kind of you to notice," I say. "And to stay, considering everything."

"What, you mean you lying to us for five years?"

"Yes, that," I say.

"Well . . ." Clown says, about to light into me. Pebble thumps his shoulder.

"Of course we'd stay, Reaper!" she says sweetly. "This our family . . ."

"But we have demands. . . ." Clown continues, wagging a finger. "If you desire our full services. But . . . for now, we must be off. I fear I have shrapnel in my ass. So I beg your leave. Come, Pebble. To the surgeons."

"Bye, boss!" Pebble says. "Glad you're not dead!"

"Squad dinner at eight!" Sevro calls after them. "Don't be late. Shrapnel in your ass is not an excuse, Clown."

"Yes, sir!"

Sevro turns to me with a grin. "Sods didn't even bat an eye when I told them you were a ruster. Came with me and Rags to fetch your family right off. Was wicked telling them what was what, though. This way."

As we pass the ship Pebble and Clown exited, I see up the ramp into its belly. Two young boys work inside, blasting the floors with hoses. The water runs brownish red down the ramp onto the hangar deck, flowing not into a drain, but down a narrow trough toward the edge of the hangar, where it disappears over the edge.

"Some dads leave ships or villas for their sons. Asshat Ares left me this wretched hive of angst and peasantry."

"*Bloodydamn,*" I whisper as I realize what exactly I'm looking at.

Beyond the hangar is an inverted forest of stalactites. It glitters in

the artificial subterranean dawn. Not only from the water that dribbles along their slick gray surfaces, but from the lights of docks, barracks, and sensor arrays that give teeth to Ares's great bastion. Supply
ships flit between the multiple docks.

"We're in a stalactite." I laugh in wonder. But then I look down at
the horror beneath and the weight on my shoulders doubles. A hundred meters below our stalactite sprawls a refugee camp. Once it was
an underground city carved into the stone of Mars. The streets are so
deep between the buildings, they're more like miniature canyons. And
the city spills over the floor of the colossal cave to the far walls kilometers away, where more honeycombed homes have been built. Streets
switchback up the sandstone. But over that a new roofless city has
spawned. One of refugees. Muddled skin and fabrics and hair all
writhing like some weird, fleshy sea. They sleep on rooftops. In the
streets. On the switchback stairs. I see makeshift metal symbols for
Gamma, Omicron, Upsilon. All the twelve clans that they divide my
people into.

I'm stunned by the sight. "How many are there?"

"Shit if I know. At least twenty mines. Lykos was small compared
to some of the ones near the larger H-3 deposits."

Four hundred sixty-five thousand. According to the logs," Ragnar
says.

"Only half a million?" I whisper.

"Seems like a hell of a lot more, right?"

I nod. "Why are they here?"

"Had to give them shelter. Poor bastards all come from mines the
Jackal has purged. Pumping achlys-9 into the vents if he even suspects
a Sons presence. It's an invisible genocide."

A chill passes through me. "The Liquidation Protocol. Board of
Quality Control's last measure for compromised mines. How do you
keep this all a secret? Jammers?"

"Yeah. And we're more than two clicks underground. Pop altered
the topographical maps in the Society's database. To the Golds, this is
bedrock that was depleted of helium-3 more than three hundred years
ago. Clever enough, for now."

"And how do you feed everyone?"

"We don't. I mean, we try, but there haven't been rats in Tinos for a month. People are sleeping toe to nose. We've started moving refugees into the stalactites. But disease is already ripping through the people. Don't have enough meds. And I can't risk my Sons getting sick. Without them. We don't have teeth. We're just a sick cow waiting to be slaughtered."

"**And they rioted,**" Ragnar says.

"Rioted?"

"Yeah, almost forgot about that. Had to cut rations by half. They were already so small. Those ungrateful shitheads down there didn't like that much."

"**Many lost their lives before I descended.**"

"The Shield of Tinos," Sevro says. "He's more popular than I am, that's for damn sure. They don't blame him for shit rations. But I'm more popular than Dancer, because I have a badass helmet and he's in charge of the nitty-gritty shit I can't do. People are so stupid. Man breaks his back for them and they think he's a dull-wit pennypincher. Least the Sons love him—and your uncle."

"It's like we've fallen back a thousand years," I say hopelessly.

"Pretty much, except for the generators. There's a river that runs underneath the stone. So there's water, sanitation, power, sometimes. And . . . there's lecherous shit too. Crime. Murders. Rapes. Theft. We have to keep the Gamma slags separate from everyone else. Some Omicrons hanged this little Gamma kid last week and carved the Gold Sigil into his chest, ripped the Red Sigils out of his arms. They said he was a loyalist, a goldy. He was fourteen."

I feel sick.

"**We keep the lights bright. Even at night.**"

"Yeah. Turn them off, it gets . . . otherworldy downstairs." Sevro looks tired as he stares down at the city. My friend knows how to fight, but this is another battle entirely.

I stare down at the city, unable to find the words I need to say. I feel like a prisoner who spent his whole life digging through the wall, only to break through and find he's dug into another cell. Except there will always be another cell. And another. And another. These people are not living. They're all just trying to postpone the end.

"This is not what Eo wanted," I say.

"Yeah . . . well." Sevro shrugs. "Dreaming's easy. War isn't." He chews on his lip thoughtfully. "You see Cassius at all?"

"Twice, at the end. Why?"

"Oh, nothing." He turns to me, eyes glittering. "It's just that he's the one who put Pops down."

10

||||||||||||||||||||||

THE WAR

66 "Our Society is at war . . ." Dancer tells me in the Sons of Ares command room. The facility is domed, skinned in rock and illuminated by pale bluish lights above, and a corona of computer terminals that glow around a central holographic display. He stands to the side of the display drenched in the blue light of Mars's Thermic Sea. With us is Ragnar, several older Sons I don't recognize, and Theodora, who greeted me with the graceful kiss on the lips popular in Luna's highColor circles. Elegant even in black utility pants, she has an air of authority in the room. Like my Howlers, she was not invited by Augustus to the garden after the Triumph. Not important enough, thank Jove. Sevro sent Pebble to get her out of the Citadel as soon as it all went down. She's been with the Sons ever since, helping Dancer's propaganda and intelligence wings.

"... Not just the Rising against Gold forces here and our other cells across the System. But *among* Gold itself. After they killed Arcos and Augustus, as well as their staunchest supporters at your Triumph, Roque and the Jackal made a coordinated play to seize the navy in orbit. They feared Virginia or the Telemanuses would rally the ships of the Golds murdered in the garden. Virginia did, not just with her father's own ships, but with those of Arcos, under the command of three of his daughters-in-law. It came to battle around Deimos. And Roque's fleet, even outnumbered, crushed Mustang's and sent them into flight."

"She's alive, then," I say, knowing they're wary of how I'd react to knowing the information.

"Yeah," Sevro says, watching me carefully, as do the rest. "Far as we know, she's alive." Ragnar seems about to say something, but Sevro cuts him off. "Dancer, show him Jupiter."

My eyes linger on Ragnar as Dancer waves his hand and the holographic display warps to show the great marbled gas giant of Jupiter. Surrounding it are the sixty-three smaller asteroidlike satellites and the four great moons of Jupiter—Europa, Io, Ganymede, and Calisto.

"The purge instituted by the Jackal and Sovereign was an impressive operation that spanned not just the thirty assassinations of the garden, but over three hundred other assassinations across the Solar System. Most carried out by Olympic Knights or Praetorians. It was proposed and designed by the Jackal to eliminate the Sovereign's key enemies on Mars, but also Luna and throughout the Society. It worked well, very well. But one grand mistake was made. In the garden, they killed Revus au Raa and his nine-year-old granddaughter."

"The ArchGovernor of Io," I say. "Sending a message to the Moon Lords?"

"Yes, but it backfired. A week after the Triumph, the children of the Moon Lords whom the Sovereign keeps on Luna as wards to ransom their parents' loyalty escaped. Two days after that, the heirs of Raa stole the entirety of *Classis Saturnus*. The whole Eighth fleet garrison in its dock at Calisto with the help of the Cordovans of Ganymede.

"The Raas declared Io's independence for the Moons of Jupiter, their new alliance with Virginia au Augustus and the heirs of Arcos, and their war on the Sovereign."

"A Second Moon Rebellion. Sixty years after the burning of Rhea," I say with a slow smile, thinking of Mustang at the head of an entire planetary system. Even if she left me, even if there's that hollowness in the pit of my stomach when I think of her, this is good news for us. We're not the Sovereign's sole enemy. "Did Uranus and Saturn join? Neptune surely did."

"All did."

"All? Then there's hope. . . ." I say.

"Yeah, you'd think. Right?" Sevro mutters.

Dancer explains. "The Moon Lords also made a mistake. They expected the Sovereign would find herself mired on Mars and would be plagued with lowColor insurrection in the Core. So they assumed she would not be able to send a fleet of sufficient size six hundred million kilometers to quash their rebellion for at least three years."

"And they were dead wrong," Sevro mutters. "The idiots. Got caught with their panties down."

"How long did it take for her to send a fleet?" I ask. "Six months?"

"Sixty-three days."

"That's impossible, the logistics on fuel alone . . ." My voice trails away as I remember the Ash Lord was on the way to reinforce House Bellona in orbit around Mars before we took the planet. He was weeks away then. He must have continued out to the Rim, following Mustang the entire way.

"You should know better than anyone the efficiency of the Society Navy. They're a war machine," Dancer says. "Logistics and systems of operation are perfect. The longer the Rim had to prepare, the harder it would have been for the Sovereign to wage a campaign. The Sovereign knew that. So the whole Sword Armada deployed straightaway to Jupiter orbit, and they've been there for nearly ten months."

"Roque did a nasty," Sevro says. "Snuck ahead of the main fleet and jacked that moonBreaker old Nero tried to steal last year."

"He stole a moonBreaker."

"Yeah. I know. He's named it the *Colossus* and chosen it as his flagship. The ponce. It's a nasty piece of hardware. Makes the *Pax* look tiny by comparison."

The holo above shows the Sovereign's fleet coming upon Jupiter, where the moonBreaker waits to welcome them. The days and weeks and months of war speed past.

"The scope of it . . . is manic," Sevro says. "Each fleet twice again as large as the coalition you summoned to pound the Bellona . . ." He says more, but I'm lost watching the months of war speed past, realizing how the worlds kept turning without me.

"Octavia wouldn't have used the Ash Lord," I say distantly. "If he even went past the asteroid belt, there would be no reconciliation. The Rim would never surrender. So who leads them? Aja?"

"Roque au Buttsucking Fabii," Sevro sneers.

"He leads the entire fleet?" I ask in surprise.

"I know, right? After the Siege of Mars and the Battle of Deimos, he's a bloodydamn godchild to the Core. Regular Iron Gold pulled from annals past. Never mind you snuck in under his nose. Or he was a joke at the Institute. He's good at three things. Whining, stabbing people in the back, and destroying fleets."

"They call him the Poet of Deimos," Ragnar says. **"He is undefeated in battle. Even against Mustang and her titans. He is very dangerous."**

"Fleet warfare is not her game," I say. Mustang can fight. But she's always been more a political creature. She binds people together. But raw tactics? That's Roque's province.

The warlord in me mourns having been kept away for so long. For having missed such a spectacle as that of the Second Moon Rebellion. Sixty-seven moons, most militarized, four with populations more than one hundred million. Fleet battles. Orbital bombardments. Asteroid hopping assault maneuvers with armies in mech suits. It would have been my playground. But the man in me knows if I hadn't been in the box, this room would be missing people.

I realize I'm internalizing too much. I force myself to communicate.

"We're running out of time. Aren't we?"

Dancer nods. "Last week, Roque took Calisto. Only Ganymede and Io hold strong. If the Moon Lords capitulate then that navy and the Legions with it return here to aid the Jackal against us. We will be the sole focus of the united military might of the Society, and they will eradicate us."

That was why Fitchner hated bombs. They bring the eyes, wake the giant.

"So what about Mars? What about our war? Hell, what is our war?"

"It's a bloodydamn mess is what it is," Sevro says. "It spilled over into open war about eight months ago. The Sons have stayed tight. Don't know where Orion is. Dead, we reckon. The *Pax* and your ships are gone. And now we've got paramilitary armies that aren't Sons-affiliated rising up in the north, massacring civilians and in turn getting wiped out by Legion airborne units. Then there's mass strikes and protests in dozens of cities. The prisons are overflowing with political prisoners, so they're relocating them to these makeshift camps where we know for a fact that they are pullin' mass executions."

Dancer pulls up some of the holos, so I see blurry images of what look like large prisons in the desert and forest. They zoom in on low-Colors disembarking transports at gunpoint and filing into the concrete structures. It switches to a view of rubble-strewn streets. Men with masks and Red armbands firing over the smoking remains of city trams. A Gold lands among them. The image cuts out.

"We been hitting them hard as we can," Sevro says. "Gotten some hardcore business done. Stole a dozen ships, two destroyers. Demolished the Thermic Command Center . . ."

"And now they're rebuilding it," Dancer says.

"Then we'll destroy it again," Sevro snaps.

"When we can't even hold a city?"

"These Reds are not warriors." Ragnar interrupts the two. **"They can fly ships. Shoot guns. Lay bombs. Fight Grays. But when a Gold arrives, they melt away."**

A deep silence follows his words. The Sons of Ares are guerilla fighters. Saboteurs. Spies. But in this war, Lorn's words haunt me. "How do sheep kill a lion? By drowning him in blood."

"Every civilian death on Mars is blamed on us," Theodora says eventually. "We kill two in a bombing of a munitions manufacturing plant, they say we killed a thousand. Every strike or demonstration, Society agents infiltrate the crowd masquerading as demonstrators to shoot at Gray officers or detonate suicide vests. Those images are dispersed to the media circus. And when the cameras are off, Grays break into homes and make sympathizers disappear. MidColors.

LowColor. Doesn't matter. They contain the dissent. In the north, like Sevro said, it's open rebellion."

"A faction called Red Legion is massacring every highColor they find," Dancer says darkly. "Old friend of ours has joined their leadership. Harmony."

"Fitting."

"She's poisoned them against us. They won't take our orders, and we've stopped sending them weapons. We're losing our moral high ground."

"The man with voice and violence controls the world," I murmur.

"Arcos?" Theodora asks. I nod. "If only he were here."

"I'm not sure he'd help us."

"Lamentably, it seems as if voice doesn't exist without violence," the Pink says. She folds a leg over the other. "The greatest weapon a rebellion has is its *spiritus*. The spirit of change. That little seed that finds a hope in the mind and flourishes and spreads. But the ability to plant that idea, and even the idea itself, has been taken from us. The message stolen. We are voiceless."

When she speaks, the others listen. Not to humor her like Golds would, but as if her position was nearly equal to Dancer's.

"None of this makes any sense," I say. "What sparked open war? The Jackal didn't publicize killing Fitchner. He would have wanted it quiet as he purged the Sons. What was the catalyst? And also, you say we're voiceless. But Fitchner had a communication network that could broadcast to the mines, to anywhere. He pushed Eo's death to the masses. Made her the face of the Rising. Did the Jackal take it out?" I look around at their concerned faces. "What aren't you telling me?"

"You didn't tell him already?" Sevro asks. "The hell were you doing when I was gone, picking your asses?"

"Darrow wanted to be with his family," Dancer says sharply. He turns to me with a sigh. "Much of our digital network was destroyed during the Jackal's purges in the month after Ares was killed and you were captured. Sevro was able to warn us before the Jackal's men hit our base in Agea. We went to ground, saved materiel, but lost massive amounts of manpower. Thousands of Sons. Trained operators. The next three months we spent trying to find you. We hijacked a transport going to Luna, but you weren't on it. We searched the prisons. Issued bribes. But you'd disappeared, like you never existed. And then the Jackal executed you on the steps of the citadel in Agea."

"I know all this."

"Well, what you don't know is what Sevro did next."

I look to my friend. "What did you do?"

"What I had to." He takes control of the hologram and wipes Jupiter away, replacing it with me. Sixteen years old. Scrawny and pale and naked on a table as Mickey stands over me with his buzzsaw. A chill trickles down my spine. But it's not even my spine. Not really. It belongs to these people. To the revolution. I feel . . . used as I realize what he's done.

"You released it."

"Damn right," Sevro says nastily, and I feel all their eyes settling on me, now understanding why my blade is painted on the roofs of Tinos's refugees. They all know I was once a Red. They know one of their own conquered Mars in an Iron Rain.

I started the war.

"I released your Carving to every mine. To every holoSite. To every millimeter of this bloodydamn Society. The Golds thought they could kill you off. That they could beat you and make your death mean nothing. I'll be damned if I'd let that happen." He thumps his hand on a table. "Damned if I'd let you disappear facelessly into the machine like my mother. There's not a Red on Mars that doesn't know your name, Reap. Not a single person in the digital world who doesn't know that a Red rose to become a prince of the Golds, to conquer Mars. I made you a myth. And now that you're back from the dead, you're not just a martyr. You're the bloodydamn messiah the Reds have been waiting for their entire lives."

11

|||||||||||||||||||||||||

MY PEOPLE

I sit with my legs dangling off the edge of the hangar, watching the city beneath teem with life. The clamor of a thousand hushed voices rises to me like a sea of leaves brushing together. The refugees know I'm alive. SlingBlades have been painted on walls. On roofs. The desperate silent cry of a lost people. For six years I've wanted to be back among them. But looking down, seeing their plight, remembering Kieran's words, I feel myself drowning in their hope.

They expect too much.

They don't understand that we can't win this war. Ares even knew we could never go toe-to-toe with Gold. So how am I supposed to lift them up? To show them the way?

I'm afraid, not just that I can't give them what they want. But that by releasing the truth, Sevro's burned the boat behind us. There's no going back for us.

So what does that mean for my family? For my friends and these people? I felt so overwhelmed by these questions, by Sevro's use of my Carving, that I stormed out without a word. It was petulant.

Behind me, Ragnar moves past my wheelchair and slides down next to me. Legs dangling off the edge like mine. His boots comically large. The breeze of a passing shuttle catches the ribbons in his beard. He says nothing, at ease with the silence. It makes me feel safe knowing he's here. Knowing he's with me. Like I thought I would feel near Sevro. But he's changed. Too much weight in that helm of Ares.

"When I was a boy, we always wanted to know who the bravest of us was," I say. "We'd sneak out of our homes at night and go down into the deeptunnels and stand with our backs to the darkness. You could hear the pitvipers if you were quiet. But you could never tell how close they were. Most boys would break and run after a minute, maybe five. I always stood the longest. Till Eo found out about our game." I shake my head. "Now I don't think I'd last a minute."

"Because you now know how much there is to lose."

Ragnar's black eyes hold the shadows of a vast history. Nearly forty, he's a man who was raised in a world of ice and magic, sold to the Gods to buy life for his people, and served as a slave longer than I've been alive. How much better does he understand life than I do?

"Do you still miss home? Your sister?" I ask.

"I do. I long for the early snow in the throes of summer, how it stuck to the fur of Sefi's boots as I carried her on my shoulders to see *Níðhǫggr* break through the spring ice."

Níðhǫggr was a dragon who lived under the world tree of the Old Norse societies and spent his days gnawing at the roots of Yggdrasil. Many Obsidian tribes believe he comes up from the deep waters of their sea to break the ice that blocks their harbors and open the veins of the pole for their spring raiding boats. In honor of him, they send the bodies of their criminals to the deep in a holiday called Ostara, the first day of true spring light.

"I sent friends to the Spires and the Ice to spread your word. To tell my people their gods are false. They are in bondage, and we will soon come to free them. They will know Eo's song."

Eo's song. It seems so fragile and silly now.

"I don't feel her anymore, Ragnar." I glance behind us to the Oranges and Reds who spare glances our direction as they work on the ripWings in the hangar. "I know they think I'm their link to her. But I lost her in the darkness. I used to think she was watching me. I used to talk to her. Now . . . she's a stranger." I hang my head. "So much of this is my fault, Ragnar. If I hadn't been so proud, I would have seen the signs. Fitchner would be alive. Lorn would be alive."

"You think you know the strands of fate?" He laughs at my arrogance. "You do not know what would have happened if they lived."

"I know I can't be what these people need."

He frowns. "And how would you know what they need when you are afraid of them? When you can't even look upon them?" I don't know how to answer. He stands abruptly and extends a hand to me. "Come with me."

The hospital was once a cafeteria. Rows of gurneys and makeshift beds now fill it along with coughs and solemn whispers as Red, Pink, and Yellow nurses in yellow scrubs move through the beds checking the patients. The back of the room is a burn ward, separated from the rest of the patients by plastic containment walls. A woman's screaming on the other side of the plastic, fighting a nurse as he tries to give her an injection. Two other nurses rush to subdue her.

I feel swallowed by the sterile sadness of the place. There's no gore. No blood dripping on the floor. But this is the aftermath of my escape from Attica. Even with a Carver as good as Mickey, they won't have the resources to mend these people. The wounded stare up at the stone ceiling wondering what life will be like now. That's what this feeling is in this room. Trauma. Not of flesh. But lives and dreams interrupted.

I'd retreat from the room, but Ragnar rolls me forward to the edge of a young man's bed. He watched me as I came in. His hair is short. His face plump and awkward with a prominent under bite.

"What's what?" I ask, my voice remembering the flavor of the mine.

He shrugs. "Just dancin' time away, hear?"

"I hear." I extend a hand. "Darrow . . . of Lykos."

"We know." His hands are so small he can't even wrap his fingers around mine. He chuckles at the ridiculousness of it. "Vanno of Karos."

"Night or day?"

"Dayshift, you pigger. I look like some saggy-faced night digger?"

"Well, you never know these days . . ."

"True enough. I'm Omicron. Third drillboy, second line."

"So that was your chaff I'd be dodging deep."

He grins. "Helldivers, always lookin' themselves in the eye." He makes a lewd motion with his hands. "Someone's gotta teach you to look up."

We laugh. "How much did it hurt?" he asks, nodding to me. At first I think he's asking about what the Jackal did. Then I realize he's referring to the Sigils on my hands. The ones I've tried to cover with my sweater. I unveil them now. "Manic shit, that." He flicks it with his finger.

I look around, suddenly aware that it's not just Vanno watching me. It's everyone. Even on the far side of the room in the burn unit Reds push themselves up in their beds to look at me. They can't see the fear inside. They see what they want. I glance at Ragnar, but he's busy speaking to an injured woman. Holiday. She nods to me. Grief still very much at home on her face for her lost brother. His pistol is on her bedside, his rifle leaning against the wall. The Sons recovered his body during the rescue so he could be buried.

"How much did it hurt?" I repeat. "Well, imagine falling into a clawDrill, Vanno. A centimeter at a time. First goes the skin. Then the flesh. Then bone. Easy stuff."

Vanno whistles and looks down at his missing legs with a tired, almost bored expression. "Didn't even feel this. My suit injected enough hydrophone to knock out one of them." He nods to Ragnar and draws air through his teeth. "And least I still got my prick."

"Ask him," a man beside him urges. "Vanno . . ."

"Shut up." Vanno sighs. "Boys have been wonderin'. Did you get to keep it?"

"Keep what?"

"*It.*" He looks at my groin. "Or did they . . . you know . . . make it proportionate?"

"You really want to know?"

"I mean . . . not for personal reasons. But I've got money riding on it."

"Well." I lean forward seriously. So do Vanno and his bedmates nearby. "If you really want to know, you should ask your mother."

Vanno stares at me intensely, then explodes into laughter. His bedmates laugh and spread the joke to the far edges of the room. And in that tiny moment, the mood shifts. The suffocating sterility cut through with amusement and crude jokes. Whispering suddenly seems ridiculous here. It fills me with energy to see the shifting tide and realize it's because of a single laugh. Instead of retreating from the eyes, from the room, I move away from Ragnar down the lines of cots to mingle more with the injured, to thank them, to ask where they're from and learn their names. And this is where I thank Jove that I've a good memory on me. Forget a man's name and he'll forgive you. Remember it, and he'll defend you forever.

Most call me sir or Reaper. And I want to correct them and tell them to call me Darrow, but I know the value of respect, of distance between men and leader. Because even though I'm laughing with them, even though they're helping heal what's been twisted inside me, they are not my friends. They are not my family. Not yet. Not until we have that luxury. For now, they are my soldiers. And they need me as much as I need them. I'm their Reaper. It took Ragnar to remind me. He favors me with an ungainly grin, so pleased to see me smiling and laughing with the soldiers. I've never been a man of joy or a man of war, or an island in a storm. Never an absolute like Lorn. That was what I pretended to be. I am and always have been a man who is made complete by those around him. I feel strength growing in myself. A strength I haven't felt in so long. It's not only that I'm loved. It's that they believe in me. Not the mask like my soldiers at the Institute. Not the false idol I built in the service of Augustus, but the man beneath. Lykos may be gone. Eo may be silent. Mustang a world away. And the Sons on the brink of extinction. But I feel my soul trickling back into me as I realize I am finally home.

|||||||||||

With Ragnar at my side I return to the command room where Sevro and Dancer are hunched over a blueprint. Theodora's in the corner exchanging correspondences. They turn as I enter, surprised to see the smile on my face and to see that I'm now standing. Not on my own, but with Ragnar's help. I left the chair in the hospital and had him guide me back to the command room I fled only an hour prior. I feel a new man. And I may not be what I was before the darkness, but perhaps I'm better for it. I have humility I didn't have before.

"I'm sorry for how I acted," I say to my friends. "This has been . . . overwhelming. I know you've done the best you can. Better than anyone could, given the circumstances. You've all kept hope alive. And you saved me. And you saved my family." I pause, making sure they know how much that means to me. "I know you didn't expect me to come back like this. I know you thought I'd come back with wrath and fire. But I'm not what I was. I'm just not," I say as Sevro tries to correct me. "I trust you. I trust your plans. I want to help in whatever way I can. But I can't help you like this." I hold up my thin arms. "So I need your help with three things."

"Always so dramatic," Sevro says. "What are your demands, Princess?"

"First I want to send an emissary to Mustang. I know you think she betrayed me, but I want her to know I'm alive. Maybe there's some chance it'll make a difference. That she'll help us."

Sevro snorts. "We already gave her the opportunity once. She almost killed you and Rags."

"But she did not," Ragnar says. "It is worth the risk, if she will help us. I will go as emissary so she does not doubt our intentions."

"Like hell," Sevro says. "You're one of the most wanted men in the System. Golds have shut down all unauthorized air traffic. And you won't last two minutes in a space port, even with a mask."

"We'll send one of my spies," Theodora says. "I have one in mind. She's good, and a hundred kilograms less conspicuous than you, Prince of the Spires. The girl's in a port city already."

"Evey?" Dancer asks.

"Just." Theodora looks my direction. "Evey's done her best to make amends for the sins of the past. Even ones that weren't hers. She's been very helpful. Dancer, I'll make the arrangements for travel and cover, if that's all right with you."

"It's all right," Sevro says quickly, though Theodora waits for Dancer to nod his agreement.

"Thank you," I say. "I also need you to bring Mickey back to Tinos."

"Why?" Dancer asks.

"I need him to make me into a weapon again."

Sevro cackles. "Now we're talking. Get some man-killing meat on your bones. No more of this anorexic scarecrow shit."

Dancer shakes his head. "Mickey's half a thousand clicks away in Varos, working on his little project. He's needed there. You need calories. Not a Carver. In the state you're in, it could be dangerous."

"Reap can handle it. We can get Mickey and his equipment here by Thursday," Sevro says. "Virany has been consulting with him anyway about your condition. He'll be tickled Pink to see you."

Dancer watches Sevro with strained patience. "And the last request?"

I grimace. "I have a feeling you're not gonna like this one."

12

||||||||||||||||||||||||

THE JULII

I find Victra in an isolated room with several Sons guarding the door. She lies with her feet sticking off the edge of a medical cot, watching a holo at the foot of her bed as Society news channels drone on about the valiant Legion attack on a terrorist force that destroyed a dam and flooded the lower Mystos River Valley. The flooding has forced two million Brown farmers out of their homes. Grays deliver aid packages from the backs of military trucks. Easily could have been Reds who blew up the dam. Or it could have been the Jackal. At this point, who knows?

Victra's white-gold hair is bound in a tight ponytail. Every limb, even the paralyzed legs, is cuffed to the bed. Not much trust here for her kind. She doesn't look up at me as the holo story kicks over to a profile on Roque au Fabii, the Poet of Deimos and the newest heart-throb of the gossip circuit. Searching through his past, conducting interviews with his Senator mother, his teachers before the Institute, showing him as a boy on their country estate.

"Roque always found the natural world to be more beautiful than cities," his mother says for the camera. "It's the perfect order in nature that he so admired. How it formed effortlessly into a hierarchy. I think that's why he loved the Society so dearly, even then. . . ."

"That woman would look much better with a gun in her mouth," Victra mutters, muting the sound.

"She's probably said his name more in the last month than she did his entire childhood," I reply.

"Well, politicians never let a popular family member go to waste. What was it Roque once said about Augustus at a party? 'Oh, how the vultures flock to the mighty, to eat the carcasses left in their wake.' " Victra looks at me with her flashing, belligerent eyes. The madness I saw in them earlier has retreated but not vanished entirely. It lingers like mine. "Might as well have been talking about you."

"That's fair," I say.

"Are you leading this little pack of terrorists?"

"I had my chance to lead. I made a mess of it. Sevro is in charge."

"Sevro." She leans back. "Really?"

"Is that funny?"

"No. For some reason I'm not surprised at all, actually. Always had a bigger bite than bark. First time I saw him, he was kicking Tactus's ass."

I step closer. "I believe I owe you an explanation."

"Oh, hell. Can't we skip this part?" she asks. "It's boring."

"Skip it?"

She sighs heavily. "Apologies. Recrimination. All the trifling shit people muddle through because they're insecure. You don't owe me an explanation."

"How do you figure?"

"We all enter a certain social contract by living in this Society of ours. My people oppress your tiny kind. We live off the spoils of your labor. Pretending you don't exist. And you fight back. Usually very poorly. Personally, I think that's your right. It's not good or evil. But it's fair. I'd applaud a mouse that managed to kill an eagle, wouldn't you? Good for it.

"It's absurd and hypocritical for Golds to complain now simply because the Reds finally started fighting well." She laughs sharply at my surprise. "What, darling? Did you expect me to scream and rant and piss on about honor and betrayal like those walking wounds, Cassius and Roque?"

"A little," I say. "I would. . . ."

"That's because you're more emotional than I am. I'm a Julii. Cold runneth through my veins." She rolls her eyes when I try to correct her. "Don't ask me to be different because you need validation, please. It's beneath the both of us."

"You've never been as cold as you pretend to be," I say.

"I've existed long before you ever came into my life. What do you really know of me? I am my mother's daughter."

"You're more than that."

"If you say so."

There's no artifice to her. No coy manipulation. Mustang's all smirks and subtle plays. Victra's a wrecking ball. She softened before the Triumph. Let her guard down. But now it's back and it's as alienating as when I first met her. But the longer we speak, the more I see her hair is shot with gray, not just pale Gold. Her cheeks are hollow, her right hand, the one on the opposite side of the cot, clenching the sheets.

"I know why you lied to me, Darrow. And I can respect it. But what I don't understand is why you saved me in Attica. Was it pity? A tactic?"

"It's because you're my friend," I say.

"Oh, please."

"I would rather have died trying to get you out of that cell than let you rot in there. Trigg did die getting you out."

"Trigg?"

"One of the Grays who were behind me when we came into your cell. The other one is his sister."

"I didn't ask to be saved," she says bitterly, her way of washing her hands of Trigg's death. She looks away from me now. "You know Antonia thought we were lovers, you and I. She showed me your Carving. She taunted me. As if it would disgust me to see what you are. To see where you came from. To see how I had been lied to."

"And did it?"

She sneers. "Why would I care what you were? I care about what people do. I care about truth. If you had told me, I wouldn't have done a single thing differently. I would have protected you." I believe her. And I believe the pain in her eyes. "Why didn't you tell me?"

"Because I was afraid."

"But I wager you told Mustang?"

"Yes."

"Why her and not me? I at least deserve that."

"I don't know."

"It's because you're a liar. You said I wasn't wicked in the hall. But you think it deep down. You never trusted me."

"No," I say. "I didn't. That's my mistake. And my friends have paid for it with their lives. That . . . that guilt was my only company in the box he kept me in for the nine months." By the look in her eyes I know she didn't know what had been done to me. "But now I've been given a second chance at life, I don't want to waste it. I want to make amends with you. I owe you a life. I owe you justice. And I want you to join us."

"Join you?" she says with a laugh. "As a Son of Ares?"

"Yes."

"You're serious." She laughs at me. Another defense mechanism. "I'm not really into suicide, darling."

"The world you know is gone, Victra. Your sister has stolen it from you. Your mother and her friends have been wiped out. Your house is now your enemy. And you're an outcast from your own people. That is the problem with this Society. It eats its own. It pits us against one another. You have nowhere to go. . . ."

"Well, you really know how to make a girl feel special."

". . . I want to give you a family that will not stab you in the back. I want to give you a life with meaning. I know you're a good person, even if you laugh at me for saying it. But I believe in you. Yet . . . all that doesn't matter—what I believe, what I want. What matters is what you want."

She searches my eyes. "What I want?"

"If you want to leave here, you can. If you want to stay in this bed, you can. Say what you want and it's yours. I owe you that."

She thinks for a moment. "I don't care about your rebellion. I don't care about your dead wife. Or about finding a family or finding meaning. I want to be able to sleep without them jacking me full of chemicals, Darrow. I want to be able to dream again. I want to forget my mother's caved-in head and her vacant eyes and her twitching fingers. I want to forget Adrius laughing. And I want to repay Antonia and Adrius for their hospitality. I want to stand above them and that piece of shit, Roque, as they weep for the end as I gouge out their eyes and pour molten gold into the sockets so they scream and writhe and spread their urine upon the floor and beg forgiveness for ever thinking they could put Victra au Julii in a gorydamn cage." She smiles ferally. "I want revenge."

"Revenge is a hollow end," I say.

"And I'm a hollow girl now."

I know she's not. I know she's more than that. But I also know better than anyone that wounds aren't healed in a day. I'm barely stitched together myself, and I have my entire family here. "If that is what you want, that is what I owe you. In three days the Carver who made me into a Gold will be here. He will make us what we were. He'll mend your spine. Give you your legs back, if you want them."

She squints at me. "And you trust me, after what trust has cost you?"

I take the magnetic key given to me by the Sons outside and press it to the inside of her cuffs. One by one they unlatch from the bed, freeing her legs, her arms.

"You're dumber than you look," she says.

"You might not believe in our rebellion. But I saw Tactus change before his future was robbed from him. I've seen Ragnar forget his bonds and reach for what he wants in this world. I've seen Sevro become a man. I've seen myself change. I truly do believe we choose who we want to be in this life. It isn't preordained. You taught me loyalty, more than Mustang, more than Roque. And because of that, I believe in you, Victra. As much as I've ever believed in anyone." I hold out my hand. "Be my family and I will never forsake you. I will never lie to you. I will be your brother as long as you live."

Startled by the emotion in my voice, the cold woman stares up at me. Those defenses she erected forgotten now. In another life we might have been a pair. Might have had that fire I feel for Mustang, for Eo. But not in this life.

Victra does not soften. Does not crumble to tears. There's still rage inside her. Still raw hate and so much betrayal and frustration and loss coiled around her icy heart. But in this moment, she is free of it all. In this moment, she reaches solemnly up to grasp my hand. And I feel the hope flicker in me.

"Welcome to the Sons of Ares."

PART II

||||||||||||||||||||||||||||||||

RAGE

"Shit escalates."

—SEVRO AU BARCA

13

||||||||||||||||||||||||

HOWLERS

"It's gorydamn infuriating being kept in the dark," Victra mutters as she helps me rack the weights on the bench press. The sound echoes through the stone gymnasium. It's bare bones in here. Metal weights. Rubber tires. Ropes. And months of my sweat.

"Don't they know who you are?" I say, sitting up.

"Oh, shut up. Didn't you found the Howlers? Don't you have any say over how they treat us?" She nudges me off the bench to take my spot, laying her spine on the padded surface and pushing her arms up to grip the barbell. I take a few weights off. But she glares at me and I put them back on as she fixes her grip.

"Technically, no," I say.

"Oh. But seriously: what's a girl got to do to get a wolfcloak?" Her powerful arms thrust the bar up off from its rack, moving it up and down as she talks. Nearly three hundred kilos. "I shot a Legate in the head two missions ago. A Legate! I've seen your Howlers. Aside from . . . Ragnar, they're tiny. They need . . . more heavies if they want to . . . take on Adrius's Boneriders or the Sovereign's . . . Praetorians." She grits her teeth as she finishes her last repetition, racking the bar without my help, and standing to point to herself in the mirror. Hers is a powerful, laconic form. Shoulders broad and swaying with a haughty walk. "I'm a perfect physical specimen, on and off my feet. Not using me is an indictment on Sevro's intelligence."

I roll my eyes. "It's probably your lack of self-confidence he's worried about."

She throws a towel at me. "You're as annoying as he is. Swear to Jove if he says one more thing about my 'nascent poverty' I'm going to cut his head off with a gorydamn spoon." I watch her for a moment, trying not to laugh. "What, you have something to say as well?"

"Not a thing, my goodlady," I say, holding up my hands. Her eyes linger on them instinctively. "Squats next?"

The ramshackle gymnasium has been our second home since Mickey Carved us. It was weeks of recovery in his ward as her nerves remembered how to walk and both of us tried to put on weight again under the supervision of Dr. Virany. A gaggle of Reds and a Green watch us from the corner of the gym. Even after two months, the novelty hasn't worn off seeing how much two chemically and genetically enhanced Peerless Scarred can lift.

Ragnar came in to embarrass us a couple weeks back. Brute didn't even say a word. Just started piling weights onto a barbell till no more would fit, power-cleaned it, and then gestured for us to do the same. Victra couldn't even get the weight off the ground. I got as far as my knees. Then we had to listen to the hundred idiots who flocked after him chant his name for an hour. Found out afterward Uncle Narol had been overseeing bets on how much more Ragnar could lift than I. Even my own uncle bet against me. But it's a good sign, even if the others don't think of it this way. Gold can't win everything.

It was with Mickey and Dr. Virany's help that Victra and I regained control of our bodies. But regaining our sense in the field has taken just as long. We started with baby steps. Our first mission out together was a supply run with Holiday and a dozen bodyguards, not for the supply run itself, but for me. We didn't do it with the Howlers. "Gotta work your way up to the A squad, Reap. Make sure you can keep up," Sevro said, patting my face. "And Julii has to prove herself." She slapped his hand when he tried petting her.

Ten supply runs, two sabotage missions, and three assassinations later Sevro was finally convinced that Holiday, Victra, and I were ready to run with the B squad: the Pitvipers, led by my own Uncle Narol—who has become a bit of a cult hero to the Reds here. Ragnar's a godlike creature. But my uncle is just a rough old man who drinks too much, smokes too much, and is uncommonly good at war. His Pitvipers are a motley collection of hardasses specializing in sabotage and thievery, about half are ex Helldivers, the rest are a spattering of other useful lowColors. We've completed three missions with them, destroying a barracks and several Legion communications installations, but I can't shake the feeling we're a snake eating our own tail. Every bombing is twisted by the Society media. Every pinprick of damage we do seems only to bring more Legions from Agea to the mines or the smaller cities of Mars.

I feel hunted.

Worse, I feel like a terrorist. I've only ever felt this way once before, and that was with a bomb on my chest walking into the gala on Luna.

Dancer and Theodora have been pressing Sevro to reach out to more allies. Trying to bridge the gap between the Sons and other factions. Reluctantly, Sevro agreed. So earlier this week, the Pitvipers and I were dispatched from the tunnels to the northern continent of Arabia Terra, where the Red Legion had carved themselves a stronghold in the port city of Ismenia. It was Dancer's hope I could bring them into the fold in a way Sevro hadn't been able to, maybe pull them away from Harmony's influence. But instead of finding allies, we found a mass grave. A gray, bombed-out city shelled from orbit. I can still see that pale bloated mass of bodies writhing on the coastline. Crabs skittering over the corpses, making meals of the dead, as a lone ribbon of smoke twirled and twirled up to the stars, the old soundless echo of war.

I'm haunted by the sight, but Victra seems to have moved past it as she plows through her workout. She's pushed it to that vast vault in the back of her mind where she compresses and locks away all the evil she's seen, all the pain she's felt. I wish I were more like her. I wish I felt less and was less afraid. But as I recall that ribbon of smoke, all I can think is that it presages something worse. As if the Universe is showing us a glimpse of the end we're rushing toward.

It's late night and the mirrors have fogged with condensation when we're done with our workout. We wash up in the showers, talking over the plastic dividers. "Take it as a sign of progress," I say. "At least she's speaking to you."

"No. Your mother hates me. She'll always hate me. Not a damn thing I can do about it."

"Well, you could try being more polite."

"I'm perfectly polite," Victra says in offense, turning off her shower and exiting the stall. Eyes closed against the water, I finish shampooing my hair, expecting her to say more. She doesn't, so I finish rinsing the shampoo out and exit the stall when I'm done. I feel something's amiss the moment before I see Victra naked on the floor, hands and legs hogtied behind her back. A hood over her head. Something moves behind me. I whirl around just in time to see a half dozen ghostCloaks slipping through the steam. Then someone inhumanly strong slams into me from behind, wrapping their arms around mine, pinning them to my sides. I feel their breath on my neck. Terror screams through me. The Jackal's found us. He's snuck in. How? "Golds!" I shout. "Golds!" I'm slick from the shower. The floor is slippery. I use it to my advantage, wriggling against my attacker's arms like an eel and lashing back with my head in his face. There's a grunt. I twist again, feet slip. I fall. Smacking my knee on the concrete floor. Scramble to my feet. Feel two attackers rushing me from the left. Cloaked. I duck under one, putting my shoulder into his knees. He catapults over my head and smashes through the plastic barriers that divide the shower behind me. I grab the other by the throat, blocking a punch, and throw him into the ceiling. Another slams into me from the side, prying at my leg with his hands to take my balance. I go with it, jumping in the air, twisting my body in a Kravat move that steals his center of gravity and puts us both on the ground, his head between my thighs. All I need do is twist and his neck breaks. But two more sets of hands are on me, thumping me in the face, more are on my legs. GhostCloaks rippling in the vapor. I'm screaming and thrashing and spitting, but there are too many, and they're nasty, punching the tendons behind my knees so I can't kick and the nerves in my shoulders so my arms feel heavy as lead. They shove a hood over my head and bind my hands behind my back. I lay there motionless, terrified, panting.

"Get them on their knees," an electronic voice growls. "On their bloodydamn knees." *Bloodydamn?* Ah, shit. As I realize who it is, I let them lift me up to my knees. Hood is removed. The lights are out. Several dozen candles have been set on the shower floor, throwing shadows about the room. Victra's to my left, eyes furious. Blood coming from her now-crooked nose. Holiday has appeared to my right. Fully clothed but similarly bound, she is carried in by two black-clad figures and forced down on her knees. A big grin splits her face.

Standing around us in the bathroom steam are ten demons with black-painted faces staring out from beneath the mouths of the wolf pelts that hang from their heads to their mid-thighs. Two lean against the wall, in pain from my rabid defense. Beneath the pelt of a bear, Ragnar towers beside Sevro. The Howlers have come for new recruits and they look bloody terrifying.

"Greetings, you ugly little bastards," Sevro growls, removing the voice synthesizer. He stalks forward through the shadows to stand before us. "It has come to my attention that you are abnormally devious, savage, and generally malicious creatures gifted in the arts of murder, mayhem, and chaos. If I am mistaken, do say so now."

"Sevro, you scared the shit out of us," Victra says. "The hell is your problem?"

"**Do not profane this moment,**" Ragnar says menacingly.

Victra spits. "You broke my nose, you oaf!"

"Technically, I did," Sevro says. He jerks his head to a lean Howler with Red Sigils on his hands. "Sleepy helped."

"You little dwarf . . ."

"You were squirming, love," Pebble says from somewhere among the Howlers. I can't tell which she is. Voice resounding off the walls.

"And if you keep talking we'll just gag you and tickle you," Clown says sinisterly. "So . . . shhhh." Victra shakes her head but keeps her mouth shut. I'm trying not to laugh at the solemnity of the moment. Sevro continues, pacing back and forth before us.

"You have been watched, and now you are wanted. If you accept our invitation to join our brotherhood, you must take an oath to be always faithful to your brothers and sisters. To never lie, never betray those under the cloak. All your sins, all your scars, all your enemies now belong to us. Our burden to share. Your loves, your family will become your second loves, your second family. We are your first. If you cannot abide this, if you cannot conscience this bond, say so now and you may leave."

He waits. Not even Victra says a word.

"Good. Now, as per the rules set forth in our sacred text . . ." He holds up a little black book with dog-eared pages and a white howling wolfhead on the front. ". . . You must be purged of your former oaths and prove your worth before you can take our vows." He holds up his hands. "So let the Purge begin."

The Howlers pitch back their heads and howl like maniacs. What comes next is a blur of kaleidoscopic oddities. Music thumps from somewhere. We're kept on our knees. Hands tied. The Howlers rush forward. Bottles are brought to our lips and we chug as they chant around some weird looping melody that Sevro leads with bawdy aplomb. Ragnar roars with satisfaction when I finish the bottle they bring me. I almost puke then and there. The liquor burns, scouring my esophagus and belly. Victra's coughing behind me. Holiday just chugs on and the Howlers cheer as she finishes her bottle. We waver there as they surround Victra, chanting as she gasps and tries to finish the liquor. It splashes over her face. She coughs.

"Is that your best, daughter of the Sun?" Ragnar bellows. **"Drink!"**

Ragnar roars with delight when she finally finishes the swill, coughing and muttering curses. **"Bring forth the snakes and the cockroaches!"** he shouts.

They chant like priests as Pebble wobbles forward with a bucket. They push us together so we surround the bucket and in the wavering light can see the bottom of it wriggling with life. Thick, shiny cockroaches with hairy legs and wings crawl around a pitviper. I reel back, terrified and drunk as our binds are cut. Holiday's already reached inside and grabs the snake; she slams it on the floor till it dies.

Victra just stares at the Gray. "What the . . ."

"Finish the bucket or get the box," Sevro says.

"What does that even mean?"

"Finish the bucket or get the box! Finish the bucket or get the box!" they chant. Holiday takes a bite of the dead snake, tearing into it with her teeth.

"Yes!" Ragnar bellows. "She has the soul of a Howler. Yes!"

I'm so drunk I can barely see. I reach into the bucket, shivering as I feel the cockroaches crawl over my hand. I snatch one up and jam it into my mouth. It's still moving. I force my jaw to chew. I'm almost crying. Victra is gagging at the sight of me. I swallow it down and grab her hand and force it into the bucket. She makes a sudden lurching movement, and I'm too slow to realize what it means. Her vomit splashes onto my shoulder. At the smell of it, I can't hold my own in. Holiday chews on. Ragnar shouts her praises.

By the time we finish the bucket, we're a huddled pathetic mass of drunk, bug- and guts-covered filth. Sevro's saying something in front of us. Keeps swaying back and forth. Maybe that's me. Is he talking? Someone shakes my shoulder from behind. Was I asleep? "This is our sacred text," my little friend is saying. "You will study this sacred text. Soon you will know this sacred text inside and out. But today, you need know only Howler Rule One."

"Never bow," Ragnar says.

"Never bow," the rest echo and Clown steps forward with three wolfcloaks. Like the fur of the wolves at the Institute, these pelts modulate to their environment and take on a dark hue in the candlelit room. He holds one out for Victra. They free her bonds and she tries to stand, but can't. Pebble reaches to help her up, but Victra ignores the hand. Tries again and tilts down to a knee. Then Sevro kneels beside her and extends a hand. Looking at it through sweat-soaked hair, Victra snorts out a laugh as she realizes what this is about. She takes his hand, and only with his help can she walk steadily enough to take her cloak. Sevro takes it from Clown and drapes it around her bare shoulders. Their eyes meet and linger for a moment before they move to the side so Holiday can be helped up by Pebble to gain her cloak. Ragnar helps me, draping mine over my shoulders.

"Welcome, brother and sisters, to the Howlers."

Together, the Howlers pitch back their heads and let loose a mighty howl. I join them, and find to my surprise that Victra does as well.

Hurling her head back in the darkness without reservations. Then suddenly the lights flare on. The howls die as we look around in confusion. Dancer trudges into the showers with Uncle Narol.

"The bloodyhell is this?" Narol asks, eying the cockroaches and the remains of the snake and the bottles. The Howlers look at the ludicrousness of one another awkwardly.

"We're performing a secret occult ritual," Sevro says. "And you are interrupting, subordinate."

"Right," Narol says, nodding, a little disturbed. "Sorry, sir."

"One of our Pinks stole a datapad from a Bonerider in Agea," Dancer says to Sevro, not amused by the display. "We found out who he is."

"No shit?" Sevro says. "Was I right?"

"Who?" I ask, drunkenly. "Who are you talking about?"

"The Jackal's silent partner," Dancer says. "It's Quicksilver. You were right, Sevro. Our agents say he's at his corporate headquarters on Phobos, but he won't be for long. He's bound for Luna in two days. We won't be able to touch him there."

"So Operation Black Market is a go," Sevro says.

"It's a go," Dancer admits reluctantly.

Sevro pumps his fist in the air. "Hell, yeah. You heard the man, Howlers. Get scrubbed. Get sober. Get fed. We've got a Silver to kidnap and an economy to crash." He looks at me with a wild grin on his face. "It's gonna be a hell of a day. A hell of a day."

14

||||||||||||||||||||||||||

THE VAMPIRE MOON

Phobos means fear. In myth, he was the offspring of Aphrodite and Ares, the child of love and war. It's a fitting name for the larger of Mars's moons.

Formed long before the age of man, when a meteorite struck father Mars and flung debris into orbit, the oblong moon floated like a cast-off corpse, dead and abandoned for a billion years. Now it is the Hive teeming with the parasitic life that pumps blood into the veins of the Gold empire. Swarms of tiny, fat-bodied cargo ships rise from Mars's surface to funnel into the two huge gray docks that encircle the moon. There, they transfer the bounty of Mars to the kilometer-long cosmos-Haulers that will bear the treasure along the great Julii-Agos trade routes to the Rim or, more likely, to the Core, where hungry Luna waits to be fed.

The barren rock of Phobos has been carved hollow by man and wreathed with metal. With a radius of only twelve kilometers at its widest, the moon is ringed by two huge dockyards, which run perpendicular to each other. They're dark metal with white glyphs and blinking red lights for docking ships. They slither with the movement of magnetic trams and cargo vessels. Beneath the dockyards, and at times rising around them in the form of spiked towers, is the Hive—a jigsaw city formed not by neoclassical Gold ideals, but by raw economics without the confines of gravity. Six centuries' worth of buildings perforate Phobos. It is the largest pincushion man has ever built. And the disparity of wealth between the inhabitants of the Needles, the tips of the buildings, and the Hollow inside the moon's rock, borders on hilarious.

"Looks larger when you're not on the bridge of a torchShip," Victra drawls from behind me. "Being disenfranchised is so damn tedious."

I feel her pain. The last time I saw Phobos was before the Lion's Rain. Then I had an armada at my back, Mustang and the Jackal at my side, and thousands of Peerless Scarred at my command. Enough firepower to make a planet tremble. Now I'm skulking in the shadows in a rickety cargo hauler so old it doesn't even have an artificial gravity generator, accompanied only by Victra, a crew of three Sons gas haulers, and a small team of Howlers in the cargo bay. And this time I'm taking orders, not giving them. My tongue plays over the suicide tooth they put in my back right molar after the Howler initiation. All the Howlers have them now. Better than being taken alive, Sevro said. I have to agree with him. Still. Feels strange.

In the aftermath of my escape, the Jackal initiated an immediate moratorium on all flights leaving Mars for orbit. He suspected the Sons would make a desperate bid to get me off planet. Fortunately, Sevro isn't a fool. If he had been, I'd likely be in the Jackal's hands. Ultimately, not even the ArchGovernor of Mars could ground all commerce for long, and so his moratorium was short-lived. But the shock waves it sent through the market were staggering. Billions of credits lost every minute the helium-3 did not flow. Sevro found it rather inspiring.

"How much of it does Quicksilver own?" I ask.

Victra pulls herself beside me in the null gravity. Her jagged hair floats around her head like a white crown. It's been bleached and her eyes have been blackened with contacts. Easier for Obsidians to move about the rougher ends of the Moon than it would be without the disguise, and being one of the largest Howlers, she hardly could pass for any other Color.

"Hard to guess," she says. "Silver ownership is a tricky thing, in the end. The man has so many dummy corporations and off-grid bank accounts I doubt even the Sovereign knows how large his portfolio is."

"Or who is in it. If the rumors of him owning Golds are true . . ."

"They are." Victra shrugs, which tips her backward. "He's got his fingers everywhere. One of the only men too rich to kill, according to Mother."

"Is he richer than she was? Than you are?"

"Were," she corrects, shakes her head. "He knew better than that." There's a pause. "But maybe."

My eyes seek the Silver winged-heel icon that is stamped on the greatest of Phobos's towers, a three-kilometer-long double helix of steel and glass tipped with a silver crescent. How many Gold eyes look on it with jealousy? How many more must he own or bribe to protect him from all the rest? Perhaps just one. Crucial to the Jackal's rise was his silent partner. A man who helped him secretly gain control of the media and telecommunications industries. For the longest time I thought that partner was Victra or her mother and he closed the loop in the garden. But it seems the Jackal's greatest ally is alive and prospering. For now.

"Thirty million people," I whisper. "Incredible."

I can feel her eyes on me. "You don't agree with Sevro's plan, do you?"

My thumb picks at a wad of pink gum stuck to the rusted bulkhead. Kidnapping Quicksilver will get us intel and access to vast weapons factories, but Sevro's play against the economy is more concerning. "Sevro kept the Sons alive. I didn't. So I'll follow his lead."

"Mhm." She eyes me skeptically. "I wonder when you started believing grit and vision were the same thing."

"*Oy, shitheads*"—Sevro squawks over the com unit in my ear—"*if you're done sightseeing or humping or whatever the hell you're doin', it's time to tuck in.*"

||||||||||||

Half an hour later, Victra and I huddle together with the Howlers in one of the helium-3 containers stacked in the back of our transport. We can feel the ship reverberate beyond the container as it links its magnetic coupling to the docks' ringed surface. Beyond the ship's hull, Oranges will be floating in mechanized suits, waiting to steer the weightless cargo containers onto magnetic trams that will in turn take them to the cosmosHaulers awaiting the journey to Jupiter. There they will resupply Roque's fleet in his war effort against Mustang and the Moon Lords.

But before the containers are transported, Copper and Gray inspectors will come to examine them. They'll be bribed by our Blues into counting forty-nine containers instead of fifty. Then an Orange bribed by our contact will lose the container we're in, a common practice for the smuggling of illegal drugs or untaxed goods. He'll deposit it in a lower-level berth for machine parts, whereupon our Sons contact will meet us and escort us to our safe house. At least, that's the plan. But for now we wait.

Eventually gravity returns, signaling we're in the hangar. Our container settles on the floor with a thud. We steady ourselves against helium-3 drums. Voices drift beyond the metal walls of the container. The hauler beeps as it decouples from us and returns out the pulse-Field to space. Then silence. I don't like it. My hand twists around the leather grip of my razor inside my jacket sleeve. I take a step forward toward the door. Victra follows. Sevro grabs my shoulder. "We wait for the contact."

"We don't even know the man," I say.

"Dancer vouched for him." He snaps his fingers at me to return to my place. "We wait."

I notice the others listening, so I nod and shut my mouth. It's ten minutes later that we hear a solitary pair of feet click against the deck outside. The lock thuds back on the container doors, and dim light seeps in as they part to reveal a clean-cut, goateed Red with a toothpick in his mouth. Half a head shorter than Sevro, he clicks his eyes over each of us in turn. One eyebrow climbing upward when he sees

Ragnar. The other follows when he looks down the muzzle of Sevro's scorcher. Somehow he doesn't step back. Man's got a spine in him.

"What can never die?" Sevro growls in his best Obsidian accent.

"The fungus under Ares's sack." The man smiles and glances over his shoulder. "Mind lowerin' the nasty? We gotta move, now. Borrowed this dock from the Syndicate. 'Cept they don't really know about it, so unless you wanna tangle with some professional uglies, we gotta box the jabber and waddle on." He claps his hands. " 'Now' means now."

Our contact goes by the name of Rollo. Stringy and wry, with sparkling, bright eyes and an easy way with the women, even though he brings up his wife, the most beautiful woman who has apparently ever walked the surface of Mars, at least twice a minute. He also hasn't seen her in eight years. He's spent that time on the Hive as a welder on the space towers. Not technically a slave like the Reds in the mines, he and his are contract labor. Wage slaves who work fourteen-hour days, six days a week, suspended between the megalithic towers that puncture the Hive, welding metal and praying they never suffer a workplace injury. Get an injury, you can't earn. Can't earn, you don't eat.

"Mighty full of himself," I overhear Sevro saying under his breath to Victra in the middle of the pack as Rollo leads on.

"I rather like his goatee," Victra says.

"The Blues call this place the Hive," Rollo's saying as we head toward a graffiti-smeared tram in a derelict maintenance level. Smells like grease, rust, and old piss. Homeless vagrants festoon the floors of the shadowy metal halls. Twitching bundles of blankets and rags that Rollo sidesteps without looking, though his hand never leaves the worn plastic hilt of his scorcher. "Might be to them. They got schools, homes here. Little airhead communes, sects, to be technic, where they learn to fly and sync up with the computers. But let me learn you what this place really is: just a grinder. Men come in. Towers go up." He nods his head at the ground. "Meat goes out."

The only signs of life from the vagrants on the floor are little gouts of breath that plume up from their lumpy rags like steam from the cracks in a lava field. I shiver beneath my gray jacket and adjust the bag of gear over my shoulder. It's freezing on this level. Old insulation, probably. Pebble blows a cloud of steam through her nostrils as she pushes one of our gear carts, looking sadly left and right at the vagrants. Less empathetic, Victra guides the cart from the front, nudging a vagrant out of the way with her boot. The man hisses and looks up at her, and up, and up, till he sees all 2.1 meters of annoyed killer. He skitters to the side, breathing through his teeth. Neither Ragnar nor Rollo seems to notice the cold.

Sons of Ares wait for us on the run-down tram platform and inside the tram itself. Most are Red, but there's a good amount of Oranges and a Green and Blue in the mix. They cradle a motley collection of old scorchers and strafe the other hallways that lead to the platform with edgy eyes that can't help but jump our direction and wonder just who the hell we are. I'm thankful more than ever for the Obsidian contacts and prosthetics.

"Expecting trouble?" Sevro asks, eying the weapons in the Sons' hands.

"Grays been sweeping down here last couple months. Not hollow-ass tinpots from the local precinct, but knotty bastards. Legionnaires. Even some Thirteenth mixed in with Tenth and Fifth." He lowers his voice. "We had a nasty month, where they shred us up real bloody-damn bad. Took our headquarters in the Hollows, stuck Syndicate toughs on us too. Paid to hunt their own. Most of us had to go to ground, hiding in secondary safe houses. Main body of Sons have been helping the Red rebels on the station, obviously, but our special ops hasn't flexed muscle till today. We didn't wanna take chances. Ya know? Ares said you lot got important business. . . ."

"Ares is wise," Sevro says dismissively.

"And a drama queen," Victra adds.

At the door to the tram, Ragnar hesitates, eyes lingering on an antiterrorism poster pasted onto a concrete support column in the tram's waiting area. "See something, say something," it reads, showing a pale Red with evil crimson eyes and the stereotypical tattered dress of a miner skulking near a door that says "restricted access."

Can't see the rest. It's covered in rebel graffiti. But then I realize Ragnar's not looking at the poster, but at the man I didn't even notice who's crumpled on the ground beneath it. His hood's up. Left leg is an ancient mech replacement. A crusted brown bandage covers half his face. There's a puff. The release of pressurized gas. And the man leans back from us, shivering, and smiling with perfectly black teeth. A plastic stim cartridge clatters to the floor. Tar dust.

"**Why do you not help these people?**" Ragnar asks.

"Help them with what?" Rollo asks. He sees the empathy on Ragnar's face and doesn't really know how to answer. "Brother, we barely got enough for flesh and kin. No good sharing with that lot, ya know?"

"**But that one is Red. They are your family . . .**"

Rollo frowns at the bare truth.

"Save the pity, Ragnar," Victra says. "That's Syndicate crank he's puffing. Most of them would slit your throat for an afternoon high. They're empty flesh."

"Empty what?" I say, turning back to her.

She's caught off guard by the sharpness of my tone, but she's loath to back off. So she doubles down instinctively. "Empty flesh, darling," she repeats. "Part of being human is having dignity. They don't. They carved it out themselves. That was their choice, not Golds'. Even if it's easy to blame them for everything. So why should they deserve my pity?"

"Because not everyone is you. Or had your birth."

She doesn't reply. Rollo clears his throat, skeptical now about our disguises. "Lady's right about the slit-your-throat part. Most of 'em were imported laborers. Like me. Not counting the wife, I've got plus three in New Thebes that I send money back to, but I can't go home till my contract's up. Got four years left. These slags have given up on tryin' to get back."

"Four years?" Victra asks dubiously. "You said you were already here eight."

"Gotta pay for my transit."

She stares at him quizzically.

"Company doesn't cover it. Shoulda read the fine print. Sure, it was my choice to come up here." He nods to the vagrants. "Was theirs too. But when the only other choice is starving." He shrugs as if we all know the answer. "These slags just got unlucky on the job. Lost legs. Arms. Company doesn't cover prosthetics, least not decent ones. . . ."

"What about Carvers?" I ask.

He scoffs. "And who the hell do you know that can afford flesh work?"

I didn't even think of the cost. Reminds me of how distant I am from so many of the people I claim to fight for. Here's a Red, one of my own more or less, and I don't even know what type of food is popular in his culture.

"What company do you work for?" Victra asks.

"Why, Julii Industries, of course."

I watch the metal jungle pass outside the dirty duroglass window as the tram pulls away from the station. Victra sits down next to me, a troubled look on her face. But I'm a world away from her, my friends. Lost in memory. I've been to the Hive before with ArchGovernor Augustus and Mustang. He brought the lancers to meet with Society economic ministers to discuss modernizing the moon's infrastructure. After the meetings she and I snuck away to the moon's famous aquarium. I'd rented it out at absurd cost and arranged a meal and wine to be served to us in front of the orca tank. Mustang always liked natural creatures more than Carved ones.

I've traded fifty-year-old wines and Pink valets for a grimmer world with rusting bones and rebel thugs. This is the real world. Not the dream the Golds live in. Today I feel the silent screams of a civilization that has been stepped on for hundreds of years.

Our path skirts around the edges of the Hollows, the center of the moon where the latticework of cage slum apartments festers without gravity. To go there would be to risk falling into the middle of the Syndicate street war against the Sons of Ares. And to go any higher into the midColor levels would be to risk Society marines and their security infrastructure of cameras and holoScanners.

Instead, we pass through the hinterlands of maintenance levels between the Hollows and the Needles, where Reds and Oranges keep the moon running. Our tram, driven by a Sons sympathizer, speeds through its stops. The faces of waiting workers blur together as we pass. A pastiche of eyes. But faces all gray. Not the color of metal, but the color of old ash in a campfire. Ash faces. Ash clothes. Ash lives.

But as the tunnel swallows our tram, color erupts around us. Graffiti and years of rage bleeding out from the ribbed and cracking walls of its once gray throat. Profanity in fifteen dialects. Golds ripped open in a dozen dark ways. And to the right of a crude sketch of a reaper's scythe decapitating Octavia au Lune is an image of Eo hanging from the gallows in digital paint, hair aflame, "Break the Chains" written diagonally. It's a single glowing flower among the weeds of hate. A knot forms in my throat.

Half an hour after we set out, our tram grinds to a halt outside a deserted lowColor industrial hub where thousands of workers should diverge from their early-morning commute from the Stacks to attend their functions. But now it's still as a cemetery. Trash litters the metal floors. HoloCans still flash with the Society's news programs. A cup sits on a table in a café, steam still rising off the top of the beverage. The Sons have cleared the way only a few minutes before. Shows the extent of their influence here.

When we leave, life will return to the place. But after we plant the bombs we've brought with us? After we destroy the manufacturing, won't all the men and women we intend to help be just as unemployed as those poor creatures in the tram station? If work is their reason for being, what happens when we take it away? I'd voice my concerns to Sevro, but he's a driven arrow. As dogmatic as I once was. And to question him aloud seems a betrayal of our friendship. He's always trusted me blindly. So am I the worse friend for having doubts in him?

We pass through several gravLifts into a garage for garbage disposal haulers, also owned by Julii Industries. I catch Victra wiping dirt off the family crest on one of the doors. The speared sun is worn and faded. The few dozen Red and Orange workers of the facility pretend not to notice our group as we file into one of the hauler bays. Inside, at the base of two huge haulers, we find a small army of Sons of Ares. More than six hundred.

They're not soldiers. Not like us. Most are men, but there's a scattering of women, mostly younger Reds and Oranges forced to migrate here for work to feed Mars-side families. Their weapons are shoddy. Some stand. Other are seated, turning from conversations to see our pack of Obsidian killers stalking across the metal deck, carrying bags of gear and pushing two mysterious carts. A small sadness grows in me. Whatever they do, wherever they go, their lives will be stained by this day. If it were my duty to address them, I'd warn them of the burden they're taking on, the evil they'll be letting into their lives. I'd say it's nicer to hear about glorious victories in war than to witness them. Than to feel the weird unreality of lying in bed every morning knowing you've killed a man, knowing a friend is gone.

But I say nothing. My place now is beside Ragnar and Victra, behind Sevro as he spits out his gum and stalks forward, giving me a wink and an elbow in the side, to stand in front of the small army. His army. He's tiny for an Obsidian male, but still scarred and tattooed and terrifying to this company of small-handed garbage men and hunched tower welders. He tilts his head forward, eyes smoldering behind his black contacts. Wolf tattoos looking evil against his pale skin in the industrial light.

"Greetings, grease monkeys." His voice rumbles, low and predatory. "You might be wondering why Ares has sent a pack of hardcore nasties like us to this tin shithole." The Sons look to one another nervously. "We aren't here to cuddle. We aren't here to inspire you or give long-ass speeches like the bloodydamn Sovereign." He snaps his fingers. Pebble and Clown wheel the carts forward and unlatch the tops. The hinges squeal open to reveal mining explosives. "We're here to blow shit up." He throws open his arms and cackles. "Any questions?"

15

||||||||||||||||||||||||||

THE HUNT

I float in the back of the trash collector with the Howlers. It's dark. The night vision of my optics shows the garbage that orbits us in shadowy green. Banana peels. Toy packaging. Coffee grounds. Victra makes a gagging sound over the com as toilet paper sticks to her face. Her mask is a demonHelm. Like mine, it's pupil black and shaped subtly like a screaming demon face. Fitchner managed to steal them from Luna's armories for the Sons more than a year back. With them, we can see most spectrums, amplify sound, track one another's coordinates, access maps, and communicate silently. My friends around me are in all black. We wear no mechanized armor, only thin scarab-Skin over our bodies that will stop knives and occasional projectiles. We have no gravBoots or pulseArmor. Nothing that will slow us, cause noise, or trip sensors. We wear oxygen tanks with air enough for forty minutes. I finish adjusting Ragnar's harness and look to my datapad. The two Reds crewing the old trash collector are giving us a countdown. When it reaches one, Sevro says, *"Tuck your sacks and pop your cloaks."*

I activate my ghostCloak and the world warps, distorted by the cloak. It's like looking through refracted, dirty water, and I already feel the battery pack heating up against my tailbone. The cloak's good for short bursts. But it burns up small batteries like the ones we pack and needs time to cool and recharge. I grope for Sevro and Victra's hands, managing to grasp them in time. The rest partner up as well. I don't remember feeling so frightened before the Iron Rain. Was I braver then? Maybe just more naïve.

"Hold tight. We're in for some chop," Sevro says. *"Popping top in three . . . two . . ."* I tighten my grip on his hand. *". . . one."*

The collector's door retracts silently, bathing us in the amber light of a holoDisplay screen on a nearby skyscraper. There's a burst of air and my world spins as the trash collector ejects its load of garbage from the back of its hold. We're like seed chaff thrown into the city. Spinning with debris through a kaleidoscope world of towers and advertisements. Hundreds of ships funneling along avenues. All a flashing, liquid blur. We continue to spin head over heel to mask our signatures.

Over the com, I hear the grousing of a Blue traffic controller, annoyed at the spilled trash. Soon there's a company Copper on the line threatening to fire the incompetent drivers. But it's what I don't hear that makes me smile. The police channels drone on their usual slant, reporting a Syndicate airjacking in the Hive, a grisly murder in the ancient art museum near the Park Plaza, a datacenter robbery in the Banking Cluster. They haven't seen us amidst the debris.

We slow our spin gradually using small thrusters in our helmets. Bursts of air bring us to a steady drift. Silent in the vacuum. We're on target. Along with the rest of the trash, we're about to impact on the side of a steel tower. Has to be a clean landing. Victra curses as we drift closer, closer. My fingers tremble. Don't bounce. Don't bounce.

"Release," Sevro orders.

I pull my hands from his and Victra's, and the three of us impact jarringly against the steel. The trash around us bounds off the metal, cartwheeling backward at odd angles. Sevro and Victra stick, compliments of the magnets in their gloves, but a piece of debris impacting in front of me bounces off the steel and hits me in the thigh, altering my trajectory. Tipping me sideways, hands windmilling for a grip, which causes me to spin.

My feet hit first and I bounce backward toward space, cursing.

"Sevro!" I shout.

"Victra. Get him."

A hand grabs my foot, jerking me to a halt. I look down and see a warped invisible form grasping my leg. Victra. Carefully, she pulls my weightless body back to the wall so I can clamp my own magnets onto the steel. Spots race across my vision. The city is all around us. It's dreadful in its silence, in its colors, in its inhuman metal landscape. It feels more like an ancient alien artifact than a place for humans.

"Slow it down." Victra's voice crackles in my helmet. *"Darrow. You're hyperventilating. Breathe with me. In. Out. In . . ."* I force my lungs to breathe in sync with her. The spots soon fade. I open my eyes, face inches from the steel.

"You shit your suit or something?" Sevro asks.

"I'm good," I say. "A little rusty."

"Ugh. Pun intended, I'm sure." Ragnar and the rest of the Howlers land thirty meters beneath us on the wall. Pebble waves up to me. *"Got three hundred meters to go. Let's climb, you pixies."*

Lights glow behind the glass of Quicksilver's double-helix towers. Connecting the double helixes are nearly two hundred levels of offices. I can make out shapes moving inside at computer terminals. I zoom in with my optics to watch the stock traders sitting in their offices, their assistants moving to and fro, analysts signaling furiously on holographic trading boards that communicate with the markets on Luna. Silvers, all. They remind me of industrious bees.

"Makes me miss the boys," Victra says. Takes me a moment to realize she's not talking about the Silvers. The last time she and I tried this tactic, Tactus and Roque were with us. We infiltrated Karnus's flagship from vacuum as he refueled at an asteroid base during the Academy's mock war. We cut through his hull with aims of kidnapping him to eliminate his team. But it was a trap and I narrowly escaped with the help of my friends, a broken arm my only reward for the gambit.

It takes us five minutes to climb from our landing place to the peak of the tower, where it becomes a large crescent. We don't go hand over hand, so climbing isn't the true term. The magnets in our gloves have fluctuating positive and negative currents that allow us to roll up the side of the tower like we have wheels in our palms. The toughest part of the ascent, or descent, or whatever you'd call it in the null grav, is the crescent slope at the extreme height or end of the tower. We have to cling to a narrow metal support beam that extends out among a ceiling of glass, much like the stem of a leaf. Beneath our bellies and through the glass lies Quicksilver's famous museum. And above us, just over the peak of Quicksilver's tower, hangs Mars.

My planet seems larger than space. Larger than anything ever could be. A world of billions of souls, of designer oceans, mountains, and more irrigable acres of dry land than Earth ever had. It's night on this side of the world. And you could never know that millions of kilometers of tunnels wind through the bones of the planet, that even as its surface glows with the lights of the Thousand Cities of Mars, there is a pulse unseen, a tide that is rising. But now it looks peaceful. War a distant, impossible thing. I wonder what a poet would say in this moment. What Roque would whisper into the air. Something about the calm before the storm. Or a heartbeat among the deep. But then there's a flash. It startles me. A spasm of light that flares white, then erodes into devilish neon as a mushroom grows in the planet's blackness.

"Do you see that?" I ask over the coms, blinking away the cigar burn the distant detonation made in my vision. Our coms crackle with curses as the others turn to see.

"*Shit,*" Sevro murmurs. "*New Thebes?*"

"No," Pebble answers. "*Farther north. That's the Aventine Peninsula. So it's probably Cyprion. Last intel said the Red Legion was moving toward the city.*"

Then comes another flash. And the seven of us hunker motionless on the crest of the building, watching as a second nuclear bomb detonates a thumb's distance away from the first.

"Bloodydamn. Is it us or them?" I ask. "Sevro!"

"*I don't know,*" Sevro says impatiently.

"*You don't know?*" Victra asks.

How could he not know? I want to shout. But I grasp the answer, because Dancer's words now haunt me. "Sevro's not running this war," he told me, weeks ago after another failed Howler mission. "He's just a man pouring gas on the fire." Maybe I didn't understand how far gone this war is, how far reaching the chaos has become.

Could I have been wrong to trust him so blindly? I watch his expressionless mask. The skin of his armor drinks in the colors of the city around, reflecting nothing. An abyss for light. He turns slowly from the explosion and begins to climb again. Already moving on.

"HoloNews has it," Pebble says. "Fast. They say Red Legion used nukes against Gold forces near Cyprion. Least that's the story."

"Bloodydamn liars," Clown snaps. "Another bait and switch."

"Where would Red Legion get nukes?" Victra asks. Harmony would use them if she had any. But I wager it was Gold using the bombs on Red Legion instead.

"Doesn't mean shit to us now. Lock it up," Sevro says. "Still got to do what we came to do. Get your asses in gear." Numbly, we obey. When we reach our entry zone on the crescent of the double helix tower, rehearsed routine takes over. I pull a small acid flask from the pack on Victra's back. Sevro releases a nanocam no larger than my fingernail into the air, where it hovers above the glass, scanning for life inside the museum. There is none—not a surprise at 03:00. He pulls out a pulseGenerator and waits for Pebble to finish her work on her datapad.

"What's what, Pebble?" he asks impatiently.

"Codes worked. I'm in the system," she says. "Just have to find the right zone. There it is. Laser grid is . . . down. Thermal cams are . . . frozen. Heartbeat sensors are . . . off. Congratulations, everyone. We're officially ghosts! So long as no one manually pulls an alarm."

Sevro activates the pulseGenerator and a faint iridescent bubble blooms around us, creating a seal, so that the vacuum of space doesn't invade the building with us. Would be a quick way to be discovered. I put a small suction cup on the center of the glass then open the acid container and apply the foam to the window in a two-meter-by-two-meter box around the suction cup. The acid bubbles as it eats through the glass, creating an opening. With a small rush of air from the building into our pulseField, the glass pane pops up where Victra grabs it to keep it from flying into space.

"*Rags first,*" Sevro says. It's a hundred meters to the museum floor below.

Ragnar clamps a rappelling winch to the edge of the glass and clips his harness to the magnetic wire. Pulling his razor out, he reactivates his ghostCloak and pushes through the hole. It's disturbing to the senses seeing his near-invisible form accelerate down to the floor, gripped by the skyhook's artificial gravity while I'm still floating. He looks a demon made of the heat that shimmers above the desert on a summer day.

"*Clear.*"

Sevro follows. "*Break an arm,*" Victra says, pushing me into the hole after him. I float forward, then feel myself gripped by gravity as I cross the boundary into the room. I slide down the wire, picking up speed. My stomach lurches at the sudden influx of weight, food sloshing around. I land hard on the ground, almost twisting my ankle as I pull up my silenced scorcher and search for contacts. The rest of the Howlers land behind me. We crouch back to back in the grand hall. The floor is gray marble. The length of the hall is impossible to gauge, because it curves according to the crescent, bowing upward and out of sight, playing with gravity and giving me a sense of vertigo. Metal relics tower around us. Old rockets from man's Pioneer Age. The coat of arms of the Luna Company marks the hull of a gray probe near Ragnar. It looks decidedly like Octavia au Lune's house crest.

"*So this is what it's like to feel fat,*" Sevro says with a grunt as he takes a small jump in the heavy gravity. "*Disgusting.*"

"*Quicksilver's from Earth,*" Victra says. "*Jacks it up even higher when he's negotiating with anyone from low-grav birthplaces.*"

It's three times what I'm used to on Mars, eight times what they prefer on Io or Europa, but in rebuilding my body, Mickey jacked the simulators up to twice Earth's gravity. It's an unpleasant sensation weighing nearly eight hundred pounds, but it works the muscles something horrible.

We strip our oxygen tanks and stow them in the engine rim of an old space shuttle painted with the flag of pre-empire America. So we're left with our small packs, scarabSkin, demonHelms, and weapons. Sevro pulls up Victra's crude maps of the tower's interior and asks Pebble if she's found Quicksilver yet.

"I can't. It's odd. The cameras are off in the top two levels. Same with biometric readers. Can't pinpoint him like we planned."

"Off?" I ask.

"Maybe he's having an orgy or wankin' off and doesn't want his Security to see." Sevro grunts with a shrug. *"Either way, he's hiding something, so that's where we're headed."*

I cue Sevro's personal line so the others can't hear us. *"We can't wander around looking for him. If we're caught in the halls without leverage—"*

"We won't wander." He cuts me off before addressing the Howlers. *"Cloaks on, ladies. Razors and silenced scorchers. PulseFists only if shit gets dirty."* He ripples transparent. *"Howlers, on me."*

We slink from the museum into a maze of otherworldly hallways, following Sevro's lead. Floors of black marble. Walls of glass. Ten-meter-high ceilings made from pulseFields, which look into aquariums where vibrant reefs of coral stretch like fungal tentacles. Reptilian mermaids one foot long with humanoid faces, gray skin, and skulls shaped like crowns swim through a kingdom of scalding blue and violent orange. Hateful little crow eyes glare down at us as they pass.

The walls are moodGlass and pulse with subtle alternating colors. Now heartbeats of magenta, soon rippling curtains of cobalt-silver. It's dreamlike. Amidst the maze are little alcoves. Miniature art galleries showcasing works of contemporary dot holographs and twenty-first century AD ostentaciousism instead of the reserved neoclassical Romanism so in vogue with Peerless Scarred. Recharging our battery packs to our ghostCloaks, we duck into a gallery where lurks a gaudy purple metallic dog shaped like a balloon animal.

Victra sighs. *"Goryhell. Man's got the taste of a tabloid socialite."* Ragnar cocks his head at the dog. ***"What is it?"***

"Art," Victra says. *"Supposedly."*

The tone of condescension Victra strikes intrigues me, as does the building. It pulses with artifice. The art, the walls, the mermaids, all so on the nose of what the Peerless Scarred would expect of a newly moneyed Silver. Quicksilver must know Gold psychology intimately in order to have been allowed to grow so wealthy. So I wonder, is this extravagance all something far more clever? A mask so obvious and easy to accept that no one would ever think to look beneath it? Quicksilver, for all his reputation, has never been called stupid. So perhaps this tawdry dreamscape isn't for him. It's for his guests.

Which makes me think something here is amiss as we reach an unlit atrium with unpolished sandstone floors perforated by pink jasmine trees and slink across the floor in a V formation toward the set of double doors that leads to Quicksilver's bedroom suite. Cloaks deactivated so we can better see. Razors rigid and held out, metal drifting centimeters above the sandstone.

This isn't a home. It's a stage. Made to manipulate. Sinister in the cold calculation with which it was constructed. I don't like it. I key Sevro's frequency again. "Something's wrong here. Where are the servants? The guards?"

"Maybe he likes his privacy . . ."

"I think it's a trap."

"A trap? Your head or your gut talkin'?"

"My gut."

He's quiet for a breath, and I wonder if he's speaking to someone else on the other line. Maybe he's speaking to all of them. *"What's your rec?"*

"Pull back. Assess the situation to see. . . ."

"Pull back?" He snaps the question out. *"For all we know, they just dropped nukes on our people. We need this."* I try to interrupt, but he steamrolls me. *"Shit, I've run thirteen ops just to get intel on this Silvery asshole. We leave now, that's all slagged. They'll know we were here. We won't have this chance again. He's the key to getting the Jackal. You gotta trust me, Reap. Do you?"*

I bite back a curse and cut the signal short, not sure if I'm angry with him or with myself, or because I know the Jackal removed the spark that made me feel different. Every opinion I have feeble, and malleable to others. Because I know, deep down, beneath the intimidating scarabSkin, beneath the demon mask, is a callow little boy who cried because he was scared of being alone in the dark.

Purple light suddenly floods the room as a luxury vessel cruises past the wall of windows at our backs. We hastily line up to either side of the door to Quicksilver's suite, preparing to breach. I watch the vessel drift along through my black optics. Lights pulse on one of its decks as several hundred Pixies writhe to some Etrurian club beat that's all the rage on far-off Luna, as if a war didn't wage on the planet beneath this moon. As if we didn't move to rupture their way of life. They'll drink champagne from Earth in clothes made on Venus in ships fueled by Mars. And they'll laugh and consume and screw and face no consequences. So many little locusts. I feel Sevro's righteous wrath burn in me.

Suffering isn't real to them. War isn't real. It's just a three-letter word for other people that they see in the digital newsfeeds. Just a stream of uncomfortable images they skip past. A whole business of weapons and arms and ships and hierarchies they don't even notice, all to shield these fools from the true agony of what it means to be human. Soon they'll know.

And on their deathbeds, they'll remember tonight. Who they were with. What they were doing when that three-letter word gripped them and never let go. This pleasure cruise, this hideous decadence is the last gasp of the Golden Age.

And what a pathetic gasp it is.

"Of course I trust you," I say, tightening my grip on my razor. Ragnar's watching us, even though he can't hear our signal. Victra's waiting to breach the door.

The light fades, and the ship disappears into the cityscape. I'm surprised to realize I don't feel satisfaction in knowing what's about to happen. In knowing their age will fall. Neither does it bring joy to think of all the lights in all the cities across this empire of man dimming, or all the ships slowing, or all the brilliant Golds fading as their buildings rust and crumble. Would that I could hear Mustang's take on this plan. Before, I've missed her lips, her scent, but now I miss the comfort that comes from knowing her mind is aligned with mine. When I was with her, I did not feel so alone. She'd probably chastise us for focusing on breaking rather than building.

Why do I feel this way now? I'm surrounded by friends, striking at

Gold as I have always wished. Yet something itches in the back of my brain. Like eyes watch me. Whatever Sevro says, something is wrong here. Not just in this building, but with his plan. Is this how I would have done it? How Fitchner would have done it? If it succeeds, what do we usher in after the dust has settled and the helium no longer flows? A dark age? Sevro is a force unto himself. His rage a thing to move mountains.

I was once like that. And look what that got me.

"*Kill his guards. Stun the Pinks. Smash, grab, and go,*" Sevro is saying to his Howlers. My hand tightens on my blade. He gives the signal, and Ragnar and Victra slip through the doors. The rest of us follow into the dark.

16

||||||||||||||||||||||||

PARAMOUR

The lights are off. It's tomb silent. The front room empty. An electric-green jellyfish floats in a tank on a table, casting weird shadows. We move through to the bedroom, smashing through the gold filigreed doors. I guard the door with Pebble, crouching on a knee, silenced railgun cradled in my hands, sheathing my razor on my arm. Behind us, a man sleeps in a four-poster bed. Ragnar grabs him by the foot and jerks him out. Clad in expensive sleepwear, he sprawls onto the floor. Waking midair and screaming silently into Ragnar's hand.

"*Shit. It's not him,*" Victra says behind me. "*It's a Pink.*" I glance back. Ragnar kneels over the Pink, blocking him from my view.

Sevro hits the bedpost, cracking it. "*It's three in the morning. Where the hell is he?*"

"*It is four P.M. market time on Luna,*" Victra says. "*Maybe he's in his office? Ask the slave.*"

"*Where is your master?*" Sevro's mask makes his voice warble like a steel cable struck by an iron rod. I keep my eyes trained on the living room until the Pink's whimper makes me look back. Sevro's got his knee in the man's groin. "*Pretty pajamas, boyo. Wanna see what they look like in red?*"

I flinch at the coldness in this voice. Knowing the tone all too well. Hearing it from the Jackal as he tortured me in Attica.

"Where is your master?" Sevro twists his knee. The Pink wails in pain, but still refuses to answer. The Howlers watch the torture in silence, bent, faceless stains in the dark room. There's no discussion. No moral question at play. I know they've done this before. I feel dirty in the realization, in hearing the Pink sobbing on the ground. This is more a part of war than trumpets or starships. Quiet, unremembered moments of cruelty.

"I don't know," he says. "I don't know."

The voice. I remember that voice from my past. I rush from my post at the door and join Sevro, pulling him off of the Pink. Because I know the man and his gentle features. His long, angular nose, rose-quartz eyes, and dark honey skin. He's as responsible for making me what I am as Mickey ever was. It's Matteo. Beautiful and fragile, now gasping on the ground, arm broken. Bleeding from his mouth, holding his groin where Sevro beat him.

"The hell's your damage?" Sevro snarls at me.

"I know him!" I say.

"What?"

Taking advantage of my distraction, and seeing nothing but the black demon visages of our helms, Matteo lunges for a datapad sitting on the bed stand. Sevro's faster. With a meaty thud the hardest bone density in the species of man meets the softest. Sevro's fist shatters Matteo's fragile jaw. He gags and falls convulsing to the floor, eyes rolling back into his head. I watch in a haze, the violence seeming unreal and yet so cold and primitive and easy. Just muscle and bone moving the way it shouldn't. I find myself reaching for Matteo, falling over his twitching body, shoving Sevro back.

"Don't touch him!" Matteo's been knocked unconscious, mercifully. I can't tell if he has spinal damage or brain trauma. I touch the gentle curls of his now-dusky hair. It has a blue sheen to it. His hand's clutched tight like a child's, a slender silver band on his ring finger. Where has he been this whole time? Why is he here? "I know him," I whisper.

Ragnar's bending beside him protectively, though there's nothing we can do here for Matteo. Clown tosses the datapad to Sevro. *"Panic switch."*

"What do you mean you know him?" Sevro asks.

"He's a Son of Ares," I say, in a daze. "Or he was. He was one of my teachers before the Institute. He taught me Aureate culture."

"Goryhell," Screwface mutters.

Victra toes his wrist where little flowers embellish his pink Sigils. *"He's a Rose of the Garden. Like Theodora."* She glances to Ragnar. *"He costs as much as you, Stained."*

"You're sure it's the same man?" Sevro asks me.

"Of course I'm bloodydamn sure. His name is Matteo."

"Then why is he here?" Ragnar asks.

"Doesn't look like a captive," Victra says. *"Those are expensive pajamas. He's probably a paramour. Quicksilver's not known for celibacy, after all."*

"He must have turned," Sevro says harshly.

"Or he was on an assignment for your father," I say.

"Then why didn't he contact us? He's defected. Means Quicksilver has infiltrated the Sons." Sevro spins to look at the door. *"Shit. He could know about Tinos. He could know about this bloodydamn raid."*

My mind races. Did Ares send Matteo here? Or did Matteo leave a sinking ship? Maybe Matteo told them about me before Harmony did. . . . It's a knife in the gut thinking that. I didn't know him long, but I cared for him. He was a kind person, and there's so few of those left. Now look what we've done to him.

"We should get the hell out of here," Clown is saying.

"Not without Quicksilver," Sevro replies.

"We don't know where Quicksilver is," I say. "There's more to this. We have to wait for Matteo to wake up. Someone have a stimshot?"

"Dose would kill him," Victra says. *"Pink circulatory system can't handle military crank."*

"We don't have time for talking," Sevro barks. *"Can't risk being pinned in here. We move now."* I try to speak, but he rolls on, looking to Clown who is using Matteo's datapad. *"Clown, waddya got?"*

"I've got a food request on the internal server's kitchen subsection.

Looks like someone has ordered a whole host of mutton and jam sandwiches and coffee to room C19."

"Reaper, what do you think?" Ragnar asks.

"It could be a trap," I say. "We need to adjust—"

Victra laughs scornfully, cutting me off. *"Even if it is a trap, look who we're packing. We'll punch through that shit."*

"Bloodydamn right, Julii." Sevro moves toward the door. *"Screwface. Bring the Pink and stow him. Fangs out. Ragnar, Victra in front. Blood's comin'."*

One level down, we meet our first security team. Half a dozen lurchers stand in front of a large glass door that ripples like the surface of a pond. They wear black suits instead of military armor. Implants in the shape of silver heels stick out from the skin behind their left ears. There's more patrolling this level, but no servants. Several Grays in similar suits took a coffee cart into the room a few minutes earlier. Strange that they wouldn't use Pinks or Browns for delivering coffee. Security is tight. So whoever is in Quicksilver's office must be important. Or at least very paranoid.

"We're flowing quick," Sevro says, leaning back around the hallway corner where we wait thirty meters from the group of Grays. *"Neutralize those shitheads, then breach fastlike."*

"We don't know who is in there," Clown says

"And there's only one way to find out," Sevro barks. *"Go."*

Ragnar and Victra go first around the corner, ghostCloaks bending the light. The rest of us follow at a dead sprint. One of the Grays squints down the hall at us. The implanted thermal optics in his irises throb red as they activate and see the heat radiating from our battery packs. "GhostCloaks!" he shouts. Six sets of practiced hands flow to scorchers. Far too late. Ragnar and Victra tear into them. Ragnar swings his razor, cutting off one's arm and severing the jugular of another. Blood sprays over the glass walls. Victra fires her silenced scorcher. Magnetically hurled slugs slam into two heads. I slide forward between falling bodies. Stick my razor through a man's rib cage. Feeling the pop and give of his heart. I retract my blade into whip form to free it. Let it stiffen again back to my slingBlade before the man drops.

The Grays haven't managed to fire a single shot. But one has pressed a button on his datapad, and the deep throbbing sound of the tower's alarm echoes down the hall. The walls pulse red, signaling an emergency. Sevro cuts the last man down.

"Breach the room. Now!" he shouts.

Something's wrong. I feel it in my gut, but Victra and Sevro are propelling this forward. And Ragnar's kicking in the door. Ever a slave to momentum, I plunge in after him.

Quicksilver's conference room is less flamboyant than the rooms above. Its ceiling is ten meters high. Its walls are of digital glass that swirls subtly with silver smoke. Two rows of marble pillars run parallel on either side of a giant onyx conference table with a dead white tree rising from its center. At the far end of the room, a huge viewing window looks out at the industry of the Hive. Regulus ag Sun, hailed from Mercury to Pluto as Quicksilver, richest man under the sun, stands before the window, mauling a glass of red wine with a fleshy hand.

He's bald. Forehead wrinkled as a washboard. Pugilist lips. Hunched simian shoulders leading to butcher fingers that sprout from the sleeves of a high-collared Venusian turquoise robe embroidered with apple trees. He's in his sixties. Skin bronzed with a marrow-deep tan. A small goatee and mustache accent his face in a vain attempt to give it shape, though it seems he's stayed away from Carvers for the most part. His feet are bare. But it's his three eyes that demand attention. Two are heavy-lidded and Silver. An earthy, efficient shade. The third is Gold and implanted in a simple silver ring the man wears on the middle finger of his fat right hand.

We've interrupted his meeting.

Nearly thirty Coppers and Silvers pack the room. They're formed into two parties and sit across from one another at a giant's onyx table littered with coffee cups, wine carafes, and datapads. A blue holo document floats in the air between the two factions, obviously the object of their attention until the door shattered inward. Now they push back from the table, most too stunned yet to feel fear, or to even see us as the Howlers enter the room in ghostCloaks. But it isn't just Coppers and Silvers at the table.

"*Oh, shit,*" Victra sputters.

Among the professional Colors rise six Golden knights in full pulseArmor. And I know them all. On the left, a dark-faced older man wearing the pure black armor of the Death Knight, on either side of him are pudgy-faced Moira—a Fury, sister of Aja—and good old Cassius au Bellona. To the right are Kavax au Telemanus, Daxo au Telemanus, and the girl who left me on my knees in the old mining tunnels of Mars nearly one year ago.

Mustang.

17

IIIIIIIIIIIIIIIIIIIIIIII

KILLING GOLDS

"Hold your fire!" I shout, pushing down Victra's weapon, but Sevro's barking orders, and Victra brings her weapon back up. We form a staggered line with our pulseFists and scorchers aimed at the Golds. We hold fire because we need Quicksilver alive, and I know Sevro's as stunned as I to see Mustang, Cassius, and the Telemanuses here.

"*On the ground or we waste you!*" Sevro screams, voice inhuman and magnified by his demonHelm. The Howlers join him, filling the air with a harpy's chorus of commands. My blood pumps cold. The alarm throbs around the roaring voices. Not knowing what to do, I point my pulseFist at the most dangerous Gold in the room, Cassius, knowing what must be going through Sevro's mind as he sees his father's killer in the flesh. My helmet syncs with the weapon, to illuminate weak points in his armor, but my eyes drink in Mustang as she sets down a cup of coffee, graceful as ever, and steps back from the table, the pulseFist implanted in the left gauntlet of her armor slowly beginning to blossom open.

My mind and heart war against each other. What the hell is she doing here? She's supposed to be in the Rim. Like her, the other Golds aren't listening to us. They don't know who we are past our helmets. No wolfcloaks today. They step back, eyes wary, judging the situation. Cassius's razor slithers on his right arm. Kavax slowly lifts himself from his chair along with Daxo. Quicksilver waves his hands frantically.

"Stop!" he shouts, voice nearly lost in the chaos. "Do not fire! This is a diplomatic meeting! Identify yourselves!" We've stumbled into the middle of some negotiation, I realize. A surrender of Mustang's forces? An alliance? Noticeably absent is the Jackal. Is Quicksilver betraying him? He must be. So must the Sovereign. That's why this place is so deserted. No servants, minimum security. Quicksilver wanted only men he trusted at this meeting held so close under his ally's nose.

My stomach lurches as I realize the rest of the room must think we're Boneriders. Which means they think we're here to kill them, and this is going to end only one way.

"*On the bloodydamn ground!*" Victra bellows.

"*What do we do?*" Pebble asks over the com. "*Reaper?*"

"I claim the Bellona," Sevro says.

"Use stun weapons!" I say. "It's Mustang—"

"*Won't do shit against that armor,*" Sevro interrupts. "*If they lift their weapons, kill the pricks. Full pulse charges. I'm not risking any of our family.*"

"Sevro, listen to me. We need to talk to—" My words cut short because he uses the master command built into his helmet to jam my com output signal. I can hear them, but they can't hear me. I curse futilely at him.

"*Bellona, stop moving!*" Clown shouts. "*I said stop.*"

Opposite Mustang, Cassius silently drifts through the Silvers, using them as cover to close the gap between us. He's only ten meters away. Getting closer. I sense Victra tensing beside me, hungry to be let loose on one of the men who she blames for her mother's death, but there's civilians between us and the Golds, and Quicksilver's a prize we can't afford to lose.

My eyes judge the plump cheeks of the Silvers and Coppers. Not a soul here is oppressed. Not a belly here has ever been hungry. These are collaborators. Sevro would scalp them one by one if given a rusty knife and a few idle hours.

"*Reaper . . .*" Ragnar says quietly, looking to me for instruction.

"*Take your hand away from the razor!*" Victra shouts at Cassius. He stays quiet. Coming forward, certain as a glacier. Moira and the Death Knight follow after him. Kavax's helmet is slithering up to cover his head. Mustang's face is already covered. Her pulseFist active and pointed at the ground.

I know death well enough to hear it gather its breath.

I activate my external speakers. "*Kavax, Mustang, stop. It's me. It's—*"

"*Stop moving, you piece of shit!*" Victra snarls. Cassius smiles pleasantly and he lunges forward. Ragnar makes a weird twisting movement to my left, and one of the two razors he carries flies through the air and skewers the Death Knight through his forehead. The Silvers gape at the famous Olympic Knight teetering to the ground.

"KAVAX AU TELEMANUS," Kavax roars and rushes forward with Daxo. Mustang breaks sideways. Moira charges, lifting her pulseFist.

"*Waste 'em,*" Sevro says with a snarl.

The room erupts. Air torn to shreds by superheated particles as the Howlers open fire at point-blank range into the crowded room. Marble turns to dust. Chairs melt into gnarled chunks of metal and kick across the floor. Meat and bone explode, filling the air with red mist, as Silvers and Coppers are caught in the crossfire. Sevro misses Cassius, who dives behind a pillar. Kavax is shot a dozen times, but he doesn't falter even as his shields overheat. He's going to smash into Sevro and Victra with his razor when Ragnar charges from the side and hits the smaller man so hard with his shoulder that Kavax is lifted clean off his feet. Daxo attacks Ragnar from behind, and three giants tumble to the side of the room, crushing two scrabbling Coppers half their size as they go. The Coppers scream on the ground, legs shattered.

Behind Kavax, Mustang takes two shots to the chest, but her pulse-Shield holds. She stumbles, fires back at us, hitting Pebble in her thigh. Pebble's lifted backward and flipped into the wall, leg shattered from the blast. She screams and clutches at it. Clown and Victra cover her, firing back at Mustang, dragging Pebble behind a pillar. Screwface and four other Howlers who guarded the door and kept Matteo outside now fire into the room from the hallway.

I stumble sideways, lost in the chaos, as the marble where I stood shatters. Silvers scramble under the table. Others kick away from their chairs, racing for the imagined safety of the columns on the fringes of the room. Hypersonic pulsefire rips between them, over their heads, through them. Buckling the columns. Quicksilver runs behind two Coppers, using them as human shields when shrapnel rips into them, and they all tumble down in a mess of limbs and blood.

Moira, the Fury, rushes Sevro to impale my friend from behind with her razor as he tries to move past Ragnar, who's fighting both Telemanuses, to get at Cassius. I fire my pulseFist point-blank into her side just before she reaches him. Her armor's pulseShield absorbs the first few rounds, rippling blue in a cocoon around her. She stumbles sideways, and if I did not continue to fire, she'd have nothing but a bruise in the morning. But my middle finger is heavy on the trigger of the weapon. She's an engineer of oppression, and one of the best minds of Gold. And she tried to kill Sevro. Bad play.

I fire till her shield buckles inward, till she falls to a knee, till she twitches and screams as the molecules of her skin and organs superheat. Boiling blood comes out her eyes and nose. Armor and flesh fuse together, and I feel the rage ride wild inside me, numbing me to fear, to sense, to compassion. This is the Reaper who laid Cassius low. Who slew Karnus. Who Gold cannot kill.

Moira's pulseFist fires wildly as the tendons of her fingers contract in the heat. Shooting into the ceiling on full automatic. Twitching sideways, whipping a stream of death across the room. Two Silvers running for cover explode. The glass of the viewport at the far end of the room, which looks out onto the space city, cracks perilously. Howlers scramble for cover till the pulseFist glows molten on Moira's left hand and the barrel overheats to melt inward with a corrupt fizzle. With that last gasp of rage, the wisest of the Sovereign's three Furies lies in a charred husk.

My only wish is that it could have been Aja.

I turn back to the room, feeling the cool hand of wrath guiding me, hungering for more blood. But all those that are left are my friends. Or once were. I shudder with hollowness as the rage leaves me as fast as it came. Replaced by panic as I watch my friends try to kill one another. The ordered lines have broken down into a hi-tech brawl. Feet sliding on glass. Shoulder blades slamming into walls. PulseFist battles between pillars. Hands and knees scrambling against the floor as pulseFists wail and blades clamor and hack.

And it's only now, only with this terrifying clarity, that I realize that there is only one common thread that binds them. It's not an idea. Not my wife's dream. Not trust or alliances or Color.

It's me.

And without me, this is what they will do. Without me, this is what Sevro has been doing. What an inevitable waste it seems. Death begets death begets death.

I have to stop it.

At the center of the room, Cassius stumbles after Victra through twisted chairs and shattered glass. Blood slicks the floor beneath them. Her damaged ghostCloak sparks on and off and she flashes between ghost and shadow like an undecided demon. Cassius cuts her again across the thigh and spins as Clown shoots at him, cutting Clown across the side of his head before bending back to dodge a shot from Pebble on the ground across the room. Victra rolls under the table to escape Cassius, slicing at his ankles. He jumps onto the table, firing his pulseFist into the onyx till it caves in the center, trapping her beneath. He's inches from killing her when Sevro shoots him from behind, the blast absorbed by Cassius's shield, but one that knocks him several meters to the side.

To the right, Ragnar, Daxo, and Kavax fight a duel of titans. Ragnar pins Kavax's arm to the wall with his razor, leaves the weapon, ducks, fires his pulseFist into Daxo at point-blank range. Daxo's shields absorb the blast, and his razor misses Ragnar and takes out a chunk of the wall instead. Ragnar hits Daxo in his joints and is about to snap his neck when Kavax skewers him through the shoulder with a razor, screaming his family name. I rush to help my Stained friend, but as I do I feel someone to my left.

I turn just in time to see Mustang flying through the air at me, her helmet covering her face, her razor arching down to cut me in two. I bring my own razor up just in time. Blades slam together. Vibrations rattle down my arm. I'm slower than I remember, much of my muscle instinct lost to the darkness despite Mickey's lab and my training bouts with Victra. Plus Mustang's gotten faster.

I'm pressed back. I try to flow around Mustang, but she moves her razor like she's been at war for the last year. I try to slip to the side, like Lorn taught me, but there's no escape. She's smart, using the rubble, the pillars, to corner me. I'm being hemmed in, corralled by the flashing metal. My defense doesn't cave, but it erodes along the edges as I protect my core.

The blade parts an inch-deep gash through my left shoulder. Stings like a pitviper bite. I curse and she slices through more flesh. I'd shout at her to stop. Shout my name, something, if I had even half a second to breathe, but it's all I can do to keep my arms moving. I bend back just in time as she cuts a shallow gash through the neck of my scarab-Skin. Three quick cuts at the tendons of my right arm follow, just missing. Building a rhythm. My back's touching the wall. Cut. Cut. Stab. Fire opening up my skin. I'm going to die here. I call for help over my com, but they're still jammed by Sevro.

We've bitten off more than we can chew.

I scream in futility as Mustang's blade scrapes through three of my ribs. She spins the blade in her hand. Swings backhanded to cut my head off. I manage to deflect the razor into the wall with mine, pinning it above my head so her helmet is near my mask. I head-butt her. But her helmet's stronger than the composite duroplastic of my mask. She reels back her own head and slams it into mine, using my own tactic. A seam of pain splinters down my skull. I nearly black out. Vision rushing out, in. Still standing. Feel part of my mask crack off and slide off my face. Nose broken again. Seeing spots. The rest of the mask crumbles and I stare at the death-eyed horse helmet of Mustang as she prepares to end me.

Her razor arm draws back to deliver the killing stroke. And it stays there above her head. Trembling as she looks at my exposed face. Her helmet slithers away to reveal her own. Sweat-soaked hair clings to her forehead, darkening the golden luster. Beneath, her eyes are wild, and I wish I could say it's love or joy I see in them, but it's not. If anything, it's fear, maybe horror that draws the blood from her face as she stumbles back, gesturing speechlessly with her off-hand.

"Darrow . . . ?"

She looks over her shoulder to see the mayhem that still grips the room, our quiet moment a little bubble in the storm. Cassius flees, disappearing through a side door, leaving the corpse of the Death Knight and Moira behind. Our eyes meet before he disappears. Victra gives chase until Sevro reels her back in. The rest of the Howlers are turning toward Mustang. I take a step toward her, and stop when the tip of her razor pricks my collarbone.

"I saw you die."

She backs away toward the main door, boots sliding over the marble, crunching on bits of glass from the walls. "Kavax, Daxo!" she calls, a vein in her neck bulging from strain. "Pull back!"

The Telemanuses scramble to separate themselves from Ragnar, confused at who the masked man they are fighting is and why they're bleeding in so many places. They try to regroup on Mustang, both men rushing for her in a hasty retreat, but as they pass me to join her near the door, I know I can't just watch her go. So I whip my razor around Kavax's neck. He gags and reels against me, but I hold on. With the press of a button, I could retract my whip and sever his head. But I've no interest in killing the man. He falls only when Ragnar sweeps his leg and puts a knee into his chest. Slamming to the floor. Screwface and the others are on him, pinning him down.

"Don't kill him," I shout. Screwface knew Pax. He's met the Telemanuses, so he holds his blade and snaps at the newer Howlers to do the same. Daxo tries to rush to his father's aid, but Ragnar and I bar his way. His bright eyes stare in confusion at my face.

"Go, Virginia!" Kavax roars from the ground. "Flee!"

"I have the *Pax*. Orion is alive," Mustang says, eying the bloody Howlers who are at my back, coming for her and Daxo. "Don't kill him. Please." And then, with a sorrowful look to Kavax, she flees the room.

18

||||||||||||||||||||||||||||

ABYSS

"What did she mean, Orion's alive?" I ask Kavax. He's as shell-shocked as I am, nervously eying the black-clad Howlers prowling through the room. We didn't lose one, but we're in shit shape. "Kavax!"

"What she said," he rumbles. "Exactly what she said. The *Pax* is safe."

"Darrow!" Sevro shouts as he reenters the room with Victra. They pursued Cassius through the blackened door on the far side of the room but return empty-handed and limping. "On me!" There's more I want to ask Kavax, but Victra's wounded. I rush to her as she leans against the shattered onyx table, hunched over a deep gash in her biceps. Her mask's off, face twisted and sweating as she injects herself with painkillers and blood coagulant to stem the flow from the wound. I see the hint of bone through the blood.

"Victra . . ."

"Shit," she says with a dark laugh. "Your boyfriend is faster than he used to be. Almost got him in the hall, but I think Aja taught him a little of your Willow Way."

"Looked like," I say. "You prime?"

"Don't worry about me, darling." She gives me a wink as Sevro calls my name again. He and Clown are bent over Moira's smoking remains. The terrorist lord is unfazed by the carnage around us.

"One of the Furies," Clown says. "Roasted."

"Good cooking, Reap," Sevro drawls. "Crispy on the edges, bloody down the middle. Just how I like. Aja's gonna be pissed—"

"You cut my coms," I interrupt angrily.

"You were acting a bitch. Confusing my men."

"Acting a bitch? The hell is wrong with you? I was using my head instead of just shooting everything. We could have done without murdering half the damn room."

His eyes are darker and crueler than those of the friend I remember. "This is war, boyo. Murder's the name of the game. Don't be sad we're good at it."

"That was Mustang!" I say, stepping close to him. "What if we killed her?" He shrugs. I poke his chest. "Did you know she would be here? Tell me the truth."

"Naw," he says slowly. "Didn't know. Now back up, boyo." He looks up at me impudently, like he wouldn't mind taking a swing. I don't back up.

"What was she doing here?"

"How the hell would I know?" He looks past me to Ragnar, who is pushing Kavax back toward the Howlers gathering in the center of the room. "Everyone prepare to squab out. We're gonna have to cut through an army to get out of this shit den. Evac point is ten floors up on the black side."

"Where's our prize?" Victra asks, eying the carnage. Bodies litter the ground. Silvers shivering in pain. Coppers crawling across the floor, dragging broken legs.

"Probably fried," I say.

"Prolly," Clown agrees, casting me a commiserating look as we move from Sevro to pick through the bodies. "It's a slaggin' mess."

"Did you know Mustang would be here?" I ask.

"Not at all. Seriously, boss." He glances back at Sevro. "What'd you mean he jammed your coms?"

"Stop jawin' and find the bloodydamn Silver," Sevro barks from the center of the room. "Somebody grab the Pink from the hall."

Clown finds Quicksilver at the opposite end of the room, farthest from the hallway door, to the right of the grand viewport that looks down onto Phobos. He's lying motionless, pinned under a pillar that broke from its place in the floor to fall sideways against the wall. The blood of others covers his turquoise tunic. Bits of glass jut from wounded knuckles. I feel his pulse. He's alive. So the mission wasn't a damn waste. But there's a contusion on his forehead from shrapnel. I call Ragnar and Victra, the two strongest of our party, to help pry the pillar off the man.

Ragnar wedges the razor he threw into the Death Knight's head under the pillar, using a rock as a fulcrum, and is about to heave upward with me when Victra calls for us to wait. "Look," she says. Where the pillar's top meets the wall, there's a faint blue glow along a seam that runs from the floor up the wall to form a rectangle in the wall. It's a hidden door. Quicksilver must have been rushing toward it when the pillar fell. Victra puts her ear against the door, and her eyes narrow.

"PulseTorches," she says. "Oh, ho." She laughs. "Silver's bodyguards are through there. Must have hid them in case things got tense. They're speaking *Nagal*." The language of the Obsidians. And they're cutting their way through the wall. We'd be dead if the pillar hadn't fallen and blocked the door.

Pure luck saved our hides. All three of us know it, and it deepens the anger I have with Sevro and calms a bit of the wildness in Victra's eyes. Suddenly she's seeing how reckless this was. We never should have rushed into this place without its blueprints. Sevro did what I would have done a year ago. Same result. The three of us share a common thought, glancing at the main door of the room. We don't have long.

Ragnar and Victra help me pry Quicksilver free. The unconscious man's legs drag behind him, broken, as Victra carries him back to the center of the room. There, Sevro is readying Clown and Pebble to push out from the room with our prisoners, Matteo and Kavax, who stares at me openmouthed. But Pebble can't even stand. We're all in shit shape.

"We've too many prisoners," I say. "We won't be able to move fast. And we don't have any EMPs this time." Not that they'd do anyone any good on a space station when all that separates us from space is inch-thin bulkheads and air recyclers.

"Then we trim the fat," Sevro says, stalking toward Kavax, who sits wounded and bound with his hands behind his back. He points his pulseFist into Kavax's face. "Nothin' personal, big man."

Sevro pulls the trigger. I shove him sideways. The pulse blast misses Kavax's head and slams into the ground near the slumped form of Matteo, nearly taking off the man's leg. Sevro wheels on me, pulseFist pointing at my head.

"Get that out of my face," I say down the barrel. Heat radiating into my eyes, causing them to sting so I have to look away.

"Who do you think that is," Sevro snarls. "Your friend? He's not your friend."

"We need him alive. He's a chip to barter. And Orion might be alive."

"Chip to barter?" Sevro snorts. "What about Moira? Had no problem frying her, but you spare him." Sevro squints at me, lowering his weapon. His lips curl back from his janky teeth. "Oh, it's for Mustang. Of course it is."

"He's Pax's father," I say.

"And Pax is dead. Why? 'Cause you let enemies live. This isn't the Institute, boyo. This is war." He jams a finger in my face. "And war is really bloodydamn simple. Kill the enemy when you can, however you can, as fast as you can. Or they kill you and yours."

Sevro turns from me, realizing now that the others are watching us with growing trepidation. "You're wrong about this," I say.

"We *can't* drag them with us."

"Halls are swarming, boss," Screwface says, returning from the main hall. "More than a hundred security personnel. We're slagged."

"We can cut through them if we go light," Sevro says.

"A hundred?" Clown says. "Boss . . ."

"Check your juice packs," Sevro says, squinting at his pulseFist.

No. I'll not let Sevro's shortsightedness ruin us.

"Slag that," I say. "Pebble, hail Holiday. Tell her evac is squabbed. Give her our coordinates. She's to park one kilometer beyond the glass, ass end our way." Pebble doesn't reach for her datapad. She glances at Sevro, torn between us, not knowing who to follow. "I'm back," I say. "Now do it."

"Do it, Pebble," Ragnar says.

Victra gives a small nod. Pebble grimaces at Sevro, "Sorry, Sevro." She nods to me and opens up her com to hail Holiday. The rest of the Howlers look to me, and it hurts knowing I've made them choose like this.

"Clown, grab Moira's datapad if it isn't fried and get the data from the console if you can. I want to know what contract they were negotiating," I say quickly, "Screwface, take Sleepy and cover the hall. Ragnar, Kavax is yours. He tries to flee, cut his feet off. Victra, you got any rappelling line left?" She checks her belt and nods. "Start tying us together. Everyone in the center of the room. Has to be tight." I turn to Sevro. "Lay charges at the door. Company's coming."

He says nothing. It's not anger behind his eyes. It's the secret seeds of self-doubt and fear coming to blossom, hate seeping into his eyes. I know the look. I've felt it on my own face too many times to count. I'm ripping away the only thing he's ever cared about. His Howlers. After all he's done, I make them choose me over him, when he doesn't trust I'm ready. It's an indictment of his leadership, a validation of the intense self-doubt I know he must feel in the wake of his father's passing.

It shouldn't have been that way. I said I'd follow and I didn't. That's on me. But this isn't the time for coddling. I tried words with him, tried using our friendship to make him see reason, but since I've been back I've seen him respond to things only with violence and force. So now I'll speak his bloodydamn language. I step forward. "Unless you want to die here, sack up and get moving."

His wrinkled little face hardens as he watches his Howlers run to do my bidding. "You get them killed, I'll never forgive you."

"Makes two of us. Now go."

He turns away, running toward the door to plant the remaining explosives from his belt. I remain looking around the broken room, finally seeing organization in the chaos as my friends work together. They'll all have deduced my plan by now. They know how manic it is. But the confidence with which they work breathes life into me. They put the trust in me that Sevro wouldn't. Still, I catch Ragnar glancing at the viewport three times now. All our suits are compromised. Not one of us will be able to stay pressurized in vacuum. I don't even have a mask. Whether we live or die is up to Holiday. I wish there was some way I could control the variables, but if the time in darkness taught me anything, it's that the world is larger than my grasp. Have to trust others. "Jammers on, everyone," I say, toggling my own on my belt. Don't want the cameras outside spotting anyone's exposed faces.

"Holiday is in position," Pebble says. I glance out the window to see the transport hovering a click beyond the window. Hardly larger than a pen tip at this distance.

"On my mark, we are going to fire at the center of the viewport," I tell my friends, making an effort to keep the fear from my voice. "Screwface! Sleepy! Get back here. Put your masks on the unconscious prisoners."

"Oh, goryhell," Victra mutters. "I was hoping you had a better plan than that."

"If you try to hold your breath, your lungs will explode. So exhale soon as the viewport shatters. Let yourself pass out. Have sweet dreams, and pray for Holiday to be as quick on the stick as Clown is in the bedroom."

They laugh and cluster tight, letting Victra wind her rappelling line through our munitions belts so we're together like grapes on a vine. Sevro's finishing laying explosives at the door, Sleepy and Screwface join us, waving at him to hurry.

"*Attention,*" a voice booms from hidden speakers in the walls as Victra leans close to me to link me with Ragnar. "*This is Alec ti Yamato. Head of Security for Sun Industries. You are surrounded. Discard your weapons. Release your hostages. Or we will be forced to fire on you. You have five seconds to comply.*"

There's no one in the room but us. The main doors are closed.

Sevro runs back to us from laying the charges. "Sevro, fastlike!" I shout. He's not halfway to us when he crumples to the ground like an empty can crushed by a boot. I'm slammed down to the floor by the same force. Knees buckling. Bones, lungs, throat all stomped down by massive gravity. My vision swims. Blood moving sluggishly to my head. I try to lift my arm. It weighs more than three hundred pounds. Security has increased the artificial gravity in the room, and only Ragnar's not on his belly. He's fallen to a knee, shoulders hunched and straining, like Atlas holding up the world.

"The hell is that . . ." Victra manages, on the floor looking past me to the door. It's opened, and through it comes not a Gray or an Obsidian or Gold. But a giant black egg the size of a small man, rolling sideways. It's smooth and glossy, and small white numbers mark its side. A robot. As illegal as EMPs. Augustus's great fear. Like reaching out of an oil spill, the metal morphs at the point of the egg to reveal a small cannon, which aims at Sevro. I try to rise. Try to aim my pulseFist. But the gravity is too much. I can't even lift my arm to point the weapon. For all her strength, Victra can't either. Sevro's grunting on the floor, crawling away from the machine.

"The viewport!" I manage. "Ragnar. Fire at the viewport."

His pulseFist is at his side. Straining, he begins to lift it against the massive gravity. Arm shaking. Throat gargling that eerie war chant that sounds like a distant avalanche. The sound rises, an otherworldy bellow till his whole body convulses with effort and his arm draws level and the smallest of stars is born in his palm as the pulseFist gathers its trembling molten charge.

The entirety of my friend shudders and his fingers release the trigger. His arm wrenches back. The pulsefire leaps forward to scream into the center of the glass pane. The many stars ripple as the pane bends outward and cracks shoot down the window.

"*Kadir njar laga . . .*" Ragnar bellows.

And the glass shatters. Space drinks the air of the room. Everything slides. A Copper flips past us, screaming. She goes silent when she hits vacuum. Others who cowered during our brawl cling to the broken table in the center of the room. They wrap themselves around pillars. Fingers bleeding, nails cracking. Legs flailing. Grips giving out. Corpses flip end over end out into space as the abyss hungers for everything the building has. Sevro's ripped into the air away from the robot, lighter than our combined group. I reach for him and grab his short Mohawk till Victra wraps her legs around him and pulls him to her body.

I'm terrified as we slide toward the broken viewport. Hands shaking. Doubting my decision as I now stare it in the face. Sevro was right. We should have pushed into the building. Killed Kavax or used him as a shield. Anything but the cold. Anything but the Jackal's darkness from which I only just escaped.

It's just fear, I tell myself. It's just fear making me panic. And it's spread through my friends. I see the horror on their faces. How they look back at me and see that fear reflected in my own. I cannot be afraid. I've spent too long being afraid. Too long being diminished by loss. Too long being everything except what I need to be. And whether I am the Reaper, or whether it's just another mask, it's one I must wear, not just for them, but for myself.

"*Omnis vir lupus!*" I shout, kicking my head back to howl, exhaling all the air in my lungs. Beside me, Ragnar's eyes widen in wild ecstasy. He opens his massive mouth and bellows out a howl to make his ancestors hear him from their icy crypts. Then Pebble joins, and Clown, and even regal Victra. It's rage and fear leaving our bodies. Though space drags us across the floor to its embrace. Though death might come for us. I am home in this weird screaming mass of humanity. And as we pretend to be brave, we become so.

All except Sevro, who remains silent as we fly into space.

19

||||||||||||||||||||||||

PRESSURE

We rip through the broken viewport into vacuum at eighty kilometers an hour. Silence swallows our howling. A shock hits my body, like I've fallen into cold water. My body twitches. The oxygen expands in my blood, forcing my mouth to hiccup for air that isn't there. Lungs don't inflate. They're collapsed fibrous sacks. My body jerks, desperate for oxygen. But as the seconds tick by and I see the inhuman metal of Phobos's skyscrapers, and watch my friends linked together in the darkness, held together by hands and bits of wire, a stillness settles over me. The same stillness that came in the snows with Mustang, that came when the Howlers and I hunkered tight in the gulches of the Institute to roast goat meat and listen to Quinn tell her stories. I sink slowly into another memory. Not of Lykos, or Eo or Mustang. But of the cold Academy hangar bay where Victra, Tactus, Roque, and I first learned from a pale Blue professor what space does to a man's body.

"Ebulism, or the formation of bubbles in body fluids due to reduced ambient pressure, is the most severe component of vacuum exposure. Water in the tissues of your body will vaporize, causing gross swelling. . . ."

"My darling airhead, I'm well accustomed to gross swelling. Just ask your mother. And your father. And your sister." I hear Tactus say in the memory. And I remember Roque's laugh. How his cheeks blushed at the crudeness of the joke, which makes me wonder why he stood so close to Tactus. Why he cared so much about our bawdy friend's drug use and then wept by Tactus's bedside when he lay dead. The teacher continues. . . .

". . . and multiplicative increase in body volume in ten seconds, followed by circulatory failure . . ."

I feel sleepy even as pressure builds in my eyes, warping my vision and distending the tissue there. Pressure builds in my freezing fingers and aching, popped eardrums. My tongue is huge and cold, like an ice serpent slithering through my mouth into my belly as liquid evaporates. Skin stretches, inflating. My fingers are plantains. Gas in my stomach ballooning my gut. Darkness coming to claim me. I glimpse Sevro beside me. His face is freakish, swollen to twice its normal size. Legs still wrapped around him, Victra looks a monster. She's awake and staring at him with cartoonish, bloodshot eyes, hiccupping for oxygen like a fish out of water. Their hands tighten around each other's.

"Water and dissolved gas in the blood forms bubbles in your major veins, which travel throughout the circulatory system, obstructing blood flow and delivering unconsciousness in fifteen seconds. . . ."

My body fades. Seconds becoming an eternal twilight, everything slowed, everything so pointless and poignant as I see how ridiculous our human strength is in the end. Take us from our bubbles of life, and what are we? The metal towers around us look carved of ice. The lights and flashing HC screens like the scales of dragons frozen inside them.

Mars is over our heads, consuming and omnipotent. But in Phobos's fast rotation, we're already nearing a place on the planet where dawn comes and light carves a crescent into the darkness. Molten wounds still glow where the two nuclear bombs detonated. And I wonder, in my last moments, if the planet does not mind that we wound her surface or pillage her bounty, because she knows we silly warm things are not even a breath in her cosmic life. We have grown and spread, and will rage and die. And when all that remains of us is our steel monuments and plastic idols, her winds will whisper, her sands will shift, and she will spin on and on, forgetting about the bold, hairless apes who thought they deserved immortality.

I'm blind.

I wake on metal. Feel plastic against my face. Gasping around me. Bodies moving. The coldness of a shuttle engine rumbling under the deck. My body seizes and shivers. I suck down the oxygen. It feels like my head has caved in. The pain is everywhere and fading with each pulse of my heart. My fingers are their normal size. I rub them together, trying to orient myself. I'm shivering, but there's a thermal blanket on me, unsentimental hands rubbing me to promote circulation. To my left, I hear Pebble calling for Clown. We'll all be blind for several minutes as our optic nerves recalibrate. He answers her groggily and she nearly breaks down crying.

"Victra!" Sevro's slurring. "Wake up. Wake up." Gear rattles as he shakes her. "Wake up!" He slaps her face. She wakes with a gasp.

". . . the hell. Did you just hit me?"

"I thought . . ."

She slaps him back.

"Who is that?" I ask the hands that rub my shoulders through the blanket.

"Holiday, sir. We scooped you popsicles up four minutes ago."

"How long . . . How long were we out there?"

"'Bout two minutes, thirty seconds. It was a shitshow. We had to empty the cargo bay and have the pilot fly backward into you, then pressurize it on the fly. These carrots can't soldier, but they can damn well steer garbage ships. Still, if you hadn't been linked, most of you would be dead as lead. There's rubble and corpses floating around the sector now. HC crews crawling everywhere."

"Ragnar?" I ask fearfully, not having heard him yet.

"I am here, my friend. The Abyss will not claim us yet." He begins to laugh. **"Not just yet."**

20

||||||||||||||||||||||||

DISSENT

We're in trouble, and Sevro knows it. Seizing command back from me as soon as we land in the dilapidated docking berth of a Sons of Ares safe house deep in industrial sector, he orders the still-unconscious Matteo and Quicksilver to the infirmary to be woken up, Kavax to a cell, and tells Rollo and the Sons to prepare for an assault. The Sons stare at us, dumbstruck. Our Obsidian disguises are obliterated. Particularly mine. The prosthetics on my face have fallen off in the battle. Contacts sucked off in the vacuum. Black hair dye thinned out from sweat. Still got my gloves, though. But these Sons don't look at a pack of Obsidians now. They're staring at a cadre of Golds, an Obsidian, a Gray, and at least one ghost.

"The Reaper . . . ," someone whispers.

"Keep your mouth shut," Clown snaps. "Not a word to anyone."

Whatever he says, soon the rumor will spread among them. The Reaper lives. Whatever the effect it'll have, it's not the right time. We may have avoided police pursuit, but such a high-profile kidnapping, not to mention the assassination of two high-level Peerless, will ensure that the full analytical weight of the Jackal's counterterrorism units is brought to bear on the evidence. Praetorian and Securitas antiterrorism tech squads will already be poring over the footage of the attack. They'll discover how we gained access to the facility, how we made our escape, and who our likely compatriots were. Every weapon, piece of equipment, ship used will be traced to its source. Society reprisals against lowColors throughout the station will be swift and brutal.

And when they analyze the visual evidence of our little vacuum escape, they'll see my face and Sevro's. Then Jackal himself will come, or he'll send Antonia or Lilath to hunt me down with their Boneriders.

The clock's ticking.

But that's supposing the authorities suspect that only Quicksilver was kidnapped. I don't know why Mustang and Cassius were meeting, but I have to assume the Jackal doesn't know about it. That's why I used our jammers. So the security cameras outside of Quicksilver's control wouldn't ID Kavax. If the Jackal saw him here, he'd know something was amiss with his alliance with the Sovereign and Quicksilver. And I want to keep that card in my pocket till I know how best to use it and can speak with Mustang.

But what will the Sovereign think when Cassius calls her to tell her Moira is dead? And what is Mustang's place here? There are too many questions. Too many things I don't know. But what haunts me as we run down metal halls, as my friends go to patch wounds and we pass armories where dozens of Reds and Browns and Oranges load weapons and buckle armor, is what she said.

"I have the *Pax*. Orion is alive."

With her, that could mean a dozen things, and the only one who will know is Kavax. I need to ask him, but Ragnar's already taken him down another hall to the Sons lockup and Sevro's stopped rattling off orders to others to address me. "Reap, they're gonna hit us, and hit us hard," he's saying. "You know Legion military procedures better than I do. Get to the datacenter, fastlike. Give me a timetable and their plan of attack. We can't stop them, but we can buy time."

"Time for what?" I ask.

"To blow the bombs and find a way out off this rock." He puts a hand on my arm, just as cognizant of those Sons watching as I am.

"Please. Get moving." He heads off down the hall with the rest of the Howlers, leaving me alone with Holiday. I turn to her.

"Holiday, you know Legion procedures. Get to the datacenter. Give the Sons the tactical support they need." She looks back down the hall to where Sevro has turned a corner. "You good with that?" I ask.

"Yes, sir. Where you going?"

I tighten my gloves. "To get answers."

"Virginia told us you were a Red after she left you. That is why we did not come to your Triumph," Kavax says up to me. He's bound to a steel pipe, legs splayed out on the floor. Still in his armor, red-gold beard dark in the low light. He cuts a menacing figure, but I'm surprised by the openness of his face. The lack of hatred. The clarity of excitement as his nostrils flare wide in recounting his tale to Ragnar and me. Sevro told the Sons that no one was to see Kavax. But apparently they don't think the rules much apply to the Reaper. Good on that. I don't yet have a plan, but I know Sevro's isn't working. I don't have time to navigate his feelings or struggle with him. The pieces are in motion, and I need information.

"She did not know yet what to do and so took our counsel as she did as a girl," Kavax continues. "We were on my ship, the *Reynard,* having roast mutton in ponzu sauce with Sophocles, though he did not like the sauce, when Agea Command called, saying the Sovereign's loyalist forces had attacked the Triumph in Agea. Virginia could not contact you or her father, and so feared a coup and sent Daxo and me from orbit with our knights.

"She stayed in orbit with the ships and finally contacted Roque when Daxo and I were already descending through atmosphere. Roque said the Sovereign had attacked the Triumph and wounded you and her father gravely. He urged her to come to one of his new ships, where he was taking you because the surface was no longer safe." I remember Roque talking on the shuttle as the Jackal leaned over me, not being able to hear him. We landed on a ship. The Sovereign was there. She never left Mars. She was hiding in Roque's fleet. Right under my nose. "But Virginia did not rush to your bedside." He grins jovially. "A fool in love would do so. But Virginia is clever. She saw through Roque's mendacity. She knew the Sovereign would not simply attack the Triumph. It would be a plan within a plan. So she sent word to Orion and House Arcos that a coup was under way. That Roque was a conspirator. So when the assassins struck, attempting to kill Orion and the loyal commanders on their bridge, they were ready. There were firefights on bridges. In staterooms. Orion was badly shot in the arm, but she survived and then Roque's ships opened fire on ours and the fleet fractured. . . ."

All this while Sevro and Ragnar were discovering that Fitchner was dead and the Sons of Ares base had been destroyed. And I lay paralyzed on the floor of Aja's shuttle as everything came apart. No. Not everything.

"She saved the crew's lives," I say.

"Yes," Kavax says. "Your crew is alive. The one you liberated with Sevro. Even many of your Legion, who we organized and managed to evacuate from Mars before the Jackal and Sovereign's forces took power."

"Where are my friends imprisoned?" I ask. "On Ganymede? Io?"

"Imprisoned?" Kavax squints at me, then bursts into laughter. "No, lad. No. Not a man or woman has left their station. The *Pax* is just as you left it. Orion commands, the rest follow."

"I don't understand. She's letting a Blue command?"

"Do you think Virginia would have let you live in that tunnel when you and Ragnar were on your knees if she did not believe in your new world?" I shake my head numbly, not knowing the answer. "She would have killed you on the spot if she thought you were her enemy. But when she sat before my hearth as a girl beside Pax and my children, what stories did I read them? Did I read them myths of the Greeks? Of strong men gaining glory for their own heads? No. I told them tales of Arthur, of the Nazarene, of Vishnu. Strong heroes who wished only to protect the weak."

And Mustang has. More than that. She's proven Eo right. And it wasn't because of me. It wasn't because of love. It was because it was the right thing to do, and because mighty Kavax was more a father to her than her own ever was. I feel the tears in my eyes.

"**You were right, Darrow,**" Ragnar says. His hand falls on my shoulder. "**The tide rises.**"

"Then why are you here today, Kavax?"

"Because we are losing," he says. "The Moon Lords will not last two months. Virginia knows what is happening on Mars. The extermination. The savagery of her brother. The Sons are too weak to fight everywhere." His large eyes show the pain of a man watching his home burn. Mars is as much their heritage as it is mine. "The cost of war is too great for a certain defeat. So when Quicksilver proposed a peace, we listened."

"And what are the terms?" I ask.

"Virginia and all her allies would be pardoned by the Sovereign. She would become ArchGovernor of Mars and Adrius and his faction would be imprisoned for life. And certain reforms would be made."

"But the hierarchy would remain."

"Yes."

"**If this is true, we must speak with her,**" Ragnar says eagerly.

"It could be a trap," I say, watching Kavax, knowing the mind at work behind his bluff face. I want to trust him. I want to believe his sense of justice is equal to my love for him, but these are deep waters, and I know friends can lie just as well as enemies. If Mustang isn't on my side, then this would be the play to make. It would expose me, and there's no doubt in my mind that however she got on this station, she's got a nasty escort.

"One thing doesn't make sense, Kavax. If this is true, why didn't you make contact with Sevro?"

Kavax blinks up at me.

"We did. Months ago. Didn't he tell you?"

The Howlers are packing up by the time Ragnar and I rejoin them in the ready room. "It's all shit," Sevro's saying as Victra patches a gash on his back with resFlesh. Acrid smoke hisses up from the cauterizing wound. He throws down his datapad. It skitters into a corner, where Screwface collects it and brings it back to Sevro. "They've grounded everything, including utility flights."

"It's all right, boss, we'll find a way out," Clown says.

I entered the room quietly, nodding to Sevro that I'd like a word. He ignored me. His plan's a mess. We were due to stow ourselves away inside one of the empty helium haulers going back to Mars. We would have been gone before anyone even knew Quicksilver was kidnapped, and then detonated the bombs off-station. Now, like Sevro says, it's all shit.

"We obviously can't stay here," Victra says, putting the resFlesh applicator down. "We left enough DNA evidence for a hundred crime scenes back there. And our faces are everywhere. Adrius will send a whole legion for us when they find out we're here."

"Or blow Phobos out of the sky," Holiday mutters. She sits on a crate of medical supplies in the corner, studying maps with Clown on her datapad. Pebble watches them from her place on the table. Her leg's compressed with a gelCast, but the bone's not set. We'll need a Yellow and a full infirmary to fix what Mustang broke with a single shot. Pebble's lucky she was wearing scarabSkin. It minimized the burn damage. Still, she's in pain. Pupils large on a high dose of narcotics. It's let her inhibitions loose, and I note how obviously the pudgy-faced Gold is watching Clown lean across Holiday to point at the map.

"Helium-3 is Adrius's lifeblood," Victra says. "He won't risk this station."

"Sevro . . ." I say. "A moment."

"Busy right now." He turns to Rollo. "Is there any other way off this damn rock?"

The Red leans against the med room's gray wall next to a glossy paper cutout of a Pink model on one of Venus's white-sand beaches. "It's just cargo haulers down here," he says, silently noting how our Obsidian guises have been discarded. If it startles him how many of us are Gold, he doesn't let on. Probably knew from the start. His eyes linger on me the longest. "But they're all grounded. They got luxury liners and private yachts in the Needles, but you go up there, you folks are caught in a minute. Two, tops. There's facial-recognition cameras at every tram door. Retina scanners in the advertisement holos. And even if you got onto one of their ships, you gotta get past the naval pickets. Ain't like you can just teleport to safety."

"That'd be convenient," Clown mutters.

"We jack a shuttle and run the pickets," Sevro says. "Done it before."

"They'll shoot us down," I say tensely. It's pissing me off that he keeps ignoring my attempts to get him to the door.

"Didn't last time."

"Last time we had Lysander," I remind him.

"And now we got Quicksilver."

"The Jackal will sacrifice Quicksilver to kill us," I say. "Count on it."

"Not if we go straight vertical burn to the surface," Sevro says. "Sons have hidden tunnel entrances. We will fall from orbit and go straight underground."

"I will not do that," Ragnar says. **"It is foolhardy. And it abandons these noble men and women to slaughter."**

"I agree with Rags," Holiday says. She scoots away from Clown and continues looking at her datapad, monitoring police frequencies.

"Say you get off. What happens to us?" Rollo asks. "The Jackal finds out the Reaper and Ares were here and he'll tear this station apart piecemeal. Any Son left behind will be dead in a week. Did you think of that?" He makes a disgusted look. "I know who you are. We knew the second Ragnar walked into the hangar. But I didn't think Howlers ran. And I didn't think the Reaper took orders."

Sevro takes a step toward him. "You got another option, shitface? Or you just gonna run your mouth?"

"Yeah, I got one," Rollo says. "Stay. Help us take the station."

The Howlers laugh. "Take the station? With what army?" Clown asks.

"His," Rollo says, turning to me. "I don't rightly know how you're alive, Reaper. But . . . I was eating noodles by myself at midnight when the Sons leaked your Carving video onto the holoNet. Society cyber police shut down the site in two minutes. But once it was out . . . could find it on a million sites before I finished my bowl. They couldn't contain that. And then the Phobos servers crashed. You know why?"

"Securitas's cyber division pulled the plug," Victra says. "It's standard protocol."

He shakes his head. "Servers crashed because thirty million people were trying to access the holoNet at the same time in the middle of the night. Servers couldn't handle the traffic. Golds pulled the plug after that. So what I'm sayin' is if you march down to the Hive and tell the lowColors there you're alive, we can take this moon."

"Easy as that?" Victra asks skeptically.

"That's right. There's round about twenty-five million lowColors here crawling over one another, fighting for square meters, protein packages, Syndicate smack, whatever. Reaper shows his mug, all that goes to vapor. All that fighting. All that scrappin'. They *want* a leader, and if the Reaper of Mars decides to come back from the dead here . . . you won't have an army, you'll have a tide at your heels. You register? This will change the war."

He sends chills down my spine. But Victra's skeptical, and Sevro's quiet. Hurt.

"Do you know what a squad of Society Legionnaires can do to a mob of rabble?" Victra asks. "The weapons you've seen are geared to taking out men in armor. PulseFists. Razors. When they use coilguns or rattlers on mobs, a single man can fire a thousand rounds a minute. It sounds like paper tearing. Human body doesn't even know that sound is supposed to be frightening. They can superheat the water in your cellular structure with microwaves. And those are just Gray anti-mob squads. What if they unleash the Obsidian? What if Golds themselves come in their armor? What if they shut off your air? Your water?"

"What if we shut off theirs?" Rollo asks.

I frown. "Can you do that?"

"Give me a reason to." He looks at Victra, and by the bite in his voice, I know he knows exactly what her last name is. "They might be soldiers, *domina*. Might be able to put enough metal in my body that I bleed out. But before I was nine, I could strip down a gravBoot and piece it together in under four minutes. Now I'm thirty-eight and I can murder the lot of 'em ten ways till Sunday with a screwdriver and an electrical kit. And I'm sick and tired of not seeing my family. Of being stepped on and charged for oxygen, for water, for living." He leans forward, eyes glassy. "And there's twenty-five million of me on the other side of that door."

Victra rolls her eyes at the bravado. "You're a welder with delusions of grandeur."

Rollo steps forward and knocks a set of wrenches off a table. They clatter on the ground, startling Clown and Holiday, who look up from the datapad. Rollo stares up indignantly at Victra. She's easily a foot taller than him, but he doesn't break his gaze. "I'm an engineer. Not a welder."

"Enough!" Sevro snarls. "This isn't a bloodydamn debate. Quicksilver will get us off this rock. Or I'll start taking off his fingers. Then blow the bombs. . . ."

"Sevro . . ." Ragnar says.

"I am Ares!" Sevro snarls. "Not you." He shoves a finger up into Ragnar's chest and then points at me. "And not you. Finish packing the bloodydamn gear. Now."

He storms from the room, leaving us in awkward silence.

"I will not abandon these men," Ragnar says. **"They have helped us. They are our people."**

"Ares is cracked," Rollo says to the room. "Off his mind. You need—"

I wheel on the small man, picking him up with one hand and pinning him against the ceiling. "Don't you say a damn thing about him." Rollo apologizes, and I set him back on the ground. I make sure all the Howlers are listening. "Everyone stay put. I'll be right back."

I catch Sevro before he enters Quicksilver's cell in a gutted old garage that the Sons use to house generators now. Sevro and the guards turn when they hear me coming. "Don't trust me alone with him?" he sneers. "Nice."

"We need to talk."

"Sure. After he does." Sevro pushes open the door. Cursing, I follow. The room's a forlorn shade of rust. Machines older than some of the gear in Lykos. One rattles behind the thick Silver, coughing out the electricity that powers the lights bathing the man in a circle of light, and blinding him to anything beyond it. Quicksilver sits with his shoulders back in the metal chair in the center of the room. Arms bound behind his back. His turquoise robe is bloody and rumpled. Bulldog eyes patient and measuring. Wide forehead's covered in a thick sheen of sweat and grease.

"Who are you?" he hisses in irritation instead of fear. The door slams shut behind us. The man seems rather irritated with his predicament. Not disrespectful or angry, but professionally peeved at the meek measure of our hospitality and the inconvenience we've thrust upon him. He's not able to distinguish our faces due to the light blaring into his eyes. "Syndicate teethmen? Moon Lord dustmakers?" When we say nothing, he swallows. "Adrius, is that you?"

Chills creep down my spine. We say nothing. Only now, as he begins to suspect that we're the Jackal's men does Quicksilver seem truly afraid. If we had time, we could use that fear, but we need information fast.

"We need off this rock," Sevro says gruffly. "You're gonna make that happen, boyo. Or I pull off your fingers one by one."

"Boyo?" Quicksilver murmurs.

"I know you have an escape vessel, contingency—"

"Barca, is that you?" Sevro's caught off guard "It is you. Damn the stars, boy. You scared the shit out of me. I thought you were the gory-damn Jackal."

"You have ten seconds to give me something I can use, or I wear your rib cage as a corset," Sevro says, thrown by Quicksilver's familiarity. It's not his best threat.

Quicksilver shakes his head. "You need to listen to me, Mr. Barca, and listen well. This is all a misunderstanding. A vast misunderstanding. I know you may not believe it. I know you may think me mad. But you must hear me. I am on your side. I am one of you, Mr. Barca."

Sevro frowns. "One of us? What do you mean?"

"What do I mean?" Quicksilver laughs gruffly. "I mean exactly as I say, young man. I, Regulus ag Sun, chevalier of the Order of Coin, chief executive officer of Sun Industries, am also a founding member of the Sons of Ares."

21

||||||||||||||||||||||||||||||

QUICKSILVER

"A Son of Ares?" Sevro repeats, stepping into the light so Quicksilver can see his face. I stay back. It's a ludicrous claim.

"That's better. I thought I recognized your voice. More like your father's than you probably like. But yes, I'm a Son. The first Son, actually."

"Well, then slag me blind as a Pinkwhore," Sevro cries. "This *is* all just a misunderstanding!" He jumps forward and crouches beside Quicksilver to straighten the man's robe. "We'll get you cleaned up. Let you call your men. Sound good?"

"Yes, good, because you've managed to muck up something rather . . ."

Sevro hits the Silver right in his fleshy lips with a jab of his fist. It's an intimate, familiar bit of violence that makes me flinch. Quicksilver's head slams back against the chair. The man tries to move away, but Sevro pins him down easily. "Your tricks won't work here, fat little toad man."

"It's not a trick—"

Sevro hits him again. Quicksilver sputters, blood dribbling down his cracked lip. Tries to blink the pain away. Probably seeing spots. Sevro hits him a third time, casually, and I think it was for me, not the tycoon, because Sevro looks back into the darkness where I stand with impudent eyes. As if dangling moral bait in front of me so we can explode into conflict again. His moral creed has always been simple: protect your friends, to hell with everyone else.

Sevro pushes a knife into Quicksilver's mouth. "I know you think you're being clever, boyo," Sevro growls. "Saying you're a Son. Thinkin' you're so smooth. Thinkin' you can talk your way clear of us dumb brutes. But I've played this game with smarter kinds than you. And I've learned hard. Keen?" He pulls the knife sideways against Quicksilver's cheek, causing the man to move his head with the blade. Still, it splits the corner of his mouth just slightly.

"So whatever your garble, you ain't coming out on top of this, shitbrain. You're a rat. A collaborator. And it's time to reap what you've sown. So you're going to tell us how to get out of here. If you've got a ship hidden. If you can get us past the navy. Then you're going to tell us about the Jackal's plans, his equipment, his infrastructure; then you're going to give us the gear to equip our army." Quicksilver's eyes dart from the knife to Sevro's face.

"Use your brains, you little savage," Quicksilver snarls when Sevro takes the knife from his mouth. "Where do you think Fitchner got the money—"

"Don't say his name." Sevro points a finger to the man's face. "Don't you dare say his name."

"I knew your father. . . ."

"Then why'd he never mention you? Why does Dancer not know you? Because you're lying."

"Why *would* they know about me?" Quicksilver asks. "You never tie two boats together in a storm."

The words are a punch to the gut. Fitchner said the exact phrase when explaining why he didn't tell me about Titus. The Sons lost much of their technical ability when he died. What if there were two bodies to the Sons of Ares body? The lowColors, and the high? Kept apart in case one was compromised? It's what I would do. He promised me better allies if I went to Luna. Allies that would help make me Sovereign. This could be one of them. One who fled when Fitchner died. Who cut himself off from the contaminated body of the Sons.

"Why was Matteo in your bedroom?" I ask carefully.

Quicksilver stares into the darkness, wondering whose voice addresses him, yet now there's fear in his eyes, not just anger. "How . . . how did you know he was in my bedroom?"

"Answer the question," Sevro says, kicking him.

"Did you hurt him?" Quicksilver asks, enraged. *"Did you hurt him?"*

"Answer the question," Sevro repeats, slapping him.

Quicksilver trembles with anger. "He was in my room because he's my husband. You son of a bitch. He's one of us! If you hurt him . . ."

"How long has he been your husband?" I ask.

"Ten years."

"Where was he six years ago? When he worked with Dancer?"

"He was in Yorkton. He was the man who trained your friend, Sevro. He trained Darrow. The Carver made the body. Matteo sculpted the man."

"He's telling the truth." I step into the light so Quicksilver can see my face. He stares at me in shock.

"Darrow. You're alive. I . . . thought . . . it can't be."

I turn to Sevro. "He's a Son of Ares."

"Because he got a few facts right?" Sevro snarls. "You're actually serious."

"You're alive," Quicksilver murmurs to himself, trying to wrap his head around what is happening. *"How? He killed you."*

"He's telling the truth," I repeat.

"Truth?" Sevro moves his mouth like he's got a cockroach in it. "What does that even bloody mean? How could you possibly know that? You think you can get the truth outta some backroom-dealing shark like this. He's in bed with half the Peerless Scarred in the Society. He ain't just their tool. He's their friend. And he's playing you like the Jackal did. If he's a Son, why'd he abandon us? Why'd he not contact us when Pops died?"

"Because your ship was sinking," Quicksilver says, still staring at me in confusion. "Your cells were compromised. I had no way of knowing how deep the contamination went. I still don't know how the Jackal discovered you, Darrow. My only contact to the lowColor cells was Fitchner. Just like I was his contact for highColor cells. How could I reach out when I didn't know if it was Dancer himself who informed on you and made a power play to get rid of Fitchner?"

"Dancer would never do that," Sevro says with a sneer.

"How would I know that?" Quicksilver says in frustration. "I don't know the man." Sevro's shaking his head, overwhelmed by the absurdity. "I have videos. Conversations between myself and your father."

"I'm not letting you near a datapad," Sevro says.

"Test him," I say. "Make him prove it."

"I met your mother once, Sevro," Quicksilver offers quickly. "Her name was Bryn. She was a Red. If I wasn't a Son, how would I know that?"

"You could know that a dozen ways. Proves piss 'n shit," Sevro says.

"I have a test," I say. "If you are a Son, you'll know it. If you belong to the Jackal, you would have used it. Where is Tinos?"

Quicksilver smiles broadly. "Five hundred kilometers south of the Thermic Sea. Three kilometers beneath the old mining nexus Vengo Station. In an abandoned mining colony, the records of which were wiped from the internal servers of the Society by *my* hackers. The stalactites were carved hollow using Acharon-19 laser drills from my factories in spiral halls to maintain structural integrity. The Atalian hydrogenerator was built with plans designed by my engineers. Tinos might be the City of Ares, but I designed it. I paid for it. I built it."

Sevro sways there in stunned silence.

"Your father worked for me, Sevro," Quicksilver says. "First for the terraforming consortium on Triton, where he met your mother. Then in . . . less legitimate ways. Back then I was not what I am today. I needed a Gold. A hard-nosed Peerless Scarred, and all the legal protection that gives. One who owed me and was willing to play rough with my competitors. Off the books, you know."

"You're saying my father played mercenary. For you?"

"I'm saying he played assassin. I was growing. There was resistance in the marketplace to that growth. So the marketplace had to make room. You think all Silvers play it safe and legal?" He chuckles. "Some, maybe. But business in a crony-capitalist society is the craft of sharks. Stop swimming, the others will take your food and feed on your body. I gave your father money. He hired a team. Worked off-site. Did what I needed him to do. Until I discovered he was using my resources for a side project. *The Sons of Ares.*"

He makes a mockery of the words.

"But you didn't report him?" I ask skeptically.

"Golds treat sedition like cancer. I'd have been cut out too. So I was trapped. But he didn't want me trapped. He wanted a co-conspirator. Gradually he made his case. And here we are."

Sevro paces away, trying to make sense of it. "But . . . we've . . . been dying like flies. And you've been up here . . . humping your Pinks. Fraternizing with the enemy. If you were one of us . . ."

Quicksilver lifts his nose up, regaining what poise he lost during the beating. "Then I would have done what, Mr. Barca? Do tell. From your extensive experience in subterfuge?"

"You would have fought with us."

"With what? Hm?" He waits for an answer. None comes. Sevro's speechless. "I have a private security force of thirty thousand for myself and my companies. But they're spread from Mercury to Pluto. I don't own those men. They are Gray contractors. Only a fraction are owned Obsidians. I have the weapons, but I don't have the muscle to tussle with Peerless Scarred. Are you crazy? I use soft power. Not hard power. That was your father's purview. Even a minor house could wipe me out in direct conflict."

"You have the largest software company in the Solar System," Sevro says. "That means hackers. You have munitions plants. Military tech development. You could have spied for us on the Jackal. Given us weapons. You could have done a thousand things."

"May I be blunt?"

I grimace. "If ever there was a time . . ."

Quicksilver leans back to peer down his humped nose at Sevro.

"I've been a Son of Ares for more than twenty years. That requires patience. A long-eyed view. You've been one for less than a year. And look what's happened. You, Mr. Barca, are a bad investment."

"A bad . . . investment?"

It sounds ridiculous coming from a man chained to a metal chair with blood dribbling down his lips. But something in Quicksilver's eyes sells his point. This isn't a victim. It's a titan of a different plane. Master of his own domain. Equal, it seems, to Fitchner's own breed of genius. And more vast a character, more nuanced than I would have expected. But I reserve any affection for the man. He's survived by lying for twenty years. Everything is an act. Probably even this.

Who is the real man beneath this bulldog face?

What drives him? What does he want?

"I watched. I waited to see what you would do," he explains to Sevro. "To see if you were cut like your father. But then they executed Darrow"—he looks up at me, still confused on that note—"or pretended to, and you acted like a boy. You began a war you couldn't win, with insufficient infrastructure, materiel, systems of coordination, supply lines. You released propaganda in the form of Darrow's Carving to the worlds, to the mines, hoping for . . . what? A glorious rise of the proletariat?" He scoffs. "I thought you understood war.

"For all his faults, your father was a visionary. He promised me something better. And what has his son given us instead? Ethnic cleansing. Nuclear war. Beheadings. Pogroms. Whole cities shredded by fractious groups of Red rebels and Gold reprisals. Disunity. In other words, chaos. And chaos, Mr. Barca, is not what I invested in. It's bad for business, and what's bad for business is bad for Man."

Sevro swallows slowly, feeling the weight of the words.

"I did what I had to," he says, sounding so small. "What no one else would."

"Did you?" Quicksilver leans forward nastily. "Or did you do what you wanted to do? Because your *feelings* were hurt? Because you wanted to lash out?"

Sevro's eyes are glassy. His silence wounding me. I want to defend him, but he needs to hear this.

"You think I haven't been fighting, but I have," Quicksilver continues. "The Sovereign's opinion of the Jackal seems to have soured of late."

"Why?" I ask.

"I couldn't guess before, but now I'd bet anything it's because you escaped the Jackal's prisons. In any case, I saw an opportunity. I brought Virginia au Augustus and the Sovereign's representatives here to broker a peace that would give Virginia the ArchGovernorship of Mars and would remove the Jackal from power and put him in prison for life. It's not the end I wanted. But if what we're seeing on the Jackal's Mars is any indication, he is the single greatest threat to the worlds and our long-term goals."

"And yet you helped him consolidate power in the first place," I say.

Quicksilver sighs. "At the time, I thought him less of a threat than his father. I was wrong. And so were you. He needs to be removed."

The Jackal's been betrayed by two allies, then.

"But your plans for an alliance are slagged now."

"Indeed. But I don't mourn the opportunity lost. You're alive, Darrow, and that means this rebellion is alive. It means Fitchner's dream, your wife's dream, is not yet gone from this world."

"Why?" Sevro asks. "Why the bloodyhell would you want war? You're the richest man in the system. You're not an anarchist."

"No. I am not an anarchist, a communist, a fascist, a plutocrat, or even a demokrat, for that matter. My boys, don't believe what they tell you in school. Government is never the solution, but it is almost always the problem. I'm a capitalist. And I believe in effort and progress and the ingenuity of our species. The continuing evolution and advancement of our kind based on fair competition. Fact of the matter is, Gold does not want man to continue to evolve. Since the conquering, they have routinely stifled advancement to maintain their heaven. They've wrapped themselves in myth. Filled their grand oceans with monsters to hunt. Cultivated private Mirkwoods and Olympuses of their very own. They have suits of armor to make them flying gods. And they preserve that ridiculous fairy tale by keeping mankind frozen in time. Curbing invention, curiosity, social mobility. Change threatens that.

"Look where we are. In *space*. Above a planet we *shaped*. Yet we live in a Society modeled after the musings of Bronze Age pedophiles. Tossing around mythology like that bullshit wasn't made up around a campfire by an Attican farmer depressed that his life was nasty, brutish, and short.

"The Golds claim to the Obsidians that they are gods. They are not. Gods create. If the Golds are anything, they are vampire kings. Parasites drinking from our jugular. I want a Society free of this fascist pyramid. I want to unchain the free market of wealth and ideas. Why should men toil in the mines when we can build robots to toil for us? Why should we ever have stopped in this Solar System? We deserve more than what we've been given. But first, Gold must fall and the Sovereign and the Jackal must die. And I believe you are the sign I've been waiting for, Mr. Andromedus."

He nods at my gloved hands. "I paid for your Sigils. I paid for your bones, your eyes, your flesh. You are my friend's brainchild. My husband's student. The sum of the Sons of Ares. So my empire is at your disposal. My hackers. My security teams. My transports. My companies. All yours. With no reservations. No strings. No insurance policy." He looks at Sevro. "Gentlemen. In other words, I'm all in."

"Quite nice." Sevro applauds, mocking Quicksilver. "Darrow, he's just trying to buy you so he can escape."

"Maybe," I say. "But we can't blow the bombs anymore."

"Bombs?" Quicksilver asks. "What are you talking about?"

"We planted explosives in the refineries and the shipping docks," I say.

"That's your plan?" Quicksilver looks back and forth at us as if we're mad. "You can't do that. Do you have any idea what that would do?"

"An economic collapse," I say. "Symptoms including a devaluation of stock assets, a freeze of commercial bank lending, a run on local banks, eventual stagflation. And a breakdown of social order. Show us some respect when you talk to us. We're not dilettantes or boys. And it *was* our plan."

"Was?" Sevro asks, stepping back from me. "So now you're letting him dictate what we do."

"Things have changed, Sevro. We need to reassess. We've new assets."

My friend stares at me as if he doesn't recognize my face. "New assets? Him?"

"Not just him. Orion," I say. "You never told me Mustang contacted you."

"Because you would have let her manipulate you," he says without apology. "Like you did before. Like you're letting him now." He considers me, pointing a finger as he thinks he figures it out. "You're afraid. Aren't you? Afraid of pulling the trigger. Afraid of making a mistake. We finally have a chance to make Gold bleed and you wanna reassess. You wanna take time to look at our options." He pulls the detonator from his pocket. "This is war. We don't have time. We can take the bastard with us, but we can't miss this chance."

"Stop acting like a terrorist," I snarl. "We're better than that."

I stare down at him, furious in the moment. He should be my simplest, strongest friendship. But because of loss, everything is twisted between us. Even with him there's so many layers to the pain. So many levels of fear and recrimination and guilt for both of us. They once called Sevro my shadow. He's not any longer. And I think I've been bitter at him these last hours because they're proof of that. He's his own man with his own tides. Just as I think he's been bitter with me because I didn't come back as the Reaper. I came back a man he didn't recognize. And now that I'm trying to be the force he wanted, the force that's making decisions, he doubts me because he senses weakness and that's always made him afraid.

"Sevro, give me the detonator," I say coldly.

"Naw." He opens the detonator's priming shield, revealing the red thumb toggle inside the protective casing. If he presses down, one thousand kilograms of high-yield explosives will detonate across Phobos. It won't destroy the moon, but it'll demolish the moon's economic infrastructure. Helium will not flow for months. Years. And all the fears of Quicksilver will be realized. Society will suffer, but so will we.

"Sevro . . ."

"You got my father killed," he says. "You got Quinn and Pax and Weed and Harpy and Lea killed because you thought you were smarter than everyone else. Because you didn't kill the Jackal when you could. Because you didn't kill Cassius when you could. But unlike you, I don't flinch."

22

||||||||||||||||||||||||

THE WEIGHT
OF ARES

Sevro's thumb twitches for the detonation switch. But before he presses down, I activate a jamfield with the jammer on my belt, blocking the signal from leaving the room. "You son of a bitch," he snarls, rushing for the door to get beyond the field.

I reach for him. He spins under my hands. My jammer's not a strong one, so he doesn't need to get far away from me. He bowls into the hallway, I scramble after.

"Sevro, stop!" I say as I push into the hallway. He's already ten meters down the hall, running at full speed to get clear of my jamming field so his signal can go out. He's quicker than I am in these small hallways. He's going to escape. I pull my pulseFist out, aim it over his head, and fire it, but my aim is off and it nearly takes off his head. His Mohawk sizzles smoke. He stops dead in his tracks and wheels back on me, face feral.

"Sevro . . . I didn't mean . . ."

With a howl of rage he charges me. Caught off guard, I stumble back from the manic man. He closes in a flurry. I block his first punch, but an uppercut smashes into my jaw, slamming my teeth together. Rocking me back. My teeth close on a corner of my tongue. I taste blood and almost fall. If Mickey hadn't made bones proper, Sevro might've shattered my jaw. Instead, he curses, gripping his fist in pain.

I move with the uppercut and lash out with my left leg, kicking him so hard in the ribs that his whole body carries sideways into the wall, denting the metal bulkhead. I throw a straight jab with my right fist. He ducks under and my punch lands on duroSteel. Pain rattles up my arm. I grunt. He flies into me under the left elbow I swing at his head, ratcheting strikes into my stomach, aiming for my balls. I twist back, manage to grab one of his arms and swing him around as hard as I can. He slams face-first into the wall, spilling to the ground.

"Where is it?" I search his body for the detonator. "Sevro . . ."

He scissor-kicks my legs. Tangling them. Dropping me to the ground so we're grappling instead of trading punches. He's the better wrestler. And it's all I can do to keep him from choking me out from behind as his legs form a triangle, heels locked in front of my face, legs pressing in on both sides of my neck. I lift him off the ground, but I can't dislodge him. He's dangling upside down behind me, spine to my spine, heels still in my face, trying to elbow my balls through my legs from behind. I can't reach for him. I can't breathe. So I grab his calves on my neck and spin my body. He slams into the metal. Once. Twice. Then he finally lets go, scrambling off. I'm on him in a flash, throwing a tight series of kravat elbows into his face. He catches my chin with the crown of his head accidentally.

"Dumb . . . son of a bitch . . ." I mutter, stumbling back. He's gripping his own head in pain.

"Stupid lanky ass . . ."

He aims a kick at my midsection. I take the blow, catching the leg with my left arm, and exchange it for a haymaker right that crashes into his skull with all my weight behind it. He goes down hard, like I'm a hammer driving a nail into the floor. He tries to rise, but I push him down with a boot. He lies under it, heaving breaths. I'm dizzy and panting. Body hating me for what I'm doing to it.

"Are you done?" I ask him. He nods. I pull back my boot and extend a hand to help him up. He rolls to his back and reaches for it, then lurches up with his left boot heel straight into my groin. I fall and dry-heave beside him. Crippling nausea swells from my lower back into my balls and my stomach. Beside me, he's panting like a dog. At first I think he's laughing, but when I look up I'm shocked to see tears in his eyes. He lies on his back. Huge sobs make his rib cage shudder. He turns away, tries to hide from me to stop the tears from coming, but it makes it worse.

"Sevro . . ."

I sit up, feeling ripped apart by the sight of him. I don't hold him, but I put a hand on his head. And he surprises me by not flinching away, but instead crawling up to put his head on my knee. I put my other hand on his shoulder. In time the sobs slow and he blows the snot from his nose. But he doesn't move. It's like the moment after a lightning storm. The air kinetic and vibrating. After several minutes, he clears his throat and pushes himself up to sit with his legs folded under him in the center of the hall. His eyes are puffy, ashamed. He plays with his hands, the tattoos and Mohawk making him look like something pulled from a deranged children's book.

"You tell anyone I cried, I'll find a dead fish, put it in a sock, hide it in your room, and let it putrefy."

"Fair enough."

The detonator lies off to the side. Close enough so we can both reach for it. Neither of us do. "I hate this," he says weakly. "People like that." He glances up at me. "I don't want him to be a Son. I don't want to be like Quicksilver."

"You aren't."

He doesn't believe that. "At the Institute, I'd wake up in the morning. And I think I was still in my dreams. Then I'd feel the cold. And I'd slowly start remembering where I was, and there's dirt and blood under my nails. And all I want to do was go back to sleep. To be warm. But I knew I had to get up and face a world that didn't give a shit." He grimaces. "That's how I feel every morning now. I'm afraid all the time. I don't want to lose anyone. I don't want to let them down."

"You haven't," I say. "If anything, I let you down." He tries to interrupt me. "You were right. We both know it. It's my fault your father's dead. It's my fault that whole night happened."

"Was still a shit thing of me to say." He raps his knuckles on the ground. "I'm always saying shit things."

"I'm glad you said it."

"Why?"

"Because we've both forgotten we didn't get here on our own. You and I should be able to say anything to each other. That's how this works. It's how we work. We don't walk on eggshells. We talk to each other. Even if we say shit that's hard to hear." I see how alone he feels. How much weight he carried. It's how I felt when Cassius stabbed me and left me for dead at the Institute. He needs to share the weight. I don't know how else to tell him that. This stubbornness, this intransigence, looks insane from the outside, but inside he felt just as I did when Roque questioned me.

"Do you know why I helped you at the Institute when you and Cassius were gonna drown in that loch?" he asks. "It's cause of how they look at you. It wasn't like I thought you were a good primus. You were as smart as a bag of wet farts. But I saw them. Pebble. Clown. Quinn. . . . Roque." He almost trips over that last name. "I'd watch you at your fires in the gulches when Titus was in the castle. Saw you teach Lea how to cut a goat's throat even when she was afraid to do it. I wanted to do that too. To join."

"Why didn't you?"

He shrugs. "Was afraid you wouldn't want me."

"They look at you that way now," I say. "Don't you see that?"

He snorts. "Nah, they don't. The whole time, I tried to be you. Tried to be Pops. Didn't work. I could tell everyone just wished it was me that the Jackal captured. Not you."

"You know that's not true."

"It is," he says intensely, leaning forward. "You're better than I am. I saw you. When you looked down at Tinos. Saw your eyes. The love in them. The urge to protect those people. I tried feeling it. But every time I looked down at the refugees, I just hated them. For being weak. For hurting each other. For being stupid and not knowing what we've gone through to help them." He swallows and picks at the cuticles of his stubby fingers. "I know it's nasty, but it's what it is."

He seems so vulnerable here in this hall, the rage taken out of us from the fight. He's not looking for a lecture. Leadership has worn him down, alienated him from even his Howlers. Right now he's looking to feel like he's not like Quicksilver or the Jackal or any of the Golds we fight against. He's mistakenly assumed I'm something better than he is. And part of that is my fault.

"I hate them too," I say.

He shakes his head. "Don't . . ."

"I do. At least, I hate that they remind me of what I was, or could have been. Shit, I was a little idiot. You would have hated me. I was comfortable and arrogant and selfish on my knees. I liked being blind to everything because I was in love. And I thought for some reason that living for love was the most valiant thing in all the worlds. Even made Eo into something in my head that she wasn't. Romanticized her and the life we had—probably because I saw my father die for some cause. And I saw all he left behind, so I tried to cling to the life he abandoned."

I trace the lines on my palm.

"It makes me feel small to think I started doing all this for her. She was everything to me, but I was just a piece of her life. When the Jackal had me, that's all I could think about. That I wasn't enough. That our child wasn't enough. Part of me hates her for that. She didn't know all this would happen, wasn't even aware that the worlds had been terraformed. All she could have known was that she was making a point to the couple thousand people in Lykos. And was that worth dying for? Was that worth killing a child for?"

I gesture down the hall. "Now all these people think she was divine or something. A perfect martyr. But she was just a girl. And she was brave, but she was stupid and selfish and selfless and romantic; but she died before she could ever be more. Think how much she could have done with her life. Maybe we could have done this together." I laugh bitterly and lean my head against the wall. "I think the shittiest part about getting old is now we're smart enough to see the cracks in everything."

"We're twenty-three, dipshit."

"Well, I feel eighty."

"You look it." I flip him the crux, earning a smile. "Do you . . ." He almost doesn't finish the thought. "Do you think she watches you? From the Vale? Does your father?"

I'm about to say I don't know when I catch the intentness of his gaze. He's not asking about my family as much as he's asking about his own, maybe even Quinn, who he always loved but never had the courage to tell. With all his savagery it's hard to remember just how vulnerable he is. He's adrift. Alienated from Red and Gold. No home. No family. No view of a world after war. Right now I'd say anything to make him feel like he's loved.

"Yes. I believe she watches me," I say with more confidence than I feel. "And my father. And yours too."

"So they have beer in the Vale."

"Don't be sacrilegious," I say, kicking his foot. "Only whiskey. Streams of it as far as the eye can see."

His laughter stitches more of me together. Bit by bit, I feel like my friends are coming back to me. Or maybe I'm coming back to them. Suppose it's the same thing, really. I always told Victra to let people in. I could never take my own advice because I knew one day I'd have to betray them, that the foundation of our friendship was a lie. Now I'm with people who know who I am, and I'm afraid to let them in because I'm afraid of losing them, disappointing them. But it's this bond that Sevro and I share that makes us stronger than we were before. It's what we have that the Jackal doesn't.

"Do you know what happens after this?" I ask. "If we kill Octavia, the Jackal? If we somehow win?"

"No," Sevro says.

"That right there is a problem. I don't have the answer. I won't pretend to. But I won't let Augustus be right. I won't bring chaos into this world without at least a plan for something better. For that we need allies like Quicksilver. We need to stop playing terrorist. And we need a real army."

Sevro picks the detonator back up and breaks it in two. "What are your orders, Reap?"

23

||||||||||||||||||||||||

THE TIDE

Sevro and I stalk back into the ready room where the Howlers are packed and prepared to depart the station. Rollo and a dozen of his people watch us tensely from their side of the room. They know they're about to be abandoned. Quicksilver follows behind me in a wheelchair, restraints left behind in his cell. He's agreed to our plan, with a few adjustments. "Well, look at this. . . ." Victra says, seeing our bruises and bloody knuckles. "You two finally talked." She looks to Ragnar. "See?"

"Shit's sorted," Sevro says.

"And the rich man?" Ragnar asks curiously. **"He wears no manacles."**

"That's because he's a Son of Ares, Rags," Sevro says. "Didn't you know?"

"Quicksilver's a Son?" Victra explodes into laughter. "And I'm secretly a Helldiver." She looks back and forth at our faces. "Wait . . . you're serious. Do you have proof?"

"I'm sorry to hear of your mother, Victra," Quicksilver says hoarsely. "But it is a pleasure to see you walking, truly. I've been with the Sons for over twenty years. I have hundreds of hours of conversations with Fitchner to prove it."

"He's a Son," Sevro says. "Can we move on?"

"Well, I'll be damned." Victra shakes her head. "Mother was right about you. Always said you had secrets. I thought it was something sexual. That you liked horses or something." Sevro shifts uncomfortably.

"So you find us a way off this rock, rich man?" Holiday asks Quicksilver.

"Not quite," he says. "Darrow . . ."

"We're not leaving," I announce. Rollo and his men stir in the corner. The Howlers exchange confused looks.

"Maybe you wanna tell us what's going on?" Screwface asks gruffly. "Let's start with who's in charge. Is it you?"

"Howler One," Sevro says, punching my shoulder.

"Howler Two," I say, patting his in turn.

"Prime?" Sevro asks. The Howlers nod in concert.

"First order of business, policy change," I say. "Who has pliers?" I look around until Holiday pulls hers from her bomb kit and tosses them to me. I open my mouth and stick the pliers to the back right molar where the achlys-9 suicide tooth was implanted. With a grunt I tear it out and set the tooth on the table. "I've been captured before. I will not be captured again. So this is worthless to me. I don't plan on dying, but if I do, I die with my friends. Not in a cell. Not on a podium. With you." I hand the pliers to Sevro. He jerks out his own back tooth. Spitting the blood on the table.

"I die with my friends."

Ragnar does not wait for the pliers. He pulls out his back tooth with his bare fingers, eyes wide with delight as he sets the huge bloody thing on the table. **"I die with my friends."** One by one, they pass around the pliers, pulling out their teeth and tossing them down. Quicksilver watches all the while, staring at us like we're a pack of mad hooligans, no doubt wondering about what he's gotten himself into. But I need my men to lose this heavy mantle they wear. With that poison in their skulls, they felt the death sentences had already been read, and they were just waiting for the hangman to come knocking.

Slag that. Death'll have to earn its bounty. I want them to believe in this. In each other. In the idea that we might actually win and live.

For the first time, I do.

After I've detailed my instructions to my men and they depart to execute the orders, I return with Sevro to the Sons of Ares control room and ask for them to prepare a direct link. "To the Citadel in Agea, please." The Sons of Ares turn to look at me to see if they've misheard. "On the double, friends. We don't have all day."

I stand in front of the holo camera with Sevro. "Think they already know we're here?"

"Probably not quite yet," I reply.

"Think he's going to piss himself?"

"Let's hope. Remember, nothing about Mustang and Cassius being here. We're keeping that one in the pocket."

The direct holoLink goes through and the face of a wan young Copper administrator looks sleepily back at us. "Citadel General Com," she drones, "how may I direct your . . ." She blinks suddenly at our images on the display. Wipes sleep from her eyes. And loses all faculty of speech.

"I would like to speak with the ArchGovernor," I say.

"And . . . may I say who is . . . calling?"

"It's the bloodydamn Reaper of Mars," Sevro barks.

"One moment, please."

The Copper's face is replaced by the pyramid of the Society. Terribly predictable Vivaldi plays as we wait. Sevro taps his fingers on his leg and murmurs his little tune under his breath. *If your heart beats like a drum, and your leg's a little wet, it's because the Reaper's come to collect a little debt.*

Several minutes later, the Jackal's pale face appears before us. He wears a jacket with a high white collar, and his hair is parted on the side. He does not leer at us. If anything, he looks amused as he continues to eat his breakfast. "The Reaper *and* Ares," he says in a low drawl, mocking his own courtesy. He wipes his mouth on a napkin. "You departed so quickly last time I didn't have time to say farewell.

I must say, you're looking positively radiant, Darrow. Is Victra with you?"

"Adrius," I say flatly. "As you're no doubt aware, there has been an explosion at Sun Industries, and your silent partner, Quicksilver, has gone missing. I know it's a mess of jurisdiction, and the evidence won't be sorted for hours, maybe days. So I wanted to call and clarify the situation. We, the Sons of Ares, have kidnapped Quicksilver."

He sets his spoon down to sip from his white coffee cup.

"I see. To what end?"

"We will be holding him for ransom until you release all political prisoners illegally detained in your jails and all lowColors concentrated in internment camps. Additionally, you are to take responsibility for the murder of your father. Publicly."

"Is that all?" the Jackal asks, not displaying a flicker of emotion, though I know he's wondering how we discovered Quicksilver was his ally.

"You also have to personally kiss my pimply ass," Sevro says.

"Lovely." The Jackal looks off the screen to someone. "My agents tell me a flight moratorium was instituted ten minutes after the attack on Sun Industries and the vessel which fled the scene disappeared into the Hollows. Am I to assume then that you're still on Phobos?"

I pause as if caught off guard. "If you do not comply, Quicksilver's life is forfeit."

"Lamentably, I do not negotiate with terrorists. Especially ones who may be recording my conversation to broadcast it for political gain." The Jackal sips his coffee again. "I listened to your proposal, now listen to mine. Run. Now. While you can. But know, wherever you go, wherever you hide, you cannot protect your friends. I'm going to kill them all and put you back in the darkness with their severed heads for company. There is no way out, Darrow. This I promise you."

He kills the signal.

"Think he'll send the Boneriders before the legions?" Sevro asks.

"Let's hope. Time to get moving."

The Hollows is a city of cages. Row upon row. Column upon column of rusty metal homes linked together in the null gravity as far as the eye can see here in the heart of Phobos. Each cage a life in miniature. Clothing floats on hooks. Little portable thermal press-grills sizzle with the foods of a hundred different regions of Mars. Paper pictures cling to iron cage walls by bits of tape, showing distant lakes, mountains, and families gathered together. Everything here is dull and gray. The metal of the cages. The limp clothing. Even the tired and wasted faces of the Oranges and Reds who are trapped here, thousands of kilometers from home. Sparks of color dance up from the datapads and holoVisor that glow through the city, bits of dream scattered on twisted scrap metal. Men and women sit penitent over their little displays, watching their little programs, forgetting where they are in favor of where they'd wish to be. Many have taped paper or blankets over the sides of their walls to give them some semblance of privacy from their neighbors. But it's the scent and the sound you cannot escape. The throaty unceasing rattle of cage doors slamming shut. Locks clicking. Men laughing and coughing. Generators humming. Public holoCans yapping and barking the dog language of distraction. All stirred and boiled together to make a thick soup of noise and shadowy light.

Rollo once lived in negative south end of the city. Now it is deep Syndicate territory. The Sons were chased out more than two months ago. I fly along the lines of plastic rope that weave through the cage canyons, passing dockworkers and tower laborers who climb back to their little cage homes. They jerk their heads toward the throaty thrum of my new gravBoots. It's an alien sound to them. One heard only over the holoVids or experiential virtual realities low world Greens hawk for fifty credits a minute. Most will never have seen a Peerless Scarred in the flesh. Much less one in full armor. I'm a terrifying spectacle.

It was seven hours ago that my lieutenants and I clustered together in the Sons of Ares ready room and I told them and Dancer back in Tinos my plan. Six hours since I learned of Kavax's escape from our detention cell—someone let him out. Five hours since Victra delivered

Quicksilver and Matteo back to their tower, where Quicksilver has spent the remainder of the night activating his own cells and contacts in the Blue Hives, making preparation for this moment. Four hours since Quicksilver joined his security teams with Sons of Ares and gave them access to his armories and his weapons depots, and we received word that two Augustus destroyers were inbound from the orbital docks. Three hours since Ragnar and Rollo took a thousand Sons of Ares to the garbage hangars on level 43C to prepare their skiffs. Two hours since one of Quicksilver's private yachts was prepped for launch. One hour since the Society destroyers deployed four troop transports to dock at the Skyresh Interplanetary Spaceport and the new coat of blood-red paint on my armor dried and I donned it to march to war.

All is ready.

Now I carve a wake of silence into the heart of the Hollows. My bone-white razor is on my arm. At my side flies Sevro, wearing the huge spiked helmet of Ares with pride. He brought it along, but the rest of his armor is borrowed from Quicksilver. It's cutting-edge tech. Better even than the suits we wore for Augustus. Holiday follows behind along with a hundred Sons of Ares.

The Sons are awkward on their gravBoots. Some carry razors. Others pulseFists. But, per my orders, not one wears a helmet as we fly. I wanted these lowColors of the stacks witnessing our treason, so that they feel emboldened by Reds and Oranges and Obsidians wearing the armor of the masters.

The faces are a blur. A hundred thousand peering from the homes in every direction. Pale and confused, most under the age of forty. Reds and Oranges brought here with false promises just like Rollo, with families down on Mars, just like Rollo.

Neighbors point in my direction. I see my name on their lips. Somewhere, the Syndicate watchmen will be dialing their superiors, relaying the news to the police or the Securitas antiterrorism apparatus that the Reaper lives and he is on Phobos.

I bait the beasts.

As I coast into the central hub of the city, I say a silent prayer, willing Eo to give me strength. There, like some pulsing electronic idol fenced in by metal bramble, a holographic display casts Society comedy programing one hundred meters long, fifty meters broad. It bathes the circle of cages around it in sickly neon light. Speakers laugh on cue. Blue light plays over my armor. Locks jingle as they're undone and cages are pushed open so their inhabitants can sit on the edge and dangle their legs off to watch me without looking through the cage bars.

Quicksilver's Greens focus their helmet cameras on me. The Sons array around, eyes smoldering out at the lowColors, my honor guard. Their red hair floating like a hundred angry torch flames. Holiday and Ares flank me to either side. Floating two hundred meters in the air. Surrounded by cages. Silence gripping the city except the laugh track of the comedy. It's sick and weird as it cackles out of the speakers. I nod to Quicksilver's Greens, and they cut the noise and somewhere in his tower, the hacker teams he's assembled hijack every broadcast on the moon and issue commands to secondary datahubs on Earth, Luna, the asteroid belt, Mercury, the moons of Jupiter, so my message will burn across the blackness of space, taking over the data web that links mankind. Quicksilver is proving his allegiance with this broadcast, using the network he helped the Jackal build. This is not like Eo's death. A viral video you have to dig for in the dark spaces of the holoNet. This is a grand roar across the Society, broadcasting on ten billion holos to eighteen billion people.

They gave these screens to us as chains. Today, we make them hammers.

Karnus au Bellona had his faults. But he was right when he said that all we have in this life is our shout into the wind. He shouted his own name, and I learned the folly in that. But before I begin the war that will claim me one way or another, I will make my shout. And it will be something far greater than my own name. Far greater than a roar of family pride. It is the dream I've carried and shepherded since I was sixteen.

Eo appears beneath me on the hologram, replacing the comedy.

A ghostly giant of the girl I knew. Her face is quiet and pale and angrier than in my dreams. Hair dull and stringy. Clothing drab and ragged. But her eyes burn out from her gray surroundings, bright as the blood on her mangled back as she looks up from the metal whipping box. Her mouth barely seems to open. Just a sliver of space between her lips, but her song bleeds from her, voice thin and fragile as a spring dream.

> *My son, my son*
> *Remember the chains*
> *When gold ruled with iron reins*
> *We roared and roared*
> *And twisted and screamed*
> *For ours, a vale*
> *Of better dreams*

She echoes across the metal city louder than she echoed in that far-off lost city of stone. Her light flickering across the pale faces watching from their cages. These Oranges and Reds who never knew her in life, but hear her in death. They're silent and sad as she is walked to the gallows. I hear my vain cries. See myself sagging against Gray hands. Feel I'm there again. The hard-packed dirt on my knees as the world falls out from under me. Augustus speaks with Pliny and Leto as frayed hemp loops around Eo's neck. Hatred radiates from the faces in the Stacks. I could no more stop Eo's death then than I can stop it now. It's as if it always has been. My wife falls. I flinch, hearing the rustling of her clothing. The creaking of the rope. And I look down at the hologram, forcing myself to watch as the boy I was stumbles forward to wrap his hands with their Red Sigils around her kicking legs. I watch him kiss her ankle and pull her feet with all his feeble strength. Her haemanthus falls, and I speak.

"I would have lived in peace. But my enemies brought me war. My name is Darrow of Lykos. You know my story. It is but an echo of your own. They came to my home and killed my wife, not for singing a song but for daring to question their reign. For daring to have a voice. For centuries millions beneath the soil of Mars have been fed lies from cradle to grave. That lie has been revealed to them. Now they've entered the world you know, and they suffer as you do.

"Man was born free, but from the ocean shores to the crater cities of Mercury to the ice waste of Pluto down to the mines of Mars, he is in chains. Chains made of duty, hunger, fear. Chains hammered to our necks by a race that we lifted up. A race that we empowered. Not to rule, not to reign, but to lead us from a world torn by war and greed. Instead, they have led us into darkness. They have used the systems of order and prosperity for their own gain. They expect your obedience, ignore your sacrifice, and hoard the prosperity that your hands create. To hold tight to their reign, they forbid our dreams. Saying a person is only as good as the Colors of their eyes, of their Sigils."

I remove my gloves and clench my right fist in the air as Eo did before she died. But unlike Eo, my hands bear no Sigils. Removed by Mickey when I was Carved in Tinos. I am the first soul in hundreds of years to walk without them. The silence in the Hollows gives way to sounds of shock, fear.

"But now I stand before you, a man unbound. I stand before you, my brothers and sisters, to ask you to join me. To throw yourselves on the machines of industry. To unite behind the Sons of Ares. Take back your cities, your prosperity. Dare to dream of better worlds than these. Slavery is not peace. Freedom is peace. And until we have that, it is our duty to make war. This is no license for savagery or genocide. If a man rapes, you kill him on the spot. If a man murders civilians, high or low, you kill him on the spot. This is war, but you are on the side of good and that carries a heavy burden. We rise not for hate, not for vengeance, but for justice. For your children. For their future.

"I speak now to Gold, to the Aureate who rule. I have walked your halls, broken your schools, eaten at your tables, and suffered your gallows. You tried to kill me. You could not. I know your power. I know your pride. And I have seen how you will fall. For seven hundred years, you have ruled over the dominion of man, and this is all you have given us. It is not enough.

"Today, I declare your rule to be at its end. Your cities are not your cities. Your vessels are not your vessels. Your planets are not your planets. They were built by us. And they belong to us, the common trust of man. Now we take them back. Never mind the darkness you spread, never mind the night you summon, we will rage against it. We will howl and fight till our last breath, not just in the mines of Mars, but on the shores of Venus, on the dunes of Io's sulfur seas, in the glacial valleys of Pluto. We will fight in the towers of Ganymede and the ghettos of Luna and the storm-stricken oceans of Europa. And if we fall, others will take our place, because we are the tide. And we are rising."

Then Sevro slams his fist against his chest. Once, twice, thumping it rhythmically. It is echoed by the two hundred Sons of Ares. Their fists pounding their chests. By the Howlers.

In the steel mesh of the cages men and women thump their fists into the walls till it sounds like the heartbeat rising through the bowels of this vampire moon; up through the Hives of Blues, where they sit drinking coffee and studying gravitational mathematics under the warm lights of their intellectual communes; through the Gray barracks in each precinct; among the Silvers at their trading desks; the Golds in their mansions and yachts.

Out through the black ink that separates our little bubbles of life before careening down into the halls of the Jackal's lonely hold on Attica, where he sits in his winter throne, surrounded by a sea of bent necks. There our sound rattles in his ears. There he hears my wife's heart beat on. And he cannot stop it as it goes down and down into the mines of Mars, playing on the screens as Reds beat on their tables and the Copper magistrates watch in swelling fear as the miners look hatefully up through the duroglass that keeps them imprisoned.

Her heart beats mutinously through the bustling oceanside promenades of the archipelagos of Venus as sailboats float proudly in the harbor and shopping bags hang in frightened hands and Golds look to their drivers, their gardeners, the men who power their cities. It beats through the tin-roofed mess halls of the wheat and soybean latfundia that cover the Great Plains of Earth, where Reds use machines to toil under the huge sun to feed mouths of people they will never meet, in places they will never be. It beats even along the spine of the empire, raging through the spiked city moon of Luna, passing by the Sovereign in her glass high refuge to thunder on down snaking electrical wires and drying clothing lines to the Lost City, where a Pink girl makes breakfast after a long night of thankless work. Where a Brown cook leans away from his stove to hear as grease spatters his apron, and a Gray watches from the window of his patrol skiff as a Violet girl smashes the front door of a Post Office and his datapad summons him back to the station for emergency riot protocols.

And it beats inside me, this terrible hope, as I know that the end has begun, and I am finally awake.

"Break the chains," I roar.

And my people roar back.

"Ragnar," I say into my com. "Bring it down."

The Greens cut to a different feed as the fists thump and the cages rattle. And we see a distant shot of the Society's military spire on Phobos. A goliath of a building with docks and vestibules for weapons. Efficient and ugly as a crab. From it, the Jackal maintains his grip on the moon. There, the Grays and Obsidians will be donning armor under pale lights, rushing through metal halls in tight lines, stocking ammunition belts, and kissing pictures of their loved ones so they can come down to the Hollows and make this heart stop beating. But they will never make it here.

Because, as fists pound even harder into cages, the lights of that military spire go black. All her power turned off by Rollo and his men with the access cards provided by Quicksilver.

We could have bombed the building, but I wanted a triumph of daring, of achievement, not destruction. We need heroes. Not another ash city.

And so, a small squadron of a dozen maintenance skiffs coasts into view. Flat, ugly fliers designed to port Reds and Oranges like Rollo to their construction work on towers. Craggy stingrays covered with barnacles. But it isn't barnacles that cling to them now. Another camera takes a closer angle, and we can see each skiff is covered with hundreds of men. Reds and Oranges in their clunky EVA suits, almost half the Sons of Ares on Phobos. Boots against the deck, harnesses latched into exterior buckles of the ship. They carry their welding gear and have Quicksilver's weapons patched onto their legs with magnetic tape.

Among them, two feet taller than the others, is their general, Ragnar Volarus, in armor freshly painted bone white, a red slingBlade painted on the chest and back.

As the skiffs near the Society military spire, they divide down the length of the building. Sons fire magnetic harpoons to tether the skiffs to the steel. And then they go with practiced ease along the lines, flying at implausible speeds as the little motors on their buckles pull them one by one along toward the building. It's like watching Reds in the mines. The grace and nimbleness even in the clunky suits dazzle.

More than a thousand welders pour onto the vast building like we did Quicksilver's spire, but they're not playing for stealth and they're better in null gravity than we were. Magnetic boots clutching metal girders, they skitter across the building, melting through the viewports and entering with extreme prejudice. Dozens are ripped to shreds as Grays inside fire railguns out the glass, but they fire back and pour inward. A ripWing patrol banks in along the outside of the building and rakes two of the skiffs with chain guns. Men turn to mist.

A Son fires a rocket at the ripWing. Fire blooms and vanishes and the ship cracks in half in a gout of purple flame.

The camera follows Ragnar as he breaches a window, enters a hall, and runs full-tilt into a trio of Gold knights, one who I recognize as the cousin of Priam, the man Sevro killed in the Passage and whose mother owns the deed to Phobos. Ragnar flows through the young knight without stopping. Swinging both his razors like scissors and ululating the war cry of his people, followed by a pack of heavily armed welders and laborers. I told him I wanted the spire. I didn't tell him how to take it. He walked off with Rollo, putting an arm around the man.

Now the worlds watch a slave become a hero.

"This moon belongs to you," Sevro says, roaring to the roiling cage city. "Rise and take it! Rise, men of Mars. Women of Mars, rise! You bloodydamn bastards! Rise!" Men and women are pulling themselves from their homes. Donning their boots and jackets. Pushing themselves toward us so that thousands clog the air avenues, crawling over the outside of the cages.

The tide has risen. And I feel a deep terror in wondering exactly what it will wash away. "Rape and murder of innocents is punishable by death. This is war, but you are on the side of good. Remember that, you little shitheads! Protect your brothers! Protect your sisters! All residents of sections 1a-4c, you are to take the armory in level 14. Residents of sections 5c-3f are to take the water-purification center on . . ."

Sevro seizes control of the battle and the Howlers and Sons disperse to organize the mob. It isn't an army but a battering ram. Many will die. And when they die, more will rise in their place. This is just one of the stack cities of Phobos. The Sons will supply them with weapons, but there won't be nearly enough to go around. Their sword is the press of flesh. Sevro will lead them, spend them, Victra in Quicksilver's spires will guide them, and the moon will fall to the rebellion.

But I will not be here to see it.

24

||||||||||||||||||||||||||

HIC SUNT LEONES

Phobos is in uproar. Detonations shake the moon as Holiday and I run through the halls. Golds and Silvers evacuate the Needles in their flashing luxury yachts as kilometers beneath, the Hollows swarms with packs of lowColor mobs armed with welding torches, fusion cutters, pipes, black-market scorchers, and old-fashioned slug throwers. The mobs are overwhelming the tram systems and passages to gain access to the midSector and Needles while the Society military garrison, caught reeling from the attack on their headquarters, rushes to stop the upward migration. The Legions have training and organization on their side. We have numbers and surprise.

Not to mention fury.

No matter how many checkpoints the Grays blockade, how many trams the Grays destroy, the lowColors will seep through the cracks because they made this place, because they have allies among the mid-Colors, thanks to Quicksilver. They open derelict transportation tunnels, hijack cargo ships in the industrial sector, pack them full of men and women, and steer them for the luxury hangars in the Needles, or even toward the public Skyresh Interplanetary Spaceport, where cruise liners and passenger ships are being loaded with evacuees.

I'm remotely jacked into Quicksilver's security grid, watching high-Colors stampede over one another. Carrying luggage and valuables and children. Martian Navy ripWings and fast-moving fighters dart through the towers, shooting down the rebel ships rising from the Hollows toward the Needles. The debris from a destroyed lowColor skif crashes through the vaulted glass and steel ceiling of a Skyresh terminal, killing civilians, and shattering any illusion I might have had that this war would be sanitary.

Ducking away from a mob of lowColors, Holiday and I arrive outside a derelict hangar in the old freight garages, which haven't been used since before the time of Augustus. It's quiet here. Abandoned. The old pedestrian entrance is welded shut. Radiation signs warn potential scavengers away. But the doors open for us with a deep groan when a modern retinal scanner built into the metal registers my irises, as Quicksilver said it would.

The hangar is a vast rectangle skinned with dust and cobwebs. In the center of the hangar's deck sits a silver seventy-meter-long luxury yacht shaped like a sparrow in flight. It's a custom-built model out of the Venusian Shipyards, ostentatious, fast, and perfect for an obscenely wealthy war refugee. Quicksilver plucked it from his fleet to help us blend in with the migrating upper class. Its rear cargo plank is down, and inside the bird is filled to capacity with black crates stamped with the Sun Industries winged heel. Inside of which are several billion credits' worth of hi-tech weapons and equipment.

Holiday whistles. "Gotta love deep pockets. The fuel would cost my annual wages. Twice over."

We cross the hangar to meet Quicksilver's pilot. The trim young Blue waits at the bottom of the ramp. She has no eyebrows and her head is bald. Winding blue lines pulse beneath the skin where subdermal synaptic links connect her remotely to the ship. She snaps to attention, eyes wide. Clearly she had no idea who she was transporting until now. "Sir, I am Lieutenant Vesta. I'll be your pilot today. And I must say, it's an honor to have you on board."

There's three levels to the yacht, the upper and bottom for Gold use. The middle for cooks, servants, and crew. There's four staterooms, a sauna, and crème leather seats with dainty little chocolates and napkins sitting primly on armrests in the passenger cabin to the far back of the cockpit. I pocket one. And then a couple more.

As Holiday and Vesta prep the ship, I strip off my pulseArmor in the passenger cabin and unpack winter gear from one of the boxes. I dress in skintight nanofiber weave that's much like scarabSkin. But instead of black, it's mottled white and looks oily except for textured grips on the elbows, gloves, buttocks, and knees. It's crafted for polar temperatures and water immersion. It's also a hundred pounds lighter than our pulseArmor, is immune to digital component failures, and has the added benefit of not needing batteries. Much as I enjoy using four hundred million credits' worth of technology to make me a flying human tank, sometimes warm pants are more valuable. And we'll always have the pulseArmor if we need it in a pinch.

I'm struck by the silence in the cargo bay and the hangar as I finish lacing my boots. There's still fifteen minutes left on my datapad's timer, so I sit on the edge of the ramp, legs dangling off, to wait for Ragnar. I pull the chocolates from my pocket and slowly peel the foil off. Taking half a bite, I let the chocolate sit on my tongue, waiting for it to melt as I always do. And as always, I lose patience and chew it before the bottom half is melted through. Eo would make candy last for days, when we were lucky enough to have it.

I set my datapad on the ground and watch the helmet cameras of my friends as they wage my war for Phobos. Their chatter trembles out of the datapad's speakers, echoing in the vast metal chamber. Sevro's in his element, rushing through the central ventilation unit with hundreds of Sons loading themselves into the air ducts. I feel guilty for sitting here watching them, but we each have our parts to play.

The door we entered through opens with a groan and Ragnar and two of the Obsidian Howlers enter the room. Fresh from the battlefield, Ragnar's white armor is dented and stained. "Did you play gently with the fools, my goodman?" I call down from the ramp in my thickest highLingo. In reply, he tosses up to me a curule: a twisted gold scepter of power given to high-ranking military officers. This one is tipped with a screaming banshee and a splash of crimson.

"The tower has fallen," Ragnar says. "Rollo and the Sons finish my work. These are the stains of subGovernor Priscilla au Caan."

"Well done, my friend," I say, taking the scepter in my hands. On it is carved the deeds of the Caan family, which owned the two moons of Mars and once followed Bellona to war. Among great warriors and statesmen, there's a young man I recognize standing by a horse.

"What is wrong?" Ragnar asks.

"Nothing," I say. "I knew her son is all. Priam. He seemed decent enough."

"Decent is not enough," Ragnar says forlornly. "Not for their world."

With a grunt, I bend the curule against my knee and toss it back to him to show my agreement. "Give it to your sister. Time to go."

Glancing back at the hangar with a frown, he checks his datapad and files past me into the cargo hold. I try to wipe the blood from the curule off of my white suit's leg. It just smears over the oily fabric, giving me a red stripe on my thigh. I close the ramp behind me. Inside, I help Ragnar out of his pulseArmor and let him slip into the winter gear as I join Holiday and Vesta as they initiate preflight launch.

"Remember, we're refugees. Aim for the largest convoy heading out of here and stick to them." Vesta nods. It's an old hangar. So it has no pulseField. All that separates us from space are five-story-tall steel doors. They rumble as the motors begin to retract them into the ceiling and floor. "Stop!" I say. Vesta sees what caught my attention a second after I do and her hand flashes to the controls, stopping the doors before they part and open the hangar to vacuum.

"I'll be damned," Holiday says, peering out the cockpit to a small figure blocking our ship's path to space. "It's the lion."

Mustang stands in front of the ship illuminated by our headlights. Her hair washed white by the blinding light. She blinks as Holiday cuts the headlights from the cockpit and I make my way to her through the dim hangar. Her dancing eyes dissect me as I come. They dart from my Sigil-barren hands to the scar I've kept on my face. What does she see?

Does she see my resolve? My fear?

In her I see so much. The girl I fell in love with in the snow is gone, replaced in the last fifteen months by a woman. A thin, intense leader of vast and enduring strength and alarming intellect. Eyes kinetic, ringed by circles of exhaustion and trapped in a face made pale from long days in sunless lands and metal halls. Everything she is dwells behind her eyes. She has her father's mind. Her mother's face. And a distant, foreboding sort of intelligence that can give you wings or crush you to the earth.

And just at her hip sits a ghostCloak with a cooling unit.

She has watched us since we arrived.

How did she get inside the hangar?

"'Lo, Reaper," she says playfully as I come to a halt.

"'Lo, Mustang." I search the rest of the hangar. "How did you find me?"

She frowns in confusion. "I thought you wanted me to come. Ragnar told Kavax where I could find you . . ." She trails off. "Oh. You didn't know."

"No." I look back up at the ship's mirror cockpit windows, where Ragnar must be watching me. The man's overstepped his bounds. Even as I arranged a war, he went behind my back and endangered my mission. Now I know exactly how Sevro felt.

"Where have you been?" she asks me.

"With your brother."

"Then the execution was a ruse meant to make us stop looking."

There's so much more to say, so many questions and accusations that could fly between us. But I didn't want to see her because I don't know where to begin. What to say. What to ask for. "I don't have time for small talk, Mustang. I know you came to Phobos to surrender to the Sovereign. Now why are you here talking to me?"

"Don't talk down to me," she says sharply. "I wasn't surrendering. I was making peace. You're not the only one with people to protect. My father ruled Mars for decades. Its people are as much a part of me as they are part of you."

"You left Mars at the mercy of your brother," I say.

"I left Mars to save it," she corrects. "You know everything is a compromise. And you know it's not Mars; you're angry at me for leaving."

"I need you to stand aside, Mustang. This is not about us. And I don't have time to bicker. I'm leaving. So either you move or we open the door and fly through you."

"Fly through me?" she laughs. "You know I didn't have to come alone. I could have come with my bodyguards. I could have lain in wait to ambush you. Or reported you to the Sovereign to salvage the peace you ruined. But I didn't. Can you stop for a single moment to think why?" She takes a step forward. "You said to me in that tunnel that you want a better world. Can't you see that I listened? That I joined the Moon Lords because I believe in something better?"

"Yet you surrendered."

"Because I could not watch my brother's reign of terror continue. I want peace."

"This is not the time for peace," I say.

"Goryhell, you're thick. I know that. Why do you think I am here? Why do you think I've worked with Orion and kept your soldiers at their stations?"

I examine her. "I honestly don't know."

"I'm here because I want to believe in you, Darrow. I want to believe in what you said in that tunnel. I ran from you because I didn't want to accept that the only answer was the sword. But the world we live in has conspired to take everything I love away. My mother, my father, my brothers. I will not let it take the friends I have left. I will not let it take you."

"What are you saying?" I ask.

"I'm saying that I'm not letting you out of my sight. I'm coming with you."

It's my turn to laugh. "You don't even know where I'm going."

"You're wearing sealSkin. Ragnar's on board. You've declared open rebellion. Now you're leaving in the middle of the largest battle the Rising has ever seen. Really, Darrow. It doesn't take a genius to deduce that now you're using this ship to pretend to be a Gold refugee to escape and go to the Valkyrie Spires to beseech Ragnar's mother to provide an army."

Damn. I try not to let my surprise show.

This is why I did not want to involve Mustang. Inviting her into the game is adding another dimension I can't control. She could destroy my gambit with a single call to her brother, to the Sovereign, telling them where I am going. Everything relies on misdirection. On my enemies thinking I am on Phobos. She knows what I'm thinking. I can't let her leave this hangar.

"The Telemanuses know as well," she says, knowing my mind. "But I'm tired of having insurance plans against you. Tired of playing games. You and I have pushed each other away because of broken trust. Aren't you tired of that? Of the secrets between us? Of the guilt?"

"You know I am. I laid my secrets bare in the tunnels of Lykos."

"Then let this be our second chance. For you. For me. For both our people. I want what you want. And when you and I are aligned, when have we ever lost? Together we can build something, Darrow."

"You're suggesting an alliance . . ." I say quietly.

"Yes." Her eyes are afire. "The might of House Augustus and Telemanus and Arcos united with the Rising. With the Reaper. With Orion and all her ships. The Society would tremble."

"Millions will die in that war," I say. "You know that. The Peerless Scarred will fight to the last Gold. Can you stomach that? Can you watch that happen?"

"To build we must break," she says. "I was listening."

Still, I shake my head. There's too much to overcome between us, between our people. It would be a qualified victory, on her terms. "How could I ask my men to trust a Gold army? How could I trust you?"

"You can't. That is why I am coming with you. To prove I believe in your wife's dream. But you have to prove something to me. That you are worthy of *my* trust, in turn. I know you can break. I need to see that you can build. I need to see what you will build. If the blood we will shed is for something. Prove that, and you have my sword. Fail, and you and I will go our separate ways." She cocks her head at me. "So what do you say, Helldiver? Do you want to give it one more go?"

25

||||||||||||||||||||||

EXODUS

I help unbuckle Mustang's pulseArmor in the cargo hold. "Cold gear is in here." I gesture to a large plastic box. "Boots in there."

"Quicksilver gave you the keys to his armory?" she asks, eying the winged heel on the boxes. "How many fingers did it cost him?"

"None," I say. "He's a Son of Ares."

"What now?"

I grin. Comforting knowing the world isn't an open book for her. The engines rumble and the ship rises underneath us. "Get dressed and join us in the cabin." I leave her behind to change in private. I was more gruff than I intended. But it felt strange smiling in her presence. I find Ragnar leaning back in his chair in the passenger cabin eating chocolates, white boots up on the adjacent armrest. "No offense, but what the hell are you doing?" Holiday asks me. She stands, arms crossed, between the cockpit and the passenger cabin. "Sir."

"Taking a risk," I say. "I know it might seem strange to you, Holiday. But I go back with her."

"She's the definition of the elite. Worse than Victra. Her father—"

"Killed my wife," I say. "So if I can stomach it, so can you." Holiday makes a whistling sound and heads back to the cabin, unhappy with our new ally.

"So the Mustang joined our quest," Ragnar says.

"She's getting dressed," I reply. "You had no right to let Kavax go. Much less tell him where we would be. What if they gave us up, Ragnar? What if they ambushed us? You would never have seen your home. If they find out we're there, they'll never let your people off the surface. They'll kill them all. Did you think of that?"

He eats another chocolate. "A man thinks he can fly, but he is afraid to jump. A poor friend pushes him from behind." He looks up at me. "A good friend jumps with."

"You've been reading *Stoneside,* haven't you?"

Ragnar nods. "Theodora gave it to me. Lorn au Arcos was a great man."

"He'd be glad you think so, but take everything with a grain of salt. The biographer took some liberties. Especially in his early life."

"Lorn would have told you that we need her. Now, in war. And after, in peace. If we do not bring her to our cause, then we will not win until every Gold is dead. That is not why I fight."

Ragnar rises to greet Mustang as she joins us. The last time they stood eye to eye, she had a gun pointed at his head. "Ragnar, you've been busy since I last saw you. Not a Gold alive doesn't know and fear your name. Thank you for releasing Kavax."

"Family is dear," Ragnar says. "But I warn you. We go to my lands. You are under my protection. If you play your tricks, if you play your games, that protection is forfeit. And even you will not survive long on the ice without me, daughter of the lion. Do you understand?"

Mustang bows her head respectfully. "I do. And I will repay your faith in me, Ragnar. I promise you that."

"Enough chatter. Time to buckle up," Holiday snaps from the cabin. Vesta's synced with the ship and pushing out of the hangar. We find our seats. There's twenty to choose from, but Mustang takes the one next to me in the left aisle. Her hand grazes my hip accidentally as she reaches for her seat harness.

Our ship departs the hangar, silently floating forward into the vacuum of the dim subcutaneous industrial world of Phobos. Pipes and loading docks and garbage bays as far as we can see. Closed off to the stars and the light of the sun. Few ships as lovely as ours have ever flown so far beneath the surface of Phobos. The word *LowSector* is rendered in white paint over an industrial transport hub where men pour into ships, and the ships trundle up out of this dim world toward the sector gates that the Sons have breached.

Our sleek yacht passes a motley fleet of slow-moving garbage haulers and freighters. Inside, men and women huddle quietly together in windowless, dirty steel cubes. Sweat drenches their backs. Their hands shake holding unfamiliar instruments: weapons. They pray they can be as brave as they've always imagined themselves to be. Then they'll land in some Gold hangar. The Sons will shout orders. The doors will open and they will meet war.

I pray silently for them, clenching my hands as I stare out the window. I feel Mustang watching me. Measuring the tides deep within.

Soon we leave the industrial Stacks behind, trading the dim recesses for the neon advertisements that bathe the space boulevards of the midSector. Manmade canyons of steel to either side. Trams. Elevators. Apartments. Every screen connected to the web has been slaved by Quicksilver's hackers, showing images of Sevro and the Sons overrunning security gates and checkpoints, painting scythes on walls.

And around us, the city of thirty million churns. Deep space commercial transports racing past little civilian taxis and skippers meant to go between the buildings here. Freighters soar from the Hollows up through the midSector toward the Needles. A flight of ripWings hunts through the streets above us. I hold my breath. With a flip of a trigger they could shred us. But they don't. They register our high-Color ship ID and hail us over the coms and offer an escort out of the warzone toward a current of yachts and skiffs that blaze quietly away from the moon.

"*Stirring speech,*" Victra purrs over the ship's com as I answer the call from Quicksilver's tower, her bored voice at odds with the warring world around us. "*Clown and Screwface just took Skyresh's main terminals. Rollo's men have seized the water cisterns for the midSector. Quicksilver's networks are broadcasting it all the way to Luna. Scythes popping up everywhere. There's riots in Agea, Corinth, every-*

where on Mars. And we're hearing the same from Earth and Luna. Municipal buildings are falling. Police stations burning. You've woken the rabble."

"They'll hit back soon."

"*As you said, darling. We massacred the first responders the Jackal sent. Got a few Boneriders, just as we wanted. No Lilath or Thistle, though.*"

"Damn. Worth a shot."

"*Martian Navy is on its way from Deimos. The Legions are coming, and we're making our final preparations.*"

"Good. Good. Victra, I need you to let Sevro know that we've added a member to our expedition. Mustang's joined us."

Silence from her. "*Am I on a private line?*"

Holiday tosses me a headset from the cockpit. I wrestle the headset on. "You are now. You don't agree."

The bitterness in her tone is acute. "*Here are my thoughts. You can't trust her. Look at her brother. Her father. Greed is in her blood. Of course she would ally with us. It fits her aims.*" I watch Mustang as Victra speaks. "*She needs us because she's losing her war. But what happens when we give her what she needs? What happens when we're in her way? Will you be able to put her down? Will you be able to pull the trigger?*"

"Yes."

Victra's words linger as we pass Phobos's giant glass spires, cockpit skimming a dozen meters above the panes of the building. Inside roil little worlds of madness. The Rising has reached the Needles in this district of the city. LowColors push inexorably through the halls. Grays and Silvers barricading doors. Pinks standing in a bedroom over a bleeding old Gold and his wife, knives in hand. Three Silver children watching Ares on a wall-sized holo as their parents speak in the library. And at last, a Gold woman in a sky-blue cocktail dress, pearls about her neck, gold hair unbound to her waist. She stands near a window as Sons of Ares spread through the building, levels beneath her penthouse. Engulfed in her own drama, she raises a scorcher to her Golden head. Body stiff in imagined majesty. Her finger tightens around the trigger.

And we're past. Leaving her life and the chaos behind to join with the flow of yachts and pleasure craft that flee the battle for the safety of the planet. Most of the refugees call Mars home. Their ships, unlike ours, are not equipped for deep space. Now they scatter over the planet's atmosphere like burning seeds, most plunging straight for the spaceport of Corinth beneath us in the middle of the Thermic Sea. Others skimming over the atmosphere, disregarding designated transit lanes, racing past the Jackal's hastily erected blockade and the satellite level toward their homes in the opposite hemisphere. RipWings and wasps from the military frigates flash after them, trying to herd them back to the designated avenues. But entitlement and chaos are a poor mix. Mania grips these fleeing Golds.

"The *Dido*," Mustang says quietly to herself, eying a glass ship the shape of a sailboat to our starboard. "Drusilla au Ran's vessel. She taught me how to paint watercolors when I was little." But my attention is farther out, where ugly dark vessels without the flashing hulls or fanciful lines of the pleasure craft race toward Phobos. It's more than half the Martian defense fleet. Frigates, torchShips, destroyers. Even two dreadnaughts. I wonder if the Jackal is on one of those bridges. Likely not. It's probably Lilath who leads the detachment, or some other praetor newly appointed in his regime. Antonia has been dispatched to aid Roque on the Rim. Their ships will be packed with lifelong soldiers. Men and women as hard as we are. Many who fell in my Iron Rain. And they will cut through the mob I've summoned inside Phobos like paper. They'll be furious and confident: the more, the better.

"It's a trap, isn't it?" Mustang asks quietly. "You never meant to hold Phobos."

"Do you know how the Inuit tribes of Earth killed wolves?" I ask. She doesn't. "Slower and weaker than the wolves, they chiseled knives till they were razor sharp, coated them in blood and stuck them upright in the ice. Then the wolves would come up and lick the blood. And as the wolf licks faster and faster, he's so ravenous he doesn't realize until it's too late that the blood he's drinking is his own." I nod to the passing military vessels. "They hate that I was one of them. How many prime soldiers do you think those ships will launch at Phobos to take me, the great abomination for their own glory? Pride will again be the downfall of your Color."

"You're trying to get them on the station," she says, understanding. "Because you don't need Phobos."

"Like you said, I'm going to the Valkyrie Spires for an army. Orion and you might still have the remnants of my fleet. But we will need more ships than that. Sevro is waiting in the ventilation system of the hangars. When the assault forces land to take back the military spire and the Needles, they'll leave their shuttles behind in those hangars. Sevro will descend from his hiding place, hijack the shuttles, and return them home to their ships, packed with all the Sons we have left."

"And you honestly believe you can control the Obsidian?" she asks.

"Not me. Him." I nod to Ragnar. "They live in fear of their 'Gods' in the Board of Quality Control's Asgard Station. Golds in suits of armor playing at Odin and Freya. Same way that I lived in fear of the Grays in the Pot. As we were cowed by the Proctors. Ragnar's going to show them just how mortal their Gods really are."

"How?"

"We will kill them," Ragnar says. "I have sent friends ahead, months ago, to spread the truth. We will return to my mother and my sister as heroes, and I will tell them their gods are false with my own tongue. I will show them how to fly. I will give them weapons and this ship will carry them to Asgard and we will conquer it as Darrow conquered Olympus. Then we will free the other tribes and carry them away from this land on Quicksilver's ships."

"That's why you have a gorydamn armory back there," Mustang says.

"What do you think?" I ask her. "Possible?"

"Insane," she says, awed by the audacity of it. "Might be possible, though. Only *if* Ragnar can actually control them."

"I will not control. I will lead." He says it with quiet certainty.

Mustang admires the man for a moment. "I believe you will."

I watch Ragnar as he looks back out the window. What passes behind those dark eyes? This is the first time I've felt like he's not telling me something. He already deceived me by releasing Kavax. What else does he plan?

We listen in tense silence to the radio waves crackle with yacht captains requesting docking clearance on the military frigates instead of continuing down to the planet. Connections are used. Bribes offered. Strings pulled. Men weep and beg. These civilians are discovering that their place in the world is smaller than they imagined. They do not matter. In war, men lose what makes them great. Their creativity. Their wisdom. Their joy. All that's left is their utility. War is not monstrous for making corpses of men so much as it is for making machines of them. And woe to those who have no use in war except to feed the machines.

The Peerless Scarred know this cold truth. And they have trained for centuries for this new age of war. Killing in the Passage. Struggling through the deprivation of the Institute so that they might have worth when war comes. Time for Pixies with deep pockets and expensive tastes to appreciate the realities of life: you do not matter unless you can kill.

The bill, as Lorn often said, comes at the end. Now the Pixies pay.

A Gold Praetor's voice cuts through the speakers of our ship, ordering the refugee ships to redirect toward authorized transit lanes and steer clear of the navy warships or they will be fired upon. The Praetor cannot afford unauthorized vessels within one hundred kilometers of her ship. They could carry bombs. Could carry Sons of Ares. Two yachts ignore the warnings and are ripped apart as one of the cruisers fires railguns into their hulls. The Praetor repeats her order. This time it is obeyed. I look over at Mustang and wonder what she thinks of this. Of me. Wishing we could be somewhere quiet where a thousand things didn't pull at us. Where I ask about her instead of the war.

"Feels like the end of the world," she says.

"No." I shake my head. "It is the beginning of a new one. I have to believe that."

The planetscape below is blue and spackled white as we pretend to follow the designated coordinates along the western hemisphere at the equator. Tiny green islands ringed with tan beaches wink up at us from the indigo waters of the Thermic Sea. Beneath, ships jerk and burn as they hit atmosphere before us. Like phosphorous firecrackers Eo and I played with as children, kicking spasmodically and glowing orange, then blue, as heat friction builds along their shields. Our Blue veers us away, following a series of other ships who depart the general flow of traffic for their own homes.

Soon, Phobos is half a planet away. The continents pass beneath. One by one the other ships descend and we're left alone on our journey to the uncivilized pole, flying past several dozen Society satellites that monitor the southernmost continent. They too have been hacked into recycling information pulled from three years ago. We're invisible, for now. Not just to our enemies but to our friends. Mustang leans from her chair, peering up into the cockpit. "What is that?" She gestures to the sensor display. A single dot follows behind us.

"Another refugee ship from Phobos," the pilot answers. "Civilian vessel. No weapons." But it's closing fast. Trailing behind us by two hundred kilometers.

"If it's a civilian vessel, why did it just appear on our sensors?" Mustang asks.

"It could have sensor shielding. Dampeners," Holiday says warily.

The ship closes to forty kilometers. Something is wrong here. "Civilian vessels don't have that sort of acceleration," Mustang says.

"Dive," I say. "Get us through the atmosphere now. Holiday on the gun."

The Blue slips into defense protocols, increasing our speed, strengthening our rear shields. We hit atmosphere. My teeth rattle together. The ship's electronic voice suggests passengers find their seats. Holiday stumbles up, rushing past us to the tailgun. Then a warning siren trills as the ship behind us morphs on the radar display, sharp contours of hidden weapons blossoming from its formerly smooth hull. It follows us into atmosphere, and it fires.

Our pilot twists her thin hands in the gel controls. My stomach lurches. Hypersonic depleted uranium shells scar the canvas of clouds and icy terrain, superheating as they streak past. The ship jerks as we hit atmosphere ourselves. Our pilot continues to juke, twitching her fingers in the electric gel, face placid and lost in her dance with the

pursuing craft. Her eyes distant from her body. A single droplet of
sweat beading on her right temple and trickling down her jaw. Then a
gray blur rips into the cockpit and she explodes in a shower of meat.
Spattering the viewports and my face with blood. The uranium shell
takes off the top half of her body, then rips through the floor. A second shell the size of a child's head screams through the ship between
Mustang and me. Punching a hole in the floor and ceiling. Wind
shrieks. Emergency masks fall into our laps. Warning sirens warble as
pressure rushes from our ship, whipping our hair. I see the blackness
of the ocean through the hole in the floor. Stars through the hole in
the ceiling as our oxygen leaks out. The pursuing ship continues to
fire into our dying ship. I huddle in terror with my hands over my
head, teeth locked together, everything human in me screaming.

Laughter evil and inhuman rumbles so loud I think it's coming
from the buffeting wind. But it comes from Ragnar, his head tilted
back as he laughs to his gods. **"Odin knows we are coming to kill
him. Even false Gods do not die easily!"** He throws himself from his
seat and runs down the hall, laughing insanely, not listening as I shout
for him to sit down. Shells whisper past him. **"I am coming, Odin! I
am coming for you!"**

Mustang dons her emergency mask and pushes the release on her
safety webbing before I can gather my thoughts. The ship bucks,
slamming her into the ceiling and the floor hard enough to crack the
skull of any but an Aureate. Blood spills over her forehead from a
gash at her hairline and she clutches to the floor, waiting till the ship
rolls again to angle herself so that she can use gravity to fall into the
co-pilot chair. She lands awkwardly against the armrests but manages
to drag herself into the seat and buckle in. More warning lights pulse
on the blood-drenched console. I look back down the hall to see if
Ragnar and Holiday are alive only to see a trio of shells savage the
room behind us. My teeth clatter in my skull. Gut vibrating with the
champagne flutes in the cabinet to my left. I can't do anything but
hold on as Mustang tries to arrest our fall through orbit. The seat's
gel webbing tightens against my rib cage. I feel the g-forces crushing
me. Time seems to slow as the world beneath swells. We're through
the clouds. On the sensor I see something small zip away from our

ship and collide into the one trailing. Light flares behind us. Snow and mountains and ice floes dilate till they're all I can see through the broken cockpit window. Wind howls, shatteringly cold against my face. "Brace for impact," Mustang shouts over it. "In five . . ."

We plummet toward a sheaf of ice floating in the middle of the sea. On the horizon, a bloody ribbon of red ties the twilight sky to the ragged coastline of volcanic rock. A giant man stands atop the rock. Black and huge against the red light. I blink, wondering if my mind is playing tricks on me. If I'm seeing Fitchner before my death. The man's mouth is an open dark chasm into which no light escapes.

"Darrow, tuck in!" Mustang shouts. I lower my head between my knees, wrap my arms around it. "Three . . . two . . . one."

Our ship punches into the ice.

26

||||||||||||||||||||||||

THE ICE

All is dark and cold as we sink into the sea. Water's rushed in through the mangled back of the ship and gurgles through the dozen gaping holes in the cockpit. We're already beneath the waves, the last air bubbling out into the darkness. The crash webbing synched tight around my body upon impact, expanding to protect my bones. But now it's killing me, dragging me down with the ship. The water is freezing needles against my face. SealSkin protects my body, though, so I cut through the webbing with my razor. Pressure building in my ears as I search frantically for Mustang.

She's alive and already working on escape. A light in her hand carves through the darkness of the flooded cockpit. Her razor's out. Cutting through her webbing like I did. I push myself through the flooded cabin toward her. The back of the ship is missing. Three levels of vessel torn off and floating elsewhere in the darkness with Ragnar and Holiday inside. My neck's locked up from whiplash. I suck at the oxygen from the mask that covers my nose and mouth.

Mustang and I communicate silently, using the signals of Gray lurcher squads. The human instinct is to flee the crash as fast as possible, but training reminds us to count our breaths. To think clinically.

There are supplies here we might need. Mustang searches in the cockpit for the standard emergency kit while I search for my equipment bag. It's missing, along with the rest of the gear in the cargo hold that we were bringing the Obsidians to seize Asgard. Mustang joins me, carrying a plastic emergency box the size of her torso, which she pulled from a cabinet behind the pilot's chair.

Taking a last breath, we leave the oxygen behind.

We swim to the edge of the torn hull, where the ship ends and the ocean begins. It is an abyss. Mustang turns off her light as I tie our belts together with a length of the crash webbing I took from my seat. Designed to keep the Obsidians trapped in their icy continent, the Carved creatures here are man-eaters. I've seen pictures of the things. Translucent and fanged. Eyes bulging. Skin pale, worming with blue veins. Light and heat attract them. To swim in open water with a flashlight would draw things from the deeper levels. Even Ragnar wouldn't dare.

Unable to see farther than a hand's breadth in front of us, we push away from the yacht's corpse in the black water. Fighting for every agonizing meter. I can't see Mustang beside me. We're sluggish in the cold water, limbs burning as they claw darkness; but my mind is locked and certain. We will not die in this ocean. We will not drown. I repeat it over and over, hating the water.

Mustang kicks my foot, disrupting our rhythm. I try to match it again. Where is the surface? There's no sun to greet us, to tell us we're near. It's wildly disorienting. Mustang kicks my leg again. Only this time I feel the ripple of the water beneath as something large and fast and cold swims in the depths below.

I slash down blindly with my razor, hitting nothing. Impossible to fight back the panic. I'm swinging at the darkness of the two kilometers of ocean that stretches beneath me and pumping my legs so desperately that I swim into the ice crust atop the water almost knocking myself out. I feel Mustang's hand on my back. Steadying me. The ice is dull gray skin that stretches above us. I stab my razor up into it. Hear Mustang doing the same beside me. It's too thick to push clear of. I grip her shoulder and draw a circle to signal my plan. I turn so my back is against hers. Together, nearly blind and out of oxygen, we cut a circle in the ice. I keep going until I feel the ice give slightly. It's too heavy to push up without traction. Too buoyant to pull down with just our arms. So I swim to the side so Mustang can savage the cylinder we've cut with her razor. Mincing the ice enough to push the emergency box through first. She follows and extends a hand to aid me. I slash blindly back down at the darkness and follow her up.

We collapse headfirst onto the rock-hard surface of the ice.

Wind rattles over our shaking bodies.

We're on the edge of an ice shelf between a savage coastline and the beginning of a cold, black sea. The sky throbs deep metallic blue, the South Pole locked in two months of twilight as it transitions to winter. The mountainous coastline dark and twisted, maybe three kilometers off, ice stretching all the way, punctured by icebergs. Wreckage burns on the coast's mountains. Wind rushes in off the open water ahead of a coming storm, whipping the waves into calamity so salt and spray hiss over the ice like sand buffeting through the desert.

Water geysers into the air fifty meters closer inland as someone fires a pulseFist from underneath the ice. Numb and frozen, we rush toward Holiday as she pulls herself free, Mustang trailing behind with the emergency box.

"Where is Ragnar?" I shout. Holiday looks up at me, face twisted and pale. Blood pools from her leg. A piece of shrapnel sticking through her thigh. Her sealSkin has kept her from the worst of the cold, but she didn't have time to don her suit's hood or gloves. She tightens a tourniquet around her leg, looking back into the hole.

"I don't know," she says.

"You don't know?" I rip free my razor and stumble for the hole. Holiday scrambles in front of me.

"Something is down there! Ragnar pulled it off of me."

"I'm going down," I say.

"What?" Holiday snaps. "It's pitch-black. You'll never find him."

"You don't know that."

"You'll die," she says.

"I won't let him go."

"Darrow, stop." She throws down the pulseFist and pulls Trigg's pistol from her leg holster and shoots it in front of my foot. "Stop."

"What are you doing?" I shout over the wind.

"I will shoot your leg out before I let you kill yourself. That's what you're doing if you go down there."

"You'd let him die."

"He's not my mission." Her eyes are hard. Unsentimental and clinical. So different from the way I fight. I know she'll pull the trigger to save my life. I'm about to lunge at her when Mustang flashes past to my left. Too fast for me to say anything or for Holiday to threaten her as she dives into the hole, a razor in her right hand, and in her left, a flare blazing bright.

27

||||||||||||||||||||||||||

BAY OF LAUGHTER

I rush to the hole. Water laps peaceably at the edge. The ice is too thick to see Mustang beneath the surface as she swims, but the flare glows gently through the meter of dirty ice, blue and wandering toward the land. I follow it. Holiday tries to drag herself after. I shout at her to stay and get the medkit for herself.

I follow Mustang's light. Razor skimming over the ice, tracing the light underneath for several minutes, till at last the light stops. It's not enough time for her to run out of breath, but it doesn't move for ten seconds. And then it begins to fade. Ice and water darkening as the light sinks into the sea. I have to get her out. I slam my razor into the ice, carving a chunk free. I roar as I jam my fingers into the cracks and lift it up, hurling it backward over my head to reveal water churning with pale bodies and blood. Mustang bursts to the surface, crying in pain. Ragnar's beside her, blue and still, pinned under her left arm as her right hacks at something pale in the water.

I stab my razor into the ice behind me and hold on to the hilt. Mustang reaches for my hand and I haul her out. Then we pull Ragnar out with a roar of effort. Mustang claws onto the ice, falling down with Ragnar. But she's not alone. A maggot white creature the size of a small man has latched itself to her back. It's shaped like a snail in full sprint, except its back is tough, hairy translucent flesh mottled with dozens of shrieking little mouths rimmed with needle teeth that gnaw into her back. It's eating her alive. A second creature the size of a large dog is stuck on Ragnar's back.

"Get it off!" Mustang snarls, slashing wildly with her razor. "Get it off of me!" The creature is stronger than it should be and crawls back toward the hole in the ice, trying to drag her back to its home. A gunshot echoes and the creature jerks as a slug from Holiday's bullet hits it square in the side. Black blood pulses out. The creature shrieks and slows enough for me to rush to Mustang and scalp the thing from her back with my razor. I kick it to the side, where it spasms as it dies. I cut Ragnar's beast in half, skinning it off his back, and hurl it to the side.

"There's more down there. And something bigger," Mustang says, struggling to her feet. Her face tightens as she sees Ragnar. I rush to him. He's not breathing.

"Watch the hole," I tell Mustang.

My massive friend looks so childish there on the ice. I start CPR. He's missing his left boot. The sock's halfway off. Foot jerks against the ice as I pump his chest. Holiday stumbles to us. Pupils huge from painkillers. Her leg's bound with resFlesh from the medkit. She collapses to the ice beside Ragnar. Tugs his sock back on his foot like it matters.

"*Come back,*" I hear myself saying. Spit freezing against my lips. Eyelids crusty with tears I didn't even know I was shedding. "*Come back. Your work isn't finished.*" The Howler tattoo is dark against his paling skin. The protection runes like tears on his white face. "*Your people need you,*" I say. Holiday holds his hand. Both of hers not equal to the size of the massive six-fingered paw.

"*Do you want them to win?*" Holiday asks. "*Wake up, Ragnar. Wake up.*"

He jerks beneath my hands. Chest twitching as his heart kicks. Water bubbles out of his mouth. Arms scrabbling at the ice in confusion as he coughs for air. He sucks it down. Huge chest heaving as he stares up at the sky. His scarred lips curl back into a mocking smile. "Not yet, Allmother. Not yet."

"We're fucked," Holiday says as we look over the meager supplies Mustang managed to scavenge from our vessel. We shake together in a ravine, finding momentary respite from the wind. It's not much. We huddle around the paltry heat of two thermal flares after having humped it across the ice shelf as eighty-kilometer winds shredded us with cold teeth. The storm darkens over the water behind us. Ragnar watches it with wary eyes as the rest of us sort through the supplies. There's a GPS transponder, several protein bars, two flashlights, dehydrated food, a thermal stove, and a thermal blanket large enough for one of us. We've wrapped it around Holiday, since her suit's the most compromised. There's also a flare gun, a resFlesh applicator, and a thumb-sized digital survival guide.

"She's right," Mustang says. "We have to get out of here or we're dead."

Our boxes of weapons are gone. Our armor and gravBoots and supplies sunken to the bottom of the sea. All that would have let the Obsidians destroy their Gods. All that would have let us contact our friends in orbit. The satellites are blind. No one is watching. No one except the men who shot us from the sky. The lone blessing is that they crashed as well. We saw their fire deeper in the mountains as we stumbled across the ice shelf. But if they survived, if they have gear, they will hunt us, and all we have to protect ourselves is four razors, a rifle, and a pulseFist with a drained charge. Our sealSkin is sliced and damaged. But dehydration will claim us long before the cold does. Black rock and ice span the horizon. Yet if we eat the ice, our core temperatures will lower and the cold will take us.

"We have to find real shelter." Mustang blows into her gloved hands, shivering. "Last I saw of the charts in the cockpit, we're two hundred kilometers from the spires."

"Might as well be a thousand," Holiday says gruffly. She chews her cracked bottom lip, still staring at the supplies as if they'll breed.

Ragnar watches us discuss wearily. He knows this land. He knows we can't survive here. And though he will not say it, he knows that he will watch us die one by one, and there will not be a thing he can do to stop it. Holiday will die first. Then Mustang. Her sealSkin is torn where the beast bit her and water leaked in. Then I will go, and he will survive. How arrogant must we have sounded, thinking we could descend and free the Obsidians in one night.

"Aren't nomads here?" Holiday asks Ragnar. "We always heard stories about marooned legionnaires. . . ."

"They are not stories," Ragnar says. "The clans seldom venture to the ice after autumn has fled. This is the season of the Eaters."

"You didn't mention them," I say.

"I thought we would fly past their lands. I am sorry."

"What are Eaters?" Holiday asks. "My Antarctic anthropology ain't for shit."

"Eaters of men," Ragnar says. "Shamed castouts from the clans."

"Bloodyhell."

"Darrow, there must be a way to contact your men for extraction," Mustang says, determined to find a way out.

"There isn't. Asgard's jamming array makes this whole continent static. The only tech for a thousand kilometers is there. Unless the other ship has something."

"Who are they?" Ragnar asks.

"Don't know. Can't be the Jackal," I say. "If he knew who we were then he would have sent his fleet after us, not just one black-ops ship."

"It's Cassius," Mustang says. "I assume he came in a disguised ship, like I did. He's supposed to be on Luna. It was one of the positives of negotiating here. They get caught going behind my brother's back, it's as bad for them as for me. Worse."

"How'd he know which ship was ours?" I ask.

Mustang shrugs. "Must have sniffed out the diversion. Maybe he followed us from the Hollows. I don't know. He's not stupid. He did catch you in the Rain as well, going under the wall."

"Or someone told him," Holiday says, eying Mustang darkly.

"Why would I tell him when I'm on the gorydamn ship?" Mustang says.

"Well, let's hope it's Cassius," I say. "If it is, then they won't just hop on gravBoots and fly to Asgard for help, because then they'll have to explain to the Jackal why they were on Phobos to begin with. How'd it go down, anyway?" I ask. "It looked like a missile signature from the back of our ship. But we don't have missiles."

"The boxes did," Ragnar says. "I fired a sarissa out the back of the cargo bay from a shoulder launcher."

"You shot a missile at them while we were falling?" Mustang asks incredulously.

"Yes. And I attempted to gather gravBoots. I failed."

"I think you did just fine," Mustang says with a sudden laugh. It infects the rest of us, even Holiday. Ragnar doesn't understand the humor. My cheer fades quickly though as Holiday coughs and cinches her hood tighter.

I watch the black clouds over the sea. "How long till that storm hits, Ragnar?"

"Perhaps two hours. It moves with speed."

"It'll get to negative sixty," Mustang says. "We won't survive. Not with our gear like this." The wind howls through our ravine and the bleak mountainside around us.

"Then there's only one option," I say. "We sack up and push across the mountains, find the downed ship. If it is Cassius in there, he'll have at least a full squad of Thirteenth legion black ops with him."

"That's not a good thing," Mustang says warily. "Those Grays are better trained for winter combat than we are."

"Better than you," Holiday says, pulling back her sealSkin so Mustang can read the Thirteenth legion tattoo on her neck. "Not me."

"You're a dragoon?" Mustang asks, unable to hide the surprise.

"Was. Point is: PFR—Praetorian field regulations—mandate survival gear in long-range mission transport enough to last each squad a month in any conditions. They'll have water, food, heat, and grav-Boots."

"What if they survived the crash?" Mustang says, eying Holiday's injured leg and our paltry weapons supply.

"Then they will not survive us," Ragnar says.

"And we're better off hitting them when they're still piecing themselves together," I say. "We go now, fast as we can, and we might get there before the storm lands. It's our only chance."

Ragnar and Holiday join me, the Obsidian gathering the gear as the Gray checks her rifle's ammunition. But Mustang's hesitant. There's something else she hasn't told us. "What is it?" I demand.

"It's Cassius," she says slowly. "I don't know for certain. What if he's not alone? What if Aja is with him?"

28

||||||||||||||||||||||

FEAST

The storm falls as we climb along a rocky arm of the mountain. Soon we can see nothing beyond our party. Steel-gray snow gnaws into us. Blotting out the sky, the ice, the mountains inland. We duck our heads, squinting through the sealSkin balaclavas. Boots scrape the ice underfoot. Wind roars loud as a waterfall. I hunch against it, putting one boot after the other, connected with Mustang and Holiday by rope in the Obsidian way so we don't lose one another in the blizzard. Ragnar scouts ahead. How he finds his way is beyond me.

He returns now, loping over the rocks with ease. He signals for us to follow.

Easier said than done. Our world is small and furious. Mountains lurk in the white. Their hulking shoulders the only shelter from the wind. We scramble over bitter black rock that slices at our gloves while the wind tries to hurl us down gulches and bottomless crevasses. The exertion keeps us alive. Neither Holiday nor Mustang slow, and after more than an hour of dreadful travel, Ragnar guides us into a mountain pass and the storm breathes. Beneath us, impaled upon a ridgeline, is the ship that shot us from the sky.

I feel a pang of sympathy for her. Sharklike lines and flared starburst tail indicate she was once a long, sleek racing vessel of the famed Ganymede shipyards. Painted proud and bold in crimson and silver by loving hands. Now she's a cracked, blackened corpse impaled upside down on a stark ridgeline. Cassius, or whoever was inside, had a nasty time of it. The rear third of the ship sheaved off half a kilometer downhill from the main body. Both parts look deserted. Holiday scans the wreck with her rifle's scope. No sign of life or movement outside.

"Something seems off," Mustang says, crouched beside me. Her father's visage watches me from the razor on her arm.

"The wind is against us," Ragnar says. **"I smell nothing."** His black eyes scan the peaks of the mountains around us, going rock to rock, looking for danger.

"We can't risk getting pinned down by rifles," I say, feeling the wind pick up again behind us. "We need to close the distance fastlike. Holiday, you lay cover." Holiday digs a small trench in the snow and covers herself with the thermal blanket. We cover that with snow so only her rifle's peeking out. Then Ragnar slips down the slope to investigate the rear half of the ship as Mustang and I press for the main wreck.

Mustang and I slink low over rocks, covered by the renewed vigor of the storm, unable to see the ship till we're within fifteen meters. We close the rest of the distance on our bellies and find a jagged hole in the aft where the back half of the fuselage was shredded by Ragnar's missile. Part of me expected a camp of warColors and Golds preparing to hunt us down. Instead, the ship's an epileptic corpse, power flickering on and off. Inside, the ship is hollow and cavernous and almost too dark to see when the lights crackle off. Something drips in the darkness as we work our way toward the middle of the craft. I smell the blood before I see it. In the passenger compartment, nearly a dozen Grays lie dead, smashed into the floor above us by the rocks that speared the ship as it landed. Mustang kneels next to the body of a mangled Gray to examine his clothing.

"Darrow." She pulls back his collar and points to a tattoo. The digital ink still moves even though the flesh is dead. Legio XIII. So it

is Cassius's escort. I manipulate the toggle on my razor, moving my thumb in the shape of the new desired design. I press down. The razor slithers in my hand, abandoning its slingBlade look for a shorter, broader blade so I can stab more easily in the cramped environs.

There's no sign of any life as we move forward, let alone Cassius. Just the wind moaning through the bones of the vessel. A strange feeling of vertigo walking along the ceiling and looking up at the floor. Seats and belt buckles hanging down like intestines. The ship convulses back to life, illuminating a sea of broken datapads and dishes and gum packages underfoot. Sewage leaks from a crack in the metal wall. The ship dies again. Mustang taps my arm and points out a shattered bulkhead window to what looks like drag marks in the snow. Smeared blood black in the dim light. She signs to me. Bear? I nod. A razorback must have found the wreckage and begun feasting on the corpses of the diplomatic mission. I shudder, thinking of noble Cassius suffering that fate.

A grisly sucking sound makes its way to us from farther on in the ship. We press forward, feeling the dread of the scene before we enter the forward passenger cabin. The Institute taught us the sound of teeth on raw meat. But still, this is a horrifying sight, even for me. Golds hang upside down from the ceiling, imprisoned in their crash webbing, legs pinned by bent paneling. Beneath them hunch five nightmares. Their fur is grim and matted, once white but now clumped with dried blood and filth. They gnaw on the bodies of the dead. Their heads are those of massive bears. But the eyes that peer through the eye sockets of those heads are black and cold with intelligence. Standing not on four legs but two, the largest of the pack turns toward us. The ship lights throb back on. Pale muscled arms, slick with seal grease to ward off the cold, dark with blood from skinning the dead Golds, move from under the bear pelts.

The Obsidian is taller than I am. A crooked iron blade sewn into his hand. Human bones strung together with dried tendon as a breastplate. Hot breath billows from under the snout of the ursine skull he wears as a helmet. Slow and measured, the deep ululation of an evil war chant blossoms from between his blackened teeth. They've seen our eyes and one screams something unintelligible.

The ship wheezes and the lights go out.

The first cannibal vaults toward us through the cluttered hall, the rest behind him. Shadows in the darkness. My pale razor lashes forward and hews through his iron knife, through his breastplate and clavicle straight into his heart. I twist aside so he doesn't crash into me. His momentum takes him past me into Mustang, who sidesteps him and cuts his head clean off. His body spills to the ground past her, twitching.

An audible grunt, and a spear with a jagged iron end flies from one of the other cannibals. I duck under it and punch upward with my left hand, deflecting it into the ceiling, just over Mustang's head. Then the Obsidian behind slams into me as I rise. As large as I am. Stronger. More creature than man. Overwhelming me with the frenzy of a lost mind, he pins me to the wall and snaps at me with blackened, sharp-filed teeth. The lights of the ship flash illuminating the sores around his mouth. My arms are pinned to my sides. He bites at my nose. I turn my face just before he rips it off. Instead, his teeth sink into the meat at the base of my lower jaw. I scream in pain. Blood flows down my neck. He chomps down again, pulling at my face. Eating me alive as the lights go out. His right hand tries to work a knife through the sealSkin to slide it between my ribs and into my heart. The fabric holds.

Then the cannibal goes slack, twitching, and his body falls to the ground, spinal cord severed by Mustang from behind.

A black missile blurs past my face and slams into Mustang. Knocking her off her feet. The fletching of an arrow sticks from her left shoulder. She grunts, scrambling on the ground. I lunge away from her, toward the three remaining Obsidian. One's nocking another arrow, the second hefts a huge axe, the third holds a huge curved horn, which the cannibal brings through the bearhelm to its mouth.

Then a terrible howl comes from outside the ship.

The lights go out.

The darkness ripples with a fourth shape. Shadowy forms lashing at one another. Metal cutting flesh. And when the lights come back on, Ragnar stands holding the head of one Obsidian as he pulls his razor out of the chest of the second. The third, bow cut in half, pulls a knife, stabbing wildly at Ragnar. He hacks her arm off. Still she rolls away, mad, immune to pain. He stalks after her and rips off her helmet. Beneath is a young woman. Face painted white, nostrils slit open so she looks a snake. Ritual scars forming a series of bars under both eyes. She can't be more than eighteen. Her mouth slurs out something as she stares at the vastness of Ragnar, large even for her people. Then her wild eyes find the tattoos on his face.

"*Vjrnak,*" she rasps, not in terror, but fevered joy. "*Tnak ruhr. Ljarfor aesir!*" She closes her eyes and Ragnar cuts off her head.

"You prime?" I ask Mustang, rushing to her. She's already on her feet. The arrow sticks out from under her collarbone.

"What did she say?" Mustang asks past me. "Your Nagal is better than mine."

"I didn't understand the dialect." It was too guttural. Ragnar knows it.

"**Stained son. Kill me. I will rise Golden,**" Ragnar explains. "**They eat what they find.**" He nods to the Golds. "**But to eat the flesh of Gods is to rise immortal. More will come.**"

"Even in the storm?" I ask. "Can their griffins fly in this?"

His lips curl in disgust. "**The beasts do not ride griffin. But no. They will seek refuge.**"

"What about the other wreck?" Mustang asks, pressing on. "Supplies? Men?"

He shakes his head. "**Bodies. Ship munitions.**"

I send Ragnar to fetch Holiday from her post. Mustang and I stay with plans to search the ship for gear. But I remain standing motionless in the cannibals' charnel house even after Ragnar's slipped out into the snow. The Golds might have been enemies, but this horror makes life feel so cheap. There's a cruel irony to this place. It is terrifying and wicked, but it wouldn't exist unless Gold made it exist to create fear, to create that need for their iron rule. These poor bastards were eaten by their own pet monsters.

Mustang stands from examining one of the Obsidian, wincing from the arrow that's still imbedded in her shoulder. "Are you all right?" she asks, noting my silence. I gesture to the broken fingernails on one of the Golds.

"They weren't dead when they started skinning them. Just trapped."

She nods sadly and holds out her palm. Something she found on the Obsidian body. Six Institute class rings. Two Pluto Cyprus trees, a Minerva owl, a Jupiter lightning bolt, a Diana stag, and one which I pick from her palm, emblazoned with the Mars wolf head.

"We should look for him," she says.

I reach up to the ceiling to examine the Golds who hang upside down from their seats. Their eyes and tongues are gone, but I can see, mangled as they are, none are my old friend. We search the rest of the upside-down ship and find several small bedroom suites. In the dresser of one, Mustang finds an ornate leather box with several watches and a small pearl earring set in silver. "Cassius was here," she says.

"Are those his watches?"

"It's my earring."

I help Mustang remove the arrow from her shoulder in Cassius's suite, away from the gore. She makes no sound as I break off the tip, push her against the wall, and jerk the arrow out by its tail end. She curls in on herself, slumping down to her heels in pain. I sit on the edge of the mattress that's fallen from the ceiling and watch her hunch there. She doesn't like being touched when she's wounded.

"Finish up," she says, standing.

I use the resGun to make a shiny patch over the hole on the front and back, just under her collarbone. It stops the bleeding and will help repair the tissue, but she'll feel the wound and it'll slow her for days. I pull her sealSkin back up over her bare shoulder. She zips the front up for herself before patching the wound on my jaw as well. Her breath fills the air. She comes so close I can smell the dampness of the snow that's melted in her hair. She presses the resGun to my jaw and paints a thin layer of the microorganisms onto the wound. They scramble into the pores and tighten to make a fleshlike antibacterial coating. Her hand lingers on the back of my head, fingers wrapped in the strands of my hair, like she wants to say something but doesn't have the words. Nor does she find them by the time Holiday and Ragnar return. Hearing Holiday calling my name, I squeeze Mustang's good shoulder and leave her there.

Most of the ship's gear is gone. Several sets of optics missing from their cases. The armory missing entirely, scattered across the mountains as the ship came apart and the cargo hold ripped open. The rest has been torn through by Obsidians or broken in the crash. All I get is static from the transponder and com gear.

Ragnar discerns that Cassius and the rest of his party, some fifteen men, departed several hours before we reached the vessel. They stripped it bare of supplies. The Eaters likely descended as soon as it landed, otherwise Cassius wouldn't have left those Golds behind to be eaten. Supporting this idea, Mustang finds several Eater bodies nearer the cockpit, which means Cassius and his men were under attack as they left. Snow's almost covered the corpses. We stack the fresher bodies outside in the snow in case worse predators than Eaters come to visit.

After scavenging the ship for supplies, I have Mustang and Holiday seal us inside the galley. Fusing the two entrances shut with welding torches found in the ship's maintenance closet. The weapons and cold gear might have been stripped clean, but the ship's cistern is full, the water inside not yet frozen. And the galley's pantries are stocked with food.

It's passingly cozy in our shelter. The insulation traps our heat inside. The light from two amber emergency lamps bathes the room in soft orange. Holiday uses the intermittent power to cook a feast of pasta with marinara sauce and sausage over the galley's electric stoves as Ragnar and I plot a course to the Spires and Mustang sorts through the stacks of scavenged provisions, filling military packs she found in storage.

I burn my tongue as Holiday brings Ragnar and me heaping portions of pasta. I didn't realize how hungry I was. Ragnar nudges me and I follow his eyes to watch quietly as Holiday brings Mustang a bowl too and leaves her with a small nod. Mustang smiles to herself. The four of us sit eating in silence. Listening to our forks against the bowls. The wind shrieking outside. Rivets groaning. Steel gray snow piles against the small circular windows, but not before we see strange shapes moving through the white to drag off the corpses we set outside.

"What was it like growing up here?" Mustang asks Ragnar. She sits cross-legged with her back against the wall. I lay adjacent to her, a backpack between, on one of the mattresses Ragnar dragged inside the room to line its floor, on my third serving of pasta.

"It was home. I did not know anything else."

"But now that you do?"

He smiles gently. **"It was a playground. The world beyond is vast, but so small. Men putting themselves in boxes. Sitting at desks. Riding in cars. Ships. Here, the world is small, but without end."** He loses himself in stories. Slow to share at first, now it seems he revels in knowing that we listen. That we care. He tells us of swimming in the ice floes as a boy. How he was an awkward child. Too slow. Bones outracing the rest of him. When he was beaten by another boy, his mother took him to the sky for his first time on her griffin. Making him hold on to her from behind. Teaching him it is his arms that keep him from falling. His will. **"She flew higher, and higher, till the air was thin and I could feel the cold in my bones. She was waiting for me to let go. To weaken. But she did not know that I tied my wrists together. That is as close to Allmother death as I have ever been."**

His mother, Alia Volarus, the Snowsparrow, is a legend among her people for her reverence for the gods. A daughter to a wanderer, she became a warrior of the Spires and rose in prominence as she raided other clans. Such is her devotion to the gods that when she rose to power, she gave four of her own children to serve them. Keeping only one for herself, Sefi.

"She sounds like my father," Mustang says softly.

"Poor sods," Holiday mutters. "My ma would make me cookies and teach me how to strip down a hoverJack."

"And what about your father?" I ask.

"He was a bad sort." She shrugs. "But bad in a boring way. A different family in every port. Stereotypical legionnaire. I got his eyes. Trigg got Ma's."

"I never knew my first father," Ragnar says, meaning his birth

father. Obsidian women are polygamous. They might have seven children from seven fathers. Those men are then bound to protect the
other children of her brood. **"He went to become a slave before I was
born. My mother never speaks his name. I do not even know if he
lives."**

"We can find out," Mustang says. "We'd have to search the Board
of Quality Control's registry. Not easy, but we can find him. What
happened to him. If you want to know."

He's stunned by the idea and nods slowly. **"Yes. I would like that."**

Holiday watches Mustang in a very different way than she did just
hours before when we were leaving Phobos, and I'm struck by how
natural this feels, our four worlds colliding together. "We all know
your father," Holiday says. "But what is your ma like? She looks
frigid, from what I've seen, just on the HC, you know?"

"That's my stepmother. She doesn't care for me. Just Adrius, actually. My real mother died when I was young. She was kind. Mischievous. And very sad."

"Why?" Holiday presses.

"Holiday . . ." I say. Her mother is a subject I've never pushed. She's
held her back from me. A little locked box in her soul that she never
shares. Except tonight, it seems.

"It's all right," she says. She pulls up her legs, hugging them, and
continues. "When I was six, my mother was pregnant with a little girl.
The doctor said there would be complications with the birth and recommended intervening medically. But my father said that if the child
was not fit to survive birth, it did not deserve life. We can fly between
the stars. Mold the planets, but father let my sister die in my mother's
womb."

"The hell?" Holiday mutters. "Why not give her cell therapy? You
got the money."

"Purity in the product," Mustang says.

"That's insane."

"That's my family. Mother was never the same. I'd hear her crying
in the middle of the day. See her staring out the window. Then one
night she went for a walk at Caragmore. The estate my father gave
her as a wedding present. He was in Agea working. She never came

home. They found her on the rocks beneath the sea cliffs. Father said she slipped. If he was alive now, he'd still say she slipped. I don't think he could have survived thinking anything else."

"I'm sorry," Holiday says.

"As am I."

"It's why I'm here, since that's what you were wondering," Mustang says. "My father was a titan. But he was wrong. He was cruel. And if I can be something else"—her eyes meet mine—"I will be."

29

||||||||||||||||||||||||||

HUNTERS

By the time we wake, the storm has cleared. We bundle ourselves with insulation taken from the ship's walls and set out into the bleakness. Not a cloud mars the marbled blue-black sky. We head toward the sun, which stains the horizon a cooling shade of molten iron. Autumn has few days left. We head for the Spires with plans of lighting fires as we go, in hopes of signaling the few Valkyrie scouts active in the area. But smoke will also bring the Eaters.

We scan the mountains as we pass, wary of the cannibal tribes and of the fact that somewhere ahead Cassius and maybe Aja trudge through the snow with a troop of special forces operators.

By midday we find evidence of their passing. Churned snow outside a rocky alcove large enough for several dozen men. They camped there to wait out the storm. A cairn of stacked stones lies near the campsite. One of the stones has been carved with a razor and reads: *per aspera ad astra.*

"It's Cassius's handwriting," Mustang says.

Pulling off the rocks, we find the corpses of two Blues and a Silver. Their weaker bodies froze in the night. Even here, Cassius had the decency to bury them. We replace the rocks as Ragnar lopes ahead, following the tracks at a speed we can't match. We follow after. An hour later, manmade thunder rumbles in the distance, accompanied by the lonely shriek of distant pulseFists. Ragnar returns soon after, eyes shining with excitement.

"I followed the tracks," he says.

"And?" Mustang asks.

"It is Aja and Cassius with a troop of Grays and three Peerless."

"Aja is here?" I ask.

"Yes. They flee on foot through a mountain pass in the direction of Asgard. A tribe of Eaters harries them. Bodies litter the way. Dozens. They sprang an ambush and failed. More come."

"How much gear do they have?" Mustang asks.

"No gravBoots. ScarabSkin only. But they have packs. They left the pulseArmor behind just two kilometers north. Out of energy."

Holiday looks at the horizon and touches Trigg's pistol on her hip. "Can we catch them?"

"They carry many supplies. Water. Food. Injured men now too. Yes. We can overtake them."

"Why are we here?" Mustang interjects. "It's not to hunt Aja and Cassius down. The only thing that matters is getting Ragnar to the Spires."

"Aja killed my brother," Holiday says.

Mustang's taken aback. "Trigg? The one you mentioned? I didn't know. But still, we can't be pulled to the side by vengeance. We can't fight two dozen men."

"What if they reach Asgard before we reach the Spires?" Holiday asks. "Then we're cooked." Mustang's not convinced.

"Can you kill Aja?" I ask Ragnar.

"Yes."

"This is an opportunity," I say to Mustang. "When else will they be so exposed? Without their Legions? Without the pride of Gold protecting them? These are champions. Like Sevro says, 'When you have the chance to waste your enemy, you do it.' This is one time I'd agree with the mad bastard. If we can take them off the board, the Sovereign loses two Furies in one week. And Cassius is Octavia's link to Mars and the great families here. And if we expose her negotiations with you to him, we fracture that alliance. We sever Mars from the Society."

"An enemy divided . . ." Mustang says slowly. "I like it."

"And we owe them a debt," Ragnar says. **"For Lorn, Quinn, Trigg. They came here to hunt us. Now we hunt them."**

The trail is unmistakable. Corpses litter the snow. Dozens of Eaters. Bodies still smoking from pulsefire near a narrow mountain pass where the Obsidians sprang an ambush on the Golds. They did not understand the firepower the Golds could bring to bear. Huge craters pock the craggy slopes. Deeper imprints in the snow mark the passing of aurochs. Huge steerlike animals with shaggy coats that the Obsidian ride.

The pass widens into a thin alpine forest that skins an expanse of rolling hills. Gradually the craters decrease and we begin seeing discarded pulseFists and rifles and several Gray bodies with arrows or axes embedded in them. The Obsidian dead are closer to the Gold trail now and bear razor wounds. There's dozens with missing limbs, clean decapitations. Cassius's band is running out of ammunition and now Olympic Knights are doing the work up close. Yet the wind still crackles with gunfire kilometers ahead.

We pass moaning Obsidian Eaters who lie dying from bullet wounds, but it's only over a wounded Gray that Ragnar stops. The man's still alive, but barely. An iron axe is buried in his stomach. He wheezes up at an unfamiliar sky. Ragnar crouches over him. Recognition goes through the Gray's eyes as he sees the Stained's uncovered face.

"Close your eyes," Ragnar says, pressing the man's empty rifle back in his hands. **"Think of home."** The man closes his eyes. And with a twist, Ragnar breaks his neck and sets his head gently back on the snow. A shrill horn echoes across the mountain range. **"They call off the hunt,"** Ragnar says. **"Immortality is not worth the price today."**

We pick up our pace. Kilometers to our right, Mounted Eaters on aurochs skirt the edges of the woods, heading for their high-mountain camps. They do not see us as we move through the pine taiga. Holiday watches the hunting party disappear behind a hill through the scope of her rifle. "They carried two Golds," she says. "Didn't recognize them. They weren't dead yet."

We all feel the chill.

It's an hour later that we spy our quarry beneath us in an uneven snowfield striped with crevasses. Two arms of forest hug the snowfield. Aja and Cassius chose an exposed route instead of continuing through the treacherous forest where they lost so many Grays. There's four left in the company. Three Golds and a Gray. They wear black scarabSkin, cloaked with pelts and extra layers they stripped from the dead cannibals. They move at a breakneck pace, the rest of their party massacred in the depths of the woods. We can't tell which is Aja or Cassius because of the masks and the similar shapes they make under the cloaks.

Initially, I wanted to lie in wait and ambush them to take the tactical initiative, but I remember how the optics were missing from their boxes and assume Aja and Cassius are both wearing them. With thermal vision, they'll see us hiding under snow. Might even see us if we hide inside the bellies of dead aurochs or seals. So instead, I have Ragnar lead me on the path he found to cut them off at a pass they must travel through and block their path to draw their eyes.

I'm panting beside Ragnar, coughing the cold out of aching lungs, when the party of four arrives on our chosen ground. They jog along the edge of a crevasse in improvised snowshoes, hunched against the weight of food and survival gear they drag behind them on little makeshift sleds. Textbook Legion survival skills, courtesy of the military schools of the Martian Fields. All four wear black optics visors with smoky glass lenses. It's eerie as they see us. No expressions on the optics or masked faces. So it feels like they expected us to be here waiting at the edge of the snowfield, blocking the pass out.

My eyes dart back and forth between them. Cassius is easy enough to distinguish by his height. But which of the four is Aja? I'm torn between two thick Golds, each shorter than Cassius. Then I see my old razormaster's weapon dangling from her belt.

"Aja!" I call, removing the sealSkin balaclava.

Cassius pulls off his mask. His hair is sweaty, face flushed. He alone carries a pulseFist, but I know its charge must be running low, based on the dispersion patterns of the dead cannibals behind them. His razor unfurls, as do the rest. They look like long red tongues, blood frozen on the blades.

"Darrow . . ." Cassius mutters, stunned by the sight of us. "I saw you sink . . ."

"I swim just as well as you. Remember?" I look past him. "Aja, you going to let Cassius do all the talking?"

Finally, she steps from the other to stand by the tall knight, removing from around her waist the rope that attaches her to her makeshift sled. She doffs her scarabSkin mask, revealing her dark face and bald head. Steam swirls. She scans the crevasses that thread their way through the snow, and the rocks and trees, the pen in the snowfield, wondering where my ambush will come from. She remembers Europa well enough, but she can't know who my crew was or how many survived.

"An abomination and a rabid dog," she purrs, eyes lingering on Ragnar before coming back to me. The scarabSkin she wears is unmarked. Can she really not have taken a single wound from the Obsidian? "I see your Carver has pieced you back together, ruster."

"Well enough to kill your sister," I say in reply, unable to keep the poison out of my voice. "Pity it wasn't you." She makes no reply. How many times have I seen her kill Quinn in memory? How many times have I seen her rob Lorn of his razor as he lay dead from the Jackal and Lilath's blades? I gesture to the weapon. "That doesn't belong to you."

"You were born to serve, not speak, abomination. Do not address me." She glances up to the sky where Phobos glitters on the eastern horizon. Red and white lights flicker around it. It's a space battle, which means Sevro has captured ships. But how many? Aja frowns and exchanges a worried look with Cassius.

"I have long awaited this moment, Aja."

"Ah, my father's favorite pet." Aja examines Ragnar. "Has the Stained convinced you he's tamed? I wonder if he told you how he liked to be rewarded after a fight in the Circada. After the applause faded and he cleaned the blood from his hands, Father would send him young Pinks to satisfy his animal lusts. How greedy he was with them. How frightened they were of him." Her voice is flat and bored of this ice, of this conversation, of us. All she wants is what we have to give her, and that is a challenge. After all the Obsidian bodies behind her, she still is not tired of blood. "Have you ever seen an Obsidian rut?" she continues. "You'd think twice about taking off their collars, ruster. They have appetites you can't imagine."

Ragnar steps forward, holding his razors in either hand. He unfastens the white fur he took from the Eaters and lets it fall behind him. It's strange being here surrounded by wind and snow. Stripped of our armies, our navies. The only thing protecting each of our lives: little coils of metal. The hugeness of the Antarctic laughs at our size and self-importance, thinking how easily it could snuff out the heat in our little chests. But our lives mean so much more than the frail bodies that carry them.

Ragnar's step forward is a sign to Mustang and Holiday in the trees.

Aim true, Holiday.

"Your father bought me, Aja. Shamed me. Made me his devil. A thing. The child inside fled. The hope vanished. I was Ragnar no more." He touches his own chest. "But I am Ragnar today, tomorrow, forever more. I am son of the Spires, brother of Sefi the Quiet, brother of Darrow of Lykos, and Sevro au Barca. I am the Shield of Tinos. I follow my heart. And when yours beats no more, foul Knight, I will pull it from your chest and feed it to the griffin of the . . ."

Cassius scans the craggy rocks and stunted trees that cup the snowfield to his left. His eyes narrow when they fall upon a cluster of broken timber at the base of a rock formation. Then, without warning, he shoves Aja forward. She stumbles, and just behind her, where she stood, the head of their remaining Gray explodes. Blood splatters the snow as the crack of Holiday's rifle echoes from the mountains. More bullets tear into the snow around Cassius and Aja. The Fury moves behind the third Gold, using his body as cover. Two bullets slam into his scarabSkin, penetrating the strong polymer. Cassius rolls on his shoulder and uses much of the last juice from his pulseFist. The hillside erupts. Rocks glowing. Exploding. Snow vaporizing.

And under that noise is the sound of a bowstring releasing. Aja hears it too. She moves fast. Spinning as an arrow fired by Mustang from the woods careens toward her head. It misses by centimeters. Cassius fires on Mustang's position on the hill, shattering trees and superheating rocks.

Can't tell if she's hit. Can't spare the seconds to look because Ragnar and I use the distraction to charge, vision narrowing, slingBlade curving into form. Closing the distance over the snow. PulseFist glowing in his hand, Cassius turns just as I bear down on him. He fires the pulseFist. It's a weak charge that I dive beneath, hitting the ground and rolling up like a Lykos tumbler. He fires again. The pulseFist is dead, battery drained from firing on the hillside. Ragnar hurls one of his razors at Aja like a huge throwing knife. It flips end over end in the air. She doesn't move. It slams into her. She spins backward. For a moment I think he's killed her. But then she turns back to us, holding the razor by the hilt in her right hand.

She caught it.

A dark fear sweeps through me as all of Lorn's warnings about Aja come rushing back. "Never fight a river, and never fight Aja."

The four of us smash together, turning into a clumsy mash of cracking whips and clattering blades. Scrambling and twisting and bending. Our razors faster than our own eyes can track. Aja swipes diagonally at my legs as I go for hers; Ragnar and Cassius aim for each other's necks in quick no-look thrusts. Identical strategies, all. It's so awkward we all almost kill one another in the first half second. Yet each gambit misses by a hair.

We separate. Stumbling backward. Humorless smiles on our faces—a bizarre kinship as we remember we all speak the same martial language. All that hateful breed of human Dancer told me about before I was Carved, the ones Lorn lived among and despised all the while.

I shatter the weird peace first. Lashing forward in a tight series of thrusts at Cassius's right side, peeling him away from Aja so Ragnar can take her down singly. Behind Cassius, Mustang stirs from among the rubble. Rushing across the snow, huge Obsidian bow in hand. Still fifty meters away. I sweep my razor whip twice at Cassius's legs, retracting it into a blade as he swings diagonally at my head. The blow rattles my arm as I catch it halfway along the razor's curve. He's stronger than I am. Faster than he was the last time we fought. And he's practiced now against the curved blade. Training with Aja, no doubt. He forces me back. I stumble, fall, between his legs I see the Fury and the Stained tearing into each other. She stabs him through his left thigh.

Another arrow whispers through the air. It slams into Cassius's back. His scarabSkin holds. Off balance, he swings again in a tight set of eight moves. I throw myself backward just as the razor hisses through the air where my head had been. I sprawl on the snow, centimeters from the edge of a huge crevasse. Scrambling up as Cassius rushes me. I block another downward swing, teetering on the edge. I fall backward and push off the edge as hard as I can so I land and clear the other side, using my agility to avoid his onslaught. Behind him, Aja spins under Ragnar's blade, slicing at his hamstrings. She's peeling him apart.

Cassius pursues me, hurdling the crevasse and swinging down at me. I block the blade. It would have opened me from shoulder to opposite hip. I throw a rock at his face. Gain my feet. He slams his blade down again in a feint, pivots his wrist, and swings to carve off my knees. I stumble to the side, barely dodging. He converts his razor to a whip, cracks it at my legs, and rips them out from under me. I fall. He kicks me in the chest. Wind gushes out of me. He stands on my wrist, pinning my razor down, and is about to plunge his razor into my heart, his face a mask of determination.

"*Stop,*" Mustang shouts. She's twenty meters away, aiming her bow at Cassius. Hand quivering from the strain of the taut string. "I will put you down."

"No," he says. "You would . . ."

The bowstring snaps. He jerks his razor up to deflect the arrow. Misses, slower than Aja. The serrated iron tip punches through the front of his throat and out the back of his neck, the feather fletching scratching the underside of his dimpled chin. There's no spray of blood. Just a meaty, wet gurgle. He flops back. Hitting the ground hard. Gagging. Hacking hideously. His feet kick as he clutches the arrow. Hissing for breath, eyes inches from my own. Mustang rushes to me. I scramble to my feet, away from Cassius, and grab my razor from the snow, pointing it at his thrashing body.

"I'm prime," I say, tearing my eyes from my old friend as blood pools beneath him and he fights for his life. "Help Ragnar."

Over Cassius's body, we see the Stained and Aja whirling at each other on the edge of a crevasse. Blood paints the snow around them. All of it coming from Ragnar. But still he presses the woman knight back, a furious song cascading out of his throat. Beating her down. Overwhelming her with his two hundred and fifty kilograms of mass. Sparks flare from their blades. She caves before him now, unable to match the anger of the banished prince of the Spires. Heels skidding on the snow. Arm shuddering. Bending back away from Ragnar. Bending like a willow. His song roars louder. "No," I murmur. "Shoot her," I tell Mustang.

"They're too close. . . ."

"I don't care!"

She fires a shot. It rips inches past Aja's head. But it does not matter. Ragnar has already fallen into the trap the woman has laid for him, Mustang doesn't see it yet. She will. It's one of the many Lorn taught me. The one Ragnar could not have learned because he never had a razormaster. He only ever had his rage and years of fighting with solid weapons, not the whip. Mustang loads another arrow. As Ragnar swings down at Aja with a blacksmith's overhead strike, Aja raises her rigid blade to meet his. She activates the whip function. Her blade goes limp. Expecting to meet the resistance of solid polyenne fiber, Ragnar's whole weight carries down on empty air. He's athletic enough to slow the movement so his blade doesn't smash into the ground, and against a lesser opponent he would have recovered with ease. But Aja was the greatest student of Lorn au Arcos. She's already spinning to the side, contracting the whip back into a blade and using her momentum to hack sideways at Ragnar as she finishes her spin. The movement is simple. Laconic. Like one of the ballerinas Mustang and Roque would watch at Agea's opera house as I studied with Lorn, pivoting through a *fouetté*. If I didn't see the blood paint her blade and spray a delicate arc of red across the snow, I could be convinced that she missed.

Aja does not miss.

Ragnar tries to turn and face her, but his legs betray him. Crumpling underneath. His gaping wound a bloody smile against the white of his sealSkin. Aja cut into his lower back, through his spinal cord, and out the front of his stomach at the belly button. He flops down at the lip of a crevasse. Razor skipping across the ice. I howl in rage, in crushing disbelief, and charge Aja as Mustang fires her bow, running with me. Aja sidesteps Mustang's arrows and stabs Ragnar twice more in the stomach as he lies grasping his wound. His body jerks. The blade slides in and out. Aja sets her feet now, preparing for me, when her eyes go wide. She steps back, marveling at something in the sky above my head. Mustang fires twice in quick succession. Aja's head jerks. She twists away from us, spinning backward to the edge of the crevasse. Ice caves beneath her foot, crumbling off into the crevasse. Her arms windmill, but she can't regain her balance as her eyes meet mine and she pitches with the ice headfirst into the darkness.

30

||||||||||||||||||||||||

THE QUIET

ja is gone. The crevasse is deep, sides narrowing away into darkness. I rush back to Ragnar as Mustang stares up at the hillside and the clouds, bow at the ready. She only has three arrows left. "I don't see anything," she says.

"**Reaper,**" Ragnar murmurs from the ground. His chest heaves. Panting heavily. Dark lifeblood pulses out of his open stomach. Aja could have finished him quickly with the two thrusts when he was on the ground. Instead, she stabbed his lower gut so he would suffer as he died. I push on the first wound, red to my elbows, but there's so much blood I don't even know what to do. A resGun can't fix what Aja has done. It can't even hold him together. The tears sting my eyes. Can hardly see. Steam billows from the wound. My frozen fingers tingling with warmth from the blood. Ragnar blanches at the blood, an embarrassed look on his face as he whispers apologies.

"It could be the cannibals," Mustang says, regarding Aja's distraction. "Can he move?"

"No," I say weakly. She glances down at him, more stoic than I am.

"We can't stay here," she says.

I ignore her. I've watched too many friends die to let Ragnar go. I led him to fight Aja. I convinced him to come home. I will not let him slip away. I owe him that much. If it is the last thing I do, foolish or not, I will defend him. I will find some way to fix him, get him to a Yellow. Even if the cannibals come. Even if it costs me my life, I will not leave him. But thinking it doesn't make it true. Doesn't give me magical powers. Whatever plan I make, it seems the world is content to undo it.

"Reaper . . ." Ragnar manages again.

"Save your strength, my friend. It's going to take all of it to get you out of here."

"She was fast. So fast."

"She's gone now," I say, though I can't know for sure.

"I always dreamed of a good death." He shudders as he realizes again that he's dying. **"This does not seem good."**

His words fishhook a sob from my chest into my throat. "It's fine," I say thickly. "It'll be fine. Once we get you patched up. Mickey will fix you proper. We'll get you to the Spires. Call in an evac."

"Darrow . . ." Mustang says.

Ragnar blinks hard up at me, trying to focus his eyes. He reaches for the sky with a hand. **"Sefi . . ."**

"No. It's me, Ragnar. It's Darrow," I say.

"Darrow . . ." Mustang presses sharply.

"What?" I snap.

"Sefi . . ." Ragnar points. I follow his finger to the sky above. I see nothing. Just the faint clouds shifting in the wind that comes in from the sea. I hear only the sound of Cassius's hacking and the creak of Mustang's bow and Holiday limping toward us over the snow. Then I see why Aja fled as three thousand kilograms of winged predator pierces the clouds. Body that of a lion. Wings, front legs, and head that of an eagle. Feathers white. Beak hooked and black. Head the size of a grown Red. The griffin is huge, underside of its wings painted with the screaming faces of sky-blue demons. They stretch ten meters wide as the beast lands in the snow in front of me. The earth shakes. Its eyes are pale blue, glyphs and wards painted along its black beak in white. Upon its back sits a lean, terrible human, who blows mournfully on a white horn.

More horns echo from the clouds above and twelve more griffins slam down into the mountain pass, some clinging to the sharp rock walls above us, others pawing at the snow. The first griffin-rider, the one who blew the horn, is cloaked head to toe in filthy white fur and wears a bone helmet crested with a single spine of blue feathers, which trail down the back of the neck. Not a rider is under two meters tall.

"Sunborn," one of them calls in their sluggish dialect as she rushes to the side of their silent leader. The speaker strips her helmet to reveal a brutish face thick with scars and piercings before falling to her knee and touching her forehead with a gloved palm in a sign of respect. A blue handprint covers her face. "We saw the flame in the sky. . . ." Her voice falters when she sees my slingBlade.

The other riders strip their helms, dismounting in a rush as they see our hair and eyes. Not a rider among them is a man. The women's faces are painted with huge sky-blue handprints, a little eye drawn in the center of each. White hair flows in long braids down their backs. Black eyes peer from hooded lids. Iron and bone piercings bridge noses and hook lips and notch ears. Only the lead rider has yet to remove her helmet or kneel. She steps toward us, in a trance.

"Sister," Ragnar manages. "My sister."

"Sefi?" Mustang repeats, eying the black human tongues on the prize-hook on the Obsidian's left hip. She wears no gloves. The backs of her hands are tattooed with glyphs.

"Do you know me?" Ragnar rasps. A tentative smile on quivering lips as the rider approaches. "You must." The rider catalogues his scars from behind her mask. Eyes dark and wide. "I know you," Ragnar continues. "I would know you if the world were dark and we were withered and old." He shudders in pain. "If the ice was melted and the wind quiet." She drifts forward, step by step. "I taught you the forty-nine names of the ice . . . the thirty-four breaths of the wind." He smiles. "Though you could only ever remember thirty-two."

She gives him nothing, but the other riders are already whispering his name, and looking at us as if by accompanying him and possessing a curved blade they've pieced together who I am. Ragnar continues, voice carrying the last of his strength.

"I carried you on my shoulders to watch five Breakings. And let you braid my hair with your ribbons. And played with the dolls you made from seal leather and threw balls of ice at old Proudfoot. I am your brother. And when the men of the Weeping Sun took me and a harvest of our kin to the Chained Lands, do you remember what I told you?"

Despite his wound, the man reeks of power. This is his land. This is his home. And he is as vast here as I was upon my clawDrill. The gravity of him draws Sefi closer. She collapses to her knees and strips away her bone helmet.

Sefi the Quiet, famed daughter of Alia Snowsparrow, is raw and majestic. Face severe. Angled like a crow's. Her eyes too small, too close together. Her lips thin, purple in the cold, and permanently pursed in thought. White hair shaved down the left side, braided and falling to the waist on the right. A wing tattoo encircled by astral runes is livid blue on the left side of her pale skull. But what makes her unique among the Obsidians, and the object of their admiration, is that her skin is without pocks or scars. The only ornament she wears is a single iron bar through her nose. And when she blinks down at Ragnar's wound, the blue eyes tattooed on the back of her eyelids pierce through me.

She extends a hand to her brother, not to touch him, but to feel the breath steam before his mouth and nose. It is not enough for Ragnar. He seizes her hand and presses it fiercely to his chest so she can feel his fading heartbeat. Tears of joy gather in his eyes. And when they spill from Sefi's down her cheeks to carve paths through her blue warpaint, his voice cracks. "I told you I would return."

Her eyes leave him to follow Aja's tracks into the crevasse. She clicks her tongue and four Valkyrie stake ropes into the snow and rappel down into the darkness to seek out Aja. The rest guard their warleader and watch the hills, elegant recurve bows at the ready. "We have to fly him to the Spires," I say in their language. "To your shaman."

Sefi does not look at me. "It is too late." Snow gathers on Ragnar's white beard. "Let me die here. On the ice. Under the wild sky."

"No," I mumble. "We can save you."

The world feels very distant and unimportant. His blood continues to leave him, but there is no more sadness in my friend. Sefi has chased it away.

"It is no great thing to die," he says to me, though I know he doesn't mean it as deeply as he wants to. "Not when one has lived." He smiles, trying to comfort me even now. But he wears the unjustness of his life and death upon his face. "I owe that to you. But . . . there is much undone. Sefi." He swallows, his tongue heavy and dry. "Did my men find you?" Sefi nods, staying hunched over her brother, her white hair flying about her in the wind. He looks to me. "Darrow, I know you think words will suffice," Ragnar says in Aureate lingo so Sefi cannot understand. "They will not. Not with my mother." This was what he did not tell me. Why he was so quiet on the shuttle, why he carried dread upon his shoulders. He was coming home to kill his mother. And now he's giving me permission to do just that. I glance over to Mustang. She heard too, and wears her heartbreak on her face. As much for my shattered, fool's dream of a better world as for my dying friend. He shudders in pain and Sefi pulls a knife from her boot, unwilling to watch him suffer any longer. Ragnar shakes his head at her and nods to me. He wants me to do it. I shake my head as if I can wake up from this nightmare. Sefi stares at me fiercely, daring me to contradict her brother's last wishes.

"I will die with my friends," Ragnar says.

I numbly let my razor slither into my hand and hold it over his chest. There's peace at last in Ragnar's wet eyes. It's all I can do to be strong for him.

"I will give Eo your love. I will make a house for you in the Vale of your fathers. It will be beside my own. Join me there when you die." He grins. "But I am no builder. So take your time. We will wait."

I nod like I still believe in the Vale. Like I still think it waits for me and for him. "Your people will be free," I say. "On my life, I promise this. And I will see you soon." He smiles as he stares up at the sky. Sefi frantically puts her axe in Ragnar's palm so that he can die as a warrior, a weapon in hand, and secure his place in the halls of Valhalla.

"No, Sefi," he says, dropping the axe and taking snow in his left hand, her hand with his right. "Live for more." He nods to me.

The wind whips.

The snow falls.

Ragnar watches the sky, where the cold lights of Phobos glitter on as I silently slide the metal into his heart. Death comes like nightfall, and I cannot tell the moment when the light leaves him, when his heart no longer beats and his eyes no longer see. But I know he's gone. I feel it in the chill that settles over me. In the sound of the lonely, hungry wind, and the dread silence in the black eyes of Sefi the Quiet.

My friend, my protector, Ragnar Volarus has left this world.

31

||||||||||||||||||||||||

THE PALE QUEEN

I'm numb with grief. Unable to think of anything but how Sevro will react when he hears Ragnar has died. How my nieces and nephews will never braid another bow into the Friendly Giant's hair. Part of my soul has departed and will never return. He was my protector. He gave so many strength. Now, without him, I cling to the back of a Valkyrie as her griffin rises away from the bloody snow. Even as we soar through the clouds on great beating wings, even as I see the Valkyrie Spires for the first time, I feel no awe. Just numbness.

The spires are a twisting, vertiginous spine of mountain peaks so ludicrous in their abrupt rise from the arctic plains that only a maniacal Gold at the controls of a Lovelock engine with fifty years of tectonic manipulation and a solar system of resources could conspire to create them. Probably just to see if they could. Dozens of stone spires weave together like spiteful lovers. Mist shrouding them. Griffins making nests on their peaks, crows and eagles in the lower reaches. Upon a high rock wall, seven skeletons hang from chains. The ice is stained with blood and the droppings of animals. This is the home of the only race to ever threaten Gold. And we come stained in the blood of its banished prince.

Sefi and her riders searched the crevasse in which Aja fell; they found nothing but boot prints. No body. No blood. Nothing to abate the rage that burns inside Sefi. I think she would have remained over her brother's body for hours more, had they not heard drums beating in the distance. Eaters who had mustered greater strength and intended to challenge the Valkyrie for possession of the fallen gods.

Wrath stained her face as she stood over Cassius, her axe in hand. He is one of the first Golds she'll ever have seen without armor. Maybe the first aside from Mustang. And I think, stained with the blood of her brother, she would have killed him there on the snow. I know I would have let her, and so too would have Mustang. But she relented at the urging of her Valkyrie. Clicking her tongue to her riders, sheathing her axe and signaling them to mount. Now Cassius is tied to the saddle of a Valkyrie to my right. The arrow missed his jugular, but death might come for him even without a kiss from Sefi's axe.

We land in a high alcove cut into the highest reach of a corkscrew spire. Slaves from enemy Obsidian clans, eyes branded into blindness, receive our griffins. Their faces painted yellow for cowardice. Iron doors groan shut behind, sealing us off from the wind. The riders jump from their saddles before we land to help carry Ragnar away from us deeper into the rock city.

There's a commotion as several dozen armed warriors push their way into the griffin stable and confront Sefi. They gesture wildly at us. Their accents thicker than the Nagal I learned with Mickey's uploads and my studies at the Academy, but I understand enough to glean that the newer group of warriors is shouting that we should be in chains, and something about heretics. Sefi's women are shouting back, saying we are friends of Ragnar, and they point feverishly to the Gold of our hair. They don't know how to treat us, or Cassius, who several of the warriors pull away from us like dogs fighting for scrap meat. The arrow's still in his neck. Whites of his eyes huge. He reaches for me in terror as the Obsidians drag him across the floor. His hand grasps mine, holds for a moment, and then he's gone down a torch-lit hall, borne away by half a dozen giants. The rest cluster around us, huge iron weapons in hand, the stink of their furs thick and nauseating.

Quieting only when an old stout woman with a hand-shaped tattoo on her forehead pushes through their ranks to speak with Sefi. One of her mother's warchiefs. She gestures upward toward the ceiling with large hand motions.

"What is she saying?" Holiday asks.

"They're talking about Phobos. They see the lights from the battle. They think the Gods are fighting. These ones think we should be prisoners, not guests," Mustang says. "Let them take your weapons."

"Like hell." Holiday steps back with her rifle. I grab the barrel and push it down, handing them my razor. "This is bloody spectacular," she mutters. They shackle our arms and legs with great iron manacles, taking care not to touch our skin or hair, and jerk us toward a tunnel by the Spires guards, away from Sefi's Valkyrie. But as we go, I catch sight of Sefi watching after us, a strange, conflicted look on her white face.

After being dragged down several dozen dimly lit stairwells, we're shoved into a windowless cell of carved stone and stifling, smoky air. Seal oil smolders in iron braziers stinging our eyes. I trip on a raised flagstone and fall to the floor. There, I slam my chains against the stone. Feeling the anger. The helplessness. All the things happening so fast, whipping me around, so I can't tell which way's up. But I can think long enough to grasp the futility of my actions, my plans. Mustang and Holiday watch me in heavy silence. One day into my grand plan and Ragnar is already dead.

Mustang speaks more softly. "Are you all right?"

"What do you think?" I ask bitterly. She says nothing in reply, not the fragile sort of person to take offense and whimper out how she's just trying to help. She knows the pain of loss well enough. "We need to have a plan," I say mechanically, trying to force Ragnar out of my mind.

"Ragnar was our plan," Holiday says. "He was the entire sodding plan."

"We can salvage it."

"And how the hell do you expect to do that?" Holiday asks. "We don't have weapons anymore. And they don't exactly look tickled Pink to see us. They're probably going to eat us."

"These ones aren't cannibals," Mustang says.

"You're willing to bet your leg on that, missy?"

"Alia is the key," I say. "We can still convince her. It will be difficult without Ragnar, but that's the only way. Convince her that he died trying to bring their people the truth."

"Didn't you hear him? He said words wouldn't work."

"They still can."

"Darrow, give yourself a moment," Mustang says.

"A moment? My people are dying in orbit. Sevro is at war, and he's depending on us to bring him an army. We don't have the luxury of taking a bloodydamn moment."

"Darrow . . ." Mustang tries to interrupt. I keep going, methodically sorting through the options, how we must hunt down Aja, rejoin with the Sons. She puts a hand on my arm. "Darrow. Stop." I falter. Losing track of where I was, slipping away from the comfort of logic and falling straight into the emotion of it all. Ragnar's blood is under my nails. All he wanted was to come home to his people and lead them out of darkness like he saw me doing with mine. I robbed him of that choice by leading the attack on Aja. I don't cry. There isn't time for it, but I sit there with my head in my hands. Mustang touches my shoulder.

"He smiled in the end," she says softly. "Do you know why? Because he knew what he was doing was right. He was fighting for love. You've made a family of your friends. You always have. It made Ragnar a better man to know you. So you didn't get him killed. You helped him live. But you have to live now." She sits next to me. "I know you want to believe the best in people. But think how long it took for you to get through to Ragnar. To win over Tactus or me. What can you do in a day? A week? This place . . . it's not our world. They don't care about our rules or our morality. We will die here if we do not escape."

"You don't think Alia will listen."

"Why would she? Obsidians only value strength. And where is ours? Ragnar even thought he would have to kill his mother. She won't listen. Do you know the word for surrender in Nagal? *Rjoga*. The word for subjugation? *Rjoga*. What's the word for slavery? *Rjoga*. Without Ragnar to lead them, what do you think is going to happen if you release them on the Society? Alia Snowsparrow is a black-blooded tyrant. And the rest of the warchiefs are no better. She might even be expecting us. Even if we've hacked the Golds' monitoring systems, the Golds know she's his mother, then they could have told her to expect him. She could be reporting to them right now."

When I looked up at my father as a boy, I thought being a man was having control. Being the master and commander of your own destiny. How could any boy know that freedom is lost the moment you become a man. Things start to count. To press in. Constricting slowly, inevitably, creating a cage of inconveniences and duties and deadlines and failed plans and lost friends. I'm tired of people doubting. Of people choosing to believe they know what is possible because of what has happened before.

Holiday grunts. "Escaping won't be that easy."

"Step one," Mustang says as she slips free of her manacles. She used a little shard of bone to pick the lock.

"Where'd you learn that?" Holiday asks.

"You think the Institute was my first school?" she asks. "Your turn." She reaches for my manacles. "As I see it, we can rush them when they open the . . . what's wrong?"

I've pulled my hands back from her. "I'm not leaving."

"Darrow . . ."

"Ragnar was my friend. I told him I would help his people. I will not run to save myself. I will not let him die in vain. The only way out is through."

"The Obsidians . . ."

"Are needed," I say. "Without them, I can't fight Gold Legions. Not even with your help."

"All right," Mustang says, not belaboring the point. "Then how do you intend to change Alia's mind?"

"I think I'll need your help with that."

||||||||||||

Hours later, we are guided to the center of a cavernous throne room built for giants. It's lit by seal oil lamps that belch out black smoke along the walls. The iron doors slam shut behind us, and we're left alone before a throne, upon which sits the largest human being I've ever seen. She watches us from the far side of the room, more statue than woman. We approach awkwardly in our chains. Boots over the slick black floor till we come before Alia Snowsparrow, Queen of the Valkyrie.

Across her lap lies the body of her dead son.

Alia glares down at us. She is as colossal as Ragnar, but ancient and wicked, like the oldest tree of some primeval forest. The kind that drinks the soil and blocks the sun for lesser trees and watches them wither and yellow and die and does nothing but reach her branches higher and dig her roots deeper. The wind has armored her face in dead skin and calluses. Her hair is stringy and long, the color of dirty snow. She sits on a cushion of furs stacked inside the rib cage of the skeleton of what must have been the largest griffin ever Carved. The griffin's head screams silently down at us from above her. The wings spread against the stone wall, ten meters across. On her head is a crown of black glass. At her feet is her fabled warchest which is locked in times of peace by a great iron device. Her knotty hands are covered in blood.

This is the primal realm, and though I would know what to say to a queen who sits upon a throne, I have no bloodydamn clue what to say to a mother who sits with her own son dead in her lap and looks at me as though I am some worm that's just slithered up from the taiga.

It seems she doesn't much care that I've lost my tongue. Hers is sharp enough.

"There is a great heresy in our lands against the gods who rule the thousand stars of the Abyss." Her voice rumbles like that of an old crocodile. But it is not her language, it is ours. HighLingo Aureate. A sacred tongue, known by few in these lands, mostly the shaman who commune with the gods. Spies, in other words. Alia's fluency startles Mustang. But not me. I know how the low rise under the power of the mighty, and this merely confirms what I've long suspected. Slaggin' Gamma are not the only favored slaves of the worlds.

"A heresy told by wicked prophets with wicked aims. For a summer and a winter it has slithered through us. Poisoning my people and the people of the Dragon Spine and the Blooded Tents and the Rattling Caves. Poisoning them with lies that spit in the eye of our people." She leans down from her throne, blackheads huge on her nose. Wrinkles deep ravines around pitch eyes.

"Lies that say a Stained son will return and he will bring a man to guide us from this land. A morning star in the darkness. I have sought these heretics out to learn of their whispers, to see if the gods spoke through them. They did not. Evil spoke through them. And so I have hunted the heretics. Broken their bones with my own hands. Peeled their flesh and set them upon the rock of the spires to be eaten as carrion by the fowl of the ice." The seven bodies who dangled from the chains outside. Ragnar's friends.

"This I do for my people. Because I love my people. Because the children of my loins are few, and those of my heart many. For I knew the heresy to be a lie. Ragnar, blood of my blood, would never return. To return would mean the breaking of oaths to me, to his people, to the gods who watch over us from Asgard on high."

She looks down at her dead son.

"And then I woke into this nightmare." She closes her eyes. Breathes deep and opens them again. "Who are you to bring the corpse of my best born to my spire?"

"My name is Darrow of Lykos," I say. "This is Virginia au Augustus and Holiday ti Nakamura." Alia's eyes ignore Holiday and twitch over to Mustang. Even at nearly two meters, she seems a child in this huge room. "We came with Ragnar as a diplomatic mission on behalf of the Rising."

"The Rising." She dislikes the taste of the foreign word. "And who are you to my son?" She eyes my hair with more disdain than a mortal should have for a god. Something deeper is at play here. "Are you Ragnar's master?"

"I am his brother," I correct.

"His brother?" She mocks the idea.

"Your son swore an oath of servitude to me when I took him from a Gold. He offered me Stains and I offered him his freedom. Since then he has been my brother."

"He . . ." Her voice catches. "Died free?"

The way she says it intones that deeper understanding. One Mustang notes. "He did. His men, the ones you have hanging on the walls outside, would have told you that I lead a rebellion against the Golds who rule over you, who took Ragnar from you as they took your other children. And they would have told you, as well as all your people, that Ragnar was the greatest of my generals. He was a good man. He was—"

"I know my son," she interrupts. "I swam with him in the ice floes when he was a boy. Taught him the names of the snow, of the storms, and took him upon my griffin to show him the spine of the world. His hands clutched my hair and sang for joy as we rose through the clouds above. My son was without fear." She remembers that day very differently than Ragnar did. "I know my son. And I do not need a stranger to tell me of his spirit."

"Then you should ask yourself, Queen, what would make him return here," Mustang says. "What would make him send his men here, if he would come here himself if he knew it meant breaking his oath to you and your people?"

Alia does not speak as she examines Mustang with those hungry eyes.

"Brother." She mocks the word again, looking back to me. "I wonder, would you use brothers as you have used my son? Bringing him here. As if he is the key to unlocking the giants of the ice?" She looks around the hall so I see the deeds carved into the stone that stretches the height of fifteen men above us. I've never met an Obsidian artisan. They send us only their warriors. "As if you could use a mother's love against her. This is the way of men. I can smell your ambition. Your plans. I do not know the Abyss, oh, worldly warlord, but I know the ice. I know the serpents that slither in the hearts of men.

"I questioned the heretics myself. I know what you are. I know you descend from a lower creature than us. A Red. I have seen Reds. They are like children. Little elves who live in the bones of the world. But you stole the body of an Aesir, of a Sunborn. You call yourself a breaker of chains, but you are a maker of them. You wish to bind us to you. Using our strength to make you great. Like every man."

She leans over my dead friend to leer at me and I see what this woman respects, why Ragnar believed he would have to kill her and take her throne, and why Mustang wanted to flee. Strength. And where is mine, she wonders.

"You know many things of him," Mustang says. "But you know nothing of me, yet you insult me."

Alia frowns. It's clear she has no idea who Mustang is, and no wish to anger a true Gold, if, indeed, Mustang is one. Her confidence wavers only a fraction. "I have laid no claims against you, Sunborn."

"But you have. By suggesting he has evil wishes in store for your people, you too suggest that I collude with him. That I, his companion, am here with the same wicked intentions."

"Then what are your intentions? Why do you accompany this creature?"

"To see if he was worth following," Mustang says.

"And is he?"

"I don't know yet. What I do know is that millions will follow him. Do you know that number? Can you even comprehend it, Alia?"

"I know the number."

"You asked my intentions," Mustang says. "I will put it plainly. I am a warlord and Queen like you. My dominion is larger than you can comprehend. I have metal ships in the Abyss that carry more men than you have ever seen. That can crack the highest mountain in two. And I am here to tell you that I am not a god. Those men and women on Asgard are not gods. They are flesh and blood. Like you. Like me."

Alia rises slowly, bearing her huge son easily in her arms, and walks him to a stone altar and lays him upon it. She pours oil from a small urn onto a cloth and drapes it over Ragnar's face. Then she kisses the cloth. Looking down at him.

Mustang presses her. "This land cannot hold seed. It is ruled by wind and ice and barren rock. But you survive. Cannibals roam the hills. Enemy clans ache for your land. But you survive. You sell your sons, your daughters to your 'gods,' but you survive. Tell me, Alia. Why? Why live when all you live for is to serve. To watch your family wither away? I've watched mine go. Each stolen from me one by one. My world is broken. And so is yours. But if you join your arms with mine, with Darrow as Ragnar wanted . . . we can make a new world."

Alia turns back to us, beleaguered. Her steps are slow and measured as she comes before us. "Which would you fear more, Virginia au Augustus, a god? Or a mortal with the power of a god?" The question hangs between them, creating a rift words cannot mend. "A god cannot die. So a god has no fear. But mortal men . . ." She clucks her tongue behind her stained teeth. "How frightened they are that the darkness will come. How horribly they will fight to stay in the light."

Her corrupt voice chills my blood.

She knows.

Mustang and I realize it at the same terrible moment. Alia knows her gods are mortal. A new fear bubbles up from the deepest part of me. I'm a fool. We traveled all this distance to pull the wool from her eyes, but she's already seen the truth. Somehow. Some way. Did the Golds come to her because she is queen? Did she discover it herself? Before she sold Ragnar? After? It's no matter. She's already resigned herself to this world. To the lie.

"There's another path," I say desperately, knowing that Alia made her judgment against us before we ever entered the room. "Ragnar saw it. He saw a world where your people could leave the ice. Where they could make their own destiny. Join me and that world is possible. I will give you the means to take the power that will let you cross the stars like your ancestors, to walk unseen, to fly among the clouds on boots. You can live in the land of your choosing. Where the wind is warm as flesh and the land is green instead of white. All you need to do is fight with me like your son did."

"No, little man. You cannot fight the sky. You cannot fight the river or the sea or the mountains. And you cannot fight the Gods," Alia says. "So I will do my duty. I will protect my people. I will send you to Asgard in chains. I will let the Gods on high decide your fate. My people will live on. Sefi will inherit my throne. And I will bury my son in the ice from which he was born."

32

||||||||||||||||||||||||||

NO MAN'S LAND

The sky is the color of blood underneath a dead nail as we fly away from the Spires. This time, we are imprisoned, chained belly down to the back of fetid fur saddles like luggage. My eyes water as the wind of the lower troposphere slashes into them. The griffin beats its wings, muscled shoulders rippling, churning the air. We bank sideways and I see the riders tilting their masked faces up to the sky to see the faint light that is Phobos. Little flashes of white and yellow mar the darkening sky as ships overhead battle. I pray silently for Sevro's safety, for Victra's and the Howlers.

Words failed with Alia, as Mustang said they would. And now we are bound for Asgard, a gift for the gods to secure the future of her people. That is what she told Sefi. And her silent daughter took my chains and, with the help of Alia's personal guards, dragged me and Mustang and Holiday to the hangar where her Valkyrie waited.

Now, hours later, we pass over a land created by wrathful gods in their youth. Dramatic and brutal, the Antarctic was designed as punishment and a test for the ancestors of the Obsidians who dared rise against the Golds in the two-hundredth year of their reign. A place so savage less than sixty percent of Obsidians reach adulthood, per Board of Quality Control quotas.

That desperate struggle for life robs them of a chance for culture and societal progress, just as the nomadic tribes of the first Dark Ages were so robbed. Farmers make culture. Nomads make war.

Subtle signs of life freckle the bald waste. Roving herds of auroch. Fires on mountain ridges, glittering from the cracks in the great doors of Obsidian cities that are carved into the rock as they gather supplies and huddle behind their walls on the eve of the long dark of winter. We fly for hours. I fall in and out of sleep, body exhausted. Not having closed my eyes since we shared the pasta with Ragnar in our cozy hole in the belly of that dead ship. How has so much changed so quickly?

I wake to the bellow of a horn. *Ragnar is dead*. It's the first thought in my head.

I am no stranger waking to grief.

Another horn echoes as Sefi's riders close their gaps, drifting together into tight formation. We rise amidst a sea of ash-gray clouds. Sefi bent over the reins in front of me. Pushing her griffin hard toward a hulking darkness. We slip free of the clouds to find Asgard hanging in the twilight. It's a black mountain ripped from the ground by the gods and hung halfway between the Abyss and the ice world below. Seat of the Aesir. Where Olympus was a bright celebration of the senses, this is a brooding threat to a conquered race.

A set of stone stairs, precarious and seemingly unsupported, rises from the mountains tethering Asgard to the world below. The Way of Stains. The path all young Obsidian must take if they wish to gain the favor of the gods, to bring honor and bounty to their tribes by becoming the servants of Allmother Death. Bodies litter the Valley of the Fallen beneath. Frozen mounds of men and women in a land where carrion never rots and only the industry of crows can make proper skeletons. It is a lonely walk, and one we must make if the Obsidian are to approach the mountain.

This is what it takes to make an Obsidian afraid. I feel that fear now from Sefi. She has never walked this path. No Stained may stay among the people of the Spires or the other tribes. All are chosen by the Golds for service. Her mother never would have let her take the tests. She needed one daughter to remain as her heir.

Unlike Olympus, Asgard is surrounded by defensive measures. Electronic high-pitched frequency emitters that would make the griffins' eardrums bleed two clicks out. A high-charged pulse shield closer in that would hyper-oscillate the molecular structure of any man or creature by boiling the water in our skin and organs. Black magic to the Obsidian. But the sensors are dead today, compliments of Quicksilver and his hackers, and the cameras and drones that monitor our approach are blind to us, showing instead the footage recorded three years before, just as with the satellites. There is only one way to seek an audience with the gods, and that is along the Way of Stains through the Shadowmouth Temple.

We set down atop the forbidding mountain peak beneath Asgard where the Way of Stains is tethered to the earth. A black temple squats over the stairs like a possessive old crone. Its skin ravaged by time. Face crumbling to the wind.

I'm pulled off the saddle and fall to the ice, legs asleep after the long journey. The Valkyrie wait for me to rise with Mustang's help. "I think it's time," she says. I nod and let the Valkyrie push us after Sefi toward the black temple. Wind pours through the mouths of three hundred and thirty-three stone faces that scream out from the temple's front façade imprisoned beneath the black rock, wild eyes desperate for release. We enter under the black arch. Snow rolls across the floor.

"Sefi," I say. The woman turns slowly back to look at me. She's not cleaned her brother's blood from her hair. "May I speak to you? Alone?" The Valkyrie wait for their quiet leader to nod before pulling Mustang and Holiday back. Sefi walks farther into the temple. I follow as best I can in my chains to a small courtyard open to the sky. I shiver at the cold. Sefi watches me there in the weird violet light, waiting patiently for me to speak. It's the first time it's occurred to me that she's as curious of me as I am of her. And it also fills me with confidence. Those small dark eyes are inquisitive. They see the cracks in things. In men, in armor, in lies. Mustang was right about Alia. She would never listen. I suspected it before we entered her throne room, but I had to give it my best. And even if she had listened, Mustang would never trust Alia Snowsparrow to lead the Obsidian in our war. I would have gained an ally and lost another. But Sefi . . . Sefi is the last hope I have.

"Where do they go?" I ask her now. "Have you ever wondered? The men and women your clan gives to the gods? I don't think you believe what they tell you. That they are lifted up as warriors. That they are given untold riches in service of the immortals."

I wait for her to reply. Of course, she does not. If I can't sway her here, then we're as good as dead. But Mustang thinks, as do I, that we have a chance with her. More than we ever did with Alia, at least.

"If you believed in the gods, you would not have sworn yourself to silence when Ragnar ascended. Others cheered, but you wept. Because you know . . . don't you." I step closer to the woman. She's just above my own height. More muscular than Victra. Her pale face is nearly the same shade as her hair. "You feel the dark truth in your heart. All who leave the ice become slaves."

Her brow furrows. I try not to lose my momentum.

"Your brother was Stained, a Son of the Spires. He was a titan. And he ascended to serve the gods but was treated no better than a prized dog. They made him fight in pits, Sefi. They wagered on his life. Your brother, the one who taught you the names of the ice and wind, who was the greatest son of the Spires in his generation, was another man's property."

She looks up at the sky where the stars blink through the black-violet twilight. How many nights has she looked up and wondered what had become of her big brother? How many lies has she told herself so she can sleep at night? Now to know the horrors he suffered, it makes all those times she looked at the stars so much worse.

"Your mother was the one who sold him," I say, seizing the opportunity. "She sold your sisters, brothers, your father. Everyone who has ever left has gone to slavery. Like my people. You know what the prophets your brother sent said. I was a slave but I have risen against my masters. Your brother rose with me. Ragnar returned here to bring you with us. To bring your people out of bondage. And he died for it. For you. Do you trust him enough to believe his last words? Do you love him enough?"

She looks back to me, the whites of her eyes red with an anger that seems to have been long dormant. As if she's known of her mother's duplicity for years. I wonder what she's heard, listening for two and a half decades. I wonder even if her mother has told her the truth. Sefi is to be queen. Perhaps that is the right of passage. Passing down the knowledge of their true condition. Perhaps Sefi even listened to our audience with Alia. Something in the way she watches me makes me believe this.

"Sefi, if you deliver me to the Golds, their reign continues and your brother will have sacrificed himself for nothing. If the world is as you like it, then do nothing. But if it is broken, if it is unjust, take a chance. Let me show you the secrets your mother has kept from you. Let me show you how mortal your gods are. Let me help you honor your brother."

She stares at the snow as it drifts across the floor, lost in thought. Then, with a measured nod, she pulls an iron key from her riding cloak and steps toward me.

The stairs of the Way of Stains are frigid and gusty, and switch back devilishly into the sky through the clouds. But they are just stairs. We climb them without chains in the guise of Valkyrie—bone riding masks painted blue, riding cloaks, and boots too big for my feet. All loaned to us by three women who stayed behind to guard the griffin at the base of the temple. Sefi leads us, eight other Valkyrie coming behind. My legs shake from exertion by the time we reach the top and see the black glass complex of the Golds that crests the floating mountain. There are eight towers in all, each belonging to one of the gods. They surround the central building, a dark glass pyramid, like wheel spokes, connected by thin bridges twenty meters above the uneven snowy ground. Between us and the Gold complex is a second temple in the shape of a giant screaming face, this one as large as Castle Mars. In front of the temple lies a little square park, at the center of which stands a gnarled black tree. Flames smolder along its branches. White blossoms perch amidst the flames, untouched by the fire. The Valkyrie whisper to each other, fearing the magic at work.

Sefi carefully plucks a blossom from the tree. The flames scorch the edges of her leather gloves, but she comes away with a small white flower the shape of a teardrop. When touched it expands and darkens to the color of blood before wilting and turning to ash. I've never seen anything like it. Nor do I particularly give a piss about the showmanship. It's too cold for that. A bloody red footprint blossoms in the snow in front of us. Sefi and her Valkyrie stay deathly still, arms outstretched with fingers crooked in a gesture of defense against evil spirits.

"It's just blood hidden in the stone," Mustang says. "It's not real."

Still, the Valkyrie are overawed when more footprints begin to appear on the ground, leading us toward the god's mouth. They look to each other in fear. Even Sefi goes to her knees when we reach the stairs at the base of the temple's mouth. We mimic her, pressing our noses to the stone as the throat opens and out waddles a withered old man. Beard white. Eyes violet and milky with age.

"You are mad!" he howls. "Mad as crows to travel the stairs on the eve of winter!" His staff thumps each individual step in his descent. Voice squeezing the lines for all they're worth. "Bone and frozen blood is all that should remain. Have you come to request a trial of the Stains?"

"No," I rumble in my best Nagal. To take the trial of the Stains now would do nothing for us. We would only see the gods when we received the facial tattoos. And surviving a test of the Stained is something even Ragnar thought I was not prepared for. There's only one other way to bring the gods to me. Bait.

"No?" the Violet says, confused.

"We come to seek an audience with the gods."

At any moment, one of the Valkyrie could give us up. All it would take is a word. The tension works its way through my shoulders. Only thing that keeps me sane is knowing Mustang's on board enough with the plan to be bent on a knee beside me at the top of this damn mountain. That has to mean I'm not totally insane. At least I hope.

"So you *are* mad!" the Violet says, growing bored of us. "The gods come and go. To the abyss, to the sea down below. But they give no audience to mortal men. For what is time to creatures such as them. Only the Stained are worth their love. Only the Stained can bear the fever of their sight. Only the children of ice and darkest night."

Well this is bloodydamn annoying.

"A ship of iron and star has fallen from the Abyss," I say. "It came with a tail of fire. And struck among the peaks near the Valkyrie Spires. Burning across the sky like blood."

"A ship?" the Violet asks, now utterly interested, as we supposed he would be.

"One of iron and star," I say.

"How do you know it was no vision?" the Violet asks cleverly.

"We touched the iron with our own hands."

The Violet is silent, mind sprinting to and fro behind those manic eyes. I'm wagering he knows that their communications systems are down. That his masters will be eager to hear of a fallen ship. The last sight he might have seen was my speech before Quicksilver shut every-thing down. Now this lowly Violet, this eager actor banished to the wastes to perform a mummer's farce for barbaric simpletons has news his masters don't. He has a prize, and his eyes, when he realizes this, narrow greedily. Now is his time to seize initiative and gain favor in the eyes of the masters.

How sad, the dependability of greed to make men fools.

"Have you evidence?" he asks eagerly. "Any man may say he has seen a ship of the gods fall." Hesitating, fearful of the deception I work but disdainful of priests, Sefi produces my razor from her bag. It is wrapped in seal skin. She lays it on the ground in whip form. The Violet smiles, so very pleased. He tries to snatch it from the ground with a rag from his pocket, but Sefi pulls it back with the seal cloth.

"This is for the gods," I growl. "Not their whelps."

33

||||||||||||||||||||

GODS AND MEN

The priest ushers us through the temple's mouth, where we wait, kneeling on a black stone antechamber inside the mountain. The stone mouth grinds closed behind us. Flames dance in the center of the room, leaping up in a pillar of fire to the onyx ceiling.

Acolytes wander through the cavernous temple, chanting softly, draped with black sackcloth hoods.

"Children of the Ice," a divine voice finally whispers from the darkness. A synthesizer, like the ones in our demonHelms, layers the voice so it seems a dozen sewn together. The invisible Gold woman doesn't even bother to use an accent. Fluent as I in their language, but disdainful of the fact and of the people to which she speaks. "You come with news."

"I do, Sunborn."

"Tell us of the ship you saw," another voice says, this one a man. Less lofty, more playful. "You may look upon my face, little child." Remaining on our knees, we glance up furtively from the ground to see two armored Golds deactivating their ghostCloaks. They stand close to us in the dark room. The temple flames dance over their metallic god faces. The man wears a cloak. The woman likely didn't have time to don hers, so eager were they to attend us.

The woman plays Freya while the man is dressed as Loki. His metal visage like that of a wolf. Animals can smell fear. Men can't. But those who kill enough can feel the vibrations in that particular silence. I feel them now from Sefi. The gods are true, she's thinking. Ragnar was wrong. We were wrong. But she says nothing.

"It bled fire across the sky," I murmur, head down. "Making great roars and crashed upon the mountainside."

"You don't say," Loki murmurs. "And is it in one piece, or lots of little itty-bitty pieces, child?"

It is risky saying we saw a ship fall. But I knew no other ruse that would draw the Golds away from their holo screens in the middle of a rebellion, past their security systems and Gray garrison to meet me here. They're Peerless Scarred, trapped here on the frontier as their world shifts beyond these walls. Once, this post would have been considered glamorous, but now it's a form of banishment. I wonder about what crimes or failings brought these Peerless Scarred here to babysit the wastes.

"The bones of the ships litter the mountain, Sunborn," I explain, looking back at the ground so they do not insist I take away the riding mask that covers my face. The more groveling I do, the less curious I am. "Broken like a fishing boat laid upon mid-stern by a Breaker. Splinters of iron, splinters of men upon the snow."

I think that's a metaphor the Obsidians would use. It passes muster.

"Splinters of men?" Loki asks.

"Yes. Men. But with soft faces. Like seal skin in firelight." Too many metaphors. "But eyes like hot coals." I can't stop. How else did Ragnar speak? "Hair like the gold of your face." The Golds' metal masks remain impassive, communicating to one another over the coms in their helmets.

"Our priest claims you have a weapon of the gods," Freya says leadingly. Sefi produces the seal cloth once more, body tense, wondering when I will dispel the magic of the gods as I promised. Her hands tremble. Both Golds move closer, the slight ripple of pulseShields evident. I touch them and I fry. They have no fear. Not here on their mountain. Closer. Closer, you dumb bastards.

"Why did you not take this to the leader of your tribe?" Loki asks.

"Or to your shaman?" Freya adds suspiciously. "The Way of Stains is long and hard. To climb all this way just to bring this to us . . ."

"We are wanderers," Mustang says as Freya bends to look at the blade. "No tribe. No shaman."

"Are you, little one?" Loki asks above Sefi, voice hardening. "Then why are there blue tattoos of the Valkyrie on the ankles of that one?" His hand drifts to the razor on his hip.

"She was cast out from her tribe," I say. "For breaking an oath."

"Is it marked with a house Sigil?" Loki asks Freya. She reaches for the weapon's hilt in front of me when Mustang laughs bitterly, drawing her attention.

"On the handle, my goodlady," Mustang says in Aureate lingo, remaining on her knees as she strips off her mask and tosses it onto the ground. "You will find a Pegasus in flight. Sigil of the House Andromedus."

"Augustus?" Loki sputters, knowing Mustang's face.

I use their surprise and slip forward. By the time they turn back to me I've snatched the razor out from under Freya's hand and activated the toggle so it is the curved question-mark shape that has burned on hillsides, been cut into foreheads, and killed so many of their kind. The same they would have seen on the holoDisplays as I made my speech.

"Reaper . . ." Freya manages, pulling up her pulseFist. I hack her arm off at the shoulder, then her head at the jaw before hurling my razor straight into Loki's chest. The blade slows as it hits his pulseShield, frozen in midair for half a second as the shield resists. Finally the blade slips through. But it's slowed and the armor beneath holds. It embeds itself in the pulseArmor plate. Harmless. Until Mustang steps forward and swivel-kicks the hilt of the razor. The blade punches through the armor and impales Loki.

Both gods fall. Freya to her back. Loki to his knees.

"Mask off," Mustang barks as Loki's hands wrap around the blade sticking from his chest. She slaps his hands away from his datapad. "No coms." Holiday strips the razor from the man's hip as his pulse-Shield shorts. I take Freya's razor from her corpse. "Do it."

Sefi and her Valkyrie stare wide-eyed from their knees at the blood pooling beneath Freya. I remove Freya's helmet from her head to reveal the mangled face of a middle-aged Peerless Scarred woman with dark skin and almond-shaped eyes.

"Does this look like a god to you, Sefi?" I ask.

Mustang snorts a dark little laugh when Loki removes his mask. "Darrow. Look who it is. Proctor Mercury!" The pudgy, cherub-faced Peerless Scarred who endeavored to recruit me into his own house at the Institute before Fitchner stole me away. When last we saw each other five years ago, he tried to duel me in the halls as my Howlers stormed Olympus. I shot him in the chest with a pulseFist. He smiled all the while. He's not smiling now as he stares at the metal in his chest. I feel a pang of pity.

"Proctor Mercury," I say. "You have to be the least lucky Gold I've ever met. Two mountains lost to a Red."

"Reaper. You have to be shitting me." He shudders in pain and laughs at his own surprise. "But you're on Phobos."

"Negative, my goodman. That'd be my diminutive psychotic accomplice."

"Gorydammit. Gorydammit." He looks at the blade in his chest, grunting as he sits on his haunches and wheezes out breaths. "How . . . did we not see you . . ."

"Quicksilver hacked your system," I say.

"You're . . . here for . . ." His voice trails away as he looks at the Valkyrie rising to gather around the dead god. Sefi bends over Freya. The pale warrior traces her fingers over the woman's face as Holiday strips off her armor.

"For them," I say. "Bloodydamn right I am."

"Oh, goryhell. Augustus," our old proctor says turning to Mustang with a bitter laugh. "You can't do this . . . it's madness. They're monsters! You can't let them out! Do you know what will happen? Don't open Pandora's box."

"If they are monsters, we should ask ourselves who made them that way," Mustang says in the Obsidian tongue so Sefi can understand. "Now, what are the codes to Asgard's armory?"

He spits. "You'll have to ask nicer than that, traitor."

Mustang is deadly cold. "Treason is a matter of the date, Proctor. Must I ask again? Or must I begin trimming your ears?"

Beside Freya's body, Sefi dips her finger into the blood and tastes it.

"Just blood," I say, crouching beside her. "Not ichor. Not divine. Human."

I hold out Freya's razor for her to take. She flinches at the idea, but forces herself to wrap her fingers around the hilt, hand trembling, expecting to be struck by lightning or electrocuted like men are who touch pulseShields with bare hands. "This button here retracts the whip. This one controls the shape."

She cradles the weapon reverently and looks up at me, furious eyes asking which shape she should conjure. I nod to mine, trying to build kinship with her. And I do. If only in this martial way. Slowly her razor takes the shape of the slingBlade. The skin on my arm prickles as the Valkyrie laugh to one another. Vibrating with excitement, they pull their own axes and long knives and look at me and Mustang.

"There's five gods left," Mustang says. "How'd you ladies like to meet them?"

34

|||||||||||||||||||||||||||

GODKILLERS

We drag the bodies of seven gods, two dead and five captured, behind us. I wear the armor of Odin. Sefi the armor of Tyr. Mustang the armor of Freya. All of which we pillaged from the armory on Asgard. Blood smears the stone of the hall. Feet slide and stumble as Sefi jerks one of the living Golds behind us by his hair. Her Valkyrie drag the rest.

We returned to the Spires on a shuttle stolen from Asgard, which we slipped through silently, using Loki's codes to access the armory and drape ourselves in the panoply of war before seeking the remaining gods out. Two we found in Asgard's mainframe leading a team of Greens attempting to purge Quicksilver's hackers from their system. Sefi with her new razor claimed the arm of one and beat the other unconscious, terrifying the Greens, two of which held up fists to me as silent acknowledgment of their sympathy for the Rising. With their help, we locked the others in a storage room as the two Green sympathizers connected me directly with Quicksilver's operations room.

We didn't reach Quicksilver himself, but Victra relayed news that Sevro's gamble worked. A little more than a third of the Martian defense fleet is under control of the Sons of Ares and Quicksilver's Blues. Thousands of the Society's best troops are trapped on Phobos, but the Jackal is hitting back hard, taking personal command of the remaining ships and recalling forces from the Kuiper Belt to reinforce his depleted fleet.

The rest of the Golds we located through the station's biometric sensor map in the lower levels. One practicing with her razor in the training rooms. She saw my face and dropped her blade in surrender. Reputation is a fine thing sometimes. The remaining two Golds we found in the monitoring bays, shifting back and forth between the cameras. They'd only just discovered that the footage was archival from three years before.

Now, all our Gold captives wear magnetic handcuffs and are tied together by long pieces of rope from Sefi's griffin, all gagged, all glancing around at the Spires like we've dragged them into the mouth of hell itself.

Obsidians of the Spires flock to us in the halls. Rushing from the deeper levels to see the strange sight. Most would only have seen their gods from a distance, as flashes of gold streaking over the spring snow at mach three. Now we come among them, our pulseShields distorting the air, our shuttle's pulse cannons melting open the huge iron doors which closed off the griffin hangar from the cold. The doors melt inward like the door on the *Pax* melted when Ragnar offered me Stains.

This is not how I intended to bring the Obsidians into my fold. I wanted to use words, to come humbly, in seal skin, not armor, putting myself at the mercy of the Obsidians to show Alia that I valued her people's worth. Valued their judgment, and was willing to put myself in peril for them. I wanted to do as I preached. But even Ragnar knew that was a fool's errand. And now I don't have time for intransigence or superstition. If Alia will not follow me to war, I'll drag her to it, kicking, screaming, like Lorn before her. For Obsidian to hear, I must speak in the only language they understand.

Might.

Sefi fires her pulseFist past my head at the doors leading to her mother's sanctuary. The ancient iron buckles. Bent and twisted hinges screaming. We flow past an army of prostrate giants who clutter the cavernous halls to either side. So much strength made frail by superstition. Once, when they were stronger, they tried to cross the seas. Built mighty knarrs to carry explorers across the oceans to seek out new lands. The Carved monsters the Golds sowed in the oceans destroyed each boat, or the Golds themselves melted them from the sea. The last boat sailed more than two hundred years ago.

We come upon Alia as she sits in council with her famed seven and seventy warchiefs. They turn to us now amidst large, smoking braziers. Huge warriors, with white hair to the waists, arms bare, iron buckles on waists, huge axes on backs. Black eyes and rings studded with precious metals glitter in the low light. But they're too stunned by the sight of the three-hundred-year-old iron doors suddenly glowing orange and melting away to speak or kneel. I draw up before them, still dragging the corpses of the Golds behind me. Mustang and Sefi hurl their captured Golds forward, kicking out their legs. They sprawl on the ground and stumble to their feet, attempting beyond all reason to maintain some dignity here surrounded by giant savages in the smoky room.

"Are these gods?" I roar through my helmet.

No one answers. Alia moves slowly through the parting warlords.

"Am I a god?" I snarl, this time removing my helmet. Mustang and Sefi remove theirs. Alia sees her daughter in the armor of her gods and she flinches back. Fear whispers over her lips. She stops near the five bound and gagged Golds as they finally find their feet. They stand over two meters tall. But, even bent and old as Alia is, she's a head taller than I. She stares down at the men and women who were once her gods before looking up at her last daughter. "Child, what have you done?"

Sefi says nothing. But the razor on her arm slithers, drawing the eyes of every Obsidian. One of their greatest daughters carries the weapon of the gods.

"Queen of the Valkyrie," I say as if we had never met. "My name is Darrow of Lykos. Blood brother of Ragnar Volarus. I am the warlord of the Rising, which rages against the false Golden gods. You have all seen the fires that rage around the moon. Those are caused by my army. Beyond this land in the abyss, a war rages between slaves and masters. I came here with the greatest son of the Spires to bring the truth to your people." I wave to the Golds, who stare at me with the hatred of an entire race. "They struck him down before he could tell you that you are slaves. The prophets he sent told it true. Your gods are false."

"Liar!" someone screams. A shaman with crooked knees and a bent spine. He babbles something else but Sefi cuts him off.

"Liar?" Mustang hisses. "I have stood upon Asgard. I have seen where your immortals sleep. Where your immortals rut and eat and shit." She twists the pulseFist in her hand. "This is not magic." She activates her gravBoots, floating in the air. The Obsidians stare at her in wonder. "This is not magic. This is a tool."

Alia sees what I have done. What I have shown her daughter and what I have now brought her people whether she wants it or not. We're the same cruel kind. I told myself I would be better than this. I failed that promise. But noble vanity can shine another day. This is war. And victory is the only nobility. I think that is what Mustang was looking for here with Obsidians. She was more afraid that I would allow my own idealism to let something loose that I could not control. But now she sees the compromise I'm willing to make. The strength I'm willing to exert. That's what she wants in an ally as much as she wants a builder. Someone wise enough to adapt.

And Alia? She sees how her people look at me. How they look at my blade, still stained with the blood of the gods, as though it were some holy relic. And she also knows I could have made her complicit in the Golds' crime. Could have accused her before her people. But instead I offer her a chance to pretend she is just learning this for the first time.

Lamentably, my friend's mother does not take the offer. She steps toward Sefi. "I carried you, birthed you, nursed you, and this is my reward? Treason? Blasphemy? You are no Valkyrie." She looks at her people. "These are lies. Free our gods from the usurpers. Kill blasphemers. Kill them all!"

But before the first warchief can even draw their blade, Sefi steps forward, lifts the razor I gave her, and decapitates her mother. Alia's

head falls to the floor, eyes still open. The woman's huge body remains standing. Slowly it tips backward and thuds to the ground. Sefi
stands over the fallen queen and spits on the corpse. Turning back to
her people, she speaks for the first time in twenty-five years.

"She knew."

Her voice is deep and dangerous. Hardly rising above the level of a
whisper. Yet it owns the room as surely as if she roared. Then tall Sefi
turns away from the Golds, walks back through the gaggle of warchiefs to the griffin throne where her mother's fabled warchest has sat
unopened for ten years. There, she bends and takes the lock in her
hands and roars gutturally, like a beast, as she pulls at the rusted iron
till her fingers bleed and the iron crumbles apart. She throws the old
lock to the ground and rips open the chest, pulling free the old black
scarabSkin her mother used to conquer the White Coast. Pulling free
the red scale cloak of the dragon her mother slew in her youth. And
hoisting high her great, black, double-headed axe of war called Throg-
mir. The rippling gleam of duroSteel catches in the light. She stalks
back to the Golds, dragging the axe on the ground behind her.

She motions to Holiday, who removes the gags from the mouths of
the Golds.

"Are you a god?" Sefi asks, her tone so different from her brother's.
Direct and cold as a winter storm.

"You will burn, mortal," the man says. "If you do not release us,
Aesir will come from the sky and rain fire upon your land. This you
know. We will wipe your seed from the worlds. We will melt the ice.
We are the mighty. We are the Peerless Scarred. And this millennium
belongs to . . ."

Sefi slays him there with one giant swing, cleaving him nearly in
twain. Blood sprays my face. I do not flinch. I knew what would happen if I brought them here. I also know there's no way I could keep
them as prisoners. The Golds built this myth, but now it must die.
Mustang moves closer to me, her sign that she accepts this. But her
eyes are fixed on the Golds. She will remember this slaughter for the
rest of her life. It is her duty and mine to make it mean something.

Part of me mourns the death of these Golds. Even as they die, they
make these other taller mortals still seem so much lesser. They stand

straight, proud. They do not quake in their last moment in this smoky room so far from their estates where they rode horses as children and learned the poetry of Keats and the wonder of Beethoven and Volmer. A middle-aged Gold woman looks back at Mustang. "You let them do this to us? I fought for your father. I met you when you were a girl. And I fell in his Rain," she glares at me and begins to recite with a loud clear voice the Aeschylus poem the Peerless Scarred use at times as a battle cry:

Up and lead the dance of Fate!
Lift the song that mortals hate . . .
Tell what rights are ours on earth,
Over all of human birth
Swift of foot to avenge are we!
He whose hands are clean and pure.
Naught our wrath to dread hath he.

One by one they fall to Sefi's axe. Until only the woman is left, her head held high, her words ringing clear. She looks me in the eye, as sure of her right as I am of mine. "Sacrifice. Obedience. Prosperity." Sefi's axe sweeps through the air and the last god of Asgard flops to the stone floor. Over her body towers the blood-spattered Princess of the Valkyrie, terrible and ancient with her justice. She bends and removes the tongue of the female Gold with a crooked knife. Mustang shifts beside me in discomfort.

Sefi smiles, noticing Mustang's unease, and walks away from us to her dead mother. She takes the woman's crown and ascends the steps to the throne, bloody axe in one hand, glass crown in the other, and sits inside the rib cage of the griffin where she crowns herself.

"Children of the Spires, the Reaper has called us to join him in his war against false gods. Do the Valkyrie answer?"

In reply, her Valkyrie raise their blue-feathered axes high above their heads to drone out the Obsidian chant of death. Even the warchiefs of fallen Alia join. It seems the ocean itself crashes through the stone hallways of the Spires, and I feel the drums of war beating inside, chilling my blood.

"Then ride, Hjelda, Tharul, Veni, and Hroga. Ride Faldir and Wrona and Bolga to the tribes of the Blood Coast, to the Bleaking Moor, the Shattered Spine and the Witch Pass. Ride to kin and enemy alike and tell them Sefi speaks. Tell them Ragnar's prophets told true. Asgard has fallen. The gods are dead. The old oaths have been broken. And tell all who will hear: the Valkyrie ride to war."

As the world swirls around us and the ecstasy of war fills the air, Mustang and I look at one another with darkened eyes and wonder just what we have unleashed.

PART III

||||||||||||||||||||||||||||||||||||||||||||

GLORY

All that we have is that shout into the wind—
how we live. How we go. And how
we stand before we fall.

—KARNUS AU BELLONA

35

||||||||||||||||||||||||||

THE LIGHT

For seven days after the death of Ragnar, I travel across the ice with Sefi, speaking to the male tribes of the Broken Spine, to the Blooded Braves of the North Coast, to women who wear the horns of rams and stand watch over the Witch Pass. Flying in gravBoots beside the Valkyrie, we come bringing the news of the fall of Asgard.

It is . . . dramatic.

Sefi and a score of her Valkyrie have begun training with Holiday and me to learn to use the gravBoots and pulse weapons. They're clumsy at first. One flew into the side of a mountain at mach 2. But when thirty land with their headdresses kicking in the wind, the left of their faces painted with the blue handprint of Sefi the Quiet and the right with the slingBlade of the Reaper, folks tend to listen.

We take the lion's share of Obsidian leaders to the conquered mountain and let them walk the halls where their gods ate and slept, and show them the cold, preserved corpses of the slain Golds. In seeing their gods slain, most, even those who knew tacitly of their true condition as slaves, accepted our olive branch. Those who did not, who denounced us, were overcome by their own people. Two warchiefs hurled themselves from the mountain in shame. Another opened her veins with a dagger and bleeds out on the floor of the Green houses.

And one, a particularly psychotic little woman, watched with great malevolence as we took her to the mountain's datahub where three Greens informed her of a planned coup against her rule, showing her video of the conspiracy. We loaned her a razor, a flight back home, and two days later she added twenty thousand warriors to my cause.

Sometimes I encounter Ragnar's legend. It has spread among the tribes. They call him the Speaker. The one who came with truth, who brought the prophets and sacrificed his life for his people. But with my friend's legend grows my own. My slingBlade's symbol burns across mountainsides to greet me and the Valkyrie when we fly to meet with new tribes. They call me the Morning Star. That star by which griffin-riders and travelers navigate the wastes in the dark months of winter. The last star that disappears when daylight returns in the spring.

It is my legend that begins to bind them. Not their sense of kinship with one another. These clans have warred for generations. But I have no sordid history here. Unlike Sefi or the other great Obsidian warlords, I am their untouched field of snow. Their blank slate on which they can project whatever disparate dreams they have. As Mustang says, I am something new, and in this old world steeped in legends, ancestors, and what came before, something new is something very special.

Yet despite our progress with gathering the clans, the difficulty we face is massive. Not only must we keep the fractious Obsidians from killing one another in honor duels, but many of the clans have accepted my invitation for relocation. Hundreds of thousands of them must be brought from their homes in the Antarctic to the tunnels of the Reds so they are beyond the reach of Gold bombardment, which will come when the Golds discover what has transpired here. All this while keeping the Jackal dumb and blind to our maneuvers. From Asgard, Mustang has led the counterintelligence efforts, with the help of Quicksilver's hackers to mask our presence and project reports consistent with those filed in previous weeks to the Board of Quality Control HQ in Agea.

With no way to move them without someone noticing, Mustang, a Gold aristocrat, has conceived the most audacious plan in the history of the Sons of Ares. One massive troop movement, utilizing thousands of shuttles and freighters from Quicksilver's mercantile fleet and the Sons of Ares navy to move the population of the pole in twelve hours. A thousand ships skimming over the Southern Sea, burning helium to set down on the ice before Obsidian cities and lower their ramps to the hundreds and thousands of giants swaddled in fur and iron who will fill their hulls with the old, the sick, the warriors, the children, and the fetid stink of animals. Then, under the cover of the Sons of Ares ships, the population will be dispersed underground and many of the warriors to our military ships in orbit. I do not think I know another person in the worlds who can organize it as fast as she does.

On the eighth day after the fall of Asgard, I depart with Sefi, Mustang, Holiday, and Cassius to join Sevro in overseeing the final preparations for the migration. The Valkyrie bring Ragnar with us on the flight, wrapping his frozen body in rough cloth and clutching him close in terror as our ship cruises just beneath the speed of sound five meters from the surface of the ocean. They watch in awe as we enter the tunnels of Mars through one of the many Sons' subterranean access points. This one an old mining colony in a southern mountain range. Sons lookouts in heavy winter jackets and balaclavas salute with their fists in the air as we pass into the tunnel.

Half a day of subterranean flying later, we arrive at Tinos. It is a hub of ship activity. Hundreds cluttering the stalactite docks, taxiing through the air. And it seems the whole city watches our shuttle as it passes through the traffic to land in its stalactite hangar, knowing it bears not just me and our new Obsidian allies, but the broken Shield of Tinos. Their weeping faces blur past. Already rumors swirl through the refugees. The Obsidians are coming. Not just to fight, but to live in Tinos. To eat their food. To share their already-crowded streets. Dancer says the place is a powder keg about to erupt. I can't say I disagree.

The disposition of the Sons of Ares is dour. They gather in silence as my ship's landing ramp unfurls. I go first down the ramp. Sevro waits beside Dancer and Mickey. He slams me into a hug. The beginnings of a goatee mark his stoic face. He holds his shoulders as square as he can, as if those bony things alone could hold up the hopes of the thousands of Sons of Ares who fill the docking bay to see the Shield of Tinos brought back to his adopted home.

"Where is he?" Sevro asks thickly.

I look back to my shuttle as Sefi and her Valkyrie carry Ragnar down the ramp. The Howlers are the first to greet them. Clown saying a respectful word to Sefi as Sevro steps past me to stand before the Valkyrie.

"Welcome to Tinos," he says to the Valkyrie in Nagal. "I am Sevro au Barca, blood brother to Ragnar Volarus. These are his other brothers and sisters." He motions to the Howlers, all of whom wear their wolfcloaks. Sevro produces Ragnar's bear cloak. "He wore this to battle. With your permission, I'd like him to wear it now."

"You were brother to Ragnar. You are brother to me," Sefi says. She clicks her tongue and her Valkyrie pass stewardship of her brother's body to Sevro. Mustang glances my way. Sefi's generosity strikes me as a promising sign. If she were a covetous creature, she would have kept his body in her lands and given him an Obsidian funeral pyre before burying his ashes in the ice. Instead, she told me she knows where his true home lies: with those who fought beside him, who helped him come back to his people.

Mustang moves closer beside me as the Howlers drape Ragnar's cloak over his body and carry him through the crowd. The Sons part for them. Hands reach to touch Ragnar. "Look," Mustang says, nodding to the thin black ribbons that the Sons have tied into their beards and hair. Her hand finds my smallest finger. A small squeeze sends me back to the woods where she saved me. Making me feel warm even as we watch Sevro leave the hangar with Ragnar's body. "Go." She nudges me his direction. "Dancer and I have a conference scheduled with Quicksilver and Victra."

"She needs a guard," I tell Dancer. "Sons you trust."

"I'll be fine," Mustang says, rolling her eyes. "I survived the Obsidians."

"She'll have the Pitvipers," Dancer says, examining Mustang without the kindness I'm used to seeing in his eyes. Ragnar's death has taken the spirit out of him today. He seems older as he waves Narol over and nods to the shuttle. "The Bellona on board?"

"Holiday's got him in the passenger cabin. His neck's still torn up so he'll need Virany to take a look at him. Be discreet about it. Give him a private room."

"Private? Place is crammed, Darrow. Captains don't even get private rooms."

"He's got intel. You want him shot before he can give it to us?" I ask.

"Is that why you kept him alive?" Dancer looks at Mustang skeptically, as if she's already compromising my decisions. Little does he know she'd have let Cassius die more readily than I ever would. Dancer sighs when I don't relent. "He'll be safe. On my word."

"Find me later," Mustang says as I depart.

I find Sevro slumped over Ragnar in Mickey's laboratory. It's a thing to hear of a friend's death, it's another to see the shadow of what they've left behind. I hated the sight of my father's old workgloves after he died. Mother was too practical to throw them away. Said we couldn't afford to. So I did it myself one day and she boxed my ears and made me bring them back.

The scent of death is growing stronger from Ragnar.

The cold preserved him in his native land, but Tinos has been suffering power outages and refrigeration units play second zither to the water purifiers and air reclamation systems in the city beneath. Soon Mickey will embalm him and make preparations for the burial Ragnar asked for.

I sit in silence for half an hour, waiting for Sevro to speak. I don't want to be here. Don't want to see Ragnar dead. Don't want to linger in the sadness. Yet I stay for Sevro.

My armpits stink. I'm tired. The scanty tray of food Dio brought me is untouched except the biscuit I chew numbly and think how ridiculous Ragnar looks on the table. He's too big for it, feet hanging off the edge.

Despite the smell, Ragnar is peaceful in death. Ribbons red as winter berries nestled in the white of his beard. Two razors rest in his hands, which are folded across his bare chest. The tattoos are darker in death, covering his arms, his chest and neck. The matching skull he gave me and Sevro seems so sad. Telling its story even though the man who wears it is dead. Everything is more vivid except the wound. It's innocuous and thin as a snake's smile along his side. The holes Aja made in his stomach seem so small. How could such little things take so large a soul from this world?

I wish he were here.

The people need him more than ever.

Sevro's eyes are glassy as his fingers glide over the tattoos on Ragnar's white face. "He wanted to go to Venus, you know," he murmurs, voice soft as a child's. Softer than I've ever heard it before. "I showed him one of the holoVids of a catamaran there. Second he put the goggles on I'd never seen anyone smile like that. Like he'd found heaven and realized he didn't have to die to go there. He'd sneak in and borrow my holo gear in the middle of the night till one day I just gave him the damn thing. Things are four hundred credits, max. Know what he did to repay me?" I don't. Sevro holds up his right hand to show me his skull tattoo. "He made me his brother." He gives Ragnar a slow, affectionate punch to the jaw. "But the big fat idiot had to run at Aja instead of away from her."

The Valkyrie still scour the wastes in vain for signs of the Olympic Knight. Her trail goes deeper into the crevasse before it is covered by the frozen black blood of some creature. I hope something found her and took her to its cave in the ice to finish her slowly. But I doubt it. A woman like that doesn't just fade. Whatever Aja's fate, if she's alive she'll find a way to contact the Sovereign or the Jackal.

"It was my fault," I say. "My shit plan to take Aja out."

"She killed Quinn. Helped kill my father," Sevro mutters. "Killed dozens of us when you were locked up. Wasn't your bad. You'd have lost me too if I were there. Even Rags couldn't have kept me from having a go at her." Sevro rolls his knuckles along the edge of the table, leaving little white creases in the skin. "Always trying to protect us."

"The Shield of Tinos," I say.

"The Shield of Tinos," he echoes, voice catching. "He loved the name."

"I know."

"I think he'd always thought himself a blade before he met us. We let him be what he wanted. A protector." He wipes his eyes and backs away from Ragnar. "Anyway. The little princeling is alive."

I nod. "We brought him on the shuttle."

"Pity. Two millimeters." He pinches his fingers together, illustrating how narrowly Mustang's arrow missed Cassius's jugular. After Sefi dispatched riders to the tribes, I took her and many of her warlords to Asgard aboard the shuttle to see the fortress there. I brought Cassius along as well and Asgard's Yellows saved his life. "Why are you keeping him alive, Darrow? If you think he's going to thank you for your generosity, you've got another thing coming."

"I couldn't just let him die."

"He killed my father."

"I know."

"Give me a reason."

"Maybe I think the world would be a better place with him in it," I say tentatively. "So many people have used him, lied to him, betrayed him. All that's defined him. It's not fair. I want him to have a chance to decide for himself what kind of person he wants to be."

"None of us get to be what we want to be," Sevro mutters. "Least not for long."

"Isn't that why we fight? Isn't that what you just said about Ragnar? He was made a blade but we gave him a chance to be a shield. Cassius deserves that same chance."

"Shithead." He rolls his eyes. "Just 'cause you're right doesn't mean you're right. Anyway, eagles are hated as much as the lions. Someone here's still going to try to pop him. And your girl too."

"She's got the Pitvipers with her. And she's not my girl."

"Whatever you say." He collapses into one of Mickey's stolen leather chairs and rubs a hand along his Mohawk's ridge. "Wish she'd taken the Telemanuses with her. If she had, you'd have slagged Aja hard." He closes his eyes and leans his head back. "Oh, hey," he remembers suddenly, "I got you some ships."

"I saw that. Thank you," I say.

"Finally." He snorts a laugh. "A sign we're making a difference. Twenty torchships, ten frigates, four destroyers, a dreadnought. You should have seen it, Reap. Martian Navy pumped Phobos full of Legionaries, emptied their ships and we just stole their assault shuttles, flew them back with the right codes, and landed them in their hangars. My squad didn't even fire a shot. Quicksilver's boys even hacked the PA systems in the navy ships. They all heard your speech. It was mutiny almost before we got on board, Reds, Oranges, Blues, even Grays. It won't work again, the PA system bit. Golds will learn to cut themselves off the network so we can't hack in, but it got 'em hard this week. When we unite with the *Pax* and Orion's other ships we'll have a real force to slag the Pixies."

It's moments like this that I know I'm not alone. Damn the world, so long as I have my mangy little guardian angel. If only I was so good at guarding him as he is at guarding me. Once again he's done all I could ask and more. As I marshaled the Obsidians, he ripped a gaping hole in the Jackal's defense fleet. Crippled a fourth of them. Forced the rest to retreat toward the outer moon of Deimos to regroup with the Jackal's reserves and await additional reinforcements from Ceres and the Can.

For a brief hour, he held naval supremacy over all of Mars's southern hemisphere. The Goblin King. Then he was forced to retreat to hunker close into Phobos, where his men eliminated the trapped loyalist marines by using Rollo's squads to cut off their air and vent them into space. I'm under no delusion. The Jackal won't let us have the moon. He might not care about its people, but he can't destroy the station's helium refineries. So another assault will come soon. It won't affect my war effort, but the Jackal will get tied down fighting the populace that we've woken. It'll drain his resources without trapping me. Worst possible situation for him.

"What are you thinking?" I ask Sevro.

His eyes are lost in the ceiling. "I'm wondering how long till it's us on the slab. And wondering why it's gotta be us on the line. You see vids and hear stories and you think of the regular people. The ones who got a chance at life on Ganymede or Earth or Luna. Can't help but be jealous."

"You don't think you've gotten a chance to live?" I ask.

"Not proper," he says.

"What's proper?" I ask.

He crosses his arms like he's a kid in a fort looking down at the real world and wondering why it can't be as magical as he is. "I dunno. Something far away from being a Peerless Scarred. Maybe a Pixie or even a happy midColor. I just want something to look at and say, that's safe, that's mine, and no one is going to try and take it. A house. Kids."

"Kids?" I ask.

"I don't know. I never thought of it till Pops died. Till they took you."

"Till Victra you mean . . . ," I say with a wink. "Nice goatee by the way."

"Shut up," he says.

"Have you two—" He cuts me off, changing the subject.

"But it'd be nice to just be Sevro. To have Pops. To have known my mother." He laughs at himself, harder than he should. "Sometimes I think about going back to the beginning and wondering what would have happened if Pops had known the Board was coming. If he'd escaped with my mother, with me."

I nod. "I always think about how life would have been if Eo never died. The children I would have had. What I would have named them." I smile distantly. "I would have grown old. Watched Eo grow old. And I would have loved her more with each new scar, with each new year even as she learned to despise our small life. I would have said farewell to my mother, maybe my brother, sister. And if I was lucky, one day when Eo's hair turned gray, before it began to fall out and she began to cough, I would hear the shift of rocks over my head on the drill and that would be it. She would have sent me to the incinerators and sprinkled my ashes, then our children would have done the same. And the clans would say we were happy and good and raised bloodydamn fine children. And when those children died, our memory would fade, and when their children died, it would be swept away like the dust we become, down and away to the long tunnels. It would have been a small life," I say with a shrug, "but I would have liked it. And every day I ask myself if I was given the chance to go back, to be blind, to have all that back, would I?"

"And what's the answer?"

"All this time I thought this was for Eo. I drove straight on like an arrow because I had that one perfect idea in my head. She wanted this. I loved her. So I'll make her dream real. But that's bullshit. I was living half a bloodydamn life. Making an idol out of a woman, making her a martyr, something instead of someone. Pretending she was perfect." I run my hand through my greasy hair. "She wouldn't have wanted that. And when I looked out at the Hollows, I just knew, I mean I guess I realized as I was talking that justice isn't about fixing the past, it's about fixing the future. We're not fighting for the dead. We're fighting for the living. And for those who aren't yet born. For a chance to have children. That's what has to come after this, otherwise what's the point?"

Sevro sits silently thinking over what I've said.

"You and I keep looking for light in the darkness, expecting it to appear. But it already has." I touch his shoulder. "We're it, boyo. Broken and cracked and stupid as we are, we're the light, and we're spreading."

36

||||||||||||||||||||||||||

SWILL

I run into Victra in the hall as I leave Sevro with Ragnar. It's late. Past midnight and she's only just arrived to help coordinate the final preparations between Quicksilver's security, the Sons, and our new navy, which I've given her command of until we're reunited with Orion. It's another decision that peeves Dancer. He's frightened I'm bestowing too much power on Golds who might have ulterior motives. Mustang's presence could be the straw that breaks the camel's back.

"How's he doing?" Victra asks regarding Sevro.

"Better," I say. "But he'll be glad to see you."

She smiles at that, despite herself, and I think she actually blushes. It's a new look for her. "Where are you going?" she asks.

"To make sure Mustang and Dancer haven't torn each other's heads off yet."

"Noble. But too late."

"What happened? Is everything prime?"

"That's relative, I suppose. Dancer's in the warroom ranting about Gold superiority complexes, arrogance, etc. Never heard him curse so much. I didn't stay long, and he didn't say much. You know he's not that sweet on me."

"And you're not that sweet on Mustang," I say.

"I've nothing against the girl. She reminds me of home. Especially considering the new allies you've brought us. I just think she's a duplicitous little filly. That's all. But it's the best horses that'll buck you right off. Don't you think?"

I laugh. "Not sure if that was innuendo or not."

"It was."

"Do you know where she is?"

Victra makes a sad little face. "Contrary to popular opinion, I don't know everything, darling." She moves past me to join Sevro, patting my head as she goes. "But I'd check the commissary on level three if I were you."

"Where are *you* going?" I ask.

She smiles mischievously. "Mind your own business."

I find Mustang in the commissary hunched over a metal bottle with Uncle Narol, Kavax, and Daxo. A dozen members of the Pitvipers lounge at the other tables, smoking burners and eavesdropping intently to Mustang, who sits with her boots up on the table, using Daxo as a backrest, as she tells a story about the Institute to the other two occupants of the table. I couldn't see them when I first entered, due to the bulk of the Telemanuses but my brother and mother sit listening to the tale.

". . . And so of course I shout for Pax."

"That's my son," Kavax reminds my mother.

". . . and he comes on over the hill leading a column of my housemembers. Darrow and Cassius feel the ground shaking and go screaming into the loch where they clung together for hours, shivering and turning blue."

"Blue!" Kavax says with a huge childish laugh that makes the Sons eavesdropping unable to keep their composure. Even if he's a Gold, it's difficult not to like Kavax au Telemanus. "Blue as blueberries, Sophocles. Isn't that right? Give him another, Deanna." My mother rolls a jelly bean across the table to Sophocles, who waits eagerly beside the bottle to gobble it up.

"What's going on here?" I ask. Eying the bottle my brother's refilling the Golds' mugs with.

"We're getting stories from the lass," Narol says gruffly through a cloud of burner smoke. "Have a dram." Mustang wrinkles her nose at the smoke.

"Such an awful habit, Narol," she says.

Kieran looks pointedly at our mother. "I've been telling both of them that for years."

"Hello, Darrow," Daxo says, standing to clasp my arm. "Pleasure to see you without a razor in your hand this time." He pokes me in the shoulder with a longer finger.

"Daxo. Sorry about all that. I think I owe you a bit of a debt for taking care of my people."

"Orion did most of the minding there," he says with a twinkle in his eye. He returns gracefully to his seat. My brother's captivated by the man and the angels tattooed on his head. And how could he not be? Daxo's twice his weight, immaculate, and more well-mannered than even a Rose like Matteo, who I hear is recovering well on one of Quicksilver's ships, and is delighted to know I'm alive.

"What happened with Dancer?" I ask Mustang.

Her cheeks are flushed and she laughs at the question. "Well, I don't think he very much likes me. But don't worry, he'll come around."

"Are you drunk?" I ask with a laugh.

"A little. Catch up." She swivels her legs down and puts her feet on the ground to clear a space on the bench beside her. "I was just getting to the part where you wrestled Pax in the mud." My mother watches me quietly, a little smile on her lips as she knows the panic that must be going through me right now. Too shocked at seeing two halves of my life collide without my supervision, I sit down uneasily and listen to Mustang finish the story. With all that's transpired, I'd forgotten the charm of this woman. Her easy, light nature. How she draws others in by making them feel important, by saying their names and letting them feel seen. She holds my uncle and brother in a spell, one reinforced by the Telemanus's admiration for her. I try not to blush when my mother catches me admiring Mustang.

"But enough of the Institute," Mustang says after she's explained in detail how Pax and I dueled in front of her castle. "Deanna, you promised me a story about Darrow as a boy."

"How about the gas pocket one," Narol says. "If only Loran was here . . ."

"No not that one," Kieran says. "What about . . ."

"I have one," mother says, cutting off the men. She begins slow, words sluggish through the lisp. "When Darrow was small, maybe three or four, his father gave him an old watch his father had given him. This brass thing, with a wheel instead of digital numbers. Do you remember it?" I nod. "It was beautiful. Your favorite possession. And years later, after his father had died, Kieran here got sick with a cough. Meds were always in short ration in the mines. So you'd have to get them from Gamma or Gray, but each has a price. I didn't know how I was going to pay, and then Darrow comes home one day with the medicine, won't say how he got it. But several weeks later I saw one of the Grays checking the time with that old watch."

I look at my hands, but I feel Mustang's eyes on me.

"I think it's time for bed," mother says. Narol and Kieran protest until she clears her throat and stands. She kisses me on the head, lingering longer than she usually would. Then she touches Mustang's shoulder and limps from the room with my brother's help. Narol's men go with them.

"She's quite a woman," Kavax says. "And she loves you very much."

"I'm glad you met like this," I say to him, then to Mustang, "Especially you."

"How's that?" she asks.

"Without me trying to control it. Like last time."

"Yes, I would say that was quite the disaster," Daxo says.

"This feels right," I say.

"I agree. It does." Mustang smiles. "I wish I could introduce you to mine. You would have liked her better than my father."

I return the smile, wondering what this is between us. Dreading the idea of having to define it. There's an easiness that comes with being around her. But I'm afraid to ask her what she's thinking. Afraid to broach the subject for fear of shattering this little illusion of peace. Kavax awkwardly clears his throat, dissolving the moment.

"So the meeting with Dancer didn't go well?" I ask.

"I fear not," Daxo says. "The resentment he harbors runs deep. Theodora was more forthcoming, but Dancer was . . . intransigent. Militantly so."

"He's a cypher," Mustang clarifies, taking another drink and wincing at the quality of proof. "Hoarding information from us. Wouldn't share anything I didn't already know."

"I doubt you were very forthcoming yourself."

She grimaces. "No, but I'm used to making others compensate for me. He's smart. And that means it's going to be difficult to convince him that I want our alliance to work."

"So you do."

"Thanks to your family, yes," she says. "You want to build a world for them. For your mother, for Kieran's children. I understand that. When . . . I chose to negotiate with the Sovereign I was trying to do the same thing. Protecting those I love." The Telemanuses share a glance. Her finger traces dents in the table. "I couldn't see a world without war unless we capitulated." Her eyes find my Sigil-barren hands, searching the naked flesh there as if it held the secret to all our futures. Maybe it does. "But I can see one now."

"You really mean that?" I ask. "All of you?"

"Family is all that matters," Kavax says. "And you are family." Daxo sets an elegant hand on my shoulder. Even Sophocles seems to understand the gravity of the moment, resting his chin on my foot beneath the table. "Aren't you?"

"Yes." I nod gratefully, "I am."

With a tight smile, Mustang pulls a piece of paper from her pocket and slides it to me. "That's Orion's com frequency. I don't know where they are. Probably in the belt. I gave them a simple directive: cause chaos. From what I've heard from Gold chatter, they're doing just that. We'll need her and her ships if we're going take down Octavia."

"Thank you," I say to them all. "I didn't think we'd ever have a second chance."

"Nor did we," Daxo replies. "Let me be blunt with you, Darrow: there is a matter of concern. It's your plan. Your design to use claw-Drills to allow the Obsidians to invade key cities around Mars . . . we think it is a mistake."

"Really?" I ask. "Why? We need to wrest the Jackal's centers of power away, gain traction with the populace."

"Father and I do not have the same faith in the Obsidians you seem to have," Daxo says carefully. "Your intentions will matter little if you let them loose on the populace of Mars."

"Barbarians," Kavax says. "They are barbarians."

"Ragnar's sister . . ."

"Is not Ragnar," Daxo replies. "She's a stranger. And after hearing what she did to the Gold prisoners . . . we can't in good conscience join our forces to a plan that would unleash the Obsidians on the cities of Mars. The Arcos women won't either."

"I see."

"And there's another reason we think the plan flawed," Mustang says. "It doesn't deal properly with my brother. Give my brother credit. He's smarter than you. Smarter than me." Even Kavax does not contest this. "Look what he's done. If he knows how to play the game, if he knows the variables, he'll sit in a corner for days running through the possible moves, countermoves, externalities, and outcomes. That's his idea of fun. Before Claudius's death and before we were sent to live in different homes, he'd stay inside, rain or shine, and piece together puzzles, create mazes on paper and beg me over and over again to try and find the center when I came back from riding with Father or fishing with Claudius and Pax. And when I did find the center, he would laugh and say what a clever sister he had. I never thought much of it until I saw him afterward one day alone in his room when he thought no one was watching. Shrieking and hitting himself in the face, punishing himself for losing to me.

"The next time he asked me to find the center of a maze I pretended I couldn't, but he wasn't fooled. It was like he knew I'd seen him in his room. Not the introverted, but pleasant frail boy everyone else saw. The real him." She gathers her breath, shrugging away the thought. "He made me finish the maze. And when I did, he smiled, said how clever I was, and walked off.

"The next time he drew a maze, I couldn't find the center. No matter how hard I tried." She shifts uncomfortably. "He just watched me try from the floor among his pencils. Like an old evil ghost inside a little porcelain doll. That's how I remember him. It's how I see him now when I think about him killing Father."

The Telemanuses listen with a foreboding silence, as afraid of the Jackal as I am.

"Darrow, he'll never forgive you for beating him at the Institute. For making him cut off his hand. He'll never forgive me for stripping him naked and delivering him to you. We are his obsession, just as much as Octavia is, as much as Father was. So if you think he's going to just forget how Sevro waltzed into his citadel with a clawDrill and stole you from under him, you're going to get a lot of people killed. Your plan to take the cities won't work. He'll see it coming a kilometer off. And even if he doesn't, if we take Mars, this war will last for years. We need to go for the jugular."

"And not just that," Daxo says, "we need assurances that you're not aiming to begin a dictatorship, or a full-demokracy in the case of victory."

"A dictatorship," I ask with a smirk. "You really think I want to rule?"

Daxo shrugs. "Someone must."

A woman clears her throat at the door. We wheel around to see Holiday standing there with her thumbs in her belt loops. "Sorry to interrupt, sir. But the Bellona is asking for you. It seems rather important."

37

||||||||||||||||||||||

THE LAST EAGLE

Cassius lies handcuffed to the rails of the reinforced medical gurney in the center of the Sons of Ares infirmary. The same place I watched my people die from the wounds they suffered to save me from his clutches. Bed after bed of injured rebels from Phobos and other operations on the Thermic fill the expanse. Ventilators whir and beep, men cough. But it's the weight of the eyes that I feel most. Hands reach for me as I pass through the rows of cots and pallets lying on the floor. Mouths whisper my name. They want to touch my arms, to feel a human without Sigils, without the mark of the masters. I let them as well as I can, but I haven't time to visit the fringes of the room.

I asked Dancer to give Cassius a private room. Instead, he's been set smack in the middle of the main infirmary among the amputees, adjacent to the huge plastic tent that covers the burn unit. There he can watch and be watched by the lowColors and feel the weight of this war the same way they do. I sense Dancer's hand at work here. Giving Cassius equitable treatment. No cruelty, no consideration, just the same as the rest. I feel like buying the old socialist a drink.

Several of Narol's boys, a Gray and two weathered ex-Helldivers, slump on metal chairs playing cards near Cassius's bedside. Heavy scorchers slung around their backs. They jump to their feet and salute as I approach.

"Heard he's been asking for me," I say.

"Most of the night," the shorter of the Reds answers gruffly, eying Holiday behind me. "Wouldn't have bothered you . . . but he's a bloodydamn Olympic. So thought we should pass the word up the chain." He leans so close I can smell the menthol of the synth tobacco between his stained teeth. *"And the slagger says he's got information, sir."*

"Can he talk?"

"Yeah," the soldier grumbles. "Doesn't say much, but the bolt missed his box."

"I need to speak with him privately," I say.

"We got you covered, sir."

The doctor and the guards wheel Cassius's gurney to the far back of the room to the pharmacy, which they keep guarded under lock and key. Inside, among the rows of plastic medication boxes, Cassius and I are left alone. He watches me from his bed, a white bandage around his neck, the faintest pinprick of blood dilating between his Adam's apple and the jugular on the right side of his throat. "It's a miracle you're not dead," I say. He shrugs. There's no tubes in his arms or morphon bracelet. I frown. "They didn't give you painkillers?"

"Not punishment. They voted," he says very slowly, taking care not to rip the stitches on his neck. "Wasn't enough morphon to go around. Low supplies. As they tell, the patients voted last week to give the hard meds to the burn victims and amputees. I'd think it noble if they didn't moan all night from pain like lonely little puppies." He pauses. "I always wondered if mothers can hear their children weeping for them."

"Can yours?"

"I didn't weep. And I don't think my mother cares much for anything other than revenge. Whatever that means at this point."

"You said you had information?" I ask, to business because I don't know what else to say. I feel an ironclad kinship with this man. Sevro asked why I saved him, and I could aspire to notions of valor and honor. But the deepspine reason is I desperately want him to be a friend again. I crave his approval. Does that make me a fool? Disloyal? Is it the guilt speaking? Is it his magnetism? Or is it that vain part of me that just wants to be loved by the people I respect. And I do respect him. He has honor, a corrupted sort, but true honor nonetheless.

"Was it her or was it you?" he asks carefully.

"What do you mean?"

"Who kept the Obsidians from boiling out my eyes and taking my tongue? You or Virginia?"

"It was both of us."

"Liar. Didn't think she'd shoot, to tell the truth of it." He reaches up to feel his neck, but the manacles jerk his hands to a halt, startling him back into the room. "Don't suppose you could take these off? It's dreadful when you've got an itch."

"I think you'll live."

He chuckles as if saying he had to try. "So, is this where you act morally superior for saving me? For being more civilized than Gold?"

"Maybe I'm going to torture you for information," I say.

"Well, that's not exactly honorable."

"Neither is letting a man put me in a box for nine months after torturing me for three. Anyway, what the hell ever made you think I give a shit about being honorable?"

"True." He frowns, creasing his brow and looking startling, like something Michelangelo would have carved. "If you think the Sovereign will barter, you're wrong. She won't sacrifice a single thing to save me."

"Then why serve her?" I ask.

"Duty." He says the words, but I wonder how deeply he means them any longer.

In his eyes I glimpse the loneliness, the longing for a life that should have been, and the glimmer of the man he wants to be underneath the man he thinks he has to be.

"All the same," I say, "I think we've done enough evil to one another. I'm not going to torture you. Do you have information or are we just going to dance around it for another ten minutes?"

"Have you wondered yet why the Sovereign was suing for peace, Darrow? Surely it must have crossed your mind. She's not one to dilute punishment unless she must. Why would she show leniency to Virginia? To the Rim? Her fleets outnumber those of the Moon Lord rebels three to one. The Core is better supplied. Romulus can't match Roque. You know how good he is. So why would the Sovereign send us to negotiate? Why compromise?"

"I already know she wanted to replace the Jackal," I say. "And she can't very well have a full-scale rebellion on the Rim while trying to cuff his ears and fight the Sons of Ares. She's trying to limit her theaters of war so she can focus all her weight on one problem at a time. It's not a complicated strategy."

"But do you know why she wanted to remove him?"

"My escape, the camps, the disruptions in helium processing . . . I could list a hundred reasons why installing a psychopath as Arch-Governor could prove burdensome."

"All those are valid," he says, interrupting. "Convincing, even. And they are the reasons we provided Virginia."

I step back toward him, hearing the implication in his voice. "What didn't you tell her?" He hesitates, as if wondering even now if he should tell me. Eventually, he does.

"Earlier this year, our intelligence agents discovered discrepancies between the quarterly helium production logs reported to the Department of Energy and the Department of Mine Management and the yield reports from our agents in mining colonies themselves. We found at least one hundred and twenty-five instances where the Jackal falsely reported helium losses due to Sons of Ares disruption. Disruptions which didn't exist. He also claimed fourteen mines destroyed by Sons of Ares attacks. Attacks which never happened."

"So he's skimming off the top," I say with a shrug. "Hardly the first corrupt ArchGovernor in the worlds."

"But he's *not* reselling it on the market," Cassius says. "He's creating artificial shortages while he stockpiles."

"Stockpiles? How much so far?" I ask tensely.

"With the surplus inventory from the fourteen mines and the Martian Reserve? At this rate, in two years he'll have more than the Imperial Reserves on Luna and Venus and the War Reserve on Ceres combined."

"That could mean a hundred things," I say quietly, realizing just how much fuel that is. Three quarters of the most valuable substance in the worlds. All under the control of one man. "He's making a play for Sovereign. Buying Senators?"

"Forty so far," Cassius admits. "More than we thought he had. But there's another kink which he's involved them in." He tries to sit up straighter in his cot, but the manacles around his hands anchor him to a half-slouched pose. "I'm going to ask you a question, and I need you to tell me the truth." I'd laugh at the idea if I didn't see how serious he is. "Did the Sons of Ares rob a deep space asteroid warehouse in March, several days after your escape? About four months ago?"

"Be more specific," I say.

"A minor main belter in the Karin Cluster. Designation S-1988. Silicate-based junk asteroid. Nearly zero mining potential. Specific enough?"

I reviewed the entirety of Sevro's tactical operations when I was making my recovery with Mickey. There were several assaults on Legion military bases within the asteroid belts, but nothing remotely like what Cassius is talking about.

"No. There were no operations on S-1988 that I know of."

"*Gorydamn,*" he mutters under his breath. "Then we judged right."

"What was in the warehouse?" I ask. "Cassius . . ."

"Five hundred nuclear warheads," he says darkly.

The blood on his bandage has spread to the size of a gaping mouth.

"Five hundred," I echo, my own voice a distant, hollow thing. "What was their yield?"

"Thirty megatons each."

"World killers . . . Cassius, why would they even exist?"

"In case the Ash Lord ever had to repeat Rhea," Cassius says. "The depot lies between the Core and the Rim."

"Repeat Rhea . . . that's who you serve?" I ask. "A woman who stores enough nuclear warheads to destroy a planet, just in case."

He ignores my tone. "All evidence pointed to Ares, but the Sovereign thought it gave Sevro too much credit. She had Moira investigate it personally, and she was able to trace the tags of the hijacker's ship to a defunct shipping line formerly owned by Julii Industries. If the Sons truly didn't steal them, then the Jackal has the weapons. But we don't know what he's doing with them." I stand there, numb. Mind racing to piece together how the Jackal might utilize so many atomics. According to the Compact, the Martian military is only permitted twenty in its arsenal, for ship-to-ship warfare. All under five megatons.

"If this is true, why would you tell me?" I ask.

"Because Mars is my home too, Darrow. My family has been there as long as yours. My mother is still there in our home. Whatever the Jackal's long-term strategy is, the judgment of the Sovereign is that he will use the weapons here if his back is to the wall."

"You're afraid we might win," I realize.

"When it was Sevro's war, no. The Sons of Ares was doomed. But now? Look what's happening." He looks me up and down. "We've lost containment. Octavia doesn't know where I am. Whether or not Aja is alive. She has no eyes on this. The Jackal might know she tried to betray him to his sister. He's a wild dog. If you provoke him, he will bite." He lowers his voice. "You might be able to survive that, Darrow, but can Mars?"

38

||||||||||||||||||||||||||

THE BILL

"Five hundred nuclear warheads?" Sevro whispers. "*Holy bloodydamn shit*. Tell me you're joking. Go on."

Dancer sits quietly at the warroom table, kneading his temples.

"It's bullshit," Holiday grunts from the wall. "If he has them, he'd have used them."

"Let's leave the deductions to the individuals who have actually met the man, shall we?" Victra says. "Adrius doesn't function like a normal human."

"That's for damn sure," Sevro says.

"Still, it is a solid question," Dancer says, annoyed at the presence of so many Golds, particularly Mustang who stands beside me. "If he has them, why hasn't he used them?"

"Because that sort of escalation will hurt him almost as much as it hurts us," I say. "And if he uses them, the Sovereign will have every excuse to replace him."

"Or he doesn't have them," Quicksilver says dismissively. He floats before us, blue holoPixels shimmering over a display panel. "It's a ploy. Bellona knows what you care about, Darrow. He's plucking your heartstrings with notions of oblivion. It's bullshit. My techs would have seen major ripples if he was moving missiles. And I would have heard about plutonium enriching if the Sovereign had them built."

"Unless they're old missiles," I say. "Lots of relics lying about."

"And it's a big solar system," Mustang says evenly.

"I've got big ears," Quicksilver replies.

"Had," Victra says. "They're whittling them down as we speak."

The leaders of the rebellion sit in a semicircle in front of a holoprojector which displays asteroid S-1988. It's a barren hunk of rock, part of the Karin subfamily of the Koronis Family of asteroids in the Main Belt between Mars and Jupiter. The Koronis asteroids are the base for heavy mining operations by an Earth-run energy consortium and home to several disreputable astral way stations for smugglers and pirates, most notably 208 Lacrimosa, where Sevro refueled on his journey from Pluto to Mars. The locals call the smuggler's cove Our Lady of Sorrows, where life is cheaper than a kilo of iced helium and a gram of demonDust, or so he says. He's unusually quiet about the place and his time there.

Gold warroom meetings are held in circles or rectangles because people facing one another are more likely to engage in intellectual conflict than people sitting side by side. Golds relish that. I'm trying a different tack, having my friends face the problem—the holoprojector, so if they want to argue with one another, they have to crane their necks to do it.

"It's a shame we don't have the Sovereign's oracles," Mustang says. "Strap one on his wrist and see how forthcoming Cassius really is."

"Sorry we don't quite have the resources you're used to, *domina*," Dancer says.

"That's not what I meant."

"We could torture him," Sevro says. He's in the middle of the table cleaning his fingernails with a blade. Victra leans against the wall behind him, flinching in annoyance with each flake of nail that falls onto the table. Dancer is to Sevro's left. The meter-tall hologram of Quicksilver glows to his right, between us. Having declared Phobos a free city on behalf of the Rising, he functions as its Governor and now hunches over a small stack of thumb-sized heart oysters with a platinum octopus shucking knife, arranging the shells in five even mounds. If he's nervous about the Jackal's reprisals against his station, he doesn't look it. Sefi sweats underneath her tribal furs as she stalks along the perimeter of the table like a trapped animal, making Dancer shift in agitation.

"You want the truth?" Sevro asks. "Just give me seventeen minutes and a screwdriver."

"Should we really be having this talk with her here?" Victra asks of Mustang.

"She's on our side," I say.

"Are you sure?" Dancer asks.

"She was crucial to recruiting the Obsidians," I say. "She's connected us with Orion." I made contact with the woman after speaking with Cassius. She's burning hard with the *Pax* and a sizable remnant of my old fleet to meet me. Seems impossible I'd ever see the ornery Blue again, or that ship which was the first place to feel like home since Lykos. "Because of Mustang, we'll have a real navy. She preserved my command. She kept Orion at the helm. Would she have done that if she didn't have the same aims as us?"

"Which are?" Dancer asks.

"Defeating Lune and the Jackal," she says.

"That's just the surface of what we want," Dancer says.

"She's working with us," I stress.

"For now," Victra says. "She's a clever girl. Maybe she wants to use us to eliminate her enemies? Place herself in a position of power. Maybe she wants Mars. Maybe she wants more." Seems only yesterday my council of Golds was discussing whether or not Victra was worth trusting. Roque spoke up for her when no one else would. The irony is apparently lost on Victra. Or maybe she remembers Mustang's vocal distrust of her intentions a year ago and has decided to repay the old debt.

"I hate to agree with the Julii," Dancer says, "but she's right in this. Augustans are players. Not one's been born that hasn't been." Apparently Dancer wasn't impressed with Mustang's lack of transparency earlier. Mustang expected this. In fact, she asked to stay in her room, away from this so she wouldn't detract from my plan. But in order for this to work, in order for there to be some way to piece things together in the end, there must be cooperation.

They expect me to defend Mustang, which shows how little they know her.

"You are all being rather illogical," Mustang says. "I don't mean that as an insult, but simply as a statement of fact. If I meant you ill, I would have hailed the Sovereign or my brother and brought a tracking device on my ship. You know what lengths she would go to in order to find Tinos." My friends exchange troubled glances. "But I didn't. I know you will not trust me. But you trust Darrow and he trusts me, and since he knows me better than any of you do, I think he's in the best position to make the call. So stop whimpering like gorydamn children and let's be about the task, eh?"

"If you have a buzzsaw I could do it in around three minutes. . . ." Sevro says.

"Will you shut the hell up?" Dancer barks at him. It's the first time I've ever seen him lose his temper. "A man will lie through his teeth, say whatever you want to hear if you're pulling off his toenails. It doesn't work." He was tortured himself by the Jackal. Just like Evey and Harmony were.

Sevro crosses his arms. "Well, that's an unfair and massive generalization, Gramps."

"We don't torture," Dancer says. "That's final."

"Oh, yeah, right," Sevro says. "We're the good guys. Good guys never torture. And always win. But how many good guys get their heads put in boxes? How many get to watch their friends' spines cut in half?"

Dancer looks to me for help. "Darrow. . . ."

Quicksilver pops open an oyster. "Torture can be effective if done correctly with confirmable information in a narrow scope. Like any tool, it is not a panacea; it must be used properly. Personally, I don't really think we have the luxury of drawing moral lines in the sand. Not today. Let Barca have a go. Pulls some nails. Some eyes if need be."

"I agree," Theodora says, surprising the council.

"What about Matteo?" I ask Quicksilver. "Sevro shattered his face."

Quicksilver's knife slips on the new oyster, punching into the meat of his palm. He winces and sucks at the blood. "And if he hadn't have passed out he would have told you where I was. From my experience, pain is the best negotiator."

"I agree with them, Darrow," Mustang says. "We have to be certain he's telling the truth. Otherwise we're letting him dictate our strategy—which is classic counterintelligence on his part. It's what you would do." And it's what I tried to do till the torture started with the Jackal.

Victra, who has been silent on the issue till now, walks abruptly around the table into the holo projection so that black space and stars play across her skin. Jagged white-blond hair drifts in front of angry eyes as she pulls her gray shirt off. She's muscled and lithe beneath and wears a compression bra. A half dozen razor scars stretch three inches at a diagonal across her flat belly. There's more than a dozen on her sword arm. A few on her face, neck, clavicle.

"Some I'm proud of," she says of the scars. "Some I'm not." She turns to show us her lower back. It's a waxy melted swath of flesh where her sister left her mark in acid. She turns back to us, raising her chin in defiance. "I came here because I didn't have a choice. I stayed when I did. Don't make me regret that."

It's startling to see the vulnerability in her. I don't think Mustang would ever let her guard down in public like this. Sevro stares intensely at the tall woman as she tugs her shirt back on and turns back to the holo. She reaches for the asteroid with both hands to stretch the hologram. "Can we get better resolution?" she asks as if the matter is settled.

"The picture was taken by a Census Bureau drone," I say. "Nearly seventy years ago. We don't have access to the current Society military records."

"My men are on it," Quicksilver says. "But they're not optimistic. We're fighting a legion of Society counterattacks right now. Gory-damn maelstrom."

"This is when having your father around would come in handy," Sevro says to Mustang.

"He never mentioned anything like this to me," she replies.

"Mother did, once," Victra says thoughtfully. "Antonia and I. Something about nasty little goody bags that Imperators could collect on the fly if the Rim went off the tracks."

"That matches with what Cassius says."

She turns back to us. "Then I think Cassius is telling the truth."

"So do I," I say to the group. "And torturing him doesn't resolve anything. Cut off his fingers one by one, and what if he still says it's true? Do we keep cutting until he says it's not? Either way it's a gamble." I get a few reluctant nods and feel relief that at least one battle's won, if a little wary knowing how savage my friends can become.

"What did he suggest we do?" Dancer asks. "I'm sure he had a proposal."

"He wants me to have a holoconference with the Sovereign," I say.

"Why?"

"To discuss an alliance against the Jackal. They give us intel, we kill him before he can detonate any bombs," I say. "That's his plan."

Sevro giggles. "Sorry. But that would be bloodydamn fun to watch." He pulls up his left hand and makes a talking motion with it. " 'Hello, you old rusty bitch, you recall when I kidnaped your grandchild?' " He pulls up his right hand. " 'Why yes, my goodman. Just after I enslaved your entire race.' " He shakes his head. "No purpose in talking to that Pixie. Not until we're knocking on her doorstep with a fleet. You should send me and the Howlers after good old Jackal. Can't press a button without a head."

"The Valkyrie will attend this mission with the Howlers," Sefi says.

"No. The Jackal will invite a personal attack," I say, glancing at Mustang, who has already warned me off that course. "He knows us too well to be surprised by things we've done in the past. I'm not throwing lives away by playing into his understanding of our strengths."

"Do you have anyone inside his inner circle, Regulus?" Dancer asks Quicksilver. Surprisingly, the two men seem to rather like one another.

"I did. Until your Grays broke Darrow out. Adrius had his chief of intelligence purge his inner circle. My men are all dead or imprisoned or scared shitless."

"What do you think, Augustus?" Dancer asks Mustang.

All eyes turn to her. She takes her time in replying.

"I think the reason you've managed to stay alive so long is because Golds are so consumed with the individual ego that they've forgotten how they conquered Earth. Each thinks they can rule. With Orion returning and Sevro's gains, your greatest strength now lies with your navy and an Obsidian army. Don't help the Sovereign. She is still the most dangerous enemy. You help her, she focuses on you. Sow more seeds of discord."

Dancer nods in agreement. "But are we sure the Jackal would actually use the nukes on the planet?"

"The only thing my brother ever wanted was my father's approval. He did not get it. So he killed my father. Now he wants Mars. What do you think he'll do if he doesn't get it?"

A menacing silence fills the room.

"I have a new plan," I say.

"I should bloodydamn hope so," Sevro mutters to Victra. "Do I get to hide inside anything?"

"I'm sure we can find something for you, darling," she says.

I nod my agreement.

He waves a hand. "Well, then let's hear it, Reaper."

"Hypothetically, assume we take half the cities of Mars," I say, standing and summoning a graphic from the table that shows a red tide flowing over the globe of Mars, claiming cities, pushing back the Golds. "Say we crush the Jackal's fleet in orbit when Orion joins us, even though we are outnumbered two to one. Say we shatter his armies. With the Valkyrie's help, we fracture the Obsidians away from the legions and have them join us, and we have a groundswell from the populace itself. The machines of industry grind to a complete halt on Mars. We've rebuffed the Society's countless reinforcements and we have insurrection in every street and we have cornered the Jackal after years of warfare. And it *will* take years. What happens then?"

"The machines of industry don't stop off of Mars," Victra says.

"They keep rolling. And they'll keep pumping men and materiel here."

"Or . . . ," I say.

"He uses the bombs," Dancer says.

"Which I also believe he'll use on the Obsidians and our army if we go ahead with operation Rising Tide," I say.

"We've been prepping the operation for months," Dancer protests. "With the Obsidians it might just work. You just want to scrap it?"

"Yes," I say. "This planet is why we fight. The strength of rebel armies throughout history is that they have less to protect. They can rove and move and are impossible to pin down. We have so much to lose here. So much to protect. This war won't be won in days or weeks. It will be a decade. Mars will bleed. And at the end, ask yourselves: What will we inherit? A corpse of what was once our home. We must fight this war, but I will not fight it here. I propose we leave Mars."

Quicksilver coughs. "Leave Mars?"

Sefi steps forward from the shadows of the stone room. "You said you would protect my people."

"Our strength is here, in the tunnels," Dancer continues. "In our population. That's where our responsibility lies, Darrow." He glances at Mustang, his suspicions clear. "Don't forget where you come from. Why you're doing this."

"I have not forgotten, Dancer."

"Are you so sure? This war is for Mars."

"It's for more than that," I say.

"For lowColors," he continues, voice gaining volume. "Win here and then spread across the Society. It's where the helium is. It is the heart of the Society, of Red. Win here, then spread. That's how Ares intended it."

"This war is for everyone," Mustang corrects.

"No," Dancer says territorially. "This is our war, Gold. I was fighting it when you were still learning how to enslave human beings at your . . ."

Sevro looks at me in annoyance as our friends descend into bickering. I give him a little nod and he pulls his razor and slams it into the table. It cuts halfway through and trembles there. "Reaper's trying to speak, you shitgobblers. Besides all this Colorism bores me." He looks around, terribly pleased with the silence. He nods to himself and waves a theatrical hand. "Reaper, please, continue. You were getting to the exciting part."

"Thank you, Sevro. I won't fall into the trap of the Jackal," I say. "The easiest way to lose any war is to let the enemy dictate the terms of engagement. We must do the thing the Jackal and the Sovereign least expect of us. Create our own paradigm so they're playing *our* game. Reacting to *our* decisions. We must be bold. Right now we've sparked a fire. Rebellions in almost all Society territories. We stay here, that means we are contained. I will not be contained."

I transfer the image on my datapad to the table so that the hologram of Jupiter floats in the air. Sixty-three tiny moons dot the periphery but the four great Jovian moons dominate its orbit. These four largest—Ganymede, Callisto, Io, and Europa—are referred to collectively as Ilium. Around those moons are two of the largest fleets in the Solar System, that of the Moon Lords, and that of the Sword Armada. Sevro looks so pleased he might faint.

I'm giving him the war he didn't even know he wanted.

"The civil war between Bellona and Augustus has exposed larger fault lines between the Core and the Outer Rim. Octavia's main fleet, the Sword Armada, is hundreds of millions of kilometers away from its nearest support. Excepting the Sceptre Armada around Luna it is the greatest weapon Octavia has. Octavia sent our good friend Roque au Fabii to bring the Moon Lords to heel. He has shattered every fleet that has been thrown against them, even with the help of Mustang, the Telemanuses, and the Arcoses, he has beaten the Rim down. On board these ships are more than two million men and women. More than ten thousand Obsidian. Two hundred thousand Grays. Three thousand of the greatest killers alive, Peerless Scarred. Praetors, Legates, knights, squad commanders. The greatest Golds of their Institutes. This fleet has been reinforced by Antonia au Severus-Julii. And it is the instrument of fear by which the Sovereign binds the planets to her will. It, like its commander, has never been defeated." I pause, allowing the words to sink in so they all know the gravity of my proposal.

"In forty days we're going to destroy the Sword Armada and rip the beating heart out of the Society war machine." I pull Sevro's razor out of the table and toss it back to him. "Now, I'll take your bloody-damn questions."

39

||||||||||||||||||||||||

THE HEART

Dancer finds me as I make final preparations to board the shuttle with Sevro and Mustang that will take us to the fleet in orbit. Tinos swarms with activity. Hundreds of shuttles and transports gathered by Dancer and his Sons of Ares leadership depart through the great tunnels to make their migration toward the South Pole, where they will still ferry the Obsidian young and old from their home to the safety of the mines, but the warriors will go to orbit to join my fleet. In twenty-four hours, they will move eight hundred thousand human beings in the greatest effort in Sons of Ares history. It makes me smile thinking how much happier Fitchner would be knowing the greatest endeavor of his legacy was to save lives instead of to take them.

After covering the evacuation with the fleet, I will burn hard for Jupiter. Dancer and Quicksilver will remain behind to continue what they started and hold the Jackal on Mars till the next evolution of the plan begins.

"It's haunting, isn't it," Dancer says, watching the sea of blue engine flares that flow past our stalactite up to the great tunnel in the ceiling of Tinos. Victra stands closely with Sevro at the edge of the open hangar, two dark silhouettes watching the hope of two peoples float away into the darkness. "The Red Armada goes to war," Dancer breathes. "Never thought I'd see the day."

"Fitchner should be here," I reply.

"Yes, he should," Dancer grimaces. "It's my greatest regret, I think. That he couldn't live to see his son wear his helm. And you become what he always knew you to be."

"And what's that?" I ask, watching a Red Howler jump twice with his gravBoots and rocket off the edge of the hangar to enter the open cargo hatch of a passing troop carrier.

"Someone who believes in the people," he says delicately.

I turn to face Dancer, glad that he's sought me out in my last moments here among my kin. I don't know if I'll ever return. And if I do, I fear he will see me as a different man. One who betrayed him, our people, Eo's dream. I've been here before. Saying goodbye on a landing pad. Harmony stood with him then, Matteo too as they said goodbye on that spire in Yorkton. How can I feel so melancholy for so terrible a past? Maybe that's just the nature of us, ever wishing for things that were and could be rather than things that are and will be.

It takes more to hope than to remember.

"Do you think the Moon Lords will really help us?" he asks.

"No. The trick will be making them think they're helping themselves. Then getting out before they turn on us."

"It's a risk, boy, but you like those, don't you?"

I shrug. "It's also the only chance we have."

Boots clomp on the metal deck behind me. Holiday moves past up the ramp carrying a bag of gear with several new Howlers. Life moves on, carrying me with it. It's been nearly seven years since Dancer and I met, yet it seems thirty on him. How many decades of war has he faced? How many friends has he said goodbye to that I've never known, that he's never even mentioned? People who he loved as much as I love Sevro and Ragnar. He had a family once, though he rarely speaks of them now.

We all had something once. We're each robbed and broken in our own way. That's why Fitchner formed this army. Not to piece us together, but to save himself from the abyss his wife's death opened in him. He needed a light. And he made it. Love was his shout into the wind. Same with my wife.

"Lorn once told me if he had been my father he would have raised me to be a good man. 'There's no peace for great men,' he said." I smile at the memory. "I should have asked him who he thinks makes the peace for all those good men."

"You *are* a good man," Dancer tells me.

My hands are scarred and brutal things. When I clench them their knuckles turn that familiar shade of white.

"Yeah?" I grin. "Then why do I want to do bad things?" He laughs at that, and I surprise him by pulling him into a hug. His good arm wraps around my hips. His head barely coming to my chest. "Sevro might've worn the helmet, but you're the heart here," I tell him. "You always have been. You're too humble to see it, but you're as great a man as Ares himself. And somehow, you're still good. Unlike that dirty rat bastard." I pull back and thump his chest. "And I love you. Just so you know."

"Oh, bloodydamn," he mutters, eyes tearing up. "I thought you were a killer. You gone soft on me, boy?"

"Never," I say, winking.

He pushes me off. "Go say goodbye to your mother before you go."

I leave him to shout at a group of Sons marines and work my way through the bustle, bumping fists with Pebble who Screwface pushes on a wheelchair toward a boarding ramp, tossing a salute to Sons of Ares I recognize, talking shit back to Uncle Narol who walks with a troop of Pitvipers. They're destined for a sabotage mission against the Jackal's deep space communication relays. My mother and Mustang stop talking abruptly when I arrive. Both look distraught.

"What's the matter?" I ask.

"Just saying goodbye," Mustang says.

My mother steps close to me. "Dio brought this from Lykos." She opens a little plastic box and shows me the dirt inside. My little mother smiles up at me. "You fly into night, and when all grows dark, remember who you are. Remember you are never alone. The hopes and dreams of our people go with you. Remember home." She pulls me down to kiss my forehead. "Remember you are loved." I hug her tight and pull back to see she has tears in her hard eyes.

"I'll be all right, Ma," I say.

"I know. I know you don't think you deserve to be happy," she says. "But you do, child. You deserve it more than anyone I know. So do what you need to do, then come home to me." She takes my hand and Mustang's. "Both of you come home. Then start living."

I leave her behind, confused and emotional. "What was that about?" I ask Mustang. Mustang looks at me as if I should know.

"She's afraid."

"Why?"

"She's your mother."

I walk up my shuttle's landing pad, with Sevro and Victra who join Mustang and I at the bottom. "Helldiver . . ." Dancer shouts before we reach the top. I turn back to find the gnarled man with his fist thrust in the air. And behind him the whole of the stalactite hangar watches me, hundreds of deckhands on mechanized loading trams, pilots, Blue and Red and Green, who stand at the ramps of their ships or on the ladders leading into their cockpits, helmets in hands, platoons of Grays and Reds and Obsidians standing side by side carrying combat gear and supplies—the scythe sewn onto shoulders, painted onto faces—as they board shuttles bound for my fleet. Men and women of Mars, all. Fighting for something larger than themselves. For our planet, for their people. I feel the weight of their love. I feel the hopes of all those people in bondage who watched as the Sons of Ares rose to take Phobos. We promised them something, and now we must deliver. One by one, my army raises their hands till a sea of fists clench as Eo's did when she held the haemanthus and fell before Augustus.

Chills run through me as Sevro and Victra and Mustang and even my mother raise their hands in union. "Break the chains," Dancer bellows. I raise my own scarred fist and step silently into the shuttle to join the Red Armada as it sails to war.

40

||||||||||||||||||||||||

YELLOW SEA

The Yellow Sea of Io rolls in around my black boots. Great dunes of sulfur-laced sand with razorback ridges of silicate rock as far as the eye can see. In the steel blue sky, the marbled surface of Jupiter undulates. One hundred and thirty times the diameter that Luna appears from the surface of Earth, it seems the vast and evil head of a marble god. War grips its sixty-seven moons. Cities hunker under pulseShields. Blackened husks of men in starShells litter moons while fighter squadrons duel and hunt troop and supply transports among the faint ice rings of the gas giant.

It's quite a sight.

I stand upon the dune flanked by Sefi and five Valkyrie in black pulseArmor waiting for the Moon Lord's shuttle. Our assault ship sits behind us, engines idling. It's shaped like a hammerhead shark. Dark gray. But the Valkyrie and Red dockworkers painted its head together on our journey from Mars, giving the ship two bulging blue eyes and a gaping mouth with ravenous bloodstained teeth. Up between the eyes, Holiday lies on her belly, sniper rifle scanning the rock formations to the south.

"Anything?" I ask, voice crackling through the breathing mask.

"Nothin'," Sevro says over the com. He and Clown scout the little settlement two clicks away on gravBoots. I can't see them with the naked eye. I fidget with my slingBlade.

"They'll come," I say. "Mustang set the time and place."

Io is a strange moon. Innermost and smallest of the four great Galilean moons, she is a belt-notch larger than Luna. It was never her destiny to be fully changed by the Golds' terraforming machines. She's a hell Dante could be proud of. The driest object in the Sol System, rife with explosive volcanism and sulfur deposits and interior tidal heating. Her surface a canvas of yellow and orange plains broken by huge thrust faults from her shifting surface. Dramatic sheer cliffs rising from the sulfur dunes to scrape the sky.

Huge stains of concentric green freckle her equatorial regions. Finding crops and animals difficult to cultivate so far from the sun, the Society Engineering Corp covered millions of acres of Io's surface with pulseFields, imported dirt and water for three lifetimes on cosmos-Haulers, thickened the planet's atmosphere to filter Jupiter's massive radiation, and used the planet's interior tidal heating to power great generators to grow foodstuffs for the entire Jupiter orbit and exportation to the Core and, more important, the Rim. She's a farm deck with the biggest breadbasket between Mars and Uranus with easy gravity and cheap land.

Guess who did all the labor.

Beyond the pulseFields is the Sulfur Sea stretching from pole to pole, interrupted only by volcanoes and lakes of magma.

I may not like Io. But I can respect the people of this land. Ionian men and women are not like humans of Earth or Luna or Mercury or Venus. They are harder, lither, eyes slightly larger to absorb the dimmed light six hundred million kilometers from the sun, skin pale, taller, and able to withstand higher doses of radiation. These people believe themselves most like the Iron Golds who conquered Earth and put man at peace for the first time in her history.

I shouldn't have worn black today. My gloves, my cloak, my jacket underneath. I thought we were going to the anti-Jupiter side of Io where sulfur dioxide snowfields crust the planet. But the Moon Lord's operation team demanded a new meeting point at the last moment, setting us on the edge of the Sulfur Sea. Temperature 120 Celsius.

Sefi walks up to stand beside me with her new optics scanning the yellow horizon. She and her Valkyrie have taken quickly to the gear of war, studying and training day and night with Holiday during our month and a half journey to Jupiter. Practicing ship-boarding and energy weapon tactics as well as Gray hand signals.

"How's the heat?" I ask.

"Strange," she says. Only her face can feel it. The rest benefits from the cooling systems in the armor. "Why would people live here?"

"We live everywhere we can."

"But Golds choose," she says. "Yes?"

"Yes."

"I would be wary of men who choose such a home. The spirits here are cruel." Sand kicks up from the wind in the low gravity, floating down in wavering columns. It's Sefi who Mustang thinks I should be wary of. On our voyage to Jupiter, she has watched hundreds of hours of holofootage. Learning our history as a people. I keep track of her datapad's activity. But what concerns Mustang isn't that Sefi is fond of rain forest videos and experientials, but that she has spent countless hours watching holos of our wars, particularly the nuclear annihilation of Rhea. I wonder what she makes of it.

"Sound advice, Sefi," I reply. "Sound advice."

Sevro lands dramatically before us, spraying us with sand. His ghostCloak ripples away. "Bloodydamn shithole."

I dust off my face, annoyed. He was incorrigible the whole journey out here. Laughing, pulling pranks, and slipping off to Victra's room whenever he thought no one was looking. Ugly little man's in love. And for what it's worth, it seems to go both ways. "What do you think?" I ask.

"The whole place smells like farts."

"That your professional assessment?" Holiday asks over the com.

"Yup. There's a Waygar settlement over the ridge." His Howler wolf pelt kicks in the wind, jingling the little chains that connect it to his armor. "Buncha Red hunched goggle heads carting distillation gear."

"You've scanned the sand?" I ask.

"Ain't my first slag, boss. I don't like this face-to-face bullshit, but it looks clear." He glances at his datapad. "Thought Moonies were supposed to be punctual. Pricklicks are thirty minutes late."

"Probably cautious. Must think we've air support," I say.

"Yeah. Because we'd be bloodydamn shitbrains for not bringing some."

"Roger that," Holiday says in agreement over the com.

"Why would I need air support when I've got you," I say, gesturing to Sevro's gravBoots. A plastic gray case sits on the ground behind him. Inside, a *sarrissa* missile launcher in foam padding. The same Ragnar used on Cassius's craft. If the need arises I've got myself a psychotic Goblin-sized fighter jet.

"Mustang said they'll be here," I say.

"Mustang said they'll be here," Sevro mocks in childish voice. "They better. Fleet can't squat for long out there without being spotted."

My fleet waits with Orion in orbit since Mustang took her shuttle to Nessus, the capital of Io. Fifty torchShips and destroyers hunkered down, shields off, engines dark on the barren moon of Sinope as the larger fleets of the Golds swim through space closer in to the Galilean Moons. Any closer and the Gold sensors will pick us up. But as it hides, my fleet is vulnerable. With one pass a measly squadron of rip-Wings could destroy it.

"The Moonies will come," I say. But I'm not sure of it.

They're a cold, proud, insular people, these Jovian Golds. Roughly eight thousand Peerless Scarred call the Galilean Moons of Jupiter home. Their Institutes are all out here. And it is only Societal service or vacations for the wealthiest among them that takes them to the Core. Luna might be the ancestral home of their people, but it's alien to most of them. Metropolitan Ganymede is the center of their world.

The Sovereign knows the danger of having an independent Rim. She spoke to me of the difficulty of imposing her power across a billion kilometers of empire. Her true fear was never Augustus and Bellona destroying one another. It was the chance that the Rim would rebel and cut the Society in half. Sixty years ago, at the beginning of her reign, she had the Ash Lord nuke Saturn's moon, Rhea, when its ruler refused to accept her authority. That example held for sixty years.

But nine days after my Triumph, the children of the Moon Lords who were kept on Luna in the Sovereign's court as insurance toward their parents' political cooperation, escaped. They were assisted by Mustang's spies which she left behind in the Citadel. Two days after that, the heirs of the fallen ArchGovernor Revus au Raa, who was killed at my Triumph, stole or destroyed the entirety of the Societal Garrison Fleet in its dock at Calisto. They declared Io's independence and pressured the other more populous and powerful moons into joining them.

Soon after, the infamously charismatic Romulus au Raa was elected Sovereign of the Rim. Saturn and Uranus joined soon after that, and the Second Moon Rebellion began sixty years, two hundred and eleven days after the first.

The Moon Lords obviously expected the Sovereign would find herself mired on Mars for a decade, maybe longer. Add to that a certain lowColor insurrection in the Core and one can see why they assumed she would not be able to devote the resources needed to send a fleet of sufficient size six hundred million kilometers to quash their nascent rebellion. They were wrong.

"We've got inbound," Pebble says from her station at the shuttle's sensor boards. "Three ships. Two-ninety clicks out."

"Finally," Sevro mutters. "Here come the bloodydamn Moonies."

Three warships emerge from the heat mirage on the horizon. Two black *sarpedon*-class fighters painted with the four-headed white dragon of Raa clutching a Jovian thunderbolt in its talons escort a fat tan *priam*-class shuttle. The ship lands before us. Dust swirls and the ramp unfurls from the belly of the craft. Seven lithe forms, taller and lankier than I, walk down into the sand. Golds all. They wear kryll, organic breathing masks made by Carvers, over nose and mouths. Looks like the shed skin of a locust, legs stretching to either ear. Their tan combat gear is lighter than Core armor and complimented with brightly colored scarves. Long-barreled railguns with personalized ivory stocks are strapped to their backs. Razors hang from their hips. Orange optics cover their eyes. And on their feet are skippers. Light-weight boots that use condensed air instead of gravity to move their user. Skipping them over the ground like stones on a lake. Can't get much height, but you can move nearly sixty kilometers an hour. They're about a quarter the weight of my boots, have battery life for a year, and are dead cold on thermal vision.

These are assassins. Not knights. Holiday recognizes the different breed of danger.

"She's not with them," she says over her com. "Any Telemanuses?"

"No," I say. "Hold. I see her."

Mustang steps out of the craft, joining the much-taller Ionians. She's dressed like them, except without a rifle. Joined by another Io-nian woman, this one with the forward hunching shoulders of a chee-tah, Mustang joins us atop the dune. The rest of the Ionians stay near the ship. Not a threat, just an escort.

"Darrow," Mustang says. "Sorry we're late."

"Where's Romulus?" I ask.

"He's not coming."

"Bullshit," Sevro hisses. "I told you, Reap."

"Sevro, it's fine," Mustang says. "This is his sister, Vela."

The tall woman stares down her smashed-flat nose at us. Her skin is pale, body adapted for the low gravity. It's hard to see her face past the mask and goggles, but she seems in her early fifties. Her voice is one even note. "I send my brother's greetings, and welcome, Darrow of Mars. I am Legate Vela au Raa." Sefi slinks around us, examining the alien Gold and the strange gear she carries. I like the way people talk when Sefi circles. Seems a little more honest.

"Well met, *legatus*." I nod cordially. "Will you be speaking for your brother? I'd hoped to make my case in person."

The skin to the side of her goggles crinkles. "No one speaks for my brother. Not even I. He wishes for you to join him at his private home on the Wastes of Karrack."

"So you can lure us into a trap?" Sevro asks. "Better idea. How 'bout you tell your bitch of a brother to honor his bloodydamn agreement before I take that rifle and shove it so far up your farthole you look like a skinny Pixie shish kebab?"

"Sevro, stop," Mustang says. "Not here. Not these people."

Vela watches Sefi circle. Taking note of the razor on the huge Obsidian's hip.

"I could give a shit and piss who this is. She knows who we are. And she ain't got a little trickle goin' down her leg standing toe to toe with the bloodydamn Reaper of Mars, then she's got less brains than a wad of ass lint."

"He cannot come," Vela says.

"Understandable," I reply.

Sevro makes a grotesque motion.

"What is that?" Vela asks, nodding to Sefi.

"That is a queen," I say. "Sister to Ragnar Volarus."

Vela is wary of Sefi, as well she should be. Ragnar is a name known. "She cannot come either. But I was speaking in regards to that hunk of metal you flew here on. Is it meant to be a ship?" She snorts and turns up her nose. "Built on Venus, obviously."

"It's borrowed," I say. "But if you care to make an exchange . . ."

Vela surprises me with a laugh before becoming serious once more. "If you wish to present yourself to Moon Lords as a diplomatic party, then you must show respect for my brother. And trust the honor of his hospitality."

"I've seen enough men and women set aside honor when it's inconvenient," I say probingly.

"In the Core, perhaps. This is the Rim," Vela replies. "We remember the ancestors. We remember how Iron Golds should be. We do not murder guests like that bitch on Luna. Or like that Jackal on Mars."

"Yet," I say.

Vela shrugs. "It is a choice you must make, Reaper. You have sixty seconds to decide." Vela steps away as I confer with Mustang and Sevro. I motion Sefi over.

"Thoughts?"

"Romulus would rather die than kill a guest," Mustang says. "I know you don't have any reason to trust these people. But honor actually means something to them. It's not like the Bellona who just toss the word around. Out here a Gold's word means as much as his blood."

"Do you know where the residence is?" I ask.

She shakes her head. "If I did I'd take you there myself. They've got equipment inside to check for radiation and electronic trackers. They've studied you. We'll be on our own."

"Lovely." But this isn't about tactics. No short-term game here. My big play was coming out to the Rim knowing I had leverage the Sovereign doesn't. That leverage will keep my head on my shoulders better than anyone's honor. Yet I've been wrong before, so I double-check and listen now.

"Do the rules governing treatment of guests extend to Reds?" Sevro asks. "Or just Golds? That's what we need to know."

I glance back at Vela. "It's a fair point."

"If he kills you, he kills me," Mustang says. "I'm not leaving your side. And if he does that, my men turn against him. The Telemanuses turn against him. Even Lorn's daughters-in-law will turn against him. That's nearly a third of his navy. It's a bloodfeud he can't afford."

"Sefi, what do you think?"

She closes her eyes so her blue tattoos can see the spirits of this waste. "Go."

"Give us six hours, Sevro. If we're not back by then . . ."

"Wank off in the bushes?"

"Lay waste."

"Can do." He bumps my fist with his and winks. "Happy diplomacy, kids." He keeps his fist out for Mustang. "You too horsey. We're in this shit together, eh?"

She happily bumps his knuckles with her own. "Bloodydamn right."

41

||||||||||||||||||||||

THE MOON LORD

The home of the most powerful man in the Galilean Moons is a simple, wandering place of little gardens and quiet nooks. Set in the shadow of a dormant volcano, it looks out over a yellow plain that stretches to the horizon where another volcano smolders and magma creeps westward. We set down in a small covered hangar in the side of a rock formation, one of only two ships. The other a sleek black racing craft Orion would die to fly next to a row of several dust-covered hover bikes. No one comes to service our vessel as we disembark and approach the home along a white stone walkway set into the sulfur chalk. It curves around to the side of the home. The entirety of the small property enclosed by a discreet pulseBubble.

Our escorts are at ease on the property. They file in ahead of us through the iron gate that leads to the grass courtyard into the home, removing their dust-caked skipper boots and setting them just inside the entryway beside a pair of black military boots. Mustang and I exchange a glance then remove our own. It takes me the longest to remove my bulky gravBoots. Each weighing nearly nine kilos and having three parallel latches around the boot that lock my legs in. It's oddly comforting to feel the grass between my toes. I'm conscious of the stink of my feet. Odd seeing the boots of a dozen enemies stacked by the door. Like I've walked in on something very private.

"Please wait here," Vela says to me. "Virginia, Romulus wishes to speak with you alone first."

"I'll scream if I'm in danger," I say with a grin when Mustang hesitates. She winks as she leaves to follow Vela, who noticed the subtlety of the exchange. I feel there's little the older woman misses, even less that she doesn't judge. I'm left alone in the garden with the song of a wind chime hanging from a tree above. The courtyard garden is an even rectangle. Maybe thirty paces wide. Ten deep from the front gate to the small white steps that lead into the home's front entrance. The white plaster walls are smooth and covered with thin creeping vines that wander into the home. Little orange flowers erupt from the vines and fill the air with a woodsy, burning scent.

The house rambles, rooms and gardens unfolding out from each other. There is no roof to the house. But there's little reason for one. The pulseBubble seals off the property from the weather outside. They make their own rain here. Little misters drip water from the morning's watering of the small citrus trees whose roots crack the bottom of the white stone fountain in the center of the garden. A little glance at a place like this was what led my wife to the gallows.

How strange a journey she'd think this was.

But also, in a way, how marvelous.

"You can eat a tangerine if you like," a small voice says behind me. "Father won't mind." I turn to find a child standing by another gate that leads off from the main courtyard to a path that winds around the left of the house. She might be eight years old. She holds a small shovel in her hands, and the knees of her pants are stained with dirt. Her hair is short-cropped and messy, her face pale, eyes a third again as large as any girl of Mars. You can see the tender length of her bones. Like a fresh-born colt. There's a wildness in her. I've not met many Gold children. Core Peerless families often guard them from the public eye for fear of assassination, keeping them in private estates or schools. I've heard the Rim is different. They do not kill children here. But everyone likes to pretend that they don't kill children.

"Hello," I say kindly. It's a fragile, awkward tone I haven't used since I saw my own nieces and nephews. I love children, but I feel so alien to them these days.

"You're the Martian, aren't you?" she asks, impressed.

"My name is Darrow," I reply with a nod. "What's yours?"

"I am Sera au Raa," she says proudly. "Were you really a Red? I heard my father speaking," she explains. "They think just because I don't have this"—she runs a finger along her cheek in an imaginary scar—"that I don't have ears." She nods up to the vine-covered walls and smiles mischievously. "Sometimes I climb."

"I still am a Red," I say. "It's not something I stopped being."

"Oh. You don't look like one."

She must not watch holos if she doesn't know who I am. "Maybe it's not about what I look like," I suggest. "Maybe it's about what I do."

Is that too clever a thing to say to a six-year-old? Hell if I know. She makes a disgusted face and I fear I've made a mistake.

"Have you met many Reds, Sera?"

She shakes her head. "I've only seen them in my studies. Father says it's not proper to mingle."

"Don't you have servants?"

She giggles before she realizes I'm serious. "Servants? But I haven't earned servants." She taps her face again. "Not yet." It darkens my mood to think of this girl running for her life through the woods of the Institute. Or will she be the one chasing?

"Nor will you ever earn them if you don't leave our guest alone, Seraphina," a low, husky voice says from the main entry to the house. Romulus au Raa leans against the doorframe of his home. He is a serene and violent man. My height, yet thinner with a twice broken nose. His right eye a third larger than mine set in a narrow, wrathful face. His left eyelid is crossed with a scar. A smooth globe of blue and black marble stares out at me in place of an eyeball. His full lips are pinched, the top lip bearing three more scars. His dark gold hair is long and held in a ponytail. Except for the old wounds, his skin is perfect porcelain. But it's how he seems more than how he looks that makes the man. I feel his steady way. His easy confidence, as if he's always been at the door. Always known me. It's startling how much I like him from the moment he winks at his daughter. And also how much I want him to like me, despite the tyrant I know him to be.

"So what do you make of our Martian?" he asks his daughter.

"He is thick," Seraphina says. "Larger than you, father."

"But not as large as a Telemanus," I say.

She crosses her arms. "Well, nothing is as large as a Telemanus."

I laugh. "If only that were true. I knew a man who was nearly as large to me as I am to you."

"No," Seraphina says, eyes widening. "An Obsidian?"

I nod. "His name was Ragnar Volarus. He was Stained. A prince of an Obsidian tribe from the south pole of Mars. They call themselves the Valkyrie. And they are ruled by women who ride griffins." I look at Romulus. "His sister is with me."

"Who ride griffins?" The notion dazzles the girl. She's not yet gotten there in her studies. "Where is he now?"

"He died, and we fired him toward the sun as we came to visit your father."

"Oh. I'm sorry . . . ," she says with the blind kindness it seems only children still have. "Is that why you looked so sad?"

I flinch, not knowing it was so obvious. Romulus notices and spares me from answering. "Seraphina, your uncle was looking for you. The tomatoes won't plant themselves. Will they?" Seraphina dips her head and gives me a farewell wave before departing back down the path. I watch her disappear and belatedly realize that my child would be her age now.

"Did you arrange that?" I ask Romulus.

He steps into the garden. "Would you believe me if I said no?"

"I don't believe much from anyone these days."

"That'll keep you breathing, but not happy," he says seriously, voice having the clipped staccato delivery of a man raised in gladiatorial academies. There's no affectations here, no purring insults or games. It's a refreshing, if estranging, directness. "This was my father's refuge, and his father's before mine," Romulus says, gesturing for me to take a seat on one of the stone benches. "I thought it a fitting place to discuss the future of my family." He plucks a tangerine from the tree and sits on an opposite bench. "And yours."

"It seems a strange amount of effort to expend," I say.

"What do you mean?"

"The trees, the dirt, the grass, the water. None of it belongs here."

"And man was never meant to tame fire. That's the beauty of it," he says challengingly. "This moon is a hateful little horror. But through ingenuity, through will we made it ours."

"Or are we just passing through?" I ask.

He wags a finger at me. "You've never been credited for being wise."

"Not wise," I correct. "I've been humbled. And it's a sobering thing."

"The box was real?" Romulus asks. "We've heard rumors this last month."

"It was real."

"Indecorous," he says in contempt. "But it speaks to the quality of your enemy."

His daughter left little muddy footprints on the stone path. "She didn't know who I was." Romulus concentrates on peeling the tangerine in delicate little ribbons. He's pleased I noticed about his daughter.

"No child in my family watches holos before the age of twelve. We all have nature and nurture to shape us. She can watch other people's opinions when she has opinions of her own, and no sooner. We're not digital creatures. We're flesh and blood. Better she learns that before the world finds her."

"Is that why there are no servants here?"

"There are servants, but I don't need them seeing you today. And they aren't hers. What kind of parent would want their children to have servants?" he asks, disgusted by the idea. "The moment a child thinks it is entitled to anything, they think they deserve everything. Why do you think the Core is such a Babylon? Because it's never been told no.

"Look at the Institute you attended. Sexual slavery, murder, cannibalism of fellow Golds?" He shakes his head. "Barbaric. It's not what the Ancestors intended. But the Coreworlders are so desensitized to violence they've forgotten it's to have purpose. Violence is a tool. It is meant to shock. To change. Instead, they normalize and celebrate it. And create a culture of exploitation where they are so entitled to sex and power that when they are told no, they pull a sword and do as they like."

"Just as they've done to your people," I say.

"Just as they've done to my people," he repeats. "Just as we do to yours." He finishes peeling the tangerine, only now it feels more like a scalping. He tears the meat of it gruesomely in half and tosses one part to me. "I won't romanticize what I am. Or excuse the subjugation of your people. What we do to them is cruel, but it is necessary."

Mustang told me on our journey here that he uses a stone from the Roman Forum itself as a pillow. He is not a kind person. Not to his enemies at least, which I am, regardless of his hospitality.

"It's hard for me to speak to you as if you were not a tyrant," I say. "You sit here and think you are more civilized than Luna because you obey your creed of honor, because you show restraint." I gesture to the simple house. "But you're not more civilized," I say. "You're just more disciplined."

"Isn't that civilization? Order? Denying animal impulse for stability?" He eats his fruit in measured bites. I set mine on the stone.

"No, it's not. But I'm not here to debate philosophy or politics."

"Thank Jove. I doubt we'd agree upon much." He watches me carefully.

"I'm here to discuss what we both know best, war."

"Our ugly old friend." He glances once at the door to the house to make sure we're alone. "But before we move to that sphere, may I ask you a question of personal note?"

"If you must."

"You are aware my father and daughter died at your Triumph on Mars?"

"I am."

"In a way it's what began all this. Did you see it happen?"

"I did."

"Was it as they say?"

"I wouldn't presume to know who they are or what they say."

"They say that Antonia au Severus-Julii stepped on my daughter's skull till it caved in. My wife and I wish to know if it is true. It's what we were told by one of the few who managed to escape."

"Yes," I say. "It is true."

The tangerine drips in his fingers, forgotten. "Did she suffer?"

I hardly remember seeing the girl in the moment. But I've dreamed of the night a hundred times, enough to wish my memory was a weaker thing. The plain-faced girl wore a gray dress with a brooch of the lightning dragon. She tried to run around the fountain. But Vixus slashed the back of her hamstrings as he walked past. She crawled and wept on the ground until Antonia finished her off. "She suffered. For several minutes."

"Did she weep?"

"Yes. But she did not beg."

Romulus watches out the iron gate as sulfur dust devils dance across the barren plain beneath his quiet home. I know his pain, the horrible crushing sadness of loving something gentle only to see it ripped apart by the hard world. His girl grew here, loved, protected, and then she went on an adventure and learned fear.

"Truth can be cruel," he says. "Yet it is the only thing of value. I thank you for it. And I have a truth of my own. One I do not think you will like . . ."

"You have another guest," I say. He's surprised. "There's boots at the door. Polished for a ship, not a planet. Makes the dust stick something awful. I'm not offended. I half expected it when you didn't meet me in the desert."

"You understand why I will not make a decision blindly or impetuously."

"I do."

"Two months ago, I did not agree with Virginia's plan to negotiate for peace. She left of her own accord with the backing of those frightened by our losses. I believe in war only insofar as it is an effective tool of policy. And I did not believe we stood in a position of strength to gain anything from our war without achieving at least one or two victories. Peace was subjugation by another word. My logic was sound, our arms were not. We never made the victories. Imperator Fabii is . . . effective. And the Core, as much as I despise their culture, produces very good killers with very good logistical supply and support. We are fighting uphill against a giant. Now, you are here. And I can achieve something with peace that I could not with war. So I must weigh my options."

He means he can leverage my presence into suing the Sovereign for better terms than she would have given if the war had continued. It's boldly self-interested. I knew it was a risk when I set this course, but I'd hoped he'd be hot-blooded after a year of war with the woman and would want to pay her back. Apparently Romulus au Raa's blood runs a special kind of cold.

"Who did the Sovereign send?" I ask.

He leans back in amusement. "Who do you think?"

42

||||||||||||||||||||||||

THE POET

Roque au Fabii sits at a stone table in an orchard along the side of the house, finishing a dessert of elderberry cheesecake and coffee. Smoke from a brooding dwarf volcano twirls up into the twilight horizon with the same indolence as the steam from his porcelain saucer. He turns from watching the smoke to see us enter. He's striking in his black and gold uniform—lean like a strand of golden summer wheat, with high cheekbones and warm eyes, but his face is distant and unyielding. By now he could drape a dozen battle glories across his chest. But his vanity is so deep that he thinks affectation a sign of boorish decadence. The pyramid of the Society, given flight with Imperator wings on either side, marks each shoulder; a gold skull with a crown burdens his breast, the Sigil of the Ash Lord's warrant. Roque sets the saucer down delicately, dabs his lips with the corner of his napkin, and rises to his bare feet.

"Darrow, it's been an age," he says with such mannered grace that I could almost convince myself that we were old friends reuniting after a long absence. But I will not let myself feel anything for this man. I cannot let him have forgiveness. Victra almost died because of him. Fitchner did. Lorn did. And how many more would have had I not let Sevro leave the party early to seek his father?

"Imperator Fabii," I reply evenly. But behind my distant welcome is an aching heart. There's not a hint of sorrow on his face, however. I want there to be. And knowing that, I know I still feel for the man. He is a soldier of his people. I'm a soldier of mine. He is not the evil of his story. He's the hero who unmasked the Reaper. Who smashed the Augustus-Telemanus fleet at the Battle of Deimos the night after my capture. He does not do these things for himself. He lives for something as noble as I. His people. His only sin is in loving them too much, as is his way.

Mustang watches me worriedly, knowing all I must feel. She asked me about him on the journey from Mars. I told her that he was nothing to me, but we both know that isn't true. She's with me now. Anchoring me among these predators. Without her I could face my enemies, but I would not hold on to so much of my self. I would be darker. More wrathful. I count my blessings that I have people like her to which I can tether my spirit. Otherwise I fear it would run away from me.

"I can't say it's a pleasure to see you again, Roque," she says, taking the attention away from me. "Though I am surprised the Sovereign didn't send a politico to treat with us."

"She did," Roque says. "And you returned Moira as a corpse. The Sovereign was deeply wounded by that. But she has faith in my arms and judgment. Just as I have faith in the hospitality of Romulus. Thank you for the meal, by the bye," he says to our host. "Our commissary is woefully militaristic, as you can imagine."

"The benefit of owning a breadbasket," Romulus says. "Siege is never a hungry affair." He gestures for us to take our seats. Mustang and I take the two facing Roque as Romulus sits at the head of the table. Two other chairs to the right and left of him are filled with the ArchGovernor of Titan and an old, crooked woman I don't know. She wears the wings of Imperator.

Roque watches me. "It does please me, Darrow, knowing you're finally participating in the war you began."

"Darrow isn't responsible for *this* war," Mustang says. "Your Sovereign is."

"For instilling order?" Roque asks. "For obeying the Compact?"

"Oh, that's fresh. I know her a bit better than you, poet. The crone is a nasty, covetous creature. Do you think it was Aja's idea to kill Quinn?" She waits for an answer. None comes. "It was Octavia's. She told her to do it through the com in her ear."

"Quinn died because of Darrow," Roque says. "No one else."

"The Jackal bragged to me that he killed Quinn," I say. "Did you know that?" Roque is unimpressed with my claim. "If he'd let her be, she would have lived. He killed her in the back of the ship while the rest of us fought for our lives."

"Liar."

I shake my head. "Sorry. But that guilt you feel in your skinny little gut. That's gonna stick around. Because it's the truth."

"You made me a mass murderer against my own people," Roque says. "My debt to my Sovereign and the Society for my part in the Bellona-Augustus War is not yet paid. Millions lost their lives in the Siege of Mars. Millions who need not have died if I had seen through the ruse and done my duty to my people." His voice quavers. I know the lost look in his eyes. I've seen it in my own in the mirror as I wake from a nightmare and stare at myself in the pale bathroom light of that same stateroom on Luna. All those millions cry to him in the darkness, asking him why?

He continues. "What I cannot understand, Virginia, is why you abandoned the talks on Phobos. Talks which would have healed the wounds that divide Gold and permit us to focus on our true enemy." He looks at me heavily. "This man wanted your father to die. He desires nothing but the destruction of our people. Pax died for his lie. Your father died because of his schemes. He's using your heart against you."

"Spare me." Mustang snorts contemptuously.

"I'm trying to . . ."

"Don't talk down to me, poet. You're the weeping sort here. Not me. This isn't about love. This is about what is right. That has nothing to do with emotion. It has to do with justice, which rests upon facts." The Moon Lords shift uncomfortably at the notion of justice. She jerks her head in their direction. "They know I believe in Rim independence. And they know I'm a Reformer. And they know I'm intelligent enough not to conflate the two or to confuse my emotions with my beliefs. Unlike you. So since your rhetorical plays here are going to fall on deaf ears, shall we spare ourselves the indignity of verbal jousting and make our propositions so we can end this war one way or another?"

Roque glowers at her.

Romulus smiles slightly. "Do you have anything to add, Darrow?"

"I believe Mustang covered it quite thoroughly."

"Very well," Romulus replies. "Then I shall say my piece and let you say yours. You are both my enemies. One has plagued me with worker's strikes. Anti-government propaganda. Insurrection. The other with war and siege. Yet here on the fringe of the darkness away from both your sources of power, you need me, and my ships, and my legions. You see the irony. My lone question is this. Who can give me more in return?" He looks first to Roque. "Imperator, please begin."

"Honorable lords, my Sovereign mourns this conflict between our people, as do I. It spawned from the seeds sown in previous disputes, but it can end now as Rim and Core remember that there is a greater, more pernicious evil than political squabbling and debate over taxes and representation. And that is the evil of demokracy. That noble lie that all men are created equal. You've seen it tear Mars apart. Adrius au Augustus has nobly fought the battle there on behalf of the Society."

"Nobly?" Romulus asks.

"Effectively. But still the contagion has spread. Now is our best chance to destroy it before it can claim a victory from which we may never be able to recover. Despite our differences, our ancestors all fell upon Earth in the Conquering. In remembrance of that, the Sovereign is willing to cease all hostilities. She requests the aid of your legions and armada in destroying the Red menace that seeks to destroy both Rim and Core.

"In return, after the war she will remove the Societal garrison from Jupiter, but not Saturn or Uranus." The ArchGovernor of Titan snorts contemptuously. "She will enter into talks in good faith regarding the reduction of taxes and Rim export tariffs. She will grant you the same licenses for Belt mining which Core companies currently hold. And she will accept your proposal for equal representation in the Senate."

"And the reformation of the Sovereign election process?" Romulus asks. "She was never meant to be an empress. She's an elected official."

"She will revise the election process after the new Senators have been appointed. Additionally, the Olympic Knights will be appointed by the vote of the ArchGovernors, not by order of the Sovereign, as you requested."

Mustang tilts her head back and laughs one hard note. "I'm sorry. Call me skeptical. But what you're saying, Roque, is that the Sovereign will say yes to everything Romulus might want until she's back in a position to say no." She blows air out of her nose comically. "Trust me, my friends, my family well knows the sting of the Sovereign's promises."

"And what of Antonia au Julii?" Romulus asks, noting Mustang's skepticism. "Will you deliver her to our justice for the murder of my daughter and father?"

"I will."

Romulus is pleased by the terms, and moved by Roque's comments about the Red menace. It doesn't help that his promises seem very plausible. Practical. Not promising too much or too little. All I can do to combat them is to embrace the fact that I offer them a fantasy, and a dangerous one at that. Romulus looks to me, waiting.

"Color notwithstanding, you and I have a common bond. The Sovereign is a politician, I am a man of the sword. I deal in angles and metal. Like you. That is my life blood. My entire purpose for being. Look how I rose in your ranks without being one of you. Look how I took Mars. The most successful Iron Rain in centuries." I lean forward. "Lords, I will give you the independence you deserve. Not half measured. Not transient. Permanent independence from Luna. No taxes. No twenty years of service to the Core for your Grays and Obsidians. No orders from the Babylon that the Core has become."

"A bold promise," Romulus says, showing the depth of his character by bearing the insult he must feel at a Red promising to deliver him
his independence.

"An outlandish promise," Roque says. "Darrow is only who he is
because of who is around him."

"Agreed," Mustang says cheerily.

"And I still have everyone around me, Roque. Who do you have?"

"No one," Mustang answers. "Just dear old Antonia, who has become my brother's quisling."

The words hit home with Roque and Romulus. I return to addressing the Moon Lords. "You have the greatest dockyard the worlds have
ever seen. But you started your war too quickly. Without enough
ships. Without enough fuel. Thinking the Sovereign would not be able
to send a fleet here so quickly. You were wrong. But the Sovereign has
made a mistake as well: all her remaining fleets are in the Core, defending moons and worlds against Orion. But Orion is not in the
Core. She is with me. Her forces joined to the ships I stole from the
Jackal to form the armada with which I will smash the Sword Armada from the sky."

"You don't have the ships for that," Roque says.

"You don't know what I have," I say. "And you don't know where I
hide it."

"How many ships does he have?" Romulus asks Mustang.

"Enough."

"Roque would have you believe I am a wildfire. Do I look wild?"
Not today, at least. "Romulus, you have no interest in the Core just as
I have no interest in the Rim. This is not my home. We are not enemies. My war is not against your race, but against the rulers of my
home. Help us shatter the Sword Armada, and you will have your
independence. Two birds with one stone. Even if I do not defeat the
Sovereign in the Core after we defeat the Poet here, even if I lose
within the year, we will cause such damage that it will be a lifetime
before Octavia can summon the ships, the money, the men, the commanders to cross the billion kilometers darkness again." The Moon
Lords lean into my words. I may yet have them.

Roque scoffs. "Do you really think this self-styled liberator will abandon the lowColors in the Rim? In the Galilean Moons alone over a hundred and fifty million are 'enslaved.' "

"If I could free them, I would," I admit. "But I cannot. I recognize that and it breaks my heart, because they are my people. But every leader must sacrifice."

This receives nods from the Golds. Even if I am the enemy, they can respect my loyalty to my people, and also the pain I must feel. It is odd having such veneration in the eyes of my enemies. I am not used to it.

Roque also sees the nods. "I know this man better than any of you," he presses. "I know him like a brother. And he is a liar. He would say whatever it took to break the bonds that bind us together."

"Unlike the Sovereign, who never lies," I say lightly, drawing a few laughs.

"The Sovereign will honor her agreement," Roque insists.

"As she did with my father?" Mustang asks scathingly. "When she planned to kill him at the Gala last year? I was her lancer and she planned it right under my nose. And why? Because he did not agree with her politics. Imagine what she'd do to men who actually went to war with her."

"Hear, hear," the ArchGovernor of Titan says, rapping his knuckles on the table.

"And instead you would trust a terrorist and a turncoat?" Roque asks. "He has conspired to destroy our Society for six years. His entire existence is deception. How could you trust him now? How could you think a Red cares more for you than a Gold?" Roque shakes his head sadly. "We are *Aureate*, my brothers and sisters. We are the order that protects mankind. Before us was a race intent on destroying the only home it had ever known. But then we brought peace. Do not let Darrow manipulate you into bringing back the Dark Age that came before. They will purge all the wonders we have made to fill their bellies and sate their lusts. We have a chance to stop him here, now. We have a chance to unite once more, as we were always meant to. For our children. What world do you want them to inherit?"

Roque puts a hand over his heart.

"I am a Man of Mars. I have no love for the Core any more than you. The appetites of Luna have pillaged my planet long before I was born. That must change. And it will change. But not at the end of *his* sword. He would burn the house to fix a broken window. No, friends, that is not the way. To change for the better, we must look past the politics of the day and remember the spirit of our Golden Age. Aureate, united over all."

The longer this plays, the more likely Roque will convince them of their patriotism. Mustang and I both know it. Just as I knew I would have to sacrifice something in coming here. I'd hoped it would not be what I'm about to offer, but I know by the looks in the eyes of the Moon Lords that Roque's message has struck home. They fear an uprising. They fear me.

It's the great dread of the Sons of Ares, the great mistake Sevro made in releasing my Carving and taking the Sons to a true war. In the shadows we could let them kill each other. We were just an idea. But Roque has made them think the thought that unites all masters who have ever been: what if the slaves take my property for their own?

When my uncle gave me my slingBlade, he said it would save my life for the price of a limb. Every miner is told that so that he knows from the first day he steps in the mine, the sacrifice is worth it. I make one now for which I may never be forgiven.

"I will give you the Sons of Ares," I say quietly. No one hears me through Roque's continued speech. Only Mustang. "I will give you the Sons of Ares," I repeat more loudly. Quiet falls over the table.

Romulus's chair creaks as he leans forward. "What do you mean?"

"I told you I have no interest in the Rim. Now I will prove it. There are over three hundred and fifty Sons of Ares cells throughout your territories," I say. "We are your dock strikes. We are the sanitation sabotage and the reason why Nessus's streets fill with shit. Even if you hand me over to the Sovereign today, the Sons will bleed you for a thousand years. But I will give you every single Sons of Ares cell in the Rim, I will abandon the lowColors here and take my crusade to the Core, never coming through the asteroid belt as long as I live if you help me kill his bloodydamn fleet."

I stab a finger at Roque, who looks horrified.

"That is insanity," Roque says, noting the effect my words have had. "He's lying."

But I'm not lying. I've given orders for the Sons of Ares cells to evacuate across the Rim. Not many will make it out. Thousands will be captured, tortured, killed. Thus is war, and the peril of leadership.

"Lords, the Imperator is asking you to bow," I reply. "Aren't you tired of that? Of groveling to a throne six hundred million kilometers from your home?" They nod. "The Sovereign says I am a threat to you. But who has bombed your cities? Who has slain a million of your people? Who kept your children hostage on Luna? Slaughtered your father and daughter on Mars? Who burned an entire moon? Was it me? Was it my people? No. Your greatest enemy is the greed of the Core. The burners of Rhea."

"That was a different time," Roque protests.

"It was the same woman," I snarl and look to the Saturnian Gold to Romulus's left who pays rapt attention. "Who burned Rhea? The Sovereign has forgotten, because her throne sits with its back toward the Rim. But you see her glassy corpse every night in your skies."

"Rhea was a mistake," Roque says, falling into the pitfall that Mustang helped me prepare. "One that must never be repeated."

"Never repeated?" Mustang asks, springing the trap shut. She turns to Vela, who watches from the steps of the house with several other Ionian Golds. "Vela, my friend, may I please have my datapad?"

"Don't play her game," Roque says.

"My game?" Mustang asks coyly. "My game is facts, *Imperator*. Are those not welcome here or is rhetoric alone permissible? Personally, I trust no man who fears facts." She looks back to Vela, amused by her own barbs. "You can operate it for me, Vela. The password is L17L6363." She grins at my surprise.

Vela looks to her brother. "She might send a message to Barca."

"Deactivate my connection," Mustang says. Romulus nods to Vela. She deactivates it. "Look in datafolders, cache number 3, please." She does. At first the quiet Gold's eyes narrow, confused at what she's looking at. Then, as she reads, her lips curl back and the skin on her arms pucker with goose bumps. The rest of the small gathering watches her reaction with growing anxiety. "Illuminating, isn't it, Vela?"

"What is it?" Romulus demands. "Show us."

Vela glares hatefully at Roque, who is as confused as anyone, and walks the device to her brother. His face manages to remain impassive as he reads the data, fingers swiping through the files. I use Cassius's information against his master now, turning his gift into an arrow aimed at her heart. Mustang and I thought it would be better coming from her, however. Lending the lie to the credibility of her friendship with Romulus.

"Put it up," Romulus says, tossing the datapad to Vela.

"What is this?" Roque asks angrily. "Romulus . . ." His words falter as an image of Asteroid S-1988, part of the Karin subfamily of the Koronis family of asteroids in the belt, blossoms in the air. It rotates slowly over the table. The green stream of data beneath it spelling the Sovereign's doom. It's a series of falsified Society communiqués detailing the delivery of supplies to an asteroid without a base. The stream continues to roll, detailing high-level Society directives for "refueling" at the asteroid. Then it shows the footage of the ship I sent away from the main fleet to investigate the asteroid as the rest of us journeyed to Jupiter. Reds float through the dark warehouse. The small jets on their suits silent in the vacuum. But their Geiger meters, which are synced to their helms, crackle at the amount of radiation in the place. A far greater amount of radiation than is present in the legal five megaton warheads which are used in space combat.

Romulus stares at Roque. "If Rhea was not to be repeated, then why did your fleet empty a nuclear weapons depot before coming to our orbit?"

"We did not visit the depot," Roque says, still trying to process what he's seen and the implications of it. The evidence is compelling. All lies are better served with a hefty helping of the truth. "The Sons of Ares pillaged it months ago. The information is falsified." He's operating off of the wrong information. Which means the Sovereign has kept the Jackal's sedition tight to her chest. And now she pays for trusting so few. He's not prepared for this argument and it shows.

"So there *is* a depot," Romulus asks. Roque realizes how devastating the admission was. Romulus frowns and continues. "Imperator Fabii, why would there be a secret depot of nuclear weapons between here and Luna?"

"That's classified."

"Surely you jest."

"The Societal Navy is responsible for the security of . . ."

"If it was for security then wouldn't it be nearer a base?" Romulus asks. "This is near the edge of the asteroid belt on the path a fleet from Luna would use when Jupiter is in closest orbit to the sun. As if it was a cache meant to be acquired by an Imperator on the way to my home . . ."

"Romulus, I realize how this looks. . . ."

"Do you, young Fabii? Because it looks as if you were considering *annihilation* to be an option against people you call brother and sister."

"This information is clearly falsified. . . ."

"Except the existence of the depot . . ."

"Yes," Roque admits. "That exists."

"And the nuclear warheads. With that much radiation?"

"They're for security."

"But the rest of it is a lie?"

"Yes."

"So you didn't, in fact, come to my home with enough nuclear weapons to make our moons glass?"

"We did not," Roque says. "The only warheads we have aboard are for ship-to-ship combat. Five megaton yield, max. Romulus, on my honor . . ."

"The same honor you had when you betrayed your friend . . ." Romulus gestures to me. "When you betrayed honorable Lorn. My ally, Augustus. My father, Revus. That honor by which you watched as my daughter's head was stomped in by a sociopathic matricide who takes orders from a sociopathic patricide?"

"Romulus . . ."

"No, Imperator Fabii. I do not believe you deserve the intimacy of using my given name any longer. You call Darrow a savage, a liar. But he came here wearing his heart on his sleeve. You came with the lies. Hiding behind manners and breeding . . ."

"ArchGovernor Raa, you must listen. There's an explanation if you will just . . ."

"Enough," Romulus screams. Surging to his feet and slamming his large hand on the table. "Enough hypocrisy. Enough schemes. Enough lies you sniveling Core sycophant." He trembles finally with the rage. "If you were not my guest, I would hurl my glove at you and cut your manhood away in the Bleeding Place. Your lost generation has forgotten what it means to be Gold. You have forsaken your heritage. Suckling at the tit of power, and why? For what? Those wings on your shoulders? *Imperator.*" He scoffs at the word. "You whelp. I pity a world where you decide if a man like Lorn au Arcos lives or dies. Did your parents never teach you?" They did not. Roque was raised by tutors, by books. "What is pride without honor? What is honor without truth? Honor is not what you say. It is not what you read." Romulus thumps his chest. "Honor is what you do."

"Then do not do this. . . ." Roque says.

"Your master did this," Romulus replies indifferently. "If she could not make us bow, she would make us burn. Again."

Mustang tries and fails to keep the smile from her face as Roque watches the Moon Lords slip through his fingers. A darkness enters his cultured voice. One which leaves my heart in tatters. To think that voice once defended me. Now he guards something far less loving. A Society that cares nothing for him.

I always wondered why Fitchner selected Roque for House Mars. Until his betrayal I had known him to be only the most gentle soul. But now the Imperator shows his wrath.

"ArchGovernor Raa, listen to me carefully," he says. "You are mistaken in believing we came here with intent to destroy you. We came to preserve the Society. Don't give in to Darrow's manipulation. You are better than that. Accept the Sovereign's terms, and we may have peace for another thousand years. *But* if you choose this path, if you renege on our armistice, there will be no quarter. Your fleet is ragged. Darrow's, wherever it hides, can be nothing more than a coalition of deserters in borrowed vessels.

"But we are the Sword Armada. We are the iron hand of the Legion and the fury of the Society. Our ships will darken the lights of your worlds. You know what I can do. You do not have a commander to match me. And when your ships burn, the knights of the Core will pour into your cities at the head flying columns and fill the air with ash enough to choke your children.

"If you betray your Color, the Compact, the Society—which is what this will be—Ilium will burn. I will acquaint you with ruin. I will hunt down every person you have ever known and I will exterminate their seed from the worlds. I will do so with a heavy heart. But I am a Man of Mars. A man of war. So know my wrath will be unending." He extends a thin hand. The wolf of House Mars' mouth is open in a silent, hungry howl. "Take my hand in kinship for the sake of your people and the sake of Gold. Or I will use it to build an age of peace upon the ashes of your house."

Romulus walks around the edge of the table so that he is facing Roque, the younger man's outstretched hand between them. Romulus draws his razor from where it is coiled on his hip. It rasps into rigid form. A blade etched with visions of Earth and of the Conquering. His family is as old as Mustang's, as old as Octavia's. He uses that blade to slice open his hand and suck the scarlet blood from the wound before drawing up and spitting it into Roque's face.

"This is a bloodfeud. If ever again we meet, you are mine or I am yours, Fabii. If ever again we draw breath in the same room, one breath shall cease." It is a formal, cold declaration that requires one thing of Roque. He nods. "Vela, see the Imperator to his shuttle. He has a fleet to prepare for battle."

"Romulus, you can't let him leave," Mustang says. "He's too dangerous."

"I agree," I say, but for another reason. I'd spare Roque from this battle. I do not want his blood on my hands. "Hold him prisoner until the battle is over, then release him unharmed."

"This is my home," Romulus says. "This is how we conduct ourselves. I promised him safe passage. He shall have it."

Roque dabs the blood and spit away with the same napkin he used for the cheesecake and follows Vela away from the table toward the steps that lead back into the home. He pauses there before turning back to face us. I cannot say if he speaks to me or the Golds gathered but when he recites his last words, I know they are for the ages:

"Brothers, sisters, till the last
Woe that this has come to pass,
By your grave, I shall weep
For it was I who made you sleep."

Roque bows minutely. "Thank you for the hospitality, ArchGovernor. I will see you shortly." As Roque leaves the assembly, Romulus instructs Vela to hold him until I am safely off Io.

"Hail my Imperators and Praetors," he tells one of his lancers. "I want them on holos in twenty minutes. We have a battle to plan. Darrow, if you would like to link in your Praetors . . ." But my mind is on Roque. I may never see him again. Never have a chance to say so many things which swarm my chest now. But so too do I know what letting him go could mean for my people.

"Go," Mustang says, reading my eyes. I rise abruptly, excusing myself and manage to catch Roque as he finishes tying his boots in the garden. Vela and several others are moving him toward the iron gate.

"Roque." He hesitates. Something in my voice causing him to turn and watch me approach. "When did I lose you?" I ask.

"When Quinn died," he says.

"You planned to kill me even when you thought I was a Gold?"

"Gold. Red. It doesn't matter. Your spirit is black. Quinn was good. Lea was good. And you used them. You are ruin, Darrow. You drain your friends of life, and leave them spent and wasted in your wake, convincing yourself each death is worth it. Each death brings you closer to justice. But history is littered with men like you. This Society is not without fault, but the hierarchy . . . this world, it is the best man can afford."

"And it's your right to decide that?"

"Yes. It is. But beat me in space, and it will be yours."

43

||||||||||||||||||||

HERE AGAIN

lood drips from Mustang's hand.

The voices of children drift through the air.

"My son, my daughter, now that you bleed, you shall know no fear." A young virgin girl with hair of white and feet bare on cold metal panels walks through the lines of kneeling giants carrying an iron dagger that drips with Aureate blood. "No defeat."

Gold armor etched with deeds of their ancestors. The boy's cloak innocent as snow. "Only victory." She slices the already-injured hand of Romulus au Raa, whose eyes are closed, his dragon armor white and smooth as ivory as his other hand holds his eldest son's hand. The boy is no older than seventeen, only just having won his year at the Ganymede Institute. His eyes are flashing and wild for the day. If only his intrepid young soul knew what waited on the other side of the hour. His older cousin kneels by his side, her hand on his knee. Her brother beside her. The family forming a chain across the bridge. "Your cowardice seeps from you." Behind the girl, more children walk through the fold, carrying the four standards of Gold—a scepter, a sword, and a scroll crowned with a laurel. "Your rage burns bright." She holds up the dripping dagger before Kavax au Telemanus and his youngest daughter Thraxa, a wild haired, freckle-faced, squat girl with her father's laugh and Pax's simple kindness. "Rise, children of Ilium, warriors of Gold, and take with you your Color's might."

Two hundred Gold Praetors and Legates rise. Mustang and Romulus at their head, flanked by the Telemanuses and House Arcos. Mustang lifts up her hand and smears the blood upon her own face. Two hundred killers join her, but I do not. I watch from the corner with Sefi as the combined officer corps of my Gold allies honors their Ancestors. Martian Reformers, Rim tyrants, old friends, old enemies clutter the bridge of Mustang's flagship, the two-hundred-year-old dreadnought *Dejah Thoris*.

"The battle today is to decide the fate of our Society. Whether we live under the rule of a tyrant or whether we carve our own destiny." Mustang catalogues the list of enemies for the day's hunt. "Roque au Fabii, Scipia au Falthe, Antonia au Severus-Julii, Cyriana au Tanus." Thistle. "These are wanted lives."

I've been here before, witnessing this benediction, and I can't help but feel I will be here again. It has lost none of its luster. None of the grandeur that so sheathes this remarkable people. They go to death not for the Vale, not for love, but for glory. We have never seen a race quite like them, nor will we again. After months surrounded by the Sons of Ares I see these Golds less as demons than falling angels. Precious, flaring so brilliantly across the sky before disappearing beyond the horizon.

But how many more days like this can they afford?

In the halls of our enemies, Roque will be reciting our names, and the names of my friends. He who kills the Reaper will have glory unending, bounty and renown. Young beasts with wide shoulders and angry eyes straight from the halls of the Core's schools will hunt me. Ready to make their name.

So too will the old Gray legionnaires hunt me. Those who see my rebellion as the great threat against mother Society. Against that union which they have loved and fought for their entire lives. And Obsidian will seek me, led by masters who promised them Pinks in exchange for my head. They will hunt my friends. They will say Sevro's name, and Mustang's, and Ragnar's because they do not yet know he is gone from us. They will hunt the Telemanuses and Victra, Orion, and my Howlers. But they cannot have them. Not today.

Today I take.

I stand looking down at my Gold allies. I am encased in militarized metal. Two point one meters tall, one hundred and sixty kilograms of death in a pulseArmor suit of blood-red. My slingblade is coiled around my right vambrace just above the wrist. A gravFist on my left hand. Built for collisions in corridors today, not speed. Sefi is just as monstrous as I in her brother's armor. Hate in her eyes seeing this host of enemies.

My allies needed to see her. To see me. To know beyond a shadow of a doubt that the Reaper is more alive than ever. Many of the Martians fell with me in the Rain. Some look at me with hate. Others with curiosity. And some—a very few—salute. But from most there's a contempt that will never be washed away. That's why I brought Sefi. Absent love, fear will do nicely in a pinch.

Upon hearing news that Roque's fleet has begun its journey from Europa, I make my farewell to Romulus and his coterie of Praetors who helped devise our battle plan. Romulus's handshake is firm. Respect between us, but no love. In the hangar, I say goodbye to Mustang and the Telemanuses. The floor vibrates as shuttles ferry the hundreds of Peerless back to their ships. "It seems like we're always saying farewell," I say to Kavax after he says his goodbyes to Mustang, lifting her up easy as he might a little doll and kissing her head.

"Farewell? It is not farewell," he rumbles with a toothy grin. "Win today and it becomes just a long hello. Much life left for the both of us, I think."

"I don't know how to thank you," I say.

"What for?" Kavax asks, confused, as per usual.

"The kindness . . ." I don't know how else to say it. "For watching over my friends when I'm not even one of you."

"One of us?" His ruddy face smirks. "A fool. You speak like a fool. My boy made you one of us." He looks across the hangar where Mustang speaks with one of Lorn's daughters-in-law near a transport. "She makes you one of us." It's all I can do to keep the tears from my eyes. "And if we damn all that, I say you're one of us. So one of us you are."

He lets Sophocles down from his shoulder perch to lope onto the floor. Circling, the fox jumps up onto my leg to dig something out of a joint in my armor. A jellybean. Thraxa puts a finger to her lips behind her father. The big man's eyes light up. "What fresh deliciousness is this, Sophocles? Oh, your favorite kind! Watermelon." The fox returns, jumping up onto his shoulder. "See! You have his benediction as well."

"Thank you, Sophocles," I say, reaching to scratch him behind the ears.

Kavax slams me into a hug before departing. "Take care, Reaper." He trundles up the ramp. "Fishing?" he booms down at me before he's gone ten meters.

"What?"

"Do Reds fish?"

"I never have."

"There is a river through my estate on Mars. We will go, you and I, when this is done and sit by the bank and toss our lines and I will teach you how to tell a pike from a trout."

"I'll bring the whiskey," I say.

He points a finger at me. "Yes! And we will be drunk together. Yes!" He disappears into the ship, throwing his arm around Thraxa and calling to his other daughters about a miracle he just witnessed. "I think he might be the luckiest of us," I say as Mustang comes up from behind me to watch the Telemanus ship depart.

"Is it ridiculous if I ask you to be careful?" she asks.

"I promise not to do anything rash," I reply with a wink. "I'll have the Valkyrie with me. I doubt anyone will want to tangle with us for long." She glances over my shoulder to where Sefi waits by my own shuttle, admiring the engines of other ships as they fly away. Mustang looks like she wants to say something, but is wrestling with how.

"You're not invincible." She touches the armor of my chest. "Some of us might want you around after all of this. After all, what's the point of all this if you go and die on me? You hear?"

"I hear."

"Do you?" She looks up at me. "I don't want to be left alone again. So come back." She raps her knuckles on my chest and turns to go to her ship.

"Mustang." I chase after her and grab her arm, pulling her back toward me. Before she can say anything, I kiss her there surrounded by metal and engine roar. Not some delicate kiss, but a hungry one, where I pull her head to mine and feel the woman beneath the weight of duty. Her body presses against me. And I feel the shudder of fear that this will be the last time. Our lips part and I sink into her, rocking there, smelling her hair and gasping at the tightness in my chest. "I'll see you soon."

44

||||||||||||||||||||||||||||

THE LUCKY ONES

I pace my bridge like a caged wolf, his meal just beyond the bars. The kindness of me hidden again behind the Reaper's savage face. "Virga, are the Howlers in position?" I ask. Behind and below me, the skeleton crew of Blues chatter in their sterile pit. Faces illuminated by holoscreens. Subdermal implants pulsing as they sync with the ship. The captain, Pelus, a waifish gentleman who was a former lieutenant aboard the *Pax* when I first took the ship, awaits my orders.

"Yes, sir," Virga says from her station. "Forward elements of the enemy fleet will be within long-range guns in four minutes."

The arrogant might of Gold unfolds across the black of space. An unending sea of pale white splinters. I'd give anything to be able to reach out and shatter them. My own capital ships cluster in three groups around our powerful dreadnoughts above the north pole of Io. Mustang and Romulus marshal their forces around the south. And together, eight thousand kilometers apart, we watch Roque's fleet cross the void between Europa and Io to bring us battle.

"Enemy cruisers at ten thousand kilometers," a Blue intones.

There is no preamble for my fleet. No benediction or rite that we perform before battle like the Golds. For all our right, we seem so pale and simple compared with them. But there's a kinship here on my ship. One I saw in the engine rooms, in the gunnery stations, on the bridge. A dream that links us together and makes us brave.

"Give me Orion," I say without turning.

A holo of the overweight, ornery Blue ripples into life in front of me. She's half a hundred kilometers away in the heart of *Persephone's Howl,* one of my other four dreadnoughts, sitting in a command chair synced with every ship captain in my fleet save those of my strike force. Much of today relies upon her and the pirate fleet she's assembled in the months since last we saw one another. She's been raiding Core shipping lines. Drawing Blues to her cause. Enough to help the Sons staff the ships we stole from the Jackal with loyal men and women.

"*Big fleet,*" Orion says of our enemy, impressed. "*I knew I never should have answered your call. I was rather enjoying being a pirate.*"

"I can tell," I say. "Your stateroom's gaudy enough to a make a Silver blush." The *Pax* has been her home for the last year and a half. She took over my old quarters and filled it right up with the booty of her raids. Rugs from Venus. Paintings from private Gold collections. I found a Titian jammed behind a bookcase.

"*What can I say? I like pretty things.*"

"Well, pull this off today, and I'll find you a parrot for your shoulder. How about that?"

"*Ah! Pelus told you I was looking for one. Good man, Pelus.*" The waifish captain tilts his head genteelly behind me. "*Damn hard to find parrots when you can't dock planetside anywhere. We found a hawk, a dove, an owl. But no parrot. If you make it a red one I'll personally shoot a hole in Antonia au Severus-Julii's bridge.*"

"Red parrot it is," I say.

"*Good. Good. I suppose now I should go be about the battle.*" She laughs to herself and takes a tea from a valet on her bridge. "*Just want to say, thank you, Darrow. For believing in me. For giving me this. After today, Blue will have no master. Goodspeed, boy.*"

"Goodspeed, Admiral."

She vanishes. I glance back at the central sensor projection. The tactical readout floats before the windows as a to-scale globe of the Jupiter system. Four tiny inner moons orbit Jupiter more closely than the four huge Galilean Moons. My eyes focus on Thebe, the outermost of them and closest to Io. It's a small mass. Barely larger than Phobos. Long since mined for valuable minerals, and now the home of a military base that was blasted apart in the early days of the war.

"Sixty ticks till Howler coms go black," Virga intones from her station as Victra enters the bridge, wearing thick golden armor painted with a Red slingBlade on the chest and back.

"The hell are you doing here?" I ask.

"You're here," she replies innocently.

"You're supposed to be on the *Shout of Mykos*."

"This isn't the *Mykos*?" She bites her lip. "Well, I suppose I got lost. I'll just follow you around so that doesn't happen again. Prime?"

"Sevro sent you. Didn't he?"

"His heart's a black little thing. But it can break. I'm here to make sure it doesn't by keeping you nice and cozy. Oh, and I want to say hello to Roque."

"What about your sister?" I ask.

"Roque first. Then her." She elbows me. "I can be a team player too."

Grinning, I turn back to the pit. "Virga, give me a helmet patch to the Howlers."

"Aye, sir."

The com in my ear crackles. I activate my armor's helmet. The transparent heads up display shows me the tags on my crew, ranks, names, everything that's logged into the central ship register. I activate the com holo function and a semi-translucent collage of my friends' faces appears over the sight of my ship's bridge. *"'Sup boss?"* Sevro asks, his face is painted Red with warpaint but bathed in blue light from his mech's HUD display. *"Need a goodbye kiss or something?"*

"Just checking to make sure you're all tucked in."

"Your kin could've carved us a bigger nook," Sevro mutters. *"It's foot to face to fartbox in here."*

"*So you're saying Tactus would've liked it?*" Victra asks. She's patched into the panel so I hear her voice in link.

I laugh. "What didn't he like?"

"*Clothing, predominantly,*" Mustang replies from her own bridge. She wears her battle armor as well. Pure Gold with a red lion roaring on her chest.

"*And sobriety,*" Victra adds.

"*This moon smells like royal shit,*" Clown mumbles from his own starShell mech. "*Worse than a dead horse.*"

"*You're in a mech in vacuum,*" Holiday drawls. I hear the clang and shouts of the people behind her in the hangar bay of my ship. She wears a huge blue handprint on her face. Given to her by one of her Obsidians. "*It's likely not the moon.*"

"*Oh. Then it must be me,*" Clown says. He sniffs. "*Oh, ho. It's me.*"

"*I told you to shower,*" Pebble mutters.

"*Howler Rule 17. Only Pixies shower before battle,*" Sevro says. "*I like my soldiers savage, stinky, and sexy. I'm proud of you, Clown.*"

"*Thank you, sir.*"

"*Threka! Put your safety on,*" Holiday shouts. "*Now! Sorry. Bloodydamn Obsidians walking around with their fingers on the bloodydamn triggers. Shit is terrifying.*"

"Why do we laugh and speak like children?" Sefi booms over the com, so loud my eardrums rattle.

"*Bloodyshit in a handbasket,*" Sevro yelps. There's a chorus of curses at Sefi's volume.

"*Turn down your output volume!*" Clown snaps at the queen.

"I do not understand. . . ."

"*Your output . . .*"

"What is output . . . ?"

"'*The Quiet' is a bit of a misnomer, eh?*" Victra asks. Mustang snorts a laugh.

"*Sefi, bend down,*" Holiday barks. "*I can't reach. Bend down.*" Holiday's found Sefi in the hangar and helps her turn down her output volume. The Obsidian queen sleeps with her new pulseFist every night, but she's a bit behind on her understanding of telecommunication equipment.

"So, like the big girl asked, was there a reason for this little tête-à-tête?" Holiday says.

"Tradition, Holi," Sevro says, mimicking her twang. *"Reap's a sentimental sap. He's probably going to give a speech."*

"No speech," I say.

My odd little family whines and catcalls. *"You're not going to admonish us to rage, rage against the dying of the light?"* Sevro asks. But the joke feels strange, knowing it is what Roque would have said. My chest tightens again. I feel so much love for this band of misfits and oathbreakers. So much fear. I wish that I could protect them from this. Find some way to spare them the coming hell.

"Whatever happens, remember we're the lucky ones," I say. "We get to make a difference today. But you're my family. So be brave. Protect each other. And come home."

"You too boss," Sevro says.

"Break the chains," Mustang says.

"Break the chains," my friends echo.

Sevro's face becomes a snarl as he booms out: "Howlers go . . ."

"Ahhhwwwooooo." They howl like fools, cracking up. One by one, their images flicker away, and I'm left in the solitude of my helmet. I breathe and say a silent prayer to whoever is listening. Keep them safe.

I let the helmet slither back into the neck of my armor. My Blues watch me from their displays. A small coterie of Red and Gray marines stand by the door, waiting to escort me to the hangar. The strings of so many lives from so many worlds all intersecting here, at this moment around mine. How many will fray? How many will end this day? Victra smiles at me, and it seems I'm too lucky already for this day to end in joy. She should not be here. She should be across the void at the helm of an enemy battle cruiser. Yet she's here with us, seeking the redemption she thought she could never have.

"Once more unto the breach," she says.

"Once more," I reply. I address the crew. "How do you all feel?"

Awkward silence. They exchange nervous glances. Unsure of how to answer. Then a young Blue woman with a bald head bursts up from her console. "We're ready to kill some bloodydamn Golds . . . sir."

They laugh, tension broken.

"Anyone else?" Victra booms. They roar in reply. Marines as young as eighteen and as old as Lorn would be now slam their steel-heeled boots against the ground.

"Patch me through to the fleet," I command. "Broadcast on an open frequency to Quicksilver. Make sure the Golds can hear me so they know where to find me." Virga gives me a nod. I'm live.

"My friends, this is the Reaper." My voice echoes over the master com in all one hundred and twelve capital ships in my fleet, in the thousands of ripWings, in the leechCraft and the engine rooms and the medbays where doctors and newly appointed nurses walk through empty beds with crisp white sheets, waiting for the flood. Thirty-eight minutes from now Quicksilver and the Sons of Ares on Mars will hear it, and they'll boost the signal to the core. Whether we're alive at that time will depend on my dance with Roque.

"In mine, in space, in city and sky, we have lived our lives in fear. Fear of death. Fear of pain. Today, fear only that we fail. We cannot. We stand upon the edge of darkness holding the lone torch left to man. That torch will not go out. Not while I draw breath. Not while your hearts beat in your chests. Not while our ships yet have menace in them. Let others dream. Let others sing. We chosen few are the fire of our people." I beat my chest. "We are not Red, not Blue or Gold or Gray or Obsidian. We are humanity. We are the tide. And today we reclaim the lives that have been stolen from us. We build the future we were promised.

"Guard your hearts. Guard your friends. Follow me through this evil night, and I promise you morning waits on the other side. Until then, break the chains!" I pull my razor from my arm and let it take the shape of my slingBlade. "All ships, prepare for battle."

45

||||||||||||||||||||||||||

THE BATTLE
OF ILIUM

Red tribal drums played in the belly of one of my ships, *The Evening Tide,* beat through the speakers in a martial rendition of the Forbidden Song. A steady undulation of defiance as we roll toward the Sword Armada. I've never seen a fleet so large. Not even when we stormed Mars. That was just two rival houses summoning allies. This is the conflict of peoples. And it is appropriately massive.

Unfortunately, Roque and I studied under the same teachers. He knows the battles of Alexander, of the Han armies, and Trafalgar. He knows the greatest threat to an overwhelming power is miscommunication, chaos. So he does not overestimate the power of his force. He subdivides into twenty smaller mobile divisions, giving relative autonomy to each Praetor to create speed and flexibility. We face not one huge hammer, but a swarm of razors.

"It's a nightmare," Victra murmurs.

I thought Roque would do this, but I still curse as I see it. In any space engagement, you must decide if you're killing enemy ships or capturing them. It seems he's intent on boarding. So we cannot slug it out with them and hope for the best. Nor can we lure his fleet into my trap from the first. They'll muscle through it and kill the Howlers. Everything depends on the one advantage we do have. And it's not our ships. It is not our hundred thousand Obsidians I have packed in leechCraft. It is the fact that Roque thinks he knows me, and so his entire strategy will be predicated on how I would behave.

So I decide to overshoot his estimation of my insanity and show him how little he really understands the psychology of Reds. Today I lead the *Pax* on a suicide mission into the heart of his fleet. But I don't begin the battle. Orion does, soaring forward ahead of me on *Persephone's Howl* with three quarters of my fleet. They cluster in spheres, the smallest corvettes still four hundred meters long. Most are half-kilometer-long torchShips, some destroyers, and the four huge dreadnoughts. Long-range missiles slither out from the Gold ships and from our own. Miniature computer-guided countermeasures are deployed. And then Roque's fleet flashes into motion and the black space between the two fleets erupts with flack, missiles, and long-range railgun munitions. Billions of credits' worth of munitions spent in seconds.

Orion shrinks the distance to Roque's fleet as Mustang and Romulus's ships hurtle toward the southern edge—per Io's pole—of Roque's formation, attempting to hit the only vulnerable place on a ship, the engines. But Roque's fleet is nimble and ten squadrons divide from the rest, orientating themselves so their bristling broadsides face the bows of the Moon Lord ships coming up from the planet's south pole and rake them with railgun fire. A hundred thousand guns go off simultaneously.

Metal shreds metal. Ships vomit oxygen and men.

But ships are made to take a beating. Huge hulks of metal subdivided into thousands of interlocking honeycombed compartments designed to isolate breaches and prevent ships from venting with one railgun shot. From these floating castles stream thousands of tiny one-man fighter craft. They swarm in small squadrons through the no-man's-land between our fleet and Roque's. Some packed with miniature nukes meant for killing capital ships. Helldivers and drillboys trained night and day in sims by the Sons of Ares fly with squadrons of synced Blues. They slash into the Society's war-hardened pilots led by ripWings striped with Gold.

Romulus's force peels away from Mustang's to link with Orion, while Mustang continues toward the heart of the enemy formation, preparing the way for my thrust.

We close to three hundred kilometers, and the mid-range rail guns open up. Huge barrages of twenty kilogram munitions hurtling through space at mach eight. Flak shields plume over the entire Gold formation. Closer to the ships, PulseShields throb iridescent blue as munitions crack into them and career off into space.

My strike force lingers behind the main battle. Soon it will become a war of boarding parties. LeechCraft launching by the hundreds. Aggressive Praetors will empty their ships of their marines and Obsidians to claim enemy vessels, which they will then keep after the battle, per rules of naval law. Conservative Praetors will hoard their men till the last, keeping them to repel boarding parties and use their ships as their main weapon of war.

"Orion's given the signal," my captain says.

"Set course for the *Colossus*. Engines to ramming speed." My ship rumbles under my feet. "Pelus, the trigger's yours. Ignore torchShips. Destroyers or larger are the order of the day." The ship groans as we hurtle forward from the back of Orion's fleet. "Escorts keep tight. Match velocity."

We pass the artillery ships, then the four-kilometer-long *Persephone's Howl* as we emerge out the center of Orion's front with the enemy like a hidden spear, now driving into the fifty kilometers of no-man's-land, aiming for the heart of the enemy. Orion's ships fire chaff, creating a corridor to protect our mad approach. Roque will see what I intend now, and his capital ships drift back from mine, inviting me into the center of his huge formation as they rain fire down on my strike force.

Our shields flicker blue. Enemy munitions sneak through the chaff and punish us. We return fire. Raking a destroyer as we pass with a full broadside. It loses power. LeechCraft pour out of it to try and slip through our chaff tunnel, but our escorts shred the small craft. Still, we're hit by the guns of a dozen ships. Red glows around our shields. They fail in stages, local generators shorting out on our starboard side. Instantly, our hull is punctured in seven places. The honeycomb network of pressurized doors activates, shutting the compromised levels of my ship off from the rest. I lose a torchShip. Half a click off bow, a full barrage of rail-munitions rake her from stem to stern, fired by Antonia's dreadnaught the *Pandora*.

"Seems my sister is enjoying my ship," Victra says.

Bodies erupt out of the torchShip's bridge, but Antonia continues to fire on the much-smaller ship until the nuclear core of her engines implodes. Pulsing white twice before devouring the ship's back half. The shock wave pushes our craft sideways. Our EMP and pulse shielding holds, lights flickering just once. Something huge slams into the ten-meter-thick bulkhead beyond the bridge. The wall bends inward to my right. The shape of a railgun munition stretching the metal inward like an alien baby. Our gunners rip apart the 1.5-kilometer destroyer that fired on us, loosing eighty of our railguns directly into her bridge. Two hundred men gone. We're taking no prisoners at this stage. It's staggering the amount of violence the *Pax* can deal out. And staggering the amount we're taking. Antonia dissects another part of my strike force.

"*Hope of Tinos* is down," my Blue sensor officer says quietly. "*The Cry of Thebes* is going nuclear."

"Tell *Tinos* and *Thebes* helmsman to punch negative forty-five their midline and abandon ship," I snap. The ships obey and alter course to ram Antonia's flagship. She reverses her engines and my dying ships carry on harmlessly into space. One goes nuclear.

We're outmatched and outgunned here in the heart of the enemy formation. Trapped. No escape. A sphere forming around us. I only have four torchships left. Make that three.

"Multiple deck fires," an officer intones.

"Munitions detonations on deck seventeen."

"Engines one through six are down. Seven and eight are at forty percent capacity."

The *Pax* dies around me.

Roque's MoonBreaker looms ahead. Twice the length of my ship, three times the girth. A floating military dock city eight kilometers long. With a huge crescent bow, like a shark with an open mouth swimming sideways. She retreats from us at the same pace we advance. Making sure we cannot ram her as she punishes us with her superior weaponry. Roque thought I would pull a Karnus. Try to slam into their capital ship with my own. That's now impossible. Our engines are nearly done. Our hull compromised.

"All forward guns target their railguns and missile launchers on their top deck, carve us a shadow." I pull up a hologram of the ship and circle the area of fire with my fingers, directing the fire as Victra gives commands to the fighter groups which we've held on to till now. The ripWings scream out into space. The *Pax* rotates to present her main gunbanks to the *Colossus* to open a broadside.

It doesn't matter what we do at this stage. We're a wolf pinned to the ground by a bear and it's smashing our legs one by one, carving off our ears, our eyes, our teeth but keeping our belly nice and ready for a raking. My ship shudders around me. Blues rip out of sync, vomiting in the pits as the datanerves in the ships, to which they're linked, die one by one. My helmsman, Arnus, has a seizure as the engines are shredded.

"*The Dancer of Faran* is gone," Captain Pelus says. "No escape pods." It was a skeleton crew, but still forty die. Better than a thousand. Only two torchShips of my initial sixteen remain. They race around Antonia's *Pandora* behind us, but that ship is a black, hulking monster. She shreds the fastmovers till they're dead metal. And when escape pods launch from the quiet ships, she shoots them down. Victra watches the murder quietly. Adding it to Antonia's debt.

Roque is inviting us to launch our leechCraft, drawing the *Colossus* closer to my dead ship. A kilometer away now. I accept the invitation. "Launch all leechCraft at the surface of the MoonBreaker," I say. "Now. Fire the spitTubes."

Hundreds of empty suits fire out the spitTubes as they would in an Iron Rain. Two hundred leechCraft launch from the four hangars of my ship. Spewed out in a stream of ugly metal, each could carry fifty men to pump into the guts of the MoonBreaker. Controlled remotely by Blue pilots on board *Persephone's Howl,* they race fast as they can to cross the dangerous space between the two capital ships. And they're wiped away before they make it half the distance as Roque detonates a series of low-yield nuclear warheads.

He guessed my move.

And now my flight of ships is nothing but debris floating between the two vessels. Emergency sirens flash on the ceiling of my bridge. Our long-range sensors are down. Our guns smashed. Multiple deck breaches.

"Hold together," I murmur. "Hold together, *Pax*."

"We're receiving a transmission," Virga says.

Roque appears in the air before me. "Darrow." He sees Victra too. "Victra, it is done. Your ship is dead in the water. Tell your fleet to surrender and I will spare your lives." He thinks he can end this rebellion without putting us in the grave. The entitlement of it rankles me. But we both know he needs my body to show the worlds. If he destroys my ship and kills me, they'll never find me in the wreckage. I look at Victra. She spits on the ground in challenge. "What is your answer?" Roque demands.

I bend my fingers crudely. "Fuck you."

Roque looks off screen. "Legate Drusus, launch all leechCraft. Tell the Cloud Knight to bring me the Reaper. Dead or alive. Just make sure he's recognizable."

46

|||||||||||||||||||||||||||

HELLDIVER

I look to the Blues at their stations. Most were here when I took this
ship. When I renamed her. They became pirates with Orion, rebels
with me. "You all heard him," I say. "Well done. You did the *Pax* proud.
Now say goodbye, get to your shuttle, and I'll see you soon. There's no
shame in this." They salute and Captain Pelus opens the hatches in the
bottom of the pit. The Blues begin their slide down the narrow shaft
into the berth where there should be escape pods, but we replaced
them with heavily armored shuttles. My own escape pod is built into
the side of the bridge. But Victra and I aren't escaping. Not today.

"Time to go, baby boy," Victra says. "Now."

I pat the doorframe of the bridge. "Thank you, *Pax*." I say to the
ship. One more friend lost to the cause. I follow Victra and the marines in a sprint down the empty halls. Red lights pulse. Sirens wail.
Small thumps reverberate through the hull as we go. Roque's leech-
Craft will be swarming the *Pax* by now. Melting holes through her
sides and pumping in boarding parties of Grays and Obsidians led by
Gold knights. Instead of me, they'll find an abandoned ship. A molten circle throbs on the hallway wall beside a gravLift as we board. I

watch the orange deepen till it is the color of the sun. The drums still beat through the speakers. *Thump. Thump. Thump.*

Victra leaves a mine behind as a present for the boarding party.

We hear it detonate ten levels above us as the gravLift deposits us on level negative three in the auxiliary hangar. Here my true assault force waits. Thirty heavy assault shuttles with their ramps down. Blues performing flight checks in the cockpits. Orange mechanics working furiously to prime engines, fill fuel tanks. Each ship is filled with a hundred Valkyrie in full smart armor. Reds and Grays accompany them in equal number for special weapons tasks. The Obsidians stomp their pulseAxes and razors as I run past, a thunderous chanting of my name. I find Holiday in the center of the hangar standing with Sefi and a coterie of Valkyrie who will be my personal squad. With them, praying in a small group, are the Helldivers I requested from Dancer. They're less than half the size of the Obsidians.

"Ship is breached," I say to Holiday. She jerks her head at a squad of Reds, who rush off to cover our back. "Distance is less than a click."

"No . . ." Holiday says with an elated laugh. "That close?"

"I know," I reply excitedly. "They want to get close so we can't shoot down their leechCraft."

"So now we give them a kiss," Victra says with a little purr for Holiday. "And some tongue."

Holiday bobs her cinderblock head up and down. "Then let's stop jawin'."

Sefi pulls a handful of dried mushrooms from a satchel. "God's bread?" she asks. "You will see dragons."

"War's scary enough, darling," Victra says. Then as an aside: "I one time tripped on that shit with Cassius for a week on the Thermic." She catches my look. "Well, it was before I met you. And have you ever seen him with his shirt off? Don't tell Sevro, by the way."

Holiday and I abstain from the mushrooms as well. Automatic weapons fire rattles from a hall just beyond the hangar. "The hour is here!" I boom to the three thousand Obsidian in the assault shuttles. "Sharpen your axes! Remember your training! *Hyrg la,* Ragnar!"

"*Hyrg la,* Ragnar!" they roar.

It means "Ragnar lives." The Queen of the Valkyrie salutes her razor to me and begins the Obsidian war chant. It spreads through the black armored assault craft. A horrible dread sound, this time it is on my side. I've brought the Valkyrie to the heavens, and now I let them loose.

"Victra, you prime?" I ask, worried about Antonia being so near. Is my friend distracted by her sister?

"I'm gorydamn splendid, baby boy," the tall woman says. "Take care of that pretty little ass of yours." She slaps my butt before back-pedalling, blowing me an obnoxious kiss and jogging to her shuttle. "I'll be right behind." I'm left with the Helldivers. They're smoking burners, watching me with evil red eyes.

"First one through gets the bloodydamn laurel," I say. "Helmets on."

Little needs to be said to such men. They nod their heads and grin. We depart. I fly thirty meters upward on my gravBoots to land atop of one of the four clawDrills we confiscated from the platinum mining company in the inner asteroid belt. They stand in a row on the hangar deck, each fifty meters apart. Like grasping hands, the cockpit where elbow would be, the dozen drill bits on the deck where fingers would reach. Each is retrofitted by Rollo to have thrusters on the back and thick plates of armor extend down the sides. I slide into the cockpit, enlarged for my frame and armor, and slip my hands into the digital control prism.

"Fire them up," I say. A familiar thrum of energy goes through the drill, vibrating the glass around me. I grin like a madman. Perhaps I am one. But I knew I could not win this battle without altering the paradigm. And I knew Roque would never be driven into a trap or lured into an asteroid belt, for fear of exposing his larger force to ambushes. So I had only one recourse: hide my ambush in a flaw of character. He always preached for me to step back, to find peace. Of course he thought he knew how to beat me. But I'm not fighting as the man he knew today, as a Gold.

I'm a bloodydamn Helldiver with an army of giant, mildly psychotic women behind me and a fleet of state-of-the-art warships crewed by pissed-off pirates, engineers, techs, and former slaves. And he thinks he knows how to fight me? I laugh as the clawDrill shakes my seat. Filling me with a dormant, crazed sort of power. An enemy boarding party breaches the hangar from the same gravLift we took. They stare up at the huge claw drills and evaporate as Victra's shuttle fires a railgun at them from point-blank range.

"Remember the words of our Golden leader," I say to the Helldivers. "Sacrifice. Obedience. Prosperity. These are the better parts of humanity."

"*Bloodydamn slag,*" one says over the com. "*I'll show her the better part of my humanity.*"

"Drills hot," I order. They echo confirmation one by one. "Helmets up. Let's burn."

I flip the rotation toggle on my clawDrill clockwise. Beneath, the drill whirs. I plunge both hands forward in the control prism. Existence shakes. Teeth rattle. The metal deck sags under me. Molten metal peels back. I lurch ten meters down into the ship. Carving through the deck in five seconds. And the one after that. I sink again, falling through the floor of the hangar bay completely. Chewed metal around the cockpit. Then the next deck goes. Then the next. Heat builds along the drill as I slam through more of the ship, leaving the Valkyrie behind. Slow, the drill jams, slow and you die. And this speed is the pulse of my people. Momentum flowing into more momentum.

My clawDrill is building up a hell of a pace. Slamming through decks. Murdering metal with molten tungsten carbide teeth. I glimpse fractured sights of the other clawdrills ripping through the heart of the ship as we fall through the dimly lit barracks. Each drill glowing with heat and then slamming into the next deck. It is a glorious, horrible sight. Going through a mess hall. Through a water tank, then a hallway where a boarding party stumbles back from the debris and stares at the megalithic drills carving through the ship like the molten hands of some hilarious metal god.

"Don't slow," I roar, entire body convulsing in the seat. I'm out of control, going too fast, drill too hot. Then . . . nothing. I breach the belly of the *Pax*. Silence of space grips me. Weightless. I float like a spear through water toward the huge *Colossus*. LeechCraft bound for the *Pax* streak past me, one close enough I can see the captain's wide eyes inside the cockpit. Another flies straight into my superheated drill's mouth. Shredded in seconds. Men and debris cartwheel to the side. The other drills exit farther down the *Pax*'s belly, bursting into space, diving for the MoonBreaker. Around us, the battle rages. Blue explosions, huge fields of flak. Mustang's group racing along the edge of Roque's formations, exchanging punishing broadsides. Sevro still waits, hiding.

I can feel the confusion in the enemy gunners. I'm in the center of their leechCraft assault teams. They can't fire. Their computers won't even register the vessel classification. It'll look like a hunk of debris shaped like an arm from the elbow down. I doubt the bridge will even know what it is without seeing it with their naked eye.

"Blast engines," I say. The engines of the retrofitted clawDrill kick behind me and hurl me down at the black surface of the *Colossus*. Recognizing my threat, a ripWing sprays me with chain gun rounds. Thumb-sized bullets slam silently into the drill. The armor holds. Not so on the clawDrill beside mine. When a railgun round fired from a five-meter gun along the top-crest of the MoonBreaker punches through the cockpit, murdering the Helldiver in it, his ship shatters. One of his drillbits slams into my glass cockpit, cracking it. A dozen more rounds shred the leechCraft beside me. Roque might not know what the 30 meter projectiles coming from my ship are, but he's willing to kill his own men to stop their approach.

Gray metal blurs toward me. A railgun slug fired from the *Colossus* punches through three leechCraft in front of my ship before striking the bottom of my clawDrill, at the "wrist." It tears up the length of the drill, erupts up through the floor of my cockpit, between my legs, inches from my balls, scraping along my chest, almost taking my head off at the jaw. I jerk back and the slug slams into the metal support of the cockpit. Shattering the glass and bending the bar outward like a melting plastic straw. I gasp, knocked half unconscious by the kinetic energy transference.

White spots flash across my vision.

I shake myself. Trying to bring my senses back.

I've spun off course. This rig isn't meant for steering. About to slam into the MoonBreaker's deck. Instinct doesn't save me. My friends do. The clawDrill's engines are slaved to the bank of Blues back on Orion's ship. Someone reverses the thrusters at the last moment so I don't crash. I'm slammed back in my seat as the clawDrill slows and then lands gently onto the surface of the *Colossus*. I jerk in my seat, laughing in fear.

"Bloodydamn" I whoop to my distant saviors, whoever they are. "Thank you!"

But the clawDrill itself is all manual. Blues can't operate the digits any better than I can plot slingshots around a planet. My hands dance over the controls, flowing into my old mode of labor. I reactivate the drill, using my engines to push me down like a nail into the surface of the ship. Metal wheezes. Bolts rattle. And I begin to gnaw through the top layer of armor, which they said no leechCraft could penetrate.

Pressure hisses out around my drill. I ramp up the revolutions, my hands dancing through the controls, shifting the drill bits as they overheat, cycling through cooled units. Space disappears. I burrow into the warship. Carving not in a straight line, but a tunnel toward the front of the ship. One deck. Two decks. Chewing through halls and barracks and generators and gas lines. It's hideous and as savage a thing as I've ever done. I just pray I don't hit a munitions store. Men and women and debris fly out into space through the hole I've carved like autumn leaves sucked from the various deck levels I penetrate. Bulkheads will seal off the wound, but those caught between the bulkheads and the tunnel are good as dead.

Three hundred meters into the ship, my clawDrill breaks down. Drill bits spent and engine overheating. I reach down to pop my cockpit canopy to abandon the drill, but my hand slips on the lever. Blood coats it. I search my body frantically. But my armor isn't punctured. The blood isn't from me. It floats off the right cockpit wall, slick around the round railgun slug that pierced the three leechCraft to imbed itself in the support beam of my clawDrill. Bits of hair and a fragment of bone clump in the clotting blood.

I leave my clawDrill behind for the vacuum of the tunnel I carved. Air no longer gushing from the ship. It's calm now, the pressure already vented and the emergency bulkheads closed to quarantine the compromised hull. The gravity generator in this section of the ship must have been hit. My hair floats in my helmet.

I look up. At the end of the tunnel, where I penetrated the hull, is a little keyhole to the stars. A dead man drifts just beyond it, slowly spiraling. A shadow grips him as Antonia's flagship passes beyond, blocking the light reflected from Jupiter's surface. Like the man, I'm left in darkness. Alone in the belly of the *Colossus*. My com a flood of war-chatter. Victra is launching from our hangar. Orion and the Moon Lords are in flight, knocked off the poles of Io and bound for Jupiter. Mustang's flagship is now under assault by Roque's ship as Antonia leads the rest of his fleet after the retreating Telemanuses and Raas.

Still, Sevro waits.

Thirty meters above me, something moves out from one of the levels I carved through, peering into the twenty-meter-wide tunnel. My helmet identifies an active weapon. I fly upward, activating my pulse-Shield as I go only to find a young Gray staring at me through the plastic faceplate of an emergency oxygen mask. He floats, one arm holding a ragged length of metal wall. Blood coats him. Not his own. The body of one of his friends floats behind him. He's shaking. My drill must have gone through his entire platoon, and then space pulled their bodies out, leaving him alone here. The terror of me is reflected in his eyes. He raises his scorcher and I react without thinking. Putting my razor into the side of his heart, I make him a carcass. He dies wide-eyed and young and he floats there, upright till I put my foot on his chest so I can pull my blade out. We drift away from each other. Little droplets of blood dancing off my blade in the zero gravity.

Then the gravity generators reboot and my feet clomp to the floor. The blood splatters over them. His body flops to the ground. Light floods in behind me from the tunnel shaft. I pull myself away from the dead man and peer up into the tunnel to see a shuttle ripping in out of space. More follow. A whole cavalcade of assault craft led by Victra. RipWings chase them, but mounted guns on the back of the assault craft spray high-energy fist-sized rounds at them. Shredding the ripWings. More will come. Hundreds more. We must move fast. Speed and aggression our only advantage here.

Victra's transport slows dramatically in the tunnel beyond my level, just above the clawDrill. Valkyrie pour out to join me. More transports unload on levels above. Holiday and several Reds with battle armor move with the Obsidians, carrying breaching equipment across the airless room toward the bulkhead door that seals us off from the rest of the ship. They slam the thermal drill onto the metal. It begins glowing red. They deploy a pulseBubble over the metal hatch so that when we breach, we don't activate more bulkheads.

"Breach green in fifteen," Holiday says.

Victra stands to the side listening to enemy chatter. "Response teams inbound. More than two thousand mixed units." She's also patched to the strategic command on Orion's ship, so she can gather battle data from the huge sensor arrays on the flagship. Looks like Roque launched more than fifteen thousand men at us in his leech-Craft. Most will be in the *Pax* by now. Burrowed through to find me. Silly bastards. Roque gambled big, bet wrong. And I've just brought three thousand crazed Obsidian berserkers to a mostly empty warship.

The Poet is going to be pissed.

"Ten," Holiday says.

"Valkyrie, on me," I boom, lifting my hands in a triangle formation.

The hundred Obsidians step over the debris of the commissary and gather behind me, just as we trained them to do on the journey from Jupiter. Sefi's on my left hip, Victra's on my right and Holiday behind. The superheated metal door sags. The Reds and Grays back away. All along the tunnel on the ten levels I carved through, teams like this will be preparing to breach just like us. Two of the other clawDrills hit home. Two thousand Obsidians are breaching there as well. Grays, Reds, and a scattering of sympathizer Golds will lead them against the security forces who take trams and gravLifts to ferry themselves to the new battlefront inside the ship.

This is going to be a firestorm. Close quarters combat. Smoke. Screams. The worst of war.

"Full power to shields," I say in Nagal, facing the Valkyrie. They ripple iridescent as shields play over their armor. "Kill anything with a weapon. Harm nothing without one. Doesn't matter the Color. Remember our target. Clear me a path. *Hyrg la,* Ragnar!"

"*Hyrg la,* Ragnar!" they roar, beating their chests, embracing the madness of war. Most will have taken their beserker fungus in the shuttlecraft. They'll feel no pain. They move foot-to-foot, eager for the succor of battle. Victra vibrates next to me. I remember sitting with her in Mickey's lab as she told me how she loves the smell of battle. The old sweat in the gloves. The oil on the guns. The pulled muscles and shaking hands afterward. It's the honesty of it, I realize. That's what she loves. Battle never lies.

"Victra, stay at my side," I say. "Pair up for the Hydra if we encounter Golds."

"*Njar la tagag . . .*" Sefi says from behind me.

". . . *syn tjr rjyka!*"

"There is no pain. Only joy," they chant, deep in the embrace of the god's bread. Sefi begins the war bellow. Her voice higher than Ragnar's. Her two wing-sisters join her. Then their wing-sisters, until dozens fill the com with their song, giving me a sense of grandeur as my mind tells my body to flee. This is why the Obsidians chant. Not to sow terror. But to feel brave, to feel kinship, instead of isolation and fear.

Sweat drips down my spine.

Fear is not real.

Holiday deactivates her safety.

"*Njar la tagag . . .*"

My razor goes rigid.

PulseWeapon shudders and whines, priming.

Body trembles. Mouth full of ashes. Wear the mask. Hide the man. Feel nothing. See everything. Move and kill. Move and kill. I am not a man. They are not men.

The chanting swells. . . . "*Syn tjr rjyka!*"

Fear is not real.

If you're watching, Eo, it's time to close your eyes.

The Reaper has come. And he's brought hell with him.

47

||||||||||||||||||||||||

HELL

"Breach!" Holiday roars. The door falls open. I rush into the pulseField surrounding the breach point. Everything condenses. Sights, sounds, the movement of my own body. All a haze. Holiday's scatterFlash cackles through the two-meter opening in the bulkhead, frying any unshielded optic nerves on the other side. A secondary fusion grenade detonates. I jump through the hole into smoke, going right, Victra comes with. Sefi goes left. Enemy fire hits us immediately. My shield cackles with the sound of hail hitting a tin roof. The end of the hall a chaos of muzzle flashes and pulse fire. Superheated projectiles slice through the smoke.

I fire my pulseFist, arm jerking spasmodically. Ducking and moving so I don't block the entrance. Something slams into me. I stumble to the left wall, superheated particles screaming from my fist. My shield crackles with coilgun rounds that impact the energy barrier and fall, flattened to the ground at my feet. More Obsidian fill the hall behind me. They move so fast. It's a cacophony of sound. My tactical mind shoves the facts to the front. We're pinned down. Men die in the breach. Must move forward.

Something whizzes past my head. It detonates behind at the entrance. Limbs and armor slop onto the floor. The helmet mutes the massive noise, saving my eardrums. I stumble forward, trying to get out of the killzone. Another grenade lands among us. Detonating after an Obsidian dives upon it. More meat for the grinder. Must close the distance. Can't see anything in front of me. So much smoke. Fire.

To hell with this.

With a roar of frustration, I activate my gravBoots and rocket down the narrow hall eighty kilometers an hour toward our assailants, firing as I go. Flying a meter above the floor. Victra follows. It's a whole squad of twenty Grays led by a Gold legate in brilliant silver armor. I crash into the Gold. Razor outstretched, piercing his shield and spearing his brain. Crash to the ground. Arm pinned under me. The Gray response team separates from one another, keeping me at the center as I struggle to my feet. One shoots an ion-charge into my back. Blue lightning spasms over my shields, killing them. I stab one Gray through the neck with my razor. Two others fire into my chest. My armor dents with a dozen rounds. I stumble back. A heavy railgun with a boring round in the chamber levels at my head. I dip and dodge to the side, slipping on blood. Going down. The gun goes off and opens a hole the size of a man's head in the floor.

Then Victra smashes into the Grays. Bursting side to side with her gravBoots, an angry wrecking ball. Shattering bones between the walls and her heavily armored body. Then the Obsidians are among the Grays, hacking them to pieces with their pulseAxes. The Grays are screaming, falling back around the corner where they have fire support. A Gray's leg is slashed off by Sefi and he stumbles, firing his weapon into the wall. She rips his head clean off from behind.

This is horror.

The smoke. The twitching bodies and evaporation of blood as it boils out of charred wounds. A dying man's urine pools around my armor, hissing against the superheated barrel of my pulseFist as Victra helps me up.

"Thanks."

Her frightening bird helmet nods to me without expression.

As the rest of my platoon files through the breach, I move forward to the corner around which several of the Grays escaped. Another enemy response squad hastily sets up a heavy weapon mounted on a floating gravPod about thirty meters down near a gravLift entrance. When it fires, a quarter of the wall above me melts. I order Holiday take my place at the corner with Trigg's ambi-rifle.

"Four tins, one Gold," I say. "They've got a mounted QR-13. Slag 'em."

She adjusts her rifle's multi-use barrel. "Yessir."

At our breach point, six Valkyrie are down. A huge woman's helmet peels back into her armor. She vomits blood. Half her torso smokes, molten armor still melting her flesh. She tries to stand, laughing at the pain, high on god's bread. But this is a new type of war to these women with new injuries. Unable to support herself, the Obsidian slumps against a sister who calls to Sefi. The young Queen looks at the wounds and sees Victra shake her head. A quicker learner than the rest of them, Sefi knew well what this war would cost her people. But staring it in the face is something different altogether. She says something of home to the woman, something of the sky and the feathers at summer's twilight. I don't see the blade she slips into the base of the dying woman's skull until she pulls it back out.

A hologram of Mustang's face flashes in the corner of my screen. I open the link. *"Darrow, have you breached?"*

"We're in. Double for my teams. Pressing to bridge now. What's what?"

"You need to hurry. My ship's under heavy fire."

"We're in. You're supposed to bug out. Head to Thebe."

"Roque used EMPs." Her voice is tense. *"Our shielding kept us up, but half my fleet's engines are squabbed. We're sitting dead, punching it out with him. Soon as your clawDrill hit, the* Colossus *started shooting to kill. They're ripping us apart. We're outgunned, hard. Main batteries are already at half strength."* A sick feeling rises in my gut. Roque can see us on the cameras in his ship. He knows the strength of my boarding party. It's only a matter of time till I reach the bridge. Soon he'll make an announcement over the com for me to surrender or he'll kill her. *"Get to the gorydamn bridge and put him down. Register?"*

"Register." I turn to face my troops, "We gotta move," I say. "Victra, take squad command. I'm going digital. Sefi, range ahead."

"Holiday, anytime," Victra says eagerly, pacing back and forth in the hall. "The little lion needs our help. Come on! Come on!"

"Hold your tits," Holiday mutters, adjusting her rifle and toggling the corner-shot feature. The barrel joints rotate so it peeks around the wall and feeds the visual link directly into her bionic eye. Four quick bursts tear out of the gun. Thirty rounds each from the ammo magazine in the back of her armor. "Go."

Victra and I burst around the corner, eating up meters as a Gray tries to take his companion's place at the gun. I cut him down with my pulseFist and Victra exchanges a four move kravat set with the Gold, before skewering him with a thrust to the chest. I finish him with a stab to the throat. Holiday has her commandos haul the QR-13 with us, only able to keep pace with our long legs because of our heavy armor.

As we press for the bridge at a full-sprint, other elements of my invasion force make for vital ship functions with a new frantic speed. It's a lightning strike. Grays can't move with this speed because they rely on tactics, leapfrog maneuvers, corner-shots and sly tech. The Obsidian are straight battering rams. It's tempting to surge ahead, focus only on getting to the bridge. But I can't abandon my plan. My platoons need me to guide them using the battlemap on my HUD. Speaking to Red and Gray platoon leaders, I coordinate on the run as Victra leads us through the maze of metal halls and ambushes. As the platoons are pinned down, I use my com to maneuver other platoons through gravLifts and halls to flank entrenched security teams. It's an intricate dance. Not only are we racing against the destruction of Mustang's ship. But we're racing against the return of the leechCraft.

Roque knows this. And less than three minutes into our insertion, the ship goes into full lockdown protocol. All gravLifts and trams and bulkheads sealed off, creating a honeycomb of obstacles throughout the ship. We can only advance fifty meters at a time. It's a devilish system, pins down boarding forces as security teams with digital keys run about the ship at ease, flanking and creating deadly killboxes and cross-fires that can shred even a boarding party like mine. There's no way to combat it. This is the grind of war. No matter the tech or the tactics, it all comes down to terrifying moments crouching chalk-mouthed at a corner as a friend lays down cover fire and you try not to trip over the hi-tech gear that's wrapped around your body as you advance, head lowered, legs churning. It's not bravery, it's fear of shaming yourself in the eyes of your friends that keeps you moving.

As we melt our way through bulkhead after bulkhead, Sefi's Valkyrie feed the grinder. We're ambushed from every side. Some of the best warriors I've ever seen fall with smoking holes in the back of their helmets from Gray marksmen. They melt under pulseFist fire. They fall to a Gold knight flanked by seven Obsidian till Victra, Sefi, and I put them down with razors.

All this to reach the bridge. All this to reach a man who I could have reached out and touched the day before. If this is the cost of honor, give me a shameful murder. If I'd have stabbed Roque in the throat then, Valkyrie would not litter the ground now.

"Men and women of the Society Navy, this is the Reaper. Your ship has been boarded by the Sons of Ares . . ." I hear my voice over the ship's general com unit. One of my platoons has reached the com-munication mainframe in the back half of the ship. Every boarding party in my fleet has copies of the speech Mustang and I recorded together to upload to boarded enemy vessels. It exhorts lowColors to aid my units, to deactivate lockdown protocol if they can, to unlock doors manually if they cannot, and to storm the armories. Most of these men and women are veterans. It's unrealistic to expect the same sort of conversion as I had on the *Pax*'s crew, but every little bit helps.

The announcement works partially on the *Colossus*. It buys us pre-cious time as we bypass several doors in seconds instead of the min-utes it would take to melt through. Roque also turns off the artificial gravity, realizing by watching their tactics that my Obsidians don't have zero g experience.

Society Grays push their way through halls like seals under water, taking their revenge on my floating Obsidians, robbed of their closing speed, who've mauled so many of their friends. In the end, one of my teams reactivates the gravity. I have them decrease it to one-sixth

Earth standard so that my force is not encumbered by the heavy armor we wear. It's a blessing on our lungs and legs.

After cutting through a security team of Grays, we finally reach the bridge, battered and bloody. I crouch, panting, and increase the oxygen circulation in my armor. Swimming in sweat, I activate a stim injection in my gear to keep me from feeling the gash in my biceps where a Gold's razor caught me. The needle bites into my thigh. Reports come from my other platoons that they've lost contact with the enemy, which means they're being consolidated by Roque, redirected, likely to us. Back to the bridge door, I stare across the circular, exposed antechamber to the bridge and remember how my instructor at the Academy demonstrated the geometric deadliness of the space for anyone besieging a starburst bridge design like this. Three halls from three directions lead to the circular room, including a gravLift in the center. It's indefensible, and Roque's marines are coming.

"Roque, darling," Victra calls up to the cameras in the ceiling as Holiday and her team set up the drill on the door. "How I have pined for you since the garden. Are you there?" She sighs. "I'll just assume you are. Listen, I understand. You think we must be wroth with you, what with the murder of my mother, the execution of our friends, the bullets in the spine, the poison, and a year of torture for dear Reaper and I, but that's not so. We just want to put you in a box. Maybe several. Would you like that? It's very poetic."

Holiday's remaining three commandos are attaching magnetic clamps to the door and mounting their thermal drill. She taps a few commands and the eye of the drill begins to spin.

Sefi returns from her scouting. Her helmet slithers back into her armor. "Many enemies come from tunnel." She points to the middle hall. "I killed their leader, but more Golds follow." She didn't just kill the leader. She brought his head back. But she's limping and her left arm bleeds.

"Oh, hell. That's Flagilus," Victra says, regarding the head. "He was in my school house. Very sweet fellow actually. Wonderful cook."

"How many are coming, Sefi?"

"Enough to give us a good death."

"Shit. Shit. Shit." Holiday punches the door behind me.

"It's too thick isn't it?" I ask.

"Yeah." She pulls her assault helmet off. Her Mohawk is mashed to the side. Tense face dripping with sweat. "Door's not VDY specs like the rest of the ship. It's Ganymede Industries. Custom. At least twice as thick."

"How long will it take to get through?" I repeat.

"At full burn? Fourteen minutes?" she guesses.

"Fourteen?" Victra repeats.

"Maybe more."

I turn, hissing the anger out. The women know as well as I that we don't have even five minutes. I hail Mustang's coms. No answer. Her ship must be dying. Bloodydamn. Stay alive. Just stay alive. Why did I ever let her out of my sight?

"We charge them," Victra's saying. "Straight down the middle hall. They'll run like foxes from hounds."

"Yes," Sefi says, finding a more kindred spirit in Victra than either might have thought prior to shedding blood together. "I will follow you, daughter of the sun. To glory."

"Piss on glory," Holiday says. "Let the drill do its work."

"And sit here to die like Pixies?" Victra asks.

Before I can say a word or do much of anything, there's a metallic wheeze behind me from the hydraulics in the wall as the door to the bridge opens.

48

||||||||||||||||||||||||||

IMPERATOR

We surge onto the bridge, expecting an ambush. Instead, it's calm. Clean, lights dimmed, just as Roque prefers it. Beethoven streams out from hidden speakers. Everyone is still at their stations. Wan faces illuminated by pale light. Two Golds walk along the wide metal path that leads over the pits toward the front of the bridge where Roque stands orchestrating his battle before a thirty-meter-wide holographic projection. Ships dance among the sensors. Framed by fire, he cycles through images, issuing commands like a great conductor summoning the passion of an orchestra. His mind a beautiful, terrible weapon. He's destroying our fleet. Mustang's *Dejah Thoris* leaks flame from her oxygen stores as the *Colossus* and her three escort destroyers continue to hammer her with railguns. Men and debris float through space. This is just one part of the larger battle. The great host of his force, including Antonia, has pursued Romulus, Orion and the Telemanuses toward Jupiter.

To our left, twenty meters away, near the bridge's armory, a tactical squad of Obsidian and Grays secure their heavy weapons and listen intently to their Gold commanders, preparing to defend their bridge against me.

And just to our right, at the control panel by the now open door, unseen and unnoticed by anyone else on the bridge, trembles a small Pink in a white valet's uniform. The passcode display glows green under her hands. Her thin figure is frail against the backdrop of war. But the woman's face is set defiantly, her finger on the door's release button, her mouth spreading into the most delightful little smile as she shuts the door behind us.

All this in three seconds. The Gold infantry commander sees us.

Wolves, lovely as they are when they howl, kill best in silence. So I point to the left and the Obsidian surge toward the soldiers listening to the Gold. He shouts for them to turn, but Sefi is already on his men before they can lift their weapons. Dancing through them with her blades fluttering into faces and knees. Her Valkyrie smash into the rest. Only two guns go off by the time the Gold's body slides off the end of Sefi's razor and thumps to the floor.

Grays fire at us from the other side of the pit. Holiday and her commandos pick them off. My helmet slithers away. "Roque," I snarl as my men continue to kill.

He's turned now from his battle to see me. All the nobility in him, all the cold-blooded Imperator melting away, leaving him a stunned, startled man. Victra and I stalk across the bridge, Blues beneath us to every side, staring up at us in confusion and fear even as their ship is engaged in battle. Silently, Roque's two Praetorians come at us. Both wear black and purple armor adorned with the silver quarter moon of House Lune. We pair off on the metal bridge in the hydra. Victra taking the right, me the left. My Praetorian is shorter than I. Her helmet off, hair in a tight bun, ready to proclaim the grand laurels of her family. "My name is Felicia au . . ." I feint a whip at her face. She brings her blade up, and Victra goes diagonal and impales her at the belly button. I finish her off with a neat decapitation.

"Bye, Felicia," Victra spits, turning to the last Praetorian. "No substance these days. Are you of the same fiber?" The man drops his razor and goes to his knees, saying something about surrender. Victra's about to cut his head off anyway, when she glimpses me out of the corner of her eye. Grudgingly, she accepts his surrender, kicking him in the face and hands him over to our Obsidians who secure the bridge. "You like the clawDrills?" Victra asks, pacing to Roque's left. Hungry for the kill. "That's some poetic justice for you, you little backstabbing bitch."

The Blues still watch on, unsure of what to do. The boarding party that came for us now fills our place in the corridor outside the bridge. We left the drill, but it would take them ten minutes at least to breach the door.

The com on Roque's head buzzes with requests for orders. Squadrons he'd sent on attack runs now drift, overexposed. Their commanders used to being guided by the invisible hand now fight blind to the overall battle. It's the flaw in Roque's strategy. The individual initiative now creates chaos, because the central intelligence has just gone silent.

"Roque, tell your fleet to stand down," I demand. I'm soaked with sweat. Hamstring pulled. Hand trembling with exhaustion. I take a heavy step forward. Boot clomping on the steel. "Do it."

He stares past me, at the Pink who let us onto the bridge. Voice thick with the betrayal of a lover instead of that of a master. "Amathea . . . even you?" The young woman is not shamed by his sadness. She pulls her shoulders back, anchoring herself to the spot. She removes the rose badge on her collar that marks her the property of the gens Fabii and drops it to the ground.

A tremor passes through my friend. "You romantic sop." Victra laughs. I close the distance between myself and Roque. Boots tracking blood over his gray steel deck. I point to the display behind him where Mustang's ship is dying. I can see the stars glittering through holes in her hull, but still the destroyers punish her. They're orientated off the bow of the *Pax,* thirty kilometers closer than her ship.

"Tell them to stop firing!" I say, pointing my razor at him. His own is on his hip. He knows how little it means to draw it against me. "Do it now."

"No."

"That's Mustang!" I say.

"She chose her fate."

"How many men did you send?" I ask coldly. "How many did you send to the *Pax* to bring me back here? Fifteen thousand? How many are on those destroyers?" I slide back the protective sheath over my datapad on my left forearm and summon the reactor diagnostics of the *Pax*. It pulses red. We've reversed the coolant flow to let the reactor overheat. A slight increase in the output demand and it goes thermal. "Tell them to cease fire or their lives are forfeit."

He lifts his gentle chin. "According to my conscience I can give no such order."

He knows what it means.

"Then this is on both of us."

His head snaps toward his comBlue. "Cyrus, tell the destroyers to take evasive action."

"Too late," Victra says as I raise the output on the generator. It throbs an evil crimson on my datapad, washing us with its light. And on the hologram behind Roque, the *Pax* begins to release gouts of blue flame. Frantically responding to their Imperator, the destroyers halt their barrage on Mustang and try to jet away, but a bright light implodes in the center of the *Pax,* enveloping the metal decks and crumpling the hull as energy spasms outward. The shock wave hits the destroyers and, crumpling their hulls, smashes them into one another. The *Colossus* shudders around us and we're knocked through space as well, but her shielding holds. The *Dejah Thoris* drifts, lights dark. I can only pray that Mustang is alive. I bite the inside of my cheek to make me focus.

"Why didn't you just use our guns," Roque says, shaken by the loss of his men, of his destroyers, at being so outmaneuvered. "You could have crippled them. . . ."

"I'm saving these guns," I say.

"They won't save you." He turns back to me. "My fleet has yours in flight. They will decimate the remainder and return here and take the *Colossus* back. Then we'll see how well you hold a bridge."

"Silly Poet. Haven't you wondered where Sevro is?" Victra asks. "Don't tell me you lost track of him in all this." She nods to the screen where his fleet pursues the routed forces of the Moon Lords and Orion toward Jupiter. "He's about to make his entry."

When the battle began, the outermost of the inner four moons of Jupiter, Thebe, was in far rotation. But as the battle dragged on, her orbit brought her closer, and closer, taking her across the path of my now-retreating navy, just under twenty thousand kilometers from Io. Led by Antonia's flagship, Roque's fleet pursued, as they should have, to complete the destruction of my forces. What they did not anticipate was that my ships had always planned to bring them to Thebe, the proverbial dead horse.

While I negotiated with Romulus, teams of Helldivers were melting caverns into the face of barren Thebe. Now, as Roque's battlecruisers and torchShips pass the moon, Sevro and six thousand soldiers in starShells pour out of the caverns. And out the other side of the moon pours two thousand leechCraft packed with fifty thousand Obsidians and forty thousand screaming Reds. Railguns spray. Flak deploys last minute. But my forces envelope the enemy, latching onto their hulls like a cloud of Luna gutter mosquitos to burrow into their guts and claim the ships from the inside.

Yet even my victory carries betrayal. Romulus had Gold leechCraft of his own prepared to launch from the surface of the moon, so that he could capture ships as well to balance my gains. But I need the ships more than he. And my Reds collapsed the mouth of their tunnels at the same time Sevro launches. By the time he realizes the sabotage, my fleet will outnumber his.

"I could not lure you to an asteroid field, so I brought one to you," I say to Roque as we watch the battle unfold.

"Well played," Roque whispers. But we both know the plan works only because I have a hundred thousand Obsidian and he does not. At most, his entire fleet has ten thousand. Probably more like seven. Worse, how could he have known that I had so many when every other Sons of Ares attack has rested on the backs of Reds? Battles are won months before they are fought. I never had enough ships to beat him. But now my ships will continue to flee, continue to run away from his guns as my men carve his battlecruisers apart from the inside. Slowly his ships will become my ships and fire on the very vessels they're in formation with. You can't defend against that. He can vent the ships, but my men will have magnetic gear, breathing masks. He'll only kill his own.

"The day is lost," I say to the thin Imperator. "But you can still save lives. Tell your fleet to stand down."

He shakes his head.

"You're in a corner, Poet," Victra says. "There's no getting out. Time to do the right thing. I know it's been a while."

"And destroy what's left of my honor?" he asks quietly as a group of twenty men in starShells penetrate the rear hangar of a nearby destroyer. "I think not."

"Honor?" Victra sneers. "What honor do you think you have? We were your friends and you gave us up. Not just to be killed. But to be put in boxes. To be electrocuted. Burned. Tortured night and day for a year." Here in armor, it's hard to imagine the blond warrior to have ever been a victim. But in her eyes there's that special sadness that comes from seeing the void. From feeling cut away from the rest of humanity. Her voice is thick with emotion. "We were your friends."

"I swore an oath to protect the Society, Victra. The same oath you both swore the day we stood before our betters and took the scar upon our faces. To protect the civilization that brought order to man. Look upon what you've done instead." He eyes the Valkyrie behind us in disgust.

"You don't live in a bedtime story, whimpering little sod," she snaps. "You think any of them care about you? Antonia? The Jackal? The Sovereign?"

"No," he says quietly. "I have no such illusions. But it's not about them. It's not about me. Not every life is meant to be warm. Sometimes the cold is our duty. Even if it pulls us from those we love." He looks pityingly at her. "You'll never be what Darrow wants. You have to know that."

"You think I'm here for him?" she asks.

Roque frowns. "Then it's revenge?"

"No," she says angrily. "It's more than that."

"Who are you trying to fool?" Roque asks, jerking his head toward me. "Him or yourself?" The question catches Victra off guard.

"Roque, think of your men," I say. "How many more have to die?"

"If you care so much for life, tell yours to stop firing," Roque replies. "Tell them to fall in line and understand that life isn't free. It isn't without sacrifice. If all take what they want, how long will it be till there's nothing left?"

It breaks me to hear him say those words.

My friend has always had his own way of things. His own tides that come in and out. It is not in his nature to hate. Nor was it in mine. Our worlds made us what we are, and all this pain we suffer is to fix the folly of those who came before, who shaped the world in their image and left us the ruin of their feast. Ships detonate in his irises. Washing his pale face with furious light.

"All this . . . ," he whispers, feeling the end coming. "Was she so lovely?"

"Yes. She was like you," I say. "A dreamer." He's too young to look so old. Were it not for the lines on his face and the world between us, it would seem only yesterday that he crouched before me as I shivered on the floor of the Mars Castle after killing Julian and he told me that when you're thrown in the deep, there's only one choice. Keep swimming or drown. I should have loved him more. I would have done anything to keep him at my side and show him the love he deserves.

But life is the present and the future, not the past.

It's as if we look at each other from distant shores and the river between widens and roars and darkens till our faces are pale shards of the moon in the deep night. More ideas of the boys we were than the men we are. I see the resolve forming in his face. The determination pulling him away from this life.

"You don't have to die."

"I have lost the invincible armada," he says, stepping back, his hand tightening on his razor. Behind him, the display shows Sevro's trap ruining the main body of his fleet. "How can I go on? How can I bear this shame?"

"I know shame. I watched my wife die," I say. "Then I killed myself. Let them hang me to end it all. To escape the pain. I've felt that guilt every day since. This is not the way out."

"My heart breaks for who you were," he says. "For that boy who watched his wife die. My heart broke in that garden. It breaks now knowing all you suffered. But the only solace was my duty, and now that has been robbed from me. All the remittance I've attempted to make . . . gone. I love the Society. I love my people." His voice softens. "Can't you see that?"

"I can."

"And you love yours." It's not judgment, not forgiveness that he gives me. It's just a smile. "I cannot watch mine fade. I cannot watch it all burn."

"It won't."

"It will. Our age is ending. I feel the days shortening. The brief light dimming upon the kingdom of man."

"Roque . . ."

"Let him do it," Victra says from behind me. "He chose his fate." I hate her for being so cold even now. How can she not see that beneath his deeds, he's a good man? He's still our friend, despite what he's done to us.

"I'm sorry for what happened, Victra. Remember me fondly."

"I won't."

He favors her with a sad smile as he strips the Imperator badge from his left shoulder and clutches it in his hand, drawing his strength from it. But then he tosses it to the ground. There's tears in his eyes as he strips away the other. "I do not deserve these. But I shall have glory by losing this day. More than you by vile conquest shall attain."

"Roque, just listen to me. This not the end. This is the beginning. We can repair what's broken. The worlds need Roque au Fabii." I hesitate. "I need you."

"There is no place for me in your world. We were brothers, but I would kill you, if only I had the power."

I'm in a dream. Unable to change the forces that move around me. To stop the sand from slipping through my fingers. I set this into motion but didn't have the heart or strength or cunning or whatever the hell I needed to stop it. No matter what I do or say, Roque was lost to me the moment he discovered what I am.

I step toward him, thinking I can take his razor from his hand without killing him, but he knows my intention and he holds up his off hand plaintively. As if to comfort me and beg me the mercy of letting him die as he lived. "Be still. Night hangs upon mine eyes." He looks to me, eyes full with tears.

"Keep swimming, my friend," I tell him.

With a gentle nod, he wraps his razor whip around his throat and stiffens his spine. "I am Roque au Fabii of the *gens* Fabii. My ancestors walked upon red Mars. They fell upon Old Earth. I have lost the day, but I have not lost myself. I will not be a prisoner." His eyes close. His hand trembles. "I am the star in the night sky. I am the blade in the twilight. I am the god, the glory." His breath shudders out. He is afraid. "I am the Gold."

And there, on the bridge of his invincible warship as his famous fleet falls to ruin behind him, the Poet of Deimos takes his own life. Somewhere the wind howls and the darkness whispers that I'm running out of friends, running out of light. The blood slithers away from his body toward my boots. A shard of my own reflection trapped in its red fingers.

49

||||||||||||||||||||

COLOSSUS

Victra is less shaken than I. She assumes command as I linger over Roque's corpse. His lifeless eyes stare at the ground. Blood thunders in my ears. Yet the war rages on. Victra's standing over the Blue operations pit, face drawn in determination.

"Does anyone contest that this ship now belongs to the Rising?" Not a sailor says a word. "Good. Follow orders and you'll keep your post. If you can't follow orders, stand up now and you'll be a prisoner of war. If you say you can follow orders but don't, we shoot you in the head. Choose." Seven Blues stand. Holiday escorts them out of the pit. "Welcome to the Rising," Victra says to the remainders. "The battle is far from won. Give me a direct link to *Persephone's Howl* and *Reynard*. Main screen."

"Belay that," I say. "Victra, make the call on your datapad. I don't want to broadcast the fact that we have taken this ship just yet."

Victra nods and punches her datapad several times. Orion and Daxo appear on the holo. The dark woman speaks first. *"Victra, where is Darrow?"*

"Here," Victra says quickly. "What's your status? Have you heard from Virginia?"

"*A third of the enemy fleet is boarded. Virginia is aboard an escape pod, about to be picked up by the* Echo of Ismenia. *Sevro's in the halls of their secondary flagship. Periodic reports. He's making headway. Telemanuses and Raa are pinching. . . .*"

"*An even match,*" Daxo says. "*We'll need the* Colossus *to tilt the odds. My father and sisters have boarded the* Pandora. *They're striking for Antonia. . . .*"

Their conversation feels a world away.

Through my grief, I feel Sefi approach me. She kneels beside Roque. "This man was your friend," she says. I nod numbly. "He is not gone. He is here." She touches her own heart. "He is there." She points to the stars on the holo. I look over at her, surprised by the deep current she reveals to me. The respect she gives Roque now doesn't heal my wounds, but it makes them feel less hollow. "Let him see," she says, nodding to his eyes. The purest gold, they stare now at the ground. So I unscrew my gauntlet and close them with my bare fingers. Sefi smiles and I gain my feet beside her.

"Pandora *is moving lateral to sector D-6,*" Orion says of Antonia's ship. On the display, the Severus-Julii ships are separating from the Sword Armada and firing at each other to try and skin away the leech-Craft which festoon them. She's shifting power to engines and away from shields and angling away from the engagement. "*Now D-7.*"

"She's abandoning them," Victra says, dumbfounded. "The little shit is saving her own hide." The Society Praetors must not believe what they're seeing. Even if I brought the *Colossus* to bear on them, the fleets would be evenly matched. The battle would last another twelve hours and exhaust both our fleets. Now it crumbles apart.

Whether by cowardice or betrayal, I don't know, but Antonia just gave us the battle on a silver platter.

"*She's left us a gap,*" Orion says. Her eyes go distant as she syncs with her ship captains and her own vessel, thrusting the huge capital ships into the region formerly occupied by Antonia, which brings them into the flank of the main enemy body.

"Do not let her escape!" Victra snarls.

But neither Daxo nor Orion can spare the ships to pursue Antonia. They're too busy taking advantage of her absence. "We can catch her," Victra says to herself. "Engines, prepare to give us sixty percent thrust, escalate by ten percent over five. Helmsman, set our course for the *Pandora*."

I make a quick assessment. Of our small battle at the rear of the warzone, we're the only ship still battle-ready. The rest are drifting rubble. But the *Colossus* has not yet made an action or a declaration that its bridge has been taken by the Rising. Which means we have an opportunity.

"Belay that," I snap.

"What?" Victra wheels on me. "Darrow, we have to catch her."

"There's something else that needs doing."

"She'll escape!"

"And we'll hunt her down."

"Not if she gets enough of a lead. We'll be tied here for hours. You promised me my sister."

"And I'll deliver. Think beyond yourself," I say. "Bridge shield down." I ignore the wrathful woman's glare and walk past Roque's body to peer into the blackness of space as the metal shielding beyond the glass viewports slides into the wall. In the far distance ships flicker and flash against the marble backdrop of Jupiter. Io is beneath us, and far to our left, the city moon of Ganymede glows, large as a plum.

"Holiday, recall all available infantry to protect the bridge and make safe the vessel. Sefi make sure no one gets through that door. Helmsman, set course for Ganymede. Do not make any Society ships aware the bridge is taken. Do I make myself clear? No broadcasts." The Blues follow my instructions.

"To Ganymede?" Victra asks, eying her sister's ship. "But Antonia, the battle . . ."

"The battle is won. Your sister made sure of that."

"Then what are we doing?"

Our ship's engines throb and we untangle ourselves from the wreckage of the *Pax* and Mustang's devastated strike group. "Winning the next war. Excuse me."

I wipe blood from my armored kneecap onto my face and let my helmet slither over my head. The HUD display expands. I wait. And then, as expected, a call from Romulus comes. I let it flash on the left-hand side of my screen, altering my breathing so it seems I've been running. I accept the call. His face expands over the left eighth of my visor's vision. He's in a firefight, but my vision is as constricted as his. All I can see is his face in his helmet. *"Darrow. Where are you?"*

"In the halls," I say. I pant and crouch on a knee as if taking respite. "Pressing for the *Colossus*'s bridge."

"You're not in yet?"

"Roque initiated lockdown protocol. It's thick going," I say.

"Darrow, listen carefully. The Colossus *has altered trajectory and is headed for Ganymede."*

"The docks," I whisper intensely. "He's going for the docks. Can any ships intercept?"

"No! They're out of position. If Octavia can't win, she'll ruin us. Those docks are my people's future. You must take that bridge at all cost!"

"I will . . . but Romulus. He has nukes on board. What if it's not just the docks he's going for?"

Romulus pales. *"Stop him. Please. Your people are down there too."*

"I'll do my best."

"Thank you, Darrow. And good luck. First cohort, on me . . ."

The connection dies. I remove my helmet. My men stare at me. They haven't heard the conversation, but they know what I'm doing now. "You're going to destroy Romulus's dockyards around Ganymede," Victra says.

"Holy shit," Holiday mutters. "Holy shit."

"I'm not destroying anything," I reply. "I'm fighting my way through corridors. Trying to reach the bridge. Roque is ordering this move as his last act of violence before I claim his command." Victra's eyes light up, but even she has reservations.

"If Romulus finds out, if he even suspects, he'll fire on our forces and everything we've won today goes to ash."

"And who will tell him?" I ask. I look around the bridge. "Who will tell him?" I look to Holiday. "If anyone sends a signal out, shoot them in the head. Wipe the video memory from the whole ship."

If I ruin Ganymede's dockyards the Rim won't be able to threaten us for fifty years. Romulus is an ally today, but I know he will threaten the core if the Rising succeeds. If I must give Roque for this victory, if I must give the Sons on these moons, I will take something in return. I look down. Red bootprints follow my path. I didn't even realize I'd stepped in Roque's blood.

We carve our way free of the debris formed by Mustang's fleet and mine and break away from Jupiter toward Ganymede, leaving her behind. I feel the pulsing desperation as the Moon Lords send their fastest craft to intercept us. We shoot them down. All the pride and hope of Romulus's people are in the rivets and assembly lines and electric shops of that dull gray ring of metal. All their promises of power and future independence are at my mercy.

When I reach the sparkling gem that is Ganymede, I bring the *Colossus* parallel to the monument of industry they've built in orbit at her equator. The Valkyrie gather behind us at the viewport. Sefi staring in awe at the majesty and triumph of Gold will. Two hundred kilometers of docks. Hundreds of haulers and freighters. Birthplace of the greatest ships in the Sol System including the *Colossus* herself. Like any good monster of myth, the girl must eat her mother before being free to pursue her true destiny. That destiny is leading the assault on the Core.

"Men built this?" Sefi asks with quiet reverence. Many of her Valkyrie have fallen to a knee to watch in wonder.

"My people built it," I say. "Reds."

"It took two hundred fifty years . . . It's how old the first dock there is," Victra says, shoulder to shoulder with me. Hundreds of escape pods flower out from her metal carapace. They know why we're here. They're evacuating the senior administrators, the overseers. I'm under no delusion. I know who will die when we fire.

"There's still going to be thousands of Reds on there," Holiday says quietly to me. "Oranges, Blues . . . Grays."

"He knows that," Victra says.

Holiday doesn't leave my side. "You sure you want to do this, sir?"

"Want to?" I ask hollowly. "Since when has any of this been about what we want?" I turn to the helmsman, about to give the order when Victra puts a hand on my shoulder.

"Share the load, darling. This one's on me." Her Aureate voice rings clear and loud. "Helmsman, open fire with all port batteries. Launch tubes twenty-one through fifty at their center-line."

Together, we stand shoulder to shoulder and watch the warship lay ruin to the defenseless dock. Sefi stares out in profound awe. She has watched the holos of ship warfare, but her war until now has been narrow halls and men and gunfire. This is the first time they see what a vessel of war can do. And for the first time, I see her frightened.

It's a crime that the marvel should die like this. No song. Nothing but silence and the unblinking gaze of the stars to herald the end of one of the great monuments of the Golden Age. And I hear in the back of my mind, that age-old truth of darkness whispering to me.

Death begets death begets death . . .

The moment is sadder than I wanted. So I turn to Sefi as the dock continues to fall apart. The shattered bits drifting down to the moon, where they will fall into the sea or upon the cities of Ganymede.

"The ship must be renamed," I say. "I would like you to choose."

Her face is stained with white light.

"Tyr Morga," she says without hesitation.

"What's that mean?" Holiday asks.

I look back out the viewport as explosions ripple through the dock and her escape pods flare against the atmosphere of Ganymede. "It means Morning Star."

PART IV

||||||||||||||||||||||||||||||||||

STARS

My son, my son

Remember the chains

When Gold ruled with iron reins

We roared and roared

And twisted and screamed

For ours, a vale

Of better dreams

—Eo of Lykos

50

||||||||||||||||||||||||

THUNDER AND
LIGHTNING

The Sword Armada is shattered. More than half destroyed. A quarter seized by my ships. The remainder fled with Antonia or in little ragged bands, rallying around the remaining Praetors to sprint for the Core. I sent Thraxa and her sisters in fast-moving corvettes out under Victra's command to reel Antonia in and recapture Kavax, who was captured by Antonia's forces while attempting to board the *Pandora*. I asked Sevro to go with Victra, thinking to keep the two of them together, but he went to her ship then returned a half hour before it departed, wrathful and quiet, refusing to discuss whatever it was that transpired.

For her part, Mustang is beside herself with worry for Kavax, though she makes a brave face. She'd lead the rescue mission herself if she weren't needed in the main fleet. We make repairs where we can to make the ships fit for travel. We scuttle the ships we can't save, and search the naval debris for survivors. A tentative alliance exists between the Rising and the Moon Lords, one that will not last long.

I've not slept since the battle two days ago. Neither, it seems, has Romulus. His eyes are dark with anger and exhaustion. He's lost an arm and a son on the day and more, so much more. Neither one of us could risk meeting in person. So all we have left between us is this holo conference.

"As promised, you have your independence," I say.

"And you have your ships," he replies. Marble columns stretch up behind him, carved with Ptolemaic effigies. He's on Ganymede, in the Hanging Palace. The heart of their civilization. "But they will not be enough to defeat the Core. The Ash Lord will be waiting for you."

"I hope so. I have plans for his master."

"Do you sail on Mars?"

"Perhaps."

He allows a thoughtful silence. "There's one thing I find curious about the battle. Of all the ships my men boarded, not one nuclear weapon over five megatons was found. Despite your claims. Despite your . . . evidence."

"My men found plenty enough," I lie. "Come aboard if you doubt me. It's hardly curious that they would store them on the *Colossus*. Roque would want to keep them under tight watch. We're only lucky that I managed to take bridge when I did. Docks can be rebuilt. Lives cannot."

"Did they ever have them?" Romulus asks.

"Would I risk the future of my people on a lie?" I smile without humor. "Your moons are safe. You define your own future now, Romulus. Do not look the gift horse in the mouth."

"Indeed," he says, though he sees through the lie now. Knows he was manipulated. But it is the lie he must sell to his own people if he wants peace. They cannot afford to go to war with me now, but their honor would demand it if they knew what I'd done. And if they went to war with me, I would likely win. I have more ships now. But they'd hurt me bad enough to ruin my real war against the Core. So Romulus swallows my lies. And I swallow the guilt of leaving hundreds of millions in slavery and personally signing the death warrants of thousands of Sons of Ares to Romulus's police. I gave them warning. But not all will escape. "I would like your fleet to depart before end of day," Romulus says.

"It will take three days to search the debris for our survivors," I say. "We will leave then."

"Very well. My ships will escort your fleet to the boundaries we agreed upon. When your flagship crosses into the asteroid belt, you may never return. If one ship under your command crosses that boundary, it will be war between us."

"I remember the terms."

"See that you do. Give my regards to the Core. I'll certainly give yours to the Sons of Ares you leave behind." He terminates the signal.

We depart three days after my conference with Romulus, making additional repairs as we travel. Welders and repairmen dot hulls like benevolent barnacles. Though we lost more than twenty-five capital ships during the battle, we've gained over seventy more. It is one of the greatest military victories in modern history, but victories are less romantic when you're cleaning your friends off the floor.

It's easy to be bold in the moment, because all you have is what you can process: see, smell, feel, taste. And that's a very small amount of what is. But afterward, when everything decompresses and uncoils bit by bit, and the horror of what you did and what happened to your friends hits you. It's overwhelming. That's the curse of this naval war. You fight, then spend months waiting, engaged only by the tedium of routine. Then you fight again.

I've not yet told my men where we sail. They don't ask me themselves, but their officers do. And again I give them the same answer.

"Where we must."

The core of my army is the Sons of Ares, and they are experienced in hardship. They organize dances and gatherings and force jubilation down war-weary throats. It seems to take. Men and women whistle in the halls as we distance ourselves from Jupiter. They sew unit badges onto uniforms and paint starShells in wild colors. There's a vibrancy here different from the cold precision of the Society Navy. Still they keep mostly to their Color, blending only when assigned to do so. It's not as harmonious as I thought it would be, but it's a start.

I feel disconnected from it all even as I smile and lead as best I know. I killed ten men in the corridors. Killed another thirteen thousand of my own when we destroyed the docks. Their faces don't haunt me. But that feeling of dread is hard to lose.

We have not yet been able to contact the Sons of Ares. Communications are blacked out across all channels. Which means Narol succeeded in destroying the relays as he promised. Gold and Red are just as blind now.

I give Roque the burial he would have wanted. Not in the soil of some foreign moon, but in the sun. His casket is made of metal. A torpedo with a hatch through which Mustang and I slip his body. The Howlers smuggled him from the overflowing morgue so we could say goodbye to him in secret. With so many of our own dead, it would not do to see me honor an enemy so deeply.

Few mourn the death of my friend. Roque, if he is remembered by his people, will forever be known as The Man Who Lost the Fleet. A modern Gaius Terentius Varro, the fool who let Hannibal encircle him at Cannae. Or Alfred Jones. The American general who went mad and lost his Imperium's dreaded mech division in the Conquering. To my people, he is just another Gold who thought himself immortal till the Reaper showed him otherwise.

It's a lonely thing carrying the body of someone dead and loved. Like a vase you know will never again hold flowers. I wish he believed as firmly in the afterlife as I once did, as Ragnar did. I'm not sure when I lost my faith. I don't think it's something that just happens. Maybe I've been worn down bit by bit, pretending to believe in the Vale because it's easier than the alternative. I wish Roque would have thought he was going to a better world. But he died believing only in Gold, and anything that believes only in itself cannot go happily into the night.

When it is my turn to say goodbye, I stare at his face and see nothing but memories. I think of him on the bed reading before the Gala, before I stabbed him with the sedative. I see him in his suit, pleading with me to come along with him and Mustang to the Opera in Agea, saying how much I'd delight in the plight of Orpheus. I see him laughing by the fire at her estate after the Battle of Mars. His arms around me as he sobbed after I came home to House Mars when we were hardly more than boys.

Now he is cold. Eyes ringed with circles. All the promise of youth fled. All the possibilities of family and children and joy and growing old and wise together are gone because of me. I'm reminded of Tactus now, and I feel tears coming.

My friends, the Howlers in particular, do not much like that I've let Cassius come to the funeral. But I could not stand the idea of sending Roque to the sun without the Bellona kissing him farewell. His legs are chained. Hands manacled behind his back with magnetic cuffs. I un-cuff them so he can say goodbye properly. Which he does. Leaning to kiss Roque farewell on the brow.

Sevro, pitiless even now, slams shut the metal lid after Cassius is done. Like Mustang, the little Gold came for me, in case I needed him. He has no love for the man, no heart for someone who betrayed me and Victra. Loyalty is everything to him. And, in his mind, Roque had none. So too with Mustang. Roque betrayed her as readily as he betrayed me. He cost her a father. And though she can understand Augustus was not the best of men, he was her father nonetheless.

My friends wait for me to say something. There's nothing I can say that will not anger them. So, as Mustang recommended, I spare them the indignity of having to listen to compliments about a man who signed their death warrants, and instead recite the most relevant lines of one of his old favorites.

Fear no more the heat o' the sun
Nor the furious winter's rages,
Thou thy worldly task hast done,
Home art gone, and ta'en thy wages;
Golden lads and girls all must
As chimney sweepers come to dust

"*Per aspera, ad astra,*" my Golden friends whisper, even Sevro. And with a press of a button, Roque disappears from our lives to begin his last journey to join Ragnar and generations of fallen warriors in the sun. I remain behind. The others leave. Mustang lingers with me, eyes following Cassius as he's escorted away.

"What are your plans for him?" she asks me when we're left alone.

"I don't know," I say, angry she would ask that now.

"Darrow, are you all right?"

"Fine. I just need to be alone right now."

"OK." She doesn't leave me. Instead, she steps closer. "It's not your fault."

"I said I want to be alone."

"It's not your fault." I look over at her, angry she won't leave, but when I see how gentle her eyes are, how open to me they are, I feel the tension in my ribs release. The tears come unbidden. Streaking down my cheeks. "It's not your fault," she says, pulling me close as I feel the first sob rattle my chest. She wraps her arms around my waist and puts her forehead into my chest. "It's not your fault."

Later that night my friends and I have supper together in the state-room I've inherited from Roque. It's a quiet affair. Even Sevro doesn't have much to say. He's been quiet since Victra left, something gnawing in the back of his mind. The trauma of the past few days weighs heavy on all of us. But these few men and women know where we travel, and it's that knowledge that adds even more weight than the regular soldier carries.

Mustang wants to stay behind with me, but I don't want her to. I need time to think. So I quietly click the door shut behind her. I am alone. Not just at the table in my suite, but in my grief. My friends came to Roque's funeral for me, not him. Only Sefi was kind about his passing, because over the course of our journey to Jupiter she learned of Roque's prowess in battle and so respected him in a pure way the others can't. Still, of my friends, only I loved Roque as much as he deserved in the end.

The Imperator's stateroom still smells like Roque. I leaf through the old books on his shelves. A piece of blackened ship metal floats in a display case. Several other trophies hang on the wall. Gifts from the

Sovereign "For heroism at the Battle of Deimos" and from the Arch-Governor of Mars for "The Defense of Aureate Society." *Sophocles's Theban Plays* lies open on the bedside. I've not changed the page. I've not changed anything. As if by preserving the room I can keep him alive. A spirit in amber.

I lie down to sleep, but can only stare at the ceiling. So I rise and pour three fingers of scotch from one of his decanters and watch the holoTube in the lounge. The web is down thanks to the hacking war. Creates an eerie feeling being disconnected from the rest of humanity. So I search the old programs on the ship's computer, skimming through vids of space pirates, noble Golden knights, Obsidian bounty hunters and a troubled Violet musician on Venus, till I find a menu with recently played vids catalogued. The most recent dates to the night before the battle.

My heart thumps heavily in my chest as I sort through the vids. I look over my shoulder, like I'm going through someone else's journal. Some are Aegean renditions of Roque's favorite opera, *Tristan and Isolde,* but most are feeds from our time at the Institute. I sit there, my hand in the air, about to click on the feed. But instead I feel compelled to wait. I call Holiday on my com.

"You up?"

"Now I am."

"I need a favor."

"Don't you always."

Twenty minutes later, Cassius, chained hand and foot, shuffles in from the hall to join me. He's escorted by Holiday and three Sons. I excuse them. Nodding my thanks to Holiday. "I can take care of myself."

"Begging your pardon, sir, that's not exactly a fact."

"Holiday."

"We'll be right outside, sir."

"You can go to bed."

"Just shout if you need anything, sir."

"Ironclad discipline you have here," Cassius says awkwardly after she's left. He stands in my circular marble atrium, eying the sculptures. "Roque always did dress up a place. Unfortunately he's got the taste of a ninety-year-old orchestra first chair."

"Born three millennia late, wasn't he?" I reply.

"I rather think he would have hated the toga of Rome. Distressing fashion trend, really. They made an effort to bring it back in my father's day. Especially during drinking bouts and some of the breakfast clubs they had back then. I've seen the pictures." He shudders. "Dreadful stuff."

"One day they'll say it about our high collars," I say, touching mine.

He eyes the scotch in my hand. "This a social occasion?"

"Not exactly." I lead him into the lounge. He's slow and loud in the forty kilogram prisoner boots they've sealed his feet inside, but is still more at home in the room than I am. I pour him a scotch as he sits on the couch, still expecting some sort of trap. He raises his eyebrows at the glass.

"Really, Darrow? Poison isn't your style."

"It's a cache of Lagavulin. Lorn's gift to Roque after the Siege of Mars."

Cassius grunts. "I never was fond of irony. Whisky, on the other hand . . . we never had a quarrel we couldn't solve." He looks through the whisky. "Fine stuff."

"Reminds me of my father," I say, listening to the soft hum of the air vents above. "Not that the stuff he drank was good for anything more than cleaning gears and killing brain cells."

"How old were you when he died?" Cassius asks.

"About six, I reckon."

"Six." He tilts his glass thoughtfully. "My father wasn't a solitary drinker. But sometimes I'd find him on his favorite bench. Near this eerie path on the spine of the Mons. He'd have a whisky like this." Cassius chews the inside of his cheek. "Those were my favorite moments with him. No one else around. Just eagles coasting in the distance. He'd tell me what sort of trees were on the hillside. He loved trees. He'd ramble on about what grew where and why and what birds liked to roost there. Especially in winter. Something about how they looked in the cold. I never really listened to him. Wish I had."

He takes a drink. He'll find the spirit in the glass. The peat, the grapefruit on the tongue, the stone of Scotland. I can never taste anything but the smoke. "Is that Castle Mars?" Cassius asks, nodding to the hologram above Roque's console. "By Jove. It looks so small."

"Not even the size of the engines on a torchShip," I say.

"Boggles the mind, the exponential expectations of life."

I laugh. "I used to think Grays were tall."

"Well . . ." He smiles mischievously. "If your metric is Sevro . . ." He chuckles before growing serious. "I wanted to say thank you . . . for inviting me to the funeral. That was . . . surprisingly decent of you."

"You'd have done the same."

"Hmm." He's not sure of that. "This was Roque's console?"

"Yeah. I was going through his vids. He's rewatched most of these dozens of times. Not the strategies or the battles against other houses. But the quieter bits. You know."

"Have you watched them?" he asks.

"I wanted to wait for you."

He's struck by that, and suspicious of my hospitality.

So I press play and we fall back into the boys we were in the Institute. It's awkward at first, but soon the whisky dispels that and the laughs come easier, the silences stretch deeper. We watch the nights when our tribe cooked lamb in the northern gulch. When we scouted the highlands, listening to Quinn's stories by the campfire. "We kissed that night," Cassius says when Quinn finishes a story about her grandmother's fourth attempt to build a house in a mountain valley a hundred kilometers from civilization without an architect.

"She was climbing into her sleeping roll. I told her I heard a noise. We investigated. When she found out I was just throwing rocks into the dark to get her alone, she knew what I wanted. That smile." He laughs. "Those legs. The kind meant to be wrapped around someone, you know what I mean?" He laughs. "But the lady did protest. Put her hand in my face, shoved me away."

"Well, she wasn't an easy one," I say.

"No. But she did wake me up near morning to give me a kiss or two. On her terms, of course."

"And that is the first time throwing stones has ever worked on a woman."

"You'd be surprised."

There's moments I never knew existed. Roque and Cassius try to catch fish together only for Quinn to push Cassius in from behind. He takes a deep drink beside me now as his younger self splashes in the water and tries to pull Quinn in. We watch private moments where Roque fell in love with Lea, where they scouted the highlands in the dark. Their hands brushing innocently together as they stop for water. Fitchner surveying them from a copse of trees, taking notes on his datapad. We watch the first time they sleep snuggled under the same blankets in the gate's keep, and as Roque takes her off to the highlands to steal his first kiss only to hear boots on rocks and see Antonia and Vixus emerge from the mist, eyes glowing with optics.

They took Lea and when Roque fought, threw him off a cliff. He broke his arm and was swept down the river. By the time he returned, after three days of walking, I was supposedly dead by the Jackal's hand. Roque mourned for me and visited the cairn I built atop Lea only to find that wolves dug in and had stolen the body. He wept there by himself. Cassius grows somber witnessing this, reminding me of the distress on his face when he returned with Sevro to discover what had happened to Lea and Roque. And perhaps feeling guilty for ever allying himself with Antonia.

There's more videos, more little truths I discover. But the one viewed the most according to the holodeck was the time Cassius said he'd found two new brothers and offered us places as lancers to House Bellona. He looked so hopeful then. So happy to be alive. We all did, even I, despite what I felt inside. My betrayal feels all the more monstrous watching it from afar.

I refill Cassius's tumbler. He's quiet under the glow of the hologram. Roque's riding his dappled gray mare away from us, looking pensively down at his reins. "We killed him," he says after a moment. "It was our war."

"Was it?" I ask. "We didn't make this world. And we're not even fighting for ourselves. Neither was Roque. He was fighting for Octavia. For a Society that won't even notice his sacrifice. They'll play politics with his death. Blame him. He died for them and he'll just be a punch line." Cassius feels the disgust I intended. That's his greatest fear. That no one will care that he goes. This noble idea of honor, of a good death . . . that was for the old world. Not this one.

"How long do you think this goes on?" he asks pensively. "This war."

"Between us or everyone?"

"Us."

"Till one heart beats no more. Isn't that what you said?"

"You remembered." He grunts. "And everyone?"

"Until there are no Colors."

He laughs. "Well, good. You've aimed low."

I watch him tilt the liquor around in his glass. "If Augustus did not put me with Julian, what do you think would have happened?"

"Doesn't matter."

"Say it does."

"I don't know," he says sharply. He downs his whisky and pours himself another, surprisingly agile in his cuffs. He considers the glass in irritation. "You and I aren't like Roque or Virginia. We're not nuanced creatures. All you have is thunder. All I have, lightning. Remember that dumb shit we used to say when we would paint our faces and ride about like idiots? It's the deepspine truth. We can only obey what we are. Without a storm, you and I? We're just men. But give us this. Give us conflict . . . how we rattle and roar." He mocks his own grandiloquence, a dark irony staining his smile.

"You really think that's true?" I ask. "That we're stuck being one thing or another."

"You don't?"

"Victra says that about herself." I shrug. "I'm betting a hell of a lot that she's not. That we're not." Cassius leans forward and pours me a drink this time. "You know, Lorn always talked about being trapped by himself, by the choice he made, till it felt like he wasn't living his own life. Like something was behind him beating him on, something to the sides winnowing his path. In the end, all his love, all his kindness, family, it didn't matter. He died as he lived."

Cassius sees more than just the doubt in my own theory. He knows I could talk about Mustang, or Sevro, or Victra changing. Being different, but he sees the undercurrent because in many ways his thread in life is the most like my own. "You think you're going to die," he says.

"As Lorn used to say, the bill comes at the end. And the end is on its way."

He watches me gently, his whisky forgotten, the intimacy deeper than I intended. I've touched a part of his own mind. Maybe he too has felt like he's marching toward his own burial. "I never thought about the weight on you," he says carefully. "All that time among us. Years. You couldn't talk to anyone, could you?"

"No. Too risky. Kind of a conversation killer. Hello, I'm a Red spy."

He doesn't laugh. "You still can't. And that's what kills you. You're among your own people and you feel a stranger."

"There it is," I say, raising a glass. I hesitate, wondering how much to confide in him. Then whisky talks for me. "It's hard to talk to anyone. Everyone is so fragile. Sevro with his father, with the weight of a people he hardly knows. Victra thinks she's wicked and keeps pretending like she just wants revenge. Like she's full of poison. They think I know the path here. That I've had a vision of the future because of my wife. But I don't feel her like I used to. And Mustang—" I stop awkwardly.

"Go on. What about her? Come on, man. You killed my brothers. I killed Fitchner. It's already awkward."

I grimace at the weirdness of this little moment.

"She's always watching me," I say. "Judging. Like she's keeping a tally of my worth. Whether I'm fit."

"For what?"

"For her? For this? I don't know. I felt like I proved myself on the ice, but it hasn't gone away." I shrug. "It's the same for you, isn't it? Serving at the Sovereign's pleasure when Aja killed Quinn. Your mother's . . . expectations. Sitting here with the man who took two brothers from you."

"You can have Karnus."

"He must have been a treat at home."

"He was actually fond of me as a child," Cassius says. "I know. Hard to believe, but he was my champion. Included me in sports. Took me on trips. Taught me about girls, in his way. He was not so kind to Julian, though."

"I have an older brother. His name's Kieran."

"Is he alive?"

"He's a mechanic with the Sons. Got four kids."

"Wait. You're an uncle?" Cassius says in surprise.

"Several times over. Kieran married Eo's sister."

"Did he? I was an uncle once. I was good at that." His eyes go distant, smile fading, and I know the suspicions that rest heavy on his soul. "I'm tired of this war, Darrow."

"So am I. And if I could bring Julian back to you, I would. But this war is for him, or men like him. The decent. It's for the quiet and gentle who know how the world should be, but can't shout louder than the bastards."

"Aren't you afraid you're going to break everything and not be able to put it back together?" he asks sincerely.

"Yes," I say, understanding myself better than I have for a long time. "That's why I have Mustang."

He stares at me for a long, odd moment before shaking his head and chuckling at himself or me. "I wish it was easier to hate you."

"There's a toast if I ever heard one." I raise my glass and he his, and we drink in silence. But before he parts with me that night, I give him a holocube to watch in his cell. I apologize in advance for its contents, but it's something he needs to see. The irony is not lost on him. He'll watch it later in his cell, and he will weep and feel lonelier still, but the truth is never easy.

51

||||||||||||||||||||||||

PANDORA

Hours after Cassius has left me, I'm woken from a restless dream by Sevro. He calls my datapad with an urgent message. Victra has engaged Antonia in the Belt. She requests reinforcements, and Sevro's already got his gear and has Holiday mustering a strike team.

Mustang, the Howlers and I hitch a ride on the remaining Telemanus torchShip, the fastest left in the fleet. Sefi tried to come along, eager for more combat, but even after the victory at Io my fleet rides on a razor's edge. Her leadership is needed to keep the Obsidians in line. She's a peacemaker, and the punch line of Sevro's favorite new joke: what do you say when a seven-and-a-half-foot-tall woman walks into a room with a battle axe and tongues on a hook? Absolutely nothing.

Personally, I'm more worried that only a handful of strong personalities bind this alliance together. If I lose one, the whole thing might crumble.

We go full burn, straining the ships to reach Victra, but an hour before we arrive at her coordinates amidst a thicket of sensor-disrupting asteroids, we receive a brief encoded message that is patented Julii: *Bitch captured. Kavax free. Victory mine.*

We shuttle over from the lean Telemanus torchShip toward Victra's waiting fleet. Sevro picks nervously at his pant leg. Victra's won a great victory. She set out in pursuit with twenty strike craft. Now she possesses nearly fifty black ships—fast, nimble, expensive craft. Just the sort you'd expect of a trading family. None of the hulking behemoths the Augustuses and Bellona favor. All the black ships bear the weeping spear-pierced sun of the Julii family.

Victra waits for us on the deck of her mother's old flagship, the *Pandora*. She's splendid and proud in a black uniform with the Julii sun upon her right breast, a fiery orange line burning down the black pants, gold buttons sparkling. She's found her old earrings. Jade hangs from her ears. Her smile is broad and enigmatic.

"My goodmen, welcome aboard the *Pandora*."

Beside her stands Kavax, injured yet again, with a cast on his right arm and resFlesh coating the right side of his face. The daughters who raced ahead to find him flank him now and laugh as Kavax bellows a hello to Mustang. She tries to maintain propriety as she rushes to him and tosses her arms around his neck. She kisses him once on his bald head.

"Mustang," he says happily. He pushes her back and lowers his head. "Apologies. Deepest apologies. I cannot stop being captured."

"Just a damsel in distress," Sevro says.

"It seems the case," Kavax replies.

"Just promise me this is the last time, Kavax," Mustang says. He does. "And you're injured again!"

"A scratch! Just a scratch, my liege. Don't you know I've magic in my veins?"

"I have someone who has been dying to see you," Mustang says, looking back up the ramp. She whistles and inside the shuttle Pebble lets Sophocles go. Claws clatter behind me, then under me as he races through Sevro's legs, almost knocking my friend down, to jump onto Kavax's chest. Kavax kisses the fox with open mouth. Victra cringes.

"Thought you were in trouble," Sevro grunts up at her.

"I told you I had it under control," she says. "How far behind is the rest of the fleet, Darrow?"

"Two days."

Mustang looks around. "Where's Daxo?"

"Daxo is dealing with rats on the upper decks. Still some hardcore Peerless left. It's been a bitch digging them out," Victra says.

"There's barely any wreckage . . ." I say. "How did you do this?"

"How? I am the true heir of House Julii," Victra says proudly. "According to mother's will and according to birth. Antonia's ships—legally *my* ships—were run by stool pigeons, paid allies. They contacted me, thought the whole fleet was right behind my little harrying party. They *begged* me to spare them from the big bad Reaper . . ."

"And where are your sister's men now?" I ask.

"I executed three and destroyed their ships as an example to the rest. The disloyal Praetors which I could capture are rotting in cells. My loyalists and mother's friends have taken command."

"And will they follow us?" Sevro asks gruffly.

"They follow me," she says.

"That's not the same thing," I say.

"Obviously. They're *my* ships." She's one step closer to taking back her mother's empire. But the rest can only be done in peace. Still, it gives her an eerie independence. Just like Roque had when he gained ships after the Lion's Rain. It will test her loyalty, a fact Sevro does not seem entirely comfortable with. Mustang and I frown at one another.

"Property is a funny thing these days," Sevro says. "Tends to have opinions." Victra bristles at the challenge.

Mustang inserts herself. "I think Sevro means to say: now that you have your revenge, do you still intend to come with us to the Core?"

"I don't have my revenge," Victra says. "Antonia still breathes."

"And when she does not?" Mustang asks.

Victra shrugs. "I'm not good with commitment."

Sevro's mood sours even more.

Dozens of prisoners fill the ward's cells. Most Gold. Some Blue and Gray. All high ranking and loyal to Antonia. A canyon of enemies who glare out at me from the bars. I walk alone down the hall, enjoying the feeling of so many Golds knowing I'm their captor.

I find Antonia in the second to last cell. She sits against the bars of the cell that separate her from the adjacent one. Aside from a bruised cheek, she's as beautiful as ever. Mouth sensual, eyes smoldering behind thick eyelashes as she broods under the brig's pale lights. Her willowy legs are folded under her, black-nailed hands picking at a blister on her big toe.

"I thought I heard the Reaper swing," she says with a seductive little smile. Her eyes drift slowly up the length of me, eating every centimeter up. "You've been downing your protein, haven't you, darling? All big again. Don't fret. I'll always remember you as a weeping little worm."

"You're the only Boneriders left alive in the fleet," I say looking at the cell adjacent hers. "I want to know what the Jackal's planning. I want to know his troop positions, his supply routes, his garrison strengths. I want to know what information he has on the Sons of Ares. I want to know what his plans are with the Sovereign. Are they colluding? Is there tension? Is he making a move against her? I want to know how to beat him. And most of all, I want to know where the bloodydamn nuclear weapons are. If you give me this, you live. If you do not, you die. Am I clear?"

She didn't flinch at the mention of the weapons. Neither did the woman in the adjacent cell.

"Crystal clear," Antonia says. "I'm more than willing to cooperate."

"You're a survivor, Antonia. But I wasn't just talking to you." I slam my hand on the bars of the cell next to hers where a shorter, dark-faced Gold sits watching me with raw eyes. Her face is sharp, like her tongue used to be. Hair curly and more golden than last time I saw her—artificially lightened, same with her eyes. "I'm talking to you too, Thistle. Whichever of you gives us more information gets to live."

"Devilish ultimatum." Antonia applauds from the ground. "And you call yourself a Red. I think you were more at home with us than you are with them. Isn't that right?" She laughs. "It is isn't it?"

"You have an hour to think it over."

I walk away from them, letting them stew in it. "Darrow," Thistle calls after me. "Tell Sevro I'm sorry. Darrow, please!" I turn and walk back to her slowly.

"You dyed your hair," I say.

"Little Bronzie just wanted to fit in," Antonia purrs, stretching her long legs. She's more than a head and a half taller than Thistle. "Don't blame the runt, unrealistic expectations."

Thistle stares out at me, hands clutching the bars. "I'm sorry, Darrow. I didn't know it would go so far. I couldn't have . . ."

"Yes, you did. You're not an idiot. And don't be pathetic and claim to be one. I understand how you could do it to me," I say slowly. "But Sevro was supposed to be there. So were the Howlers." She looks at the ground, unable to meet my gaze. "How could you do that to him? To them?"

She has no answer. I touch her hair with my hand. "We liked you the way you were."

52

||||||||||||||||||||||||

TEETH

I join Sevro, Mustang, and Victra in the brig's monitoring room. Two techs lean back in ergonomic chairs, several dozen holos floating around them at once. "They said anything yet?" I ask.

"Not yet," Victra answers. "But pot's stirred and I've cranked the heat."

Sevro's watching Thistle on the holoDisplay. "Did you want to talk with Thistle?" I ask.

"Who?" he asks, raising his eyebrows. "Never heard of her." I can tell he's wounded by seeing her again. Wounded even more because he tells himself to be hard, but this betrayal—by one of his own Howlers—cuts at his core. Still he plays it off. Not sure if it's for Victra, for me, or for himself. Probably all three.

After several minutes, Antonia and Thistle drip with sweat. Per my recommendation, we've made the cells forty degrees Celsius to amp up their irritability. Gravity is jacked up a fraction too. Just outside the realm of perception. So far, Thistle's done nothing but weep and Antonia has been touching the bruise on her cheek to see if any lasting damage has been done to her face. "You need to come up with a plan," Antonia says idly through the bars.

"What plan?" Thistle asks from the far corner of her own cell. "They're going to kill us even if we give them information."

"You weeping little cow. Pick your chin up. You're embarrassing your scar. You're House Mars, aren't you?"

"They know we're listening," Sevro says. "Least, Antonia does."

"Sometimes it doesn't matter," Mustang replies. "Highly intelligent prisoners often play games with their captors. It's the self-confidence that can make them even more vulnerable to psychological manipulation because they think they're still in control."

"You know this from your own extensive personal experience being tortured?" Victra asks. "Do tell me about that."

"Quiet," I say, turning up the holo's volume.

"I'm going to tell them everything," Thistle's saying to Antonia. "I don't give a shit about this anymore."

"Everything?" Antonia asks. "You don't know everything."

"I know enough."

"I know more," Antonia says.

"Who would ever trust you?" Thistle snaps. "Matricidal psychopath! If you even knew what people really thought about you . . ."

"Oh, darling, you can't really be so stupid." Antonia sighs sympathetically. "You are. So sad to watch."

"What do you mean?"

"Use your head, you little simpleton. Just try, please."

"Slag you, bitch."

"I'm sorry, Thistle," Antonia says, arching her back against the bars. "It's the heat."

"Or syphilitic madness," Thistle mutters, now pacing, arms wrapped around herself.

"How . . . base. It's in the upbringing really."

I consider pulling Thistle out, extracting the information she's willing to give. "Could be a ruse," Mustang says. "Something Antonia designed in case they were captured. Or maybe my brother's play. That'd be like him to sow misinformation. Especially if they just let themselves be captured."

"Let themselves be captured?" Victra asks. "There's over fifty dead

Golds in the morgues of this ship who would disagree with that statement."

"She's right," Sevro says. "Let it play. Might make Antonia open up more when we get her in a room."

Antonia closes her eyes, resting her head against the bars, knowing Thistle will ask what she meant by "use her head." And sure enough, Thistle does. "What did you mean when you said if I tell them everything, I'd have no more use?"

Antonia looks back at her through the bars. "Darling. You really haven't thought this through. I'm dead. You said it yourself. I can try to deny it, but . . . my sister makes me look like the village cat. I shot her in the spine and played acid drip with her back for almost a year. She's going to peel me like an onion."

"Darrow wouldn't let her do that."

"He's Red, we're just devils in crowns to him."

"He wouldn't *do* that."

"I know a Goblin that would."

"His name's Sevro."

"Is it?" Antonia couldn't care less. "Point's the same. I'm dead. You might have a chance. But they only need one of us alive for information. The question you have to ask yourself is if you tell them everything, will they still keep you alive? You need a strategy. Something to hold back. To barter incrementally."

Thistle approaches the bars that separate the women. "You're not fooling me." Her voice becomes brave. "But you know what, you *are* done. Darrow is going to win and maybe he should. And you know what? I'm going to help him." Thistle looks up at the camera in the corner of her cell, taking her eyes off Antonia. "I'll tell you what he's planning, Darrow. Let me make . . ."

"Get her out," Mustang says. "Get her out now."

"No . . ." Victra murmurs beside me, seeing what Mustang sees. Sevro and I look at the women in confusion, but Victra's already halfway to the door. "Open cell 31!" she shouts to the techs before disappearing through into the hall. Realizing what's happening, Sevro and I rush after her, knocking over a Green who's adjusting one of the holoscreens. Mustang follows. We break into the hallway and run to the brig security door. Victra's hammering on the door, shouting to be let in. The door buzzes and we fly in behind her, past the confused security guards who are gathering their gear, and into the cell block.

Prisoners are shouting. But even then I hear the wet *thwop, thwop, thwop* before we make it to Antonia's cell and see her hunched over Thistle. Her hands through the bars that separate their cells, drenched in blood. Fingers gripping Thistle's curly hair. The shattered remnants of the top of the Howler's skull bend around the bar as Antonia jerks Thistle's head toward her and against the bars between them one last time. Victra shoves open the magnetized cell door.

Antonia rises, grisly deed finished, bloody hands held in the air innocently as she bestows a little smirk upon her older sister. "Careful," she taunts. "Careful, Vicky. You need me. I'm the only one left with information to sell. Unless you want to stumble into the Jackal's maw you'll . . ."

Victra breaks Antonia's face. I can hear the brittle snap of bone from ten meters away. Antonia reels back, trying to escape. Victra pins her to the wall and beats her. Machinelike and eerily quiet. Elbow pumping back, driving from her legs, just as they teach us. Antonia's fingers claw at Victra's muscled arms, then go limp as the sound becomes wet and muddy. Victra doesn't stop. And I don't stop her, because I hate Antonia, and that dark little part of me wants her to feel the pain.

Sevro shoves past me and launches himself at Victra, pinning her right arm back and choking her with his left. He sweeps her legs and takes her backward to the floor, locking his legs around her waist, immobilizing her. Released from Victra's hold, Antonia flops sideways. Mustang lunges forward to keep her head from cracking on the sharp edge of the welded metal bed pallet. I kneel and reach through the bars to feel Thistle's pulse though I don't know why I bother. Her head is caved in. I stare at it. Wondering why I'm not horrified at the scene.

Some part of me has died. But when did it die? Why did I not notice?

Mustang is shouting for a Yellow. The guards picking up the call. I shake myself.

Sevro's letting go of Victra. She coughs from where he restrained her, shoving him away angrily. Mustang bends over Antonia, who's now snoring through her shattered nose. Face a ruin. Bits of teeth littering mashed lips. Except for her hair and Sigils, you can't even tell she's a Gold. Victra leaves the room without looking at her, pushing through the Gray guards so hard two of them fall down.

"Victra . . ." I call after her like there's something to say.

She turns back to me, eyes red, not with rage, but a fathomless sadness. Knuckles frayed open. "I used to braid her hair," she says forcefully. "I don't know why she's like this. Why I am." Half of one of her sister's broken teeth protrudes from the meat between her middle and ring knuckle. She pulls the tooth from her knuckles, and holds it up to the light like a child discovering sea glass on the beach before shivering in horror and letting it clatter to the steel deck. She looks past me to Sevro. "Told you."

Later that day, as the doctors tend to Antonia, the Sons go through Thistle's personal effects in her suite aboard the torchShip, the *Typhon*. Under a false bottom in a cabinet, they find the stinking, cured fur of a wolf. Sevro chokes up when Screwface brings it to him.

"Thistle cut her down," Clown says as the remaining original Howlers loiter around the room. Mustang gives them space, watching from the wall. Pebble, Screwface, and Sevro are with us. "When Antonia was crucified by the Jackal at the Institute, Thistle cut her down."

"I'd forgotten," I say from her desk.

Sevro snorts. "What a world."

"Remember when you had her fight Lea when Lea couldn't skin the sheep? Trying to make her tough," Pebble says with a little laugh. Sevro laughs too.

"Why are you laughing?" Clown asks. "You were still off eating mushrooms and howling at the moon back then."

"I was watching," Sevro says. "I was always watching."

"That's creepy, boss," Screwface says drolly. "What were you doing while you were watching?"

"Wanking in the bushes, obviously," I say.

Sevro grunts. "Only when everyone was asleep."

"Gross." Pebble wrinkles her nose and tucks the Howler cloak in her pack. "Howl on, little Thistle." The kindness in her eyes is almost too much to bear. There's no recrimination. No anger. Just the absence of a friend. Reminds me how much I love these people. Clown and Pebble leave hand in hand, Screwface taunting them all the while. I smile at the sight as Sevro and I linger behind. Mustang still hasn't moved from her place at the wall.

"What did Victra mean when she said 'told you'?" I ask.

Sevro glances at Mustang. "Ah it doesn't matter anymore." He acts like he's going to leave, but hesitates. "She called it off."

"It?" I ask.

"*Us.*"

"Oh."

"I'm sorry, Sevro," Mustang says. "She's going through a lot right now."

"Yeah." He leans against the wall. "Yeah. It's my fault, prolly. Told her . . ." He makes a face. "I told her I . . . *loved* her before the battle. Know what she said?"

"Thank you?" Mustang guesses.

He flinches. "Naw. She just said I was an idiot. Maybe she's right. Maybe I just read too much into it. Just got excited, you know." He looks at the ground, thinking. Mustang nods at me to say something.

"Sevro, you're a lot of things. You're smelly. You're small. Your tattoo taste is questionable. Your pornographic proclivities are . . . uh, eccentric. And you've got really weird toenails."

He swivels to look at me. "Weird?"

"They're really long, mate. Like . . . you should trim them."

"Nah. They're good for hanging on to things."

I squint at him, not sure if he's joking, and carry on as best I can. "I'm just saying, you're a lot of things, boyo. But you are not an idiot."

He makes no sign of having heard me. "She thinks she had poison in her veins. That's what she was talking about in the brig. Said she'd just ruin everything. So better just to cut it off."

"She's just scared," Mustang says. "Especially after what just happened."

"You mean what's happening . . ." He sits against the wall and leans his head back against it. "Startin' to feel like a prophecy. Death begets death begets death. . . ."

"We won at Jupiter . . . ," I say.

"We can win every battle and still lose the war," Sevro mutters. "The Jackal's got something up his sleeve and Octavia's only wounded. Scepter Armada is bigger than the Sword Armada, and they'll pull the fleets from Venus and Mercury. We'll be outnumbered three to one. People are gonna die. Probably most of the people we know."

Mustang smiles. "Unless we change the paradigm."

53

||||||||||||||||||||||

SILENCE

After Mustang details the broad strokes of her plan to us and we finish laughing, analyzing and dissecting its flaws, she leaves us to ruminate on it and departs to rejoin the rest of the fleet with the Telemanuses. We stay behind with Victra and the Howlers to interrogate Antonia and oversee ship repair.

The beautiful Antonia is a thing of the past. The damage she suffered was superficially catastrophic. Left orbital bone pulverized. Nose flattened, crushed so brutally they had to pull it out of her nasal cavity with forceps. Mouth so swollen it makes a hissing sound as air goes between her shattered front teeth. Whiplash and severe concussion. The ship doctors thought she was in a ship crash until they found the imprint of House Jupiter's lightning crest in several places on her face.

"Marked by justice," I say. Sevro rolls his eyes. "What? I can be funny."

"Keep practicing."

When I question Antonia, her left eye is a swollen black mass. The right peers out at me in rage, but she cooperates. Perhaps now because she thinks threats against her carry a bit of merit, and that her sister is just waiting to finish the job.

According to her, the Jackal's last communiqué stated he was making preparations for our attack on Mars. He gathers his fleet around retaken Phobos and recalls Society ships from The Can and other naval depots. Similarly, there's an exodus of Gold, Silver, and Copper ships away from Mars to Luna or Venus, which have become refugee centers for disenfranchised patricians. Like London during the first French Revolution or New Zealand after the Third World War when the continents brimmed with radioactivity.

The problem with Antonia's information is that it's difficult to verify. Impossible really, with long range and intra-planetary communication essentially back to the stone age. For all we know the Jackal might have prepared contingency information for her to give us in case she was captured under duress. If she uses that information and we act on it, we could easily be falling into a trap. Thistle would have been crucial to our understanding of information. Antonia's murder of her was horrific, but tactically very efficient.

Holiday joins me on the bridge of the *Pandora* as I try to make that contact. I sit cross-legged on the forward observation post attempting to log in to Quicksilver's digital dataDrop again. It's late night shiptime. Lights dimmed. Skeleton crew of Blues manning the pit below guiding us back to the rendezvous with the main fleet. Shadowy asteroids rotate in the distance. Holiday plops down beside me.

"Fortify thyself," she says, handing me a tin coffee mug.

"That's nice of you," I say in surprise. "Can't sleep either?"

"Nah. Hate ships actually. Don't laugh."

"That's gotta be inconvenient for a legionnaire."

"Tell me about it. Half of being a soldier is being able to sleep anywhere."

"And the other half?"

"Being able to shit anywhere, wait, and to accept stupid orders without going manic." She taps the deck. "It's the engine hum. Reminds me of wasps." She wiggles off her boots. "You mind?"

"Go on." I sip the coffee. "This is whiskey."

"You catch on quick." She winks at me boyishly.

She nods to the datapad in my hands. "Still nothin'?"

"Asteroids are bad enough, but Society is jamming everything they can."

"Well, Quicksilver gave them a run for it."

We sit quietly together. Hers isn't a naturally soothing presence, but it's the easy one of a woman raised in the agriculture backcountry where your reputation's only as good as your word and your hunting dog. We're not alike in many ways, but there's a chip on her shoulder I understand.

"Sorry about your friend," she says.

"Which one?"

"Both. You know the girl long?"

"Since school. She was a bit nasty. But loyal . . ."

"Till she wasn't," she says. I shrug in reply. "Julii is rattled."

"She talk to you?" I ask.

She laughs lightly. "Not a chance." She pops a laced burner into her mouth and lights up, I shake my head when she offers me a drag. The ship's air ducts hum. "Silence is a bitch, isn't it?" she says after a while. "But I guess you'd know that after the box."

I nod. "No one ever asks me about it," I say. "The box."

"No one asks me about Trigg."

"Do you want them to?"

"Nah."

"I never used to mind it," I say. "The silence."

"Well, you fill it with more things when you get older."

"Wasn't much to do in Lykos, 'cept sit around and watch the darkness in Lykos."

"Watch the darkness. That's so badass sounding." Smoke jets out of her nose. "We grew up near corn. Bit less dramatic. Shitloads of it far as you could see. I'd go stand in the middle of it at night sometimes and pretend it was an ocean. You can hear it whispering. It's not peaceful. Not like you'd think. It's malevolent. I always wanted to be somewhere else. Not like Trigg. He loved Goodhope. Wanted to enlist at the local precinct for policing duty or be a game warden. He'd be happy kicking it in the backwater till he was old, drinking with those idiots at Lou's, going hunting in early morning frost. I was the one who wanted out. Who wanted to *hear the ocean, see the stars.* Twenty years of service to the Legion. Cheap price."

She mocks herself, but it's curious to me that she's choosing to open up now. She found me here. At first I thought it was because she came to console me. But there's already whiskey on the squat woman's breath. She didn't want to be alone. And I'm the only one who knew Trigg even a little. I set my datapad down.

"I told him he didn't have to come with, but I knew I was draggin' him along. Told mom that I'd take care of him. Haven't even been able to tell her he's dead. Maybe she thinks we both are."

"Were you able to tell his fiancé?" I ask. "Ephraim, right?"

"You remembered."

"Of course. He was from Luna."

She watches me for a moment. "Yeah, Eph's a good one. Was with a private security firm in Imbrium City. Specialized in high-value property recovery—art, sculptures, jewels. A real pretty boy. They met at one of those themed bars when we were on leave from the Thirteenth. Venusian beach regalia. Eph didn't know about Trigg and me, that we were with the Sons and all. But I got a hold of him after we rescued you from Luna when I was out on a supply run. Used a web café. About a week after I told him Trigg was gone, he sent a message saying he was going off-grid, joining the Sons on Luna. Haven't heard from him since."

"I'm sure he's all right," I say.

"Thanks. But we both know Luna's a cluster of shit right now." She shrugs. After a moment of picking the weightlifting calluses on her palms, she nudges me. "I want you to know, you're doing good. I know you didn't ask. And I'm just a grunt. But you are."

"Trigg would approve?"

"Yeah. And he'd piss his pants if he knew were we marching on—"

She's cut short as the holo above us beeps softly and one of the comBlues calls up to me. I scramble to pick up my datapad. A single message is being broadcast across all frequencies into the belt. Our first contact with Mars since we went through the asteroid belt the first time. "Play it!" Holiday says. I do and a recording appears. It's a gray interrogation room. A man's covered in blood, shackled to a chair. The Jackal walks into frame to stand behind him.

"Is that . . ." Holiday whispers beside me.

"Yes," I say. The man is Uncle Narol.

The Jackal holds a pistol in his hand. *"Darrow. My Boneriders found this one sabotaging beacons in deep space. Really is tougher than he looks. Thought he might know your mind. But he tried to bite off his own tongue instead of talking to me. Irony for you."* He walks behind my uncle. *"I don't want a ransom. I don't want anything from you. I just want you to watch."* He lifts up the pistol. It's a slender gray slip of metal the size of my hand. The Blues in the pit gasp. Sevro rushes onto the bridge just as the Jackal points the gun at the back of my uncle's head. My uncle lifts his eyes to look into the camera.

"Sorry, Darrow. But I'll say hello to your father for—"

The Jackal pulls the trigger, and I feel another part of me slip away into the darkness as my uncle slumps in his chair. "Turn it off," I say numbly, the past flooding into me—Narol putting a frysuit helmet on my head as a boy, tussling with him at Laureltide, his sad eyes as we sat beneath the gallows after Eo's hanging, his laugh . . .

"Timestamp puts it at three weeks ago, sir," Virga, the comBlue says quietly. "We didn't receive it because of the interference."

"Did the rest of the fleet get this?" I ask quietly.

"I don't know, sir. Interference is marginal now. And it's on a pulse frequency. They've probably already seen it."

And I told Orion to keep all ships scanning in case we got lucky. It will leak.

"Oh, shit," Sevro mutters.

"What?" Holiday asks.

"We just set fire to our own fleet," I say mechanically. The fragile alliance between the highColors and low will shatter from this. My uncle was nearly as beloved as Ragnar. Narol is gone. Just like that. I feel helpless. I shudder inside. It's not real yet.

"What do we do?" Sevro asks. "Darrow?"

"Holiday, wake the Howlers," I say. "Helmsman, max thrust to rear engines. I want to be with the main fleet in four hours. Get me Mustang and Orion on the com. Telemanuses too."

Holiday snaps to attention. "Yes, sir."

Despite the interference, I reach Orion over the com and tell her to seal off all the ship bridges and to isolate control of the guns in case anyone decides to take a potshot at our Gold allies. It takes nearly thirty minutes for the Blues to connect me with Mustang. Sevro and Victra are with me now along with Daxo. The rest of his family is on their ships. The signal is weak. Interference causing static that wavers across Mustang's face. She's moving through a hall. Two Golds with her. *"Darrow, you've heard?"* she says, seeing the others behind me.

"Thirty minutes ago."

"I'm so sorry . . ."

"What's happening?"

"We received the communiqué. Some jackass tech pimped it to all the sensor chiefs," Mustang confirms. *"It's on the ship hubs throughout the fleet. Darrow . . . there's already movement against highColors on several of our ships. Three Golds on* Persephone *were killed fifteen minutes ago by Reds. And one of my lieutenants opened up on two Obsidian who tried to take her. They're dead."*

"Shit's hitting the fan," Sevro says.

"I'm evac-ing all my personnel back to our ships." There's gunshots in the background behind Mustang.

"Where are you?" I ask.

"On the Morning Star."

"What the hell are you doing there? You have to get off."

"I still have men on here. There's seven Golds in the engine deck for logistical support. I'm not leaving them behind."

"Then I'm sending my father's guard," Daxo growls from his family's torchShips. *"They'll get you out."*

"That's stupid," Sevro says.

"No," Mustang snaps. *"You send Gold knights in here, and this turns into a bloodbath we don't recover from. Darrow, you have to get back here. That's the only thing that might stop this."*

"We're still hours out."

"Well, do your best. There's one more thing . . . they've stormed the prison. I think they're going to execute Cassius."

Sevro and I exchange a look. "You need to find Sefi and stay with her," I say. "We'll be there soon."

"Find Sefi? Darrow . . . she's leading them."

54

||||||||||||||||||||||||

THE GOBLIN AND
THE GOLD

My assault shuttle lands on the auxiliary deck of the *Morning Star* where Mustang was supposed to meet us. She's not there. Neither are the Golds she was rescuing. A coterie of Sons of Ares waits for us instead, led by Theodora. She carries no weapon and looks out of place surrounded by the armored men, but they defer to her. She tells me what's happened. My uncle's death sparked several small fights that escalated into shootings on both sides. Now several ships roil with conflict.

"Mustang has been taken by Sefi's men, along with Cassius and the rest of the highColor prisoners, Darrow," Theodora announces, assessing the rest of my lieutenants.

"Gorydamn savages," Victra mutters. "If they kill her this is done."

"They won't kill her," I say. "Sefi knows Mustang's on her side."

"Why would she do this?" Holiday asks.

"Justice," Victra says, drawing a look from Sevro.

"No," I say. "No I think it's something else altogether."

"Gorydamn marvelous." Victra nods back to space. "Looks like the Telemanuses are intent on slagging this all up." Another shuttle taxis into the hangar behind us. We gather as it lands. Storming down the ramp before it even sets down, jumping to deck is the whole Te-lemanus clan. Daxo, Kavax, Thraxa, two other sisters I haven't met land heavily behind them. Armed to the teeth, though Kavax's arm is still in a sling. Behind them come thirty more of their House Golds. It's a bloodydamn army.

"They're going to get us all killed," Holiday says. At my side, Sevro blinks up at the disembarking war party.

"Death begets death begets death . . . ," he murmurs.

"Kavax, what the hell are you doing?" I ask as his family crosses the hangar.

"Virginia needs our help," he booms, not breaking his pace until I cut him off, blocking his way deeper into the ship. For a moment I think he'll go through me. "We will not leave her to the mercy of savages."

"I told you to stay on your ship."

"Unfortunately we take orders from Virginia, not you," Daxo says. "We know the ramifications of being here. But we will do what we must to protect our family."

"Mustang even told you not to storm in here with knights."

"The situation has changed," Kavax rumbles.

"You want this to turn into a war? You want our fleet to shatter? The fastest way you do that is marching in there with a show of Gold force."

"We will not let her die," Kavax says.

"And what if they kill her because of you?" I ask. That's the only thing that gives him pause. "What if they cut her throat when you storm in there?" I step close so he can see the fear on my face too and I can speak just loud enough for Daxo to hear as well. "Listen to me, Kavax, the problem with that is that you leave the Obsidian only one choice. Fight back. And you know they can. Let me handle this and we'll get her back. Don't and we'll be standing over her casket tomorrow."

Kavax looks back to his lean son, always the moderating influence, to see what he thinks. And to my relief Daxo nods. "Very well," Kavax says. "But I will go with you, Reaper. Children, await my summons. If I fall, come with all fury."

"Yes, father," they say.

Breathing a sigh of relief, I turn back to my men. "Where's Sevro?"

Sevro snuck away while we argued, to what purpose I don't know. We rush after him through the corridors, Victra behind us. Holiday leads, taking information from other Sons of Ares in through the optic implant in her eye. Her men have spotted the mob in the main hangar. They're holding a trial for Cassius for the murder of several dozen Sons of Ares, and, of course, Ares himself. No sign of Mustang. Where is she? She was supposed to stay out of sight. Meet us if she could. Did they catch her? Worse? When we reach the corridor that leads to the hangar, there's such a press of people we can barely get through, shoving Reds and Obsidians out of the way as I pass.

They're all shouting and pushing. Over their heads, near the center of the hangar, I see several dozen Obsidian and Reds astride the twenty-meter-high walkway that spans part of the hangar, high over the crowd. Sefi's at their center. Seven Golds hang dead from the walkway, suspended by rubber cable ligature, feet dangling five meters above the crowd, scalps hewn off. Aureate spines are tougher than average humans. Each of these men and women would have died horribly over several minutes from cerebral anoxia, watching the crowd beneath them curse and spit at them and hurl lugnuts and wrenches and bottles. Blood clots in a long ribbon cover their chins to their chests. Tongues removed by Sefi the Quiet. Cassius and several other prisoners await their own executions upon the walkway, kneeling beside their captors, bloody and beaten. Mustang is not with them, thank Jove. They've stripped Cassius to the waist and carved a bloody SlingBlade across his broad chest.

"Sefi!" I shout, but I can't be heard. Can't see Sevro anywhere. There's more than twenty-five thousand in a space meant for ten. Many are armed. Some wounded from the battle the week prior. All pressing into the hangar to watch the execution. The Obsidian stand titanic amidst the masses, like great boulders amidst a sea of lowColors. I never should have condensed most of the wounded and rescued crews into this hotbed of grief. The crowd has realized I'm here now and they part for me and begin to chant my name as if they think I've come to see justice done. The barbarity of it chills me. One of the men holding Cassius down is a Green tech who gave me coffee on Phobos. Most of the others I don't recognize.

One by one those Sons nearby recognize my presence. The quiet spreads around me.

"Sefi!" I snarl. "Sefi." At last she hears me. "What are you doing?"

"What you will not," she calls down in her own language, not in wrath, but acceptance that she performs an unsavory but necessary deed. Like a spirit of vengeance has drifted up from Hel. Her white hair hangs long behind her. Her knife is bloody from the tongues it has claimed. And to think I vouched for her. Let her name this ship. But just because a lion lets you pet it doesn't mean it's tame. Kavax is horrified by the scene. He's almost ready to call to his children, and would if Victra did not grip his arm and talk him down. There's fear in her eyes, too. Not just at the sight above, but at what could happen to her here. I shouldn't have brought the Golds with me.

There's moments in life where you're walking ahead so intent on your task that you forget to look down until you feel knee-deep in quicksand. I'm right there now. Surrounded by an unpredictable mob, looking up at a woman with the blood of Alia Snowsparrow running through her veins. My only defense a small circle of Sons of Ares and Golds. Holiday's pulling a scorcher. Victra's razor moves beneath her sleeve. I was too brash in storming in here. All this could go so wrong so quickly.

"Where is Mustang?" I call up to Sefi. "Did you kill her?"

"Kill her? No. The daughter of the Lion brought us from the Ice. But she stood in the way of justice, so she is in chains." Then she's safe.

"That's what this is?" I call up. "Justice? Is that what was given to Ragnar's friends who your mother hanged from the chains of the Spires?"

"This is the code of the Ice."

"You're not on the Ice, Sefi. You're on *my* ship."

"Is it yours?" This doesn't sit well with the lowColors among the crowd. "We paid for it in our blood."

"As did we all," I say. "What about the Ice was good? You left that place because you knew it was wrong. You knew your ways were shaped by your masters. You said you'd follow me. Are you a liar now?"

"Are you? You promised my people they would be safe," Sefi bellows down to me, pointing her axe, the weight of loss heavy upon her. "I have seen the works of these people. I have seen the war they make. The ships they sail. Words will not suffice. These Golds speak one language. And that is the language of blood. And so long as they live. So long as they speak, my people will not be safe. The power they have is too great."

"Do you think this is what Ragnar wanted?"

"Yes."

"Ragnar wanted you to be better than them. Than this. To be an example. But maybe the Golds are right. Maybe you are just killers. Savage dogs. Like they made you to be."

"We will never be anything more until they are gone," she says down to me, voice echoing around the hangar. "Why defend them?" She drags Cassius toward her. "Why weep over one who helped kill my brother?"

"Why do you think Ragnar gripped your hand instead of the sword when he died? He didn't want you to make your life about vengeance. It's a hollow end. He wanted more for you. He wanted a future."

"I have seen the heavens, I have seen the hells, and I know now that our future is war," Sefi says. "War until they fade in the night." She drags Cassius toward her and lifts her knife to carve out his tongue. But before she does, a pulseFist fires and knocks the weapon from her hands and Ares, lord of this rebellion, slams down on the walkway wearing his spiked helmet of war. The Obsidians recoil from him as he straightens, dusts off his shoulders and lets the helmet slither back into his armor.

"What is he doing?" Victra asks me.

"You dumb shits," Sevro sneers. "You're touching my property." He stalks across the bridge toward Sefi. "Tsst. Get away." Several Valkyrie bar his way. He stands nose to chest with them. "Move, you albino sack of pubic hair."

The Obsidian moves only when Sefi tells her to. Sevro walks past the bound Golds tapping their heads playfully as he goes. "That one's mine," he says, pointing at Cassius. "Get your hands off him, lady." She doesn't move her knife. "He cut my father's head off and put it in a box. And unless you want me to do the same to you, you'll do me the courtesy of letting go my property."

Sefi backs away but does not sheath her knife. "It is your blood debt. His life belongs to you."

"Obviously." He shoos her away. "Stand up, you little Pixie," he barks at Cassius, kicking him with his boot and hauling him up by the cable around his neck. "Have some dignity. Stand up." Cassius rises to his feet, awkwardly. Hands behind his back. Face swollen from the beatings. The slingBlade livid on his chest. "Did you kill my father?" Sevro flicks him on his broad chest. "Did you kill my father?"

Cassius looks down at him. No measure of humor to the man, just pride, not the vain sort I've seen in him over the years. War and life have drained that vigorous spirit from him. This is the face, the bearing of a man who wants nothing more than to die with a little dignity. "Yes," he says loudly. "I did."

"Glad we cleared that up. He's a murderer," Sevro shouts to the crowd. "And what do we do to murderers?"

The crowd roars for Cassius's life. And Sevro, after making a show of cupping his ear, gives it to them. He shoves Cassius off the edge of the walkway. The Gold plummets till the cable around his neck snaps taut, arresting his fall. He gags. Feet kick. Face reddens. The crowd roars hungrily, chanting Ares's name.

Mobs are soulless things that feed on fear and momentum and prejudice. They do not know the spirit in Cassius, the nobility of a man who would have given his life for his family, but was cursed to live while they all died. They see a monster. A seven-foot-tall former god now mostly naked, humbled, strangling on his own hubris.

I see a man trying his best in a world that doesn't give a shit. It breaks my heart.

Yet I do not move, because I know I'm not witnessing the death of a friend as much as I'm seeing the rebirth of another. My company does not understand. Horror stains Kavax's face. Victra's too—even though she held little pity for Cassius all this time, I think she mourns the savagery she sees in Sevro. It's an ugly thing for any man to bear. Holiday pulls her weapon, eying the Reds nearby who point to Kavax. But they're missing the show.

I watch in awe of Sevro as he bounds up onto the railing, arms wide, embracing his army. Beneath, Cassius dangles and dies and the crowd beneath makes a game of seeing who can launch themselves high enough to pull his feet. None succeed.

"My name is Sevro au Barca," my friend cries out. "I am Ares!" He thumps his chest. "I have killed forty-four Golds. Fifteen Obsidian. One hundred and thirteen Grays with my razor." The crowd roars in approval, even the Obsidians. "Jove knows who else with ships, rail-guns, and pulseFists. With nukes, knives, sharp sticks . . ." He trails off dramatically.

They slam their feet.

He beats his chest again. "I am Ares! I am a murderer too!" He puts his hands on his hips. "And what do we do to murderers?"

This time no one answers.

He never expected them to. He grabs the cable from the neck of one of the kneeling Golds, wraps it around his own neck, and looking to Sefi with a demented little smile, winks and backflips off the railing.

The crowd screams, but Victra's stunned gasp is the loudest. Sevro's rope snaps taut. He kicks, choking beside Cassius. Feet scrambling. Silent and horrible. Face turning red, on its way to purple like Cassius's. They swing together, the Goblin and the Gold, suspended above the swirling crowd that's now stampeding trying to get up the ladder to the walkway to cut Sevro down, but in their madness they overload the ladder and it bends away from the wall. Victra's about to launch herself into the air on her gravBoots to save him. I hold her down. "Wait."

"He's dying!" she says frantically.

"That's the point."

It is not a boy who dangles on that line. It is not a brokenhearted orphan who needs me to pick him up. It's a man who has been through hell and now believes in the dream of his father, in the dream of my wife. It's a man I would die to protect even as he dies to save the soul of this rebellion.

Kavax is transfixed, watching Sefi who stares down at the curious scene. Her Obsidian are just as confused. They glance to her, searching for leadership. Ragnar believed in his sister. In her capacity to be better than the world that was given them, one in which there is no such thing as mercy, no such thing as forgiveness. Silently, she hefts her axe and swings it into Sevro's cable and then, reluctantly, Cassius's. Somewhere, Ragnar is smiling.

Both men tumble through the air to be caught by the swirling crowd beneath.

Kavax has not moved since Sevro jumped, watching Sefi with a profound look of confusion. Still with his hand on the com to call his children, but I lose him in the crowd. The Sons of Ares and Howlers have formed a tight circle around their leader, shoving others back. Sevro hacks for breath on all fours. I rush to him and kneel as Holiday helps Cassius, who wheezes on the ground to my left. Pebble drapes her Howler cloak over his body.

"Can you talk?" I ask Sevro. He nods, lips trembling from the pain, but his eyes are all fire. I give my arm and help him stand. I hold up a fist, demanding silence. Sons shout the others down till the twenty-five thousand breaths balance on the beating heart of my little friend. He looks out at them, startled by the love he sees, the reverence, the wet eyes.

"Darrow's wife . . ." Sevro croaks, larynx damaged. "His wife," he says more deeply. "And my father never met. But they shared a dream. One of a free world. Not built on corpses, but on hope. On the love that binds us, not the hate that divides. We have lost many. But we are not broken. We are not defeated. We fight on. But we do not fight for revenge for those who have died. We fight for each other. We fight for those who live. We fight for those who don't yet live.

"Cassius au Bellona killed my father. . . ." He stands over the man, swallowing before looking back up. "But I forgive him. Why? Because he was protecting the world he knew, because he was afraid."

Victra pushes her way to the front of the circle, watching Sevro who speaks now as if it was meant for her and her alone. "We are the new age. The new world. And if we're to show the way, then we better damn well make it a better one. I am Sevro au Barca. And I am no longer afraid."

55

||||||||||||||||||||||

THE IGNOBLE
HOUSE BARCA

"You're bloodydamn manic," I tell Sevro when we're alone in Virany's infirmary. Sevro's holding his neck laughing at himself. I kiss the top of his head. "Bloodydamn insane, you know that?"

"Yeah well I stole that one from your playbook; what does that say about you?"

"That he's insane as well," Mickey says from the corner. He's smoking his laced-burners. Purple smoke slithering from nostrils.

Sevro winces. "That slagging hurt. I can't even look sideways."

"You sprained your neck, damaged the cartilage, lacerations in your larynx," Dr. Virany says from behind her biometric scanner. She's a lithe, tan woman with that special small silence inside her reserved for people who have seen both sides of hardship.

"Just as I said when you came in. All these tools you use, Virany. Really where's the art in it?"

Virany rolls her eyes. "Another ten kilos on your body and you would have broken your neck, Sevro. Count yourself lucky."

"Good thing I took a shit before," he grumbles.

"Darrow's neck would have held up under the strain of fifty more kilos," Mickey brags idly. "The tensile rating of his cervical—"

"Really?" Virany says tiredly. "Can't you brag later Mickey?"

"Merely observing my own mastery," Mickey replies, giving me a little wink. He enjoys pushing the gentle Virany's buttons. Since he's employed her help in his project they've been spending most waking moments in his laboratory, much to Virany's chagrin.

"Ow!" Sevro yelps as she prods the back of his spine. "That's my body."

"Sorry."

"Pixie," I say.

"I almost broke my neck," Sevro complains.

"Been there, done that. At least you didn't have to get whipped."

"I'd rather have been whipped," he mutters, wincing as he tries to turn his neck. "Be better than this."

"Not being whipped by Pax," I reply.

"I saw the video, he wasn't swinging that hard."

"Have you ever been whipped? Did you see my back?"

"You see my bloodydamn eye at the Institute? Jackal had it plucked out with a knife, didn't see me whining."

"I had my whole bloodydamn body carved open," I say as the doors hiss open and Mustang enters. "Twice."

"Oh, it always comes back to the slagging Carving," Sevro mutters, wiggling his fingers in the air. "I'm so bloodydamn special, I had my bones peeled. My DNA spliced."

"Do they always do this?" Virany asks Mustang.

"Seems like," Mustang says. "Any chance I could bribe you to suture their mouths shut till they learn not to swear so much?"

Mickey perks up. "Well, it's interesting you ask . . ."

Sevro interrupts him. "How's the Gold holding up?" he asks Mustang. "You know?"

"Happy he still has a tongue," Mustang says. "They're suturing his chest in the infirmary. He has some internal bleeding from blunt trauma, but he'll live."

"You finally went to see him?" I ask.

"I did." She nods thoughtfully to herself. "He was . . . emotional. He wanted me to thank you, Sevro. He says he knows he didn't deserve it."

"Damn right he didn't," Sevro mutters.

"Sefi says the Obsidian will leave him be," I say.

"The Obsidian?" Mustang asks, my statement pulling her from her thoughts. "All of them."

I laugh suddenly. "I didn't even think about that."

"What's that?" Sevro asks.

"She spoke for the Obsidian now, not just the Valkyrie. Wasn't a slip of the tongue. Pan-tribalism wasn't in place before the riot," I say. "Must have used it to unite the other warchiefs under her direction."

"So . . . she pulled a coup?" Sevro asks.

I laugh. "Seems like."

"We'll see if it holds. Still . . . impressive," Mustang says. "They always told us never to let a good crisis go to waste."

Mickey shivers. "Obsidians playing politics . . ."

"So all that out there . . . was that strategy or was it real?" Mustang asks Sevro.

"Dunno." Sevro shrugs. "I mean, gotta stop the cycle somewhere. Sucks, but dad's gone. No sense burning down the world to try and bring him back. You know? Cassius didn't kill dad because he hated him. They were both soldiers doing what soldiers do."

Mustang shakes her head, at a loss for words. So she sets a hand on his shoulder, and he knows how impressed she is. The compliment of silence is as deep a one as she can give, and Sevro favors her with a rare un-ironic smile. One that disappears when the door opens and Victra comes in. She's red-eyed and agitated.

"I need to talk to you," she says to Sevro.

"Get out," Sevro says when we don't move. "Everyone."

We wait outside the door as Victra and Sevro speak inside. "How long do you think it will take to make the voyage?" Mustang asks.

"Forty-nine days," I say, pulling Mickey back from the door where he cups his ear in an attempt to hear the happenings inside. "Key is keeping the Blues quiet."

"Forty-nine days is a long time for my brother to make plans."

Beyond our hull the worlds continue to turn. Reds are hunted. And though we've woken the spirit of the lowColors, and given this rebellion another victory, every day we spend crossing the distance to Core is another day that the Jackal can hunt our friends and the Sovereign can squelch the rebellions that plague her. My uncle's already gone. How many more will die before I return?

"This won't heal everything," Mustang says. "The Obsidians still killed seven prisoners. My people are wary of this war. The consequences. Particularly if Sefi now has united the tribes. That makes her dangerous."

"And more useful," I say.

"Until she disagrees with you again. This could go wrong at any moment."

She straightens as Mickey skitters back and the door to the infirmary opens. Sevro and Victra come out, both wearing smiles. "What are you two grinning about?" I ask.

"Just this." Sevro thrusts out a House Jupiter Institute ring. It's loose on his finger. I squint at it, not understanding right away. His own ring is missing and then I see it awkwardly jammed onto Victra's pinky. "She proposed," he says with delight.

"What?" I sputter.

Mustang's eyebrows shoot up. "Proposed . . . as in . . ."

"Yeah, boyo!" Sevro beams. "We're gettin' hitched."

Sevro and Victra marry seven nights later in a small ceremony in the auxiliary hangar of the *Morning Star*. When Victra asked me to give her away after they broke the news to us, I couldn't speak. I hugged her then as I hug her now before taking her arm and walking her through the small line of scrubbed and washed Howlers and towering Telemanuses. It's the cleanest I've ever seen Sevro, his unruly Mohawk combed to the side as he stands before Mickey. It is custom to have a

White give the benediction. But Victra laughed at the idea of tradition and asked Mickey.

The Violet's face glows now. Too much makeup on the day, but he's a ray of light all the same. From Carver to slaver to slave to wedding officiant, he's not had an easy road, but he's lovelier for it. He was delighted when Clown and Screwface asked him to join us for Sevro's bachelor night, and he howled along with us as we kidnapped Sevro from his room the night before and dragged him to the mess hall where the Howlers gathered to drink.

The animosity stemming from the riot has not abated entirely, but the wedding brings a sense of nostalgic normalcy. Surrounded by the insanity of war, it's a special hope given knowing life can go on. Though some Sons gripe about the marriage of the Red leader to a Gold, Victra's done enough to merit respect from the leaders within the Sons. And the bravery she showed in storming the *Morning Star* with Sefi and me around Ilium has bought her their respect. She shed blood for them, with them, so my fleet is quiet, at peace. At least for tonight.

I've never seen Sevro so happy. Nor so nervous as he was the hour before the ceremony when he combed his hair in my washroom. Not that you can do much with a Mohawk. "Is this insane? It seemed like a good idea yesterday," he asked, staring at himself in the mirror.

"And it's a good idea today too," I told him.

"You're not just saying that. Tell me the truth, man. I feel sick."

"Before I married Eo, I threw up."

"Bullshit."

"Got it all over my uncle's boots." A twinge of pain as I remember he's gone. "Wasn't that I was afraid of making the wrong decision. I was afraid she was. Afraid of not living up to her expectations . . . But my uncle told me that it's women who see us better than we see ourselves. That's why you love Victra. That's why you fight with her. And that's why you deserve this."

Sevro squinted at me in the mirror. "Yeah, but your uncle was crazy. Everyone knows that."

"Even company then. We're all a little manic. Especially Victra. I mean she'd have to be to marry you?"

He grinned. "Bloodydamn right." And I rumpled his hair, hoping beyond all hope that they can have this little moment of happiness and maybe more after that. It's the best any of us can hope for, really. "Wish Pops was here, though."

"I think he's laughing his ass off somewhere that you have to stand on your tiptoes to kiss your bride," I said.

"Always was a prick."

Now Sevro shifts from foot to foot as I hand Victra over to him and he looks up into her eyes. I'm not even there. None of us are, not to them. The gentleness I see from the raging woman now is all it takes to know how much she loves him. It's not something she'd ever talk about. It's not her way. But the sharp edge she has for everything and everyone is dull tonight. Like she sees Sevro as a refuge, a place where she can be safe.

I rejoin Mustang as Mickey begins his flowery speech. It's not half so grandiloquent as I might have expected. The way Mustang nods along to the words, I know she must have helped him edit it down. Reading my mind, she leans over. "You should have heard the first draft. It was a spectacle." She sniffs me. "Are you drunk?" She looks back at the flushed Howlers and teetering Telemanuses. "Are they all drunk?"

"Shhh," I say and hand her a flask. "You're too sober."

Mickey is finishing the ceremony. ". . . a compact that can be broken only by death. I pronounce you Sevro and Victra Barca."

"Julii," Sevro corrects quickly. "Hers is the elder house."

Victra shakes her head down at him. "He said it right."

"But you're a Julii," he replies, confused.

"Yesterday I was. Today I'd rather be a Barca. Presuming you don't have a problem with that and I don't have to become proportionally diminutive."

"It'd be lovely," Sevro says, cheeks glowing as Mickey continues and Sevro and Victra turn to face their friends. "Then I present you to your fellows and the worlds as Sevro and Victra of the Martian House Barca."

||||||||||

The ceremony may have been small, but the celebration is anything but. Fleet-spanning, even. If my people know one thing it is how to survive hardship with celebration. Life's not just a matter of breathing, it's a matter of being. Word of Sevro's speech and his hanging spread through the ships, stitching the wounds back together.

But this day is the one that matters. The one that reaffirms the joy of life throughout my fleet. Dances are held on the smallest corvettes, on the destroyers and torchShips and the *Morning Star*. Flights of ripWings buzz bridges in celebratory formation. Swill and Society liquors flow among the milling crowds, which gather in hangars to sing and dance around weapons of war. Even Kavax, so stubborn in his fear of chaos and his prejudice against the Obsidians, dances with Mustang. Drunkenly hugging Sevro and Victra and clumsily attempting to forget the ballroom dreck of Gold dances and learn those of my people from a full-figured Red with a laughing face and a mechanic's grease under her nails. With them is Cyther, the awkward Orange who so impressed me a year and a half ago in the garages of the *Pax*. He only just finished Mustang's special project this morning. Now he's drunk and turning his ungainly body around on the dance floor as Kavax roars approval.

Daxo shakes his head at his father's antics while sitting in reserve on the side, as always. I share a drink with him. "It's wine," I say.

"Thank Jove," he replies, delicately taking the glass. "Your people keep trying to give me some kind of engine solvent." He scans his datapad warily.

"I've got Holiday on security," I say. "This isn't a Gold party."

He laughs. "Thank Jove for that then as well." Finally he takes a sip from his wine. "Venusian Atolls," he says. "Very nice."

"Roque had good taste. Your father is a sight," I say, nodding to the dance floor where the big man sways along with two Reds.

"He's not the only one," Daxo replies shrewdly, following my eyes to Mustang who's now being spun about by Sevro. The woman's face is aglow with life, or maybe it's the alcohol. Hair sweaty and plastered on her forehead. "She loves you, you know," Daxo says. "She's just afraid of losing you, so she holds you far away." He smiles to himself. "Funny how we are, isn't it?"

"Daxo why aren't you dancing?" Victra says, striding up to him. "So proper all the time. Up! Up!" She hauls him up and pushes him onto the dance floor then collapses into his chair. "My feet. Raided Antonia's closet. Forgot she's got pigeon feet."

I laugh and Clown stumbles up to us, heavily drunk.

"Victra, Darrow. A question. Do you think Pebble is interested in that man?" he asks me, leaning against one of the tables as he chugs down another glass of wine. His teeth are already purple.

"The tall one?" Victra asks. Pebble's dancing with a Gray captain. "She seems to fancy him."

"He's terribly handsome," Clown says. "Good teeth too."

"I suppose you could always cut in," I say.

"Well, I wouldn't want to seem desperate."

"Jove forbid," Victra says.

"I think I'll cut in."

"I think it's a good idea," she says. "But you should bow first. To be polite."

"Oh. Then it's settled. I'll go right now." He pours another glass of wine. "After another drink."

I take the wine from him and push him on his way. Holiday appears in the doorframe to watch Clown's awkward interruption. He's bowing to Pebble and sweeping back his hand dramatically. "Oh, hell. He actually did it." Victra snorts champagne through her nose. "You should do the same with Mustang. Think she's trying to steal my husband away. *Husband.* That's a weird word."

"It's a weird world."

"Isn't it, though. *Wife.* Who'd have thought?"

I look her up and down. "On you, it seems to fit." I put my arm around her. "It seems to fit perfectly." She smiles radiantly.

"Sir," Holiday says, coming up to us.

"Holiday, come to have a drink?" I glance over at her, smile dying when I see the expression that marks her face. Something has happened. "What is it?"

She motions me away from Victra.

"It's the Jackal," she says quietly so as not to spoil the mood. "He's on the com for you. Direct link."

"What's the delay?" I ask.

"Six seconds."

On the dance floor, Sevro's spinning with Mustang clumsily, laughing because neither knows the dance the Reds around them perform. Her hair is dark from sweat on her temples, her eyes alight with the joy of the moment. None of them feel the sudden dread in me, in the world beyond. I don't want them to. Not tonight.

56

||||||||||||||||||||||||

IN TIME

He sits in a simple chair in the center of my circular training room wearing a coat of white with a gold lion to either side of his high collar. The stars above his glowing hologram are cold stains of light through the duroglass dome. This room was built to train for war and so it is here that I will grant my enemy an audience. I will not let him pervert this ship where Roque lived and where my friends celebrate by seeing or being anyplace else.

Even though he's millions of kilometers away, I can nearly smell the pencil-shaving scent of him. Hear the vast silence with which he fills rooms as I stand before his digital image. It's so lifelike if it did not glow I would think him here. The background behind him is blurred. He watches me enter the room. No smile on his face. No false pleasantness, but I can tell he's amused. His silver stylus spins in his one hand. The only sign of his agitation.

"Hello, Reaper. How are the festivities?" I try not to let my discomfort show. Of course he knows of the wedding. He has spies in our fleet. How close they are to me, I cannot tell. But I don't let the thought spread malignantly through me. If he could reach out and hurt us here, he already would have.

"What do you want?" I ask.

"You called me last time. I thought I should return the favor, particularly considering the message I sent of your uncle. Did you receive it?" I say nothing. "After all, when you arrive at Mars the cannons will speak for us. We may never see each other again. Strange, isn't that? Did you see Roque before he died?"

"I did."

"And did he weep for your forgiveness?"

"No."

The Jackal frowns. "I thought he would. It's easy to fool a romantic. To think he was right there when I took his girl. You went running by in the hall screaming Tactus's name, and he looked up in confusion. I pushed a sliver of Quinn's skull deeper into her brain with my scalpel. I thought about letting her live with brain damage. But the thought of her drooling everywhere made me sick. You think he still would have loved her if she drooled?"

There's a sound at the door, out of the camera's capture range. Mustang's followed me from the wedding. Taking in the scene, she watches quietly. I should turn off the holo. Leave this creature to himself, but I can't seem to part with him. The same curiosity that brought me here now anchors me to this spot.

"Roque wasn't perfect, but he cared about Gold. He cared about humanity. He had something he would die for. And that makes him a better man than most," I say.

"It's easy to forgive the dead," the Jackal replies. "I'd know." A tiny spasm of humanity moves across his lips. He may never say it, but the very tone of his voice tells me he is not without regret. I know he wanted his father's approval. But could it actually be that he misses the man? That he's forgiven his father in death and now mourns him?

He pulls a short gold baton up from his lap. With the press of a button, the baton extends to a scepter. One with the skull of a jackal overtop the pyramid of the Society. I had it commissioned for him more than a year ago. "I've not parted with your gift," he says. He traces the head of the jackal. "All my life I've been given lions. Nothing of my own. What does it say about me that my greatest enemy knows me better than any friend?"

"You the scepter, I the sword," I say, ignoring his question. "That was the plan." I gave it to him because I wanted him to feel loved. To feel like I was his friend. And I would have been, then. I would have helped him change like Mustang did. Like Cassius might. "Is it what you thought it would be?" I ask.

"What?"

"Your father's seat."

He frowns, considering which tack to take. "No," he says eventually. "No it is not what I expected."

"You want to be hated. Don't you?" I ask. "That's why you killed my uncle when you didn't need to. It gives you purpose. That's why you called me. To feel important. But I don't hate you."

"Liar."

"I don't."

"I killed Pax and your uncle and Lorn . . ."

"I pity you."

He recoils. "Pity?"

"ArchGovernor of all Mars, one of the most powerful men in all the worlds. With the might to do anything you like. And it's not enough. Nothing has ever been enough for you, nor will it be. Adrius, you're not trying to prove yourself to your father, to me, to Virginia, to the Sovereign. You're trying to matter to yourself. Because you're broken inside. Because you hate what you are. You wish you were born like Claudius. Like Virginia. You wish you were like me."

"Like you?" he asks with a sneer. "A filthy Red?"

"I'm no Red." I show him my hands, bare of Sigils. It disgusts him.

"Not even evolved enough to have a Color, Darrow? Just a *homo sapiens* playing in the realm of gods."

"Gods?" I shake my head. "You're no god. You're not even a Gold. You're just a man who thinks a title will make him great. Just a man who wants to be more than he actually is. But all you really want is love. Isn't that right?"

He snorts in derision. "Love is for the weak. The only thing you and I have in common is our hunger. You think that I cannot be satisfied. That I always yearn for more. But look in the mirror and you'll see the same man staring back at you. Tell your little Red friends what you like. But I know you lost yourself among us. You yearned to be Gold. I saw it in your eyes at the Institute. I saw that fever on Luna when I proposed that we should rule. I saw it when you rode that triumphal chariot up to the steps of the citadel. It's that hunger that makes us forever alone."

And there he strikes the core of me. That abyssal fear that the darkness made my reality. The fear of being alone. Of never finding love again. But then Mustang steps out to join me. "You're wrong, brother," she says.

The Jackal leans back at the sight of his sister.

"Darrow had a wife. A family he loved. He had just a little bit and he was happy. You had everything, and you were miserable. And you always will be because you covet." His foundation of calm begins to crumble. "That's why you killed Father and Quinn. Why you killed Pax. But this isn't a game, brother. This isn't one of your mazes. . . ."

"Do not call me brother, whore. You are no sister of mine. Opening your legs for a mongrel. For a beast of burden. Are the Obsidians next? I bet they are all queued up already. You are a disgrace to your Color and to our House."

I move angrily toward his holo, but Mustang puts a hand in the center of my chest and turns back to her brother. "You think you never had love, *brother*. But mother loved you."

"If she loved me why didn't she stay?" he asks sharply. "Why did she leave?"

"I don't know," Mustang says. "But I loved you too, and you threw that away. You were my twin. We were bound for life." There are tears in her eyes. "I defended you for years. Then I find out that it was you who had Claudius killed." She blinks through the tears, shaking her head as she finds her resolve. "I cannot forgive that. I cannot. You had love and you lost it, brother. That is your curse."

I step forward till I'm even with Mustang. "Adrius, we are coming for you. We will break your ships. We will storm Mars. We will burrow through the walls of your bunker. We will find you and we will bring you to justice. And when you hang from the gallows, when the door beneath you opens, when your feet do the Devil's Dance, then you will realize in that moment that this has all been for nothing, because there will be no one left to pull your feet."

The pale light of the holo vanishes as we close the connection, leaving us to the glass ceiling and stars beyond. "Are you all right?" I ask Mustang. She nods, wiping her eyes.

"Didn't expect to start crying like that. Sorry."

"To be fair, I think I cry more. But, forgiven."

She tries a smile. "Do you actually think we can do this, Darrow?"

Her eyes are red, the mascara she wore for the wedding stained by the tears. Her running nose is a ruddy pink, but I've never seen beauty as deep as hers is now. All the rawness of life flows through her. All the cracks and fears that make her who she is worn in her eyes. So imperfect and rough that I want to hold her and love her as long as I can. And for once, she lets me.

"We have to. You and I have a whole life ahead of us," I say, pulling her into me. It seems impossible a woman like this could ever want to be held by me, but she puts her head on my chest as I wrap my arms around her and I remember how perfectly we fit together as we hold each other and the stars and minutes pass distantly.

"We should return to the party," she eventually says to me.

"Why? I have everything I need right here." I look down at the crown of her golden head and see the darkness of her roots. I breathe in the full scent of her. If it ends tomorrow or in eighty years, I could breathe her the rest of my life. But I want more. I need more. I tilt her slender jaw up with my hand so that she's looking at me. I was going to say something important. Something memorable. But I've forgotten it in her eyes. That gulf that divided us is still there, filled with questions and recrimination and guilt, but that's only part of love, part of being human. Everything is cracked, everything is stained except the fragile moments that hang crystalline in time and make life worth living.

57

||||||||||||||||||||||||||

LUNA

The Rubicon Beacons are a sphere of transponders, each as large as two Obsidian, floating in space one million kilometers beyond Earth's core, encircling the innermost domain of the Sovereign. For five hundred years, no foreign fleet has passed beyond their borders. Now, two months and three weeks after news of the destruction of the invincible Sword Armada reaches the Core, eight weeks after I proclaimed that we sailed on Mars, seventeen days after the Sovereign's declaration of martial law in all Society cities, the Red Armada approaches Luna, sailing past the Rubicon Beacons without firing a shot.

Telemanus torchShips race ahead at the vanguard to clear mines and scan for any traps left by Society forces. They're followed by Orion's Obsidian-filled heavy destroyers, painted with the all-seeing eyes of the ice spirits, then by the Julii fleet with Victra's weeping sun adorning the heavy dreadnought, the *Pandora,* the forces of the Reformers—the daughters-in-law of Lorn au Arcos come for justice and the gold and black ships bearing the lion of Augustus led by the battle-scarred *Dejah Thoris.* And finally my own vessels led by the greatest ship ever built and stolen, the indomitable white *Morning Star* painted with a seven-kilometer-long red scythe on her port and starboard sides. The holes we carved in her with our clawDrills are not mended all through the ship. But the armor has been replaced along the outer hull. The *Pax* died to give her to us. And what a prize she is. We ran out of paint on the bottom scythe, so it's a sloppy crescent moon, the symbol of House Lune. The men think it's a good omen. An accidental promise to Octavia au Lune that we have her marked.

War has come to the Core.

For three days they've known I was coming. We could not cover our entire approach from their sensors, but the chaos around the planet shows how unprepared they are for it. It is a civilization in turmoil. The Ash Lord has arrayed the Scepter Armada, the pride of the Core, around Luna in defensive formation. Caravans of trading vessels from the Rim clutter the Via Appia above the northern Lunar hemisphere, while backlogs of civilian vessels stagger their way back along the Via Flaminia, waiting to pass through inspection on the colossal Flaminius astroDock before their descent into Earth's atmosphere. But as we cross the Rubicon Beacons and encroach farther into Luna space, the vessels hurl themselves into a frenzy. Many bursting from their ordered queue to race for Venus, others trying to pass the Docks entirely and burn for Earth. They flare as silver and white Society fighters and fast-moving gun frigates shred engines and hulls. Dozens of vessels die to maintain order.

We're outnumbered, still vastly outgunned, but initiative is on our side, and so is the fear that all civilizations have of barbarian invaders.

The first dance of the Battle of Luna has begun.

"Attention unidentified fleet . . ." A brittle Copper voice echoes through an open frequency. *"This is Luna Defense Command: you are in possession of stolen property and in violation of Societal deep-space boundary regulations. Identify yourself and intentions with all haste."*

"Fire a long range missile at the Citadel," I say.

"That's a million kilometers away . . . ," the gunBlue says. "It'll be shot down."

"He bloodywell knows that," Sevro says. "Follow the order."

It took a campaign of counterintelligence not just in our transmissions to Sons cells throughout the Core, but among our ships and commanders to bring us here unnoticed. The Jackal will not be in position to help the Sovereign, nor will the *Classis Venetum,* the 4th Fleet of Venus. Or the *Classis Libertas,* the 5th Fleet of the inner Belt, which the Sovereign sent to Mars to aid the Jackal. At full burn all the ships will be three weeks away at current orbit. The lie worked. The spies in my ship leaked misinformation about our plans, just as I'd hoped.

That is the peril of a solar empire: all the power in all the worlds means nothing if it is in the wrong place.

Twenty minutes later, my missile is shot down by orbital defense platforms.

"New direct link incoming," the comBlue says behind me. "It's got Praetorian tags."

"Main holo," I say.

A Gold Praetorian with an aquiline face and gray at the temples of his short-cropped hair materializes in front of me. The image will appear on all bridges and holoscreens in the fleet. "Darrow of Lykos," he asks in an impeccably well-bred Luna accent. "Are you in possession of *imperium* over this war fleet?"

"What need have I of your traditions?" I ask.

"Very well," the Gold says, maintaining propriety even now. "I am ArchLegate Lucius au Sejanus of the Praetorian Guard, First Cohort." I know of Sejanus. He's an eerie, efficient man. "I am come with a diplomatic envoy to your coordinates," he says dryly. "I request you stay further aggression and give my shuttle access to your flagship so we might relate the Sovereign and Senate's intentions in . . ."

"Denied," I say.

"I beg your pardon?"

"If any Society ship comes toward my fleet, they will be fired upon. If the Sovereign wishes to speak with me, then let her do it herself. Not through a lackey's mouth. Tell the hag we're here for war. Not words."

|||||||||||||

My ship throbs with activity. Told only three days ago of our true destination, the men are filled with madcap excitement. There's something immortal to attacking Luna. Win or lose, we've forever stained the legacy of Gold. And in the minds of my men, and in the chatter we pick up over the coms from the Core planets and moons, there is real fear in the air. For the first time in centuries, Gold has shown weakness. Breaking the Sword Armada has spread the rebellion faster than my speeches ever could.

Soldiers salute as they pass me in the hall, making their way to their troop carriers and leechCraft. The squads are predominantly Red and defected Grays, but I see Green battletechs, Red machinists, and Obsidian scouts and heavy infantry in each capsule as well. I resend the shuttle flight clearance order to the *Morning Star*'s flight controller with my authorization code. It's accepted and cleared. Most days I'd trust the order to stand on its own, but today I want to be sure, so I make my way to the bridge to confirm in person. The Red marine captain responsible for the security of the bridge shouts his men to attention when I enter. More than fifty armored soldiers salute me. The Blues in their pits continue in their operations. Orion's at the forward observation post where Roque once stood. Meaty hands clasped behind her back. Skin nearly as dark as her black uniform. She turns to me with those large pale eyes and that nasty white smile.

"Reaper, the fleet is nearly ready."

I greet her warmly and join her in looking out through the glass viewports. "How does it look?"

"The Ash Lord is pulled up in defensive array. He seems to think we intend an Iron Rain before moving him off the moon. Sharp assumption. He has no reason to come to us. All the rest of the ships in Core will be headed here. When they get here we'll be the cockroach pinned between the ground and the hammer. He's assumed correctly we'll rush the engagement."

"The Ash Lord knows war," I say.

"That he does." She glances at her datapad. "What's this I hear about a flight clearance for a *sarpedon*-class shuttle from HB Delta?"

I knew she'd notice. And I don't want to explain myself to her now. Not everyone is as compassionate toward Cassius as I, even with Sevro sparing his life.

"I'm sending an emissary to meet with a group of Senators," I lie.

"We both know you're not," she says. "What's going on?"

I step closer so no one can overhear us. "If Cassius remains in the fleet while we go to war, someone will try to get past the guards and slit his throat. There's too much hate for the Bellona for him to stay here."

"Then hide him in another cell. Don't release him," she says. "He'll just go back to them. Rejoin the war."

"He won't."

She looks behind me to ensure we're not being overheard. "If the Obsidians find out . . ."

"This is exactly why I didn't tell anyone," I say. "I'm releasing him. You clear that shuttle. You let it go. I need you to promise me." Her lips make a thin, hard line. "Promise me." She nods and looks back to Luna. As always, I feel she knows more than she lets on.

"I promise. But you be careful, boy. You still owe me a parrot, remember."

I meet Sevro in the hall outside the high security prisoner lockup. He's sitting atop the orange cargo crate and its floating gravRig drinking from a flask, left hand rested on the scorcher in his leg holster. The hall's quieter than it should be given its guests, but it's in the main hangars and gun stations and engines and armories where my ship pulses with activity. Not here on the prison deck. "What took you?" Sevro asks. He's in his black fatigues too, stretching uncomfortably against his new combat vest. His boots click together as his legs dangle.

"Orion was asking questions on the bridge about the flight clearance."

"Shit. She figure out we were letting the eagle fly?"

"She promised to let it go."

"She better. And she better keep her trap shut. If Sefi finds out . . ."

"I know," I say. "And so does Orion. She won't tell her."

"If you say so." Sevro wrinkles his face and downs the last of his flask as he glances down the hall. Mustang approaches.

"Guards are redeployed," she says. "Marine patrols are diverted from hall 13-c. Cassius is clear to the hangar."

"Good. You sure about this?" I ask, touching her hand. She nods.

"Not entirely, but that's life."

"Sevro? You still prime?"

Sevro hops down from the crate. "Obviously. I'm here, ain't I?"

Sevro helps me maneuver the gravRig through the brig's doors. The guard station is deserted. Food wrappers and tobacco dip cups all that remain of the Sons team who guarded the prisoners. Sevro follows me from the entrance down into the decagon room of duroglass cells, whistling the tune he made for Pliny.

"If your leg's a little wet . . . ," he sings as we stop before Cassius's cell. Antonia's cell is across from his. Her face swollen from her beating, she watches us hatefully without moving from her cell's cot. Sevro knocks on the duroglass separating us from Cassius.

"Wakey wakey, Sir Bellona."

Cassius wipes his eyes of sleep and sits up from his bed, taking in Sevro and I, but addressing Mustang. "What's going on?"

"We've arrived at Luna," I say.

"Not Mars?" Cassius asks in surprise. Antonia shifts in her cot behind us, just as startled by the news as Cassius appears to be.

"Not Mars."

"You're actually attacking Luna?" Cassius murmurs. "You're insane. You don't have the ships. How do you even plan to get past the shields?"

"Don't you worry about that, sweetheart," Sevro says. "We got our ways. But soon hot metal's gonna be sliding through this ship. And someone's likely gonna come in here and pop you in the head. Darrow here gets all sad thinkin' of that. And I don't like sad Darrow." Cassius just stares at us like we're mad. "He still doesn't get it."

"When you said you were done with this war, did you mean it?" I ask.

"I don't understand. . . ."

"It's pretty bloodydamn simple, Cassius," Mustang says. "Yes or no?"

"Yes," Cassius says from his cot. Antonia sits up to watch. "I am. How could I not be? It's taken everything from me. All for people who only care about themselves."

"Well?" I ask Sevro.

"Oh, please." Sevro snorts. "You think that's going to satisfy me?"

"What game are you playing at?" Cassius asks.

"Ain't no game, boyo. Darrow wants me to let you out." Cassius's eyes widen. "But I needa know you aren't gonna come try to kill us. You're all about honor and blood debts, so I need you to swear an oath so I can sleep soundly."

"I killed your father. . . ."

"You really should stop reminding me of that."

"If you stay here, we can't protect you," I say. "I believe the worlds still need Cassius au Bellona. But there's no place for you here. And there's no place for you with the Sovereign. If you give me your oath, on your honor that you will leave this war behind you, I'll give you your freedom."

Antonia bursts out laughing behind us. "This is hilarious. They're toying with you, Cassi. Just plucking you like a harp."

"Be quiet, you poisonous little brat," Mustang snaps.

Cassius eyes Mustang, judging our proposal. "You agreed to this?"

"It was my idea," she says. "None of this is your fault, Cassius. I was cruel to you, and I'm sorry for that. I know you wanted revenge on Darrow. On me . . ."

"Not on you, not ever on you."

Mustang flinches. ". . . but I know you've seen what revenge brings. I know you've seen what Octavia really is. What my brother really is. You're only guilty of trying to protect your family. You don't deserve to die here."

"You really want me to go?" he asks.

"I want you to live," she says. "And yes. I want you to go, and never come back."

"But . . . go where?" he asks.

"Anywhere but here."

Cassius swallows, searching himself. Not just seeking to understand what he owes honor or duty, but trying to imagine a world without her. I know the horrible loneliness he feels now even as we give him freedom. Life without love is the worst prison of all. But he licks his lips and nods to Mustang, not to me. "On my father, on Julian, I promise not to raise arms against any of you. If you let me go, I will leave. And I will never come back."

"You coward." Antonia punches the glass of her cell. "You gorydamn sniveling little whipped worm . . ."

I nudge Sevro. "Still your call."

He tugs the hairs of his little goatee. "Ah hell, you better be right about this, you pricklicks." Digging into his pocket he pulls out a magnetic key card and Cassius's cell door unlocks with a heavy *thunk*.

"Then there's a shuttle waiting for you in the auxiliary hangar on this level," Mustang says evenly. "It's been cleared to fly. But you have to go now."

"That means *now*, shithead," Sevro says.

"They'll pop you in the back of the head!" Antonia is saying. "You traitor."

Cassius puts a tentative hand on the cell door, as if he's afraid he'll push and find it locked and we'll laugh at him and all the hope we've given him will be ripped away. But he has faith and, steeling his face, he pushes. The cell's door swings outward. Cassius walks out to join us. He holds out his hands to be cuffed.

"You're free, man," Sevro slurs, rapping the orange box heavily with his knuckles, "but you gotta get in the box so we can wheel you outta here without anyone seeing."

"Of course." He pauses and turns back to me to extend a hand. I take it, a strange feeling of kinship rising in me. "Goodbye, Darrow."

"Good luck, Cassius."

And for Mustang he pauses, wanting to reach out and wrap his arms around her, but she merely sticks out a hand, cold even now to him. He looks at her hand and shakes his head, not accepting her gesture. "We'll always have Luna," he says.

"Goodbye, Cassius."

"Goodbye."

He goes to the crate, which Sevro has opened and looks inside. Hesitating there, wanting to say something to Sevro, perhaps thank him one last time. "I don't know if your father was right. But he was brave." He extends a hand to Sevro as he did me. "I'm sorry that he's not here."

Sevro blinks hard at the hand, wanting to hate it. This does not come easy for him. He's never been a gentle soul. But he does his best and he takes the outstretched hand. They shake. But something feels wrong. Cassius won't let go. His face is cold, eyes unforgiving. His body rotates. So fast I can't stop him from jerking back on Sevro's hand, pulling my friend's smaller body forward toward him just as he swivels his hip, bringing Sevro to his right armpit like they're dancing, so he can strip Sevro's pistol from his leg holster. Sevro stumbles, fumbling for the weapon but it is already gone. Cassius shoves him off and stands behind him with the scorcher pressed to his spine. Sevro's eyes are huge, staring at me in fear. "Darrow . . ."

"Cassius no!" I shout.

"This is my duty."

"Cassius . . ." Mustang takes a step forward. Outstretched hand trembling. "He saved your life . . . Please."

"On your knees," Cassius says to us. "On your gorydamn knees." I feel myself teetering on the edge of a precipice, the darkness spreading out before me. Whispering to have me back. I can't reach for my razor. Cassius could easily shoot me down before I even pull it. Mustang goes to her knees and motions me to get down. Numbly, I follow her lead.

"Kill him!" Antonia's shouting. "Shoot the bastard!"

"Cassius, listen to me . . . ," I beg.

"I said on your knees," Cassius repeats to Sevro.

"My knees?" Sevro smiles wickedly. A mad gleam in his eye. "Stupid Gold. You forgot Howler rule number one. Never bow." He snatches up his razor from his right wrist, tries to spin around. But he's too slow. Cassius shoots him in the shoulder, jerking him sideways. The combat vest cracks. Blood sprays onto the metal wall. Sevro stumbles forward, eyes wild.

"For Gold," Cassius whispers and fires six more shots point-blank into Sevro's chest.

58

FADING LIGHT

Blood erupts from Sevro's chest. Spraying my face. He stumbles. Drops his razor. Collapses to his knees, gasping in shock. I rush to him under the muzzle of Cassius's smoking weapon. Sevro's grasping at his chest, confused. Blood dribbles from his mouth. Bubbling out through his vest, staining my hands. He coughs it onto me. He's desperate to rise. To laugh it off. But nothing's working. His arms tremble. His breath ragged. Eyes huge, fear wild and deep and primal in him as Antonia cackles in delight from her cell.

"Don't die," I say frantically. "Don't die. Sevro." He shivers in my arms. "Sevro. Please. *Please.* Stay alive. Please. Sevro . . ." Without a final word, without a plea or a flicker of personality, he goes still, leaking red. Pulse fading away as tears stream down my face and Antonia howls in mockery.

I cry out in horror.

At the bleak evil I feel in the world.

Rocking there on the floor with my best friend.

Overwhelmed by this darkness and the hate and the helplessness.

Cassius stares pitilessly down at me.

"Reap what you sow," he says.

I rise with a horrible sob. He strikes me in the side of the head with the scorcher. I don't go down. I take the blow and pull my razor. But he hits me twice more and I fall. He takes my razor from me, holding it to Mustang's throat as she tries to rise. He points the gun at my forehead as I look up at him and is about to pull the trigger.

"The Sovereign will want him alive!" Mustang says.

"Yes." Cassius replies quietly, overcoming his anger. "Yes, you're right. So she can peel him apart till you tell us your battle plans."

"Cassius, get me out of this damn cell," Antonia hisses.

Cassius moves Sevro's body over with his foot and pulls out the passcard to open her door. When Antonia exits her cell, she does so like a queen. Prisoner slippers making little tracks in Sevro's fresh blood. She knees Mustang in the face. Mustang goes down. My own vision wavers in and out. Nausea in my gut from a concussion. Warmth from Sevro's blood leaking through my shirt along the belly. Antonia sighs above me. "Ugh. The Goblin's still leaking everywhere."

"Guard them and get their datapads," Cassius orders. "We need a map."

"Where are you going?"

"Getting manacles." He tosses her the scorcher.

As he disappears around the corner, Antonia crouches over me, considering. She pushes the gun against my lips. "Open." She punches my testicles. "Open." Eyes rolling in pain, I open my mouth. She shoves the scorcher barrel inside. The alien metal presses against the back of my throat. Teeth scrape along the black steel. I gag. Feel bile coming up. She stares me hatefully in the eyes, crouched over my head, the barrel down my throat as my body convulses, only pulling it out as I vomit on the ground. "Worm."

She spits on me and takes our datapads and razors, tossing Sevro's to Cassius when he returns from the guard station. They fit me in a prisoner harness, a metallic muzzle-and-vest combination that interlocks the arms and pins them to my chest so that my fingers are touching the opposite shoulder, and dump me into the container we brought for him, forcing my knees to bend so I fit. I am unable to arrest my fall with my hands, and my head slams on the plastic at the bottom. Then they pile Sevro and Mustang in atop me like garbage and slam shut the crate. Sevro's blood drips down my face. My own leaks from the gash on the side of my head. Too dazed to weep or move.

"*Darrow* . . ." Mustang murmurs. "Are you all right?"

I don't answer her.

"You find a map?" I hear Cassius ask Antonia through the crate.

"And a jammer for cameras," she says. "I'll push. You range, if you can manage."

"I can manage. Let's go."

The jammer *pops* and the gravRig moves, taking us along with them. If Sevro and Mustang were not atop me, I could crouch and put my back into the lid, but their weight pins me down in the small container. It's hot. Smells like sweat. Hard to breathe. I'm helpless in here. Unable to stop them as they use the path I cleared for Cassius. Unable to stop them as they push us across the deserted hangar, up the ramp into the ship and begin preflight checks. "*Shuttle S-129, you are clear for departure, stand by for pulseShield deactivation,*" the flight officer says over the com from the distant bridge as the engines prime. "*You are go for launch.*"

Out from the belly of the war ship, my enemies smuggle me away from the comfort of my friends, the safety of my people, and the might of my army as it prepares for war. I hold my breath, expecting Orion's voice to come over the com. To ground the ship. For ripWings to shoot her engines out. None do. Somewhere, my mother will be making tea, wondering where I am, if I am safe. I pray she cannot feel this pain across the void, this fear that consumes me despite all my vaunted strength and foolish bluster. I'm afraid, despite what I know. Not just for myself, but for Mustang.

I hear Antonia and Cassius speaking beyond the crate. Cassius has broadcast an emergency signal from the craft. A few moments later, a cold voice crackles over the com.

"*Sarpedon shuttle, this is the LDC assault-runner Kronos; you have transmitted an Olympic distress signal. Please identify yourself.*"

"*Kronos,* this is the Morning Knight. Clearance code 7-8-7-Echo-

Alpha-9-1-2-2-7. I have escaped from imprisonment aboard the enemy's flagship and am requesting escort and docking clearance. Antonia au Severus-Julii is with me. We have valuable cargo. The enemy is in pursuit."

There's a pause.

"Register, code accepted. Hold on the com. The next voice you hear will be the Protean Knight's." A moment later Aja's voice rumbles through the ship, filling me with dread. So she did survive the waste to find her way back home.

"Cassius? You're alive."

"For now."

"What is your cargo?"

"The Reaper, Virginia, and the body of Ares," Antonia says excitedly.

"The body . . . I want to see them."

Boots thud toward my container. The top opens and Cassius hauls Mustang out. Then he hauls me out and tosses me to the ground before the hologram. Small and dark in the holographic projector, Aja watches us with otherworldly calm. Antonia keeps Sevro's gun trained on my head as Cassius pulls up Sevro's head by his Mohawk to show his face.

"Goryhell, Bellona," Aja says, excitement entering her voice. *"Goryhell. You've done it. The Sovereign will want to see you in the citadel."*

"Before I do, I need you to assure me that no harm will come to Virginia."

"What are you talking about?" Antonia asks, wary how close Cassius stands near her with his razor. "She's a traitor."

"And she'll be imprisoned," Cassius says. "Not executed. Not tortured. I need your word, Aja. Or I turn this ship around. Darrow killed your sister. Do you want vengeance or not?"

"You have my word," Aja says. *"No harm will befall her. I am sure Octavia will agree. We need her to settle things with the Rim. We're sending squadrons to intercept your pursuit. Re-direct to vector 41'13'25, circle the moon and await contact from the* Lion of Mars *for*

docking instructions. We can't clear your ship to land moonside. But ArchGovernor Augustus will be joining the Sovereign in the Citadel within the hour. I don't think he'll mind offering you a ride down."

"The ArchGovernor is here?" Cassius asks. "I don't see his ships."

"Of course he's here," Aja replies. *"He knew Darrow was never going to Mars. His entire fleet is on the far side of Luna, waiting for them to attack my father's. This is his trap."*

59

||||||||||||||||||||||||

THE LION OF MARS

Mustang and I are dragged down the cargo plank of the shuttle by Obsidians in black armor, each nearly as large as Ragnar and wearing the badge of the lion. I try to kick up at them, but they jam two-meter-long ionPikes down into my stomach, electrocuting me. My muscles cramp. Electricity screaming through me. They toss me down to the deck, pulling me up by my hair so I'm on my knees staring down at the body of Sevro. Mercifully his eyes are shut. His mouth pink from smeared blood. Mustang tries to rise. A muffled thump as an Obsidian hits her in the stomach. Putting her back on her knees, gasping for breath. Cassius has been forced to his knees as well.

Antonia joins Lilath, who stands before us in black armor. A screaming gold skull on either shoulder and another in the center of the breastpiece. Down her sides are human rib-bones embedded in the armor. The first bonerider in all her barbaric finery. The Jackal's Sevro. Head shaved. Quiet eyes sunken in a small, pinched face that likes little of what it sees in the world. Behind her tower ten young Peerless Scarred, heads shaved like hers for war. "Scan them," she orders.

"What the hell is this?" Cassius asks.

"Jackal's orders." Lilath watches carefully as the Golds scan me. Cassius suffers the indignity as Lilath continues. "Boss doesn't want tricks."

"I have the Sovereign's warrant," he says. "We're to take the Reaper and Virginia to the Citadel."

"Understood. We received the same orders. Bound there soon." She motions Cassius to stand as her men clear them. No bugs or devices or radiation tracking. Cassius dusts his knees off. I remain on mine as Lilath peers at Sevro, who one of the Obsidians has dragged down the ramp. She feels his pulse and smiles. "A fine kill, Bellona."

One Bonerider, a lofty, striking man with blazing eyes and a statue's cheekbones makes a little cooing noise. Tattooed fingers with painted nails tap his bottom lip. "How much for Barca's bones?" he asks.

"Not for sale," Cassius replies.

The man flashes an arrogant smile. "Everything's for sale, my goodman. Ten million credits for a rib."

"No."

"One hundred million. Come now, Bellona . . ."

"My title, *Legate Valii-Rath,* is Morning Knight. You may address me as sir or not at all. Ares's body is property of the state. It's not mine to sell. But if you ask me about it again, I will have more than words with you, sir."

"Will you have a rut?" Tactus's elder brother asks. "Is that what you mean?" I've never met the annoyingly aristocratic creature before, and I'm glad for it. Tactus seems the better of the bunch.

"You gorydamn savage," Mustang says through bloody teeth.

"Savage?" Tactus's brother asks. "Such a pretty mouth. That's not how you should use it." Cassius takes a step toward the man. The other Boneriders reach for their blades.

"Tharsus. Shut up." Lilath tilts her head, listening to a com in her ear as he returns to her side, lifting his nose. "Yes, my liege," she says into her com. "Barca is dead. I checked."

Antonia steps forward. "Is that Adrius? Let me speak with him."

She holds up a hand to the taller woman. "Antonia wants to speak with you." She pauses. "He says it can wait. Tharsus, Novas, uncuff the Reaper and spread his arms."

"What about Virginia?" Tharsus asks.

"Touch her, you die," Cassius says. "That's all you need to know." There's fear behind Cassius's eyes, even if he doesn't show it. He never would have brought her here if he could have helped it. Unlike the Sovereign's men, the Jackal is liable to do anything at anytime. Aja's guarantee of safety suddenly feels very frail. Why would the Sovereign send us here?

"No one will touch your prizes," Lilath says, voice that eerie one note. "Except the Reaper."

"I'm to deliver him . . ."

"We know. But my master requires compensation for past grievances. The Sovereign granted him permission while you were landing. Precautionary measures." She flashes her datapad. Cassius reads the order and goes a little pale, looking back at me. "Now may we proceed, or do you care to fuss further?"

Cassius has no choice. He depresses the remote. The metal cuffs locking my hands to my chest open. Tharsus and Novas are there to grab my arms and haul them to the sides, wrapping their whip form razors around each wrist, pulling taut till my shoulders grind in their sockets.

"You're going to let them do this?" Mustang snarls at Cassius. "What happened to your honor? It is as false as the rest of you?" He's about to say something, but she spits at his feet.

Antonia smiles repugnantly, captivated by the sight of me in pain. Lilath takes my razor from Cassius and walks away toward the rip-Wings that escorted us into the hangar. There, she holds my sling-Blade up into one of the smoldering engines.

"Tell me, Reaper, did you piddle my baby brother? Is that why he was so besotted?" Tharsus asks as we wait. His perfumed locks fall over his eyes. He alone has not shaved his head. "Well, you're not the first to plow that field, if you catch my flow."

I stare straight ahead.

"Is he right or left handed?" Lilath calls over.

"Right," Cassius replies.

"Pollox, tourniquet," Lilath instructs.

I realize what they intend and my blood runs cold. It feels like it's happening to someone else. Even when the rubber tightens around my right forearm and the needle-pricks of sensation tingle through the tips of my fingers.

Then I hear my enemy.

The clicking of his black boots.

The delicate shift in everyone's mannerisms.

The fear.

The Boneriders part to watch their master enter out of the mouth of the main hall to the hangar bay, flanked by a dozen more towering Gold bodyguards with shaved heads. Each tall as Victra. Gold skulls laugh on their collars, on the handles of their razors. Bones rattle on their shoulders, finger joints taken from their enemies. Taken from Lorn, from Fitchner, from my Howlers. These are the killers of my time. Their arrogance drips from them. As they look at me, it isn't hate I see in their violent eyes, but a fundamental absence of empathy.

I told the Jackal I didn't hate him. That was a lie. It's all I feel watching him walk across the deck, the pistol he killed my uncle with hanging on a magnetic strip holster on his thigh. His armor gold. Roaring with Gold lions. Human ribs implanted along the sides of the torso, each carved with details I cannot make out. Hair combed and parted on the side. His silver stylus in his hand, twirling, twirling. Antonia takes a step toward him, but stops herself when she sees he's walking to Sevro and not to her.

"Good. The bones are intact." After he's examined Sevro's bloody body, he stands over his sister. "Hello, Virginia. Nothing to say?"

"What is there to say?" she asks through gritted teeth. "What words have I for a monster?"

"Hm." He takes her jaw between his forefingers, causing Cassius's hand to drift to his razor. Lilath and the Boneriders would cut him to pieces if he even drew it. "It is us against the world," the Jackal says softly. "Do you remember telling me that?"

"No."

"We were young. Mother had just died. I couldn't stop crying. And you said you'd never leave me. But then Claudius would invite you somewhere. And you'd forget all about me. And I'd stay home in a big old house and cry, because I knew even then I was alone." He taps her nose. "These next hours are going to test who you are as a person, sister. I'm excited to see what's beneath all the bluster."

He moves on to me, loosening my muzzle. Even on my knees my physicality dwarfs him. Fifty kilograms heavier. Still, his presence is like the sea: strange and vast and dark and full of hidden depths and power. His silence, his roar. I see his father in him now. He tricked me, guessing my play on Luna, and now I'm afraid all I've done is going to unravel.

"And here we are again," he says. I do not reply. "Do you recognize these?"

He runs his stylus down the ribs in his armor, coming closer so I can see the details. "My dear father thought a man's deeds make him. I rather think it's his enemies. Do you like it?" He steps even closer. One of the ribs shows a helmet with a spiked sunburst. Another rib shows a head in a box.

The Jackal is wearing Fitchner's rib cage.

Anger roars out of me and I try to bite his face, bellowing like a wounded animal, startling Mustang. I strain against the men holding me, trembling with rage as the Jackal watches me squirm. Cassius stares at the ground, avoiding Mustang's gaze. My voice croaks out of me, hardly my own. That deeper demon only the Jackal can summon from me. "I'm going to skin you," I say.

Bored of me, he rolls his eyes and snaps his fingers. "Put the muzzle back on." Tharsus binds my mouth. The Jackal opens his arms as if welcoming two long-lost friends to a party. "Cassius! Antonia!" he says. "Heroes of the hour. My dear . . . what happened?" he asks when he sees Antonia's face. They were lovers during my imprisonment. Sometimes I'd smell her on him as he came to visit me before the box. Or she'd drag a nail along his neck as she passed. He goes close to her now, taking her jaw in his hand, tilting her head to examine the damage done to her. "Did Darrow do this?"

"My sister," she corrects, disliking his examination. She mourned her face in our captivity more than she mourned her own mother's death. "The bitch will pay. And I'll have it fixed, don't worry." She pulls her head back from him.

"Stop," the Jackal says sharply. "Why fixed?"

"It's disgusting."

"Disgusting? My dear, scars are what you are. They tell your story."

"This is Victra's story, not mine."

"You're still beautiful." He pulls her down gently by her chin and kisses her lips delicately. He doesn't care for her. Like Mustang said, we're just sacks of meat to him. But while Antonia's as wicked a thing as I've ever met, she wants to be loved. To be valued. The Jackal knows how to use that.

"This was Barca's," Antonia says, handing the Jackal Sevro's pistol. The Jackal runs a thumb over the howling wolves engraved in the hilt.

"Fine work," he says. He strips his own gun from his magnetic holster and tosses it to a bodyguard before holstering Sevro's. Of course he takes my friend's pistol as a trophy.

His datapad flashes and he holds up a hand for silence. "Yes, Imperator?"

The grotesque Ash Lord appears in the air before the Jackal as a disembodied, gigantic head. Dark Gold eyes peer out from beneath twin thickets of eyebrows. His jowls hang over the high black collar of his uniform. *"Augustus, the enemy is under way. TorchShips in front."*

"They're coming for him," Cassius says.

"How many?" the Jackal asks.

"More than sixty. Half bearing the red fox."

"Do you wish me to spring the trap?"

"Not yet. I will assume command of your ships."

"You know the arrangement."

The Ash Lord's wide mouth makes a straight line. *"I do. You are to continue to join the Sovereign as planned. Escort the Morning Knight and his package to the Citadel. My daughter will take custody of him there. Go now, for Gold."*

"For Gold."

The head disappears.

The Jackal glances over to the Obsidians who pulled me down the cargo ramp. "Slaves, attend to Praetor Licenus on the bridge. You are no longer needed." The Obsidians leave without question. When they are gone, he eyes the thirty Boneriders. "The Morning Knight has given us an opportunity to win this war today. The Telemanuses will come for my sister. The Howlers and the Sons of Ares will come for the Reaper. They will not have them. It is upon our shoulders to deliver them to our Sovereign and her strategists in the Citadel."

He addresses Antonia and Cassius. "Set aside your little grievances. Today we are Gold. We can bicker when the Rising is ash. Most of you lived the darkness of the caves with me. You watched by my side as this . . . creature stole what was ours. They will take everything from us. Our homes. Our slaves. Our right to rule. Today we fight to keep what is ours. Today we fight against the dying of our Age."

They lean into his words, awaiting his orders hungrily. It's terrifying to see the cult he's built around himself. He's taken bits of me, of my speaking pattern, and transposed it onto his own behavior. He continues to evolve.

The Jackal turns from his men as Lilath brings back my slingBlade, red-hot from engine's heat, and hands it to him hilt first. "Lilath, you're to stay with the fleet."

"You're sure?"

"You're my insurance plan."

"Yes, my liege."

Antonia's not sure what they're talking about, and she doesn't like it one bit. The Jackal twirls my razor in his hand. And then looking between me and Mustang he's struck by a thought. "How long were you imprisoned by Darrow, Cassius?"

"Four months."

"Four months. Then I believe you should do the honors." He flips the red-hot razor to Cassius, who smoothly catches it by its hilt. "Cut off Darrow's hand."

"The Sovereign wants him . . ."

"Alive, yes. And he will be. But she doesn't want him coming in to her bunker with his sword arm attached to his body, now does she?

We're to take all his weapons. Neuter the beast and let's be on our way. Unless . . . there's a problem?"

"No problem," Cassius says. Stepping forward, he lifts high the razor, metal throbbing with heat.

"Is this what you've become?" Mustang asks. Cassius suffers her gaze, shame on his face. "Look at me, Darrow," Mustang says. "Look at me."

I will myself to forget the blade. To watch her, taking strength from her. But as the superheated metal cleaves through the skin and bone of my right wrist, I forget her. I scream in pain, looking back where my hand was to see a stump lazily dripping blood through charred capillaries. Smoke from my burning flesh slithers into the air. And through the agony I can see the Jackal picking my hand up from the ground and holding it in the air. His newest trophy.

"Hic sunt leones," he says.

"Hic sunt leones," echo his men.

60

||||||||||||||||||||||||

DRAGON'S MAW

I think of my uncle as I cradle the charred stump of my right arm, shivering from pain. Is he with my father now? Does he sit with Eo by a woodfire listening to the birds? Do they watch me? Blood weeps through the blackened flesh at my wrist. The pain is blinding. Overtaking my entire body. I'm strapped beside Mustang into a seat in two parallel rows in the back of the military assault craft amidst thirty Boneriders. The overhead light pulses an alien green. The ship shudders from turbulence. Luna is in storm. Huge thunderheads swaddling the cities. Black towers penetrating the murky clouds. All along the rooftops, motes of light dance from the headlamps of Oranges and highReds, my own brethren, who slave under the military yoke, preparing weapons that will fell their Martian kin. Brighter flood lamps bathe military scenes. Black shapes trimmed with evil red beacons zip and float between towers as squadrons of ripWings patrol the sky and Golds in gravBoots jump between towers kilometers apart, checking on defenses, preparing for the storm above, saying last words to friends, to schoolmates, to lovers.

Passing the Elorian Opera House, I see a line of Golds perched on its highest crenellation, staring up at the sky, their glorious war helms spiked with horns so they look a troupe of gargoyles balanced there, silhouetted by lightning, waiting for hell to rain.

We drive toward the cauldron of clouds that swirls around the highest skyscrapers. Beneath the cloud layer, the interlocked skin of cityscape is quiet. Dark in anticipation of orbital bombardment, except for the veins of flame that bleed across the horizon from riots in Lost City. Flashing emergency vehicles dive toward the blazes. The city has gathered its breath for hours, for days, and, with exhalation bare moments away, her seams strain and her lungs stretch to bursting.

We taxi onto a circular landing pad atop the Sovereign's spire. There, Aja and a cohort of Praetorians meet us. The Boneriders unload with gravBoots before we land, covering the craft as it settles onto the pad. Cassius comes out, manhandling me along. He drags Sevro with his other hand like a deer carcass. Antonia shoves Mustang along. The weary winter rain of the city-moon drips down Aja's dark face. Steam rises from her collar and a brilliant white smile slashes the night.

"Morning Knight, welcome home. The Sovereign awaits."

A kilometer beneath the surface of the moon, the great gravLift known only in military myth as the Dragon Maw stops, hissing open to lead down a dimly lit concrete hall to another door emblazoned with the pyramid of the Society. There, blue light scans Aja's irises. The pyramid fractures in half, gears and huge pistons whirring. Technology here older than the Citadel above, ancient, from a time when Earth stood the only enemy Luna knew, and the great American railguns were the fear of all Luneborn. It's a testament to the architecture and the discipline of the Praetorians that the great bunker of the Sovereign has not had to change substantially for more than seven hundred years.

I wonder if Fitchner knew its inner workings. Doubtful. Seems a secret Aja would hoard. But I wonder if she even knows all the secrets of this place. Tunnels to the left and right of the narrow hall we pass through are long-ago collapsed, and I can't help but wonder who once walked through them, who collapsed them and why.

We pass heavily guarded rooms aglow with holo lights. Synced Blues and Greens lying back in tech beds, IVs hooked into their bodies as data streams through their brains via uplink nodes embedded in their skulls, eyes lost to some distant plane. It's the central nervous system of the Society. Octavia can wage a war from here even if the moon falls to ruin around her.

The Obsidians here wear black helmets with draconic shaped skulls and dark purple on their body armor. Gold letters spelling *cohors nihil* wind along the short-swords at their sides. Zero Legion. I've never heard of them, but I see what they guard: one last door of solid, unadorned metal, the deepest refuge of the Society. It dilates open with a groan and only then, a year and a half since I jumped out the back of her assault shuttle, do I see the silhouette of the Sovereign.

Her patrician voice echoes down the hall. ". . . Janus, who cares about civilian casualties? Does the sea ever run out of salt? If they manage an Iron Rain, you shoot them down, whatever the cost. The last thing we desire is for the Obsidian Horde to land here and link with the riots in Lost City. . . ."

The ruler of all I've ever fought against stands in a depressed circle at the center of a large gray and black room bathed in blue light from the Praetors and Ash Lord who surround her in holographic form. There's more than forty in a semicircle, the veterans of her wars. Pitiless creatures watching me enter the room with the dark, smug contentment of cathedral statues, as if they always knew it would come to this. As if they earned this end of mine and didn't luck into it just as they lucked into their birth.

They know what my capture means. They've been broadcasting it nonstop to my fleet. Trying to take our coms with hacking attacks to spread the word among my ships. Spreading it to Earth to quell the uprisings there, pimping the signal to the Core to forestall any more civil unrest. They'll do the same with my execution. The same with Sevro's dead body. And maybe Mustang, despite the deal Cassius thinks he's struck. Look what befalls those who rise against, they will say. Look how even these mighty beasts fall before Gold. Who else can stand against them? No one.

Their grip will tighten.

Their reign will strengthen.

If we lose today, a new generation of Gold will rise with vigor un-seen since the fall of Earth. They will see the threat to their people and they will breed creatures like Aja and the Jackal by the thou-sands. They'll build new Institutes, expand their military, and throttle my people. That is the future that could be. The one Fitchner feared the most. The one I fear is coming as I watch the Jackal move past me into the room.

"His Obsidians are not trained in extraplanetary warfare," one of the Praetors is saying.

"You want to tell that to Fabii?" the Sovereign asks. "Or perhaps to his mother? She's with the other Senators who I had to corral in the Chamber before they could flee like little flies and take their ships with them."

"Politico cravens . . ." someone murmurs.

Aside from the glowing holographs, the room is occupied by a small host of martial Golds. More than I expected. Two Olympic Knights, ten Praetorians, and Lysander. Ten years of age now, he has grown nearly half a foot since last I saw him. He carries a datapad to take copious notes of his grandmother's conversation and smiles to Cassius as we enter, watching me with the wary interest you'd watch a tiger through duroglass. His crystal Gold eyes take in my bindings, Aja, and my missing hand. Mentally tapping the glass with a nail to see just how thick it is.

The two Olympic Knights greet Cassius quietly as we enter, so as not to disturb the Sovereign in her debriefing, though she's noted my presence with an emotionless glance. Both knights are heavily ar-mored and ready to defend their Sovereign.

Above the Sovereign, a globular holo dominates the domed ceiling of the room, showing the moon in perfect detail. The Ash Lord's fleet is spread out like a screen to cover Luna's darkside, where the Citadel is, like a concave shield. The battle is well under way. But my forces have no way of knowing that the Jackal is just waiting to swing around their flank and hammer them against the Ash Lord's anvil. If only I could reach Orion, she might find some way to salvage this.

The Jackal quietly takes a seat to the side, patiently watching the Ash Lord give instructions to a sphere of torchShips.

"Cassius, you gorydamn hound," the Truth Knight says, voice a deep baritone. His eyes narrow and Asiatic. He's from Earth, and he's more compact than us Martians. "Is it really him?"

"Bones and heart. Took him from his flagship," Cassius says, kicking me to my knees and hauling back my head by my hair so they can better see my face. He tosses Sevro on the ground and they inspect the kill. The Joy Knight shakes his head. He's thinner than Cassius and twice again as aristocratic, from an old Venusian family. Met him once at a duel on Mars.

"Augustus too? Don't you just have all the luck. And Aja bagged the Obsidian. Fear and Love are going to get Victra and that White Witch. . . ."

"I'd kill to snag Victra," Truth says, walking around me. "That'd be a dance. Say, didn't you bed her, Cassius?"

"I never kiss and tell." Cassius nods to the battle. "How do we fare?"

"Better than Fabii. They're tenacious. Hard to pin down, keep trying to close so they can use their Obsidian, but the Ash Lord's keeping them at a distance. The ArchGovernor's fleet will be the hammer that wins this. They're already coming around their flank. See?" The knight looks longingly at the holo. Cassius notices.

"You could always join," Cassius says. "Order a shuttle."

"That would take hours," Truth replies. "We've four knights in engagement already. Someone has to protect Octavia. And my ships are being held in reserve protecting the dayside. If they make landfall, which is doubtful at this point, we'll need martial men on the ground. We'll have to wash his face."

"What?"

"Barca's face. It's too bloody. We'll make the broadcast soon, if we're not hacked again. Saboteurs were wrecking operations. More of Quicksilver's boys. All sorts of tech-head demokratic filth with delusions of grandeur. But we hit one of their dens last night with a lurcher squad."

"Best way to stop a hacker? Hot metal," Joy adds.

"The enemy is brave, I'll give them that," the Ash Lord is saying in the center of the room, his hologram twice again the width of his adjuncts'. *"Cutting off their escape but still they're standing toe-to-toe."* He's on a corvette in the back of his fleet, his signal being re-routed through dozens of other ships. The Ash Lord's fleet moves with beautiful precision, never allowing my ships within fifty kilometers.

Roque cared about casualties. Cared about not destroying the beautiful three-hundred-year-old ships I'd captured. The Ash Lord has no such restraint. He thuggishly smashes ships to oblivion. Damn their heritage, damn the lives, damn the expense, he's a destroyer. Here with his back to the wall he will win at all cost. It aches to see my fleet suffer.

"Report when you have further news," the Sovereign says. "I want Daxo au Telemanus alive, if possible. All others are expendable, including his father and the Julii."

"Yes, my liege." The old killer salutes and disappears. With a tired sigh, the Sovereign turns to look at her Morning Knight and extends her arms as if greeting a long-lost child. "Cassius." She embraces him after he bows, kissing his forehead with the same familiarity she once had for Mustang. "My heart broke when I heard what happened on the ice. I thought you were slain."

"Aja was right to think I was. But I'm sorry it took so long for me to return from the dead, my liege. I had unfinished business to attend."

"So I see," the Sovereign says, caring little for me. Focusing on Mustang instead. "I do believe you've won the war, Cassius. The both of you." She nods without a smile to the Jackal. "Your ships will make this a short battle."

"It is our pleasure to serve," the Jackal replies with a knowing smile.

"Yes," the Sovereign says in a strange, almost nostalgic way. Her fingers trace the scars on Cassius's broad neck. "Did they hang you?"

"Oh, they tried. It didn't quite take." He grins.

"You remind me of Lorn when he was young." I know she once said to Virginia that she reminded her of herself. The affection is more real than the Jackal has for his men, but she's still a collector. Still using love and loyalty as a shield to protect herself. The Sovereign gestures to me, wrinkling her nose at the metal muzzle around my face. "Do you know what he's planning? Anything that will compromise our endgame . . ."

"From what I glean he's planning an attack on the Citadel."

"Cassius, stop. . . ." Mustang snaps. "She doesn't care about you."

"And you do?" the Sovereign asks. "We know exactly what you care about, Virginia. And what you'll do to get it."

"By air or ground?" the Jackal asks. "The attack."

"Ground, I believe."

"Why didn't you mention this in space?"

"You were more concerned with chopping off Darrow's hand."

The Jackal ignores the barb. "How many clawDrills are there on Luna?"

"None working, not even in the abandoned mines," the Sovereign says. "We made sure of that."

"If he has a team coming, it'll be Volarus and Julii," the Jackal says. "They're his best weapons and helped him take the Moon-Breaker."

"Volarus is the Obsidian?" the Sovereign asks. "Yes?"

"Queen of the Obsidian," Mustang says. "You should meet her. You'd remind Sefi of her mother."

"Queen of the Obsidian . . . they are united?" the Sovereign asks Cassius warily. "Is that right? My politicos said pan-tribal leadership was impossible."

"And they were wrong," Cassius says.

Antonia seizes a moment to stand out in the Sovereign's eyes. "It's only the Obsidian in Darrow's fold, my liege. An alliance of the southern tribes."

The Sovereign ignores her. "I don't like it. We have hundreds of Obsidians in the citadel alone. . . ."

"They're loyal," Aja says.

"How do you know?" Cassius asks. "Are any from Mars?"

Octavia looks to Aja for confirmation. "Most," Aja admits. "Even Zero Legion. Martian Obsidians are the best."

"I want them out of the bunker," Octavia says. "Now."

One of the Praetorians moves to do her bidding.

"Is she as formidable as her brother?" Aja asks Cassius.

"Worse," Mustang says from her knees with a laugh. "Far worse and far brighter. She fights with a pack of warrior women. She has sworn a blood oath to find you, Aja. To drink your blood and use your skull as her chalice in Valhalla. Sefi is coming. And you cannot stop her."

Aja and Octavia exchange a wary look. "They would have to land first before making an assault on the citadel," Aja says. "It's impossible."

"How are they coming?" Cassius asks me. I shake my head and laugh at him behind my muzzle. Aja kicks the stump of my right hand. I almost black out as I curl around the wound in pain. "How are they coming?" Cassius asks. I don't reply. He motions to the Joy Knight. "Hold out his other arm." Joy grabs my left arm and pulls it out. "How are they coming?" he asks not me, but Mustang. "I will cut his other hand off if you do not tell me. Followed by his feet and nose and eyes. How is Volarus coming?"

"You're going to kill him anyway," Mustang sneers. "So fuck you."

"How slowly he dies is up to you," Cassius says.

"Who said they didn't already land?" Mustang asks.

"What?"

"They came in the grain ships from Earth, compliments of Quicksilver. Landed hours ago. And they're pressing for the Citadel now. Ten thousand strong. Didn't you know?"

"Ten thousand?" Lysander murmurs from his chair to the side of the holopit. His grandmother's Dawn Scepter lies on the table before him. A meter long length of gold and iron, it's tipped with the triangle of the Society and the withered heart of the Obsidian warlord who led the Dark Revolt nearly five hundred years ago. "The Legions are deployed to halt an invasion. The Obsidians will overrun our defenses before they can return."

"I will make ready the Praetorians and recall two legions," Aja says, striding for the door.

"No." Octavia stands motionless, thinking. "No, Aja, you stay with me." She turns to the Praetorian captain. "Legatus, go reinforce the surface. Take your platoon. There's no need for them here. I have my knights. Any ship approaching the Citadel should be fired upon. I don't care if it claims to carry the Ash Lord himself. Do you understand?"

"It will be done." Legatus and the remaining Praetorians rush out, leaving the room deserted save for Cassius, the three Olympic Knights, Antonia, the Jackal, the Sovereign, three Praetorian guards, and us prisoners. Aja presses her palm into a console near the door. The sanctum seals behind the Praetorians. A second, thicker door appears from the walls in a corkscrew, slowly locking us off from the world beyond.

"I'm sorry, Aja," Octavia says as the woman returns to her side. "I know you want to be with your men, but we already lost Moira. I couldn't risk losing you too."

"I know," Aja replies, but her disappointment is obvious. "The Praetorians will deal with the Horde. Shall we attend the other matter?"

Octavia glances over to the Jackal and he gives her the barest of nods. "Severus-Julii, come forward," Octavia says.

Antonia does, surprised to have been singled out. A hopeful smile works its way onto her lips. No doubt she's to receive a commendation for her efforts today. She clasps both hands behind her back and waits before her Sovereign.

"Tell me, Praetor, you were conscripted to join the Sword Armada as it subjugated the Moon Lords in June of this year, were you not?"

Antonia frowns. "My liege, I do not understand. . . ."

"It's a fairly simply question. Answer it to the best of your abilities."

"I was. I led my family's ships and the Fifth and Sixth Legions."

"Under the pro tem command of Roque au Fabii?"

"Yes, my liege."

"Then tell me, how is it that you are still alive and your Imperator is not?"

"I only barely managed to escape the battle," Antonia says, seeing the danger in the line of questioning. Her voice modulates accordingly. "It was a . . . terrible calamity, my liege. With the Howlers hidden in Thebe, Roque . . . Imperator Fabii, fell into the trap twofold, through no fault of his own. Any would have done the same. I made an effort to rescue his command, to rally our ships. But Darrow had already reached his bridge. And torchShips were burning all around us. We did not know friend from foe. It's haunted my dreams, the sounds of the Obsidian Horde pouring through their ships. . . ."

"Liar." Mustang snorts her derision.

"And so you retreated."

"At grave cost, yes, my liege. I saved as many ships for the Society as I could. I saved my men, knowing they would be needed for the battle to come. It was all I could do."

"It was a noble thing, saving so many," the Sovereign says.

"Thank—"

"At least it would be if it were true."

"I beg your pardon?"

"I don't believe I have ever stuttered, girl. I do, however, believe you fled the battle, abandoning your post and your Imperator to the enemy."

"You are calling me a liar, my liege?"

"Obviously," Mustang says.

"I will not stand aspersions against my honor," Antonia snaps at Mustang, puffing up her chest. "It is beneath . . ."

"Oh, be still, child," the Sovereign says. "You're in deep waters here, with larger fish than you. You see, others escaped the battle, others who transmitted their battle analytics to us so we would know what happened. So we could assess the calamity and see how Antonia of the Severus-Julii disgraced her name and lost us the battle, abandoning her Praetor when he called for aid, fleeing for the belt to save her own hide, where she then lost her ships."

"Fabii lost the battle," she says vindictively. "Not I."

"Because his allies abandoned him," Aja purrs. "He might still have saved his command had you not thrown his formation to chaos."

"Fabii made mistakes," the Sovereign says. "But he was a noble creature and as loyal a servant to his Color. He was even honorable enough to take his own life, to accept that he had failed and to pay justly for it and ensure he would not be interrogated or bartered. His last act in destroying the rebel docks was the act of a hero. An Iron Gold. But you . . . you scurrilous craven, you fled like a little girl who pissed her Whiteday dress. You abandoned him to save yourself. Now you slander him in front of all. In front of his friend." She gestures protectively to Cassius. "Your men saw the reptile underneath, that is why they turned on you. Why you lost your ships to your better sister."

"I would see whoever lays these claims against me in the Bleeding Place," Antonia says, trembling with anger. "My honor will not be smeared by faceless, jealous creatures. It is sad that they would manufacture evidence to smear my good name. No doubt they have ulterior motives. Perhaps intentions against my company or my holdings or they seek to undermine Gold as a whole. Adrius, tell the Sovereign how ridiculous this all is."

But Adrius remains quiet. "Adrius?"

"I'd rather have the loyalty of a dog than that of a coward," he says. "Lilath was right. You are weak. And that is dangerous."

Antonia looks about like a drowning woman, feeling the water coming over her head, undertow pulling her down, nothing to grab onto, nothing to save her. Aja swells behind her like a dark wave as Octavia denounces her formally. "Antonia au Severus-Julii, matron of House Julii and Praetor First Class of the Fifth and Sixth Legions, by the power vested in me by the Compact of the Society, I find you guilty of treason and dereliction of duty in a time of war and hereby sentence you to death."

"You bitch," Antonia hisses at her, then to the Jackal, "You can't afford to kill me. Adrius . . . please." But she has no ships anymore. No face. Tears stream out of swollen eyes as she seeks some hope here, some way out. There is none, and when she meets my gaze, she knows what I am thinking. *Reap what you sow.* This is for Victra, and Lea, and Thistle, and all the others she would sacrifice so she could live. "Please . . . ," she whimpers.

But there is no mercy here.

Aja grasps Antonia's neck from behind. She shivers in horror, shrinking to her knees, not even attempting to fight as the huge woman slowly closes her hands and begins to strangle her to death. Antonia snorts, wriggles, and takes a full minute to die. When she has, Aja completes the execution by snapping her neck with a violent twist and tossing her atop Sevro's corpse.

"What an odious creature," the Sovereign says, turning from Antonia's body. "At least her mother had spine. Cassius, your shoes are filthy." Blood crusts the rubber soles of his prison slippers and spatters the green jumpsuit's legs. "There's a complex of sleeping quarters through there, a kitchen, showers. Clean yourself. My valet has been attempting to foist a meal on me for hours. I'll have him serve it here for you. You won't miss the battle. The Ash Lord has promised it will last another several hours, at the very least. Lysander, will you show him the way?"

"I won't leave your side, my liege," Cassius says very nobly. "Not till this is through and these monsters are put down." The Truth Knight rolls his eyes at the display.

"You're a good lad," she says before turning toward me. "Now it's time we dealt with the Red."

61

||||||||||||||||||||||||||

THE RED

Aja drags me to the Sovereign's feet at the center of the holo-pad. The cold sneer of command is etched deeply into the tyrant's marble face. Her shoulders are weary though, pressed down by the weight of empire and the shadowy mass of a hundred years of sleepless nights. Her tightly bound hair is shot with deep rivers of gray. Tendrils of blue worm through the corners of her eyes from relapsed cellular rejuvenation therapy. She's had no peace from me. Kneeling and bleeding though I am, it does my soul good to know I've haunted her nights.

"Remove his muzzle," she tells Aja, who stands behind me, preparing to administer the Sovereign's justice. The Truth Knight and the Joy Knight flank Octavia. Cassius stands over Mustang to the side in his prisoner greens among the Praetorians while the Jackal watches from his chair near Lysander, sipping a coffee brought by the valet. I stretch my jaw as the muzzle comes off.

"Imagine a world without the arrogance of the young," Octavia says to her Fury.

"Imagine a world without the greed of the old," I reply hoarsely.

Aja slams the side of my head with her fist. The world flashes black and I almost keel over.

"Why'd you take off his muzzle if you wanted him to be silent?" Mustang asks.

The Jackal laughs. "A fair point, Octavia!"

Octavia scowls at him. "Because we executed a puppet last time and the worlds know it. This is flesh and blood. The Red who rose. I want them to know it is he who falls. I want them to know that even their best is insignificant."

"Give him words and he'll just make another slogan," the Jackal warns.

"Octavia, do you really think my brother won't kill you?" Mustang asks. "He won't rest until you're dead. Until you're all dead. Till he takes your scepter and sits on your throne."

"Of course he wants my throne, who wouldn't?" the Sovereign says. "What is my charge, Lysander?"

"To defend your throne. To create a union where it is safer for subjects to follow than to fight. That is the role of Sovereign. Be loved by a few, be feared by the many, and always know thyself."

"Very good, Lysander," she says sadly.

"The purpose of a Sovereign isn't to rule. It's to lead," I say.

Not even hearing me, she turns to the Joy Knight, who is at the controls of the holodeck preparing her broadcast. "Is it ready?"

"Yes, my liege. Greens have restored the links. It'll go out live to the Core."

"Say your goodbyes to the Red . . . *Mustang*," Aja says, patting Mustang's head.

"Can't even do it yourself?" I ask the Jackal. "What a man you are."

He frowns. "I want to do it, Octavia," the Jackal says suddenly, rising from his seat and walking out to the holodeck.

"Olympic Knights carry out executive executions," Aja says. "It's not your place, ArchGovernor."

"I don't remember asking for your permission." Aja bares her teeth at the insult, but the Sovereign's hand on her shoulder restrains her tongue.

"Let him do it," the Sovereign says. Strange, the Sovereign's deference to the Jackal. It's out of character, but in keeping with the oddness I've felt between them on the day. Why would he be here, I wonder. Not Luna. That's obvious enough. But why would he come to a place where the Sovereign has absolute power over him? At any moment, she could kill him. He must have something over her, to buy himself immunity. What is his play here? I sense Mustang trying to divine the same answer as Aja moves away from me. The Joy Knight offers the Jackal a scorcher, but Adrius refuses. Instead, he picks Sevro's gun from his holster and twirls it around his index finger.

"He's no Gold," the Jackal explains. "He doesn't deserve a razor or a state death. He'll go like his uncle. In any matter, I very much would like to begin the transition as the hand of justice. Plus, offing Darrow with Sevro's gun is . . . more poetic, don't you think, Octavia?"

"Very well. Is there anything else you would like?" the Sovereign asks tiredly.

"No. You've been most accommodating." The Jackal takes Aja's place beside me as the Sovereign transforms before our eyes. The exhaustion burning away from her face as she adopts the serene, matronly visage I remember telling me: "Obedience. Sacrifice. Prosperity," time and time again from the HC in Lykos. Then, Octavia seemed a goddess so far beyond mortal ken that I would have given my life to please her, to make her proud of me. Now I'd give my life to end hers.

The Joy Knight nods to the Sovereign. A light glows softly above her, empowering the woman with the fury and warmth of the sun. It's just a spotlight. The lamp deepens its glow. The Jackal brushes an errant strand from his fastidiously parted hair and smiles fondly at me.

The broadcast begins.

"Men and Women of the Society," Octavia says. "This is your Sovereign. Since the dawn of man, our saga as a species has been one of tribal warfare. It has been one of trial, one of sacrifice, one of daring to defy nature's natural limits. Then, after years of toiling in the dirt, we rose to the stars. We bound ourselves in duty. We set aside our own wants, our own hungers to embrace the Hierarchy of Color, not to oppress the many for the glory of the few, as Ares and this . . . terrorist would have you believe, but to secure the immortality of the human race on principles of order and prosperity. It was an immortality that was assured before this man tried to steal it from us."

She points a long, elegant finger at me.

"This man, once a noble servant of you, of your families, should have been the brightest son of his Color. He was lifted up as a youth. Awarded merits of honor. But he chose vanity. To extend his own ego across the stars. To become a conqueror. He forgot his duty. He forgot the reason for order and has fallen into darkness, dragging the worlds with him.

"But we will not fall into that darkness. No. We will not bend to the forces of evil." She touches her heart. "We . . . we are the Society. We are Gold, Silver, Copper, Blue, White, Orange, Green, Violet, Yellow, Gray, Brown, Pink, Obsidian, and Red. The bonds that bind us together are stronger than the forces that pull us apart. For seven hundred years, Gold has shepherded humanity, brought light where there was dark, plenty where there was famine. Today we bring peace where there is war. But to have peace, we must destroy outright this murderer who has brought war to each and every one of our homes."

She turns to me with a callousness that reminds me of how she watched my duel with Cassius. How she would have let me die then sipped her wine and been about her dinner. I am a speck to her, even now. She's thinking past this moment. Past the time where my blood cools on the floor and they drag me off to be dissected.

"Darrow of Lykos, by the power entrusted in me by the Compact, I hereby find you guilty of conspiracy to incite acts of terror." I stare directly into the holoCam's optic lens, knowing how many countless souls watch me now. How many countless eyes will watch me long after I have gone. "I find you guilty of mass murder upon the citizens of Mars." I barely listen to her. My heart thunders in my chest. Rattling the fingers of my left hand. Pushing up into my throat. This is it. The end swarming toward me. "I find you guilty of murder." This moment, this fragment of time is my life in summary. It is my shout into the void. "And I find you guilty of treason against your Society. . . ."

But I want no shout.

Let that be for Roque. Let that be for the Golds. Give me something more. Something they cannot understand. Give me the rage of my people. The wrath of all people in bondage. As the Sovereign recites her sentence, as the Jackal waits to deliver it, as Mustang kneels on the ground, as Cassius watches me from among the Praetorians and Knights, waiting, and as Aja sees me look to the tall blond knight, she steps forward in trepidation because she knows something is wrong, I throw my head back and I howl.

I howl for my wife, for my father. For Ragnar and Quinn and Pax and Narol. For all the people I've lost. For all they would take.

I howl because I am a Helldiver of Lykos. I am the Reaper of Mars. And I have paid for access to this bunker with my flesh, all so I could come before Octavia, all so that I might either die with my friends or see our enemies brought to justice.

The Sovereign nods to the Jackal to execute the sentence. He presses the barrel to the back of my head and he squeezes the trigger. The gun kicks in his hand. Fire spits, scorching my scalp. Deafening sound ringing through my right ear. But I do not fall. No bullet carves through my head. Smoke swirls out of the barrel. And as the Jackal looks down at the gun, he knows.

"No . . ." He steps away from me, dropping the gun, trying to pull out his razor.

"Octavia . . . ," Aja shouts, lunging forward.

But just then, in that beat of the heart, the Sovereign hears something behind the camera and turns to see a Praetorian guard with his head tilted, his pulseRifle thumping to the floor as a grisly red tongue protrudes from his mouth. Only it's not a tongue. It's Cassius's bloody razor that entered through the back of the Praetorian's skull and out between his teeth. It disappears back into the mouth. The three guards fall before the Sovereign can say a bloodydamn word. Cassius stands behind the slaughtered men, his head lowered, his razor red, his left hand holding the remote control to my restraints and Mustang's.

"Bellona?" is all the Sovereign can say before he presses the button. Mustang's steel vest unbuckles and falls to the ground. Mine follows suit. She dives for a dead Praetorian's pulseRifle. Unshackled, I rise, jerking my arms free and pulling the knife hidden inside the metal vest. I lunge toward the Sovereign. Faster than she can blink, I jam the blade through her black jacket into the softness of her lower belly. She gasps. Eyes huge. Inches from mine. I smell the coffee on her breath. Feel the flutter of her eyelashes as I stab her six more times in the gut and on the last, rip the metal up toward her sternum. Hot blood pours over my knuckles and chest as she spills open.

"Octavia!" Aja's charging me. Makes it halfway before Mustang, firing from her knees, shoots her in the armored side with the pulse-Rifle. The blast lifts Aja off her feet, slapping her across the room into the wooden conference table beside Sevro and Antonia's bodies, nearly crushing Lysander. Seeing their Sovereign stumbling backward, gut ripped open, the Truth Knight and the Joy Knight both wheel on Cassius, pulling their razors from their hips, their shields thrumming to life. Unarmored, wearing only his blood-spattered prison greens, Cassius flashes forward, skewering the surprised Truth Knight through his eye socket up through the roof of his skull.

The Jackal pulls my razor from his hip and slashes at me. I sidestep, coming at him. He swings again, screaming in rage, but I catch his arm and head butt him in the face before sweeping his legs and tackling him to the floor. I take my razor and stake his left arm to the floor so that he has no free hand. He screams. His spit spattering my face. Thrashing at me with his legs. I drop a knee into his forehead and leave him stunned and pinned to the floor.

"Darrow!" Cassius calls to me as he duels the Joy Knight. "Behind!"

Behind me, Aja's rising from the shattered remains of the table. Eyes wide with rage. I run from her to help Cassius and Mustang, knowing she'd kill me in seconds with my right hand gone. Blood darkens Cassius's green jumpsuit. His left leg has been slashed badly by the better-armored Joy Knight, who is using his weight and the pulsing aegis shield on his left arm to overwhelm Cassius. Mustang grabs two razors from the dead Praetorian and tosses one to me. I catch it on the run with my left hand. Toggle the hilt. Razor leaps to killing length. Cassius takes another slash to the leg and stumbles over a body, going down, blocking the second strike with the pulse-Fist, ruining the weapon. The Joy Knight's back is to me. He feels me coming, but it's too late. Silently, I jump through the air and swing a huge looping strike down at him from behind, left arm slowing as it meets the throbbing resistance of the pulseShield centimeters from the armor, then jerking as it cleaves into his sky-blue plate and through muscle and bone. Carrying from left shoulder to the right pelvis, parting his body at a diagonal. His body drips to the ground.

Silence in the room as the bodies hit the floor.

Mustang rushes to my side. She sweeps her golden mess of hair back, a fevered grin splitting her face. I help Cassius up from the ground.

"How was my acting?" he asks, wincing.

"Not quite as good as your swordwork," I say, looking at the bodies around him. He grins, more alive in battle than anywhere else. I feel a pang, knowing this is always how it should have been. Missing the days where we rode together in the highlands pretending we were lords of the earth. I grin back at him, wounded, bleeding, but almost whole for the first time I can remember.

"Will you two save the flirting for later," Mustang says.

Side by side with her, we turn together to face the deadliest human being in the Solar System. She's crouched over a terribly wounded Octavia, who has crawled to the edge of the holodeck and pants on her back, holding her stomach together with both hands. Octavia is pale and shivering. Tears stream down Aja's face and Lysander's, who has rushed into the pit to help his grandmother.

"Aja!" the Jackal screams from the floor. "Kill them! Open the door or kill them!" He's lost his mind. Thrashing about, trying to reach the whip toggle on the razor with his stump. It's three and a half feet above him and he just can't quite reach. "Open it!" he says through gnashing teeth.

But to open the door she must reach it. And to reach it, she must go through me and my friends then present her back to us while she enters the code. She's trapped in here till we're dead or she is.

"Aja, give us the Sovereign. Her justice is due," I say, knowing what Aja's reply to that will be, but minding the holodeck is still active. Still broadcasting as Gold blood wets the floor. Aja does not turn to look at us. Not yet. Her huge hands caress Octavia's face. She cradles the older woman like a mother holding her own child. "Stay alive," she tells her. "I will get you out of here. I promise. Just stay alive, Octavia."

Octavia nods weakly. Lysander touches Aja's arm. "Hurry. Please."

"Wear her down," Mustang whispers. "She's the one with the ticking clock."

"Don't let her pin you in a corner," I say. "Move laterally like we planned. Cassius, you can still take point?"

"Just try to keep up," he says.

Aja rises from her crouch to her full height, a brooding mass of muscle and armor, the greatest student of the greatest razormaster the Society has ever known. Face dark, unreadable. The deep blue Protean armor moving subtly with sea dragons. Shoulders nearly as broad as Ragnar's. I wish I could have brought Sefi here. A meter and a half of killing silver slithers out before Aja and she takes the winter stance of the Willow Way, sword raised like a torch off to the side, left foot forward, hips sunken, knees slightly bent. Mustang and I slide apart taking the right and left. Cassius, the best swordsman of us now, takes the middle. Aja's hungry eyes devour our weaknesses. The drag in Cassius's step, my missing right hand, Mustang's size, the arrangement of obstacles on the floor. And she attacks.

There are two strategies when fighting multiple opponents. The first is use them against one another. But Cassius and I have always been of one mind in battle, and Mustang is adaptable. So Aja chooses the second option: an all out attack on me before Cassius or Mustang can come to my aid. She deems me the weakest enemy. And she is right. Her whip cracks toward my face faster than I can bring my blade up. I flinch back, almost losing my eye. Throwing off my center of balance. She's on me, blade rigid, poking at me in a poetic frenzy of carefully constructed movements to bring my blade out of position across my body, so she can perform Lorn's maneuver called the Wing Scalp. Where she tries to lever her blade atop mine to touch the tip to my sword arm's shoulder and scrape down to the outside of my wrist to peel off the muscle and tendons along the way. I dance back, robbing her of the leverage, navigating the corpses behind me as Cassius and Mustang close on Aja. Cassius is rushed in his approach, and he overextends, like I almost did.

But Aja doesn't use her razor. She activates her gravBoots in a quick burst and launches back at him, two hundred kilograms of armor and Peerless Scarred propelled by gravBoots crashes into flesh and bones. You can almost hear his skeleton creak. His body wraps around her, forehead smashing against her armored shoulder. He drips off her and she spikes him to the ground. Mustang rushes her flank to stop her from finishing Cassius off. But Aja was expecting the rush from Mustang and used Cassius to bait her. She slashes Mustang shallowly across the stomach, nearly opening her lower intestine.

I hurl my razor at Aja from behind. She somehow hears or feels it coming and bends sideways as it passes and sticks into the wall of the holodeck that separates it from the sitting room above. Aja's leg shoots out at Mustang, impacting her kneecap and jamming it backward. Can't tell if it dislocates, but Mustang stumbles back, razor outstretched and Aja turns back toward me, because I have no weapon.

"Shit shit shit shit shit," I hiss, scrambling toward the Praetorians to pick up one of their razors. I gain a pulseRifle and fire blindly behind me. Aja's pulseShield absorbs the munitions, throbbing crimson as she sprints at me and slashes the weapon from my hand. I escape again, rolling backward, taking a long burning gash on the back of my hamstrings, but gaining a razor as I jump out of the holodeck ring up to the sitting level several feet above. She picks up a pulseFist and shoots it at me. I dive down so she loses her shot. The steel ceiling above me bubbles and drips down. I roll to the side.

Razors keen on the deck bellow. I scramble back to the lip to get back in the fight. Aja's cutting us to ribbons and all fleeing does is allow her to turn back to Cassius and Mustang. She bears down on him, using his limp and the new wound in his shoulder against him. Mustang attacks from behind before he's cut down, but Aja bends when Mustang slashes, moving like she's studied the fight before it ever happened.

We're not going to put her down, I realize. This was our fear. Losing my hand was never part of the plan, either. One by one she's going to kill us.

I have a brief moment of hope when Mustang and Cassius finally pin Aja between them. I jump down to help the assault. The woman pivots and twirls like a willow caught among three tornadoes. She knows her armor will take our glancing blows but our skin can't take hers. She goes for shallow cuts, bleeding us out methodically, aiming for the tendons in our knees, arms, like Lorn taught us both. A sage digging the roots.

Her blade cuts deep into my forearm, lacerates my knuckles, taking off a corner of my pinky. I roar anger, but anger isn't enough. My instincts aren't enough. We're too spent, too overwhelmed by the monstrosity of her. Lorn trained her too well. Spinning, she delivers a two-handed thrust up into the right side of my rib cage. My world rocks. She lifts me up with a horrible bellow. My feet dangle half a meter above the deck. Cassius charges her and she flings me off the edge of her blade to parry his attack. I crash to the ground, my chest feeling like it is caving in on itself. Gasp for air, barely able to draw breath. Cassius and Mustang put themselves between Aja and me.

"Do not touch him," Mustang hisses.

The blade missed my organs, wedging itself between two of the reinforced ribs Mickey gave me, but I'm bleeding all over myself. Trying to stand, scrambling across the deck. The Jackal watches me from his place on the ground, exhausted from trying to free himself. He's grinning, despite the horror of bodies all around us, knowing Aja is going to kill me. The Sovereign's face distant and fading she watches too, propped up against the lip of the holodeck as it rises to the rest of the room, Lysander's hands holding her together. Aja looks at her in fear, knowing she has not long to live.

"How could you choose him over us?" Aja shouts in rage to Mustang and Cassius.

"Easily," Mustang replies.

Cassius pulls the syringe from the holster on his leg and tosses it across the room to me. "Do it before she kills us, man." I stumble to my feet as Aja tries furiously to get at me, but Cassius and Mustang have strength enough to batter her away. She roars in frustration. The three slipping on blood, my friends not long for this world standing toe-to-toe with her. I make it to the edge of the holodeck, opposite the Sovereign, and climb toward Sevro's body.

"You cannot run!" Aja shouts. "I will carve your eyes out. There's nowhere to run, you rusty coward!" But I am not running. I fall to my knees beside Sevro. The front of his chest is a chaos of laboratory blood and torn fabric from the entry wounds of Cassius's execution. I cut open his shirt with my razor. Six holes stare up at me from the combat vest Cyther made him, bits of Carved flesh looking so real. His face is quiet and peaceful. But peace isn't in his nature, and we haven't earned it yet. I pop open the syringe filled with Holiday's snakebite. Enough to wake the dead. Even those faking eternal sleep from Narol's wicked cocktail of haemanthus extract. I pull off his vest.

"Wakey, wakey, Goblin," I say as I lift high the syringe, praying the silent prayer that his heart doesn't fail, and plunge it straight into my best friend's chest. His eyes burst open.

"Fuuuuuuuuck."

62

||||||||||||||||||||||||||

OMNIS VIR LUPUS

Exploding upward out of the coma induced by the haemanthus oil in the flask he was drinking from before we freed Cassius, he flails past me, gaining his feet, looking around with manic, wild eyes, hands vibrating. Holding his heart, gasping in pain as I did when Trigg and Holiday brought me from my prison. The last thing he saw was my face in the brig, now to wake here, to be thrust into the battle, blood and bodies littering the floor. He stares at me with crazed, bloodshot eyes, pointing at my belly. "You're bleeding! Darrow! You're bleeding!"

"I know."

"Where is your hand? You're missing a fucking hand!"

"I know!"

"Bloodydamn." His eyes dart around, seeing the Jackal pinned and Octavia on the ground, Aja beating Cassius and Mustang back. "It worked! It fucking worked! We've got to help the Goldbrows, shit-head. Get up! *Get up!*" He hauls me to my feet and shoves my razor back into my hand, rushing into the holopit, howling the hideous battle cry we made as children among the frozen pines. "I'm going to kill you, Aja! I'm going to kill you in your face!"

"It's Barca!" the Jackal screams from the ground. "Barca's alive!"

On the run, Sevro scoops up a pulseFist from a dead Praetorian and tramples over the Jackal's body, stomping on his face as he grabs the razor that pins the young ArchGovernor to the ground without stopping. He flies into Aja, firing with the pulseFist. Insane with the drugs and the victory he can smell.

The pulse blasts ripple over Aja's shield, spreading crimson around her silhouette, impairing her vision enough to finally let Cassius slip his razor through her guard. Still, she twists as it comes so it only takes her in the shoulder, but then Sevro is on her, stabbing her twice in the small of her back. She grunts in pain, backing away. I join the fray as Aja gains separation, stumbling back from us. But on the ground behind her, she leaves something few humans have seen: a thin ribbon of blood. It coats Sevro's razor. He wipes it from the tip of the blade and smears it between his fingers.

"Hahaha. Well look at that. You *do* bleed. Let's see how much more ya got in there." He hunches like an animal, stalking toward her as Mustang, Cassius, and I pin her between us, making a square around the greatest living Olympic Knight, like a wolfpack come upon a great panther of the forest. Shrinking before it as it charges, striking at its hindquarters, slashing its flanks. Bleeding it out. We're a prison of four. Sevro swishes his razor through the air, howling rabidly.

"Shut up!" Aja says, lashing out at him. But Sevro dances back and Cassius and I dart forward, stabbing at her. She parries Cassius's thrust at her neck and his two successive moves, but not in time to counter me. I feign a thrust at her abdomen and slash her shin instead, raking through the metal. Metal sparks and blood coats my blade. Mustang stabs her calf. I dart back as she wheels on me, making her overextend so Sevro can strike again. He does, furiously slashing the Achilles tendon on her right leg. She grunts and stumbles before lashing at him. He dances back.

"You're gonna die," he says with an evil little hiss. "You're gonna die."

"Shut up!"

"That one's for Quinn," he hisses as Cassius cuts through the tendons of her left knee. "This one's for Ragnar." I impale her right thigh with an underhanded thrust. "This one's for Mars." Mustang takes her arm off at the elbow. Aja looks down at the appendage on the ground, as if wondering if it belongs to her.

But she's given no respite. Sevro tosses aside his pulseFist, picks the Truth Knight's razor from the ground and jumps in the air to bring both his swords down into her chest, hanging there, a foot off the ground. Their faces inches from one another, noses nearly touching as Aja sinks to her knees, setting Sevro back on his feet.

"Omnis vir lupus."

He kisses her nose and jerks his razors out of her chest, letting them slither back into whips around his forearms. Arms outstretched, he backs away from the dying Protean Knight, greatest of her age as she pulses her last blood onto the cold floor. Still on her knees Aja's eyes drift hopelessly to the Sovereign, the woman who became mother to her sisters, who raised her, loved her as truly as any who rules the Solar System can love, and now dies along with her.

"I'm sorry . . . my liege." Aja wheezes wet breaths.

"Never be," Octavia manages from her place on the ground. "You burned bright, my Fury. Time itself . . . will remember you."

"Nah, prolly not," Sevro says pitilessly. "Nighty night, Grimmus."

He lops off her head and kicks her in the chest. Her body teeters back and collapses to the floor, where he jumps atop it on all fours and howls. A deep moan escapes the Sovereign's mouth at the hideous sight. She shuts her eyes, leaking tears as we make our way to her and Lysander. Cassius and I limping together, his arm around my shoulders to take pressure off the leg he drags behind him. Mustang follows us. Sevro secures the Jackal by sitting on his chest and juggling a razor over his head.

Soaked in his grandmother's blood, Lysander grabs Octavia's razor from the ground and bars our way. "I won't let you kill her."

"Lysander . . . don't," Octavia says. "It's too late."

The boy's eyes are swollen with tears. The razor trembles in his hands. Cassius steps forward and extends a hand. "Drop the weapon, Lysander. I don't want to kill you." Mustang and I exchange a glance. One Octavia notices, and must make her soul shiver. Lysander knows he cannot fight us. His sense overcomes his grief and he drops the razor, stepping back to watch us hollowly.

Octavia's eyes are distant and dark, already halfway to that other world where even she does not reign. I thought there'd be spite in the end from her, or begging like Vixus or Antonia. But there's nothing weak in her even now. It's sadness and love lost that come in the end. She did not create the hierarchy, but she was its keeper in her time. And for that, she must be held accountable.

"Why?" Octavia asks Cassius, shaking from sorrow. "Why?"

"Because you lied," he says.

Wordlessly Cassius pulls the small holocube, a thumb-sized triangular prism, from his ammunition belt and sets it in her bloody hands. Images dance across its surfaces before floating into the air above the Sovereign's hands. The scene of Cassius's family dying plays, bathing her in blue light. Shadows move through a hall, becoming men in scarabSkin. They cut down his aunt in a hallway and the men move through and appear a moment later dragging children, which they kill with the razors and boots. More bodies are dragged and piled up, then lit on fire so there would be no survivors. More than forty children and non-scarred family members died that night. They thought they could heap the sin upon the shoulders of a fallen man. But it was the Jackal's work. He finished the war between the Bellona and the Augustuses, and the Sovereign's cooperation and silence was his price for my Triumph.

"You ask me why?" Cassius's voice is barely above a whisper. "It is because you are without honor. I swore an oath as an Olympic Knight to honor the Compact, to bring justice to the Society of Man. You swore the same, Octavia. But you forgot what that meant. Everyone has. That is why this world is broken. Maybe the next one can be better."

"This world is the best we can afford," Octavia whispers.

"Do you really believe that?" Mustang asks.

"With all my heart."

"Then I pity you," Mustang says.

And so does Cassius. "My heart was my brother. And I no longer believe in a world that says he was too weak to deserve life. He would have believed in this. In the hope for something new." Cassius looks over at me. "For Julian, I can believe that too."

Cassius hands me the two other holocubes from his pouch. The first is the murder of my friends at my Triumph. The second is for the Rim; when they see this recording, they will know I have struck a blow for them. Politics never rests. I set the two holocubes in the Sovereign's hands to join the first. Rhea glows before her. A blue and white moon, gorgeous beside its brothers Iapetus and Titan as they orbit giant Saturn. Then over the moon's north pole, tiny slivers which you'd hardly notice flicker several innocent times, and mushrooms of fire bloom upon the surface of the blue and white planet.

As the nuclear fire blazes in the Sovereign's eyes, Mustang moves aside so I can crouch before the dying woman, speaking softly so she will know that justice, not vengeance, has found her in the end.

"My people have a legend of a being who stands astride the road leading to the world after. He will judge the wicked from the good. His name is the Reaper. I am not him. I'm just a man. But soon you will meet him. Soon he will judge you for all the sins you hold."

"Sins?" Octavia shakes her head, looking back to the three holos dancing in her hands, these drops in her ocean of sins. "These are sacrifices. What it takes to rule," she says, her hands closing around them. "I own them as I own my triumphs. You will see. You will be the same, Conqueror."

"No. I will not."

"In the absence of a sun, there can be only darkness." She shudders, cold now. I fight off the urge to put something over her. She knows what's being left behind. When she dies, the succession struggle will begin. It'll tear Gold apart. "Someone . . . someone must rule, or a thousand years from now, children will ask, 'Who broke the worlds? Who put the light out,' and their parents will say it was you." But I already know this. I knew this when I asked Sevro if he knew how this would end. I will not replace tyranny with chaos. There must be order, even if it is a compromise. But I don't tell her that. She swallows painfully, a struggle to even breathe. "Listen to me. You must stop him. You must . . . stop Adrius . . ."

Those are the last words of Octavia au Lune. And as they fade, the fire of Rhea cools in her eyes and life leaves a cold pupil surrounded by gold, staring into infinite dark. I close her eyes for her. Chilled by her passing, by her words, her fear.

The Sovereign of the Society, who has ruled for sixty years, is dead.

And I feel nothing but dread, because the Jackal has begun to laugh.

63

||||||||||||||||||||||

SILENCE

His laughter rattles through the room. His face pale under the glow of the holo of the moon and the fleets pummeling one another in the darkness. Mustang has turned off the holodeck's broadcast and is already analyzing the Sovereign's data center as Cassius moves toward Lysander and I rise above Octavia's body. My body burns from wounds.

"What did she mean, stop him?" Cassius asks me.

"I don't know."

"Lysander?"

The boy's too traumatized by the horror around him to speak.

"Video went out to the ships and the planets," Mustang says. "People are seeing Octavia's death. Communiqué boards are flooding. They don't know who is in control. We have to move now before they marshal behind someone."

Cassius and I approach the Jackal. "What did you do?" Sevro's asking. He shakes the small man. "What was she talking about?"

"Get your dog off me," the Jackal says from under Sevro's knees. I pull Sevro back. He paces around the Jackal, still vibrating with adrenaline.

"What did you do?" I ask.

"There's no point in talking with him," Mustang says.

"No point? Why do you think the Sovereign let me in her presence," the Jackal asks from the ground. He comes up to a knee, holding his wounded hand to his chest. "Why she did not fear the gun on my hip, unless there was a greater threat keeping her in line?"

He looks up at me from under disheveled hair. His eyes calm despite the butchering we've done.

"I remember the feeling of being under the ground, Darrow," he says slowly. "The cold stone under my hands. My Pluto housemembers around me, hunched in the darkness. The steam on their breaths, looking to me. I remember how afraid I was of failing. Of how long I had prepared, how little my father thought of me. All my life weighed in those few moments. All of it slipping away. We'd run from our castle, fleeing Vulcan. They came so fast. They were going to enslave us. The last of our housemembers were still running through the tunnel by the time I rigged the mines to blow, but so were Vulcan. I could hear my father's voice. Hear him telling me how he was not surprised I failed so quickly. It was a week before we killed a girl and ate her legs to survive. She begged us not to. Begged us to choose someone else. But I learned then in that moment if no one sacrifices, then no one survives."

Cold fear wells in me, beginning in the deep hollow of my stomach and spreading upward. "Mustang . . ."

"They're here," she says, horrified.

"What's happening? What's here?" Sevro hisses.

"Darrow . . ." Cassius whispers.

"The nukes aren't on Mars," I say. "They're on Luna."

The Jackal's smile stretches. Slowly, he gains his feet and not one of us dares touch him. It all falls into place. The tension between him and the Sovereign. The subtle threats. His boldness in coming here into the Sovereign's place of power. His ability to mock Aja without consequence.

"Oh, shit. *Shit. Shit. Shit.*" Sevro pulls his Mohawk. "Shit."

"I never wanted to nuke Mars," the Jackal says. "I was born on

Mars. It is my birthright, the prize from which all things flow. Her helium is the blood of the empire. But this moon, this skeleton orb is, like Octavia, a treacherous old crone sucking at the marrow of the Society, crowing about what was instead of what can be. And Octavia let me ransom it. Just as you will, because you are weak and you did not learn what you should have at the Institute. To win, you must sacrifice."

"Mustang, can you find the bombs?" I ask. "Mustang!"

She's been struck dumb. "No. He would have masked the radiation signatures. Even if we could, we couldn't deactivate them. . . ." She reaches for the com to call our fleet.

"If you make the call, then I detonate a bomb every minute," the Jackal says, tapping his ear where a little com has been implanted. Lilath must be listening. She must have the trigger. That's what he meant. She's his insurance. "Would I really tell you my plan if you could do anything about it?" He straightens his hair and wipes blood from his armor. "The bombs were installed weeks ago. The Syndicate smuggled the devices across the moon for me. Enough to create nuclear winter. A second Rhea, if you will. When they were in place, I told Octavia what I had done and I told her my terms. She would carry on as Sovereign until the Rising was put down, which . . . has taken a surprising twist . . . obviously. And afterward, on the day of victory, she would convene the Senate, abdicate the Morning Throne and name me her successor. In return, I would not destroy Luna."

"That's why Octavia has the Senate rounded up," Mustang says in disgust. "So you could be Sovereign?"

"Yes."

I stand back from him, feeling the weight of the fight on my shoulders, the weakness in my body from the strain, the loss of blood, now this . . . this evil. This selfishness, it's overwhelming.

"You're bloodydamn mad," Sevro says.

"He's not," Mustang says. "I could forgive him if he were mad. Adrius, there are three billion people on this moon. You don't want to be that man."

"They don't care for me. So why should I care for them?" he asks. "This is all a game. And I have won."

"Where are the bombs?" Mustang asks, taking a threatening step toward him.

"Uh-uh," he says, scolding her. "Touch a hair on my head, Lilath detonates a bomb." Mustang's beside herself.

"These are people," she says. "You have the power to give three billion people their lives, Adrius. That is power beyond anything anyone should ever want. You have the chance to be better than Father. Better than Octavia . . ."

"You condescending little bitch," he says with a small laugh of disbelief. "You really think you can still manipulate me. This one is on you. Lilath, detonate the bomb on the southern Mare Serenitatis." We all look to the hologram of the moon above our heads, hoping beyond hope that somehow he's bluffing. That somehow the transmission won't go through. But a little red dot glows on the cool hologram, blossoming outward, a small almost insignificant little animation that envelops ten kilometers of city. Mustang rushes to the computer. "It's a nuclear event," she whispers. "There's more than five million people in that district."

"Were," the Jackal says.

"You freak . . ." Sevro shrieks, rushing the Jackal. Cassius gets in his path, knocking him back. "Get out of my way!"

"Sevro, calm down."

"Careful, Goblin! There's hundreds more," the Jackal says.

Sevro's overwhelmed, clutching his chest where his heart must be wrenching from the drugs. "Darrow, what do we do?"

"You obey," the Jackal says.

I force myself to ask: "What do you want?"

"What do I want?" He wraps a bit of cloth around his bleeding arm, using his teeth. "I want you to be what you always wanted, Darrow. I want you to be like your wife. A martyr. Kill yourself. Here. In front of my sister. In return, three billion souls live. Isn't that what you've always wanted? To be a hero? You die, and I will be crowned Sovereign. There will be peace."

"No," Mustang says.

"Lilath, detonate another bomb. Mare Anguis, this time."

Another red blossom erupts on the display. Nuclear fire ends the lives of millions. "Stop!" Mustang says. "Please. Adrius."

"You just killed six million people," Cassius says, not comprehending.

"They'll think it's us," Sevro sneers.

The Jackal agrees. "Each bomb looks like part of an invasion. This is your legacy, Darrow. Think of the children burning now. Think of their mothers screaming. How many you can save by simply pulling a trigger."

My friends look at me, but I'm in a distant place, listening to the moan of the wind through the tunnels of Lykos. Smelling the dew on the gears in the early morning. Knowing Eo will be waiting for me when I come home. Like she waits for me now at the end of the cobbled road, as Narol does, as Pax and Ragnar and Quinn and, I hope, Roque, Lorn, Tactus and the rest of them do. It would not be the end to die. It would be the beginning of something new. I have to believe that. But my death would leave the Jackal here in this world. It would leave him with power over those I love, over all I've fought for. I always thought I would die before the end. I trudged on knowing I was doomed. But my friends have breathed love into me, breathed my faith back into my bones. They've made me want to live. They've made me want to build. Mustang looks at me, her eyes glassy, and I know she wants me to choose life, but she will not choose for me.

"Darrow? What is your answer?"

"No." I punch him in the throat. He croaks. Unable to breathe. I knock him down and jump atop him, pinning his arms to the ground with my knees so his head is between my legs. I jam my hand into his mouth. His eyes go wild. Legs kicking. His teeth cut my knuckles, drawing blood.

The last time I pinned him down, I took the wrong weapon. What are hands to a creature like him? All his evil, all his lies, are spun with the tongue. So I grab it with my helldiver hand, pinning it between forefinger and thumb like the fleshy little baby pitviper it is. "This is always how the story would end, Adrius," I say down to him. "Not with your screams. Not with your rage. But with your silence."

And with a great pull, I rip out the tongue of the Jackal.

He screams beneath me. Blood bubbling from the mutilated stump at the back of his throat. Splashing over his lips. He thrashes. I shove off him and stand in dark rage, holding the bloody instrument of my enemy as he wails on the ground, feeling the hatred rolling through me and seeing the stunned eyes of my friends. I leave the com in his ear so Lilath can hear him wailing and I stalk to the holocontrols and hail Victra's ship. Her face appears, eyes widening at the sight of my face.

"*Darrow . . . you're alive . . .*" she manages. "*Sevro . . . The nukes . . .*"

"You need to destroy the *Lion of Mars*," I say. "Lilath is detonating the bombs on the surface. There's hundreds more hidden in the cities. Kill that ship!"

"*It's at the center of their formation,*" she protests. "*We'll destroy our fleet trying to get to it. It will take hours if we even manage.*"

"Can we jam their signal?" Mustang asks.

"*No.*"

"EMPs?" Sevro asks, coming up behind me. Victra's face brightens at the sight of him, before she shakes her head.

"*They have shielding,*" she says.

"Use the EMPs on the bombs to short-circuit their radio transmitters," I say. "Fire an Iron Rain and drop EMPs on the city till they're out."

"And plunge three billion people into the Middle Ages?" Cassius asks.

"*We'll be slaughtered,*" Victra says. "*We can't drop a Rain. We'll lose our army. And Gold will just keep the moon.*"

Another bomb detonates. This one nearer the southern pole. And then a fourth at the equator. We know the consequences to each one. "Lilath doesn't know exactly what's happened to Adrius," Cassius says quickly. "How loyal is she? Will she detonate all of them?"

"Not when he's still whimpering," I say. Least that's my hope.

"Excuse me," a small voice says. We turn to see Lysander standing behind us. We forgot about him in the mayhem. His eyes are shot red from tears. Sevro raises a pulseFist to shoot him. Cassius knocks it aside.

"Call my godfather," Lysander says bravely. "Call the Ash Lord. He will see reason."

"Oh, like hell . . ." Sevro says.

"We just killed the Sovereign and his daughter," I say. "The Ash Lord . . ."

"Destroyed Rhea," Lysander interrupts. "Yes. And it haunts him. Call him and he will help you. My grandmother would have wanted him to. Luna is our home."

"He's right," Mustang says, pushing me from the console. "Darrow, move." She's in that locked zone of concentration. Unable to relate her own thoughts as she starts opening direct com channels to the Gold Praetors in the fleet. The towering men and women appear around us like silvery ghosts, standing among the corpses they watched us make. Last to appear is the Ash Lord. His face stricken with rage. His daughter and master both dead by our hands.

"Bellona, Augustus," he growls, seeing Lysander among us. "Is it not enough . . ."

"Godfather, we have no time for recrimination," Lysander says.

"Lysander . . ."

"Please listen to them. Our world depends on it."

Mustang steps forward and raises her voice. "Praetors of the fleet, Ash Lord. The Sovereign is dead. The nuclear blasts you see destroying your home are not Red weapons. They come from your own arsenal which was stolen by my brother. His Praetor, Lilath, is overseeing the detonation of more than four hundred nuclear warheads from the bridge of *The Lion of Mars*. They will continue until Lilath is dead. My fellow Aureate, embrace change or embrace oblivion. The choice is yours."

"You are a traitor. . . ." one of the Praetors hisses.

Lysander walks off the holopad to the table where he sat earlier. He picks up his grandmother's scepter and returns as the Praetors are issuing threats to Mustang.

"She is no traitor," Lysander says, handing her the scepter. The blood of his grandmother staining his hands. "She is our conqueror."

64

||||||||||||||||||||||||

HAIL

The *Lion of Mars* dies an ignoble death, fired upon from all sides by loyalist and rebel alike. Watching Luna crackle with nuclear explosions did more to kill the bloodlust between the two navies than any peace or truce ever did. Few men truly like seeing beauty burn. But burn it does. Before the *Lion* is put to rest, more than twelve bombs detonate, carving new cities of fire and ash among those of steel and concrete. The moon is in turmoil.

As is the Gold Armada. With news of the Sovereign's death and the detonation of the bombs, the Society shudders beneath our feet. Wealthy Praetors are taking their personal ships and fracturing away, heading home to Venus, Mercury, or Mars. They do not stand together, because they do not know where to stand.

For sixty years Octavia has ruled. For most living, she is the only Sovereign they have ever known. Our civilization teeters on the brink. Electrical grids are down across the moon. Riots and panic spread as we prepare to leave the Sovereign's sanctum. There is an escape ship, but there is no escaping what we've done. We've carved the heart out of the Society. If we leave, what takes its place?

We knew we could never win Luna by force of arms. But that was never the goal. Just as it was not Ragnar's desire to fight until all Golds perished. He knew Mustang was the key. She always has been. That's why he risked our lives to let Kavax go. Now Mustang stands beneath the holo of the wounded moon, hearing the silent screams of the city as keenly as I. I step close to her.

"Are you ready?" I ask.

"What?" She shakes her head. "How could he do this?"

"I don't know," I say. "But we can fix it."

"How? This moon will be pandemonium," she says. "Tens of millions dead. The devastation . . ."

"And we can rebuild it, together."

The words flood her with hope, as if she's only just remembered where we are. What we've done. That we're together, alive. She blinks quickly and smiles at me. Then she looks at my arm, where my right hand used to be and touches my stomach where Aja stabbed me. "How are you still standing?"

"Because we're not yet done."

Battered and bloody, we join Cassius, Lysander, and Sevro before the door leading out of the Sovereign's inner sanctum as Cassius types in the Olympic code to open the doors. He pauses to sniff the air. "What's that smell?"

"Smells like a sewer," I say.

Sevro stares intensely at the razors he's taken from Aja, including the one belonging to Lorn. "I think it smells like victory."

"Did you shit your pants?" Cassius squints at him. "You did."

"Sevro . . ." Mustang says.

"It's an involuntary muscle reaction when you're fake executed and swallow massive amounts of haemanthus oil," Sevro snaps. "You think I would do that on purpose?"

Cassius and I look at each other.

I shrug. "Well, maybe."

"Yeah, actually."

He flips us the crux and makes a face, twisting his lips till it looks like he's going to explode. "What's happening?" I ask. "Are you . . . still . . ."

"No!" He throws his water bottle at me. "You stuck a needle full of adrenaline into my chest, asshole. I'm having a heart attack." He swats our hands as we try to help him. "I'm good. I'm good." He wheezes for a moment before straightening with a grimace.

"Are you sure you're prime?" Mustang asks.

"Left arm's numb. Probably need a Yellow."

We snort laughs. We look like walking corpses. Only thing keeping me up are the stim packs we found on the Praetorians. Cassius hobbles like an old man, but he's kept Lysander close to him, vetoing Sevro's offers to end the Lune bloodline here and now by drawing his razor. "The boy is under my protection," Cassius sneered. And now he walks with us as a sign of our legitimacy.

"I love you all," I say as the door begins to groan open. I adjust the unconscious Jackal, who I carry on my shoulder as a prize. "No matter what happens."

"Even Cassius?" Sevro asks.

"Especially me, today," Cassius says.

"Stay close," Mustang says to us, clutching the scepter tight.

The first great door parts. Mustang squeezes my hand. Sevro vibrates with fear. Then the second rumbles and dilates open to reveal a hall filled with Praetorians, their weapons drawn and pointed into the mouth of the bunker. Mustang steps forward bearing two symbols of power, one in each hand.

"Praetorians, you serve the Sovereign. The Sovereign is dead. A new star rises."

She continues walking toward them, refusing to break her step when she nears their line of bristling metal. I think a young Gold with furious eyes might pull the trigger. But his old captain puts a hand on the man's weapon, lowering it.

And they break for her. Parting and lowering their weapons one by one. They back away to let her pass. Their helmets slithering back into their armor. I've never seen a woman so glorious and powerful as she is now. She is the calm eye of the storm and we follow in her wake. Riding the Dragon Maw lift up in silence. More than four dozen of the Praetorians have come with us.

We find the Citadel in chaos. Servants ransacking rooms, guards leaving their posts in two and threes, worried for their families or their friends. The Obsidians we said were coming are still in orbit. Sefi is with the ships. We only created the ruse to draw men from the room. But it seems word has spread. The Sovereign is dead. The Obsidians are coming.

Amidst the chaos there is only one leader. And as we move through the Citadel's black marbled halls, past towering Gold statues and departments of state, soldiers gather behind us, their boots stamping over the marble halls to flock to Mustang, the one symbol of purpose and power left in the building. She lifts both her symbols of power high in the air, and those who first raise weapons against us see them and me and Cassius and the swelling mass of soldiers behind us and realize they're fighting the tide. They join us, or they run. Some take shots at us, or rush forward in small bands to halt our progress, but they're cut down before they get within ten meters of Mustang.

By the time we come before the great ivory-white doors to the Senate Chambers, behind which Senators have been sequestered inside by Praetorians, an army of hundreds is at our backs. And only a thin line of Praetorians bars our way to the Senate Chamber. Twenty in number.

An elegant Gold Knight steps forward, leader of the men guarding the chamber. He eyes the hundred behind us, seeing the purple adherents Mustang has gathered, the Obsidians, the Grays, me. And he makes a decision. He salutes Mustang sharply.

"My brother has thirty men in the Citadel," Mustang says. "The Boneriders. Find them and arrest them, Captain. If they resist, kill them."

"Yes, Lady Augustus." He snaps his fingers and departs with a fist of soldiers. The two Obsidians guarding the doors push them open for us and Mustang strides into the Senate Chamber.

The room is vast. A tiered funnel of white marble. At the bottom center is a podium from which the Sovereign presides over the ten levels of the chamber. We enter on the north side, causing a disruption. Hundreds of beady Politico eyes turn their entitled focus toward us. They will have watched the broadcast. Seen Octavia die. Seen the bombs wrecking their moon. And somewhere in the room, Roque's mother will stand up from her seat on her marble bench and crane her neck to watch our bloody band stomping down the white marble stairs to the bottom center of the great chamber, passing Senators to our right and left, bringing silence with us instead of shouts or protests. Lysander trails behind Cassius.

You can hear the rasping panicked breath of the Senate Majority Speaker as his Pink attendants help his withered form down from the podium where he was presiding over something of great importance. They were holding an election. Here, now, in the middle of chaos. And now they look like children who've been caught with their hands in the biscuit jar. Of course they would never suspect that the Praetorians guarding them would support rebels. Or that we could walk from the Sovereign's bunker unimpeded. But they've created a Society of fear. Where men and women must attach themselves to a rising star to survive. That's all this is. That simple human directive that allows for this coup to work. The old power is dead. See how they flock to the new.

Mustang takes the podium with the rest of us flanking her. I toss the Jackal to the ground so the Senate can see what has become of him. He's unconscious and pale from blood loss. Mustang looks at me. This is a moment she never wanted. But she accepts it as her burden just as I have accepted mine as Reaper. I see how it troubles her. How she will need me as I've needed her. But I could never stand where she stands or hold what she holds. Not without destroying everyone in this room. They would never accept it. If I am the bridge to the lowColors, she's the bridge to the high. Only together can we bind these people. Only together can we bring peace.

"Senators of the Society," Mustang proclaims, "I stand before you, Virginia au Augustus. Daughter of Nero au Augustus of the Lion House of Mars. You may know me. Sixty years ago Octavia au Lune stood before you with the head of a tyrant, her father, and laid her claim on the post of Sovereign to this Society."

Her keen eyes scour the room.

"I stand before you now with the head of a tyrant." She lifts her left hand to show the head of Octavia. One of the two objects which granted us passage here. Gold respects only one thing. And to change, they must be tamed by that one thing. "The Old Age has brought nuclear holocaust to the heart of the Society. Millions burned for Octavia's greed. Millions burn now for my brother's. We must save ourselves from ourselves before the inheritance of humanity is ash. Today I declare the beginning of a new age." She looks at me. "With new allies. New ways. I have the Rising at my back. A navy made of great Golden Houses which holds the Obsidian Horde in orbit. You have a choice before you." She tosses the head on the stone podium and raises her other hand. In it is the Dawn Scepter, bestowing upon the bearer the right to rule Society. "Bend. Or break."

A silence fills the chamber. So vast I feel it might swallow us all into itself and begin the war anew. No Gold will be the first to bend. I could make them. But better I bend for them. I fall to my knee before Mustang. Looking up into her eyes, I put my stump over my heart and feel myself swept away by the impossible joy of the moment. "Hail, Sovereign," I say. Then Cassius falls to his knee. And Sevro. Then Lysander au Lune and the Praetorians, and then one by one the Senators fall to their knees till all but fifty kneel and break the silence together, shouting with a single riotous voice: "Hail, Sovereign. Hail, Sovereign!"

A week after Mustang's ascension, I stand beside her to watch her brother hang. But for Valii-Rath and some ten men, the Jackal's Boneriders have been found and executed. Now their leader walks past me through the crowded Luna square. His hair is feathery and combed. His prisoner jumpsuit lime green. The lowColors around us watch in silence. A light dusting of snow falls from a thin skin of gray clouds. I'm nauseous from my radiation medication. But I came for her as she came for me to watch Roque buried. She's quiet and serene beside me. Face pale as the marble beneath our feet. The Telemanuses stand beside her, watching impassively as the Jackal climbs the stairs of the metal scaffold to where the White hangwoman waits.

The woman reads the sentence. Jeers are shouted from the crowd. A bottle shatters at the Jackal's feet. A stone splits his forehead. But he does not blink or buckle. He stands proud and vain as they loop the noose around his neck. I wish this would bring Pax back to us. That Quinn and Roque and Eo could live again, but this man has carved his mark in the world. The Jackal of Mars will never be forgotten.

The White moves for the lever, snow gathering on Adrius's hair. Mustang swallows. And the trapdoor opens. On Mars there's not much gravity, so you have to pull the feet to break the neck. They let the loved ones do it. On Luna there's even less. But no one comes forward from the crowd as the White extends the invitation. Not a soul lifts a finger as the Jackal's legs kick and his face purples. There's a stillness in me watching the sight. As if I'm a million kilometers away. I cannot feel for him. Not now. Not after all he's done. But I know Mustang does. I know this tears her apart. So I lightly squeeze her hand and guide her forward. She moves across the snow in a daze to grip her twin brother's feet. Looking up at him as if this were a dream. She whispers something and, lowering her head, she pulls down, showing him he was loved, even at the end.

65

||||||||||||||||||||||||

THE VALE

In the weeks following the bombing of Luna and the ascension of Mustang, the world has changed. Millions lost their lives, but for the first time there is hope. In the aftermath of her speech to the Senate, dozens of Gold ships defected, joining the forces of Orion and Victra. The Ash Lord did his best to rally his navy, but with Luna burning, his fleet fracturing, and Mustang as Sovereign, it was all he could do to keep his own ships from falling into enemy hands. He retreated to Mercury with the core of his forces.

In his absence, Mustang has secured the cooperation of much of the military, particularly the Gray Legions and Obsidian slave-knights. She has used this political muscle to take the first steps to dismantling the Color Hierarchy and the Gold grip on military power. The Senate has been disbanded. The Board of Quality Control has been dissolved. Thousands face charges of crimes against humanity. Justice will not be so quick as it was with the Jackal, or so clean, but we will do the best we can.

I thought I might be able to rest after Octavia was dead, but we are not without enemies. Romulus and the Moon Lords remain on the

Rim. The Ash Lord aims to rally Mercury and Venus. Gold warlords have begun carving out claims. And Luna itself is a disaster. Overrun by riots and shortages of food and spreading radiation. She will survive, but I doubt she will ever look the same, no matter how much Quicksilver promises to rebuild the city to even greater heights.

My own body is in recovery. Mickey and Virany reattached my hand, which I retrieved from the Jackal's shuttle that set down on Luna. It will be months before I can write again, much less use a blade. Though I hope I have less cause for that in the coming days.

In my youth, I thought I would destroy the Society. Dismantle its customs. Shatter the chains and something new and beautiful would simply grow from the ashes. That's not how the world works. This compromised victory is the best mankind could hope for. Change will come slower than Dancer or the Sons want, but it will come without the price of anarchy.

So we hope.

Under the supervision of Holiday, Sefi has set off to Mars to begin the slow process of freeing the rest of her people, visiting the poles with medicine instead of weapons. I remember how dark her eyes seemed when she looked at one of the Jackal's nuclear craters in person. For now, she's embraced the legacy of her brother, and plans to settle on warmer land set aside for her people on Mars. Though she wishes to keep her people from the alien cities, I think she knows deep down that she will not be able to control them. The Obsidians will leave their prisons. They will grow curious, spread, and assimilate. Their world will never be the same. Nor will that of my people. Soon I will return to Mars to help Dancer lead the migration of Reds to the surface. Many will stay and continue the lives they know. But for others, there will be a chance for life under the sky.

I said farewell to Cassius the day before last as he departed Luna. Mustang wanted him to stay and help us shape a new, fairer system of justice. But he's had enough of politics. "You don't have to go," I told him as I stood with him on the landing pad.

"There's nothing for me here but memories," he said. "I've been living my life too long for others. I want to see what else is out there. You can't fault me for that."

"And the boy?" I asked, nodding to Lysander, who moved into the ship carrying a satchel of belongings. "Sevro thinks it's a mistake to let him live. What were his words? 'It's like leaving a pitviper egg under your seat. Sooner or later it's gonna hatch.'"

"And what do you think?"

"I think it's a different world. So we should act like it. He's got Lorn's blood in his veins as much as he's got Octavia's. Not that blood makes a difference anymore."

My tall friend smiled fondly at me. "He reminds me of Julian. He's a good soul, despite everything. I'll raise him right. Away from all this." He extended a hand, not to shake mine, but to give me the ring he took from my finger the night Lorn and Fitchner died. I closed his hand back around it.

"That belongs to Julian," I said.

He nodded softly. "Thank you . . . brother." And there, on a citadel landing platform in what was once the heart of Gold power, Cassius au Bellona and I shake hands and say farewell, almost six years to the day since we first met.

Weeks later, I watch the waves lap at the shore as a gull careens overhead. Whitecaps mark the dark water that lashes the northern beach's sea stacks. Mustang and I set our little two-person flier down on the east-northeast coast of the Pacific Rim, at the edge of a rain forest on a great peninsula. Moss grows on the rocks, on the trees. The air is crisp. Just cold enough to see your breath. It is my first time on Earth, but I feel like my spirit has come home. "Eo would have loved it here, wouldn't she?" Mustang asks me. She wears a black coat with the collar pulled up around her neck. Her new Praetorian bodyguards sit in the rocks a half kilometer off.

"Yes," I say. "She would have." A place like this is the beating heart of our songs. Not a warm beach or a tropical paradise. This wild land is full of mystery. It holds its secrets covetously behind arms of fog and veils of pine needles. Its pleasures, like its secrets, must be earned. It reminds me of my dreams of the Vale. The smoke from the fire we made of driftwood rises diagonally across the horizon.

"Do you think it will last?" Mustang asks me, watching the water from our place in the sand. "The peace."

"It would be the first time," I say.

She grimaces and leans into me, closing her eyes. "At least we have this."

I smile, reminded of Cassius as an eagle skims low over the water before rising up through the mist and disappearing in the trees that jut from the top of a sea stack. "Have I passed your test?"

"My test?" she asks.

"Ever since you blocked my ship from leaving Phobos, you've been testing me. I thought I passed on the ice, but it didn't stop there."

"You noticed," she says with a mischievous little grin. It fades and she brushes hair from her eyes. "I'm sorry that I couldn't just follow you. I needed to see if you could build. I needed to see if my people could live in your world."

"No, I understand that," I say. "But there's more to it. Something changed when you saw my mother. My brother. Something opened up in you."

She nods, eyes still on the water. "There's something I have to tell you." I look over at her. "You lied to me for nearly six years. Since the moment we met. In the Lykos tunnel you broke what we had. That trust. That feeling of closeness we built. Piecing that together takes time. I needed to see if we could find what we lost. I needed to see if I could trust you."

"You know you can."

"I do, now," she says. "But . . ."

I frown. "Mustang, you're shaking."

"Just let me finish. I didn't want to lie to you. But I didn't know how you would react. What you would do. I needed you to make the choice to be more than a killer not just for me, but for someone else too." She looks past me to the blue sky where a ship coasts lazily down. I hold my hand up against the autumn sun to watch it approach.

"Are we expecting company?" I ask warily.

"Of a sort." She stands. I join her. And she goes to her tiptoes to kiss me. It is a gentle, long kiss that makes me forget the sand under our boots, the smell of pine and salt in the breeze. Her nose is cold against mine. Her cheeks ruddy. All the sadness, all the hurt in the past making this moment all the sweeter. If pain is the weight of being, love is the purpose. "I want you to know that I love you. More than anything." She backs away from me, pulling me along. "Almost."

The ship skims over the evergreen forest and sets down on the beach. Its wings fold backward like a settling pigeon. Sand and salt spray kicked up by its engines. Mustang's fingers twine through mine as we trudge through the sand. The ramp unfurls. Sophocles sprints out onto the beach, running toward a group of seagulls. Behind him comes the voice of Kavax and the sweet sound of a child laughing. My feet falter. I look over at Mustang in confusion. She pulls me on, a nervous smile on her face. Kavax exits the ship with Dancer. Victra and Sevro come with, waving over to me before looking expectantly back up the ramp.

I used to think the life strands of my friends frayed around me, because mine was too strong. Now I realize that when we are wound together, we make something unbreakable. Something that lasts long after this life ends. My friends have filled the hollow carved in me by my wife's death. They've made me whole again. My mother joins them now on the ramp, walking with Kieran to set foot on Earth for the first time. She smiles like I did when she smells the salt. The wind kicks her gray hair. Her eyes are glassy and full of the joy my father always wanted for her. And in her arms she carries a laughing child with golden hair.

"Mustang?" I ask. My voice trembling. "Who is that?"

"Darrow . . ." Mustang smiles over at me. "That is our son. His name is Pax."

EPILOGUE

Pax was born nine months after the Lion's Rain, as I lay in the Jackal's stone table. Fearing that our enemies would seek the boy out if they knew of his existence, Mustang kept her pregnancy a secret on the *Dejah Thoris* until she was able to give birth. Then, leaving the child to be guarded by Kavax's wife in the asteroid belt, she returned to war.

That peace she intended to make with the Sovereign was not just for her and her people, but for her son. She wanted a world without war for him. I can't hate her for that. For keeping this secret from me. She was afraid. Not just that she could not trust me, but that I was not prepared to be the father my son deserves. That was her test, all this time. She almost told me in Tinos, but after conferring with my mother, she decided against it. Mother knew if I realized I had a son, I would not be able to do what needed to be done.

My people needed a sword, not a father.

But now, for the first time in my life, I can be both.

This war is not over. The sacrifices we made to take Luna will haunt our new world. I know that. But I am no longer alone in the dark. When I first stepped through the gates of the Institute, I wore the weight of the world on my shoulders. It crushed me. Broke me, but my friends have pieced me together. Now they each carry a part of Eo's dream. Together we can make a world fit for my son. For the generations to come.

I can be a builder, not just a destroyer. Eo and Fitchner saw that when I could not. They believed in me. So whether they wait for me in the Vale or not, I feel them in my heart, I hear their echo beating across the worlds. I see them in my son, and, when he is old enough, I will take him on my knee and his mother and I will tell him of the rage of Ares, the strength of Ragnar, the honor of Cassius, the love of Sevro, the loyalty of Victra, and the dream of Eo, the girl who inspired me to live for more.

ACKNOWLEDGMENTS

I was afraid to write *Morning Star*.

For months I delayed that first sentence. I sketched ship schematics, wrote songs for Reds and Golds, histories of the families and the planets and the moons that make up the savage little world I'd stumbled onto in my room above my parents' garage almost five years ago.

I wasn't afraid because I didn't know where I was going. I was afraid because I knew exactly how the story would end. I just didn't think I was skillful enough to take you there.

Sound familiar?

So I put myself in seclusion. I packed my bags, my hiking boots, and left my apartment in Los Angeles for my family's cabin on the wind-ripped coast of the Pacific Northwest.

I thought isolation would help the process, that somehow I would find my muse in the quiet and the fog of the coast. I could write sunup to sundown. I could walk among the evergreens. Channel the spirits of mythmakers past. It worked for *Red Rising*. It worked for *Golden Son*. But it didn't work for *Morning Star*.

In my isolation, I felt shuttered, trapped by Darrow, trapped by the thousand paths he could follow and the congestion in my own brain.

I wrote the initial chapters in that mental space. I suppose it helped their formation, giving Darrow a weird, sad mania behind his eyes. But I couldn't see beyond his rescue from Attica.

It wasn't until I returned from the cabin that the story began to find its voice and I began to understand that Darrow wasn't the focus anymore. It was the people around him. It was his family, his friends, his loves, the voices that swarm and hearts that beat in tune with his own.

How could I ever expect to write something like that in isolation? Without the coffee powwows with Tamara Fernandez (the wisest person I know without white hair), the early dawn breakfasts with Josh Crook where we conspire to take over the world, the Hollywood Bowl concerts with Madison Ainley, the hours of debate about Roman military warfare with Max Carver, the ice cream crusades with Jarrett Llewelyn, the Battlestar nerdouts with Callie Young, and the maniacal plotting with Dennis "the Menace" Stratton?

Friends are the pulse of life. Mine are wild and vast and full of dreams and absurdity. Without them, I'd be a shade, and this book would be hollow between the covers. Thank you to each and every one of them, named and unnamed, for sharing this wonderful life with me.

Every upstart needs a wise wizard to guide his path and show him the proverbial ropes. I count myself lucky to have a titan of my youth become a mentor in my twenties. Terry Brooks, thank you for all the words of encouragement and advice. You're the man.

Thank you to the Phillips Clan for always giving me a second home where I could dream aloud. And Joel in particular for sitting on that couch with me five years ago and wildly planning to make maps for a book that hadn't yet been written. You're a wonder and a brother in all but name. Thank you to my other brohirim: Aaron for making me write, and Nathan for always liking what I write, even when you shouldn't.

Thank you also to my agent, Hannah Bowman, who found *Red Rising* amidst the slush. Havis Dawson for guiding the novels into more than twenty-eight different languages. Tim Gerard Reynolds for giving me chills with his audiobook narration. My foreign publishers for their tireless efforts in trying to translate Bloodydamn or ripWing or anything Sevro says into Korean or Italian or whatever the local tongue.

Thank you to the peerless team at Del Rey for believing in *Red Rising* from the moment it first passed across your desks. I could not ask for a better House. Scott Shannon, Tricia Narwani, Keith Clayton, Joe Scalora, David Moench, you've got the hearts of Hufflepuffs and the courage of Gryffindors as far as I'm concerned.

Thank you to my family for always suspecting that my strangeness was a quality and not a liability. For making me explore forests and fields instead of the channels on the tube. My father for teaching me the grace of power unused, and mother for teaching me the joy of power used well. My sister for her tireless efforts on behalf of the Sons of Ares fan page, and for understanding me better than anyone else.

The most profound thanks must go to my editor, Mike "au Telemanus" Braff. If he didn't fully understand the extent of my neurosis before this book, he sure as hell does now. Few authors are as lucky as I am to have an editor like Mike. He's humble, patient, and diligent, even when I'm not. That this book was brought to you only a year after *Golden Son* is a miracle of his making. I doff my cap to you, my goodman.

And to each and every reader, thank you. Your passion and excitement have allowed me to live my life on my own terms, and for that I am ever grateful and humbled. Your creativity, humor, and support come through in every message, tweet, and comment. Getting to meet you and hear your stories at conventions and signings is one of the perks of being an author. Thank you, Howlers, for all that you do. Hopefully we'll have a chance to howl together soon.

Once I thought that writing this book would be impossible. It was a skyscraper, massive and complete and unbearably far off. It taunted me from the horizon. But do we ever look at such buildings and assume they sprung up overnight? No. We've seen the traffic congestion that attends them. The skeleton of beams and girders. The swarm of builders and the rattle of cranes . . .

Everything grand is made from a series of ugly little moments. Everything worthwhile by hours of self-doubt and days of drudgery. All the works by people you and I admire sit atop a foundation of failures.

So whatever your project, whatever your struggle, whatever your dream, keep toiling, because the world needs your skyscraper.

Per aspera, ad astra!

—*Pierce Brown*

THE
RED RISING SAGA
CONTINUES

RED RISING

GOLDEN SON

MORNING STAR

AVAILABLE NOW

FIND OUT MORE AT **PIERCEBROWNBOOKS.COM**

PHOTO: © JOAN ALLEN

PIERCE BROWN is the #1 *New York Times* bestselling author of *Red Rising, Golden Son, Morning Star,* and *Iron Gold*. His work has been published in thirty-three languages and in thirty-five territories. He lives in Los Angeles, where he is at work on his next novel, *Dark Age*.

piercebrownbooks.com

Facebook.com/PierceBrownAuthor

Twitter: @Pierce_Brown

Instagram.com/PierceBrownOfficial

To inquire about booking Pierce Brown for a speaking engagement, please contact the Penguin Random House Speakers Bureau at speakers@penguinrandomhouse.com.

ENEMY OF ROME

BEN KANE

St. Martin's Griffin ☙ New York

HANNIBAL: ENEMY OF ROME. Copyright © 2011 by Ben Kane. All rights reserved. Printed in the United States of America. For information, address St. Martin's Press, 175 Fifth Avenue, New York, NY 10010.

www.stmartins.com

The Library of Congress has cataloged the hardcover edition as follows:

Kane, Ben.
    Hannibal : enemy of Rome / Ben Kane. — First U.S. edition.
        p. cm.
    ISBN 978-1-250-00115-3 (hardcover)
    ISBN 978-1-4668-4963-1 (e-book)
    1. Hannibal, 247–182 B.C.—Fiction.   2. Punic War, 2nd, 218–201 B.C.—Fiction.
3. Carthage (Extinct city)—Fiction.   4. Rome—History—Republic, 265–30 B.C.—
Fiction   I. Title.
    PR6111.A536H36 2014
    823'.92—dc23   2014008048

ISBN 978-1-250-06851-4 (trade paperback)

St. Martin's Griffin books may be purchased for educational, business, or promotional use. For information on bulk purchases, please contact the Macmillan Corporate and Premium Sales Department at 1-800-221-7945, extension 5442, or write to specialmarkets@macmillan.com.

First published in the United Kingdom in 2011 by Preface Publishing

Previously published as *Hannibal: Enemy of Rome*

First St. Martin's Griffin Edition: July 2015

10   9   8   7   6   5   4   3   2   1

For Ferdia and Pippa, my wonderful children

GAUL

Alps

Rhodanus

Taurasia • Placentia **CISALPINE**

Padus **GAUL**

Genua •

Massilia • Pisae •

Pyrenees

Iberus

IBERIA

Tagus

Saguntum •

Balearic Islands **CORSICA**

SARDINIA

Gades • New Carthage •

NUMIDIA Carthage •

M A R E

CARTHAGE

N

0   100   200   300   400   500

Miles

The Mediterranean World in 219 BC

ILLYRICUM

Danuvius

PONTUS EUXINUS

THRACE

GREECE

ASIA MINOR

SELEUCID EMPIRE

Adriaticum

Syracuse

CYPRUS

Tyre

INTERNUM

CRETE

Alexandria

EGYPT

LIBYA

Nilus

Rubrum Mare

ENEMY OF ROME

I

HANNO

Hanno!" His father's voice echoed off the painted stucco walls. "It's time to go."

Stepping carefully over the gutter that carried liquid waste out to the soakaway in the street, Hanno looked back. He was torn between his duty and the urgent gestures of his friend, Suniaton. The political meetings his father had recently insisted he attend bored him to tears. Each one he'd been to followed exactly the same path. A group of self-important, bearded elders, clearly fond of the sound of their own voices, made interminable speeches about how Hannibal Barca's actions in Iberia were exceeding the remit granted to him. Malchus—his father—and his closest allies, who supported Hannibal, said little or nothing until the graybeards had fallen silent, when they would stand forth one by one. Invariably, Malchus spoke last of all. His words seldom varied. Hannibal, who had been commander in Iberia for just three years, was doing an outstanding job in cementing Carthage's hold over the wild native tribes, forming a disciplined army and, most importantly, filling the city's coffers with the silver from his mines. Who else was pursuing such heroic and worthy endeavors while simultaneously enriching Carthage? In defending the tribes who had been attacked by Saguntum, a city allied to Rome, he was merely reinforcing their people's sovereignty in Iberia. On these grounds, the young Barca should be left to his own devices.

Hanno knew that what motivated the politicians was fear, partly assuaged by the thought of Hannibal's forces, and greed, partly satisfied by the shiploads of precious metal from Iberia. Malchus' carefully chosen words therefore normally swayed the Senate in Hannibal's favor, but only after endless hours of debate. The interminable politicking made Hanno want to scream, and to tell the old fools what he really thought of them. Of course he would never shame his father in that manner, but nor could he face yet another day stuck indoors. The idea of a fishing trip held too much appeal.

One of Hannibal's messengers regularly came to bring his father news from Iberia, and had visited not a week since. The nighttime rendezvous were supposed to be a secret, but Hanno had soon come to recognize the cloaked, sallow-skinned officer. Sapho and Bostar, his older brothers, had been allowed to stand in on the meetings for some time. Swearing Hanno to secrecy, Bostar had filled him in afterward. Now, if he was able, Hanno simply eavesdropped. In a nutshell, Hannibal had charged Malchus and his allies with the task of ensuring that the politicians continued to back his actions. A showdown with the city of Saguntum was imminent, but conflict with Rome, Carthage's old enemy, was some way off yet.

The deep, gravelly voice called out again, echoing down the corridor that led to the central courtyard. There was a hint of annoyance in it now. "Hanno? We'll be late."

Hanno froze. He wasn't afraid of the dressing down his father would deliver later, more of the disappointed look in his eyes. A scion of one of Carthage's oldest families, Malchus led by example, and expected his three sons to do the same. At seventeen, Hanno was the youngest. He was also the one who most often failed to meet these exacting standards. For some reason, Malchus expected more of him than he did of Sapho and Bostar. At least that's how it seemed to Hanno. Yet farming, the traditional source of their wealth, interested him little. Warfare, his father's preferred vocation, and Hanno's great fascination, was barred to him still, thanks to his youth. His brothers would be sailing for Iberia any day. There, no doubt, they would cover themselves in glory in the taking of Saguntum. Frustration and resentment filled Hanno. All he could do was practice his riding and weapons skills. Life as ordained by his father was so boring, he thought, choosing to ignore Malchus' oft-repeated statement: "Be patient. All good things come to those who wait."

"Come on!" urged Suniaton, thumping Hanno on the arm. His gold earrings jingled as he jerked his head in the direction of the harbor. "The fishermen found huge shoals of tunny in the bay at dawn. With Melqart's blessing, the fish won't have moved far. We'll catch dozens. Think of the money to be made!" His voice dropped to a whisper. "I've taken an amphora of wine from Father's cellar. We can share it on the boat."

Unable to resist his friend's offer, Hanno blocked his ears to Malchus' voice, which was coming closer. Tunny was one of the most prized fish in the Mediterranean. If the shoals were close to shore, this was an opportunity too good to miss. Stepping into the rutted street, he glanced once more at the symbol etched into the stone slab before the flat-roofed house's entrance. An inverted triangle topped by a flat line and then a circle, it represented his people's preeminent deity. Few dwellings were without it. Hanno asked Tanit's forgiveness for disobeying his father's wishes, but his excitement was such that he forgot to ask for the mother goddess's protection.

"Hanno!" His father's voice was very near now.

Without further ado, the two young men darted off into the crowd. Both their families dwelled near the top of Byrsa Hill. At the summit, reached by a monumental staircase of sixty steps, was an immense temple dedicated to Eshmoun, the god of fertility, health and well-being. Suniaton lived with his family in the sprawling complex behind the shrine, where his father served as a priest. Named in honor of the deity, Eshmuniaton—abbreviated to Suniaton or simply Suni—was Hanno's oldest and closest friend. The pair had scarcely spent a day out of each other's company since they were old enough to walk.

The rest of the neighborhood was primarily residential. Byrsa was one of the richer quarters, as its wide, straight thoroughfares and right-angled intersections proved. The majority of the city's winding streets were no more than ten paces across, but here they averaged more than twice this width. In addition to wealthy merchants and senior army officers, the suffetes—judges—and many elders also called the area home. For this reason, Hanno ran with his gaze directed at the packed earth and the regular soakaway holes beneath his feet. Plenty of people knew who he was. The last thing he wanted was to be stopped and challenged by one of Malchus' numerous political opponents. To be dragged back home by the ear would be embarrassing and bring dishonor to his family.

As long as they didn't catch anyone's eye, he and his friend would pass unnoticed. Bareheaded and wearing tight-fitting red woolen singlets, with a central white stripe and a distinctive wide neckband, and breeches that reached to the knee, the pair looked no different from other well-to-do youths. Their garb was far more practical than the long straight wool tunics and conical felt hats favored by most adult men, and more comfortable than the ornate jacket and pleated apron worn by those of Cypriot extraction. Sheathed daggers hung from simple leather straps thrown over their shoulders. Suniaton carried a bulging pack on his back.

Although people said that they could pass for brothers, Hanno couldn't see it most of the time. While he was tall and athletic, Suniaton was short and squat. Naturally, they both had tightly curled black hair and a dark complexion, but there the resemblance ended. Hanno's face was thin, with a straight nose and high cheekbones, while his friend's round visage and snub nose were complemented by a jutting chin. They did both have green eyes, Hanno conceded. That feature, unusual among the brown-eyed Carthaginians, was probably why they were thought to be siblings.

A step ahead of him, Suniaton nearly collided with a carpenter carrying several long cypress planks. Rather than apologize, he thumbed his nose and sprinted toward the citadel walls, now only a hundred paces away. Stifling his desire to finish the job by tipping over the angry tradesman, Hanno dodged past too, a grin splitting his face. Another similarity he and Suniaton shared was an impudent nature, quite at odds with the serious manner of most of their countrymen. It frequently got both of them in trouble, and was a constant source of irritation to their fathers.

A moment later, they passed under the immense ramparts, which were thirty paces deep and nearly the same in height. Like the outer defenses, the wall was constructed from great quadrilateral blocks of sandstone. Frequent coats of whitewash ensured that the sunlight bounced off the stone, magnifying its size. Topped by a wide walkway and with regular towers, the fortifications were truly awe-inspiring. Yet the citadel was only a small part of the whole. Hanno never tired of looking down on the expanse of the sea wall that came into view as he emerged from under the gateway's shadow. Running down from the north along the city's perimeter, it swept southeast to the twin harbors, curling protectively around them before heading west. On the steep northern and eastern sides, and to the south, where the sea gave its added protection, one wall was deemed sufficient, but on the western, landward side of the peninsula, three defenses had been constructed: a wide trench backed by an earthen bank, and then a huge rampart. The walls, which were in total over 180 stades in length, also contained sections with two-tiered living quarters. These could hold many thousands of troops, cavalry and their mounts, and hundreds of war elephants.

Home to nearly a quarter of a million people, the city also demanded attention. Directly below lay the Agora, the large open space bordered by government buildings and countless shops. It was the area where residents gathered to do business, demonstrate, take the evening air, and vote. Beyond it lay the unique ports: the huge outer, rectangular merchant harbor, and the inner, circular naval docks with its small, central island. The first contained hundreds of berths for trading ships, while the second could hold more than ten-score triremes and quinqueremes in specially constructed covered sheds. To the west of the ports was the old shrine of Baal Hammon, no longer as important as it had previously been, but still venerated by many. To the east lay the Choma, the huge man-made landing stage where fishing smacks and small vessels tied up. It was also their destination.

Hanno was immensely proud of his home. He had no idea what Rome, Carthage's old enemy, looked like, but he doubted it matched his city's grandeur. He had no desire to compare Carthage with the Republic's capital, though. The only view he ever wanted of Rome was when it fell—to a victorious Carthaginian army—before seeing it burned to the ground. As Hamilcar Barca, Hannibal's father, had inculcated a hatred of all things Roman in his sons, so had Malchus in Hanno and his brothers. Like Hamilcar, Malchus had served in the first war against the Republic, fighting in Sicily for ten long, thankless years.

Unsurprisingly, Hanno and his siblings knew the details of every land skirmish and naval battle in the conflict, which had actually lasted for more than a generation. The cost to Carthage in loss of life, territory and wealth had been huge, but the city's wounds ran far deeper. Her pride had been trampled in the mud by the defeat, and this ignominy was repeated just three years after the war's conclusion. Carthage had been unilaterally forced by Rome to give up Sardinia, as well as paying more indemnities. The shabby act proved beyond doubt, Malchus would regularly rant, that all Romans were treacherous dogs, without honor. Hanno agreed, and looked forward to the day hostilities were reopened once more. Given the depth of anger still present in Carthage toward Rome, conflict was inevitable, and it would originate in Iberia. Soon.

Suniaton turned. "Have you eaten?"

Hanno shrugged. "Some bread and honey when I got up."

"Me too. That was hours ago, though." Suniaton grinned and patted his belly. "Best get a few supplies."

"Good idea," Hanno replied. They kept clay gourds of water in their little boat with their fishing gear, but no food. Sunset, when they would return, was a long way off.

The streets descending Byrsa Hill did not follow the regular layout of the summit, instead radiating out like so many tributaries of a meandering river. There were far more shops and businesses visible now: bakers, butchers and stalls selling freshly caught fish, fruit and vegetables stood beside silver- and coppersmiths, perfume merchants and glass blowers. Women sat outside their doors, working at their looms, or gossiping over their purchases. Slaves carried rich men past in litters or swept the ground in front of shops. Dye-makers' premises were everywhere, their abundance due to the Carthaginian skill in harvesting the local *Murex* shellfish and pounding its flesh to yield a purple dye that commanded premium prices all over the Mediterranean. Children ran hither and thither, playing catch and chasing each other up and down the regular sets of stairs that broke the street's steep descent. Deep in conversation, a trio of well-dressed men strolled past. Recognizing them as elders, who were probably on their way to the very meeting he was supposed to be attending, Hanno took a sudden interest in the array of terra-cotta outside a potter's workshop.

Dozens of figures—large and small—were ranked on low tables. Hanno recognized every deity in the Carthaginian pantheon. There sat a regal, crowned Baal Hammon, the protector of Carthage, on his throne; beside him Tanit was depicted in the Egyptian manner: a shapely woman's body in a well-cut dress, but with the head of a lioness. A smiling Astarte clutched a tambourine. Her consort, Melqart, known as the "King of the City," was, among other things, the god of the sea. Various brightly colored figures depicted him emerging from crashing waves riding a fearful-looking monster and clutching a trident in one fist. Baal Saphon, the god of storm and war, sat astride a fine charger, wearing a helmet with a long, flowing crest. Also on display was a selection of hideous, grinning painted masks—tattooed, bejeweled demons and spirits of the underworld—tomb offerings designed to ward off evil.

Hanno shivered, remembering his mother's funeral three years before. Since her death of a fever his father, never the most warm of men, had become a grim and forbidding presence who lived only to gain his revenge on Rome. For all his youth, Hanno knew that Malchus was portraying a controlled mask to the world. He must still be grieving, as surely as he and his brothers were. Arishat, Hanno's mother, had been the light to Malchus' dark, the laughter to his gravitas, the softness to his strength. The center of the family, she had been taken from them in two horrific days and nights. Harangued by an inconsolable Malchus, the best surgeons in Carthage had toiled over her to no avail. Every last detail of her final hours was engraved in Hanno's memory. The cups of blood drained from her in a vain attempt to cool her raging temperature. Her gaunt, fevered face. The sweat-soaked sheets. His brothers trying not to cry, and failing. And lastly, her still form on the bed, tinier than she had ever been in life. Malchus kneeling alongside, great sobs racking his muscular frame. That was the only time Hanno had ever seen his father weep. The incident had never been mentioned since, nor had his mother. He swallowed hard and, checking that the elders had passed by, moved on. It hurt too much to think about such things.

Suniaton, who had not noticed Hanno's distress, paused to buy some bread, almonds and figs. Keen to lift his somber mood, Hanno eyed the blacksmith's forge off to one side. Wisps of smoke rose from its roughly built chimney, and the air was rich with the smells of charcoal, burning wood and oil. Harsh metallic sounds reached his ears. In the recesses of the open-fronted establishment, he glimpsed a figure in a leather apron using a pair of tongs to carefully lift a piece of glowing metal from the anvil. There was a loud hiss as the sword blade was plunged into a vat of cold water. Hanno felt his feet begin to move.

Suniaton blocked his path. "We've got better things to do. Like making money," he cried, shoving forward a bulging bag of almonds. "Carry that."

"No! You'll eat them all anyway." Hanno pushed his friend out of the way with a grin. It was a standing joke between them that his favorite pastime was getting covered in ash and grime while Suniaton would rather plan his next meal. He was so busy laughing that he didn't see the approaching group of soldiers—a dozen Libyan spearmen—until it was too late. With a thump, Hanno collided with the first man's large, round shield.

This was no street urchin, and the spearman bit back an instinctive curse. "Mind your step," he cried.

Catching sight of two Carthaginian officers in the soldiers' midst, Hanno cursed. It was Sapho and Bostar. Both were dressed in their finest uniforms. Bell-shaped helmets with thick rims and yellow-feathered crests covered their heads. Layered linen *pteryges* hung below their polished bronze cuirasses to cover the groin, and contoured greaves protected their lower legs. No doubt they too were on their way to the meeting. Muttering an apology to the spearman, Hanno backed away, looking at the ground in an attempt not to be recognized.

Oblivious to Sapho and Bostar's presence, Suniaton was snorting with amusement at Hanno's collision. "Come on," he urged. "We don't want to get there too late."

"Hanno!" Bostar's voice was genial.

He pretended not to hear.

"Hanno! Come back!" barked a deeper, more commanding voice, that of Sapho.

Unwillingly, Hanno turned.

Suniaton tried to sidle away, but he had also been spotted.

"Eshmuniaton! Get over here," Sapho ordered.

With a miserable expression, Suniaton shuffled to his friend's side.

Hanno's brothers shouldered their way forward to stand before them.

"Sapho. Bostar," Hanno said with a false smile. "What a surprise."

"Is it?" Sapho demanded, his thick eyebrows meeting in a frown. A short, compact man with a serious manner like Malchus, he was twenty-two. Young to be a midranking officer, but like Bostar, his ability had shone through during his training. "We're all supposed to be heading to listen to the elders. Why aren't you with Father?"

Flushing, Hanno looked down. Damn it, he thought. In Sapho's eyes, duty to Carthage was all-important. In a single moment, their chances of a day on the boat had vanished.

Sapho gave Suniaton a hard stare, taking in his pack and the provisions in his hands. "Because the pair of you were skiving off, that's why! Fishing, no doubt?"

Suniaton scuffed a toe in the dirt.

"Cat got your tongue?" Sapho asked acidly.

Hanno moved in front of his friend. "We were going to catch some tunny, yes," he admitted.

Sapho's scowl grew deeper. "And that's more important than listening to the Council of Elders?"

As usual, his brother's high-handed attitude rankled with Hanno. This type of lecture was all too common. Most often, it felt as if Sapho was trying to be their father. Unsurprisingly, Hanno resented this. "It's not as if the graybeards will say anything that hasn't been said a thousand times before," he retorted. "Just about every one is full of hot air."

Suniaton sniggered. "Like someone else not too far away." He saw Hanno's warning look and fell silent.

Sapho's jaw clenched. "You pair of impudent—" he began.

Bostar's lips twitched, and he lifted a hand to Sapho's shoulder.

"Peace," he said. "Hanno has a point. The elders *are* rather fond of the sound of their own voices."

Hanno and Suniaton tried to hide their smiles.

Sapho missed Bostar's amusement, but he lapsed into a glowering silence. He was acutely aware, and resentful, that he was not the senior officer present. Although Sapho was a year older, Bostar had been promoted before him.

"It's not as if this meeting will be a matter of life and death," Bostar continued reasonably. His wink—unseen by Sapho—told Hanno that all hope was not lost. He slyly returned the gesture. Like Hanno, Bostar resembled their mother, Arishat, with a thin face and piercing green eyes. Where Sapho's nose was broad, his was long and narrow. Rangy and athletic, his long black hair was tied in a ponytail, which emerged from under his helmet. Hanno had far more in common with the gentle Bostar than he did with Sapho. Currently, his feelings for his eldest brother often verged on dislike. "Does our father know where you are?"

"No," admitted Hanno.

Bostar turned to Suniaton. "I would assume, therefore, that Bodesmun is also in the dark?"

"Of course he is," Sapho butted in, eager to regain control. "As usual where these two are concerned."

Bostar ignored his brother's outburst. "Well?"

"Father thinks I'm at home, studying," Suniaton revealed.

Sapho's expression grew a shade more self-righteous. "Let's see what Bodesmun and Father have to say when they discover what you were both really up to. We have enough time to do that before the Council meets." He jerked a thumb at the spearmen. "Get in among them."

Hanno scowled, but there was little point arguing. Sapho was in a particularly zealous mood. "Come on," he muttered to Suniaton. "The shoals will be there another day."

Before they could move a step, Bostar spoke. "I don't see why they shouldn't go fishing."

Hanno and Suniaton stared at each other, amazed.

Sapho's brows rose. "What do you mean?"

"Such activities will shortly be impossible for both of us, and we'll miss them." Bostar made a face. "That same day will come for Hanno soon enough. Let him have his fun while he can."

Hanno's heart leaped; the gravity of Bostar's words was lost on him.

Sapho's face grew thoughtful. After a moment, though, his sanctimonious frown returned. "Duty is duty," he declared.

"Lighten up, Sapho. You're twenty-two, not fifty-two!" Bostar threw a glance at the spearmen, who were uniformly grinning. "Who would notice Hanno's absence apart from us and Father? And you're not Suni's keeper any more than I am."

Sapho's lips thinned at the teasing, but he relented. The idea of Bostar pulling rank on him was too much to bear. "Father won't be happy," he said gruffly, "but I suppose you're right."

Hanno could hardly believe what he was hearing. "Thank you!" His cry was echoed by Suniaton.

"Go on, before I change my mind," Sapho warned.

The friends didn't need any further prompting. With a grateful look at Bostar, who threw them another wink, the pair disappeared into the crowd. Broad grins creased both their faces. They would still be held to account, thought Hanno, but not until that evening. Visions of a boat full of tunny filled his mind once more.

"Sapho's a serious one, isn't he?" Suniaton commented.

"You know how he is," Hanno replied. "In his eyes, things like fishing are a waste of time."

Suniaton nudged him. "Just as well I didn't tell him what I was thinking, then." He grinned at Hanno's inquiring look. "That it would do him good to relax more—perhaps by going fishing!"

Hanno's mouth opened with shock, before he laughed. "Thank the gods you didn't say that! There's no way he would have let us go."

Smiling with relief, the friends continued their journey. Soon they had reached the Agora. Its four sides, each a stade in length, were made up of grand porticoes and covered walkways. The beating heart of the city, it was home to the building where the Council of Elders met, as well as government offices, a library, numerous temples and shops. It was also where, on summer evenings, the better-off young men and women would gather in groups, a safe distance apart, to eye each other up. Socializing with the opposite sex was frowned upon, and chaperones for the girls were never far away. Despite this, inventive methods to approach the object of one's desire were constantly being invented. Of recent months, this had become one of the friends' favorite pastimes. Fishing beat it still, but not by much, thought Hanno wistfully, scanning the crowds for any sign of attractive female flesh.

Instead of gaggles of coy young beauties, though, the Agora was full of serious-looking politicians, merchants and high-ranking soldiers. They were heading for one place. The central edifice, within the hallowed walls of which more than three hundred elders met on a regular basis as, for nearly half a millenium, their predecessors had done. Overseen by the two suffetes—the rulers elected every year—they, the most important men in Carthage, decided everything from trading policy to negotiations with foreign states. Their range of powers did not end there. The Council of Elders also had the power to declare war and peace, even though it no longer appointed the army's generals. Since the war with Rome, that had been left to the people. The only prerequisites for candidature of the council were citizenship, wealth, an age of thirty or more, and the demonstration of ability, whether in the agricultural, mercantile, or military fields.

Ordinary citizens could participate in politics via the Assembly of the People, which congregated once a year, by the order of the suffetes, in the Agora. During times of great crisis, it was permitted to gather spontaneously and debate the issues of the day. While its powers were limited, they included electing the suffetes and the generals. Hanno was looking forward to the next meeting, which would be the first he'd attend as an adult, entitled to vote. Although Hannibal's enormous public popularity guaranteed his reappointment as the commander-in-chief of Carthage's forces in Iberia, Hanno wanted to show his support for the Barca clan. It was the only way he could at the moment. Despite his requests, Malchus would not let him join Hannibal's army, as Sapho and Bostar had done after their mother's death. Instead, he had to finish his education. There was no point fighting his father on this. Once Malchus had spoken, he never went back on a decision.

Following Carthaginian tradition, Hanno had largely fended for himself from the age of fourteen, although he continued to sleep at home. He'd worked in a forge, among other places, and thus earned enough to live on without committing any crimes or shameful acts. This was similar to, but not as harsh, as the Spartan way. He had also taken classes in Greek, Iberian and Latin. Hanno did not especially enjoy languages, but he had come to accept that such a skill would prove useful among the polyglot of nationalities that formed the Carthaginian army. His people did not take naturally to war, so they hired mercenaries, or enlisted their subjects, to fight on their behalf. Libyans, Iberians, Gauls and Balearic tribesmen were among those who brought their differing qualities to Carthage's forces.

Hanno's favorite subject was military matters. Malchus himself taught him the history of war, from the battles of Xenophon and Thermopylae to the victories won by Alexander of Macedon. Central to his father's lessons were the intricate details of tactics and planning. Particular attention was paid to Carthaginian defeats in the war with Rome, and the reasons for them. "We lost because of our leaders' lack of determination. All they thought about was how to contain the conflict, not win it. How to minimize cost, not disregard it in the total pursuit of victory," Malchus had thundered during one memorable lesson. "The Romans are motherless curs, but by all the gods, they possess strength of purpose. Whenever they lost a battle, they recruited more men, and rebuilt their ships. They did not give up. When the public purse was empty, their leaders willingly spent their own wealth. Their damn Republic means everything to them. Yet who in Carthage offered to send us the supplies and soldiers we needed so badly in Sicily? My father, the Barcas, and a handful of others. No one else." He'd barked a short, angry laugh. "Why should I be surprised? Our ancestors were traders, not soldiers. To gain our rightful revenge, we must follow Hannibal. He's a natural soldier and a born leader—as his father was. Carthage never gave Hamilcar the chance to beat Rome, but we can offer it to his son. When the time is right."

A red-faced, portly senator shoved past with a curse. Startled, Hanno recognized Hostus, one of his father's most implacable enemies. The self-important politician was in such a hurry that he didn't even notice whom he'd collided with. Hanno hawked and spat, although he was careful not to do it in Hostus' direction. He and his windbag friends complained endlessly about Hannibal, yet were content to accept the shiploads of silver sent from his mines in Iberia. Lining their own pockets with a proportion of this wealth, they had no desire to confront Rome again. Hanno, on the other hand, was more than prepared to lay down his life fighting their old enemy, but the fruit of revenge wasn't ripe. Hannibal was preparing himself in Iberia, and that was good enough. For now, they had to wait.

The pair skirted the edge of the Agora, avoiding the worst of the crowds. Around the back of the Senate, the buildings soon became a great deal less grand, looking as shabby as one would expect close to a port. Nonetheless, the slum stood in stark contrast to the splendor just a short walk away. There were few businesses, and the single- or twin-roomed houses were miserable affairs made of mud bricks, all apparently on the point of collapse. The iron-hard ruts in the street were more than a handspan deep, threatening to break their ankles if they tripped. No work parties to fill in the holes with sand here, thought Hanno, thinking of Byrsa Hill. He felt even more grateful for his elevated position in life.

Snot-nosed, scrawny children wearing little more than rags swarmed in, clamoring for a coin or a crust, while their lank-haired, pregnant mothers gazed at them with eyes deadened by a life of misery. Half-dressed girls posed provocatively in some doorways, their rouged cheeks and lips unable to conceal the fact that they were barely out of childhood. Unshaven, ill-clad men lounged around, rolling sheep tail bones in the dirt for a few worn coins. They stared suspiciously, but none dared hinder the friends' progress. At night it might be a different matter, but already they were under the shadow of the great wall, with its smartly turned-out sentries marching to and fro along the battlements. Although common, lawlessness was punished where possible by the authorities, and a shout of distress would bring help clattering down one of the many sets of stairs.

The tang of salt grew strong in the air. Gulls keened overhead, and the shouts of sailors could be heard from the ports. Feeling his excitement grow, Hanno charged down a narrow alleyway, and up the stone steps at the end of it. Suniaton was right behind him. It was a steep climb, but they were both fit, and reached the top without breaking sweat. A red concrete walkway extended the entire width of the wall—

thirty paces—just as it did for the entire length of the defensive perimeter. Strongly built towers were positioned every fifty steps or so. The soldiers visible were garrisoned in the barracks, which were built at intervals below the ramparts.

The nearest sentries, a quartet of Libyan spearmen, glanced idly at the pair but, seeing nothing of concern, looked away. In peacetime, citizens were allowed on the wall during the hours of daylight. Perfunctorily checking the turquoise sea below their section, the junior officer fell back to gossiping with his men. Hanno trotted past, admiring the soldiers' massive round shields, which were even larger than those used by the Greeks. Although fashioned from wood, they were covered in goatskin, and rimmed with bronze. The same demonic face was painted on each, and denoted their unit.

Trumpets blared one after another from the naval port, and Suniaton jostled past. "Quick," he shouted. "They might be launching a quinquereme!"

Hanno chased eagerly after his friend. The view from the walkway into the circular harbor was second to none. In a masterful feat of engineering, the Carthaginian warships were invisible from all other positions. Protected from unfriendly eyes on the seaward side by the city wall, they were concealed from the moored merchant vessels by the naval port's slender entrance, which was only just wider than a quinquereme, the largest type of warship.

Hanno scowled as they reached a good vantage point. Instead of the imposing sight of a warship sliding backward into the water, he saw a purple-cloaked admiral strutting along the jetty that led from the periphery of the circular docks to the central island, where the navy's headquarters were. Another fanfare of trumpets sounded, making sure that every man in the place knew who was arriving. "What has he got to swagger about?" Hanno muttered. Malchus reserved much of his anger for the incompetent Carthaginian fleet, so he had learned to feel the same way. Carthage's days as a superpower of the sea were long gone, their fleet smashed into so much driftwood by Rome during the two nations' bitter struggle over Sicily. Remarkably, the Romans had been a nonseafaring race before the conflict. Undeterred by this major disadvantage, they had learned the skills of naval warfare, adding a few tricks of their own in the process. Since her defeat, Carthage had done little to reclaim the waves.

Hanno sighed. Truly, all their hopes lay on the land, with Hannibal.

⁓

Some time later, Hanno had forgotten all his worries. Half a mile off-shore, their little boat was positioned directly over a mass of tunny. The shoal's location had not been hard to determine, thanks to the roiling water created by the large silver fish as they hunted sardines. Small boats dotted the location and clouds of seabirds swooped and dived overhead, attracted by the prospect of food. Suniaton's source had been telling the truth, and neither youth had been able to stop grinning since their arrival. Their task was simple: one rowed, the other lowered their net into the sea. Although they had seen better days, the plaited strands were still capable of landing a catch. Pieces of wood along the top of the net helped it to float, while tiny lumps of lead pulled its lower edge down into the water. Their first throw had netted nearly a dozen tunny, each one longer than a man's forearm. Subsequent attempts were just as successful, and now the bottom of the boat was calf-deep in fish. Any more, and they would risk overloading their craft.

"A good morning's work," pronounced Suniaton.

"Morning?" challenged Hanno, squinting at the sun. "We've been here less than an hour. It couldn't have been easier, eh?"

Suniaton regarded him solemnly. "Don't put yourself down. I think our efforts deserve a toast." With a flourish, he produced a small amphora from his pack.

Hannibal laughed; Suniaton was incorrigible.

Encouraged, Suniaton went on talking as if he were serving guests at an important banquet. "Not the most expensive wine in Father's collection, I recall, but a palatable one nonetheless." Using his knife, he prized off the wax seal and removed the lid. Raising the amphora to his lips, he gulped a large mouthful. "Acceptable," he declared, handing over the clay vessel.

"Philistine. Sip it slowly." Hanno took a small swig and rolled it around his mouth as Malchus had taught him. The red wine had a light and fruity flavor, but little undertone. "It needs a few more years, I think."

"Now who's being pompous?" Suniaton kicked a tunny at him. "Shut up and drink!"

Grinning, Hanno obeyed, taking more this time.

"Don't finish it," cried Suniaton.

Despite his protest, the amphora was quickly drained. At once the ravenous pair launched into the bread, nuts and fruit that Suniaton had bought. With their bellies full, and their work done, it was the most natural thing in the world to lie back and close their eyes. Unaccustomed to consuming much wine, before long they were both snoring.

———

It was the cold wind on his face that woke Hanno. Why was the boat moving so much? he wondered vaguely. He shivered, feeling quite chilled. Opening gummy eyes, he took in a prone Suniaton opposite, still clutching the empty amphora. At his feet, the heaps of blank-eyed fish, their bodies already rigid. Looking up, Hanno felt a pang of fear. Instead of the usual clear sky, all he could see were towering banks of blue-black clouds. They were pouring in from the northwest. He blinked, refusing to believe what he was seeing. How could the weather have changed so fast? Mockingly, the first spatters of rain hit Hanno's upturned cheeks an instant later. Scanning the choppy waters, he could see no sign of the fishing craft that had surrounded theirs earlier. Nor could he see the land. Real alarm seized him.

He leaned over and shook Suniaton. "Wake up!"

The only response was an irritated grunt.

"Suni!" This time, Hanno slapped his friend across the face.

"Hey!" Suniaton cried, sitting up. "What's that for?"

Hanno didn't answer. "Where in the name of the gods are we?" he shouted.

All semblance of drunkenness fell away as Suniaton turned his head from side to side. "Sacred Tanit above," he breathed. "How long were we asleep?"

"I don't know," Hanno growled. "A long time." He pointed to the west, where the sun's light was just visible behind the storm clouds. Its position told them that it was late in the afternoon. He stood, taking great care not to capsize the boat. Focusing on the horizon, where the sky met the threatening sea, he spent long moments trying to make out the familiar walls of Carthage, or the craggy promontory that lay to the north of the city.

"Well?" Suniaton could not keep the fear from his voice.

Hanno sat down heavily. "I can't see a thing. We're fifteen or twenty stades from shore. Maybe more."

What little color there had been in Suniaton's face drained away. Instinctively, he clutched at the hollow gold tube that hung from a thong around his neck. Decorated with a lion's head at one end, it contained tiny parchments covered with protective spells and prayers to the gods. Hanno wore a similar one. With great effort, he refrained from copying his friend. "We'll row back," he announced.

"In these seas?" screeched Suniaton. "Are you mad?"

Hanno glared back. "What other choice have we? To jump in?"

His friend looked down. Both were more confident in the water than most, but they had never swum long distances, especially in conditions as bad as these.

Seizing the oars from the floor, Hanno placed them in the iron rowlocks. He turned the boat's rounded bow toward the west and began to row. Instantly, he knew that his attempt was doomed to fail. The power surging at him was more potent than anything he'd ever felt in his life. It felt like a raging, out-of-control beast, with the howling wind providing its terrifying voice. Ignoring his gut feeling, Hanno concentrated on each stroke with fierce intensity. Lean back. Drag the oars through the water. Lift them free. Bend forward, pushing the handles between his knees. Over and over he repeated the process, ignoring his pounding head and dry mouth, and cursing their foolishness in drinking all of the wine. *If I had listened to my father, I'd still be at home,* he thought bitterly. *Safe on dry land.*

Finally, when the muscles in his arms were trembling with exhaustion, Hanno stopped. Without looking up, he knew that their position would have changed little. For every three strokes' progress, the current carried them at least two farther out to sea. "Well?" he shouted. "Can you see anything?"

"No," Suniaton replied grimly. "Move over. It's my turn, and this is our best chance."

Our last chance, Hanno thought, gazing at the darkening sky.

Gingerly, they exchanged places on the little wooden thwarts that were the boat's only fittings. Thanks to the mass of slippery fish underfoot, it was even more difficult than usual. While his friend labored at the oars, Hanno strained for a glimpse of land over the waves. Neither spoke. There was no point. The rain was now drumming down on their backs, combining with the wind's noise to form a shrieking cacophony that made normal speech impossible. Only the sturdy construction of their boat had prevented them from capsizing thus far.

At length, his energy spent, Suniaton shipped the oars. He looked at Hanno. There was a glimmer of hope in his eyes.

Hanno shook his head once.

"It's supposed to be the summer!" Suniaton cried. "Gales like this shouldn't happen without warning."

"There would have been signs," Hanno snapped back. "Why do you think there are no other boats out here? They must have headed for the shore when the wind began to get up."

Suniaton flushed and hung his head. "I'm sorry," he muttered. "It's my fault. I should never have taken Father's wine."

Hanno gripped his friend's knee. "Don't blame yourself. You didn't force me to drink it. That was my choice."

Suniaton managed a half-smile. That was, until he looked down. "No!"

Hanno followed his gaze and saw the tunny floating around his feet. They were shipping water, and enough of it to warrant immediate action. Trying not to panic, he began throwing the precious fish overboard. Survival was far more important than money. With the floor clear, he soon found a loose nail in one of the planks. Removing one of his sandals, he used the iron-studded sole to hammer the nail partially home, thereby reducing the influx of seawater. Fortunately, there was a small bucket on board, containing spare pieces of lead for the net. Grabbing it, Hanno began bailing hard. To his immense relief, it didn't take long before he'd reduced the water to an acceptable level.

A loud rumble of thunder overhead nearly deafened him.

Suniaton moaned with fear, and Hanno jerked upright.

The sky overhead was now a menacing black color, and in the depths of the clouds a flickering yellow-white color presaged lightning. The waves were being whipped into a frenzy by the wind, which was growing stronger by the moment. The storm was approaching its peak. More water slopped into the boat, and Hanno redoubled his efforts with the bucket. Any chance of rowing back to Carthage was long gone. They were going one direction. East. Into the middle of the Mediterranean. He tried not to let his panic show.

"What's going to happen to us?" Suniaton asked plaintively.

Realizing that his friend was seeking reassurance, Hanno tried to think of an optimistic answer, but couldn't. The only outcome possible was an early meeting for them both with Melqart, the marine god.

In his palace at the bottom of the sea.

II

QUINTUS

Quintus woke soon after dawn, when the first rays of sunlight crept through the window. Never one to linger in bed, the sixteen-year-old threw off his blanket. Wearing only a *licium*, or linen undergarment, he padded to the small shrine in the far corner of his room. Excitement coursed through him. Today he would lead a bear hunt for the first time. It was not long until his birthday, and Fabricius, his father, wanted him to mark his transition to manhood in fitting fashion. "Assuming the toga is all well and good," he'd said the night before, "but you have Oscan blood in your veins too. What better way to prove one's courage than by killing the biggest predator in Italy?"

Quintus knelt before the altar. Closing his eyes, he sent up his usual prayers requesting that he and his family remain healthy and prosperous. Then he added several more. That he would be able to find a bear's trail, and not lose it. That his courage would not fail him when it came to confronting the beast. That his spear thrust would be swift and true.

"Don't worry, brother," came a voice from behind him. "Today will go well."

Surprised, Quintus turned to regard his sister, who was peering around the half-open door. Aurelia was almost three years younger than he, and loved her sleep. "You're up early," he said with an indulgent smile.

She yawned, running a hand through her dense black hair, a longer version of his own. Sharing straight noses, slightly pointed chins and gray eyes, they were clearly siblings. "I couldn't sleep, thinking about your hunt."

"Are you worried for me?" he teased, glad to be distracted from his own concerns.

Aurelia came a little farther into the room. "Of course not. Well, a little. I've prayed to Diana, though. She will guide you," she declared solemnly.

"I know," Quintus replied, expressing a confidence that he did not entirely feel. Bowing to the figures on the altar, he rose. Ducking his head into the bronze ewer that stood by the bed, he rubbed the water from his face and shoulders with a piece of linen. "I'll tell you all about it this evening." He shrugged on a short-sleeved tunic, and then sat to lace up his sandals.

She frowned. "I want to see it for myself."

"Women don't go hunting."

"It's so unfair," she protested.

"Many things are unfair," Quintus answered. "You have to accept that."

"But you taught me how to use a sling."

"Maybe that wasn't such a good idea," Quintus muttered. Much to his surprise, Aurelia had proved to be a deadly shot, which had naturally redoubled her desire to partake of forbidden activities. "We've managed to keep our secrets safe so far, but imagine Mother's reaction if she found out."

"You're on the brink of womanhood," said Aurelia, mimicking Atia, their mother. "Such behavior does not befit a young lady. It must come to an immediate end."

"Precisely," Quintus replied, ignoring her scowl. "Never mind what she'd say if she knew you were riding a horse." He didn't want to lose his favorite companion, but this matter was beyond his control. "That's how life is for women."

"Cooking. Weaving. Taking care of the garden. Supervising the slaves. It's so boring," Aurelia retorted hotly. "Not like hunting or learning to use a sword."

"It's not as if you're strong enough to wield something like a spear anyway."

"Isn't it?" Aurelia rolled up one sleeve of her nightdress and flexed her biceps. She smiled at his surprise. "I've been lifting stones like you do."

"Eh?" Quintus' jaw dropped farther. Keen to get as fit as possible, he'd been doing extra training in the woods above the villa. He'd clearly failed to conceal his tracks. "You've been spying on me? And copying me?"

She grinned with delight. "Of course. Once my lessons and duties are over, it's easy enough to slip away without being noticed."

Quintus shook his head. "Determined, aren't you?" Persuading her to give it all up would be harder than he had thought. He was glad that the duty wouldn't fall to him. Guiltily, Quintus remembered hearing his parents talking about how it would soon be time to find her a husband. He knew how Aurelia would take that announcement. Badly.

"I know that it can't go on forever," she declared gloomily. "They'll be looking to marry me off shortly, no doubt."

Quintus hid his shock. Even if Aurelia hadn't heard that particular conversation, it wasn't surprising that she was aware of what would happen. Maybe he could help, then, rather than pretending it would never come to pass? "There's a lot to be said for arranged marriages," he ventured. It was true. Most nobles arranged unions for their children that were mutually beneficial to both parties. It was how the country ran. "They can be very happy."

Aurelia gave him a scornful look. "Do you expect me to believe that? Anyway, our parents married for love. Why shouldn't I?"

"Their situation was unusual. It's not likely to happen to you," he countered. "Besides, Father would keep your interests at heart, not just those of the family."

"Will I be happy, though?"

"With the help of the gods, yes. Which is more than might happen to me," he added, trying to lighten the mood. "I could end up with an old hag who makes my life a misery!" Quintus was glad, though, to be male. No doubt he would eventually wed, but there would be no unseemly rush to marry him off. Meanwhile, his adolescent libido was being satisfied by Elira, a striking slave girl from Illyricum. She was part of the household, and slept on the floor of the atrium, which facilitated sneaking her into his room at night. Quintus had been bedding her for two months, ever since he'd realized that her sultry looks were being directed at him. As far as he was aware, no one else had any idea of their relationship.

Finally, she smiled. "You're far too handsome for that to happen."

He laughed off her compliment. "Time for breakfast," he announced, continuing to move away from the awkward subject of marriage.

To his relief, Aurelia nodded. "You'll need a decent meal to give you energy for the hunt."

A knot of tension formed in Quintus' belly, and what appetite he'd had vanished. He would have to eat something, though, even if it was only for appearance's sake.

——

Leaving Aurelia chatting to Julius, the avuncular slave who ran the kitchen, Quintus sloped out of the door. He had barely eaten, and he hoped that Aurelia hadn't noticed. A few steps into the peristyle, or courtyard, he met Elira. She was carrying a basket of vegetables and herbs from the villa's garden. As usual, she gave him a look full of desire. It was wasted on Quintus this morning. He gave her a reflex smile and brushed past.

"Quintus!"

He jumped. The voice was one of the most recognizable on the estate. Atia, his mother. Quintus could see no one, which meant that she was probably in the atrium, the family's primary living space. He hurried past the pattering fountain in the center of the colonnaded courtyard, and into the cool of the *tablinum*, the reception room that led to the atrium, and thence the hallway.

"She's a good-looking girl."

Quintus spun to find his mother standing in the shadows by the doors, a good vantage point to look into the peristyle. "W-what?" he stammered.

"Nothing wrong with bedding a slave, of course," she said, approaching. As always, Quintus was struck by her immense poise and beauty. Oscan nobility through and through, Atia was short and slim and took great care with her appearance. A dusting of ochre reddened her high cheekbones. Her eyebrows and the rims of her eyelids had been finely marked out with ash. A dark red *stola*, or long tunic, belted at the waist, was complemented by a cream shawl. Her long raven-black hair was pinned back by ivory pins, and topped by a diadem. "But don't make it so frequent. It gives them ideas above their station."

Quintus' face colored. He'd never discussed sex with his mother, let alone had his activities commented upon. Somehow, he wasn't surprised that it was she who had brought it up, though, rather than his father. Fabricius was a soldier, but as he often liked to say, his wife had only been prevented from being one by virtue of her sex. Much of the time, Atia was sterner than he was. "How did you know?"

Her gray eyes fixed him to the spot. "I've heard you at night. One would have to be deaf not to."

"Oh," Quintus whispered. He didn't know where to look. Mortified, he studied the richly patterned mosaic beneath his feet, wishing it would open up and swallow him. He'd thought they'd been so discreet.

"Get over it. You're not the first noble's son to plow the furrow with a pretty slave girl."

"No, Mother."

She waved her hands dismissively. "Your father did the same when he was younger. Everyone does."

Quintus was stunned by his mother's sudden openness. It must be part of becoming a man, he thought. "I see."

"You should be safe enough with Elira. She is clean," Atia announced briskly. "But choose new bed companions carefully. When visiting a brothel, make it an expensive one. It's very easy to pick up disease."

Quintus' mouth opened and closed. He didn't ask how his mother knew that Elira was clean. As Atia's *ornatrix*, the Illyrian had to help dress her each morning. No doubt she'd been grilled as soon as Atia had become aware of her involvement with him. "Yes, Mother."

"Ready for the hunt?"

He twisted beneath her penetrating scrutiny, wondering if she could see his fear. "I think so."

To his relief, his mother made no comment. "Have you prayed to the gods?" she asked.

"Yes."

"Let us do it again."

They made their way into the atrium, which was lit by a rectangular hole in the ceiling. A downward-sloping roof allowed rainwater to fall into the center of the room, where it landed in a specially built pool. The walls were painted in rich colors, depicting rows of columns that led on to other, imaginary chambers. The effect made the space seem even bigger. This was the central living area of the large villa, and off it were their bedrooms, Fabricius' office, and a quartet of storerooms. A shrine was situated in one of the corners nearest to the garden.

There a small stone altar was decorated with statues of Jupiter, Mars, or Mamers as the Oscans called him, and Diana. Guttering flames issued from the flat, circular oil lamps sitting before each. Effigies of the family's ancestors hung on the wall above. Most were Fabricius' ancestors: Romans, the warlike people who had conquered Campania just over a century before, but, in a real testament to his father's respect for his wife, some were Atia's forebears: Oscan nobility who had lived in the area for many generations. Naturally, Quintus was fiercely proud of both heritages.

They knelt side by side in the dim light, each making their silent requests of the deities.

Quintus repeated the prayers he'd made in his room. They eased his fear somewhat, but could not dispel it. By the time he had finished, his embarrassment about Elira had subsided. He was still discomfited, however, to find his mother's eyes upon him as he rose.

"Your ancestors will be watching over you," she murmured. "To help with the hunt. To guide your spear. Do not forget that."

She *had* seen his fear. Ashamed, Quintus nodded jerkily.

"There you are! I've been looking for you." Fabricius came into the room from the hall. Short and compact, his close-cut hair was more gray now than brown. Clean-shaven, he had a ruddier complexion than Quintus, but possessed the same straight nose and strong jawline. He was already wearing his hunting clothes—an old tunic, a belt with an ivory-handled dagger, and heavy-duty leather sandals. Even in civilian dress, he managed to look soldier-like. "Made your devotions?"

Quintus nodded.

"We had best get ready."

"Yes, Father." Quintus glanced at his mother.

"Go on," Atia urged. "I will see you later."

Quintus took heart. She must think I'll succeed, he thought.

"It's time to choose your spear." Fabricius led the way to one of the storerooms, where his weapons and armor were stored. Quintus had only entered the chamber a handful of times, but it was his favorite place in the house. A ripple of excitement flowed through him as his father produced a small key and slipped it into the padlock. It opened with a quiet click. Undoing the latch, Fabricius pulled wide the door, allowing the daylight in.

A dim twilight still dominated the little room, but Quintus' eyes were immediately drawn to a wooden stand upon which was perched a distinctively shaped, broad-brimmed Boeotian helmet. What made it stand out was its flowing red horsehair crest. Now faded by time, its effect was dramatic nonetheless. Quintus grinned, remembering the day his father had left the door ajar, and he'd illicitly tried the helmet on, imagining himself as a grown man, a cavalryman in one of Rome's legions. He longed for the day when he'd possess one himself.

A pair of simple bronze greaves made from the same material lay on the floor beneath the helmet. A round cavalry shield, made from ox-hide, was propped up nearby. Leaning against it was a long, bone-handled sword in a leather scabbard bound with bronze fastenings: a *gladius hispaniensis*. According to his father, the weapon had been adopted by Rome after they had encountered it in the hands of Iberian merce-naries fighting for Carthage. Although it was unusual still for a caval-ryman to bear one, virtually every legionary was now armed with a similar sword. Possessing a straight, double-edged blade nearly as long as a man's arm, the gladius was lethal in the right hands.

Quintus watched in awe as Fabricius traced his fingers affectionately over the helmet, and touched the hilt of the sword. This evidence of his father's former life fascinated him; he also yearned to learn the same martial skills. While Quintus was proficient at hunting, he had undergone little in the way of weapons training. Romans received this when they joined the army, and that couldn't happen until he was seventeen. His lessons, which included military history and tactics, and hunting boar, would have to do. For now.

Finally, Fabricius moved to a weapons rack. "Take your pick."

Quintus admired the various types of javelin and hoplite thrusting spears before him, but his needs that day were quite specific. Bringing down a charging bear was very different from taking on an enemy soldier. He needed far more stopping power. Instinctively, his fingers closed on the broad ash shaft of a spear that he had used before. It had a large, double-edged, leaf-shaped blade attached to the rest of the weapon by a long hollow shank. A thick iron spike projected from each side of the base of this. They were designed to prevent the quarry from reaching the person holding the spear. Him, in other words. "This one," he said, trying to keep his mind clear of such thoughts.

"A wise choice," his father said, sounding relieved. He clapped Quintus on the shoulder. "What next?"

He was being given complete control of the hunt, Quintus realized with a thrill. The days and weeks he'd spent learning to track over the previous two years were over. He thought for a moment. "Six dogs should be enough. A slave to control each pair. Agesandros can come too: he's a good hunter, and he can keep an eye on the slaves."

"Anything else?"

Quintus laughed. "Some food and water would be a good idea, I suppose."

"Very good," agreed his father. "I'll go to the kitchen and organize those supplies. Why don't you select the slaves and dogs you want?"

Still astonished by their role reversal, Quintus headed outside. For the first time he felt the full weight of responsibility on his shoulders. It was critical that he make the correct decisions. Bear hunting was extremely dangerous, and men's lives would depend on him.

Not long after, the little party set off. In the lead was Quintus, with his father walking alongside. Both were unencumbered except for their spears and a water bag each. Next came Agesandros, a Sicilian Greek who had belonged to Fabricius for many years. Trusted by his master, he also carried a hunting spear. A pack hung from his back, containing bread, cheese, onions and a hunk of dried meat.

Through sheer hard work, Agesandros had worked his way up to become the *vilicus*, the most important slave on the farm. He had not been born into captivity, though. Like many of his people, Agesandros had fought alongside the Romans in the war against Carthage. Captured after a skirmish, he had been sold into slavery by the Carthaginians. It was ironic, thought Quintus, that the Sicilian had become the slave of a Roman. Yet Fabricius and Agesandros got on well. In fact, the overseer had a good relationship with the entire family. His genial manner and willingness to answer questions meant that he had been a favorite with Quintus and Aurelia since they were tiny children. Although he was now aged forty or more, the bandy-legged vilicus was in excellent physical shape, and ruled over the slaves with an iron grip.

Last came three sturdy Gauls, chosen by Quintus because of their affinity with the hunting dogs. One in particular, a squat, tattooed man with a broken nose, spent all his free time with the pack, teaching them new commands. Like the other slaves, the trio had been toiling in the fields under Agesandros' supervision that morning. It was sowing time, when they had to work from dawn till dusk under the hot sun. The diversion of a bear hunt was therefore most welcome, and they chatted animatedly to each other in their own tongue as they walked. In front of each man ran a pair of large brindle dogs, straining at the leather leashes tied around their throats. With broad heads and heavily muscled bodies, they were the opposite of Fabricius' smaller dogs, which had tufted ears and feathered flanks. The former were scent hounds, while the latter relied on sight.

The sun beat down from a cloudless sky as they left behind the fields of wheat that surrounded the villa. The sundial in the courtyard had told Quintus it was only just gone *hora secunda*. The characteristic whirring sound of cicadas was starting up, but the heat haze that hung in the air daily had not yet formed. He led the way along a narrow track that twisted and wound through the olive trees dotting the slopes above the farm.

Having traversed an area of cleared earth, they entered the mixed beech and oak woods that covered most of the surrounding countryside. Although the hills were much lower than the Apennines, which ran down Italy's spine, they were home to an occasional bear. It was unlikely that he would find traces this near the farm, however. Solitary by nature, the large creatures avoided humans if at all possible. Quintus scanned the ground anyway, but seeing nothing, he picked up speed.

Like every other large town, Capua held its own *ludi*, or games, affording Quintus the opportunity to see a bear fight once before. It had not been a pretty sight. Terrified by the alien environment and baying crowds, the beast had had little chance against two trained hunters armed with spears. He had vivid memories, though, of the tremendous power in its strong jaws and slashing claws. Facing a bear in its own territory, alone, would be an entirely different prospect to the one-sided spectacle he'd witnessed in Capua. Quintus' stomach clenched into a knot, but his pace did not slacken. Fabricius, like all Roman fathers, held the power of life and death over his son, and he had chosen the task. Quintus could not let down his mother either. It was his duty to succeed. By sunset, I'll be a man, he thought proudly. Quintus couldn't help imagining, however, that he might end his days bleeding to death on the forest floor.

They climbed steadily, leaving the deciduous woods behind. Now they were surrounded by pines, junipers and cypress trees. The air grew cooler and Quintus began to worry. He'd seen piles of dung, and tree trunks with distinctive claw marks scratched into the bark, in this area before. Today, he saw nothing that wasn't weeks, even months, old. He kept going, praying to Diana, the goddess of the hunt, for a sign, but his request was in vain. Not a single bird called; no deer broke from cover. Finally, not knowing what else to do, he stopped, forcing everyone else to do the same. Acutely aware of his father at his back, Agesandros staring, and the Gauls giving each other knowing looks, Quintus racked his brains. He knew this ground like the back of his hand. Where was the best place to find a bear on such a warm day?

Quintus glanced at his father, who simply stared back at him. He would get no help.

Attempting to conceal his laughter, one of the Gauls coughed loudly. Quintus flushed with anger, but Fabricius did nothing. Nor did Agesandros. He looked at his father again, but Fabricius' gaze was set. He would get no sympathy, and the Gaul no reprimand. Today of all days he had to earn the vilicus' and the slaves' respect. Again Quintus pondered. At last an idea popped into his mind.

"Blackberries," he blurted. "They love blackberries." Higher up, in the clearings on the south-facing slopes, were sprawling bramble bushes, which fruited far earlier than those growing on slopes with a different orientation. Bears spent much of their life in search of food. It was as good a place to look as any.

Right on cue, the staccato sound of a woodpecker broke the silence. A moment later, the noise was repeated from a different location. His pulse racing, Quintus searched the trees, finally seeing not one, but two black woodpeckers. The elusive birds were sacred to Mars, the warrior god. Good omens. Turning on his heel, Quintus headed in an entirely different direction.

His smiling father was close behind, followed by Agesandros and the Gauls.

None was laughing now.

Not long after, Quintus' prayers were answered in royal style. He'd checked several glades, with no luck. Finally, though, in the shade of a tall pine tree, he found a lump of fresh dung. Its shape, size and distinctive scent were unmistakable, and Quintus could have cheered at the sight. He stuck a finger into the dark brown mass. The center had not grown completely cold, which meant that a bear had passed by in the recent past. There were also plenty of brambles nearby. Jerking his head at the tattooed man, Quintus pointed at the ground. The Gaul trotted up, and his two dogs instantly converged on the pile of evidence. Both began whining frantically, alternately sniffing the dung and the air. Quintus' pulse quickened, and the Gaul gave him an inquiring look.

"Let them loose," ordered Quintus. He glanced at the other slaves. "Those too."

―――

Aurelia's foul mood crept up on her after Quintus and their father had left. The reason for her ill humor was simple. While her brother went hunting for a bear, she had to help her mother, who was supervising the slaves in the garden outside the villa. This was one of the busiest times of the year, when the plants were shooting up out of the ground. Lovage sat alongside mustard greens, coriander, sorrel, rue and parsley. The vegetables were even more numerous, and provided the family with food for most of the year. There were cucumbers, leeks, cabbages, root vegetables, as well as fennel and brassicas. Onions, a staple of any good recipe, were grown in huge numbers. Garlic, favored for both its strong flavor and its medicinal properties, was also heavily cultivated.

Aurelia knew that she was being childish. A few weeks earlier, she had enjoyed setting the lines where the herbs and vegetables would grow, showing the slaves where to dig the holes and ensuring that they watered each with just the right amount of water. As usual, she had reserved the job of dropping the tiny seeds into place for herself. It was something she'd done since she was little. Today, with the plants growing well, the main tasks consisted of watering them and pulling any weeds that had sprouted up nearby. Aurelia couldn't have cared less. As far as she was concerned, the whole garden could fall into rack and ruin. She stood sulkily off to one side, watching her mother direct operations. Even Elira, with whom she got on well, could not persuade her to join in.

Atia ignored her for a while, but eventually she had had enough. "Aurelia!" she called. "Come over here."

With dragging feet, she made her way to her mother's side.

"I thought you liked gardening," Atia said brightly.

"I do," muttered Aurelia.

"Why aren't you helping?"

"I don't feel like it." She was acutely aware that every slave present was craning their neck to hear, and hated it.

Atia didn't care who heard her. "Are you ill?" she demanded.

"No."

"What is it then?"

"You wouldn't understand," Aurelia mumbled.

Atia's eyebrows rose. "Really? Try me."

"It's . . ." Aurelia caught the nearest slave staring at her. Her furious glare succeeded in making him look away, but she got little satisfaction from this. Her mother was still waiting expectantly. "It's Quintus," she admitted.

"Have you had an argument?"

"No." Aurelia shook her head. "Nothing like that."

Tapping a foot, Atia waited for further clarification. A moment later, it was clear that it would not be forthcoming. Her nostrils flared. "Well?"

Aurelia could see that her mother's patience would not last much longer. In that moment, however, she caught sight of a buzzard hanging overhead on the thermals. It was hunting. Like Quintus. Aurelia's anger resurged and she forgot about their captive audience. "It's not fair," she cried. "I'm stuck here, in the *garden*, while he gets to track down a bear."

Atia did not look surprised. "I wondered if that was what this is about. So you would also hunt?"

Glowering, Aurelia nodded. "Like Diana, the huntress."

Her mother frowned. "You're not a goddess."

"I know, but . . ." Aurelia half turned, so the slaves could not see the tears in her eyes.

Atia's face softened. "Come now. You're a young woman, or will be soon. A beautiful one too. Consequently, your path will be very different to that of your brother." She held up a finger to quell Aurelia's protest. "That doesn't mean your destiny is without value. Do you think I am worthless?"

Aurelia was aghast. "Of course not, Mother."

Atia's smile was broad, and reassuring. "Precisely. I may not fight or go to war, but my position is powerful nonetheless. Your father relies on me for a multitude of things—as your husband will one day. Maintaining the household is but one small part of it."

"But you and Father chose to marry each other," Aurelia protested. "For love!"

"We were lucky in that respect," her mother acknowledged. "Yet we did so without the approval of either of our families. Because we refused to follow their wishes not to wed, they cut us off." Atia's face grew sad. "It made life quite difficult for many years. I never saw my parents again, for example. They never met you or Quintus."

Aurelia was flattered. She'd never heard any of this before. "Surely it was worth it?" she pleaded.

There was a slow nod. "It may have been, but I would not want the same hard path for you."

Aurelia bridled. "Better that, surely, than being married to some fat old man?"

"That won't happen to you. Your father and I are not monsters." Atia lowered her voice. "But realize this, young lady: we *will* arrange your betrothal to someone of our choice. Is that clear?"

Seeing the steel in her mother's eyes, Aurelia gave in. "Yes."

Atia sighed, glad that her misgivings had gone unnoticed. "We understand each other then." Seeing Aurelia's apprehension, she paused. "Do not fear. You will have love in your marriage. It can develop over time. Ask Martialis, Father's old friend. He and his wife were betrothed to each other by their families, and ended up devoted to one another." She held out her hand. "Now, it's time to get stuck in. Life goes on regardless of how we feel, and our family relies on this garden."

With a faint smile, Aurelia reached out to grasp her mother's fingers. Maybe things weren't as bad as she'd thought.

All the same, she couldn't help glancing up at the buzzard, and thinking of Quintus.

⁓

Quintus had followed the pack for perhaps a quarter of an hour before there was any hint that the quarry had been found. Then a loud yelping bark rang out from the trees ahead. It quickly died away to a shrill, repetitive whine. With a racing heart, Quintus came to a halt. The dogs' role was merely to bring the bear to bay, but there was always one more eager than its fellows. Its fate was unfortunate, but unavoidable. What mattered was that the bear had been found. In confirmation, a renewed succession of growls was met by a deep, threatening rumble.

The terrifying sound made a hot tide of acid surge up Quintus' throat. Another piercing yelp told him that a second dog had been hurt, or killed. Ashamed of his fear, Quintus willed away his nausea. This was no time for holding back. The dogs were doing their job, and he must do his. Muttering more prayers to Diana, he pounded toward the din.

As he burst into a large clearing, Quintus frowned in recognition. He had often picked berries here with Aurelia. A sprawl of thorny brambles, taller than a man, ran across the floor of the glade, which was bathed in dappled sunlight. A stream pattered down the slope toward the valley below. Fallen boughs lay here and there amidst a profusion of wildflowers, but what drew Quintus' eyes was the struggle going on in the shadow cast by a nearby lofty cypress. Four dogs had a bear cornered against the tree's trunk. Growling with fury, the creature made frequent lunges at its tormentors, but the hounds dodged warily to and fro, just beyond reach. Each time the bear moved away from the tree, the dogs ran in to bite at its haunches or back legs. It was a stalemate—if the bear left the tree's protection, the dogs swarmed in from all sides, but if the beast remained where it was, they could not overcome it.

Two motionless shapes lay outside the semicircle, the casualties Quintus had heard. A cursory glance told him that one dog might survive. It was bleeding badly from deep claw wounds on its rib cage, but he could see no other injuries. The second, on the other hand, would definitely not make it. Shallow movements of its chest told him it still lived, but half its face had been torn off, and shiny, jagged ends of freshly broken bone protruded from a terrible injury to its left foreleg, the result of a bite from the bear's powerful jaws.

Quintus approached with care. Rushing in would carry a real risk of being knocked over, and the Gauls would soon be here. Once they called off the hounds, his task would begin in earnest. He studied the bear, eager for any clue that might help him kill it. Preoccupied with the snapping dogs, it paid him little notice. Its sheer size meant that it had to be a male. The creature's dense fur was yellowish-brown, and it had a typical large, rounded head and small ears. Massive shoulders and a squat body at least three times bigger than his own reinforced Quintus' awareness of just how dangerous his prey was. He could feel his pulse hammering in the hollow at the base of his throat, its speed reminding him that he was not in total control. Calm down, he thought. Breathe deeply. Concentrate.

"Thinking of the berries was a good idea," said Fabricius from behind him. "You've found a big bear too. A worthy foe."

Startled, Quintus turned his head. The others had arrived. All eyes were on him. "Yes," he replied, hoping that the growling and snarling a dozen steps away would hide the fear in his voice.

Fabricius moved closer. "Are you ready?"

Quintus quailed mentally. His father had seen his anxiety, and was prepared to step in. A fleeting look at Agesandros and the slaves was enough to see that they also understood the question's double meaning. A trace of disappointment flashed across the Sicilian's visage, and the Gauls slyly eyed each other. Damn them all, Quintus thought, his guts churning. Have they never been scared? "Of course," he replied loudly.

Fabricius gave him a measured stare. "Very well," he said, coming to a halt.

Quintus wasn't sure that his worried father would obey. There was more at stake than his life now, though. Killing the bear would prove nothing if the Sicilian and the slaves thought he was a coward, who relied on Fabricius for backup. "Do not interfere," he shouted. "This is my fight. I must do this on my own, whatever the outcome." He glanced at his father, who did not immediately respond.

"Swear it!"

"I swear," Fabricius said reluctantly, stepping back.

Quintus was satisfied to see the first signs of respect return to the others' faces.

A dog howled as the bear caught it with a sweeping arm. It was thrown through the air by the powerful blow, landing with an ominous thud by Quintus' feet. He squared his shoulders and prepared himself. Three hounds weren't enough to contain the quarry. If he didn't act at once, it had a chance of escaping. "Call them back," he shouted.

With shrill whistles, the Gauls obeyed. When the enraged dogs did not comply, the tattooed man ran in. Ignoring the bear, and using a leash as a whip, he beat them backward, out of the way. His actions worked for two of the hounds, but the largest, its lips and teeth reddened with the bear's blood, did not want to withdraw. Cursing, the Gaul half turned, trying to kick it out of the way. He missed, and it darted past him, intent on rejoining the fray.

Aghast, Quintus watched as the dog jumped, sinking its teeth into the side of the bear's face. Rearing up in pain, the bear lifted it right into the air. At once this allowed it to use its front legs, raking the dog's body repeatedly with its claws. Far from releasing its grip, the hound clamped its jaws tighter than ever. It had been bred to endure pain, to hold on no matter what. Quintus had heard of such dogs having to be knocked unconscious before their mouths could be prized open. Yet this stubborn courage would not be enough: it needed help from its companions, which were now restrained. Or from him. The Gaul was in the way, though, screaming his anger and distress. He swung the useless leash across the bear's head, once, twice, three times. It harmed the beast not at all, but would hopefully distract it from killing his favorite dog. That was the theory, anyway.

The Gaul's plan failed. With the skin and hair on both sides of the hound's abdomen ripped away, the bear eviscerated it with several powerful rakes of its claws. Slippery loops of pink bowel tumbled out into the air, only to be sheared off like so many fat sausages. Sensing the dog's grip on its face weaken, the bear redoubled its efforts. Quintus felt his gorge rise as purple lumps of liver tissue cascaded to the ground. Finally a claw connected with a major blood vessel, tearing it asunder. Gouts of dark red blood sprayed from the ruin of the dog's belly, and its jaws loosened.

A moment later, it dropped lifelessly away from the bear.

"Get back!" Quintus screamed, but the Gaul ignored him.

Instead, the wild-eyed slave launched another attack. The loss of his canine friend had driven him into battle rage, which Quintus had often heard of, but never seen. The Romans and Gauls were enemies of old and had fought numerous times. More than a hundred and seventy years before, Rome itself had been sacked by the fierce tribesmen.

Just six years previously, more than seventy thousand of them had invaded northern Italy again. They had been defeated, but stories still abounded of berserker warriors who, fighting naked, threw themselves at oncoming legionaries with complete disregard for their own safety.

This man was no such enemy, however. He might be a slave, but his life was still worth saving. Quintus jumped forward, shoving his spear at the bear. To his horror, the animal moved at the last moment, and his blade ran deep into its side rather than its chest, as he had intended. His blow was not mortal, nor was it enough to stop the beast reaching up to seize the Gaul by the neck. A short choking cry left the man's lips, and the bear shook him as a dog would a rat.

Not knowing what else to do, Quintus thrust his spear even deeper. The only reaction was an annoyed growl. In his haste, he'd stabbed into the creature's abdomen. It was potentially a mortal wound, but not one that would stop it quickly. Satisfied that the Gaul was dead, the bear flung him to one side. Naturally, its gaze next fell upon Quintus, who panicked. Although his spear was buried in its flesh, the creature's deep-set eyes showed no fear, just a searing anger. Bears normally avoided conflict with humans, but when aroused they became extremely aggressive. This individual was irate. It snapped at his spear shaft and splinters flew into the air.

There was nothing for it. Quintus took a deep breath and pulled his spear free. Roaring with pain, the bear revealed a genuinely fearsome set of teeth, the largest of which were as long as Quintus' middle fingers. Its red, gaping mouth was big enough to fit his entire head inside, and was well capable of crushing his skull. Quintus wanted to move away, but his muscles were paralyzed by terror.

The bear took a step toward him. Gripping his spear in both hands, Quintus aimed the point at its chest. Advance, he told himself. Go on the attack. Before he could move, the animal lunged at him. Catching the end of the spear, it swept the shaft to one side as though it were a twig. With nothing between them, they stared at each other for a breathless moment. In slow motion, Quintus saw its muscles tense in preparation to jump. He nearly lost control of his bladder. Hades was a whisker away, and he could do nothing about it.

For whatever reason, however, the bear did not leap at once, and Quintus was able to bring down his spear again.

His relief was momentary.

As Quintus moved to the attack, he slipped on a piece of intestine. Both of his feet went from under him, and he landed flat on his back. With a rush, all the air left his lungs, winding him. Quintus was vaguely aware of the butt of his spear catching in the dirt and wrenching itself free of his grasp. Frantically, he lifted his head. To his utter horror, he could see the bear not five paces away, just beyond his sandals. It roared again, and this time Quintus received the full force of its fetid breath. He blinked, knowing that death was at hand.

He had failed.

III

CAPTURE

THE MEDITERRANEAN SEA

Hours passed in a blur of driving rain and pounding waves. Darkness fell, which increased the magnitude of the friends' terror manyfold. The small boat was tossed up and down, back and forth, helpless before the sea's immense power. It took all of Hanno's energy just to stay on board. Both of them were sick multiple times, vomiting a mixture of food and wine over themselves and the vessel's floor. Eventually there was nothing left but bile to come up. Flashes of lightning regularly illuminated the pathetic scene. Hanno wasn't sure which was worse: not being able to see his hand in front of his face, or looking at Suniaton's wan, terrified features and puke-spattered clothes.

Slumped on the bench opposite, his friend alternated between hysterical bouts of weeping, and praying to every god he could think of. Somehow Suniaton's distress helped Hanno to remain in control of his own terror. He was even able to take some solace from their situation. If Melqart had wanted to drown them, they would already be dead. The storm had not reached the heights it would have done in winter, nor had their boat capsized. Besides these minor miracles, there had been no further leaks. Sturdily built from cypress planks, its seams were sealed with lengths of tightly packed linen fiber as well as a layer of beeswax. They had not lost the oars, which meant that they could row to land, should the opportunity arise. Moreover, every stretch of coastline had its Carthaginian trading post. There they could make themselves known, promising rich reward for a passage home.

Hanno pinched himself out of the fantasy. Don't get your hopes up, he thought bitterly. The bad weather showed no signs of letting up. Any one of the waves rolling in their direction was capable of flipping the boat. Melqart hadn't drowned them yet, but deities were capricious by nature, and the sea god was no different. All it would take was a tiny extra surge in the water for their craft to overturn. Hanno struggled to hold back his own tears. What real chance had they? Even if they survived until sunrise and their families worked out where they had gone, the likelihood of being found on the open sea was slim to none. Adrift with no food or water, they would both die, painfully, within a few days. At this stark realization Hanno closed his eyes and asked for a quick death instead.

Despite the heavy rain which had soaked him to the skin, Malchus had returned from the meeting with the Council of Elders in excellent humor. He stood now, a cup of wine in hand, under the sloping portico that ran around the house's main courtyard, watching the raindrops splashing off the white marble mosaic half a dozen steps away. His impassioned speech had gone down as he'd wished, which relieved him greatly. Since Hannibal's messenger had given him the weighty task a week before of announcing to the elders and suffetes that the general planned to attack Saguntum, Malchus had been consumed by worry. What if the council did not back the Barca? The stakes were higher than he'd ever known.

Saguntine reprisals against the tribes allied to Carthage were purportedly the reason for Hannibal's assault, but, as everyone knew, its intent was to provoke Rome into a response. Yet, thanks to the general's perfect timing, that response would not be militaristic. Severe unrest in Illyricum meant that the Republic had already committed both consuls and their armies to conflict in the East. For the upcoming campaign season, Rome would only be able to issue empty threats. After that, however, retribution would undoubtedly follow. Hannibal was not worried. He was convinced that the time for war with their old enemy was ripe, and Malchus agreed with him. Nonetheless, bringing those who led Carthage round to the same opinion had been a daunting prospect.

It was a pity, thought Malchus, that Hanno had not been there to witness his finest oratory yet. By the end, he'd had the entire council on their feet, cheering at the idea of renewed conflict with Rome. Meanwhile Hanno had most likely been *fishing*. News of the huge shoals of tunny offshore that day had swept the city. Now Hanno was probably spending the proceeds of his catch on wine and whores. Malchus sighed. A moment later, hearing Sapho and Bostar's voices in the corridor that led to the street, his mood lifted. At least two of his sons had been there. They soon emerged into view, wringing out their sodden cloaks.

"A wonderful speech, Father," said Sapho in a hearty tone.

"It was excellent," agreed Bostar. "You had them in the palm of your hand. They could only respond in one way."

Malchus made a modest gesture, but inside he was delighted. "Finally, Carthage is ready for the war that we have been preparing for these years past." He moved to the table behind him, upon which sat a glazed red jug and several beakers. "Let us raise a toast to Hannibal Barca."

"Shame Hanno didn't hear your speech too," said Sapho, throwing a meaningful glance at Bostar. Busily pouring wine, their father didn't see it.

"Indeed," Malchus replied, handing each a full cup. "Such occasions do not come often. For the rest of his life, the boy will regret that he was playing truant while history was made." He swallowed a mouthful of wine. "Have you seen him?"

There was a short, awkward silence.

He looked from one to the other. "Well?"

"We ran into him this morning," Sapho admitted. "On our way to the Agora. He was with Suniaton."

Malchus swore. "That must have been just after he'd scarpered out of the house. The little ruffian ignored my shouts! Did the pair of them give you the slip?"

"Not exactly," Sapho replied awkwardly, giving Bostar another pointed stare.

Malchus caught the tension between his sons. "What's going on?"

Bostar cleared his throat. "We talked, and then let them go." He rephrased his words. "*I* let them go."

"Why?" Malchus cried angrily. "You knew how important my speech was."

Bostar flushed. "I'm sorry, Father. Perhaps I acted wrongly, but I couldn't help thinking that, like us, Hanno will soon be at war. For the moment, though, he's still a boy. Let him enjoy himself while he can."

Tapping a finger against his teeth, Malchus turned to Sapho. "What did you say?"

"Initially, I thought that we should force Hanno to come with us, Father, but Bostar had a point. As he was the senior officer present, I gave way to his judgment." Bostar tried to interrupt, but Sapho continued talking. "In hindsight, it was possibly the wrong decision. I should have argued with him."

"How dare you!" Bostar cried. "I made no mention of rank! We made the decision together."

Sapho's lip curled. "Did we?"

Malchus held up his hands. "Enough!"

Throwing each other angry looks, the brothers fell silent.

Malchus thought for a moment. "I am sorely disappointed in you, Sapho, for not protesting more at your brother's desire to let Hanno do as he wished." He regarded Bostar next. "Shame on you, as a senior officer, for forgetting that our primary purpose is to gain revenge on Rome. In comparison, frivolities such as fishing are irrelevant!" Ignoring their muttered apologies, Malchus raised his cup. "Let us forget Hanno and his wastrel friend, and drink a toast to Hannibal Barca, and to our victory in the coming war with Rome!"

They followed his lead, but neither brother clinked his beaker off the other's.

Hanno's wish for an easy death was not granted. Eventually the storm passed, and the ferocious waves died down. Dawn arrived, bringing with it calm seas and a clear sky. The wind changed direction; it was now coming from the northeast. Hanno's hopes rose briefly, before falling again. The breeze was not strong enough to carry them back home, and the current continued to carry their small vessel eastward. Silence reigned; all the seabirds had been driven off by the inclement weather. Suniaton's exhaustion had finally got the better of him, and he lay slumped on the boat's sole, snoring.

Hanno grimaced at the irony of it. The peaceful scene could not have been more at odds with what they had endured overnight. His sodden clothes were drying fast in the warm sunshine. The boat rocked gently from side to side, wavelets slapping off the hull. A pod of dolphins broke the surface nearby, but the sight did not bring the usual smile to Hanno's face. Now, their graceful shapes and gliding motion were an acute reminder that he belonged on the land, which was nowhere to be seen. Apart from the dolphins, they were utterly alone.

Regret, and an unfamiliar feeling, that of humility, filled Hanno. I should have done my duty, he thought. Gone to that meeting with Father. The idea of listening to dirtbags like Hostus and his cronies was now most appealing. Hanno stared bleakly at the western horizon, knowing that he would never see his home, or his family, again. Suddenly, his sorrow became overwhelming. Hanno's eyes filled with tears, and he was grateful that Suniaton was asleep. Their friendship ran deep, but he had no wish to be seen crying like a child. He did not despise Suni for his extreme reaction during the storm, though. Thinking that a calm mien might help his friend was all that had prevented him from acting similarly.

A short time later, Suniaton awoke. Hanno, who was still feeling fragile, was surprised and irritated to see that his spirits had risen somewhat.

"I'm hungry," Suniaton declared, glancing around with greedy eyes.

"Well, there's nothing to eat. Or drink," Hanno replied sourly. "Get used to it."

Hanno's foul mood was obvious and Suniaton had the wisdom not to reply. Instead he busied himself by bailing out the handbreadth of water in the bottom of the boat. His housekeeping complete, he lifted the oars and placed them in their rowlocks. Squinting at the horizon and then the sun, he began rowing due south. After a moment, he started whistling a ditty that was currently popular in Carthage.

Hanno scowled. The tune reminded him of the good times they had spent carousing in the rough taverns near the city's twin ports. The pleasurable hours he had spent with plump Egyptian whores in the room above the bar. "Isis," as she called herself, had been his favorite. He pictured her kohl-rimmed eyes, her carmine lips framing encouraging words, and his groin throbbed. It was too much to bear. "Shut up," he snapped.

Hurt, Suniaton obeyed.

Hanno was spoiling for a fight now. "What are you doing?" he demanded, pointing at the oars.

"Rowing," Suniaton replied sharply. "What does it look like?"

"What's the point?" Hanno cried. "We could be fifty miles out to sea."

"Or five."

Hanno blinked, and then chose to ignore his friend's sensible answer. He was so angry he could hardly think. "Why choose south? Why not north, or east?"

Suniaton gave him a withering glance. "Numidia is the nearest coastline, in case you hadn't realized."

Hanno flushed and fell silent. Of course he knew that the southern shore of the Mediterranean was closer than Sicily or Italy. In the circumstances, Suniaton's plan was a good one. Nonetheless, Hanno felt unwilling to back down, so he sat and stared sulkily at the distant horizon.

Stubbornly, Suniaton continued to paddle southward.

Time passed, and the sun climbed high in the sky.

After a while, Hanno found his voice. "Let me take a turn," he muttered.

"Eh?" Suniaton barked.

"You've been rowing for ages," said Hanno. "It's only fair that you have a break."

" 'What's the point?' " Suniaton angrily repeated his friend's words.

Hanno swallowed his pride. "Look," he said. "I'm sorry, all right? Heading south is as good a plan as any."

Suniaton's nod was grudging. "Fair enough."

They changed position, and Hanno took control of the oars. A more comfortable atmosphere fell, and Suniaton's good humor returned. "At least we're still alive, and still together," he said. "How much worse would it have been if one of us had been washed overboard? There'd be no one to throw insults at!"

Hanno grimaced in agreement. He lifted his gaze to the burning disc that was the sun. It had to be nearly midday. It was baking hot now, and his tongue was stuck to the roof of his dry mouth. *What I'd give for a cup of water,* he thought longingly. His spirits reached a new low, and a moment later, he shipped the oars, unable to work up the enthusiasm to continue rowing.

"My turn," said Suniaton dutifully.

Hanno saw the resignation he was feeling reflected in his friend's eyes. "Let's just rest for a while," he murmured. "It looks set to remain calm. What does it matter where we make landfall?"

"True enough." Despite the lie, Suniaton managed to smile. He didn't vocalize what they were both thinking: if, by some miracle, they did manage to reach the Numidian coastline, would they find water before succumbing to their thirst?

Some time later, they both took another turn at the oars, applying themselves to the task with a vigor born of desperation. Their exertions produced no discernible result: all around, the horizon was empty. They were totally alone. Lost. Abandoned by the gods. At length, exhausted by thirst and the extreme heat, the friends gave up and lay down in the bottom of the boat to rest. Sleep soon followed.

Hanno dreamed that he was on one side of a door while his father was on the other, hammering on the timbers with a balled fist and demanding he open it at once. Hanno was desperate to obey, but could find no handle or keyhole on the door's featureless surface. Malchus' blows grew heavier and heavier, until finally Hanno became aware that he was dreaming. Waking to a pounding headache and a feeling of distinct disorientation, he opened his eyes. Above, the limitless expanse of the blue sky. Beside him, Suniaton's slumbering form. To Hanno's amazement, the thumping in his head was replaced by a regular, and familiar, cadence: that of men singing. There was another voice too, shouting indistinct commands. It was a sailor, calling the tune for the oarsmen, thought Hanno disbelievingly. A ship!

All weariness fell away, and he sat bolt upright. Turning his head, Hanno searched for the source of the noise. Then he spotted it: a low, predatory shape not three hundred paces distant, its decks lined with men. It had a single mast with a square sail supported by a complex set of rigging, and two banks of oars. The red-colored stern was curved like a scorpion's tail, and there was a small forecastle at the prow. Amidst his exultation, Hanno felt the first tickle of unease. This didn't look like a merchant vessel; it was clearly no fishing smack either. However, it was not large enough to be a Carthaginian, or even a Roman, warship. These days, Carthage had very few biremes or triremes, relying instead on the bigger, more powerful quinqueremes and, to a lesser extent, quadriremes. Rome possessed some smaller ships, but he could see none of their standards. Yet the craft had a distinctly military air.

He nudged Suniaton. "Wake up!"

His friend groaned. "What is it?"

"A ship."

Suniaton shot into a sitting position. "Where?" he demanded.

Hanno pointed. The bireme was beating a northward course, which would bring it to within a hundred paces of their little boat. It was in a hurry to be using both its sail and the power of its oars, and it seemed no one had seen them. Hanno's stomach lurched. If he didn't act, it might pass them by.

He stood up. "Here! Over here," he began shouting in Carthaginian. Suniaton joined in, waving his arms like a man possessed. Hanno repeated his cry in Greek. For a few heart-stopping moments, nothing happened. Finally, a man's head turned. With the sea almost flat calm, it was impossible not to see them. Guttural shouts rang out, and the chanting voices halted abruptly. The oars on the port side, which was facing them, slowed and stopped, reducing the bireme's speed at once. Another set of bellowed commands, and the sail was reefed, allowing the ship to bear away from the wind. The nearest banks of oars began to back water, turning the bireme toward them. Soon they could see the base of the bronze ram that was attached to the bow. Carved in the shape of a creature's head, it was only possible to make out the top of the skull and the eyes. Now pointing straight at them, the vessel gave off a most threatening air.

The two friends looked at each other, suddenly unsure.

"Who are they?" whispered Suniaton.

Hanno shook his head. "I don't know."

"Maybe we should have kept quiet," said Suniaton. He began muttering a prayer.

Hanno's certainty weakened, but it was far too late now.

The sailor who led the oarsmen's chant began a slower rhythm than before. In unison, the oars on both sides lifted and swept gracefully through the air before arcing down to split the sea's surface with a loud, splashing sound. Encouraged by the shouts of their overseer, the oarsmen sang and heaved together, dragging their oars, carved lengths of polished spruce, through the water.

Before long, the bireme had drawn alongside. Its superstructure was decorated red like the stern, but around each oar hole a swirling blue design had been painted. It was still bright and fresh, showing the work had been done recently. Hanno's heart sank as he studied the grinning men—a mixture of nationalities from Greek and Libyan to Iberian—lining the rails and forecastle. Most were clad in little more than a loincloth, but all were armed to the teeth. He could see catapults on the deck as well. He and Suniaton had only their daggers.

"They're fucking pirates," Suniaton muttered. "We're dead meat. Slaves, if we're lucky."

"Would you rather die of thirst? Or exposure?" Hanno retorted, furious at himself for not seeing the bireme for what it was. For not keeping silent.

"Maybe," Suniaton snapped back. "We'll never know now, though."

They were hailed by a thin figure near the prow. With black hair and a paler complexion than most of his dark-skinned comrades, he could have been Egyptian. Nonetheless, he spoke in Greek, the dominant language of the sea. "Well met. Where are you bound?"

His companions snorted with laughter.

Hanno decided to be bold. "Carthage," he declared loudly. "But, as you can see, we have no sail. Can we take passage with you?"

"What are you doing so far out to sea in just a rowing boat?" the Egyptian asked.

There were more hoots of amusement from the crew.

"We were carried away by a storm," Hanno replied. "The gods were smiling, however, and we survived."

"You were lucky indeed," agreed the other. "Yet I wouldn't give much for your chances if you stay out here. By my reckoning, it is at least sixty miles to the nearest landfall."

Suniaton gestured toward the south. "Numidia?"

The Egyptian threw back his head and laughed. It was an unpleasant, mocking sound. "Have you no sense of direction, fool? I talk of Sicily!"

Hanno and Suniaton gaped at one another. The storm had carried them much farther than they could have imagined. They had been mistakenly rowing out into the Mediterranean. "We have even more reason to thank you," said Hanno boldly. "As our fathers will, when you return us safely to Carthage."

The Egyptian's lips pulled up, revealing a sharp set of teeth. "Come aboard. We can talk more comfortably in the shade," he said, indicating the awning in the forecastle.

The friends exchanged a loaded glance. This hospitality was at odds with what their eyes were telling them. Every man in sight looked capable of slitting their throats without even blinking. "Thank you," said Hanno with a broad smile. He rowed around to the back of the bireme. There they found a jolly boat about the same size as theirs tied to an iron ring. A knotted rope had already been lowered to their level from above. A pair of grinning sailors waited to haul them up.

"Trust in Melqart," Hanno said quietly, tying their boat fast.

"We didn't drown, which means he has a purpose for us," Suniaton replied, desperate for something to believe in. Yet his fear was palpable.

Struggling not to lose his own self-control, Hanno studied the planks before him. This close, he could see the black tar that covered the hull below the waterline. Telling himself that Suniaton was right, Hanno took hold of the rope. How else could they have survived that storm? It *must* have been Melqart. Helped by the sailors, he ascended, using his feet to grip on the warm wood.

"Welcome," said the Egyptian as Hanno reached the deck. He raised a hand, palm outward, in the Carthaginian manner.

Pleased by this, Hanno did the same.

Suniaton arrived a moment later, and the Egyptian greeted him similarly. Leather water bags were then proffered, and the two drank greedily, slaking their fierce thirst. Hanno began to wonder if his gut instinct had been wrong.

"You're from Carthage?" The question was innocent enough.

"Yes," replied Hanno.

"Do you sail there?" asked Suniaton.

"Not often," the Egyptian replied.

His men sniggered, and Hanno noticed many were lustfully eyeing the gold charms that hung from their necks. "Can you take us there?" he asked boldly. "Our families are wealthy, and will reward you well for our safe return."

The Egyptian rubbed his chin. "Will they indeed?"

"Of course," Suniaton asserted.

A prolonged silence fell, and Hanno grew more uneasy.

At last the Egyptian spoke. "What do you think, boys?" he asked, scanning the assembled men. "Shall we sail to Carthage and collect a handsome prize for our efforts?"

"No bloody way," snarled a voice. "Just kill them and have done."

"Reward? We'd all be crucified, more like," shouted another.

Suniaton gasped, and Hanno felt sick to the pit of his stomach. Crucifixion was one of the punishments reserved for lawbreakers of the worst kind. Pirates, in other words.

Raising his eyebrows mockingly, the Egyptian lifted a hand, and his companions relaxed. "Unfortunately, people like us aren't welcome in Carthage," he explained.

"It doesn't have to be Carthage itself," Hanno said nonchalantly. Beside him, Suniaton nodded in nervous agreement. "Any town on the Numidian coast will do."

Raucous laughter met his request, and now Hanno struggled not to despair. He glanced at Suniaton, but he had no inspiration to offer.

"Supposing we agreed to that," said the grinning Egyptian, "how would we get paid?"

"I would meet you afterward with the money, at a place of your choosing," Hanno replied, flushing. The pirate captain was playing with him.

"And you'd swear that on your mother's life, I suppose?" the Egyptian sneered. "If you had one."

Hanno swallowed his anger. "I did, and I would."

Catching him off guard, the Egyptian swung forward and delivered a solid punch to his solar plexus. The air shot from Hanno's lungs, and he folded over in complete agony. "Enough of this shit," the Egyptian announced abruptly. "Take their weapons. Tie them up."

"No!" Hanno mumbled. He tried to stand upright, but strong hands grabbed his arms from behind, pinioning them to his sides. He felt his dagger being removed, and a moment later the gold charm around his neck was torn away. Weaponless and without the talisman he had worn since infancy, Hanno felt utterly naked. Alongside, the same was happening to Suniaton, who screamed as his earrings were ripped out. Greedy hands pulled and tugged at their valuables as the pirates fought for a share of the spoils. Hanno glared at the Egyptian. "What are you going to do with us?"

"You're both young and strong. Should fetch a good price on the slave block."

"Please," begged Suniaton, but the pirate captain had already turned away.

Hanno hawked and spat after him, and received a heavy blow across the head for his pains. They then had their arms tied tightly behind their backs and were bundled unceremoniously below decks, into the cramped space where the slaves sat on two tiers of benches. Slumped over their oars, and with barely enough room to sit erect, they sat twenty-five to each row, fifty on each side of the bireme. At the base of the steps, on a central walkway, stood a lone slave, the man whose chant had woken Hanno. Near the stern, a narrow iron cage contained a dozen or so prisoners. Hanno and Suniaton glanced at each other. They weren't alone.

It was hot outside, but here the presence of more than a hundred sweating men increased the temperature to that of an oven. Countless pairs of deadened eyes stared at the newcomers, but not a single slave spoke. The reason soon became apparent. Bare feet slapped off the timbers as a short barrel of a man approached. The friends stood head and shoulders over him, but the crop-haired newcomer's muscles were enormous, reminding Hanno of Greek wrestlers he'd seen. His only garment was a leather skirt, but he exuded authority, not least because of the knotted whip dangling from his right fist. His scarred features were roughly hewn, as if from granite, his lips a mere slit in the stone.

Still winded, Hanno couldn't stop himself from meeting the overseer's cold, calculating eyes.

"Fresh meat, eh?" His voice was nasal and irritating.

"Two more for the slave market, Varsaco," answered one of the men holding Hanno.

"Consider yourself lucky. Most prisoners end up on the benches, but we have a full complement at the moment." Varsaco gestured at the long-haired wretches all around them. "So you get to stay in our select accommodation." He jerked a thumb at the cage and laughed.

Hanno felt a thrill of dread. Their fate would be no better than that of the oarsmen. They would be totally at the mercy of whoever bought them.

Suniaton's eyes were pools of terror. "We could end up anywhere," he whispered.

His friend was right, thought Hanno. The Carthaginians' weakened navy no longer had the power to keep the western Mediterranean free of pirates, and thus far the Romans had not bothered to police the high seas. The bireme could roam wherever it wanted. There were few ports indeed where the security inspection was more than cursory. Sicily, Numidia or Iberia were possibilities. As was Italy. Every decent-sized town had a slave market. Hanno felt as if he was drowning in an ocean of despair.

The Egyptian's voice carried from the deck above. "Varsaco!"

The overseer answered straightaway. "Captain?"

"Resume former course and speed."

"Yes, sir."

Hanno and Suniaton were ignored as Varsaco bellowed orders at the oarsmen on the starboard side. Leaning into the task, the slaves used their oars to back water until the overseer gestured at them to stop. At once the figure on the walkway began singing a chant that set the oarsmen into a steady rhythm.

His duties in hand, Varsaco returned. There was a predatory look in his eyes that had not been there before. "You're a handsome boy," he said, running his stubby fingers down Hanno's arm. He slipped a hand under Hanno's tunic and tweaked a nipple. Hanno shuddered and tried to pull away, but with a man either side of him, he could not go far. "I prefer those with a bit more meat on their bones, though," Varsaco confided. He moved to Suniaton's side and roughly squeezed his buttocks. Suniaton twisted away, but the pirates holding him tightened their grip. "But look, you're hurt." Varsaco touched one of Suniaton's still oozing earlobes, then, to Hanno's horror, licked the blood off his fingertip.

Suniaton wailed with fear.

"Leave him alone, you whoreson," Hanno roared, struggling uselessly to free himself.

"Or what?" teased Varsaco. Abruptly, his voice hardened. "I am the master belowdecks. I do as I please. Take him over there!"

Tears of rage streamed down Hanno's face as he watched his friend being dragged to a large block of wood nailed down near the bow. Its surface, approximately the length of a man's torso, was covered in irregular, dark patches, and heavy iron fetters were in place at each corner at floor level. Releasing Suniaton from his bonds, the pirates slammed him facedown on to the wood. He kicked and struggled, but his captors were too many. An instant later, the manacles clicked shut around his wrists and ankles.

Varsaco moved to stand behind him and, realizing what was about to happen, Suniaton began to scream. His protests intensified as the overseer was handed a knife and used it to slit his breeches from waistband to crotch. Varsaco did the same to Suniaton's undergarment, laughing as the tip of the blade snagged in his flesh, causing him to moan with pain. Finally, the overseer pulled apart the cut fabric, and his face twisted with lust. "Very nice," he muttered.

"No!" cried Suniaton.

It was too much for Hanno to bear. Summoning every reserve of his strength, he twisted and bucked like a wild horse. Engrossed by the spectacle, the two men holding him were caught unawares, and he slipped their grasp. Sprinting forward, he reached Varsaco in a dozen steps. The overseer's broad back was toward him, and he was busily unbuckling the belt that held up his leather skirt. It dropped to the floor and he sighed with satisfaction, shuffling forward to complete the outrage.

Panting with fury, Hanno steadied himself and did the only thing he could think of. Drawing back his right leg, he swung it through the air and between Varsaco's thighs. With a meaty thump, the front of his sandal connected with the soft mass of the overseer's dangling scrotum. Letting out a high-pitched scream, Varsaco collapsed to the deck in a heap. Hanno snarled with delight. "How do you like that?" he screamed, stamping his iron-studded sole on the side of Varsaco's head for good measure. He managed to deliver several more kicks before the men who had been holding him came barrelling in. Hanno saw one raising the butt of his sword. He half turned, awkward because of the ropes binding his arms, but was unable to avoid the blow. Stars exploded across Hanno's vision as the hilt connected with the back of his head. His knees buckled and he toppled forward to land on the semiconscious Varsaco. A rain of blows followed and he slipped into the darkness.

"Wake up!"

Hanno felt someone nudge him in the back. Slowly, he came to. He was lying on his side, still trussed up like a hen for the pot. Every part of his body hurt. His head, belly and groin had obviously received special attention, however. It was agony to breathe in, and Hanno suspected that two or three of his ribs were cracked. He could taste blood, and warily he used his tongue to check that all his teeth were still in place. They were, thankfully, although two felt loose, and his top lip was bruised and swollen.

He was prodded again.

"Hanno! It's me, Suniaton."

Finally, Hanno focused on his friend, who was lying only a few steps away. To his surprise, they were on the forecastle deck, under the cloth awning he had spied earlier. As far as he could tell, they were alone.

"You've been unconscious for hours." Suniaton's voice was concerned.

The temperature had dropped significantly, Hanno realized. In the gap between the gunwale and the awning, he could see an orange tinge to the sky. It was nearly sunset. "I'll live," he croaked. His last memories came flooding back. "What about you? Did Varsaco...?" He couldn't finish the question.

Suniaton screwed up his face. "I'm fine," he muttered. Amazingly, he grinned. "Varsaco couldn't stand for a long time, you know."

"Good! The fucking bastard." Hanno frowned. "Why didn't his men kill me?"

"They were going to," whispered Suniaton. "But—"

Hearing the stairs that led to the main deck creak, he fell silent. Someone was approaching. A moment later, the Egyptian stooped over Hanno. "You've come back to us," he said. "Good. A man who sleeps too long after a beating like that often doesn't wake."

Hanno glared.

"Don't give me that look," said the Egyptian reproachfully. "If it wasn't for me, you'd be dead by now. Raped before you died, like as not."

Suniaton flinched, but Hanno's fury knew no bounds. "Am I supposed to be grateful?"

The Egyptian squatted down alongside him. "Spirited, aren't you? A different prospect to your friend." He nodded in approval. "I hope to sell you as a gladiator. You'd be wasted as an agricultural or household slave. Are you able to get up?"

Hanno let the other help him to a sitting position. A stabbing pain from his chest made him grimace in pain.

"What is it?"

Hanno was disconcerted by the Egyptian's concern. "It's nothing. Just a couple of broken ribs."

"That's all?"

"I think so."

The Egyptian smiled. "Good. I thought I'd come too late. It wouldn't be the first time that one of Varsaco's little games got out of hand."

"'Little games'?" Suniaton asked faintly.

The Egyptian made an offhand gesture. "Usually, he's content to screw whichever poor bastard takes his fancy. Several times a day, normally. As long as that's it, I don't mind. It doesn't affect their sale value. After what you did, though, he would have killed you both. I don't mind him having his fun, but there's no point destroying valuable merchandise. That's why you're up here, where I sleep. Varsaco has a key to the cage, and I wouldn't trust him not to slip a knife between your ribs one night."

Hanno longed to wrap his fingers around the captain's throat, choking the life out of him, ridding his face of its perpetual smug expression. It stung that their lives had been saved for purely financial reasons. Deep down, though, Hanno was unsurprised by the Egyptian's action. He'd once seen his father stop a slave from beating a mule for much the same reason.

"This is the best place on the ship. You're out of the sun here, and it catches the evening breeze as well." The Egyptian got to his feet. "Make the most of it. We're on course for Sicily, and then Italy," he said, disappearing from view.

"At least in Iberia or Numidia, we might have had a chance of getting word to Carthage," muttered Suniaton despairingly.

Hanno's nod was bitter. Instead, they were to be sold to their people's worst enemies, as gladiators. "Melqart can't be solely responsible for this ill fortune. There's more to it." He cast his mind about, wondering why they should suffer such a terrible fate. All at once, the memory of how he had left home came crashing back. Hanno cursed. "I'm a fool."

Suniaton threw him a confused look. "What is it?"

"I didn't ask for Tanit's blessing as I walked out of the front door."

Suniaton's face paled. Although she was a virginal mother figure, Tanit was the most important Carthaginian deity. She was also the goddess of war. Angering her carried the risk of severe punishment. "It's not a crime to forget," he said, before quickly adding, "but you could ask pardon of her anyway."

In a cold sweat, Hanno did as his friend advised.

Great Mother, he pleaded. Forgive me. Do not forget us, please.

———

The next morning, Hanno had not returned home. In itself, that was not particularly unusual. But the hours passed, and still there was no sign of him. At midday, Bostar began to look worried. He paced up and down the corridor from the courtyard, checking the street for his youngest brother. By the early afternoon, he could take it no more. "Where is Hanno?"

"Nursing a hangover somewhere, probably," Sapho growled.

Bostar pursed his lips. "He's never been this late before."

"Maybe he heard about Father's speech, and got even drunker than normal." Sapho looked at their father for approval. Surprisingly, he got none.

Malchus' face now also registered concern. "You're right, Bostar. Hanno always comes back in time for his lessons. I'd forgotten, but this afternoon, at his request, we were to discuss the battle of Ecnomus again."

Sapho frowned. "He wouldn't miss it then."

"Precisely."

Suddenly, the situation felt very different.

A familiar voice cut through their dismay. "Malchus? Are you at home?"

All three turned to see a stout, bearded man appearing in the courtyard's entrance. A long cream linen robe reached almost to his feet, and a headcloth concealed his hair.

Bowing, Malchus hurried forward. "Bodesmun. I am honored by your presence."

Behind him, Sapho and Bostar were also making obeisance. Eshmoun was not their family's favored god, but he was an important deity. His temple at the top of Byrsa Hill was the largest in Carthage, and Bodesmun was one of the senior priests there.

"Can I offer you refreshment?" asked Malchus. "Some wine or pomegranate juice? Bread and honey?"

Bodesmun waved a podgy hand in dismissal. His round, gentle face was worried. "Thank you, but no."

Malchus was nonplussed. He had little in common with a peace-loving priest. "How can I help you?" he inquired awkwardly.

"It's about Suniaton."

Malchus' response was instant. "What's Hanno made him do?"

Bodesmun managed a weak grin. "It's nothing like that. Have you seen Suni today?"

Malchus' heart gave an involuntary leap. "No. I could ask you the same about Hanno."

The smile left Bodesmun's face. "He hasn't returned yet either?"

"No. Apparently, the tunny were running in their thousands yesterday. Any fool with a net could catch a boatload, and I'm sure they did the same. When Hanno didn't return, I presumed they had gone out to celebrate," Malchus replied heavily, his imagination already running riot. "It's odd that you should arrive when you did. I was just starting to get worried. Hanno has never skipped a lesson on tactics before."

"Suni has never missed the devotions in the temple at midday either."

Bostar's face fell. Even Sapho frowned.

The two older men stared at each other in disbelief. All at once, they had a great deal in common. Bodesmun was close to tears. "What should we do?" he asked in a quavering voice.

Malchus refused to let the panic that had flared in his breast grow. He was a soldier. "There'll be some easy explanation to this," he declared. "We might have to check every inn and whorehouse in Carthage, but we'll find them."

Bodesmun's normal commanding demeanor had disappeared. He nodded meekly.

"Sapho! Bostar!"

"Yes, Father," they replied in unison, eager to be given something to do. By now, Bostar was distraught. Sapho didn't look happy either.

"Rouse as many soldiers as you can from the barracks," Malchus ordered. "I want the city combed from top to bottom. Concentrate on their favorite haunts around the ports. You know the ones."

They nodded.

Despite his best efforts, Malchus' temper frayed. "Go on, then! When you're done, find me here, or in the Agora."

Bostar turned at the entrance to the corridor. "What are you going to do?"

"Talk to the fishermen at the Choma," Malchus answered grimly. His mind was full of the storm that had battered the city the previous night. "I want to know if anyone saw them yesterday." He glanced at Bodesmun. "Coming?"

The priest pulled himself together. "Of course."

With a sinking feeling in their bellies, they left the house.

On the Choma, Malchus and Bodesmun found scores of the fishermen who plied the waters off the city. Their day's work was long done. With their boats tied up nearby, they lounged about, gossiping and repairing holes in their nets. Unsurprisingly, the appearance of a noble and a high-ranking priest filled them with awe. Most went their entire lives without ever being in the presence of someone so far up the social scale. Their guttural argot was also quite hard to understand. Consequently, it was hard to get a word of sense out of them.

"We're wasting our time. They're all idiots," Malchus muttered in frustration. He forced himself not to scream and lash out with rage. Losing his temper would be completely counterproductive. The best chance of discovering anything about their sons' disappearance was surely to be found here.

"Not all, perhaps." Bodesmun indicated a wiry figure sitting on an upturned boat, whose silver hair marked him out as older than his companions. "Let's ask him."

They strolled over. "Well met," Bodesmun said politely. "The blessings of the gods be upon you."

"The same to you and your friend," replied the old man respectfully.

"We come in search of answers to some questions," Malchus announced.

The other nodded, unsurprised. "I was thinking that you were after more than fresh fish."

"Were you out on the water yesterday?"

There was a faint smile. "With the tunny running like they were? Of course I was. It's just a shame that the weather changed so early, or it would have been the best day's catch in the last five years."

"Did you see a small skiff, perhaps?" Malchus asked. "With two crew. Young men, well dressed."

His urgent tone and Bodesmun's anxious stance would have been obvious to all but an imbecile. Nonetheless, the old man did not answer immediately. Instead, he closed his eyes.

Each instant that went by felt like an eternity to Malchus. He clenched his fists to stop himself from grabbing the other by the throat.

It was Bodesmun who cracked first. "Well?"

The old man's eyes opened. "I did spot them, yes. A tall lad and a shorter, stockier one. Well dressed, as you say. They're out here regularly. A friendly pair."

Malchus and Bodesmun gave each other a look full of hope, and fear.

"When did you last see them?"

The old man's expression became wary. "I'm not sure."

Malchus knew when he was being lied to. A tidal wave of dread swamped him. There was only one reason for the other to withhold the truth. "Tell us," he commanded. "You will come to no harm. I swear it."

The old man studied Malchus' face for a moment. "I believe you." Taking a deep breath, he began. "When the wind rose sharply, I saw that a storm was coming. I quickly pulled my net on board and headed for the Choma. Everyone else was doing the same. Or so I thought. When I was safe on dry land, I saw one skiff still over the tunny. I knew it for the young men's craft by its shape. At first I imagined that they had been consumed by greed and were trying to catch even more fish, but as it was carried out of sight, I realized I was mistaken."

"Why?" Bodesmun's voice was strangled.

"The boat appeared to be empty. I wondered if they'd fallen overboard and drowned. That seemed improbable, for the sea was still not that rough yet." The old man frowned. "I came to the assumption that they were asleep. Oblivious to the weather."

"What do you take us for?" cried Malchus. "One dozing, maybe, but both of them?"

The old man quailed before Malchus' wrath, but Bodesmun laid a restraining hand on his arm. "That is a possibility."

Wild-eyed, Malchus turned on Bodesmun. "Eh?"

"A flask of good wine is missing from my cellar."

Malchus gave him a blank look. "I don't understand."

"Suniaton is the likely culprit," Bodesmun revealed sadly. "They must have drunk the wine and then fallen asleep."

"When the wind began to rise, they didn't even notice," Malchus whispered in horror.

Tears formed in Bodesmun's eyes.

"So they were just washed out to sea?" Malchus muttered in disbelief. "You are old. I can understand why you might have held back, but those?" Furiously, he indicated the younger fishermen. "Why did none of them help?"

The old man found his voice once more. "They were your sons, I take it?"

Anguish overtook Malchus' fury, and he nodded.

The other's eyes filled with an unhealed sorrow. "I lost my only child to the sea ten years hence. A son. It is the gods' way." There was a short pause. "The rules of survival are simple. When a storm strikes, it is every craft for itself. Even then, death is quite likely. Why would those men risk their own lives for two youths they barely knew? Otherwise Melqart would likely have had more corpses entering his kingdom." He fell silent.

Part of Malchus wanted to have every person in sight crucified, but he knew that it would be a pointless gesture. Glancing back at the old man, he was struck by his calm manner. All his deference had vanished. Looking once more into the other's eyes, Malchus understood why. What difference would threats make here? The man's only son was dead. He felt strangely humbled. At least he still had Sapho and Bostar.

Beside him, silent sobs racked Bodesmun's shoulders.

"Two deaths is enough," Malchus acknowledged with a heavy sigh. "I'm grateful for your time." He began fumbling in his purse.

"I need no payment," the old man intoned. "Such terrible news is beyond a price."

Mumbling his thanks, Malchus walked away. He was barely aware of a weeping Bodesmun following him. While he retained his composure, Malchus too was riven by grief. He had expected to lose one son—perhaps more—in the impending war with Rome, but not beforehand, and so easily. Had Arishat's death not been enough unexpected tragedy for one lifetime? At least he'd been able to say good-bye to her. With Hanno, there hadn't even been that chance.

It all seemed so cruel, and so utterly pointless.

———

Several days went by. The friends were kept on the forecastle and given just enough food to keep them alive: crusts of stale bread, a few mouthfuls of cold millet porridge and the last, brackish drops from a clay water gourd. Their bonds were untied twice a day for a short period, allowing them to stretch the cramped muscles in their arms and upper backs. They soon learned to answer calls of nature at these times, because at others their guards would laugh at any request for help. On one occasion, desperate, Hanno had been forced to soil himself.

Fortunately, Varsaco was not allowed near them, although he sent frequent murderous glances in their direction. Hanno was pleased to note that the overseer walked with a decided limp for days. Other than making sure Hanno was recovering from his injuries, the Egyptian ignored them, even moving his blankets to the base of the mast. Strangely, Hanno felt some pride at this clear indication of their value. Their solitude also meant that the pair had plenty of occasions to confer with each other. They spent all their time plotting ways to escape. Of course both knew that their fantasies were merely an attempt to keep their spirits up.

The bireme reached the rugged coastline of Sicily, traveling past the walled towns of Heraclea, Acragas and Camarina. Keeping a reasonable distance out to sea meant that any Roman or Sicilian triremes could be avoided. The Egyptian made sure that the friends saw Mount

Ecnomus, the peak off which the Carthaginians had suffered one of their greatest defeats to the Romans. Naturally, Hanno had heard the story many times. Sailing over the very water where so many of his countrymen had lost their lives nearly forty years before filled him with a burning rage: partly against the Egyptian for his lascivious telling of the tale, but mainly against the Romans, for what they had done to Carthage. The *corvus*, a spiked boarding bridge suspended from a pole on every enemy trireme, had been an ingenious invention. Once dropped on to the Carthaginian ships' decks, it had allowed the legionaries to storm across, fighting just as they would on land. In one savage day, Carthage had lost nearly a hundred ships, and her navy had never recovered from the blow.

A day or so after rounding Cape Pachynus, the southernmost point of Sicily, the bireme neared the magnificent stronghold of Syracuse. Originally built by the Corinthians more than five hundred years before, its immense fortifications sprawled from the triangular-shaped plateau of Epipolae on the rocky outcrop above the sea, right down to the island of Ortygia at the waterline. Syracuse was the capital of a powerful city-state, which controlled the eastern half of Sicily and was ruled by the aged tyrant Hiero, a long-term ally of the Republic, and enemy of Carthage. The Egyptian took his ship to within half a mile of the port before deciding not to enter it. Large numbers of Roman triremes were visible, the captains of which would relish crucifying any pirates who fell into their hands.

It mattered little to Hanno and Suniaton where they landed. In fact, the longer their journey continued, the better. It delayed the reality of their fate.

Rather than make for the towns located on the toe or heel of Italy, the Egyptian guided the bireme into the narrow strait between Sicily and the mainland. Only a mile wide, it afforded a good view of both coasts.

"It's easy to see why the Romans began the war with Carthage, isn't it?" Hanno muttered to Suniaton. Sicily dominated the center of the Mediterranean, and, historically, whoever controlled it, ruled the waves. "It's so close to Italy. Our troops' presence must have been perceived as a threat."

"Imagine if our people hadn't lost the war," Suniaton replied sadly.

"We would have stood a chance of being rescued by one of our ships now."

It was another reason for Hanno to hate Rome.

In the port of Rhegium, on the Italian mainland, the pirate captain prepared to sell his captives. The street gossip soon changed his mind. The forthcoming games at Capua, farther up the coast, had produced an unprecedented demand for slaves. It was enough to make the Egyptian set sail for Neapolis, the nearest shore town to the Campanian capital.

As the end of their voyage drew near, Hanno found that his increasing familiarity with the pirates was, oddly, more comforting than the unknown fate that awaited him. But then he remembered Varsaco: remaining on the bireme was an impossibility for it would only be a matter of time before the brutal overseer took his revenge. It was with a sense of relief, therefore, that two days later Hanno clambered on to the dock at Neapolis. The walled city, formerly a Greek settlement, had been one of the *socii*, allies of the Republic, for over a hundred years. It possessed one of the largest ports south of Rome, a deep-water harbor filled with warships, fishing boats and merchant vessels from all over the Mediterranean. The place was jammed, and it had taken the Egyptian an age to find a suitable mooring spot.

With Hanno were Suniaton and the other captives, a mixture of young Numidians and Libyans. The Egyptian and six of his burliest men accompanied the party. To prevent any attempt at escape, the iron ring around each captive's neck was connected to the next by a length of chain. Enjoying the solidity of the quayside's broad stone slabs beneath his feet, Hanno found himself beside a heap of roughly cut cedar planks from Tire. Alongside those lay golden mounds of Sicilian grain and bulging bags of almonds from Africa. Beyond, stacked higher than a man, were wax-sealed amphorae full of wine and olive oil. Fishermen bantered with each other as they hauled their catch of tunny, mullet and bream ashore. Off-duty sailors in their striking blue tunics swaggered along the dock in search of the town's fleshpots. Laden down by their equipment, a squad of marines prepared to embark on a nearby trireme. Spotting them, the sailors filled the air with jibes. Bristling, the marines began shouting back. The groups were only stopped from coming to blows by the intervention of a pug-nosed *optio*.

Hanno couldn't help himself from drinking the hectic scene in. It was so reminiscent of home, and his heart ached with the pain of it. Then, amidst the shouts in Latin, Greek and Numidian, Hanno heard someone speaking Carthaginian, and being answered in turn. Complete shock, then joy, filled him. At least two of his countrymen were here! If he could speak with them, word might be carried to his father. He glanced at Suniaton. "Did you hear that?"

Stricken, his friend nodded.

Hanno frantically stood on tiptoe, but the press on the quay was too great.

With a brutal yank, the Egyptian pulled on the chain, forcing his captives to follow. "It's only a short walk to the slave market," he announced with a cruel smile.

Hanno dragged his feet, but the pull around his neck was inexorable. To his immense distress, within a dozen paces he could no longer discern his mother tongue from the plethora of other languages being spoken. It was as if the last window of opportunity had been shut in their faces. It felt a crueler blow than anything that had befallen them thus far.

A tear rolled down Suniaton's cheek.

"Courage," Hanno whispered. "Somehow we will survive."

How? his mind screamed. *How?*

IV

MANHOOD

The bear lunged at his feet, and Quintus lashed out, delivering a flurry of kicks in its direction. He had to bite his tongue not to scream in terror. At this rate, the animal would seize him by the thigh, or groin. The pain would be unbelievable, and his death lingering, rather than the swift end suffered by the Gaul. Quintus could think of no way out. Desperately, he continued flailing out with his *caligae*. Confused, the animal growled, and it batted at him with a giant paw. It half ripped off one of Quintus' sandals.

A moan of fear ripped free of his lips at last.

Footsteps pounded toward Quintus, and relief poured through his veins. His life might not be over. He was simultaneously consumed by shame. He did not want to live the rest of his days known as the coward who had had to be rescued from a bear.

"HOLD!" shouted his father.

"But Quintus—" Agesandros protested.

"He must do this on his own. He said so himself," Fabricius muttered. "Stand back!"

Waves of terror washed over Quintus. In obeying his wishes, his father was consigning him to certain death. He closed his eyes. Let it be quick, please. A moment later, he realized that the bear had not pressed home its attack. Quintus peered at the animal, which was still only a few steps away. Was it Agesandros' charge, or his father's voice that had caused it to hesitate? He wasn't sure, but it gave him an idea. Taking a deep breath, Quintus let out a piercing cry. The animal's small ears flattened, which encouraged him to repeat the shrill sound. This time, he waved his arms as well.

To Quintus' immense relief, the bear backed off a pace. He was able to climb to his feet, still shrieking his head off. Unfortunately, his spear was beyond his reach. It lay right beneath the animal's front paws. Quintus knew that without it, he had no chance of success. Nor would there be any pride to be had in driving off the bear with noise. He had to regain his weapon and kill it. Swinging his arms like a mad-man, he took a step toward it. The animal's head swung suspiciously from side to side, but it gave way. Remembering Agesandros' advice about what to do if confronted by a bear in the forest, Quintus re-doubled his efforts. His damaged sandal was still attached to his calf by its straps, and he had to take great care how he placed his feet. De-spite this hindrance, it wasn't long before he regained his spear.

Quintus could have cheered. The animal was now looking all around it, searching for a way to escape, but there was no easy way. Fabricius had directed the others to spread out. They formed a loose circle around the pair. The remaining dogs filled the air with an eager clamor. His courage renewed, Quintus went on the offensive. After all, the bear was wounded. It had to be within his ability to kill it now.

He was mistaken.

Every time he stabbed his spear at the animal, it either snapped at the blade, or swept it out of the way with its massive arms. Quintus' heart thumped off his ribs. He would have to go a lot closer. How, though, could he deliver a death stroke without coming within range of its deadly claws? The bear's reach was prodigious. He could think of only one way. He'd seen pigs slaughtered many times in the farm-yard, had even wielded the knife himself on occasion. With their tough skin and thick layer of subcutaneous fat, they were difficult animals to kill, quite unlike sheep or oxen. The best way was to run the blade into their flesh directly under the chin, cutting the major vessels that exited the heart. Quintus prayed that bears' anatomy was similar, and that the gods granted him a chance to finish the matter like this.

Before he could carry out his plan, the animal lunged forward on all fours, catching Quintus off guard. He backed away hastily, forgetting his damaged sandal. Within a few steps, the studded sole snagged on a protruding root. They pulled the straps attached to his calf taut, in the process unbalancing him. Quintus fell heavily, landing this time on his backside. Somehow, he hung on to his spear, which landed flat on the glade floor beside him. That didn't stop his heart from shriveling with fear. The bear's attention focused in on him and, moving incredibly fast, it swarmed in his direction.

Quintus' eyes flickered to one side. The shocked expression on his father's face said it all. He was about to die.

Despite his horror, Fabricius kept his oath. He did not budge from his position.

Quintus' gaze returned to the bear. Its gaping mouth was no more than a handbreadth from his feet. He had but the briefest instant to react before it ripped one of his legs off. Fortunately, the end of his spear protruded beyond his sandals. Gripping the shaft, he raised it off the ground. Sunlight flashed off the polished iron tip, and bounced into the bear's eyes, distracting it, and causing it to snap irritably at the blade. Swiftly, Quintus pulled his legs to one side. At the same time, he jammed the weapon's butt into the earth by his elbow and gripped it fiercely with both hands.

When the bear closed in, he aimed the sharp point at the flesh below its wide-open jaws. Intent on seizing him, it paid no attention. Lowering its head, it lunged at his legs. Desperately, Quintus slid them away as fast as he could. The movement brought the animal right on to his spear, and its momentum was great enough for the razor-sharp iron to slice through the skin. There was a grating feeling as it pushed over the larynx before running onward into the deeper, softer tissues. Fully capable of tearing him apart yet, the bear bucked and reared, its immense strength threatening to rip Quintus' weapon from his hands. He hung on for dear life as, half suspended above him, the animal clawed furiously at the thick wooden shaft. It was so close that his nostrils were filled with its pungent odor. He could almost touch the fangs that had torn apart the Gaul and three of the dogs.

It was utterly terrifying.

The animal's immense weight eventually worked against it, forcing the deadly blade farther into its flesh. Quintus was far from happy, however. The bear was very much alive, and it was drawing ever nearer. It filled his entire range of vision—a great angry mass of teeth and claws. Any closer and it would rip him to shreds. Could the protruding spikes at the base of the iron shank take the strain? Quintus' mouth was bone dry with fear. *Die, you whoreson. Just die.*

It lurched a further handbreadth down the spear shaft.

He thought his heart would stop.

Abruptly, the bear gagged, and a bright red tide of blood sprayed from its mouth, covering the ground beyond Quintus. He had sliced through a large artery! Jupiter, let its heart be next, he prayed. *Before it reaches me.* The shaft juddered as the iron spikes slammed against the creature's neck, and it came to an abrupt stop. It snarled in Quintus' face, and he closed his eyes. There was no more he could do.

To his immense relief, the bear stopped struggling. Another torrent of blood poured from its gaping jaws, covering Quintus' face and shoulders. Disbelieving, he looked up, stunned to see the light in its amber eyes weaken, and then go out. All at once, the bear was a dead weight on the end of his spear. Quintus' exhausted muscles could take the pressure no longer, and he let go.

The animal landed on top of him.

To Quintus' immense relief, it did not move. And although he could barely breathe, he was alive.

An instant later, he felt the bear's body being hauled off.

"You're unhurt," his father cried. "Praise be!"

Agesandros growled his agreement.

Quintus sat up gingerly. "Someone was watching over me," he muttered, wiping some of the bear's blood away from his eyes.

"They were indeed, but that doesn't take away from what you've done," said Fabricius. There was tangible relief in his voice. "I was sure you were going to be killed. But you held your nerve! Few men can do that when faced with certain death. You should be proud. Not only have you proved your courage, but you've honored our ancestors in the finest way possible."

Quintus glanced at Agesandros and the two slaves, who were regarding him with new respect. His chin lifted. He had succeeded! Thank you, Diana and Mars, he thought. I will make a generous offering to you both. Inevitably, though, Quintus' eyes were drawn to the tattooed slave's body. Guilt seized him. "I should have saved him too," he muttered.

"Come now!" Fabricius replied. "You are not Hercules. The fool should have known better than to risk his life for a dog. Your achievement is worthy of any Roman." He drew Quintus to his feet and embraced him warmly.

Quintus' emotions suddenly became overwhelming: sadness at the Gaul's death mixed with relief that he had triumphed over his fear. He struggled not to cry. During the fight, he'd forgotten about becoming a man. Somehow, he had achieved the task set out by his father.

At last they drew apart.

"How does it feel?" Fabricius asked.

"No different," Quintus replied with a grin.

"Are you sure?"

Quintus stared at the bear and realized that things *had* changed. Before, he'd been unsure of his ability to kill such a magnificent creature. Indeed, he'd nearly failed because of his terror. Staring death in the face was a lot worse than he'd imagined. Yet wanting to survive had been a gut instinct. He looked back to find Fabricius studying him intently.

"I saw that you were afraid," his father said. "I would have intervened, but you had made me promise not to."

Quintus flushed, and opened his mouth to speak.

Fabricius raised a hand. "Your reaction was normal, despite what some might say. But your determination to succeed, even if you died in the attempt, was stronger than your fear. You were right to make me swear not to step in." He clapped Quintus on the arm. "The gods have favored you."

Quintus remembered the two woodpeckers he'd seen, and smiled.

"As you are to be a soldier, we shall have to visit the temple of Mars as well as that of Diana." Fabricius winked. "There's also the small matter of buying a toga."

Quintus beamed. Visits to Capua were always to be looked forward to. Living in the countryside afforded few opportunities for socializing or pleasure. They could visit the public baths and his father's old comrade, Flavius Martialis. Flavius' son, Gaius, was the same age as he was, and the two got along famously. Gaius would love to hear the story of the bear hunt.

First, though, he had to tell Aurelia and his mother. They would be waiting eagerly for news.

While Agesandros and the slaves stayed to bury the tattooed Gaul and to fashion carrying poles for the bear, Quintus and his father headed for home.

———

It didn't take the Egyptian long to sell the friends. Thanks to the impending games at Capua, sales at the Neapolis slave market were brisk. There were few specimens on sale to compare with the two Carthaginians' muscular build, or the Numidians' wiry frames, and buyers crowded around the naked men, squeezing their arms and staring into their eyes for signs of fear. Although Hanno's miserable demeanor was not that of a combatant, he impressed nonetheless. Cleverly, the Egyptian refused to sell them except as a pair. Several dealers bid against each other to purchase the two friends, and the eventual victor was a dour Latin by the name of Solinus. He also bought four of the Egyptian's other captives.

Hanno took little notice of what was going on in the noisy market place. Suniaton's efforts to revive his spirits with whispers of encouragement were futile. Hanno felt more hopeless than he ever had in his life. Since surviving the storm, every possible chance of redemption had turned to dust. Unknowingly, they had rowed out to sea rather than toward the land. Instead of a merchant vessel, fate had brought them the bireme. In a heaven-sent opportunity, Carthaginians had been present at Neapolis, but he hadn't been able to speak to them. Lastly, they were to be sold as gladiators rather than the more common classes of slaves, which guaranteed their death. What more proof did he need that the gods had forgotten them completely? Hanno's misery coated him like a heavy, wet blanket.

Along with an assortment of Gauls, Greeks and Iberians, the six captives were marched out of the town and on to the dusty road to Capua. It was twenty miles from Neapolis to the Campanian capital, a long day's walk at most, but Solinus broke the journey with an overnight stop at a roadside inn. As the prisoners watched miserably, the Latin and his guards sat down to enjoy a meal of wine, roast pork and freshly baked bread. All the captives got was a bucket of water from the well, which afforded each man no more than half a dozen mouthfuls. At length, however, a servant delivered several stale loaves and a platter of cheese rinds. However paltry the portions, the waste food tasted divine, and revived the captives greatly. As Suniaton bitterly told Hanno, they would be worth far less if they arrived in Capua at death's door. It was therefore worth spending a few coppers on provisions, however poor.

Hanno didn't respond. Suniaton soon gave up trying to raise his spirits, and they sat in silence. Deep in their own misery, and strangers to each other, none of the other slaves spoke either. As it grew dark, they lay down side by side, staring at the glittering vista of stars illuminating the night sky. It was a beautiful sight, reminding Hanno again of Carthage, the home he would never see again. His emotions quickly got the better of him, and, grateful for the darkness, he sobbed silently into the crook of an elbow.

Their current suffering was nothing. What was to come would be far worse.

In the morning, Quintus had his first hangover. During the celebratory dinner the previous night, Fabricius had plied him with wine. Although he had often taken surreptitious tastes from amphorae in the kitchen, it had been the first time Quintus was officially permitted to drink. He had not held back. His approving mother had not protested. With Aurelia hanging on his every word, Elira casting smoldering glances each time she delivered food and his father throwing him frequent compliments, he'd felt like a conquering hero. Agesandros too had been full of praise when, after dinner, he had brought the freshly skinned bear pelt to the table. Flushed with success, Quintus rapidly lost count of how many glasses he'd downed. While the wine was watered down in the traditional manner, he was not used to handling its effects. By the time the plates were cleared away, Quintus had been vaguely aware that he was slurring his words. Atia had swiftly moved the jug out of his reach and, soon after, Fabricius had helped him to bed. When a naked Elira had slipped under the covers a short time later, Quintus had barely stirred; he hadn't noticed her leave either.

Now, with the early morning sun beating down on his throbbing head, he felt like a piece of metal being hammered on a smith's anvil. It was little more than an hour since his father had woken him, and even less since they had set off from the farm. Nauseous, Quintus had refused the breakfast proffered him by a sympathetic Aurelia. Encouraged by a grinning Agesandros, he'd drunk several cups of water, and mutely accepted a full clay gourd for the journey. There was still a foul taste in Quintus' mouth, though, and every movement of the horse between his knees threatened to make him vomit yet again. So far, he'd done so four times. The only things keeping him on the saddle blanket were his vice-like hold on the reins, and his knees, which were tightly gripping the horse's sides. Fortunately, his mount had a placid nature. Eyeing the uneven track that stretched off into the distance, Quintus muttered a curse. Capua was a long distance away yet.

They traveled in single file, with his father at the front. Dressed in his finest tunic, Fabricius sat astride his gray stallion. His gladius hung from a gilded baldric, necessary protection against bandits. Also armed, Quintus came next. The tightly rolled bear pelt was tied up behind his saddle blanket. It needed to dry out, but he was determined to show it to Gaius. His mother and his sister were next, sitting in a litter carried by six slaves. Aurelia would have ridden, but Atia's presence precluded that. Despite the tradition that women did not ride, Quintus had given in to his sister's demands years before. She had turned out to be a natural horsewoman. Their father had happened to see them practicing one day, and had been amazed. Because of her ability, Fabricius had chosen to indulge her in this, but Atia had been kept in the dark. There was no way that she would have agreed to it. Knowing this, Aurelia had not protested as they'd left.

Taking up the rear was Agesandros, his feet dangling either side of a sturdy mule. He was to visit the slave market and find a replacement for the dead Gaul. A metal-tipped staff was slung over his back, and his whip, the badge of his office, was jammed into his belt. The Sicilian had left his deputy, a grinning Iberian with little brain but plenty of brawn, to supervise the taking in of the harvest. Last of all came a pair of prize lambs, bleating indignantly as Agesandros dragged them along by their head ropes.

Time passed and gradually Quintus felt more human. He drained the water gourd twice, refilling it from a noisy stream that ran parallel to the road. The pain in his head was lessening, allowing him to take more of an interest in his surroundings. The hills where they had hunted the bear were now just a hazy line on the horizon behind them. On either side sprawled fields of ripe wheat, ground which belonged to their neighbors. Campania possessed some of the most fertile land in Italy, and the proof lay all around. Groups of slaves were at work everywhere, wielding their scythes, gathering armfuls of the cut stalks, stacking sheaves. Their activities were of scant interest to Quintus, who was beginning to feel excited about wearing his first adult toga.

Aurelia drew the curtain as the litter came alongside. "You look better," she said brightly.

"A little, I suppose," he admitted.

"You shouldn't have drunk so much," Atia scolded.

"It's not every day a man kills a bear," Quintus mumbled.

Fabricius turned his head. "That's right."

Aurelia's lips thinned, but she didn't pursue the issue.

"A day like yesterday comes along only a few times in a lifetime. It is right to celebrate it," Fabricius declared. "A sore head is a small price to pay afterward."

"True enough," Atia admitted from the depths of the litter. "You have honored your Oscan, as well as your Roman, heritage. I'm proud to have you as my son."

⁓

Shortly after midday, they reached Capua's impressive walls. Surrounded by a deep ditch, the stone fortifications ran around the city's entire circumference. Watchtowers had been built at regular intervals, and six gates, manned by sentries, controlled the access. Quintus, who had never seen Rome, loved it dearly. Originally built by the Etruscans more than four hundred years before, Capua had been the head of a league of twelve cities. Two centuries previously, however, marauding Oscans had swept in, seizing the area for their people. My mother's race, thought Quintus proudly. Under Oscan rule, Capua had grown into one of the most powerful cities in Italy, but was eventually forced to seek aid from Rome when successive waves of Samnite invaders threatened its independence.

Quintus' father was descended from a member of the Roman relief force, which meant that his children were citizens. Campania's association with the Republic meant that its people were also citizens, but only the nobility were allowed to vote. This distinction was still the cause of resentment among many Campanian plebeians, who had to present themselves for military service alongside the legions, despite their lack of suffrage. The loudest among them claimed that they were remaining true to their Oscan ancestors. There was even some talk of Capua regaining its independence, which Fabricius decried as treason. Quintus felt torn if he thought about their protests, not least because his mother conspicuously remained silent at such times. It seemed hypocritical that local men who might fight and die for Rome were not permitted to have a say in who ran the Republic. It also brought Quintus to the thorny question of whether he was denying his mother's heritage in favor of his father's. It was a point that Gaius, Flavius Martialis' son, loved to tease him about. Although they had Roman citizenship and could vote, Martialis and Gaius were Oscan nobility through and through.

Their first stop was the temple of Mars, which was located in a side street a short distance from the forum. While the family watched, one lamb was offered up for sacrifice. Quintus was relieved when the priest pronounced good omens. The same assertion was made at Diana's shrine, delighting him further.

"No surprise there," Fabricius murmured as they left.

"What do you mean?" asked Quintus.

"After hearing what happened on the hunt, the priest was hardly going to give us an unfavorable reading." Fabricius smiled at Quintus' shock. "Come now! I believe in the gods too, but we didn't need to be told that they were pleased with us yesterday. It was obvious. What was important today was to pay our respects, and that we have done." He clapped his hands. "It's time to clean up at the baths, and then buy you a new toga."

An hour later, they were all standing in a tailor's shop. Thanks to its proximity to the fullers' workshops, the premises reeked of stale urine, increasing Quintus' desire to get on with the matter in hand. Workers were busy in the background, raising the nap on rolls of cloth with small spiked boards, trimming it with cropping shears to give a soft finish, and folding the finished fabric before pressing it. The proprietor, an obsequious figure with greasy hair, laid out different qualities of wool for them to choose from, but Atia quickly motioned at the best. Soon Quintus had been fitted in his toga *virilis*. He shifted awkwardly from foot to foot while a delighted Atia fussed and bothered, adjusting the voluminous folds until they met with her approval. Fabricius stood in the background, a proud smile on his lips while Aurelia bobbed up and down excitedly alongside.

"The young master looks very distinguished," gushed the shopkeeper.

Atia gave an approving nod. "He does."

Feeling proud but self-conscious, Quintus gave her a tight smile.

"A fine sight," Fabricius added. Counting out the relevant coinage, he handed it over. "Time to visit Flavius Martialis. Gaius will want to see you in all your glory."

Leaving the proprietor bowing and scraping in their wake, they walked outside. There Agesandros, who had taken their mounts to a stables, was waiting. He bowed deeply to Quintus. "You are truly a man now, sir."

Pleased by the gesture, Quintus grinned. "Thank you."

Fabricius looked at his overseer. "Why don't you go to the market now? You know where Martialis' house is. Just come along when you've bought the new slave." He handed over a purse. "There's a hundred *didrachms*."

"Of course," Agesandros replied. He turned to go.

"Wait," Quintus cried on impulse. "I'll tag along. I need to start learning about things like this."

Agesandros' dark eyes regarded him steadily. "'Things like this'?" he repeated.

"Buying slaves, I mean." Quintus had never really given much thought to the process before, which, for obvious reasons, still impacted on Agesandros. "You can teach me."

The Sicilian glanced at Fabricius, who gave an approving nod.

"Why not?" Atia declared. "It would be good experience for you."

Agesandros' lips curved upward. "Very well."

Aurelia rushed to Quintus' side. "I'm coming too," she declared.

Agesandros arched an eyebrow. "I'm not sure . . ." he began.

"It's out of the question," said Fabricius.

"There are things in the slave market which are not fitting for a girl to see," Atia added.

"I'm almost a woman, as you keep telling me," Aurelia retorted. "When I've been married off, and I'm mistress of my own house, I will be able to visit such places whenever I choose. Why not now?"

"Aurelia!" Atia snapped.

"You do what I say!" interrupted Fabricius. "I am your father. Remember that. Your husband, whoever he may be, will also expect you to be obedient."

Aurelia dropped her eyes. "I'm sorry," she whispered. "I just wanted to accompany Quintus as he walked through the town, looking so fine in his new toga."

Disarmed, Fabricius cleared his throat. "Come now," he said. He glanced at Atia, who frowned.

"Please?" Aurelia pleaded.

There was a long pause, before Atia gave an almost imperceptible nod. Fabricius smiled. "Very well. You may go with your brother."

"Thank you, Father. Thank you, Mother." Aurelia avoided Atia's hard stare, which promised all kinds of dressing-down later.

"Go on, then." Fabricius made a benevolent gesture of dismissal.

As Agesandros silently led them down the busy street, Quintus gave Aurelia a reproving look. "It's not only my exercises that you've been spying on, eh? You're quite the conspirator."

"You're surprised? I have every right to listen in to your little conversations with Father." Her blue eyes flashed. "Why should I just play with my toys while you two discuss possible husbands? I may be able to do nothing about it, but it's my right to know."

"You're right. I should have told you before," Quintus admitted. "I'm sorry."

Suddenly, her eyes were full of tears. "I don't want an arranged marriage," she whispered. "Mother says that it won't be that bad, but how would she know?"

Quintus felt stricken. Such a bargain might help them climb to the upper level of society. If so, their family's fate would be changed forever. The price required made him feel very uncomfortable, however. It didn't help that Aurelia was right beside him, waiting for his response. Quintus didn't want to tell an outright lie, so, ducking his head, he increased his pace. "Hurry," he urged. "Agesandros is leaving us behind."

She saw through his pretense at once. "See? You think the same."

Stung, he stopped.

"Father and Mother married for love. Why shouldn't I?"

"It is our duty to obey their orders. You know that," said Quintus, feeling awful. "They know best, and we must accept that."

Agesandros turned to address them, abruptly ending their conversation. Quintus was relieved to see that they had reached the slave market, which was situated in an open area by the town's south gate. Already it was becoming hard to make oneself heard above the din. Aurelia could do little but fall into an angry silence.

"Here we are," the Sicilian directed. "Take it all in."

Mutely, the siblings obeyed. Although they had seen the market countless times, neither had paid it much heed before. It was part of everyday life, just like the stalls hawking fruit and vegetables, and the butchers selling freshly slaughtered lambs, goats and pigs. Yet, Quintus realized, it *was* different here. These were people on sale. Prisoners of war or criminals for the most part, but people nonetheless.

Hundreds of naked men, women and children were on display, chained or bound together with rope. Chalk coated everyone's feet. Black-, brown- and white-skinned, they were every nationality under the sun. Tall, muscular Gauls with blond hair stood beside short, slender Greeks. Broad-nosed, powerfully built Nubians towered over the wiry figures of Numidians and Egyptians. Full-breasted Gaulish women clustered together beside rangy, narrow-hipped Judaeans and Illyrians. Many were sobbing; some were even wailing with distress. Babies and young children added their cries to that of their mothers. Others, catatonic from their trauma, stared into space. Dealers stalked up and down, loudly extolling the qualities of their merchandise to the plentiful buyers who were wandering between the lines of slaves. On the fringes of the throng, groups of hard-faced, armed men lounged about, a mixture of guards and *fugitivarii*, or slave-catchers.

"The choice is enormous, so you have to know what you want in advance. Otherwise, it would take all day," said Agesandros. He looked inquiringly at Quintus.

Quintus thought of the tattooed Gaul, whose primary duty had been working in the fields. His skill with the hunting dogs had merely been an added bonus. "He needs to be young and physically fit. Good teeth are important too." He paused, thinking.

"Anything else?" Agesandros barked.

Quintus was surprised by the change in the Sicilian, whose usual genial manner had disappeared. "There should be no obvious infirmities or signs of disease. Hernias, poorly healed fractures, dirty wounds and so on."

Aurelia screwed up her face in distaste.

"Is that it?"

Irritated, Quintus shook his head. "Yes, I think so."

Agesandros pulled out his dagger, and Aurelia gasped. "You're forgetting the most important thing," the Sicilian said, raising the blade. "Look in his eyes, and decide how much spirit he has. Ask yourself: will this whoreson ever try to cut my throat? If you think he might, walk away and choose another. Otherwise you might regret it one dark night."

"Wise words," Quintus said, levelly. Now, put him on the back foot, he thought. "What did my father think when he looked in your eyes?"

It was Agesandros' turn to be surprised. His eyes flickered, and he lowered the dagger. "I believe he saw another soldier," he answered curtly. Turning on his heel, he plunged into the crowd. "Follow me."

"He's just playing games, that's all. Trying to impress me," Quintus lied to Aurelia. He actually reckoned that Agesandros had been trying to scare him. It had partially worked too. The only reply he got, though, was a scowl. His sister was still angry with him for not telling her what he thought of her chances of happiness in an arranged marriage. Quintus walked off. *I'll sort it out later.*

The Sicilian ignored the first slaves on offer, and then stopped by a line of Nubians, poking and prodding several, and even opening the mouth of one. Their owner, a scrawny Phoenician with gold earrings, instantly scuttled to Agesandros' side, and began waxing lyrical about their quality. Quintus joined them, leaving Aurelia to simmer in the background. After a moment, Agesandros moved on, ignoring the Phoenician's offers. "Every tooth in that Nubian's head was rotten," he muttered to Quintus. "He wouldn't last more than a few years."

They wandered up and down for some time. The Sicilian said less and less, allowing Quintus to decide which individuals fitted the bill. He found several, but with each Agesandros found a reason not to buy. Quintus decided to stand his ground when he found the next suitable slave. A moment later, two dark-skinned young men with tightly curled black hair caught his eye. He hadn't noticed them before. Neither was especially tall, but both were well muscled. One kept his gaze firmly directed at the ground, while the other, who had a snub nose and green eyes, glanced at Quintus, before looking away. He paused to assess the pair. There was enough spare chain for the slaves to step out of line. Beckoning the first forward, Quintus began his examination, watched closely by the Sicilian.

The youth was about his age, in excellent physical condition, with a good set of teeth. Nothing he did made the slave look at him, which increased his interest. Agesandros' warning was still fresh in his mind, so Quintus grabbed the other's chin and lifted it. Startlingly, the slave's eyes were a vivid green color, like those of his companion. Quintus saw no defiance there, just an inconsolable sadness. *He's perfect,* he thought. "I'll take this one," he said to Agesandros. "He meets your requirements."

The Sicilian glanced the youth up and down. "Where are you from?" he demanded in Latin.

The slave blinked, but did not answer.

He understood that question, thought Quintus with surprise.

Agesandros appeared not to have noticed, though. He repeated his question in Greek.

Again no reply.

Sensing their interest, the dealer, a dour Latin, moved in. "He's Carthaginian. His friend too. Strong as oxen."

"Guggas, eh?" Agesandros spat on the ground. "They'll be no damn use."

Quintus and Aurelia were both shocked at the change in his demeanor. The abusive term meant "little rat." Immediately, Agesandros' past came to Quintus' mind. It was Carthaginians who had sold the Sicilian into slavery. That wasn't a reason not to buy the slave, however.

"There's been a lot of interest in them this morning," said the dealer persuasively. "Good gladiator material, they are."

"You haven't managed to sell them, though," replied Quintus sarcastically; beside him, Agesandros snorted in agreement. "How much are you asking?"

"Solinus is an honest man. 150 didrachms each, or 300 for the pair."

Quintus laughed. "Nearly twice the price of a farm slave." He made to leave. His face a cold mask, Agesandros did too. Then Quintus paused. He was growing tired of the Sicilian's negative attitude. The Carthaginian *was* as good as any of the others he'd seen. If he could barter the Solinus down, why not buy him? He turned. "We only need one," he barked. The slaves glanced fearfully at each other, confirming Quintus' hunch that they spoke Latin.

Solinus grinned, revealing an array of rotten teeth. "Which?"

Ignoring Agesandros' frown, Quintus pointed at the slave he'd examined.

The Latin leered. "How does 140 didrachms sound?"

Quintus made a dismissive gesture. "One hundred."

Solinus' face turned hard. "I have to make a living," he growled. "130. That's my best price."

"I could go ten didrachms more, but that's it," said Quintus.

Solinus shook his head vehemently.

Quintus was incensed by Agesandros' delighted look. "I'll give you 125," he snapped.

Agesandros leaned in close. "I haven't got that much," he muttered sourly.

"I'll sell the bear pelt, then. That's worth at least twenty-five didrachms," Quintus retorted. He'd planned on using it as a bed cover, but winning this situation came first.

Suddenly keen, Solinus stepped forward. "It's a fair price," he said.

Agesandros' fists closed over the purse.

"Give it to him," ordered Quintus. When the Sicilian did not react, his anger boiled over. "I am the master here. Do as I say!"

Reluctantly, Agesandros obeyed.

The small victory pleased Quintus no end. "That's a hundred. My man here will bring the rest later," he said.

Even as he pocketed the money, Solinus' mouth opened in protest.

"My father is Gaius Fabricius, an equestrian," Quintus growled. "The balance will be paid before nightfall."

Solinus backed off at once. "Of course, of course." Pulling a bunch of keys from his belt, he selected one. He reached up to the iron ring around the Carthaginian's neck. There was a soft click, and the slave stumbled forward, freed.

For the first time, Aurelia looked at him. *I have never seen anyone so handsome*, she thought, her heart pounding at the sight of his naked flesh.

The Carthaginian's dazed expression told Quintus that he hadn't quite taken in what was happening. It was only when his companion muttered something urgent in Carthaginian that the realization sank in. Tears welled in his eyes, and he turned to Quintus.

"Buy my friend as well, please," he said in fluent Latin.

I was right, thought Quintus triumphantly. "You speak my language."

"Yes."

Agesandros glowered, but the siblings ignored him.

"How come?" Aurelia asked.

"My father insisted I learn it. Greek too."

Aurelia was fascinated, while Quintus was delighted. He had made a good choice. "What's your name?"

"Hanno," the Carthaginian answered. He indicated his comrade. "That's Suniaton. He's my best friend."

"Why didn't you answer the overseer's question?"

For the first time, Hanno met his gaze. "Would you?"

Quintus was thrown by his directness. "No . . . I suppose not."

Encouraged, Hanno turned to Aurelia. "Buy us both—I beg you. Otherwise my friend could be sold as a gladiator."

Quintus and Aurelia glanced at each other in surprise. This was no peasant from a faraway land. Hanno was well educated, and from a good family. So was his friend. It was a bizarre, and uncomfortable, feeling.

"We require one slave. Not two." Agesandros' clarion voice was a harsh call back to reality.

"We could come to some arrangement, I'm sure," said Solinus ingratiatingly.

"No, we couldn't," the Sicilian snarled, cowing him into submission. He addressed Quintus. "The last thing the farm needs is an extra mouth to feed. Your father will already want to know why we spent so much. Best not blow any more of his money, eh?"

Quintus wanted to argue, but Agesandros was right. They only needed one slave. He gave Aurelia a helpless look. Her tiny, anguished shrug told him she felt the same way. "There's nothing I can do," he said to Hanno.

The smirk of satisfaction that flickered across Agesandros' lips went unnoticed by all except Hanno.

The two slaves exchanged a long glance, laden with feeling. "May the gods guide your path," Hanno said in Carthaginian. "Stay strong. I will pray for you every day."

Suniaton's chin trembled. "If you ever get home, tell my father that I am sorry," he said in an undertone. "Ask him for his forgiveness."

"I swear it," vowed Hanno, his voice choking. "And he will grant it, you may be sure of that."

Quintus and Aurelia could not speak Carthaginian but it was impossible to misunderstand the overwhelming emotion passing between the two slaves. Quintus took his sister's arm. "Come on," he said. "We can't buy every slave in the market." He led her away, without looking at Suniaton again.

Agesandros waited until they were out of earshot, then he whispered venomously in Hanno's ear, in Carthaginian. "It wasn't my choice to buy a gugga. But now you and I are going to have a pleasant time on the farm. Don't think you can run away either. See those types over there?"

Hanno studied the gang of unshaven, roughly dressed men some distance away. Every one was heavily armed, and they were watching the proceedings like hawks.

"They are fugitivarii," Agesandros explained. "For the right price, they'll track down any man. Bring him back alive, or dead. With his balls, or without. Even in little pieces. Is that clear?"

"Yes." A leaden feeling of dread filled Hanno's belly.

"Good. We understand each other." The Sicilian grinned. "Follow me." He strode off after Quintus and Aurelia.

Hanno turned to look at Suniaton one last time. His heart felt as if it was going to rip apart. It hurt even to breathe. Whatever his fate, Suni's would undoubtedly be worse.

"You can't help me," Suniaton mouthed. Remarkably, his face was calm. "Go."

Hot tears blinded Hanno at last. He turned and stumbled away.

V

MALCHUS

In what had become his daily routine, Malchus finished his break-fast and left the house. Although Bostar had already shipped for Iberia, Sapho was still at home. However, he mostly stayed at his rooms in the garrison's quarters. When Sapho did call by, it was rare for him even to mention Hanno, which Malchus found slightly odd. It was his eldest son's way of dealing with bereavement, he supposed. His was to shun all human contact. It meant that apart from the rare occasions when he had visitors, Malchus' only companions were the domestic slaves. It had been thus since Hanno's disappearance a few weeks before. Scared of Malchus' fierce temper and obvious sorrow, the slaves tiptoed around, trying not to attract his attention. In consequence, Malchus was even more aware of—and annoyed by—them. While he longed to lash out, the slaves were not to blame, so he bit down on his anger, bottling it up. Yet he could not bear to stay indoors, staring at the four walls, obsessed with thoughts of Hanno, his beloved youngest son—his favorite son—whom he would never see again.

Malchus headed toward the city's twin harbors. Alone. The adage that one's grief eased with time was utter nonsense, he thought bitterly. In fact, it grew by the day. Sometimes he wondered if his sorrow would overcome him. Render him unable to carry on. A moment later, Malchus caught sight of Bodesmun. He cursed under his breath. He found it increasingly hard even to look at Suniaton's father. The opposite seemed true of the priest, who sought him out at every opportunity.

Bodesmun raised a solemn hand in greeting. "Malchus. How are you today?"

Malchus scowled. "The same. And you?"

Bodesmun's face crumpled with anguish. "Not good."

Malchus sighed. The same thing happened every time they met. Priests were supposed to lead by example, not crack under pressure. He had enough problems of his own without having to deal with Bodesmun's too. Was he not carrying the weight of two losses on his shoulders? Malchus' rational side knew that he was not responsible for the death of either Arishat, his wife, or Hanno, but the rest of him did not. During the frequent nights when he lay awake, Malchus had become painfully aware that his self-righteousness was partly to blame for Hanno's bad behavior. After Arishat's death, he had become somewhat of a fanatic, interested in nothing except Hannibal Barca's plans for the future. There had been no brightness or light in the house, no laughter or fun. Sapho and Bostar, already adult men, had not been so affected by his melancholy, but it had hit Hanno hard. Since that realization, guilt had clawed at Malchus constantly. I should have spent more time with him, he thought. Even gone fishing, instead of droning on about ancient battles. "It's hard," he said, doing his best to be sympathetic. He ushered the priest out of the way of a passing cart. "Very hard."

"The pain," Bodesmun whispered miserably. "It just gets worse."

"I know," Malchus agreed. "There are only two things I know of that make it ease somewhat."

A spark of interest lit in Bodesmun's sorrowful brown eyes. "Tell me, please."

"The first is my loathing of Rome and everything it stands for," Malchus spat. "For years, it seemed that the opportunity for revenge would never come. Hannibal has changed all this. At last, Carthage has a chance at settling the score!"

"It's more than two decades since the war in Sicily ended," Bodesmun protested. "More than a generation."

"That's right." Malchus could remember how weakened the flames of his hatred had been before Hannibal's emergence on to the scene. Now, they had been fanned white-hot by his grief for Hanno. "Even greater reason not to forget."

"That can be of no help to me. Begetting violence is not Eshmoun's way," Bodesmun murmured. "What's your other means of coping?"

"I scour the streets near the merchant port, listening to conversations and studying faces," Malchus answered. Seeing the confusion on the other's face, he explained. "Looking for a clue, the smallest snippet of information, anything that might help to ascertain what happened to Hanno and Suni."

Bodesmun looked baffled. "But we know what took place. The old man told us."

"I know," Malchus muttered, embarrassed at having to reveal his innermost secret. He had spent a fortune on sacrifices to Melqart, the "King of the City," his sole request being that the god had somehow seen a way to prevent the boys' boat from sinking. Of course, he'd had no answer, but he wouldn't give up. "It's just possible that they might be alive. That someone found them."

Bodesmun's eyes widened. "That's a dangerous thing to go on believing," he said. "Be careful."

Malchus' nod was brittle. "How do you go on?"

Bodesmun looked up at the sky. "I pray to my god. I ask him to look after them both in paradise."

That was too much for Malchus. Too final. "I have to go," he muttered. He strode off, leaving a forlorn Bodesmun in his wake.

A short while later, Malchus reached the Agora. Seeing large numbers of senators and politicians, he cursed. He'd forgotten that there was an important debate on this morning. He considered changing his plans and attending, but decided against it. The majority in the Senate now backed Hannibal solidly, and this was unlikely to change in the foreseeable future. As well as restoring Carthaginian pride with his conquests of Iberian tribes and intimidation of Saguntum, a Roman ally, Hannibal had helped to restore the city's wealth. Although his long-term plans weren't common knowledge, there could be few elders who didn't suspect the truth.

Catching sight of Hostus, Malchus' lip curled. He for one thought war against Rome was coming, and was forever speaking out against it. The fool, thought Malchus. As Carthage's prosperity and pride returned, so conflict with Rome was inevitable. The annexation of Sardinia was a primary reason, and just one example of the wrongs visited upon his people by the Republic. In recent years it had continued to treat them in a disrespectful manner. Constantly sending snooping embassies to Iberia, where it had no jurisdiction, Rome had forged an alliance with Saguntum, a Greek city many hundreds of miles from Italy. It had then had the effrontery to impose a unilateral treaty on Carthage, forcing it not to expand its territories northward toward Gaul.

Deep in thought, Malchus did not see Hostus recognize him. By the time the fat man had waddled self-importantly to his side, it was too late to get away. Cursing his decision to take the shorter route to the harbors, Malchus gave Hostus a curt nod.

Hostus flashed a greasy smile. "Not coming to the debate this morning?"

"No." Malchus tried to brush past.

Moving adroitly for his size, Hostus blocked the way. "We have noted your absence in the chamber of late. Missed your valuable insights."

Malchus stopped in his tracks. Hostus wouldn't care if he died, let alone wasn't present at council meetings. He fixed the other with a flinty stare. "What do you want?"

"I know that of late you have had more important things than Carthage on your mind." Hostus leered. "Family matters."

Malchus wanted to choke Hostus until his eyeballs popped out, but he knew that would be rising to the bait. "Of course you always act for the good of Carthage," he snapped. "Never for the silver from the Iberian mines."

A tinge of color reddened Hostus' round cheeks. "The city has no more loyal servant than I," he blustered.

Malchus had had enough. He elbowed past without another word.

Hostus wasn't finished. "If you tire of visiting Melqart's temple, there is always the Tophet of Baal Hammon."

Malchus spun around. "What did you say?"

"You heard me." Hostus' smile was more of a grimace. "You may have only livestock to offer, but there are plenty in the slums who will sell a newborn or young child for a handful of coins." Seeing Malchus' temper rising, Hostus gave him a reproving look. "Such sacrifices have saved Carthage before. Who is to say a suitable offering would not please Baal Hammon and bring your son back?"

Hostus' barbed taunt sank deep, but Malchus knew that the best form of defense was attack. Give the dog no satisfaction. "Hanno is dead," he hissed. "Any fool knows that."

Hostus flinched.

Malchus poked a finger in his chest. "Unlike you, I would not murder another's child to make a request of a god. Nor would I have ever offered my own, unlike some around here. To do so is the mark of a savage. Not of someone who truly loves Carthage and would lay down his own life for it." Leaving Hostus gaping in his wake, Malchus stalked off.

His patrol of the port area that morning yielded nothing. It was little more than Malchus had come to expect. He had overheard talk of the weather conditions between Carthage and Sicily, the most auspicious place to make an offering to the Scylla, and an argument over which of the city's whorehouses was best. He'd seen merchant captains holding guarded conversations, trying to glean information from each other without giving away any of their own, and drunken sailors singing as they weaved back to their ships. Housewives sat in the open doorways of their houses, working their spinning wheels, but the whores had gone to bed. Trickles of smoke rose from the chimneys of the pottery kilns a short distance away. The open-fronted taverns that dotted the streets weren't busy at this time of day, but the stalls selling fresh bread were a different story. Stopping to buy a loaf, Malchus ran into an acquaintance, a crippled veteran of the war in Sicily whom he paid to listen out for any interesting news. So far, the man had provided him with nothing.

Nonetheless, Malchus paid for the other's bread. It didn't cost much to retain the goodwill of the poor, something Hostus would never understand. Together they walked down the street, ignoring the urchins who pestered them for a crust. Malchus watched as the cripple devoured his food before silently handing over his own. This too disappeared rapidly. Studying the man's lined, weary face, Malchus wondered if he had ever had a wife and family. Been faced with an offer from a creature like Hostus for one of his children. It didn't bear thinking about, and Malchus was grateful that the dark practices that went on in the Tophet were no longer practiced by many.

"Thank you, sir," mumbled the veteran, wiping crumbs from his lips.

Malchus inclined his head. He waited, out of habit rather than any expectation, for any information.

The veteran coughed uneasily, and scratched at the shiny red stump that was the only remnant of his lower right leg. "I saw something last night," he said. "It was probably nothing."

Malchus stiffened. "Tell me."

"Down on the docks, I noticed a bireme I've never seen before." The veteran paused. "That in itself is nothing unusual, but I thought the crew were a bit sharp-looking for ordinary traders. Seemed like they were trying too hard, if you know what I mean, sir? Talking loudly about their goods, and the prices they hoped to get for them."

Malchus felt his heart begin to beat faster. "Could you point the ship out?"

"Better than that, sir. I happened to spot the captain and some of his crew this morning. They were in a tavern, maybe four streets away. Much the worse for wear too." The veteran hesitated, looking awkward.

Even the poorest can have pride, thought Malchus. "You will be well rewarded."

Clutching his homemade crutch with renewed vigor, the smiling veteran hobbled off.

Malchus was one step behind him.

A short time later, they had arrived at the hostelry, a miserable low-roofed brick structure with crudely hewn benches and tables arrayed outside. Although it was early, this tavern was packed. Sailors, merchants and lowlifes of every nationality under the sun sat cheek by jowl with each other, swigging from clay cups or singing out of tune. Prostitutes with painted faces were sitting on men's laps, whispering in their ears in an attempt to win some business. Amidst the pieces of broken pottery littering the sawdust-covered ground, scrawny mongrels fought over half-gnawed bones. Malchus' stomach turned at the stench of cheap wine and urine, but he followed the veteran to an empty table. They both took a seat. Neither looked at the other customers. Instead they occupied themselves by trying to attract the attention of the tavern keeper or his assistant, a rough-looking woman in a low-cut dress.

Finally, they succeeded. A glazed red jug and two beakers arrived at the table soon after, borne by the owner. He cast an idle glance at the mismatched pair, but was called away before he could decide what to make of them. The veteran poured the wine, and handed a cup to Malchus.

He took a sip, and wrinkled his face with disgust. "This is worse than horse piss."

The veteran took a deep swallow. He gave an apologetic shrug. "Tastes fine to me, sir."

There was silence then, and the customers' din washed over them.

"They're right behind me," whispered the veteran at length. "Four men. One looks like an Egyptian. Another is the ugliest man you've ever seen, with scars all over his mug. The others could be Greek. Do you see them?"

Casually, Malchus glanced over the other's shoulder. At the next table, he saw a thin, pale-skinned figure with black hair sitting beside a barrel of a man whose scarred features could have been carved from granite. Their two companions had their backs toward Malchus, but he could see from their dark skin and raven hair that the veteran's guess at their nationality was probably correct. Dressed in ochre and gray woolen tunics, with daggers at their belts, the quartet were similar to many of the other customers. And yet they weren't. Malchus studied them carefully from the corner of his eye. Their faces were cruel, almost hatchet-like. Not the faces of merchants.

Gradually, Malchus began to discern their voices from the others around them. They were speaking in Greek, which was not unusual when individuals of more than one nationality crewed together. It was, after all, the predominant language used at sea. "It's good to visit a big city at last," mumbled one of the men with his back to Malchus. "Not like where we usually berth. At least here there's more than one tavern to visit."

"Plenty of whorehouses too, with decent-looking women," growled the figure beside him.

"And boys," added the scarred man with a leer.

The Egyptian laughed unpleasantly. "Never change, do you, Varsaco?"

Varsaco smirked. He lowered his voice slightly. "I just want a piece of Carthaginian arse."

The Egyptian wagged a reproachful finger.

One of their companions sniggered, and Varsaco scowled.

"You've got a long memory," said the last man. "Is this revenge for the one that got away?"

"Watch your mouth," the Egyptian snarled, confirming Malchus' suspicion that he was the leader of the group. A subdued silence fell for a moment before Varsaco and the Egyptian began whispering to each other. They cast frequent glances at the other tables.

At once, Malchus looked down. Carefully, he considered what he'd heard and seen. The men did not visit cities often. They looked a lot tougher than merchants should do. The veteran thought the same of their shipmates. Tellingly, they had had a Carthaginian crewmember in the recent past. Or had he been a prisoner? Alarm bells were now ringing in Malchus' mind. Not once since Hanno's disappearance had he had anything to go on like this. It wasn't much, but Malchus didn't care. Sliding a coin across the table with a fingertip, he watched the veteran's eyes widen. "Stay here," he whispered. "If I haven't returned by the time they leave, follow them. Use a street urchin to bring me news of their location."

"Where are you going?"

Malchus' smile was mirthless. "To get some help."

Malchus went straight to Sapho's commanding officer. His status was such that the captain fell over himself to be of assistance. At once, a dozen Libyan spearmen were put at Malchus' disposal. Although they had little idea of their mission, the men liked the sound of escaping weapons drill.

Sapho had been asleep when Malchus arrived, but the mention of possible news about Hanno sent him leaping from his bed. While Bostar had the guilt of knowing he should have made Hanno and Suniaton stay in the city, Sapho was saddled with the fact that he should not have given way. His darkest secret was that part of him was glad that Hanno was gone. Hanno had never done what Malchus wanted, while he, Sapho, did everything according to the book. Yet it was Hanno who had made their father's eyes light up. Of course Bostar knew nothing of Sapho's feelings. Unsurprisingly, the two brothers had fallen out over the matter anyway, and it hadn't been long before they were barely speaking. The issue had only subsided with Bostar's recent departure for Iberia. Hearing Malchus' news scraped raw Sapho's guilt. As he threw on his long tunic and bronze muscled cuirass, and donned his Thracian helmet and greaves, he bombarded his father with questions. Malchus had the answers to almost none of them.

"The sooner we get down there, the sooner we'll find out something," he growled.

Half an hour after he'd left the tavern, Malchus returned with Sapho and the spearmen in tow. The Libyans wore simple conical bronze helmets, and each was clad in a beltless, knee-length red tunic. They were armed with short thrusting spears.

Malchus was mightily relieved to see that the veteran and the four men he'd been watching over were still at their respective tables. The Greeks were dozing; Varsaco was talking to the Egyptian. As Malchus and his companions came to a halt outside the tavern, the two sailors looked around. Their faces twisted briefly with concern, but they did not move a muscle.

"Where are they?" demanded Sapho.

There was no need for concealment any longer. Malchus pointed. He was delighted when the Egyptian and Varsaco jumped to their feet and tried to escape. "Seize them," he shouted.

The soldiers swarmed forward and surrounded the pair with a circle of threatening spear points. The two sleeping men were kicked awake and heaved into the ring with their companions. All four were forced to throw down their daggers. Ignoring the bleary stares of the other customers, Malchus stalked forward and into view.

"What's this about?" asked the Egyptian in fluent Carthaginian. "We've done nothing wrong."

"I'll be the one to decide on that," replied Malchus. He jerked his head.

"Back to the barracks," Sapho ordered. "Quickly!"

The veteran looked on in amazement as the captives were escorted away. A metallic clunk drew his attention back to the table surface. On it lay four gold coins, their faces decorated with the image of Hannibal Barca.

"One for each of the whoresons," said Malchus. "If they turn out to be the right men, I'll give you the same again." Leaving the veteran stuttering his thanks, he followed Sapho and the soldiers.

There was urgent business to attend to.

— ⁓⁓⁓ —

It didn't take long to reach the Libyans' quarters, which were located east of the Agora, in the wall that faced on to the sea. Whole series of rooms, on two tiers, stretched for hundreds of paces in either direction. Dormitories led to eating and bathing areas. Officers' quarters were situated beside armories, administrative and quartermasters' offices. Like any military base, there were also cells. It was to these last that Sapho guided the spearmen. Nodding in a friendly manner at the jailers, he directed the party into a large room with a plain concrete floor. It was empty apart from the sets of manacles that hung from rings on the wall, a glowing brazier and a table covered in a variety of lethal-looking metal instruments and tools.

As the last man entered, Sapho slammed the door shut and locked it.

"Chain them up," ordered Malchus.

As one, the soldiers placed their spears aside, and turned on the prisoners. Struggling uselessly, the four were restrained side by side. Terror filled the two Greeks' eyes, and they began to wail. Varsaco and the Egyptian tried to maintain their composure, filling the air with questions and pleas. Studying the implements on the table, Malchus ignored them until silence fell.

"What are you doing in Carthage?"

"We're traders," muttered the Egyptian. "Honest men."

"Really?" Malchus' tone was light and friendly.

The Egyptian looked confused. "Yes."

Malchus stared at the faces of the Egyptian's companions. He turned to Sapho. "Well?"

"I think he's lying."

"So do I." Malchus' intuition was screaming at him now. These were definitely no merchants. The idea that they might know something about Hanno became all-consuming. Malchus wanted information. Fast. How they obtained it was immaterial. He indicated one of the Greeks. "Break his arms and legs."

Clenching his jaw, Sapho picked up a lump hammer. He moved to stand in front of the man Malchus had indicated, who was now moaning in fear. Silently, Sapho delivered a flurry of blows, smashing first the Greek's arms, and then his lower legs, against the wall. His victim's screams made a thin, cracked sound that reverberated throughout the room.

It took a long time, but Malchus waited until the man's cries had died to a low moaning. "A different question this time," he said coldly. "Who was the Carthaginian you were talking about earlier?"

The Egyptian shot a venomous glance at Varsaco.

A surge of adrenaline surged through Malchus. He waited, but there was no response. "Well?"

"He was nobody, just one of the crew," muttered Varsaco fearfully. "He didn't like my attentions, so he deserted at some shithole settlement on the Numidian coast."

Again Malchus looked at his son.

"Still lying," growled Sapho.

"It's the truth," Varsaco protested. He glanced at the Egyptian. "Tell him."

"It is as he says," the Egyptian agreed with a nervous laugh. "The boy ran away."

"What kind of fool do you take me for? There's far more to it than that," snapped Malchus. He pointed at Varsaco. "Cut his balls off."

Sapho laid down his hammer and picked up a long, curved dagger.

"No," pleaded Varsaco. "Please."

Stone-faced, Sapho unbuckled Varsaco's belt and threw it to the floor. Next, he cut away the bottom of his tunic, exposing his linen undergarment. Sliding the blade underneath the fabric on each side of Varsaco's groin, Sapho slit it from top to bottom. The garment dropped to the floor, leaving Varsaco naked from the waist down, and gibbering with fear. "There were two of them," he babbled, squirming this way and that. "They were adrift off the coast of Sicily."

The Egyptian's visage twisted with fury. "Shut up, you fool! You'll only make things worse."

Varsaco ignored him. Tears were running down his scarred cheeks. "I'll tell you everything," he whispered.

Sapho began to feel very guilty indeed. Taking in a shuddering breath, he looked over his shoulder.

Malchus motioned his son to stand back. Volcanic emotions swept through him. The walls came pressing in, and he could feel the blood rushing in his ears. "Speak," he commanded.

Varsaco nodded eagerly. "There was a bad storm a few weeks back. We were caught in it, and our bireme nearly sank. We didn't, thank the gods. The next day, we came across an open boat, with two young men in it."

Sapho leaped up and placed his dagger across Varsaco's throat. "Where were they from?" he screamed. "What were their names?"

"They came from Carthage." Varsaco's eyes flickered like those of a cornered rat. "I don't remember what they were called."

Malchus grew very calm. "What did they look like?" he asked quietly.

"One was tall, and had an athletic build. The other was shorter. Both had black hair." Varsaco thought for a moment. "And green eyes."

"Hanno and Suniaton!" Sapho's face twisted with anguish. Despite his relief at Hanno's disappearance, he couldn't bear that this might be the dreadful truth.

Malchus felt physically sick. "What did you do with them?"

Varsaco turned a pasty shade of gray. "Naturally, we were going to return them to Carthage," he stammered. "But the ship had sprung a leak during the storm. We had to make for the nearest land, which was Sicily. They disembarked there, in Heraclea, I think it was." He looked to the Egyptian and received a nod of confirmation. "Yes, Heraclea."

"I see." An icy calm blanketed Malchus. "If that's the case, why have they not returned? Finding a ship to Carthage from the south coast of Sicily should pose a problem to no man."

"Who knows? Young lads who have just left home are all the same. Only interested in wine and women." Varsaco shrugged as nonchalantly as he could.

"'Just left home'?" Malchus shouted. "You make it sound as if they had chosen to be washed out to sea. That it was a matter of no consequence. If you let them off in Heraclea, then my name is Alexander of Macedon." He glanced at Sapho. "Castrate him."

Sapho lowered his knife.

"Not that, please, not that," Varsaco shrieked. "I'll tell the truth!"

Malchus raised his hand, and Sapho paused. "You've probably guessed by now that you and these other sewer rats are dead men. You have condemned yourself with your own words." Malchus paused to let his sentence sink in. "Tell me honestly what you did with my son and his friend, and you'll keep your manhood. Receive a quick death too."

Varsaco nodded dully in acceptance of his fate. "We sold them as slaves," he whispered. "In Neapolis. We got an excellent price for both, according to the captain. That's why we came to Carthage. To abduct more."

Malchus took a deep breath. It was much as he had suspected. "Whom did you sell them to?"

"I don't know," Varsaco stuttered. "I wasn't there. The captain did it." His gaze turned to the Egyptian, who spat contemptuously on the floor.

"So you are the one who is responsible for this outrage?" Cold fury bathed Malchus once more. "Cut *his* balls off instead," he roared.

At once Sapho stripped the Egyptian of his clothing. Grabbing hold of the moaning pirate captain's scrotum, he tugged down to draw it taut. Sapho threw a quick glance at Malchus, and received a nod. "This is for my brother," he muttered, lining his blade up, praying that the act would assuage his guilt.

"Varsaco was the one who would have raped them," shouted the Egyptian. "I stopped him."

"How good of you," Malchus snarled. "You had no problem selling them, though, did you? Who bought them?"

"A Latin. I didn't get his name. He was going to take both to Capua. Sell them as gladiators. I don't know any more." The Egyptian looked down at Sapho, and then toward Malchus. All he saw from both was an implacable hatred. "Give me a quick death, like Varsaco," he pleaded.

"You expect me to keep my word after what you have done to two innocent boys? Those who engage in piracy merit the most terrible fate possible." Malchus' voice dripped with contempt. He turned to the soldiers. "You've heard what these scum have done to my boy and his friend."

An angry growl left the Libyans' throats, and one stood forth. "What shall we do with them, sir?"

Malchus let his gaze linger on the four pirates, one by one. "Castrate them all, but cauterize the wounds so they do not bleed to death. Break their arms and legs, and then crucify them. When you're done, find the rest of their crew and do the same to every last one."

To a background of terrified protests, the spearman snapped off a salute. "Yes, sir."

Malchus and Sapho watched impassively as the soldiers set about their task. Dividing into teams of three, they stripped the prisoners with grim purpose. Light flashed off knife blades as they rose and fell. The screaming soon grew so loud that it was impossible to talk, but the soldiers did not pause for breath. Blood ran down the pirates' legs in great streams to congeal in sticky pools on the floor. Next, the stench of burning flesh filled the air as red-hot pokers were used to stem the flow from the prisoners' gaping wounds. The pain of the castration and cautery was so severe that all the pirates passed out. Their respite was brief. A moment later, they were woken by the agony of their bones breaking beneath the blows of hammers. Low repetitive thuds mingled with their shrieks in a new, dreadful cacophony.

Malchus pressed his lips to Sapho's ear. "I've seen enough. Let's go."

Even in the corridor outside, with the door closed, the din was incredible. Although it was now possible to talk, father and son looked at each other in silence for long moments.

Malchus spoke first. "He could still be alive. They both could." Rare tears glinted in his eyes.

Sapho felt bad for Hanno. Drowning was one thing, but fighting as a gladiator? He hardened his heart. "They won't be for long. It's a mercy in a way."

Unaware of Sapho's motivations, Malchus clenched his jaw. "You're right. We can do no more than to hope that they died well. Let us join Hannibal Barca's army in Iberia, and wage war on Rome. One day, we will bring ruination, fire and death to Capua. Then, vengeance will be ours."

Sapho looked stunned. "Hannibal would invade Italy?"

"Yes," replied Malchus. "That is his long-term plan. To defeat the enemy on their own soil. I am one of only a handful of men who know this. Now you are another."

"The secret is safe with me," whispered Sapho. Obviously, he and Bostar had not been party to all of the information carried by Hannibal's messenger. Finally, he understood his father's threat to raze Capua. "Our revenge will come one day," he muttered, thinking of the golden opportunities to prove his worth that would arise.

"Speak after me," ordered Malchus. "Before Melqart, Baal Saphon and Baal Hammon, I make this vow. With all my might, I will support Hannibal Barca on his quest. I will find Hanno, or die avenging him."

Slowly, Sapho repeated the words.

Satisfied, Malchus led the way outside.

The screaming continued unabated behind them.

VI

SERVITUDE

NEAR CAPUA, CAMPANIA

Hanno trudged despondently behind Agesandros' mule, swallowing the clouds of dust sent up by those in front. Ahead of the Sicilian was the litter containing Atia and Aurelia, and beyond that, in the lead, were Fabricius and Quintus. It was the morning following his purchase by Quintus, and, after spending the night at Martialis' house, the family was returning to their farm. During their short stay, Hanno had been left in the kitchen with the resident household slaves. Dazed, still unable to believe that he had been separated from Suniaton, he had simply slumped in a corner and wept. Other than placing a loincloth, a beaker of water and a plate of food beside him, no one had offered him any comfort. Hanno would remember their curious stares afterward, however. No doubt it was something they had all seen countless times before: the new slave, who realizes that his life will never be the same again. It had probably happened to most of them. Mercifully, sleep had finally found Hanno. His rest had been fitful, but it had provided him with an escape of sorts: the possibility of denying reality.

Now, in the cold light of day, he had to face up to it.

He belonged to Quintus' father, Fabricius. Like his family, Suni was gone forever.

Hanno still didn't know what to make of his master. Since a cursory examination when they had first returned to Martialis' house, Fabricius had paid him little heed. He had accepted his son's explanation that, because of his literacy and skill with languages, the Carthaginian was worth his high purchase price, the balance of which Quintus was paying anyway. "It's your business the way you spend your money," he'd said. He seemed decent enough, thought Hanno, as did Quintus. Aurelia was but a child. Atia, Fabricius' wife, was an unknown quantity. So far, she'd barely even looked at him, but Hanno hoped that she would prove a fair mistress.

It was strange to be considering people whom he'd always considered evil as normal, yet it was Agesandros whom Hanno was most concerned about. The Sicilian had taken a set against him from the beginning. For all his concerns, at least his own situation had a positive side to it, for which he felt immensely guilty. Suniaton's fate still hung by a thread, and Hanno could only ask every god he knew to intercede on his friend's behalf. At the worst, to let him die bravely.

Hearing the word "Saguntum" mentioned, he pricked his ears. A Greek city in Iberia, allied to the Republic, it had been the focus of Hannibal's attention for months. Indeed, it was where the war on Rome would start.

"I thought that the Senate had decided there was no real threat to Saguntum?" asked Quintus. "After the Saguntines had demanded recompense for the attacks on their lands, all Hannibal did was to send them a rudely worded reply."

Hanno hid his smirk. He'd heard that insult several weeks before, at home. "Scabby, flea-bitten savages," Hannibal had called the city's residents. As everyone in Carthage knew, the rebuttal presaged his real plan: an attack on Saguntum.

"Politicians sometimes underestimate generals," said Fabricius heavily. "Hannibal has done far more than issue threats now. According to the latest news, Saguntum is surrounded by his army. They've started building fortifications. It's going to be a siege. Carthage has finally regained its bite."

Quintus threw an angry glance at Hanno, who looked down at once. "Can nothing be done?"

"Not this campaigning season," Fabricius replied crossly. "Hannibal couldn't have picked a better moment. Both the consular armies are committed to the East, and the threat there."

"You mean Demetrius of Pharos?" asked Quintus.

"Yes."

"Wasn't he an ally of ours until recently?"

"He was. Then the miserable dog decided that piracy is more profitable. Our entire eastern seaboard has been affected. He's been threatening Illyrian cities under the Republic's protection too. But the trouble should be over by the autumn. Demetrius' forces have no chance against four legions and double that number of socii."

Quintus couldn't hide his disappointment. "I'll miss it all."

"Never fear. There'll always be another war," said his father with an amused smile. "You'll get your turn soon enough."

Quintus was partly mollified. "Meanwhile, Saguntum just gets left to hang in the wind?"

"It's not right, I know," his father replied. "But the main faction in the Senate has decided that this is the course we shall follow. The rest of us have to obey."

So much for Roman *fides*, thought Hanno contemptuously.

Father and son rode in silence for a few moments.

"What will the Senate do if Saguntum falls?" probed Quintus.

"Demand that the Carthaginians withdraw, I imagine. As well as hand over Hannibal."

Quintus' eyebrows rose. "Would they do that?"

Never, thought Hanno furiously.

"I don't think so," Fabricius replied. "Even the Carthaginians have their pride. Besides, their Council of Elders will have known about Hannibal's plan to besiege Saguntum. They're hardly going to offer their support on that only to withdraw it immediately afterward."

Unseen, Hanno spat on to the road. "Damn right they're not," he whispered.

"Then war is unavoidable," Quintus cried. "The Senate won't take an insult like that lying down."

Fabricius sighed. "No, it won't, even though it's partly to blame for the whole situation. The indemnities forced on Carthage at the end of the last war were ruinous, but the seizure of Sardinia soon after was even worse. There was no excuse for it."

Hanno could scarcely believe what he was hearing: a Roman express regret for what had been done to his people. Perhaps they weren't all monsters? he wondered for the second time. His gut reaction weighed in at once. *They are still the enemy.*

"That conflict was a generation ago," said Quintus, bridling. "This is now. Even if it comes late, Rome has to defend one of her allies who has been attacked without due cause."

Fabricius inclined his head. "She does."

"So war with Carthage is coming, one way or another," said Quintus. He threw a further look at Hanno, who affected not to notice.

"Probably," Fabricius replied. "Not this year perhaps, but next."

"I could be part of that!" Quintus cried eagerly. "But I want to know how to use a sword properly first."

"You're proficient with both bow and spear," admitted Fabricius. He paused, aware that Quintus was hanging on his every word. "Strictly speaking, of course, it's not necessary for the cavalry, but I suppose a little instruction in the use of the gladius wouldn't go amiss."

Quintus' grin stretched from ear to ear. "Thank you, Father." He raised a hand to his mouth. "Mother! Aurelia! Did you hear that? I am to become a swordsman."

"That's good news indeed." Coming from the depths of the litter, Atia's voice was muffled, but Quintus thought he detected a tinge of sadness in it.

Aurelia lifted the cloth and stuck her head outside. "How wonderful," she said, forcing a smile. Inside, she was consumed by jealousy.

"We'll start tomorrow," said Fabricius.

"Excellent!" Instantly, Quintus forgot both his mother and Aurelia's reactions. His head was full of images of him and Gaius serving in the cavalry, winning glory for themselves and Rome.

Despite his guilt over Suniaton, Hanno's spirits had also risen. While he had Agesandros to contend with, he was not destined to die as a gladiator. And, although he might not be able to take part, his people were about to take on Rome again, with Hannibal Barca to lead them. A man whom his father reckoned to be the finest leader Carthage had ever seen.

For the first time in days, a spark of hope lit in Hanno's heart.

———

One summer morning, word came from the port that Malchus and Sapho had landed. Bostar shouted with delight at the news. As he hurried through the streets of New Carthage, the city founded by Hasdrubal nine years before, he couldn't stop grinning. Catching a glimpse of the temple of Aesculapius, which stood on the large hill to the east of the walls, Bostar offered up a prayer of thanks to the god of medicine and his followers. If it hadn't been for the injury to his sword arm, sustained in overexcited training with naked blades, he would have already set out for Saguntum with the rest of the army. Instead, on the orders of Alete, his commanding officer, Bostar had had to stay behind. "I've seen too many wounds like that turn bad," Alete had muttered. "Remain here, in the care of the priests, and join us when you've recovered. Saguntum isn't going to fall in a day, or a month." At the time, Bostar had not been happy. Now, he was overjoyed.

It wasn't long until he'd reached the port, which looked out over the calm gulf beyond New Carthage. The city's location was second to none. Situated at the point of a natural, enclosed bay which was furthest from the Mediterranean, it was surrounded on all sides by water. To the east and south lay the sea, while to the north and west was a large, saltwater lagoon. The only connection with the mainland was a narrow, heavily fortified causeway, which made the city almost impregnable. It was no surprise that New Carthage had replaced Gades as the capital of Carthaginian Iberia.

Bostar sped past the ships nearest the quay. New arrivals would have to moor farther away. As always, the place was extremely busy. The vast majority of the army might have left with Hannibal, but troops and supplies were still coming in daily. Javelins clattered off each other as they were laid in piles, and stacks of freshly made helmets glinted in the sun. There were wax-sealed amphorae of olive oil and wine, rolls of cloth and bags of nails. Wooden crates of glazed crockery stood beside bulging bags of nuts. Gossiping sailors coiled ropes and swept the decks of their unloaded vessels. Fishermen who had been out since before dawn sweated as they hauled their catch on to the dock.

"Bostar!"

He craned his head, searching for his family among the dense forest of masts and rigging. Finally, Bostar spotted his father and Sapho on the deck of a trireme that was tied up two vessels from the quay. He vaulted on to the first craft's deck and made his way to meet them. "Welcome!"

A moment later, they had been reunited. Bostar was shocked by the change in both. They were different men since he'd last seen them. Cold. Hard-faced. Ruthless. He bowed to Malchus, trying not to let his surprise show. "Father. It is wonderful to see you at last."

Malchus' severe expression softened briefly. "Bostar. What happened to your arm?"

"It's a scratch, nothing more. A stupid mistake during training," he replied. "Lucky it happened, though, because it's the only reason I'm still here. I receive treatment daily at Aesculapius' temple." He turned to Sapho, and was surprised to see that his brother looked downright angry. Bostar's hopes for a reconciliation vanished. The rift caused by their argument over releasing Hanno and Suniaton was clearly still present. As if he didn't feel guilty enough, thought Bostar sadly. Instead of an embrace, he saluted. "Brother."

Stiffly, Sapho returned the gesture.

"How was your journey?"

"Pleasant enough," Malchus answered. "We saw no Roman triremes, which is a blessing." His face twisted with an unreadable emotion. "Enough of that. We have discovered what happened to Hanno."

Bostar blinked with shock. "What?"

"You heard," snapped Sapho. "He and Suni didn't drown."

Bostar's mouth opened. "How do you know?"

Malchus took over. "Because I never lost faith in Melqart, and because I had eyes and ears in the port, who looked and listened out day and night for any clues." He smiled sourly at Bostar's bafflement. "A couple of months ago, one of my spies struck gold. He overheard a conversation he thought might interest me. We took the men in for questioning."

Bostar was riveted by his father's story. Hearing that Hanno and Suniaton had been captured by pirates, he began to weep. Neither of the others did, which only increased his grief. His anguish grew deeper with the revelation of the pair's sale into slavery. *I thought it was a kind gesture to let them go fishing. How wrong I was!* "That's a worse fate than drowning. They could have been taken anywhere. Bought by anyone."

"I know," Sapho snarled. "They were sold in Italy. Probably as gladiators."

Bostar's eyes filled with horror. "No!"

"Yes," Sapho shot back venomously, "and it's all your fault. If you had stopped them, Hanno would be standing here beside us today."

Bostar swelled with indignation. "That's rich coming from you!"

"Stop it!" Malchus' voice cut in like a whiplash. "Sapho, you and Bostar came to the decision together, did you not?"

Sapho glowered. "Yes, Father."

"So you are both responsible, just as I am for not being easier on him." Malchus ignored his sons' surprise at his admission of complicity. "Hanno is gone now, and fighting over his memory will serve none of us. I want no more of this. Our task now is to follow Hannibal, and take Saguntum. If we are lucky, the gods will grant us vengeance for Hanno afterward, in the fight against Rome. We must put everything else from our minds. Clear?"

"Yes, Father," the brothers mumbled, but neither looked at the other.

Bostar had to ask. "What did you do to the pirates?"

"They were castrated, and then their limbs were broken. Lastly, the scum were crucified," Malchus replied in a flat tone. Without another word, he climbed up on to the dock and headed for the city's center.

Sapho held back until they were alone. "It was too good for them. We should have gouged out their eyes too," he added viciously. Despite his apparent enthusiasm, the horror of what he'd seen still lingered in his eyes. Sapho had thought that the punishments would stop him feeling relief at Hanno's disappearance, but he'd been wrong. Seeing his younger brother again rammed that home. *I will be the favorite!* he thought savagely. "Just as well that you weren't there. You wouldn't have been up to any of it."

Despite the implication about his courage, Bostar retained his composure. He wasn't about to pull rank here, now. He was also uncertain what his own reaction might have been if he'd been placed in the same situation, handed the opportunity for revenge on those who had consigned Hanno to a certain death. Deep down, Bostar was glad that he had not been there. He doubted that either his father or Sapho would understand. Melqart, he prayed, I ask that my brother had a good death, and that you allow our family to put aside its differences. Bostar gained small consolation from the prayer, but it was all he had at that moment.

That, and a war to look forward to.

~~~

Checking that Agesandros was nowhere in sight, Hanno pulled the mules to a halt. The sweating beasts did not protest. It was nearly midday, and the temperature in the farmyard was scorching. Hanno jerked his head at one of the others who was threshing the wheat with him. "Water."

The Gaul made a reflex check for the Sicilian before putting down his pitchfork, and fetching the leather skin that lay by the storage shed. After drinking deeply, he replaced the stopper and tossed it through the air.

Hanno nodded his thanks. He swallowed a dozen mouthfuls, but was careful to leave plenty of the warm liquid for the others. He threw the bag to Cingetorix, another Gaul.

When he was done, Cingetorix wiped his lips with the back of his hand. "Gods, but it's hot." He spoke in Latin, which was the only language he and his countrymen had to communicate with Hanno. "Does it never rain in this cursed place? At home . . ." He wasn't allowed to finish.

"We know," growled Galba, a short man whose sunburned torso was covered with swirling tattoos. "It rains much more. Don't remind us."

"Not in Carthage," said Hanno. "It's as dry there as it is here."

Cingetorix scowled. "You must feel right at home then."

Despite himself, Hanno grinned. For perhaps two months after his arrival, the Gauls, with whom he shared sleeping quarters, had ignored him completely, speaking their own rapid-fire, guttural tongue at all times. He'd done his best to win them over, but it had made no difference. When it came, the change had been gradual. Hanno wasn't sure whether the extra, unwanted attention he received from Agesandros was what had prompted the tribesmen to extend the hand of friendship to him, but he no longer cared. The camaraderie they now shared was what made his existence bearable. That, and the news that Hannibal's iron grip on Saguntum had tightened. Apparently, the city would fall before the end of the year. Hanno prayed for the Carthaginian army's success every night. He also asked that one day he be granted an opportunity to kill Agesandros.

There were five of them in the yard altogether, continuing the work that had begun weeks previously with the harvest. It was late summer, and Hanno had grown used to life on the farm, and the immense labor expected of him every day. Things were made much harder by the heavy iron fetters that had been attached to his ankles, preventing him moving at any speed faster than a shuffle. Hanno had thought he was fit beforehand, but soon realized otherwise. Working twelve or more hours a day in summer heat, wearing manacles and fed barely enough, he was a taut, wiry shadow of his former self. His hair fell in long, shaggy tresses either side of his bearded face. The muscles on his torso and limbs now stood out like whipcord, and every part of exposed skin had darkened to a deep brown color. The Gauls looked no different. We're like wild beasts, Hanno thought. It was no wonder that they rarely saw Fabricius or his family.

Catching sight of Agesandros in the distance, he whistled the agreed signal to alert his companions. Swiftly, the skin was hurled back to its original position. Hanno dragged his mules into action again, pulling a heavy sledge over the harvested wheat, which had been laid right across the hard-packed dirt of the large farmyard. The Gauls began winnowing the threshed crop, tossing it into the air with their pitchforks so that the breeze could carry away the unwanted chaff. Their tasks were time-consuming and mind-numbing, but they had to be done before the wheat could be shoveled into the back of a wagon and deposited in the nearby storage sheds, which were built on brick stilts to prevent rodent access.

When Agesandros arrived a few moments later, he stood in the shade cast by the buildings and watched them silently. Uneasy, the five slaves worked hard, trying not to look in the Sicilian's direction. Soon a fresh coat of sweat coated their bodies.

Every time he turned the sledge, Hanno caught a glimpse of Agesandros, who was staring relentlessly at him. He was unsurprised when the overseer stalked in his direction.

"You're walking the mules too fast! Slow down, or half the wheat won't come off the stalks."

Hanno tugged on the nearest animal's lead rope. "Yes, sir," he mumbled.

"What's that? I didn't hear you," Agesandros snarled.

"At once, sir," Hanno repeated loudly.

"Stinking gugga. You're all the damn same. Useless!" Agesandros drew his whip.

Hanno steeled himself. It didn't seem to matter what he did. The mules' speed was just the latest example. His technique with the scythe and pitchfork, and how long he took to fetch water from the well had also recently been called into question. Everything he did was wrong, and the Sicilian's response was the same every time.

"You're all idle bastards." Lazily, Agesandros drew the long rawhide lash along the ground. "Motherless curs. Cowards. Vermin."

Hanno clicked his tongue at the mules, trying to block out the insults.

"Maybe you did have a mother," Agesandros admitted. He paused. "She must have been the most diseased whore in Carthage, though, to spawn something that looks like you."

Hanno's knuckles tightened with fury on the lead rope, and his shoulders bunched. From the corner of his eye, he saw Galba, who was behind the Sicilian, shaking his head in a gesture that said "No." Hanno forced himself to relax, but Agesandros had already seen his barb's effect.

"Didn't like that?" The Sicilian laughed, and raised his right arm. A heartbeat later, the whip came singing in to wrap itself across Hanno's back and under his right armpit. *Crack* went the tip as it opened the skin under his right nipple. The pain was intense. Hanno stiffened, and his pace decreased a fraction. It was all Agesandros needed. "Did I tell you to slow down?" he screamed. The whip was withdrawn, only to return. Hanno counted three, six, a dozen lashes. Although he did his utmost not to make a sound, eventually he couldn't help but moan.

The overseer smiled at this proof of Hanno's weakness, and ceased. His skill with the lash was such that Hanno was always left in extreme pain, but still able to work. "That should keep you moving at the right speed," he said.

"Yes, sir," Hanno muttered.

Satisfied, Agesandros gave the Gauls a hard stare and made as if to go.

Hanno did not relax. There was always more.

Sure enough, Agesandros turned. "You'll find your bed softer tonight," he confided.

Slowly, Hanno raised his gaze to meet that of the Sicilian.

"I've pissed in it for you."

Hanno did not speak. This was even worse than Agesandros spitting in his food, or halving his water ration. His anger, which had been reduced to a tiny glow in the center of his soul, was suddenly fanned to a white-hot blaze of outrage and indignation. With supreme effort, he kept his face blank. Now is not the time, he told himself. Wait.

Agesandros sneered. "Nothing to say?"

I won't give the bastard what he wants, thought Hanno furiously. "Thank you, sir."

Cheated, Agesandros snorted and walked away.

"Dirty fucker," whispered Galba when he was out of earshot. There was a rumble of agreement from the others. "You can have some of our bedding. We'll replace the wet stuff in the morning in case he checks up on you."

"Thanks," muttered Hanno absently. He was imagining running after the overseer and killing him. Thanks to Agesandros' expert needling, his warrior spirit had just reawakened. If he was to meet Suniaton in the next world, he wanted to be able to hold his head up high.

Things would come to a head soon, Hanno realized. But it didn't matter. Death would be better than this daily indignity.

———

Unusually, Quintus found himself at a loose end one fine morning. It had rained overnight, and the temperature was cooler than it had been for many months. Invigorated by the crisp, fresh air, he decided to make amends with Aurelia. Over the previous few months, much to her displeasure, Aurelia had been put in the care of a strict tutor, a sour-faced Greek slave loaned to Atia by Martialis. Rather than roaming the farm as she pleased, nowadays Aurelia had to sit demurely and learn Greek and mathematics. Atia continued to teach her how to weave and sew, and how to comport herself in polite company. Aurelia's protests fell on deaf ears. "It's time you learned to be a lady, and that's an end to it," Atia had snapped a number of times. "If you keep protesting, I'll give you a good whipping." Aurelia dutifully obeyed, but her stony silences at the dinner table since revealed her true opinion.

Fabricius knew better than to intervene in his wife's business, which left Quintus as Aurelia's only possible ally. However, he felt caught in the middle. While he felt guilty at his sister's plight, he also knew that an arranged marriage was the best thing for the family. All his attempts to lighten her mood failed, and so Quintus began to avoid her company when his day's work was done. Hurt, Aurelia spent more and more time in her room. It was a vicious circle from which there seemed no way out.

Meanwhile Quintus had been fully occupied with the work his father set him: paperwork, errands to Capua and regular lessons in the use of the gladius. Despite the time that had passed, Quintus still missed his sister keenly. He made a snap decision. It was time to make her an apology and move on. They did not have forever. Although Fabricius had found no suitable husband for Aurelia yet, he had begun the search during his visits to Rome.

Throwing some food into a pack, Quintus headed for the chamber off the courtyard where Aurelia took her lessons. Barely pausing to knock, he entered. The tutor glanced up, a small frown of disapproval creasing his brow. "Master Quintus. To what do we owe the pleasure?"

Quintus drew himself up to his full height. He was now three fingers' width taller than his father, which meant that he towered over most people. "I am taking Aurelia on a tour of the farm," he announced grandly.

The tutor looked taken aback. "Who sanctioned this?"

"I did," Quintus replied.

The tutor blew out his cheeks with displeasure. "Your parents—"

"Would approve wholeheartedly. I will explain everything to them later." Quintus made an airy gesture. "Come on," he said to Aurelia.

Her attempt to look angry faded away, and she jumped to her feet. Her writing tablet and stylus clattered unnoticed to the floor, drawing reproving clucks from the tutor. Yet the elderly Greek did not challenge Quintus further, and the siblings made their way outside unhindered.

Since killing the bear, Quintus' confidence had grown leaps and bounds. It felt good. He grinned at Aurelia.

Abruptly, she remembered their feud. "What's going on?" she cried. "I haven't seen you for weeks, and then suddenly you barge into my lessons unannounced."

He took Aurelia's hand. "I'm sorry for deserting you." To his horror, tears formed in her eyes, and Quintus realized how hurt she had been. "Nothing I said seemed to make any difference," he muttered. "I couldn't think of a way to help you. Forgive me."

She smiled through her grief. "I was at fault too, staying in a mood for days. But come, you're here now." A mischievous look stole across her face. "A tour of the farm? What have I not seen a thousand times before?"

"It was all I could think of," he replied, embarrassed. "Something to get you out of there."

Grinning, she nudged him. "It was enough to shut up the old fool. Thank you. I don't care where we go."

Arm in arm, they strolled along the path that led to the olive groves.

Hanno could see that Agesandros was in a bad mood. Any slave who so much as missed a step was getting a tongue-lashing. Ten of them were walking ahead of the Sicilian, carrying wicker baskets. Fortunately,

Hanno was near the front, which meant that Agesandros was paying him little attention. Their destination was the terraces containing plum trees, the fruit of which had lately, and urgently, become ripe. Picking the juicy crop would be an easy task compared to the work of the previous weeks, and Hanno was looking forward to it. Agesandros could only be so vigilant. Before the day was over, plenty of plums would have ended up in his grumbling belly.

A moment later, he cursed his optimism.

Galba, the man behind him, missed his footing and fell heavily to the ground. There was a grunt of pain, and Hanno turned to see a nasty gash on his comrade's right shin. It had been caused by a sharp piece of rock protruding from the earth. Blood welled in the wound, running down Galba's muscular calf and on to the dry soil, where it was soaked up at once.

"That's your day over," Hanno said in a low voice.

"I doubt Agesandros would agree," Galba replied, grimacing. "Help me up."

Hanno bent to obey, but it was too late.

Shoving past the other slaves, the Sicilian had reached them in a dozen strides. "What in the name of Hades is going on?"

"He fell and hurt his leg," Hanno began to explain.

Agesandros spun around, his eyes like chips of flint. "Let the piece of shit explain for himself," he hissed before turning back to Galba. "Well?"

"It's as he said, sir," said the Gaul carefully. "I tripped and landed on this rock."

"You did it deliberately, to get out of work for a few days," Agesandros snarled.

"No, sir."

"Liar!" The Sicilian tugged free his whip and began belaboring Galba.

Hanno's fury overflowed at last. "Leave him alone," he shouted. "He didn't do anything."

Agesandros delivered several more strokes and a hefty kick before he paused. Nostrils flaring, he glared at Hanno. "What did you say?"

"Picking plums is an easy job. Why would he try and get out of it?" he growled. "The man tripped. That's it."

The Sicilian's eyes opened wide with disbelief and rage. "You dare to tell me what to do? You piece of maggot-blown filth!"

Hanno would have given anything for a sword in that instant. He had nothing, though, but his anger. In the rush of adrenaline, it felt enough. "Is that what I am?" he spat back. "Well, you're nothing but low-born Sicilian scum! Even if my feet were covered in shit, I wouldn't wipe them on you."

Something inside Agesandros snapped. Raising his whip, he smashed the metal-tipped butt into Hanno's face.

There was a loud crunch and Hanno felt the cartilage in his nose break. Half blinded by the intense pain, he reeled backward, raising his hands protectively against the blow he knew would follow. He had no opportunity to pick up a rock, anything to defend himself. Agesandros was on him like a lion on its prey. Down came the whip across Hanno's shoulders, its tip licking around to snap into the flesh of his back. It whirled away but came singing back a heartbeat later, lacing cut after cut across his bare torso. He backed away, but the laughing Sicilian followed. When Hanno stumbled on a tree root, Agesandros shoved him in the chest, sending him sprawling. Winded, he could do nothing as the other loomed over him, his face twisted in triumph. A mighty kick in the chest followed, and the ribs broken by Varsaco cracked for the second time. The pain was unbearable and, hating himself, Hanno screamed. Worse was to follow. The beating went on until he was barely conscious. Finally, Agesandros rolled him on to his back. "Look at me," he ordered. Prompted by more kicks, Hanno managed to open his eyes. The moment he did, the Sicilian lifted his right leg high, revealing the hobnailed sole of his sandal. "This is for all my comrades," he muttered. "And my family."

Hanno had no idea what Agesandros was talking about. The bastard is going to kill me, he thought dazedly. Strangely, he didn't really care. At least his suffering would be over. He felt a numbing sense of sorrow that he would never see his family again. There would be no opportunity to apologize to his father either. Let it be so. Resigned, Hanno closed his eyes and waited for Agesandros to end it.

The blow never fell.

Instead, a commanding voice shouted, "Agesandros! Stop!"

Initially, Hanno didn't grasp what was going on, but when the order was repeated, and he sensed the Sicilian back away, the realization sank in. Someone had intervened. Who? He lay back on the hard ground, unable to do anything more than draw shallow breaths. Each movement of his rib cage stabbed knives of pain through every part of his being. It was the only thing that kept him from lapsing into unconsciousness. He was aware of Agesandros throwing hate-filled glances in his direction, but the Sicilian did nothing further to him.

A heartbeat later, Quintus and Aurelia, Fabricius' children, appeared at the edge of Hanno's vision. Outrage filled both their faces.

"What have you done?" Aurelia cried, dropping to her knees by Hanno's side. Although the bloodied Carthaginian was almost unrecognizable, her stomach still fluttered at the sight of him.

Hanno tried to smile at her. After Agesandros' cruel features, she resembled a nymph or other suchlike creature.

"Well?" Quintus' voice was stony. "Explain yourself."

"Your father leaves the running of the farm, and the care of the slaves, to me," Agesandros blustered. "That's the way it has been since before you were born."

"And if you killed a slave? What would he say then?" Aurelia challenged.

Agesandros was taken aback. "Come now," he said in a placating manner. "I was administering a beating, nothing more."

Quintus' laugh was derisory. "You were about to stamp on his head. On this rocky ground, a blow like that could stave a man's skull in."

Agesandros did not reply.

"Couldn't it?" Quintus demanded. His fury at the Sicilian, who had looked intent on murder, had doubled when he realized the victim's identity. Any residual awe he felt toward Agesandros had evaporated. "Answer me, by all the gods."

"I suppose so," Agesandros admitted sullenly.

"Was that your intention?" Aurelia demanded.

The Sicilian glanced at Hanno. "No," he said, folding his arms across his chest. "My temper got the better of me, that's all."

Liar, thought Hanno. Above him, Aurelia's face twisted with disbelief, reinforcing his conviction.

Quintus could also see that Agesandros was lying, but to accuse him further would bring the situation into completely uncharted waters. He didn't feel quite that confident. "How did it happen?"

Agesandros indicated Galba. "That slave fell deliberately and injured his leg. He was trying to get off work. It's an old trick, and I saw through it at once. I laid a few blows into the dog to teach him a lesson, and the gugga told me to stop, that it had been a genuine accident." He snorted. "Such defiance cannot be tolerated. He needed to be taught the error of his ways on the spot."

Quintus looked down at Hanno. "I think you succeeded," he said sarcastically. "He's halfway to Hades."

One corner of Agesandros' mouth tugged upward.

The only one to see it was Hanno. *Agesandros wants me dead. Why?*

It was the last coherent thought he had.

Quintus' confidence was bolstered by his success over Agesandros. Rather than let the injured Hanno be carried back to the villa like a sack of grain as the Sicilian wanted, he insisted that a litter be fetched. Galba could limp alongside. Scowling, Agesandros could do little but obey his command, sending a slave off at the run. The overseer watched with a surly expression as, using a strip of cloth, Aurelia cleaned the worst of the blood from Hanno's face. Tears poured down her cheeks, but she did not make a sound. She would not give Agesandros the satisfaction.

A short time later, when Hanno had been carefully transferred into the litter, she finally stood. A mixture of blood and dust covered the lower half of her dress, from where she had knelt in the dirt. Though reddened, her eyes were full of anger, and her face was set. "If he dies, I will see that Father makes you pay," she said. "I swear it."

Agesandros tried to laugh it off. "It takes more than that to kill a gugga," he declared.

Aurelia glared at him, afraid and yet unafraid.

"Come," said Quintus, gently leading her away. Agesandros made to follow, but Quintus had had enough. "Go about your business," he barked. "We will care for the two slaves."

They installed Hanno on blankets and a straw mattress in an empty stable off the farmyard, where he lay as still as a corpse. Quintus was concerned by his pale face. If the Carthaginian died, his father would be severely out of pocket, so he ordered hot water to be fetched from the kitchen, along with strips of linen and a flask of *acetum*, or vinegar. When they arrived, he was surprised by Aurelia's reaction. She would suffer no other to clean the Carthaginian's wounds. Meanwhile Elira treated Galba, with Quintus watching appreciatively. The Illyrian's medical knowledge was good, courtesy of her upbringing. As she'd told Quintus, her mother had been the woman to whom everyone in the tribe came with their ailments. First she washed the wound with plenty of hot water. Then, ignoring Galba's hisses of discomfort, she sluiced the area with *acetum* before patting it dry and applying a dressing. "Two days' rest, and light duties for a week," Quintus said when she was done. "I'll make sure Agesandros knows."

Muttering his gratitude, the Gaul shuffled off.

There was a moan from behind him, and Quintus turned. Hanno's face twisted briefly at whatever Aurelia was doing, before relaxing again. "He's alive," he said with relief.

"No thanks to Agesandros," Aurelia shot back vehemently. "Imagine if we hadn't come along! He might still die." Her voice tailed off as she bit back a sob.

Quintus patted her shoulder, wondering why she was so upset. Hanno was only a slave, after all.

Elira moved to the bed. "Let me take a look at him," she said.

To Quintus' surprise, Aurelia moved aside. They watched in silence as the Illyrian ran expert hands over Hanno's battered body, gently probing here and there. "I can find no head injury apart from his broken nose," she said eventually. "He has three cracked ribs, and all these flesh wounds from the whip." She pointed to his prominent rib cage and concave belly. "Someone hasn't been feeding him enough either. He's strong, though. Some good nursing and decent food, and he could be up and about inside a week."

"Jupiter be thanked," Aurelia cried.

Quintus smiled his own relief and went in search of Fabricius. Agesandros' cruelty must be reported at once. He suspected that his father would not seriously punish the Sicilian, who, no doubt, would deny everything if challenged. He could hear Fabricius' voice already. Discipline was part of the overseer's remit, and no slave had the right to question his authority as Hanno had. This was the first time that Agesandros had gone overboard. In Fabricius' eyes, it would be a one-off occurrence. Quintus knew what he had seen, however. His jaw hardened.

Agesandros would have to be watched from now on.

—⁓—

Hanno was woken by the pain radiating from his ribs each time he took a breath. The dull throbbing from his face reminded him of his broken nose. He lifted his hands, feeling the heavy strapping that circled his chest. The manacles around his ankles had been removed. This could hardly be Agesandros' work. Quintus must have insisted I be treated, Hanno thought. His surprise grew when he opened his eyes. Instead of the damp straw in his miserable cell, he was lying on blankets in an empty stable. Occasional whinnies told him that there were horses nearby. He eyed the stool alongside him. Someone had been keeping vigil.

A shadow fell across the threshold and Hanno looked up to see Elira carrying a clay jug and two beakers.

Her face lit up. "You're awake!"

He nodded slowly, drinking her beauty in.

She rushed to his side. "How do you feel?"

"Sore all over."

She reached down and lifted a gourd from the floor. "Drink some of this."

"What is it?" he asked suspiciously.

Elira smiled. "A dilute solution of *papaverum*." Seeing his confusion, she explained. "It will dull the pain."

He was too weak to argue. Taking the gourd, Hanno took a deep swallow of the painkilling draft, screwing up his face at the bitter taste of the liquid within.

"It won't take long to work," Elira murmured reassuringly. "Then you can sleep some more."

Abruptly, the Sicilian came to mind, and he tried to sit up. The small effort felt exhausting. "What about Agesandros?"

"Don't worry. Fabricius has seen your injuries, and warned him to leave you alone. The gods must have been in good humor, because he also agreed to let me care for you. It took a bit of persuasion, but Aurelia won him over," Elira said. She raised a hand to his sweating face. "Look, you are as weak as a kitten," she scolded. "Lie down."

Hanno obeyed. Why would Aurelia care what happened to him? he wondered. Feeling the papaverum begin to take effect, he closed his eyes. It was a huge relief to know that one of his owner's children was on his side, but Hanno doubted that Aurelia could shield him from Agesandros' ill will. She was only a girl. Still, he thought wearily, his situation was better now than it had been. Perhaps the gods were showing him favor once more? Keeping that idea uppermost, Hanno relaxed and let sleep take him.

VII

A GRADUAL SHIFT

Hanno did little more than sleep and eat for the next three days. Under Elira's approving eyes, he devoured plate after plate of food from the kitchen. His strength returned, and the pain of his injuries subsided. Soon he insisted that the strapping around his chest be removed, complaining that it was restricting his breathing. By the fourth day, he felt alert enough to venture outside. Fear stopped him, however. "Where's Agesandros?"

Elira's full lips flattened. "The whoreson is in Capua, thankfully."

Relieved, Hanno shuffled outside. The yard was empty. All the slaves were at work in the fields. They sat down together in the sunshine and rested their backs against the cool stone of the stable walls. Hanno didn't mind that there was no one around. It meant he could be alone with Elira, whose physical attractions were daily becoming more obvious. As the ache in his groin constantly told him, he hadn't had a woman for many months. Yet merely to entertain such thoughts was dangerous. Even if Elira was willing, slaves were forbidden from having sexual relations with each other. What's more, Hanno had seen the way she and

Quintus looked at one another. Stay well away, he told himself sternly. Screwing the master's son's favorite slave would not be clever. There was a simpler way of satisfying himself. Less enjoyable, but far safer.

He needed something to take his mind off sex. "How did you come to be a slave?"

Elira's surprise was instantly replaced by sadness. "That's the first time anyone has asked me such a question."

"I guess it's because we all have the same miserable story," said Hanno gently. He raised his eyebrows in an indication that she should continue.

Elira's eyes took on a distant look. "I grew up in a little village by the sea in Illyricum. Most people were fishermen or farmers. It was a peaceful place. Until the day that the pirates came. I was nine years old." Her face darkened with anger, and sorrow. "The men fought hard, but they weren't warriors. My father and my older brother, they . . ." Her voice wobbled for a moment. "They were killed. But what happened to Mother was just as bad." Tears formed in her eyes.

Horrified, Hanno reached out to squeeze Elira's hand. "I'm sorry," he whispered.

She nodded, and the movement made the tears spill down her cheeks. "We were taken to their ships. They sailed to Italy and sold us there. I haven't seen Mother or my sisters since."

As Elira wept, Hanno cursed himself for opening his mouth. Yet the Illyrian's sorrow made her even more attractive. It was hard not to imagine wrapping her in his arms to comfort her. He was therefore relieved to see Aurelia approaching from the direction of the villa. Nudging Elira, he scrambled to his feet. The Illyrian had barely enough time to pull her hair down around her face and wipe away her tears.

Aurelia felt a tinge of jealousy at seeing Elira so close to Hanno. "You're up and about!" she said tartly.

He bobbed his head. "Yes."

"How do you feel?"

Hanno touched his ribs. "Much better than I did a few days ago, thank you."

Aurelia's sympathy surged back at the sight of Hanno wincing. "It's Elira you should be grateful to. She's a marvel."

"She is," agreed Hanno, giving Elira a slanted grin.

The Illyrian blushed. "Julius will be wondering where I am," she muttered, before hurrying off.

Aurelia's annoyance returned, but, irritated with herself for even feeling it, she dismissed it at once. "You're Carthaginian, aren't you?"

"Yes," Hanno replied warily. He'd never yet had a proper conversation with Fabricius or any of his family. In his mind, they were still very much the enemy.

"What's Carthage like?"

He couldn't help himself. "It's huge. Perhaps a quarter of a million people live there."

Despite herself, Aurelia's eyes widened. "But that's far bigger than Rome!"

Hanno had the sense not to utter the sarcastic response that rose to his lips. "Indeed." Aurelia seemed interested, so he launched into a description of his city, picturing it in his mind's eye as he did. Realizing eventually that he had lost the run of himself, Hanno fell silent.

"It sounds beautiful," Aurelia admitted. "And you looked so happy while you were talking."

Feeling utterly homesick, Hanno stared at the ground.

"It's not surprising, I suppose," said Aurelia kindly. Looking curious, she tipped her head to one side. "I remember that you speak Greek as well as Latin. In Italy, only nobles learn that tongue. It must be much the same in Carthage. How did someone so well educated end up as a slave?"

Balefully, Hanno lifted his gaze to hers. "I forgot to ask a blessing of our most powerful goddess before I went on a fishing trip with my friend." He saw her inquiring expression. "Suni, the one you saw in Capua. After catching plenty of tunny, we drank some wine and fell asleep. A sudden storm took us far out to sea. Somehow, we survived the night, but the next day a pirate ship found us. We were sold in Neapolis, and taken to Capua to be sold as gladiators. Instead I was bought by your brother." Hanno hardened his voice. "Who knows what happened to my friend, though?" He was pleased to see her flinch.

Annoyed, Aurelia recovered quickly. Handsome or not, he's still a slave, she thought. "Everyone at the slave market has a sad story. That doesn't mean that we can buy them all. Consider yourself lucky," she snapped.

Hanno bowed his head. *She might be young, but she's got spirit.*

An awkward silence fell.

It was broken by Atia's voice. "Aurelia!"

Aurelia's face took on a hunted look. "I'm in the yard, Mother."

Atia appeared a moment later. She was wearing a simple linen stola and elegant leather sandals. "What are you doing here? We were supposed to be practicing the lyre." Her gaze passed over Hanno. "Isn't this the slave whom Agesandros beat? The Carthaginian?"

"Yes, Mother." A touch of color appeared in Aurelia's cheeks. "I was checking with Elira that his recovery was satisfactory."

"I see. It's good that you are taking an interest in things like that. It's all part of running the household." Atia eyed Hanno with more interest. "That broken nose isn't healed, but otherwise he looks fine."

Hanno shifted from foot to foot, uncomfortable with being talked about as if he weren't present.

Aurelia became a little flustered. "I suppose . . . Elira didn't say when he'd be ready to return to work."

"Well?" Atia demanded. "Are you sufficiently recovered?"

Hanno couldn't exactly refuse. "Yes, mistress," he murmured.

"He's got three cracked ribs," Aurelia protested.

"That's no reason to stop him working in the kitchen," Atia replied. She stared at Hanno. "Is it?"

It would be far less effort than toiling in the fields, thought Hanno. He bowed his head. "No, mistress."

Atia nodded. "Good. Follow us back to the house. Julius will have plenty for you to do."

Secretly delighted, Aurelia followed her mother. She would no longer need an excuse to come and see Hanno.

"Quintus wants us to watch him sparring with your father," said Atia in a proud yet wistful tone.

"Oh." Aurelia managed to convey all of her disapproval and jealousy in one word.

Atia turned. "Enough of that attitude! Would you rather spend the time playing the lyre or talking Greek with your tutor?"

"No, Mother," Aurelia muttered furiously.

"Fine." Atia's frown eased. "Come on then."

Hanno was fascinated. All the girls he'd ever met were perfectly happy to stick with womanly pursuits. Aurelia was made from a different mold.

They entered the house via a small postern gate. It was incorporated into one of the two large timber doors that formed the entrance. Hanno looked around keenly. It was the first time he had been in the villa proper. The simple elegance of its design did not fail to impress him. Carthaginian homes were typically built for functionality, rather than beauty. Elegant mosaics and colorful wall paintings were the exception, not the rule.

In the courtyard, they found Fabricius and Quintus moving carefully around each other. Both were clad in simple belted tunics, and carrying wooden swords and round cavalry shields.

Seeing Atia and Aurelia, they paused.

Fabricius raised his weapon in salute to Atia, who smiled.

"Finally," said Quintus drolly to his sister.

Aurelia did her best to look enthusiastic. This *is* better than music lessons, she told herself. "I'm here now."

Quintus looked to his father. "Ready?"

"When you are."

The two stepped closer, raising their swords. The points met with a dull clunk. Both remained still for a moment, trying to gauge when the other would move.

Atia clapped her hands. "Fetch some fruit juice," she ordered Hanno. She pointed. "The kitchen is over there."

He tore his eyes away from the contest. "Yes, mistress." Adopting the preferred slave walk, slow and measured, Hanno did as he was told. Happily, he was able to continue observing.

Quintus was first to act. He swept his gladius down, carrying his father's blade toward the ground. In the same movement, he drew back his right arm and thrust forward, straight at the other's chest. Fabricius quickly met the attack with his shield. With a great heave, he lifted it in the air. Quintus' sword was also carried up by the move, which exposed his right armpit. Knowing that his father would strike at his weak point, Quintus desperately twisted to the left and retreated several steps. Fabricius was on him like a striking snake. Despite his father's ferocity, Quintus managed to hold off the assault. "Not bad," Fabricius said at length, pulling back. They paused to catch their breath before renewing the engagement.

To Quintus' delight, he drew first blood. His success came thanks to an unexpected shoulder charge at his father that enabled him to thrust his gladius around their shields. The point snagged in the left side of Fabricius' tunic. Despite the fact that the blade was wooden, it tore a great hole in the fabric, raked along his ribs and broke the skin. He bellowed in pain, and staggered backward. Knowing that his father would now find it agonizing to lift his sword, Quintus prepared to follow through and win the bout.

"Are you all right?" Aurelia cried.

Fabricius did not answer. "Come on," he growled at Quintus. "Think you can finish me?"

Stung, Quintus lifted his gladius and ran forward. When he was only a step away, he feinted to the right and then to the left. A backward slash at Fabricius' head followed, and his father's response was barely enough to prevent the blow from landing. Quintus crowed with triumph and pushed on, keen to press home his advantage. Surprising him utterly, Fabricius backed away so fast that Quintus overbalanced and fell. As he landed, Fabricius spun round and placed his sword tip at the base of Quintus' neck. "Dead meat," he said calmly.

Furious and embarrassed, Quintus got to his feet. Catching sight of Hanno, he scowled. "What are you looking at?" he yelled. "Get about your business!"

Ducking his head to conceal his own anger, Hanno headed for the kitchen.

"Don't take it out on a slave," cried Aurelia. "It's not his fault."

Quintus glared at his sister.

"Calm down," said Fabricius. "You were undone because you were overconfident."

Now Quintus' face went beetroot.

"You did well until then," reassured his father. In the background, Atia was nodding in agreement. "If you'd just taken your time, I would have had no chance." He lifted his left arm and showed Quintus the long bloody graze along the side of his chest. "Even a scratch like this slows a man right down. Remember that."

Pleased, Quintus smiled. "I will, Father."

At that moment, Hanno emerged with a polished bronze tray. Perched upon it were a fine glass jug and four cups of the same style. Seeing him, Quintus beckoned peremptorily. "Get over here! I'm thirsty."

Arrogant little shit, thought Hanno as he hurried to obey.

Fabricius waited until the whole family had a drink before raising his cup. "A toast! To Mars, the god of war. That his shield always remains over us both."

Hanno blocked out the words as best he could and prayed silently to his own martial god. Baal Saphon, guide Hannibal's army to victory over Saguntum. And Rome.

Gulping down his juice, Fabricius indicated that Hanno should pour him a refill. He frowned in recognition. "Fully recovered?"

"Very nearly, master," Hanno replied.

"Good."

"I was impressed to find Aurelia checking up on his progress," Atia added. "He's not up to field work yet, but I didn't see any reason why Julius couldn't put him to use in the kitchen."

"Fair enough. He's ready to go back to his cell then." Aurelia's mouth opened in protest, and Fabricius raised a hand. "He's not a horse," he said sternly. "That stable is needed. His manacles should be replaced too." Seeing the apprehension in Hanno's face, Fabricius' face softened. "Obey orders, and Agesandros will not lay a hand on you. You have my word on that."

Hanno muttered his thanks, but his mind was racing. Despite Fabricius' reassurance, his troubles were far from over. Agesandros would undoubtedly be holding a grudge against him. He would constantly have to be on his guard. Without thinking, Hanno remained where he was, close to the family.

An instant later, Quintus turned and their eyes met. I'd love to take you on in a sword fight, thought Hanno. Teach you a lesson. Almost as if he understood, Quintus' top lip curled. "What are you still doing here? Get back to the kitchen."

Hanno quickly retreated. He was grateful for the smile Aurelia threw in his direction.

The conversation resumed behind him.

"Can we practice again tomorrow, Father?" Quintus' voice was eager.

"The enthusiasm of youth!" Touching his side, Fabricius grimaced. "I doubt that my ribs would permit it. But I can't anyway."

"Why not?" Quintus cried.

"I must travel to Rome. The Senate is meeting to consider how it will respond when Saguntum falls. I want to hear for myself what they plan."

War, thought Hanno fervently. I hope they decide on war. Because that's what they're going to get in any case.

Quintus was crestfallen, but he didn't argue further. "How long will you be gone?"

"At least ten days. Maybe more. It depends on the success of my other mission," Fabricius replied. He fixed Aurelia with his gray eyes. "To find a suitable husband for you."

Aurelia paled, but she did not look away. "I see. I'm not to be allowed to fall in love as you and Mother did, then?"

"You'll do as you're damn well told!" Fabricius snapped.

Atia flushed and looked down.

"Never mind, children," intervened Atia in a brisk tone. "It will be an opportunity for both of you to catch up on your studies. Quintus, the tutor reports that your grasp of geometry is not what it should be."

Quintus groaned.

Atia turned to Aurelia. "Don't think that you're going to escape either."

Even as she scowled, Aurelia was struck by an idea. Her heart leaped at its brilliance. If she could pull it off, neither of them would care about extra lessons. And it would help her not to think about her father's quest.

Like all the best plans, Aurelia's was simple. She wasn't sure if Quintus would go along with it, however, so she said nothing until their father had been gone for several days. By then, her brother's frustration at not being able to do any weapons training was reaching new highs. Aurelia picked her moment carefully, waiting until her mother was occupied with the household accounts. Quintus' morning lessons had ended a short time before, and she found him pacing around the fountain in the center of the courtyard, angrily scuffing his sandals along the mosaic.

"What's wrong?"

He glanced at her, scowling. "Nothing, apart from the fact that I've had to spend two hours trying to calculate the volume of a cylinder. It's impossible! And it's not as if I'll ever use the method again. Typical bloody Greeks for discovering how to work out something so stupid in the first place."

Aurelia made a sympathetic noise. She wasn't fond of the subject either. "I was wondering . . ." she began. Deliberately, she did not continue.

"What?" Quintus demanded.

"Oh, it's nothing," she replied. "Just a silly idea."

The first trace of interest crossed Quintus' face. "Tell me."

"You've been complaining a lot about Father being away."

He gave an irritable nod. "Yes, because I can't practice my swordplay."

Aurelia smiled impishly. "There might be a way around that."

Quintus' look was pitying. "Riding to Capua and back to train with Gaius each day isn't an option. It would take far too long."

"That's not what I've got in mind." Aurelia found herself hesitating. Say it! she thought. You've got nothing to lose. "I could be your sparring partner."

"Eh?" His eyebrows rose in shock. "But you've never used a sword before."

"I learn fast," Aurelia shot back. "You said so yourself when you taught me to use a sling." She held her breath, praying that he would agree.

A slow grin spread across Quintus' face. "We could go 'for a walk' up to the woods, to the place where I train."

"That's exactly what I was thinking," cried Aurelia delightedly. "Mother doesn't mind what we do as long as all of our homework is done, and our duties are completed."

A frown creased his brow. "What's in it for you? You'll never be able to do it again once you're . . ." He gave her a guilty look.

"That's precisely why," Aurelia said fervently. "I'll be married off within the year, most likely. Then I'll have to resign myself to child-minding and running a household for the rest of my life. What an opportunity to forget that fate!"

"Mother will kill you if she finds out," Quintus warned.

Aurelia's eyes flashed. "I'll face that day if, or when, it comes."

Quintus saw his sister's resolve, and nodded. In truth, he felt glad to be able to help her, even if it would only be a temporary affair. He wouldn't want the future she'd painted. "Very well."

Aurelia stepped in to kiss his cheek. "Thank you. It means a lot to me."

The moment that their tasks were done the following day, they met up in the atrium. Quintus slung an old sack over his shoulder; within were two of the wooden gladii, as well as a few snares. The latter could be pulled out in the event of any awkward questions from their mother. "Ready?" Aurelia whispered excitedly.

He nodded.

They had gone a dozen steps when Atia appeared from the tablinum, a roll of parchment in one hand. She threw them a curious glance. "Where are you two going?"

"For a walk," Aurelia replied lightly. She lifted the wicker basket in her right hand. "I thought you might like some mushrooms."

"I need to set some traps as well," Quintus added. He tapped his bow. "This is in case I see a deer."

"Make sure you're back well before dark." Atia had taken a few steps when she turned. "Actually, why don't you take the new slave with you? Hanno, I think he's called. While he's working in the kitchen, he might as well learn about foraging and catching game."

"That's a good idea," said Aurelia, her face lighting up. Despite the fact that Hanno now worked in the house, she had found there was still hardly ever a chance to speak to him.

"Is it?" asked Quintus, looking irritated. "He might run away."

Atia laughed. "With the manacles he's wearing? I don't think so. Besides, you can both practice your Greek with him. You'll all be learning something."

"Yes, Mother," Quintus muttered unenthusiastically.

With an absent smile, Atia left them to it.

Aurelia poked Quintus. "She didn't suspect a thing!"

Quintus grimaced. "No, but we've got to take the Carthaginian with us."

"So what? He can carry the sack."

"I suppose," Quintus admitted. "Go and get him then. Let's not hang around."

A short time later, they were following one of the narrow tracks that led through the fields to the edge of the farm. Shuffling because of his manacles, a bemused Hanno took up the rear. Aurelia's offer of a trip into the woods had come as a welcome surprise. Although his job in the kitchen kept him safe from Agesandros, Hanno had begun to miss being in the open air. He longed for the companionship of Galba, Cingetorix and the other Gauls too. Julius and the rest of the domestic slaves were pleasant, but they were soft, and did little but gossip with each other. He wouldn't see the Gauls today, but Hanno liked the sound of picking mushrooms, an activity that was unknown in Carthage, and of hunting, something he enjoyed greatly. Today he would have no time to brood.

It was when the two young Romans stopped in a large clearing that Hanno started to feel suspicious. The mushrooms that Aurelia had shown him on the way up had grown in shady areas under fallen trees, and only a fool would lay a snare or try waiting for a deer in the middle of an open space.

Quintus stalked over. "Give me the sack," he ordered.

Hanno obeyed. A moment later, he was most surprised to see two wooden swords clattering on to the soft earth. Gods, but how long it had been since he'd held a weapon! He still hadn't fully realized what was going on when Quintus tossed one of the gladii to Aurelia.

"These hurt like Hades if you land a blow, but they're not likely to spill your guts on the ground."

Aurelia moved the blade to and fro once or twice. "It feels very unwieldy."

"It's double the weight of a real sword, to build up your fitness." Quintus saw her frown. "We don't have to do this."

"Yes, we do," she retorted. "Show me how to hold the damn thing properly."

Smiling, Quintus obeyed, gripping her wrist to move it slowly through the air. "As you know, it was made to cut and thrust. But it can slash too, which is how we use it in the cavalry."

"Shouldn't we have shields too?"

He laughed. "Of course. But I think Mother might have realized what we were up to. Give me a few days. I'll take them up here on my own one evening, when she's taking her bath."

Quintus began to teach Aurelia how to thrust the gladius forward. "Keep your feet close together as you move. It's important not to over-extend yourself."

After a while, Hanno began to grow bored. He would have loved to take Aurelia's place, but that wasn't going to happen. He glanced at his nearly empty basket, and coughed to get the young Romans' attention.

Quintus turned, a frown creasing his brow. "What?"

"We didn't find many mushrooms on the way here. Should I go and pick some more?"

Quintus nodded in surprise. "Very well. You're not to go far. And don't get any ideas about running away."

Aurelia looked more grateful. "Thank you."

Hanno left them to it. He cast about the edge of the clearing, but found no mushrooms. Unnoticed by Quintus and Aurelia, he moved off into the undergrowth. The sounds of their voices became muffled and then were lost. Sunlight pierced the dense canopy above, lighting up irregular patches of the forest floor. Nonetheless, the air felt heavy. Hanno's presence made birds flit from branch to branch, sounding their alarm calls. Soon he felt as if he was the only person in the world. He felt free. Right on cue, the manacles around his ankles clanked, and reality struck. Hanno cursed. Even if he tried to run, he wouldn't get far. The moment Agesandros was alerted, he'd get out the hunting dogs. They'd track him down in no time. And of course there was the debt he owed Quintus. Sighing, Hanno got back to his task.

His luck was in. A quarter of an hour later, he returned to the clearing with a full basket.

Aurelia saw him first. "Well done!" she cried, rushing over. "Those slender mushrooms with the flat caps are delicious when fried. You'll have to try some later."

Hanno's lips turned up. "Thank you."

Quintus glanced at the basket, but didn't comment. "Race you to the stream," he said to Aurelia. "We can cool off before going back."

With a giggle, she took off toward the far side of the clearing, from where the babble of running water could be heard.

"Hey!" Quintus shouted. "That's cheating!" Aurelia didn't reply, and he sprinted after her.

Hanno looked after them wistfully, remembering similar good times with Suniaton. An instant later, though, his gaze fell on the two wooden swords, which had been left on the ground nearby. Quintus' bow and quiver lay alongside. Without thinking, Hanno walked over and picked up a gladius. As Aurelia had said, it was awkward to hold, but Hanno didn't care. Gripping the hilt tightly, he thrust it to and fro. It was the most natural thing to imagine sticking it in Agesandros' belly.

"What are you doing?"

Hanno almost jumped out of his skin. He turned to find a dripping wet Quintus regarding him with extreme suspicion. "Nothing," he muttered.

"Slaves aren't allowed to use bladed weapons. Drop it!"

With great reluctance, Hanno let the gladius fall.

Quintus picked it up. "No doubt you were thinking about murdering us all in our beds," he said in a hard voice.

"I'd never do that," Hanno protested. Agesandros is a different matter of course, he thought. "I owe you my life twice over. That's something I will never forget."

Quintus was nonplussed. "I only bought you in the first place because Agesandros didn't want me to. As for when he was beating you, well, injuring a slave badly is a waste of money."

"That's as may be," Hanno muttered. "But if it weren't for you, I'd surely be dead by now."

Quintus shrugged. "Don't pin your hopes on paying me back. There aren't too many dangers around here!" He pointed at his sack. "Pick that up. I've spotted a good place on the bank to set a snare."

Stooping so that Quintus didn't see his scowl, Hanno obeyed. Curse him and his arrogance, he thought. I should just run away. But his pride wouldn't let him. A debt was a debt.

–––

Quintus and Aurelia managed to fit in three more trips to the clearing before Fabricius' return a week later. Atia had been so pleased by the basket of mushrooms that Quintus insisted Hanno accompany him and his sister each time. Hanno was glad to obey. Aurelia was friendly, and Quintus' manner toward him had changed fractionally. He wasn't exactly warm, but his high-handed manner, which Hanno despised, was no longer so evident. Whether it was because he had revealed the debt that he owed to Quintus, Hanno could not tell.

Although Fabricius' homecoming meant that the secret trips stopped, Hanno was pleased to learn that his master was soon to return to Rome. Eavesdropping as he served food to the family, Hanno heard how the debates in the Senate about Hannibal were constant now, with some factions favoring negotiations with Carthage and others demanding an immediate declaration of war. "There's far more interest in that than the eligible daughter of a country noble," Fabricius revealed to Atia.

Aurelia was barely able to conceal her delight, but her mother pursed her lips. "Have you found no one suitable?"

"I've found plenty," Fabricius replied reassuringly. "I just need more time, that's all."

"I want to know the best candidates," said Atia. "I can write to those of their mothers who are living. Arrange a meeting."

Fabricius nodded. "Good idea."

Let it take forever, Aurelia prayed. In the meantime, I can practice with Quintus. It had been a joy to discover that handling a sword came naturally to her. She burned to train further, while she still could.

Her brother's reaction, however, was the opposite to hers. "How long will you be gone?" he asked glumly.

"I'm not sure. It could be weeks. I'll definitely be back for Saturnalia."

Quintus looked horrified. "That's months away!"

"It's not the end of the world," said Fabricius, clapping him on the shoulder. "You'll be starting your military training next spring anyway."

Quintus was about to protest further but Atia intervened. "Your father's business is far more important than your desire to train with a gladius. Be content that he is here now."

Reluctantly, Quintus held his silence.

Bending their heads together, their parents fell into a private conversation.

It was probably about her prospective husbands, thought Aurelia furiously. She kicked Quintus under the table and framed the words "We can go to the clearing more often" at him. When he raised his eyebrows, she repeated them and thrust an imaginary sword at him.

At last Quintus understood, and a happier expression replaced the sullen one.

Hanno hoped that Quintus and Aurelia would take him along too. Agesandros could not do a thing to him while he was with them. Moreover, he had come to enjoy the outings.

───※───

"Do you still think this is a good idea?" asked Atia when the children were gone.

Fabricius grimaced. "What do you mean?"

"You said yourself that no one suitable is interested in finding a bride at the moment."

"So?"

"Maybe we should leave it for six months or a year?"

His frown deepened. "Where's the benefit in that? Don't tell me that you're having second thoughts?"

"I—"

"You are!"

"Do you remember our reason for getting married, Fabricius?" she asked gently.

A guilty look stole on to his face. "Of course I do."

"Is it so surprising, then, that it's hard for me to think of forcing Aurelia into an arrangement against her will?"

"It's difficult for me too," he objected. "But you know why I'm doing it."

Atia sighed.

"I'm trying to better our family. I can't do that with a huge debt hanging over my head."

"You could always ask Martialis for help."

"I might owe thousands of didrachms to a moneylender in Capua, but I've still got my pride!" he retorted.

"Martialis wouldn't think any less of you."

"I don't care! I wouldn't ever be able to look him in the eye again."

"It's not as if you gambled the money away on chariot racing! You needed the money because of the terrible drought two years ago. There's no shame in telling him that we had no crops to sell."

"Martialis isn't a farmer," said Fabricius heavily. "He might understand if my problems were about property, but this . . ."

"You could try," Atia murmured. "He's your oldest comrade, after all."

"A friend is the worst possible person to borrow from. I'm not doing it." He fixed her with his stare. "If we don't want the farm to be repossessed in the next few years, the only way forward is to marry Aurelia into a wealthy family. That knowledge alone will keep the moneylender off our backs indefinitely."

"Maybe so, but it won't make the money appear from thin air."

"No, but with the gods' favor, I will win more recognition in this war than I did in the last. After it's over, I'll secure a local magistrate's job."

"And if you don't?"

Fabricius blinked. "It'll be down to Quintus. With the right patronage, he could easily reach the rank of tribune. The yearly pay that position brings in will make our debts seem like a drop in the ocean." He leaned in and kissed her confidently. "You see? I have it all worked out."

Atia didn't have the heart to protest any further. She couldn't make Fabricius go to Martialis, nor could she think of another strategy. She smiled bravely, trying not to think of an alternative, but entirely possible scenario.

What if Fabricius didn't come home from the war? What if Quintus never achieved the tribuneship?

Over the following weeks, it became the siblings' daily norm to go to the clearing. Pleased by the constant stream of mushrooms, hazelnuts, and the occasional deer brought down by Quintus' arrows, Atia did not protest. Because Aurelia had given Hanno the credit for their haul, he was allowed to accompany them. To Hanno's surprise, Aurelia's skill with the gladius was slowly improving, and Quintus had begun teaching her to use a shield. Not long after that, he brought two genuine swords with him. "These are just to give you an idea of what using the real thing feels like," he said, as he handed one to Aurelia. "I want no funny stuff."

Hanno eyed the long, waisted blade in Aurelia's hand with unabashed pleasure. It wasn't that different from the weapon he'd owned in Carthage.

Quintus saw his interest and frowned. "You know how to use one of these?"

Hanno jerked back to the present. "Yes," he muttered unwillingly.

"How?"

"My father used to train me." Hanno deliberately made no mention of his brothers.

"Is he a soldier?"

"He was," lied Hanno. The less Quintus knew, the better.

"Did he fight in Sicily?"

Hanno nodded reluctantly.

Quintus looked surprised. "So did mine. He spent years in the cavalry there. Father says that your people were worthy enemies, who only lacked a decent leader."

No longer, thought Hanno triumphantly. Hannibal Barca will change all that. With an effort, he shrugged at Quintus. "Maybe."

Quintus' mouth opened to ask another question.

"Let's practice!" interjected Aurelia.

To Hanno's relief, the moment passed. Quintus responded to his sister's demand, and the two began sparring gently with the gladii.

Hanno headed off to check their snares. Shortly afterward, and some distance from the clearing, he found the trail of a wild boar. He hurried back with the news as fast as his manacles would let him. Because of its rich flavor, boar meat was highly prized. The creatures were secretive too, and hard to find. An opportunity to kill one should not be passed up. Hanno's news immediately stopped Quintus practicing with Aurelia. Sheathing the gladii, he rolled them up in a blanket and stuffed them into his pack. "Come on!" he cried, sweeping up his bow.

Aurelia rushed after him. She was as keen as any to bring a boar back to the house.

Within a hundred paces, Hanno had fallen well behind. "I can't go any faster," he explained when the young Romans turned impatiently.

"We might as well give up now, then," said Quintus with a scowl. "Or you can just stay here." He had the grace to flush.

Despite this, Hanno clenched his fists. I found the damn trail, he thought. Not you.

There was a short, uncomfortable pause.

"I can help," Aurelia announced suddenly. From inside her dress she produced a small bunch of keys. Kneeling by Hanno's side, she tried several on one of his anklets before it fell apart.

"What do you think you're doing?" demanded Quintus.

Aurelia ignored him. Smiling broadly at Hanno, she opened the other. She couldn't help thinking how like the statue of a Greek athlete he looked.

Incredulous, Hanno lifted his feet one after another. "Baal Hammon's beard, that feels good."

Quintus stepped forward. "How in Hades did you get those keys?"

Aurelia swelled with pride. "You know how Agesandros likes to drink in the evenings. He's often snoring before *Vespera*. All I had to do was creep in and take an impression of each in wax, and get the smith to make them for me. I told him that they were for Father's chests, and gave him a few coins to make sure he told no one."

Quintus' eyes widened at his sister's daring, but he still wasn't happy. "Why did you do it?"

Aurelia wasn't going to admit the real reason, which was that she had come to abhor Hanno's fetters. Most slaves didn't have theirs removed until they'd been around for years and were no longer deemed a flight risk, but a small number were never trusted. Naturally, Agesandros had persuaded Fabricius that Hanno fell into this category. "For a day like this," she challenged, lifting her chin. "So we could hunt properly."

"He'll run away!" Quintus cried.

"No, he won't," Aurelia retorted hotly. She turned to Hanno. "Will you?"

Caught off guard by the bizarre situation, and stunned by Aurelia's action, Hanno stuttered to find an answer. "N-no, of course not."

"There!" Aurelia gestured in triumph at her brother.

"You believe that? He's a slave!"

Aurelia's eyes blazed. "Hanno is trustworthy, Quintus, and you know it!"

Quintus matched her gaze for a moment. "Very well." He looked at Hanno. "Do you give your word not to run away?"

"I swear it. May Tanit and Baal Hammon, Melqart and Baal Saphon be my witnesses," said Hanno in a steady voice.

"If you're lying," muttered Quintus, "I'll hunt you down myself."

Hanno stared stolidly back at him. "Fine."

Quintus gave him a curt nod. "Lead on, then."

Relishing the freedom of being able to run for the first time in months, Hanno bounded off toward the spot where he'd seen the boar's spoor. Of course he thought of escape, but there was no way Hanno would break the vow he'd just made.

Frustratingly, the boar proved elusive to the point of exasperation.

An hour later, they had still not laid eyes on it. The animal's trail had led them to a point where the forest thinned as it climbed the mountain slope above, and there it had disappeared. A large area of bare rock meant that their chances of finding it again were very slim.

Quintus looked at the darkening sky and cursed. "We'll have to give up soon. I don't fancy spending the night here. Let's spread right out. That's probably our best option."

While Aurelia walked off to Quintus' left, Hanno moved slowly to the right. He kept his eyes fixed on the ground, but saw nothing at all for a good two hundred paces. His gaze wandered to the slopes above them. Much of the ground was covered in short scrubby grass, and fit only for sheep or goats.

Hanno frowned. Some distance above them, and partially obscured by a scattering of juniper and pine trees, he could see a small wooden structure. Smoke rose lazily from a hole in the apex of its roof. Latticed fencing around it revealed the presence of sheep pens. It didn't surprise him. Like most landowners, Fabricius' flocks wandered the hills during the spring and summer, accompanied by solitary shepherds and their dogs. Makeshift huts, and enclosures for the animals, were situated regularly across the landscape, shelter in case of bad weather and protection against predators such as wolves. To his astonishment, however, Hanno heard the sound of bleating. He looked up at the sky. It was early for the animals to be back from pasture. He glanced at Quintus, who was still casting about for signs of the boar. Aurelia was visible beyond. She too appeared oblivious.

Hanno was about to give a low whistle, when something stopped him. Instead, he trotted back toward the two Romans.

Quintus grew excited as he saw Hanno approach. "Seen something?"

"The sheep up there are penned in," said Hanno. "A bit soon, isn't it?"

Quintus raised a hand to his eyes. "By Jupiter, you're right," he admitted, annoyed that he hadn't noticed first. "Libo is the shepherd around here. He's a good man, not one to avoid work."

Hanno's stomach clenched.

"I'm not happy." Quintus took off his pack and emptied it on the ground. He unrolled the cloak. Carefully shoving one gladius into his belt, he handed the other to Aurelia, who had caught up with them. "You probably won't need it," he said with a falsely confident smile. Bending the stave with his knee, Quintus slipped his bowstring into place. There were ten arrows in his quiver. Plenty, he thought.

"What's wrong?" Aurelia demanded.

"Probably nothing," replied Quintus reassuringly. "I'm just going to take Hanno and check out that hut."

Fear flared in Aurelia's eyes, but when she spoke, her voice was steady. "What shall I do?"

"Remain here," Quintus ordered. "Stay hidden. Under no circumstances are you to follow us. Is that clear?"

She nodded. "How long should I wait?"

"A quarter of an hour, no more. If we haven't reappeared by then, return to the farm as fast as you can. Find Agesandros, and tell him to bring plenty of men. Well armed."

At this, Aurelia's composure cracked. "Don't go up there," she whispered. "Let's just fetch Agesandros together."

Quintus thought for a moment. "Libo could be in danger. I have to check," he declared. He patted Aurelia's arm. "Everything will be fine, you'll see."

Aurelia saw that her brother was not to be swayed. She took a step toward Hanno, but stopped herself. "Mars protect you both," she whispered, hating the way her voice trembled.

And Baal Saphon, thought Hanno, invoking the Carthaginian god of war.

Leaving Aurelia peering from behind a large pine, the two young men began to ascend. Quintus was surprised by the imperceptible change that had already taken place in their relationship. Although they could see no human activity above, both were instinctively using the few bushes present for cover. As soldiers would. *Don't be stupid. He's a slave.* "It's bandits," Quintus muttered to himself. "What else can it be?"

"That's what it would be in the countryside around Carthage," replied Hanno.

Quintus cursed. "I wonder how many there are?"

Hanno shrugged uneasily, wishing he had a weapon. It wasn't surprising that Quintus had given the other gladius to Aurelia, but it grated on him nonetheless. "Your guess is as good as mine."

Quintus' lips had gone very dry. "What if there are too many for me to take on?"

"We try not to shit ourselves, and then crawl out of there on our bellies," Hanno answered dryly. "Before going to get help."

"That sounds like a good plan." Despite himself, Quintus grinned.

The rest of the climb was made in silence. The last point of cover before the shepherd's hut was a stunted cypress tree, and they reached it without difficulty. Recovering their breath, each took turns to peer at the pens and the miserable structure alongside, which was little more than a lean-to. His lips moving silently, Quintus counted the sheep. "I make it more than fifty," he whispered. "That's Libo's entire flock."

Be logical, thought Hanno. "Maybe he's ill?"

"I doubt it," Quintus replied. "Libo is as hard as nails. He's lived in the mountains all his life."

"Let's wait a moment then," Hanno advised. "No point rushing into a situation without assessing it first."

Hanno's observation made Quintus bridle. Slaves do not advise their masters, he told himself angrily. Yet the Carthaginian's words were wise. Biting his lip, he drew a goose-feathered arrow from his quiver. It was his favorite, and he'd killed with it many times. Never a man, he thought with a rush of fear. Taking a deep breath, Quintus exhaled slowly. It might not come to that. Nonetheless, he picked out three more shafts and stabbed them into the earth by his feet. Suddenly, an awful thought struck him. If there were bandits about, and he was outnumbered, his bow was the only advantage he had. That might not be enough. Quintus was prepared for the potential danger he'd placed himself in, but he hadn't really considered his sister. He turned to Hanno. "If anything happens to me, you're to run down and get Aurelia the hell out of here. Do you understand?"

It was too late to say that Quintus should have given him a sword, thought Hanno angrily. It would have been two of them against however many bandits might be in the hut. He nodded. "Of course."

It wasn't long before there was movement inside the building, which was perhaps twenty paces away. A man coughed, and cleared his throat in the manner of someone who has just woken. Quintus stiffened, listening hard. Hanno did likewise. Then they heard the rickety door on the far side of the hut being thrown open. A short figure wearing a sheepskin waistcoat over a homespun tunic stepped into view. Stretching and yawning, he pulled down his breeches and began to relieve himself. Glancing sunlight lit up the yellow arc of his urine.

Quintus cursed under his breath.

Despite the other's reaction, Hanno had to ask. "Is that the shepherd?" he whispered.

Quintus' lips framed the word "No." Carefully, he fitted his favorite arrow to his bowstring and drew a bead on the stranger.

"Could it be another shepherd?"

"I don't recognize him." Quintus drew back until the goose feathers at the base of the arrow nearly touched his ear.

"Wait!" Hanno hissed. "You have to be sure."

Quintus was again angered by Hanno's tone. Nonetheless, he did not release: he too had no desire to kill an innocent man.

"Caecilius? Where are you?" demanded a voice from inside the hut.

The pair froze.

With a final shake, the man pulled up his trousers. "Out here," he replied lazily. "Taking a piss on the shepherd. Making sure he's still dead."

There was a loud guffaw. "Not much chance of the whoreson being anything else after what you did to him."

"You can't talk, Balbus," added a third voice. "He screamed the most when you were using the red-hot poker."

Quintus threw Hanno a horrified glance.

Balbus laughed, a deep, unpleasant sound. "What do you think, Pollio?" There was no immediate answer, and they heard Balbus kicking someone. "Wake up, you drunken sot."

"The point of my boot up his arse should do the trick," Caecilius bellowed, heading for the door.

Desperately, Hanno turned his head to tell Quintus to loose before it was too late. He barely had time to register the arrow as it flashed past his eyes and shot through the air to plant itself in the middle of Caecilius' chest. With a stunned look, the bandit dropped to his knees before toppling sideways to the dirt. He made a few soft choking sounds and lay still.

"Well done," whispered Hanno. "Three left."

"At least." Quintus did not think about what he had done. He notched another shaft and waited. The layout of the hut was such that if the remaining bandits merely looked out of the doorway, they would see Caecilius' body without exposing themselves to his arrows. Jupiter, Greatest and Best, he begged silently, let the next scumbag come right outside.

Hanno clenched his teeth. He too could see the danger.

"Caecilius? Fallen over your own prick?" demanded Balbus.

There was no answer. A moment later, a bulky-framed man with long greasy hair emerged partially into view. It took the blink of an eye for him to notice his companion's body, to take in the arrow protruding from his chest. A strangled cry left Balbus' throat. Frantic to regain the safety of the hut, he spun on his heel.

Quintus released. His shaft flew straight and true, driving deep into Balbus' right side with a meaty thump. The bandit cursed in pain, but managed to get through the doorway. "Help me," he cried. "I'm hit."

Shouts of confusion and anger rang out from within. Hanno heard Balbus growl, "Caecilius is dead. An arrow to the chest. No, Sejanus, I don't fucking know who did it." Then, apart from low muttering, everything went silent.

"They know that I'm just outside," Quintus whispered, suddenly wondering if he'd bitten off more than he could chew. "But they have no idea that I'm on my own. How will they react?"

Hanno scowled. *You're not on your own, you arrogant fool.* "What would you do?"

"Try to get away," Quintus said, fumbling for an arrow.

In the same instant, loud cracking sounds filled the air and the back wall of the hut disintegrated in a cloud of dust. Three bandits burst into the open air, hurtling straight toward them. In the lead was a skinny man in a wine-stained tunic. He grasped a hunting spear in both hands. This had to be Pollio, thought Hanno. Beside him ran a massive figure carrying a club. Hanno blinked in surprise. It was not Balbus, because he was two steps behind, clutching the arrow in his side with one hand and a rusty sword with the other. Despite being twice Balbus' size, the big man was his spitting image. The pair had to be brothers.

The two sides goggled at each other for a heartbeat.

Pollio was the first to react. "They're only children. And one isn't even armed," he screamed. "Kill them!" His companions needed no encouragement. Bellowing with rage, the trio charged forward.

Perhaps fifteen paces now divided them. "Quick," Hanno shouted. "Take one of the bastards down."

Quintus' heart hammered in his chest, and he struggled to notch his arrow correctly. Finally it slipped on to the string, but, desperate to even the odds, he loosed too soon. His shaft flashed over Pollio's shoulder and into the wreckage of the hut. He had no time to reach for another. The bandits were virtually upon them. Dropping his bow, he pulled the gladius from his belt. "Get out of here!" he shouted. "You know what to do!"

Facing certain death if he stayed without a weapon, Hanno turned and fled.

"Let him go!" shouted Pollio. "The shitbag looks as if he can run like the wind."

Quintus had just enough time to throw up a prayer of thanks to Jupiter before Pollio, leaping over a fallen log, reached him.

"So you're the one who would murder a man while he takes a piss," the bandit snarled, lunging forward with his spear.

Quintus dodged sideways. "He got what was coming to him."

Leering, Pollio stabbed at him again. "It was a quicker death than the shepherd had."

Quintus tried not to think of Libo, or of the fact that he was outnumbered three to one. Holding his gladius with both hands, he swept the spear shaft away. Sejanus, the big man, was still a few steps away, but already there was no sign of Balbus. Where is the son of a whore? Quintus wondered frantically. He might be wounded, but he's still armed. The realization made him want to vomit. *The bastard's coming to stab me in the back.* All Quintus could think of doing was to place himself against a tree. Driving Pollio off with a flurry of blows, he sprinted toward the nearest one he could see, a cypress with a thick trunk. He could make a stand there.

To Quintus' exhilaration, he made it.

The only trouble was that, a heartbeat later, he had the grinning bandits ringed around him in a semicircle.

"Surrender now, and we'll give you an easy death," said Pollio. "Not like the poor shepherd had."

Even the wounded Balbus laughed.

What have I done? Somehow, Quintus swallowed down his fear. "You're fucking scum! I'll kill you all," he shouted.

"You think?" sneered Pollio. "It's your choice." Without warning, he thrust his spear at Quintus' midriff.

Quintus threw himself sideways. Too late, he realized that Sejanus had aimed his club at the very spot he was heading for. In utter desperation, he deliberately fell to the ground. With an almighty *crack*, the club smacked into the tree trunk. The knowledge that the blow would have brained him if it had landed drove Quintus to his feet. Seizing his opportunity, he slashed out at Sejanus' arm and was delighted when his blade connected with the big man's right arm. The flesh wound it cut was enough for Sejanus to bellow in pain and stagger backward, out of the way. Quintus' relief lasted no more than an instant. The injury wouldn't be enough to stop the brute from rejoining the fight. To survive, he immediately had to disable or kill one of the other two.

With that, a sword hilt smashed into the side of his head. Stars burst across Quintus' vision, and his knees buckled. Half-conscious, he dropped to the ground.

———

Hanno had probably run fifty paces before he glanced over his shoulder. Delighted that no one was pursuing him, he sprinted on for another fifty before looking back again. He was on his own. In the clear. Safe. So too, therefore, was Aurelia.

What of Quintus? he wondered with a thrill of dread.

You ran. Coward! Hanno's conscience screamed.

Quintus told me to, he thought defensively. The idiot couldn't bring himself to trust me with a gladius.

Does that mean you should leave him to die? his conscience shot back. What chance has he against three grown men?

Hanno screeched to a halt. Turning, he ran uphill as fast as his legs could take him. He took care to count his steps. At eighty, he slowed to a trot. Peering through the trees, he saw the three bandits standing over a motionless figure. Claws of fear savaged Hanno's guts as he took refuge behind a bush. *No! He can't be dead!* When Pollio's kick made Quintus moan, Hanno was nearly sick with relief. Quintus was alive still. Clearly, he wouldn't be for long. Hanno clenched his empty fists. *What in the name of Baal Saphon can I do?*

"Let's take him back to the hut," Pollio declared.

"Why?" complained Balbus. "We can just kill the fucker here."

"That's where the fire is, stupid! It won't have gone out yet," replied Pollio with a laugh. "I know you're injured, but Sejanus and I can carry him between us."

A cruel smile spread across Balbus' face. "Fair enough. There'll be more sport with some heat, I suppose." He watched each of his comrades take one of Quintus' arms and begin dragging him toward the hut. There was little resistance, but they retained their weapons nonetheless.

This is my chance. All three men had their backs to him, and half a dozen steps separated Balbus from the others. Hanno's mouth felt very dry. His prospects of success were tiny. Like as not, he'd end up dead, or being tortured alongside Quintus. He could still run. A wave of self-loathing swept over him. *He saved you from Agesandros, remember?*

Clenching his teeth, Hanno emerged from his hiding place. Grateful for the damp vegetation, which muffled the sound of his feet, he stole forward as fast as he could. Balbus was limping after his comrades, who were alternately grumbling about how much Quintus weighed and waxing lyrical about what they'd do to him. Hanno fixed his gaze on the rusty sword that dangled from Balbus' right hand. First, he *had* to arm himself. After that, he had to kill one of the bandits. After that . . . Hanno didn't know. He'd have to trust in the gods.

To Hanno's relief, his first target didn't hear him coming. Taking careful aim, he thumped Balbus near the point where Quintus' arrow had entered his flesh, before neatly catching the sword as it dropped from the screaming bandit's fingers. Switching it to his right hand, Hanno sprinted for the other two. "Hey!" he shouted.

Their faces twisted with alarm, but Hanno's delight turned to fear as they dropped Quintus like a sack of grain. Do not let him be hurt, Hanno prayed. Please.

"You must be a slave," Pollio growled. "You were unarmed before. Why don't you join us?"

"We'll let you kill your master," offered Sejanus. "Any way you want."

Hanno did not dignify the proposal with a reply. Sejanus was nearest, so he went for him first. The big man might have been injured, but he was still deadly with his club. Hanno ducked under one almighty swing, and dodged out of the way of another before seeing Pollio's spear come thrusting in at him. Desperate, Hanno retreated a few paces. Sejanus lumbered in immediate pursuit, blocking his comrade's view of Hanno. There was a loud curse from Pollio, and Sejanus' attention lapsed a fraction.

Hanno darted forward. As the other's eyes widened in disbelief, Hanno slid his sword deep into his belly. The blade made a horrible, sucking sound as it came out. Blood spurted on to the ground. Sejanus roared with agony; his club fell from his nerveless fingers and both his hands came up to clutch at his abdomen.

Hanno was already spinning to meet Pollio's attack. The little bandit's spear stabbed in, narrowly missing his right arm. His heart pounding, Hanno shuffled backward. His eyes flickered to the side. Despite being in obvious pain, Balbus was about to join the fray. He'd picked up a thick branch. It wouldn't kill, thought Hanno, but if Balbus landed a blow, he'd easily knock him from his feet. Panic bubbled in his throat, and his sword arm began to tremble.

Get a grip of yourself! Quintus needs you.

Hanno's breathing steadied. He fixed Balbus with a hard stare. "Want a blade in the guts as well as that arrow?"

Balbus flinched, and Hanno went for the kill. "Creating fear in an enemy's heart wins half the battle," his father had been fond of saying. "Carthage!" he bellowed, and charged forward. Even if Pollio took him down from behind, Hanno was determined that Balbus would die.

Balbus saw the suicidal look in Hanno's eyes. He dropped his length of wood and raised both his hands in the air. "Don't kill me," he begged.

Hanno didn't trust the bandit as far as he could throw him; he didn't know what Pollio was doing either. Dropping his right shoulder, he crashed into Balbus' chest, sending him flying.

When he turned to face Pollio, the skinny bandit was gone. Pumping his arms and legs as if Cerberus himself were after him, he tore up the slope and was soon lost to view among the trees. Let the bastard go, Hanno thought wearily. He won't come back. A few steps away, Balbus was in the fetal position, moaning. Further off, Sejanus was already semiconscious from the blood he'd lost.

The fight was over.

Elation filled Hanno for a moment—before he remembered Quintus.

He rushed to the Roman's side. To his immense relief, Quintus smiled up at him. "Are you all right?" Hanno asked.

Wincing, Quintus lifted a hand to the side of his head. "There's an apple-sized lump here, and it feels as if Jupiter is letting off thunderbolts inside my skull. Apart from that, I'll be fine, I think."

"Thank the gods," said Hanno fervently.

"No," replied Quintus. "Thank you—for coming back. For disobeying my orders."

Hanno colored. "I'd never have been able to live with myself if I hadn't."

"But you didn't have to do it. Even when you did, you could have taken up the bandits' offer. Turned on me." A trace of wonder entered Quintus' voice. "Instead, you took on the three of them, and won."

"I—" Hanno faltered.

"I'm only alive because of you," interrupted Quintus. "You have my thanks."

Seeing Quintus' sincerity, Hanno inclined his head. "You're welcome."

As the realization sank in that they had survived the most desperate of situations, the two grinned at each other like maniacs. These were strange circumstances for both. Master saved by his slave. Roman allied with Carthaginian. Yet both were very aware of a new bond: that of comradeship forged in combat.

It was a good feeling.

VIII

THE SIEGE

Malchus regarded the immense fortifications with a baleful eye and spat on the ground. "They're determined, you have to give them that," he growled. "They must know now that there's no help coming from Rome. But the pigheaded Greek bastards still won't give up."

"Neither will we," Sapho responded fiercely. His breath plumed in the cool, autumn air. "And when we get inside, the defenders will regret the day they slammed the gates in our faces. The whoresons won't know what hit them. Eh, Bostar?" He elbowed his brother in the ribs.

"The sooner the city falls, the better. Hannibal will find a way," Bostar replied confidently, sidestepping Sapho's needling. In the months since their argument in New Carthage, their relationship had improved somewhat, but Sapho never missed an opportunity to undermine him, or to call into question his loyalty to their cause. Just because I don't enjoy torturing enemy prisoners, thought Bostar sadly. What has he become?

In a way, though, it was unsurprising that Sapho resorted to violence in his attempts to garner intelligence that might gain them entry. Nearly six months had elapsed since Hannibal's immense army had begun the siege, and they were not much nearer to taking Saguntum. A mile from the sea, it sat on a long, naked piece of rock that towered three to four hundred paces above the plain below. The position was one of confident dominance, and made it a fearsome prospect to besiege. The only way of approaching the city, which was encircled by strongly built fortifications, was from the west, where the slope was least steep. Naturally, it was here that the defenses were strongest. Surrounded by thick walls, a mighty tower sat astride the tallest part of the rock. Hannibal had encamped the majority of his forces below this point. He had also ordered the erection of a wall that ran all the way around the base of the rock. The circumvallation was dotted with towers whose function was merely to ensure that no enemy messengers escaped.

"The gods willing, *we* are that way," Malchus added.

Both his sons nodded. Hannibal had shown their family considerable honor by picking their units to lead the impending attack. The rest of those who would take part, thousands of Libyans and Iberians, waited on the slopes below.

Sapho's face twitched, and he gestured at the massed ranks of their spearmen, who were arrayed around the massive shapes of four *vineae*, or "covered ways," attacking towers with a massive battering ram at their base. These would form the basis for their assault. "The men are nervous. It's no surprise either. We've been waiting for an hour. Where is he?"

Bostar could see that Sapho was right. Some soldiers were chatting loudly with each other, their voices a tone higher than normal. Others remained silent, but their lips moved in constant prayer. A nervous air hung over every phalanx. Hannibal will come soon, he told himself.

"Patience," advised Malchus.

Reluctantly, Sapho obeyed, but he burned to prove himself once and for all. Show his father that he was the bravest of his sons.

Moments later, their attention was drawn by murmurs of anticipation, which began spreading forward from the rear of the throng.

"Listen!" said Malchus in triumph. "Hannibal is talking to them as he passes by. There are many things that make a good general, and this is one of them. It's not just about leading from the front. You have to engage with your soldiers as well." He gave Bostar an approving nod, which made Sapho mutter something under his breath.

Bostar's temper frayed. This was an area he paid a lot of attention to. "What?" he demanded. "If you tried that instead of punishing every tiny infraction of the rules, your troops might respect you more."

Sapho's face darkened, but before he could reply, loud cheering broke out. Men began stamping their feet on the ground in a repetitive, infectious rhythm. The other officers did nothing to intervene. This was what they had all been waiting for. The noise grew and grew, until gradually a single word became audible. "HANN-I-BAL! HANN-I-BAL! HANN-I-BAL!"

Bostar grinned. One could not help but be infected by the soldiers' enthusiasm. Even Sapho was craning his neck to see.

Eventually, a small party emerged from the midst of the spearmen. It was a hollow square, formed by perhaps two dozen *scutarii*. These Iberian infantry were some of Hannibal's best troops. As always, the scutarii were wearing their characteristic black cloaks over simple tunics and small breastplates. Their fearsome array of weapons included various types of heavy throwing spear, most notably the all-iron *saunion*, as well as long, straight swords, and daggers. Within their formation walked a lone figure, partially obscured from view. This was who everyone wanted to see. Finally, nearing Malchus and his sons, the scutarii fanned out in two lines. The man within was revealed.

Hannibal Barca.

Bostar gazed at his general with frank admiration. Like most senior Carthaginian officers, Hannibal wore a simple Hellenistic gilded bronze helmet. Sunlight flashed off its surface, reflecting into the soldiers' eyes. The blinding light concealed Hannibal's face apart from his beard. A dark purple cloak hung from his broad shoulders. Under it, he wore a tunic of the same color, and an ornate muscled bronze cuirass, its details picked out in silver. Layered strips of linen guarded the general's groin, and polished bronze greaves covered his lower legs. His feet were encased in sturdy leather sandals. A hide baldric swept down from his right shoulder to his left hip, suspending a falcata sword in a well-worn scabbard. He moved forward, limping slightly.

The commander of the scutarii barked an order, and in unison his soldiers slammed their brightly painted shields on to the rock. The crashing sound instantly silenced the assembled troops. "Your general, the lion of Carthage, Hannibal Barca!" screamed the officer.

Everyone stiffened to attention and saluted.

"General!" cried Malchus. "You honor us with your presence."

The corners of Hannibal's mouth tugged up. "At ease, gentlemen." He made his way to Malchus' side. "Are you ready?"

"Yes, sir. We have checked over the siege engines twice. Every man knows his task."

Malchus' sons muttered in agreement.

Hannibal glanced at each of them in turn before giving a satisfied nod. "You will do well."

"May Baal Saphon strike us down if we do not," said Sapho fervently.

Hannibal looked a little surprised. "I hope not. The city will fall eventually, but we haven't succeeded so far. Who's to say that today will be any different? And valuable officers are hard to come by." Ignoring Sapho's obvious discomfort, he smiled at Malchus. "Understand that you're only being granted this chance because I can't run." He touched the heavy strapping on his right thigh.

"Your injury was most unfortunate, sir," said Malchus, "but we are grateful for the opportunity that it has granted us today."

Hannibal smiled. "Your eagerness is commendable."

Bostar could still picture the heart-stopping moment several weeks previously, during an assault similar to the one they were about to lead. As was his nature, Hannibal had been at the front. Bostar wished it had been he who had taken the arrow through the thigh. "How's it healing, sir?"

"Slowly enough." Hannibal grimaced. "I should be thankful, I suppose, that the defenders aren't better archers."

Father and sons laughed nervously. That eventuality was something no one wanted to entertain.

"Well, don't let me stand in your way. The Saguntines await you." Hannibal indicated the walls, which were thickly manned. He pointed back down the steep slope at the other companies of troops: reinforcements should the attack break through. "So do they."

"Yes, sir." Malchus lifted his sword.

His men, who had been watching closely, stiffened.

"Gods, but I wish Hanno were here," muttered Bostar.

Sapho's face hardened. "Eh? Why?"

"He spent his time dreaming about things like this."

"Well, he's dead," Sapho whispered back savagely. "So you're wasting your time."

Bostar gave him a furious stare. "Don't you miss him?"

Sapho had no chance to reply.

"What are you waiting for?" Malchus demanded, who had missed the exchange. "Get into position!"

With a quick salute to Hannibal, Bostar and Sapho sprinted off to join their respective phalanxes. Each was in charge of one of the vineae, and their increasingly bitter rivalry meant that both burned to command the siege engine that smashed the decisive hole in the walls, and allowed their comrades a way into Saguntum. Of course it might not be they who succeeded, thought Bostar. Their father commanded the third vinea, and Alete, a doughty veteran whom both brothers admired, had the last.

Malchus waited until they were in place before he chopped his arm downward. "Forward!" he shouted.

Using whistles, the officers encouraged the Libyans toward the walls. Dozens of men who had been selected earlier handed their spears to comrades and ran to place their shoulders against the backs of the vineae, or to stand alongside the wheels. Scores of others used their large shields to form protective screens around those who were now unprotected. More commands rang out, and the soldiers around the siege engines began to push. With loud creaks, the vineae rumbled forward, past Hannibal. When the machines were perhaps fifty paces up the slope, the remaining Libyans began to follow in tight phalanxes.

As they drew nearer, Bostar's stomach clenched. He could clearly see the faces of those above, the defenders who were waiting to rain death down upon him and his men. Upon his father and brother. Baal Saphon, let us smash the enemy's walls asunder, he prayed. Keep your shield over all of us. As the first missiles came pattering down, Bostar couldn't help wondering if Sapho was asking for similar protection for him.

He doubted it.

Taking great care, Bostar peered out at the ramparts above him. Perhaps an hour had passed, and the assault was going well. The battering rams suspended in the bottoms of the vineae were smashing great holes in the base of the wall. Thanks to the siege engines' wooden and leather roofs, which had been pre-soaked in water, the defenders' clouds of fire arrows, stones and spears were having limited effect. Bostar had lost fifteen men, which was perfectly acceptable. The phalanxes on either side, those of Sapho and Alete, looked to have suffered much the same.

Soon after, a large section of the wall collapsed. A wry grin split Bostar's face at the sight. The area lay directly between his and Sapho's positions, so neither could claim the credit. That wasn't the point now, of course. Hannibal was watching them. Bostar roared at his men to redouble their efforts. He fancied he heard Sapho's voice above the din, enjoining his soldiers to do the same. Their efforts were not in vain. Before long, two, and then three, towers had fallen outward, crushing dozens of the garrison, and spearmen, to death. But a sizable breach had now been forced, large enough to gain entry. Bostar did not wait until the dust had settled. This opportunity had to be seized by the throat, before the bewildered defenders had a chance to react. Screaming at his men to pick up their weapons and follow him, he climbed on to the mounds of broken masonry that stood before the siege engines. He was pleased to note that Sapho's soldiers were also spilling into view. Catching sight of his brother twenty paces away, Bostar raised his spear in salute. "I'll see you inside!"

"Not if I get there before you," Sapho snarled back. He turned to his soldiers, who were straining like hunting dogs on the leash. "Five gold pieces to the first man to get within the walls. Forward!"

Bostar sighed. Even this had to be a contest. So be it, he thought angrily.

The race was on.

Pursued by their men, the two brothers scrambled up toward the breach. They risked their lives with every step, not just from the continuing rain of missiles from the ramparts to either side, but from the treacherous footing beneath. Carrying a spear in one hand and a shield in the other made it even more difficult to balance. Bostar kept his gaze fixed firmly on the ground. The enemy missiles were beyond his control, but he could make sure that he didn't break an ankle in the ascent. He'd seen it happen before, consigning the unfortunates affected to being trampled by their comrades, or killed by the torrent of death being thrown by the Saguntines.

Bostar was first to reach the highest point of the smashed wall. The clouds of dust sent up by the towers' collapse formed a choking cloud that hid any defenders from sight. Perhaps there were none? wondered Bostar. His heart leaped, but then he glanced around and cursed. In his haste, he'd outstripped his soldiers. The nearest were twenty paces down the slope. "Get a move on," he roared. "This isn't a walking party!"

An instant later, Sapho arrived from the gloom. He had a dozen or more Libyans in tow; more were hauling themselves up nearby. A happy smile spread across his face when he saw that Bostar was alone. "On your own still? It's not surprising, really. Nothing like the promise of gold to speed things along."

Bostar bit back his instinctive response. "This is not the time for such bullshit," he snarled. "Let's seize the damn breach. We can argue later."

Sapho gave a nonchalant shrug. "As you wish." He leveled his spear. "Third Phalanx! On me! Form a line!"

Only four of Bostar's men had arrived. He watched in frustration as his brother led his spearmen forward. Of course he would be following in the blink of an eye, but it still rankled. A moment later, Bostar was glad that he hadn't been first into the gap. Like avenging ghosts, scores of screaming Saguntines emerged from the dust cloud. Every one of them carried a *falarica*, a long javelin with a burning ball of pitch-soaked tow wrapped around the middle of the shaft.

"Look out!" Bostar screamed, knowing that his warning was already too late.

Responding to an officer's command, the Saguntines drew back and released. They aimed short. Clouds of flaming missiles scudded through the air. Horror-struck, Sapho and his soldiers slowed down. And then the falaricae landed. Driving through shields. Maiming, killing and setting men alight.

Cursing, Bostar counted his spearmen. There were about twenty of them now. It wasn't enough, but he couldn't just stand by. If he did, Sapho would be killed, and his soldiers would run away. Their chance would be lost. "Forward!" Raising his shield, Bostar ran at the enemy. He did not look back. To his immense relief, he felt his men's presence at each shoulder. Death might take them all, thought Bostar, but at least they followed him through loyalty, not lust for gold.

He aimed for the spot where it looked as if Sapho's soldiers might be overwhelmed. Seeing him, the nearest Saguntines took aim and released their falaricae. Hunching his shoulders, Bostar ran on. Streaming flames, the javelins hummed right past him. There was a strangled scream, and he looked around. He wished he hadn't. A falarica had struck the man to his rear in the shoulder, driving deep into his flesh. In turn, the burning section had set alight the soldier's tunic. Gobbets of white-hot tow were dropping on to his face and neck. His screams were earsplitting. Bostar's nostrils filled with the stench of cooking flesh. "Leave him!" he roared at the men who instinctively went to help. "Keep moving!" Grateful it wasn't him, and hoping the soldier died quickly, he spun back to the front.

If there was one small advantage to be gained from the enemy's secret weapon, it was that after launching them, the defenders were momentarily defenseless. In addition, many weren't even wearing armor. Snarling with fury, Bostar charged at a skinny Saguntine who was frantically trying to tug free his sword. He didn't succeed. Bostar's spear took him through the chest, punching through his rib cage with ease. The man's eyes nearly popped out of their sockets with the force of the impact. He was dead before Bostar pulled free his weapon, showering the ground in gouts of blood.

Panting, Bostar rounded on the next soldier within reach, a youth who couldn't have been more than sixteen. Despite his rusty sword and bloodcurdling cries, he looked petrified.

Bostar parried his clumsy blows with little difficulty before sliding his spear into the youngster's belly. He killed two more defenders before an opportunity presented itself to assess the situation.

Perhaps a hundred of his own men were present; more were still arriving. A similar number of Sapho's soldiers were battling steadily around them. No doubt their father and Alete's phalanxes were trying to reach them too. Remarkably, however, they were being held back by the Saguntines, who were performing acts of heroism and suicidal bravery. No ground had been gained at all. Bostar realized why as he took in hundreds of civilians, who, just a few steps from the periphery of the fighting, were frantically repairing the breach with their bare hands. He could see old men, women and even children heaving rocks into place. Grudging respect filled him. Knowing that their loved ones were so close would make any man, soldier or not, fight like a demon. Bostar was not dismayed. Even now, thousands more troops would be climbing the slope to join them. Against such overwhelming numbers, even the gallant Saguntines could not hold for much longer. All they needed to do was to press home the attack.

Abruptly, his attention was drawn back to the present. Through the dust, he could make out a line of flickering flame approaching from the enemy citadel. Bostar's stomach clenched as the vision came into full focus. It was two further waves of warriors, carrying scores more burning falaricae. "Shields up!" he yelled. "Incoming javelins!"

His men hurried to obey.

Responding to a shouted order, the enemy lines came to a halt perhaps fifty paces away. Drawing back, the Saguntines threw their falaricae up in a steep arc, far over their own men. Over Bostar and Sapho's soldiers.

"Clever bastards," Bostar muttered. "They don't want to hit us." He watched in total dread as the flaming javelins turned to point downward. Like deadly shooting stars, they returned to earth to land amidst the still ascending Carthaginian troops. Thanks to the clouds of dust, these densely packed men had no idea what was about to hit them until the very last moment. Understandably, the falaricae caused utter chaos. Practically every one found a home in human flesh, running through shields and mail shirts with impunity. Yet their effect was far more profound. It was why the Saguntines had aimed at the unsuspecting soldiers to the rear, thought Bostar as the screams and wails of the injured filled his ears. The falaricae struck fear into the heart of every man who stood in their path. He knew exactly why. Who could bear to watch his comrades being turned into pillars of flame, or having the flesh blistered from their bones? No amount of training could prepare soldiers for that.

The entire advance below him had already come to a halt. As Bostar watched, the second wave of enemy javelins came rocketing down. An instant later, the Carthaginian attack became a rout. Despite the shouts of their officers, hundreds of men turned and fled. They hurled themselves down the slope with such abandon that many fell and were trampled by those following. The soldiers to either side, who had not been struck by the enemy volley, took one look at their retreating comrades and stopped dead. Then, as one, they turned on the spot and began running too.

Bostar cursed. The moment was lost. No one, even Hannibal, could turn this situation around. He caught the arm of the nearest spearman. "Pull back! Our reinforcements are withdrawing. We have to save ourselves. Spread the word." Repeating his command to every soldier he passed, Bostar fought his way through the press to Sapho's side. Oblivious to the volley's effect, his brother was urging a quartet of spearmen forward at a bunch of poorly armed defenders.

"Sapho!" Bostar yelled. "Sapho!"

Eventually his brother heard him. "What?" he snarled over his shoulder.

"We must pull back!"

Sapho's face contorted with anger. "You're crazy! Any moment, the whoresons will break, and then we'll have them. Victory is at hand!"

"No, it isn't!" Bostar bellowed. "We have to retreat. NOW."

Some of Sapho's soldiers began to look uneasy.

Sapho glared furiously at Bostar, but realized that he was serious. Shouting encouragement to his men, Sapho elbowed his way out of the front rank. With his arms and face covered in blood, he was like some creature from the underworld. "Have you entirely lost your wits?" he hissed. "The enemy is giving ground at last. Another big push, and they'll break."

"It's too late," Bostar replied in a flat tone. "Have you not seen what those fucking falaricae have done to the troops behind us?"

Sapho's rejoinder was instantaneous. "No. I keep my eyes to the front, not the back."

Bostar's fists clenched at the imputation. "Well," he muttered, "let me tell you, our entire attack has come to a halt."

Sapho bared his teeth. "So? Those motherless curs will turn and run any moment. Then we'll get a foothold inside the walls."

"Where we will be cut off and annihilated." Bostar jabbed a finger into Sapho's chest for emphasis. "Don't you understand? We're on our own up here!"

"Coward!" Sapho screamed. "You're scared of dying, that's all."

Bostar's anger surged out of control. "When the time comes, I will fight and die for Hannibal," he shouted. "What's more, I will do it proudly. But there's a difference between dying well, and like a fool. There's nothing to be gained from sacrificing your life, or those of your men, here."

Spitting on the ground, Sapho made to return to the fight.

"Stop!" Bostar's order was like the crack of a whip.

Stiff-backed, Sapho came to a halt, but he did not turn to face Bostar.

"As your superior officer, I command you to withdraw your men at once," Bostar cried, making sure that every soldier within earshot heard him.

Defeated, Sapho spun around. "Yes, *sir*," he snarled. He raised his voice. "You heard the order! Fall back!"

It didn't take long for Sapho's men to get the idea. Reenergized by the effect that their volleys had had on the ascending Carthaginian troops, the defenders were beginning to advance again. Behind them, freshly lit falaricae were being carried forward. Encouraged by this, even the civilians who were repairing the breach joined in, hurling stones and fist-sized pieces of masonry at the spearmen.

This increased the ignominy and fueled Sapho's anger to new levels, all the more because he could now see that Bostar had been right to sound the recall. "Fool," he told himself nonetheless. "It was there for the taking."

Hannibal was waiting with Malchus and Alete at the bottom of the slope. The general greeted the brothers warmly. "We were getting worried about you," he declared.

Malchus rumbled in agreement.

"Sapho here didn't want to leave the fight," said Bostar generously.

"Last on the field?" Hannibal clapped Sapho on the shoulder. "But still with the sense to withdraw. Good man! Once the whoresons had panicked your reinforcements, there was no point staying there, eh?"

Sapho flushed and hung his head. "No, sir."

"It was a good effort from both of you," said Malchus encouragingly. "But it wasn't to be."

Hannibal took Sapho's reaction to be disappointment. "Never mind, man. My spies tell me that their food is fast running out. We'll take the place soon! Now, see to your injured." He waved a hand in dismissal.

"Come on," said Bostar, leading Sapho away.

"Let go!" Sapho whispered after a few steps. "I'm not a child!"

"Stop acting like one then!" said Bostar, releasing his grip. "The least you could do is thank me. I didn't have to cover up for you there."

Sapho's lip curled. "I'm damned if I'll do that."

Bostar threw his eyes to heaven. "Of course not! Why would you recognize that I just saved your ass from a severe reprimand?"

"Fuck you, Bostar," Sapho snapped. He felt completely backed into a corner. "You're always right, aren't you? Everyone loves you, the perfect fucking officer!" Turning on his heel, he stalked off.

Bostar watched him go. Why couldn't he have gone fishing instead of Hanno? he thought. His remorse for even thinking such a thing was instant, but the feeling lingered as he began organizing rescue parties for the injured.

For the next two months, the siege went on in much the same fashion. Every full-frontal assault made by the Carthaginians was met with dogged, undying determination by the defenders. The vineae regularly smashed more holes in the outer wall, but the attackers could not press home their advantage fully, despite their overwhelming superiority of numbers. Relations between Bostar and Sapho did not improve, and the constant activity meant that it was easy to avoid each other. When they weren't fighting, they were sleeping or looking after their wounded. Malchus, who had not only his own phalanx to deal with, but the extra duties given him by Hannibal, remained unaware of the feud.

Incensed by the manner in which the siege was dragging on, Hannibal eventually ordered the construction of more siege engines: vineae, which protected the men within, and an immense multistory tower on wheels. This last, holding catapults and hundreds of soldiers on its various levels, could be moved to whichever point was weakest on a particular day. Its firepower was so great that the battlements could be cleared of defenders within a short time, allowing the wooden terraces that would protect the attacking infantry to be carried forward without hindrance. Fortunately for the Carthaginians, the ramparts had been built on a base of clay, not cement. Using pickaxes, the troops in the terraces set to work, undermining the base of the walls. In this way, a further breach was made, and the attackers' spirits were briefly lifted. Yet all was not as it seemed. Beyond the gaping hole, the Carthaginians found that a crescent-shaped fortification of earth had been thrown up in preparation for this exact eventuality. From behind its protection came repeated volleys of the terrifying falaricae.

At this point, despite the showers of burning javelins, the Carthaginians' relentless determination and superior numbers began to tell. The Saguntines did not have time to rebuild the new damage to their defenses properly, and repeated waves of attack finally smashed a passage behind the walls. Despite the defenders' heroism, the position was held. Further successes followed in the subsequent days, but then, with winter approaching, Hannibal was called away by a major rebellion of the fierce tribes that lived near the River Tagus. Maharbal, the officer he left in command, proceeded vigorously with the assault. He gained further ground, driving the weakened defenders into the citadel. The attackers' situation was strengthened by the fact that cholera and other illnesses were now causing heavy casualties among the Saguntines; their food and supplies were also running dangerously low.

By the time Hannibal had put down the uprising and returned, the end was near. The Carthaginian general offered terms to the Saguntine leaders. Incredibly, they were rejected out of hand. With the end of the year nigh, preparations were made for a final, decisive assault. Thanks to their repeated valor, Malchus, his sons and their spearmen had been chosen to be part of the last attack. Typically, Hannibal and his corps of scutarii were also present.

Long before the winter sun had tinted the eastern horizon, they assembled some fifty paces from the walls. Behind them, reaching all the way to the bottom of the slope, were units from every section of the army except the cavalry. Apart from the occasional jingle of mail or muted cough, the soldiers made little noise. The breath of thousands plumed the chill, damp air, the only manifestation of the excitement every man felt. As reward for their long struggle and because of the Saguntines' refusal to parley, Hannibal had told his troops that they had free rein when the city fell. Carthage would take some of the spoils, but the rest was theirs, including the inhabitants: men, women and children.

In serried ranks, they waited as the wooden terraces were pushed forward by torchlight. There was no longer any need for the huge tower with its slingers, spearmen and catapults. Either from lack of men, or missiles, the defenders had recently given up trying to destroy the Carthaginian siege engines. This good fortune meant that the work to undermine the fortifications had been able to proceed much faster than before. According to the engineer in charge, the citadel itself would fall by midmorning at the latest.

His prediction was accurate. As the first orange fingers of sunlight crept into the sky, ominous rumbles began to fill the air. Within moments, great clouds of smoke began to rise from the center of the citadel. The crackle of burning wood could also be heard. The Carthaginians paid it no heed. They no longer cared what the Saguntines were doing. With all possible speed, the majority of the soldiers at work in the terraces were pulled back. The danger of being crushed had grown too great. Yet, despite the extreme danger, some remained to finish the task.

They did not have to wait long. With frightening speed, a large piece of the citadel wall suddenly tumbled to the ground. In a chain reaction, it precipitated the thunderous collapse of other, bigger sections. With loud cracks, brickwork and carved stones, which had been in place for decades, even centuries, crumbled and gave way. The noise as they fell more than five stories was deafening. Inevitably, some of those in the wooden terraces failed to escape in time. A short chorus of strangled screams announced their horrifying demise. Bostar clenched his jaw at the sound. It was what he had expected. As his father had said, ordinary soldiers were expendable. The loss of a certain number meant nothing. And yet to Bostar it did, like the widespread rape, torture and killing of civilians that would shortly take place. Malchus' grim nature and Sapho's even darker personality appeared not to be affected by such things, but Bostar felt it damage his soul. He did not let his determination weaken, however. There were too many things at stake. The defeat of Rome. Revenge for his beloved younger brother, Hanno. The building of a new relationship with Sapho. Whether he would ever achieve any of them, Bostar had no idea. Somehow the last seemed the most unlikely.

Immense clouds of dust clogged the air, but as they finally began to clear, the waiting Carthaginians could see an indefensible breach had been created. A swelling cheer rippled down the slope. At last, victory was at hand.

Bostar felt his spirits rise. He threw Sapho a tight smile, but all he got in return was a scowl.

Drawing his falcata sword, Hannibal led the advance.

It was at this precise moment, because of a warning from the surviving defenders on the battlements perhaps, that the screams began. Ululating, despairing, yet still with shreds of dignity, they filled the air. The Carthaginians' heads shot up. No one could ignore such terrible sounds.

"It's the nobility burning themselves to death." Malchus' voice revealed an unusual respect. "They're too proud to become slaves. May it never fall to that in Carthage."

"Ha! That day will never come," Sapho replied.

Bostar's instinctive reaction, however, was to utter a prayer to Baal Hammon. Watch over our city forever, he prayed. Keep it safe from savages such as the Romans.

Hannibal wasn't listening to the noise. He was keen to end the matter. "Charge!" he screamed in Iberian, and then, for the benefit of the Libyans, he repeated it in his own tongue. Followed by his faithful scutarii, he trotted toward the gaping hole in the citadel. Bellowing the same command, Malchus, Sapho and Bostar sprang forward with their men. Behind them, the order rang out in half a dozen languages, and, like so many thousand ants, the host of soldiers followed.

Sapho and Bostar's rivalry resurfaced with a vengeance. Whoever reached the top of the breach first would win praise from Hannibal and the respect of the entire army. Outstripping their men, they clambered neck and neck across the uneven and treacherous piles of rubble and broken masonry. With their spears in one hand, and their shields in the other, they had no way of breaking a fall. It was lunacy, but there was no going back now. Hannibal was leading, and they must follow. Soon, the brothers had drawn alongside their leader, who was two steps in front of his scutarii. Hannibal gave them an encouraging grin, which they reciprocated, before glaring at each other.

Glancing over his shoulder an instant later, Bostar's eyes widened. The downward angle of the gradient afforded him a perfect view of the Carthaginian attack. It was a magnificent and terrible sight, guaranteed to drive terror into the hearts of the defenders who remained on the walls. Bostar doubted that any would dare. With the leaders immolating themselves rather than surrender, the ordinary soldiers would be cowering in their homes with their families, or also committing suicide.

He was wrong. Not all the Saguntines had given up the struggle.

As his gaze returned to the slope before him, his attention was drawn by movement up and to the right, on a section of the battlements that was still complete. There Bostar saw six men crouched around an enormous block of stone. Working together, they were pushing it toward the broken end of the walkway that ran along the top of the wall. Bostar followed the trajectory the block would take when it fell, and his heart leaped into his mouth. While the Saguntines' purpose was to cause as many casualties as possible, the potential cost to the Carthaginians was far greater. Bostar could see that within a few heartbeats, Hannibal would be standing full square in the stone's path. A glance at Sapho, and at Hannibal himself, told Bostar that he was the only one to have seen the danger.

When he looked up again, the irregularly shaped block was already teetering on the edge. As Bostar opened his mouth in a warning shout, it tipped forward and fell. Gathering speed unbelievably fast, the stone tumbled and bounced down the slope. Its passage sent showers of brick and masonry into the air, each piece of which was capable of smashing a man's skull. Screaming with delight, the defenders turned and fled, secure in the knowledge that their final effort would kill dozens of Carthaginians.

Bostar did not think. He simply reacted. Dropping his spear, he charged sideways at Hannibal. The air filled with a sudden thunder. Bostar did not look up, for fear of soiling himself. Several scutarii, whose advance his action was checking, mouthed confused curses. Bostar paid no heed. He just prayed that none of the Iberians would think he was trying to harm Hannibal and get in his way. Now he had covered six steps. A dozen. Sensing Bostar's approach, Hannibal turned his head. Confused, he frowned. "What in the name of Baal Hammon are you doing?" he demanded.

Bostar didn't answer. Leaping forward, he swept his right arm around Hannibal's body and drove them both to the ground, with the general trapped beneath. With his left arm, Bostar raised his shield to cover both their heads. There was a heartbeat's delay, and then the earth shook. Their ears were filled with a reverberation of sound that threatened to deafen them. Thankfully it did not last, but diminished as the block crashed down the slope.

Bostar's first concern was not for himself. "Are you hurt, sir?"

Hannibal's voice was muffled. "I don't think so."

Thank the gods, thought Bostar. Gingerly, he moved his arms and legs. To his delight, they all seemed to work. Discarding his shield, he sat up, helping Hannibal to do the same.

The general swore softly. Perhaps three steps from their position, lay a scutarius. Or at least, what had once been a scutarius. The man had not so much been broken apart as smeared across the uneven ground. His bronze helmet had provided little protection. Chunks of brain matter were spread like white paste on the rocks, providing a sharp contrast to the bright red blood that oozed from the tangled mess of tissue that had been his body. Jagged pieces of brick protruded from the scutarius' back, poking holes in his tunic. His limbs were bent at unnatural, terrible angles, exposing in multiple places the gleaming white ends of broken bones.

He was just the first casualty. Below the corpse stretched a swathe of destruction as far as the eye could see. Bostar had never witnessed anything like it. Dozens of soldiers, perhaps more, had been killed. No. Pulverized, Bostar thought. A wave of nausea washed over him, and he struggled not to be sick.

Hannibal's voice startled him. "It appears that I owe you my life."

Numbly, Bostar nodded.

"My thanks. You are a fine soldier," said Hannibal, clambering to his feet. He helped Bostar to do the same.

In the same instant, those of Hannibal's scutarii who had not been harmed came swarming in, their faces twisted with alarm. Naturally, the attack had been stalled by the Saguntines' daring action. Anxious questions filled the air as the Iberians established that their beloved commander had not been hurt. Hannibal quickly brushed them off. Picking up his falcata sword, which had fallen to the ground, he looked at Bostar. "Are you ready to finish what we started?" he asked.

Bostar was stunned by the speed at which Hannibal's composure had returned. He himself was still in shock. He managed to nod his head. "Of course, sir."

"Excellent," replied Hannibal with a brief smile. He indicated that Bostar should advance beside him.

Retrieving his spear, Bostar obeyed. He barely took in the pleased grin that Malchus gave him, and the equally poisonous expression on Sapho's face. Elation had replaced his terror, and he could try to patch things up with his brother later.

For now, it was all about following Hannibal.

A true leader of men.

IX

MINUCIUS FLACCUS

Hanno leaned against the wall of the kitchen, admiring the view as Elira bent over a table laden down with food. Her dress rode up, exposing her shapely calves and tightening over the swell of her buttocks. Hanno's groin throbbed, and he shifted position to avoid his excitement being obvious. Elira and Quintus were still lovers, but that didn't mean Hanno couldn't admire her from a distance. Alarmingly, Elira had noticed his glances, and returned them with smoldering ones of her own, but Hanno had not risked taking things any further. His newly born—and potentially valuable—friendship with Quintus was too fragile to survive a revelation like that.

Since the fight at the hut, his circumstances had become much easier. Fabricius had been impressed by Quintus' account of the fight and the physical evidence of two live, if wounded, prisoners. Hanno's reward was to be made a household slave. His manacles were removed and he was allowed to sleep in the house. Initially, Hanno was delighted. At one stroke, he had been removed from Agesandros' grasp.

Weeks later, he was not so sure. The harsh reality of his situation seemed starker than ever before.

Three times a day, Hanno had to attend the family at their meals. Naturally, he was not allowed to eat with them. He saw Aurelia and Quintus daily from morning to night, but could not talk to them unless no one else was about. Even then, conversations were hurried. It was all so different from the time they had spent together in the woods. Despite the enforced distance between them, Hanno was relieved that the palpable air of comradeship—which had so recently sprung up— had not vanished. Quintus' occasional winks and Aurelia's shy smiles now lit up his days. Lastly, there was Elira, whose bedroll was not twenty paces from his, on the floor of the atrium, and whom he dared not approach. Hanno knew that he should be grateful for his lot. On the occasions that he and Agesandros came face-to-face, it was patently clear that the Sicilian still wished him harm.

"Father!" Aurelia's delighted voice echoed from the courtyard. "You're back!"

As curious as any, Hanno followed the other kitchen slaves to the door. Fabricius hadn't been expected home for at least two weeks.

Dressed in a belted tunic and sandals, Fabricius stood by the main fountain. A broad smile creased his face as Aurelia raced up to him. "I'm filthy," he warned. "Covered in dust from the journey."

"I don't care!" She wrapped her arms around him. "It's so good to see you."

He gave her an affectionate hug. "I have missed you too."

A pang of sadness at his own plight plucked at Hanno's heart, but he did not allow himself to dwell on it.

"Husband. Thank the gods for your safe return." With a sedate smile, Atia joined her husband and daughter. Aurelia pulled away, allowing Fabricius to kiss his wife on the cheek. They gave each other a pleased look, which spoke volumes. "You must be thirsty."

"My throat's as dry as a desert riverbed," Fabricius replied.

Atia's eyes swiveled to the kitchen doorway, and the gaggle of watching slaves. She caught Hanno's gaze first. "Bring wine! The rest of you, back to work."

The doorway emptied in a flash. Every slave knew not to cross

Atia, who ruled the household with a silken yet iron-hard grip. Quickly, Hanno reached down four of the best glasses from the shelf and placed them on a tray. Julius, the friendly slave who ran the kitchen, was already reaching for an amphora. Hanno watched as he diluted the wine in the Roman fashion with four times the amount of water. "There you go," Julius muttered, placing a full jug on the tray. "Get out there before she calls again."

Hanno hurried to obey. He was keen to know what had brought about Fabricius' early return. With pricked ears, he carried the tray toward the family, who had just been joined by Quintus.

Quintus grinned broadly, before he remembered that he was now a man. "Father," he said solemnly. "It is good to see you."

Fabricius pinched his son's cheek. "You've grown even more."

Quintus blushed. To cover his embarrassment, he turned expectantly to Hanno. "Come on, then. Fill them up."

Hanno stiffened at the order, but did as he was told. His hand paused over the fourth glass, and he looked to Atia.

"Yes, yes, pour one for Aurelia too. She's practically a woman."

Aurelia's happy expression slipped away. "Have you found me a husband?" she asked accusingly. "Is that why you've come back?"

Atia frowned. "Do not be so presumptuous!"

Aurelia's cheeks flamed red and she hung her head.

"I wish it were that simple, daughter," Fabricius answered. "While I have made some progress in that regard, there are far greater events occurring on the world stage." He clicked his fingers at Hanno, whose heart raced as he moved from person to person, distributing the wine.

"What has happened?" asked Atia.

Instead of answering, Fabricius raised his glass. "A toast," he said. "That the gods, and our ancestors, continue to smile on our family."

Atia's face tightened a fraction, but she joined in the salutation.

Quintus was less ruled by decorum than his mother, and jumped in the moment his father had swallowed. "Tell us why you've returned!"

"Saguntum has fallen," Fabricius replied flatly.

Blood rushed through Hanno's ears, and he was acutely aware of Quintus spinning to regard him. Carefully, he wiped a drop of wine from the jug's lip with a cloth. Inside, every fiber of his being was rejoicing. Hannibal! his mind shouted. Hannibal!

Quintus' gaze shot back to his father. "When?"

"A week ago. Apparently, they spared virtually no one. Men, women, children. The few who survived were taken as slaves."

Atia's lips tightened. "Absolute savages."

Hanno found Aurelia staring at him with wide, horrified eyes. It's not as if your people don't do exactly the same thing when they sack a city, he thought furiously. Of course he could say nothing, so he turned his face away.

In contrast to his sister, Quintus looked angry. "It was bad enough that the Senate did nothing to help one of our allies for the last eight months. Surely they'll act now?"

"They will," Fabricius replied. "In fact, they already have."

The following silence echoed louder than a trumpet call.

"An embassy has been sent to Carthage, its mission to demand that Hannibal and his senior officers be handed over immediately to face justice for their heinous actions."

Hanno squeezed the cloth so hard that it dripped wine on to the mosaic between his feet.

No one noticed. Not that Hanno would have cared. How dare they? his mind screamed. Bastard Romans!

"They will hardly do that," said Atia.

"Of course not," Fabricius answered, unaware of Hanno's silent but fervent agreement. "No doubt Hannibal has his enemies, but the Carthaginians are a proud race. They will want redress for the humiliations we subjected them to after the war in Sicily. This grants them that opportunity."

Quintus hesitated for a moment. "You're talking about war?"

Fabricius nodded. "I think that's what it will come to, yes. There are those in the Senate who disagree with me, but I think they underestimate Hannibal. A man who has achieved what he has in a few short years would not have embarked on the siege of Saguntum without it being part of a larger plan. Hannibal wanted a war with Rome all along."

How right you are, thought Hanno exultantly.

Quintus was also jubilant. "Gaius and I can join the cavalry!"

Fabricius' obvious pride was tempered by Atia's reticence. Even she could not hide the sadness that flashed across her eyes. Her composure returned quickly. "You will make a fine soldier."

Quintus blew out his chest with satisfaction. "I must tell Gaius. Can I go to Capua?"

Fabricius gave an approving nod. "Go on. You'll need to hurry. It's not long until dark."

"I'll come back tomorrow." With a grateful smile, Quintus was gone.

Looking after him, Atia sighed. "And the other matter?"

"There is some good news." Seeing Aurelia's instant interest, Fabricius clammed up. "I'll tell you later."

Aurelia's face fell. "Everything is so unfair," she cried, and hurried off to her room.

Atia touched Fabricius' arm to still his rebuke. "Let her go. It must be hard for her."

Hanno was oblivious to the family drama. Suddenly, his desire to escape, to reach Iberia and join his countrymen in their conflict, was overwhelming. It was what he had dreamed of for so long! Yet his debt to Quintus loomed large in his mind too. Had it been repaid by what he'd done at the shepherd's hut or not? Hanno wasn't sure. Then there was Suniaton. How could he even entertain leaving without trying to find his best friend? Hanno was grateful when he heard Julius' voice calling him. The conflicting emotions in his head were threatening to tear him apart.

Time went by, and Hanno was still working in the kitchen. Although an answer regarding his obligation to Quintus evaded him yet, he could not bring himself to abandon the farm without some attempt to find Suniaton. How the quest would be achieved, Hanno had no idea. Apart from him, who knew, or even cared, where Suniaton was now? The unanswerable dilemma kept him awake at night, and even distracted him from his usual lustful thoughts about Elira. Tired and irritable, he paid little attention one day when Julius announced an exhaustive menu that Atia had ordered for the following evening. "Apparently, she and the master are expecting an important visitor," said Julius pompously. "Caius Minucius Flaccus."

"Who in the name of Hades is that?" asked one of the cooks.

Julius gave him a disapproving look. "He's a senior figure in the Minucii clan, and the brother of a former consul."

"He'll be an arrogant prick then," muttered the cook.

Julius ignored the titters this produced. "He's also a member of the embassy that has just returned from Carthage," he declared as if the matter were of some importance to him.

Hanno's stomach turned over. "Really? Are you sure?"

Julius' lips pursed. "That's what I heard the mistress saying," he snapped. "Now get on with your work."

Hanno's heart was thudding off his ribs like that of a caged bird as he went out to the storage sheds. Would Fabricius' visitor speak of what he'd seen? Hanno begged the gods that he would. Passing the entrance to the heated bathroom, he saw Quintus stripping off. Well for him, thought Hanno sourly. He hadn't had a hot bath since leaving Carthage.

Blithely unaware of Hanno's feelings, Quintus' excitement was rising by the moment. Wanting to look his best that evening, he bathed, before enjoying a massage by a slave. Sleepily imagining how Flaccus might recount everything that had gone on in Carthage, he was barely aware of Fabricius entering the room.

"This visit is very important, you know."

Quintus opened his eyes. "Yes, Father. And we will play our part in the war, if it comes."

Fabricius half smiled. "That goes without saying. When Rome calls, we answer." Clasping his hands behind his back, he walked up and down in silence.

The feel of the strigil on his skin began to irritate Quintus, and he gestured at the slave to stop. "What is it?"

"It's about Aurelia," Fabricius answered.

"You've arranged to marry her off, then," he said, shooting his father a bitter glance.

"It's not definite yet," said Fabricius. "But Flaccus liked what he heard of Aurelia when I visited him in the capital some time ago. Now he wants to see her beauty for himself."

Quintus scowled at his naïveté. Why else would a high-ranking politician pay a social visit to equestrians as lowly as they?

"Come now," said Fabricius sternly. "You knew this would happen one day. It's for the good of the family. Flaccus is not that old, and his clan is powerful and well connected. With the support of the Minucii, the Fabricii could go far." He stared at Quintus. "In Rome, I mean. You understand what I'm saying?"

Quintus sighed. "Does Aurelia know yet?"

"No." It was Fabricius' turn to look troubled. "I thought I would speak to you first."

"Make me part of it?"

"Don't take that line with me. You would also benefit," snapped his father.

Excitement flared in Quintus' breast, and he hated himself for it. He'd seen Aurelia mooning over Hanno. An impossible infatuation for her, but one he'd done nothing to end. And now this. "What made you decide on Flaccus?"

"I've been trying to organize something for the last two years," Fabricius replied. "Searching for the right man for our family, and for Aurelia. It's a tricky business, but I think Flaccus could be the one. He was going to be passing close to here anyway upon his return from Carthage. All I did was to make sure that an invitation was waiting for him when he landed."

Quintus was surprised by his father's cunning. No doubt his mother had had a hand in it, he thought. "How old is he?"

"Thirty-five or so," said Fabricius. "That's a lot better than some of the old goats who wanted to meet her. I hope she appreciates that." He paused. "One last thing."

Quintus looked up.

"Don't ask any questions about what happened in Carthage," his father warned. "It is still a matter of state secrecy. If Flaccus chooses to fill us in on some of the details, so be it. If he does not, it's none of our business to ask." With that, he was gone.

Quintus lay back on the warm stone slab, but all his enjoyment was gone. He would go to Aurelia the moment his father had finished speaking with her. What he would say, Quintus had no idea. His mood dark, he got dressed. The best place to watch Aurelia's doorway unobtrusively was from a corner of the tablinum. Quintus made his way to the large reception room. He hadn't been there long when Hanno entered, carrying a tray of crockery.

Seeing Quintus, Hanno smiled. "Looking forward to this evening?"

I am, he thought with glee.

"Not really," Quintus replied dourly.

Hanno raised his eyebrows. "Why not? You don't receive many visitors."

Quintus was surprised to find that his excitement about what Flaccus might say was muted by his friendship with Hanno. "It's hard to explain," he replied awkwardly.

At that moment, Fabricius strode from Aurelia's room, banging the door behind him. His jaw was set with anger.

Their conversation instantly came to an end. Hanno could only watch as Quintus entered his sister's chamber in turn. Hanno was genuinely fond of Aurelia. Part of him wondered what was going on, but part of him didn't care. Finally, Carthage was at war with Rome once more.

Somehow, he would be involved in it.

Quintus found Aurelia lying on her bed, huge sobs racking her body. He rushed to kneel by her side. "It will be all right," he whispered, reaching out to stroke her hair. "Flaccus sounds like a good man."

Her crying redoubled, and Quintus muttered a curse. Mentioning the man's name was the worst possible thing he could have done. Not knowing what to do, he rubbed Aurelia's shoulders comfortingly. They stayed in that position without talking for a long time. Finally, Aurelia rolled over. Her cheeks were red and blotchy, and her eyes swollen from weeping. "I must look terrible," she said.

Quintus gave her a crooked smile. "You're still beautiful," he replied.

She stuck out her tongue. "Liar."

"A bath will help," advised Quintus. He put on a jovial face. "Won't it?"

Aurelia could not keep up the pretense. "What am I going to do?" she whispered miserably.

"It was going to happen sometime," said Quintus. "Why don't you give him the benefit of the doubt? If you really hate him, Father would not make you go ahead with the marriage."

"I suppose not," Aurelia replied dubiously. She thought for a moment. "I know I have to do what Father says. It's so hard, though, especially when . . ." Her voice died away, and new tears filled her eyes.

Quintus raised a finger to her lips. "Don't say it," he whispered. "You can't." He didn't want to hear it spoken out loud.

With great effort, Aurelia regained control of her emotions. She nodded resolutely. "Better get ready, then. I have to look my best to-night."

Quintus drew her into a warm embrace. "That's the spirit," he whispered. Possessing courage was not an exclusively male quality, he realized. Nor was it confined to the battlefield or the hunt. Aurelia had just shown that she had plenty of it too.

Flaccus arrived midafternoon, accompanied by a large party of slaves and soldiers, and was immediately ushered to the best guest room to freshen up. Apart from his personal slaves, most of Flaccus' retinue stayed outside, where they were quartered in the farmyard. Hanno was busy in the kitchen and saw little of the proceedings for some time. An hour later, loud voices announced the appearance of Martialis and Gaius. They were greeted jovially by Fabricius, and guided to the banqueting hall off the courtyard where, following tradition, they were first served *mulsum*, a mixture of wine and honey. Elira performed this task, leaving Hanno to wait impatiently in the kitchen. As darkness fell, he walked around the courtyard, lighting the bronze oil lamps that hung from every pillar. At the corner farthest from the tablinum, Hanno sensed movement behind him. He turned, gaining an impression of a handsome man in a toga with thick black hair and a big nose before Flaccus disappeared into the banqueting hall. Quintus and his sister arrived soon after, wearing their best clothes. Hanno had never seen Aurelia wearing makeup before. To his surprise, he liked what he saw.

Finally, the meal was ready, and Hanno could enter the room with the other slaves. He was to remain there for the duration of the meal, serving food, clearing away plates and, most importantly of all, listening to the conversation. He waited attentively behind the left-hand couch, where Fabricius reclined with Martialis and Gaius. As an important guest, Flaccus had been given the central couch, while Atia, Quintus and an impassive Aurelia occupied the right-hand one. In customary fashion, the fourth side of the table had been left open.

Flaccus spent much of his time complimenting Aurelia on her looks and trying to engage her in conversation. His attempts met with little initial success. Finally, when Atia began to glare at her openly, she started to respond. To Hanno, it was obvious that she was being insincere, merely doing what her mother wished. Flaccus did not seem to notice this, or that apart from Fabricius, the others present did not dare to address him. Quintus and Gaius alone cast frequent glances at Flaccus, hoping in vain for news of Carthage. Quaffing large amounts of mulsum and wine, the black-haired politician seemed more and more taken by Aurelia as the night went on.

Over the sweet platters, Flaccus turned to Fabricius. "My compliments on your daughter. She is as beautiful as you said. More so, perhaps."

Fabricius inclined his head gravely. "Thank you."

"I think we should talk further on this matter in the morning," boomed Flaccus. "Come to a mutually satisfactory arrangement."

Fabricius allowed himself a small smile. "That would be a great honor."

Atia murmured her agreement.

"Excellent." Flaccus looked at Hanno. "More wine."

Hanno hurried forward, his face a neutral mask. He wasn't sure how he felt about what had just been said. Not that it mattered, he reflected bitterly. Here I am a slave. His resentment over his status surged back, stronger than ever, and he dismissed his concern about Aurelia's possible betrothal. The bonds that tied him to the farm were weakening. If Aurelia married Flaccus, she would go to live in Rome. Quintus was always talking about joining the army. When he left, Hanno would be left friendless and alone. On the spot, he resolved to begin planning his escape.

Quintus had decided that Flaccus seemed quite personable and glanced sidelong at Aurelia. He was delighted to see no sign of distress in her face, and marveled at her equanimity. Then he noted the slight flush to her cheeks, and her empty glass. Was she drunk? It wouldn't take much. Aurelia rarely consumed wine. In spite of this, Quintus found his head full of the possibilities that an alliance between the Fabricii and Minucii would create. Aurelia and Flaccus would get used to each other, he told himself. That's the way most marriages worked. He reached out to touch Aurelia's hand. She smiled, and he was reassured.

The conversation flitted about for some time, with talk of the weather, the crops and the quality of the games in Capua compared to Rome. No one mentioned the one topic that everyone wanted to know about: what had happened in Carthage?

It was Martialis who eventually broached the subject. As was his wont, he had been drinking large amounts. Draining his cup yet again, he saluted Flaccus. "They say that the Carthaginian wines are very drinkable."

"They are agreeable enough," accepted Flaccus. He pursed his lips. "Unlike the people who produce them."

Martialis was oblivious to Fabricius' frowns. "Will we be seeing such vintages in Italy more often?" he asked with a wink.

Flaccus dragged his eyes away from Aurelia. "Eh?"

"Tell us what happened in Carthage," begged Martialis. "We are all dying to know."

Hanno held his breath, and he could see Quintus doing the same.

Slowly, Flaccus took in the rapt faces around him. His features took on a self-important expression, and he smiled, pompously. "Nothing I say is to travel beyond these walls."

"Of course not," Martialis murmured. "You can be assured of our discretion."

Even Fabricius joined in with the buzz of agreement.

Satisfied, Flaccus began. "I was but a minor member of the party, although I like to think my contribution was noted. We were led by the two consuls, Lucius Aemilius Paullus and Marcus Livius Salinator. Our spokesman was the former censor Marcus Fabius Buteo." He let the important names sink in. "From the start, it seemed that our mission would be successful. The omens were good, and the crossing from

Lilybaeum uneventful. We reached Carthage three weeks ago to the day."

Hanno closed his eyes and imagined the scene. The massive fortifications gleaming in the winter sun. The magnificent temple of Eshmoun dominating the top of Byrsa Hill. The twin harbors full of ships. Home, he thought with a jolt of longing. Will I ever see it again?

Flaccus' next words brought him back to earth with a jolt. "Arrogant sons of whores," he growled. He glanced at Atia. "My apologies. But the most significant men in Rome had arrived, and who had they sent to meet us? A junior officer of the city guard."

Martialis' face went purple with rage, and he nearly choked on a mouthful of wine.

Fabricius was of a calmer disposition. "It must have been a mistake, surely," he said.

Flaccus scowled. "On the contrary. The gesture was quite deliberate. They had made up their minds before we even disembarked from our ships. Instead of being allowed time to wash and recover from the journey, we were escorted straight to the Senate."

Martialis snorted. "Typical bloody guggas. No sense of decorum."

Aurelia cast Hanno a quick, sympathetic glance.

The Carthaginian was so angry that he dared not look back at her. He longed to smash the clay jug in his hands over Martialis' head, but of course he did nothing. Punishment aside, what Flaccus had to say next was of far more importance.

"And when you got there?" asked Quintus eagerly.

"Fabius announced who we were. No one responded. They just stood there looking at us. Waiting, like so many jackals around a corpse. And so Fabius demanded to know if Hannibal's attack on Saguntum had been carried out with their approval." Flaccus paused, breathing heavily. "Do you know what they did then?" A vein pulsed in his forehead. "They laughed at us."

Martialis slammed his beaker on the table. Fabricius spat a curse, while Quintus and Gaius gaped at each other, stunned that anyone would treat the Republic's most prominent statesmen in such a manner. Atia took the opportunity to mutter something in Aurelia's ear. Hanno, meanwhile, had to bite the inside of his cheek to stop himself from laughing out loud. Carthage had not lost all of its pride when it lost Sicily and Sardinia to Rome, he reflected proudly.

"There were some who spoke out against Hannibal," Flaccus conceded. "The loudest among them was a fat man called Hostus."

Treacherous bastard! thought Hanno. What I'd give to stick a knife in his belly.

"But they were shouted down by the vast majority, who disputed the treaty signed by Hasdrubal six years ago and rejected any need to acknowledge Saguntum's links with Rome. They were shouting and hurling abuse at us," growled Flaccus. "We took counsel with each other, and decided we had only one option."

Quintus glanced at Hanno. He had had no idea that the Carthaginians would react with such force. Stunned by what he saw, he looked again. Quintus knew Hanno's body language well enough to realize that he *had* known. Flaccus' voice stopped him from dwelling on the matter further.

"Fabius walked into the middle of the chamber. That shut the guggas up," said Flaccus fiercely. "Gripping the folds of his toga, he told them that within he held both peace and war. They could have whichever they pleased. At his words, the place descended into chaos. It was impossible even to hear yourself speak."

"Did they opt for war?" demanded Fabricius.

"No," revealed Flaccus. "Instead, the presiding suffete told Fabius that he should choose."

By now everyone in the room, even Elira, was hanging on his every word.

"Fabius looked at us to confirm that we were of one mind, and then he told the guggas that he let fall war." Flaccus barked a short, angry laugh. "They've got balls, I'll grant them that. Fabius had hardly finished speaking when practically every single man in the chamber stood up and yelled, 'We accept it!'"

Hanno found he could no longer conceal his delight. Picking up two handfuls of dirty plates, he headed for the kitchen. No one except Aurelia noticed him leave. But once outside the door, Hanno's desire to hear more was so great that he lingered on, eavesdropping.

"I always hoped that another war with Carthage could be avoided," said Fabricius heavily. His jaw hardened. "But they leave us no choice.

Insulting you and your colleagues, and especially the consuls, in that manner is unforgivable."

"Absolutely right," thundered Martialis. "The curs must be taught an even better lesson than last time."

Flaccus was pleased by their reactions. "Good," he muttered. "Why don't you both come with me to Rome? Much needs to be arranged, and we will need men who have fought Carthage before."

"It would be my honor," replied Fabricius.

"And mine," added Martialis. An embarrassed look crossed his florid face, and he tapped his right leg. "Except for this. It's an old injury, from Sicily. Nowadays, I can barely walk more than a quarter of a mile without stopping for a rest."

"You have more than done your duty for Rome," said Flaccus reassuringly. "I shall just take Fabricius."

Quintus was on his feet before he knew it. "I want to fight too."

Gaius echoed his cry a heartbeat later.

Flaccus' smile was patronizing. "Both quite the dogs of war, aren't you? But I'm afraid that you're still too young. This struggle needs to be won fast, and the best men to do that are veterans."

"I'm seventeen," protested Quintus. "So is Gaius."

Flaccus' face darkened. "Remember whom you are speaking to," he snapped.

"Quintus! Sit down," Fabricius ordered. "You too, Gaius." As the two reluctantly obeyed, he turned to Flaccus. "My apologies. They're eager, that's all."

"It's of no matter. Their time will come," Flaccus replied smoothly, shooting Quintus a look of venom. It was gone so fast that no one else noticed. Quintus wondered if he'd been mistaken, but a moment later he saw something else. Aurelia made her excuses and retired for the night. Flaccus watched her retreating back as a serpent might look at a mouse. Quintus blinked, trying to clear his head, which was fuzzy from wine. When he looked again, Flaccus' expression was benevolent. I must have been imagining it, he concluded. Quintus was then disappointed to see the three older men gather in a huddle and begin muttering in low voices. Atia jerked her head at him in a clear sign of dismissal. Frustrated, Quintus beckoned Gaius outside to the courtyard.

Their appearance startled Hanno. Having hidden from Aurelia, he was only just emerging from behind an ornamental statue. Looking guilty, he scuttled off to the kitchen.

Gaius frowned. "What in Hades is he up to?"

Later, Quintus was not sure whether it was because of the wine he'd drunk or his anger at the treatment of the Roman embassy. Either way, he wanted to lash out at someone. "Who cares?" he snapped. "He's a gugga. Let him go." Quintus regretted the words the instant they left his mouth. He made to walk after Hanno, but Gaius, who was laughing, dragged him over to a stone bench by the fountain. "Let's talk," his friend muttered drunkenly.

Quintus dared not pull away. The darkness concealed his stricken face.

His shoulders stiff with repressed fury, Hanno did not look back. It was ten more steps to the kitchen, where he clattered the dishes angrily into the sink. So much for friendship with a Roman, he thought, bitterness coursing through his veins. He knew that Aurelia was sympathetic toward him, but he could not be sure of anyone else. Especially Quintus. The anger he'd heard in all the nobles' voices at Flaccus' revelation was natural, yet it changed Hanno's situation completely. In principle, he was now an enemy. His own delight at the matter would have to be buried so deeply that no one could see it. In the close confines of the house, Hanno knew how difficult this would prove. He exhaled slowly. An important decision had just been made for him. He should run away. Soon. But to Carthage or Iberia? And was there any chance of finding Suniaton before he left?

X

BETRAYAL

The next morning Quintus had another hangover, and his memories of Flaccus' facial expressions were hazy. Enough disquiet remained in his mind, however, for him to seek out his father. He found Fabricius closeted in his office with Flaccus. The pair were busily drawing up Aurelia's betrothal papers, and looked irritated by the distraction. Fabricius brushed off Quintus' muttered request for a word. Seeing his son's disappointment, he relented slightly. "Tell me later," he said.

Glumly, Quintus shut the door. He had other things on his mind too. He had insulted Hanno cruelly and he was ashamed. The Carthaginian's status meant that Quintus could treat him in any way he chose, but of course that was not the point. He saved my life. We are friends now, thought Quintus. I owe him an apology. Yet his quest to resolve this problem proved as frustrating as his attempt to speak with his father. He found Hanno easily enough, but the Carthaginian pretended not to hear Quintus' voice when he called, and avoided all attempts to make eye contact. Quintus didn't want to make a scene, and there was so much going on that he could not even find a quiet corner to explain. Fabricius' decision to accompany Flaccus to Rome and thence to war meant that the place was a flurry of activity. Every household slave was occupied in one way or another. Clothes, furniture and blankets had to be packed, armor polished and weapons sharpened.

Quintus went miserably in search of Aurelia. He wasn't sure whether he should mention anything about Flaccus. All he had to go on were two fleeting glimpses, observed while under the influence of too much wine. He decided to see what frame of mind Aurelia was in before saying a word. If she was still feeling positive about the marriage, he would say nothing. The last thing Quintus wanted to do was upset his sister's fragile acceptance of her lot.

To his surprise, Aurelia was in excellent humor. "He is so handsome," she gushed. "And not that old either. I think we will be very happy."

Burying his doubts, Quintus nodded and smiled.

"He strikes me as being quite arrogant, but what man of his position isn't? His loyalty to Rome is beyond doubt, and that is all that matters." Aurelia's face grew troubled. "I felt so sorry for Hanno last night. The horrible names they were calling his people were so unnecessary. Have you spoken with him?"

Quintus looked away. "No."

Aurelia reacted with typical female intuition. "What's wrong?" she demanded.

"Nothing," Quintus replied. "I have a hangover, that's all."

She bent to catch his eye. "Did you argue with Hanno?"

"No," he answered. "Yes. I don't know."

Aurelia raised her eyebrows, and Quintus knew that she would not leave it alone until he told her. "When I left with Gaius, it looked like Hanno had been eavesdropping outside the door," he said.

"Is that surprising? We were talking about a war between his people and ours," Aurelia observed tartly. "What does it matter anyway? He was there in the room when Flaccus told us the most important part of his story."

"I know," Quintus muttered. "It seemed suspicious, though. Gaius wanted to challenge him, but I told him not to bother. That Hanno was just a gugga."

Aurelia's hand rose to her mouth. "Quintus! How could you?"

Quintus hung his head. "I wanted to say sorry straightaway . . . but Gaius wanted to talk," he finished lamely. "I couldn't walk off and leave him."

"I hope you've apologized this morning," Aurelia said sternly.

Quintus could not get over Aurelia's level of self-assurance. It was as if her betrothal had added five years to her age. "I've tried," he answered. "But there's too much going on to get a quiet moment alone with him."

Aurelia pursed her lips. "Father is leaving in a few hours. There will be plenty of time after that."

Finally, Quintus met her gaze. "Don't worry," he said. "I'll do it."

He had cause to rethink his opinion of Flaccus later that morning. With the betrothal agreement signed, the black-haired politician suddenly started to make much of his new brother-in-law-to-be. "No doubt this war with Carthage will be over quickly—maybe even before you've completed your military training," he declared, throwing an arm around Quintus' shoulders. "Never fear. There will be other conflicts for you to win glory in. The Gauls on our northern borders are forever causing trouble. So too are the Illyrians. Philip of Macedon cannot be trusted either. A brave young officer like you could go far indeed. Perhaps even make tribune."

Quintus grinned from ear to ear. While the Fabricii were of equestrian rank, their status was not so high that it was likely he'd reach the tribuneship. Under the patronage of someone really powerful, however, the process would be much more straightforward. Flaccus' words did much to soothe Quintus' disappointment at not accompanying his father. "I look forward to serving Rome," he said proudly. "Wherever it may send me."

Flaccus clapped him on the back. "That's the attitude." Seeing Aurelia, he pushed Quintus away. "Let me talk with my betrothed before I go. It's a long time until June."

Delighted by the prospect of a glittering military career, Quintus put down Flaccus' powerful shove as nothing more than the excitement of a prospective bridegroom. Aurelia was turning into a beautiful young woman. Who wouldn't want to marry her? Leaving Flaccus alone, Quintus went in search of his father.

———

"Aurelia!" called Flaccus, entering the courtyard.

Aurelia, who had been wondering what married life would be like, jumped. She made a stiff little bow. "Flaccus."

"Walk with me." He made an inviting gesture.

Twin points of color rose in Aurelia's cheeks. "I'm not sure Mother would approve . . ."

"What do you take me for?" Flaccus' tone was mildly shocked. "I would never presume to take you outside the villa without a chaperone. I meant a stroll here in the courtyard, where everyone can see us."

"Naturally," Aurelia replied, flustered. "I'm sorry."

"The fault is all mine for not explaining," he said with a reassuring smile. "I merely thought that, with us to be wed, it would be good for us to spend a little time together. War is coming, and soon occasions such as this will be impossible."

"Yes, of course." She hurried to his side.

Flaccus drank her in. "Bacchus can make the most crab-faced crone look appealing, and the gods know I drank enough of his juice to think that last night. But your beauty is even more evident in the light of the sun," he said. "That *is* a rare quality."

Unused to such compliments, Aurelia blushed to the roots of her hair. "Thank you," she whispered.

They strolled around the perimeter of the courtyard. Awkward with the silence, Aurelia began pointing out the plants and trees that occupied much of the space. There were lemon, almond and fig trees, and vines snaking across a wooden latticework that formed an artificial shaded corridor. "This is such a bad time of year to see it," she said. "During the summer, the place is so beautiful. By the Vinalia Rustica, you can barely move for the fruit."

"I'm sure it's spectacular, but I didn't come here to talk about grapes." Seeing her embarrassment increase, Flaccus continued, "Tell me about yourself. What do you like to do?"

Anxious, Aurelia wondered what he'd want to hear. "I enjoy speaking Greek. And I'm better at algebra and geometry than Quintus."

The corners of his mouth twitched. "Are you indeed? That's wonderful. An educated girl, then."

She flushed again. "I suppose."

"You'd probably give me a run for my money. Mathematics was never my favorite subject."

Aurelia's confidence grew a little. "What about philosophy?"

He looked down his long nose at her. "The concepts of *pietas* and *officium* were being taught to me before I'd even been weaned. My father made sure that serving Rome means everything to me and my brother. We had to be schooled too, of course. Before we had any military experience, he sent us to study at the Stoic school in Athens. I didn't enjoy my time there much, however. All they did was sit around and talk in stuffy debating chambers. It reminds me a little of the Senate." Flaccus' face brightened. "Soon, though, I might be granted a senior position in one of the legions. I'm sure that will be more to my style."

Aurelia found his enthusiasm endearing. It reminded her of Quintus, which made her think of what he might achieve once she had married into such an important family. "Your brother has already served as consul, hasn't he?"

"Yes," Flaccus replied proudly. "He crushed the Boii four years ago."

Aurelia had never heard of the Boii, but she wasn't going to admit it. "I've heard Father mention that campaign," she said knowledgeably. "It was a fine victory."

"May the gods grant that I achieve the same level of success one day," Flaccus said fervently. His gaze went distant for a moment before returning to Aurelia. "Not to say I don't like ordinary pleasures like watching chariot races, or going riding, and hunting."

"So do I," Aurelia said without thinking.

He smiled indulgently. "The racing in Rome is the best in Italy. I'll take you to see it as often as you wish."

Aurelia felt slightly annoyed. "That's not what I meant."

There was a small frown. "I don't understand."

Her courage wavered for a moment. Then she thought naïvely, If he's to be my husband, we should tell each other everything. "I love riding too."

Flaccus' frown grew. "You mean watching your father or Quintus as they train their horses?"

"No. I can ride." She was delighted by his astonishment.

It was Flaccus' turn to be irritated. "How? Who taught you?" he demanded.

"Quintus. He says I'm a natural."

"Your brother taught you how to ride?"

Pinned by his direct stare, Aurelia's confidence began to seep away. "Yes," she muttered. "I made him."

Flaccus barked a short laugh. "You *made* him? Fabricius mentioned none of this when he was singing your praises."

Aurelia looked down. I should have kept my mouth shut, she thought. Lifting her head, she found Flaccus scrutinizing her. She shifted uneasily beneath his gaze.

"Do you fight also?"

Aurelia's mouth opened at his unexpected tack.

He thrust his right arm forward, mimicking a sword thrust. "Can you wield a gladius?"

Worried by what she'd already revealed, Aurelia kept her lips sealed.

"I asked you a question." Flaccus' voice was soft, but his eyes were granite hard.

What I've done isn't a crime, thought Aurelia angrily. "Yes, I can," she retorted. "I'm far better with a sling, though."

Flaccus threw his hands in the air. "I'm to be married to an Amazon!" he cried. "Do your parents know of this?"

"Of course not."

"No, I don't suppose Fabricius would be too pleased. I can only imagine what Atia's reaction might be."

"Please don't tell them," Aurelia begged. "Quintus would be in so much trouble."

He watched her for a moment, before a wolfish smile crossed his lips. "Why would I say a word?"

Aurelia couldn't believe her ears. "You don't mind?"

"No! It shows your Roman spirit, and it means that our sons will be warriors." Flaccus held up a warning finger. "Don't expect that you can carry on using weapons when we're married, however. Such behavior is not acceptable in Rome."

"And riding?" Aurelia whispered.

"We'll see," he said. He saw her face fall, and a strange look entered his eyes. "My estate outside the capital is very large. Unless I tell them, no one knows what goes on there."

Overwhelmed by Flaccus' reaction, Aurelia missed the silky emphasis he laid on the last seven words. Perhaps marriage would not be as bad as she'd thought. She took his arm. "It's your turn to tell me about yourself now," she murmured.

He gave her a pleased look, and began.

Quintus found his father outside, supervising the loading of his baggage on to a train of mules.

Fabricius smiled as he emerged. "What was it that you wanted to tell me earlier?"

"It was nothing important," Quintus demurred. He had decided to give Flaccus the benefit of the doubt. He cast a dubious eye over the pack animals, which were laden down with every piece of his father's military equipment. "How long do you think this war will last? Flaccus seems certain that it will be over in a few months."

Fabricius checked that no one was in earshot. "I think he's a little overconfident. You know what politicians can be like."

"But Flaccus is talking about getting married in June."

Fabricius winked. "He wanted to settle on a date. I obliged. What could be better than the most popular month of the year? And if it can't take place because we're still on campaign, the betrothal agreement ensures that it will happen at some stage."

Quintus grinned at Fabricius' guile. He thought for a moment, deciding that his father was more likely to be correct than Flaccus about the war's duration. "I'm already old enough to enlist."

Fabricius' face turned serious. "I know," he said. "As well as keeping an eye on you, I have asked Martialis to enrol you in the local cavalry unit, alongside Gaius. In my absence, your mother is obviously responsible for Aurelia and the care of the farm, but you will have to help her in every way possible. Yet I see no reason why you should not also begin your training."

Quintus' eyes glittered with delight.

"Don't get any madcap ideas," his father warned. "There is no question of being called up in the immediate future. The horsemen supplied by Rome and its surrounding area will be more than enough for the moment."

Quintus did his best not to look disappointed.

Fabricius took him by the shoulders. "Listen to me. War is not all valor and glory: far from it. It's about blood, filth and fighting until you can barely grip a sword. You'll see terrible things. Men bleeding to death for lack of a tourniquet. Comrades and friends dying in front of you, crying for their mothers."

It was becoming more difficult to hold his father's gaze.

"You are a fine young man," said Fabricius proudly. "Your time to fight in the front line will come. Until then, gain every bit of experience you can. If that means you miss the war with Carthage, so be it. Those initial weeks of training are vital if you want to survive more than the first few moments of a battle."

"Yes, Father."

"Good," said Fabricius, looking satisfied. "May the gods keep you safe and well."

"And you also." Despite his best effort, Quintus' voice wobbled.

———

Atia waited until Quintus had gone inside before emerging. "He's almost a man," she said wistfully. "It only seems the blink of an eye since he was playing with his wooden toys."

"I know." Fabricius smiled. "The years fly by, don't they? I can remember saying good-bye to you before leaving for Sicily as if it were yesterday. And here we are again, in much the same situation."

Atia reached up to touch his face. "You have to come back to me, do you hear?"

"I will do my best. Make sure that the altar is well stocked with offerings," he warned. "The lares have to be kept happy."

She pretended to look shocked. "You know I'll do that every day."

Fabricius chuckled. "I do. Just as you know that I'll pray daily to Mars and Jupiter for their protection."

Atia's face became solemn. "Are you still sure that Flaccus is a good choice for Aurelia?"

His brows lowered. "Eh?"

"Is he the right man?"

"I thought he came across well last night," said Fabricius with a surprised look. "Arrogant, of course, but one expects that from someone of his rank. He was plainly taken with Aurelia too, which was good. He's ambitious, presentable and wealthy." He eyed Atia. "Isn't that enough?"

She pursed her lips.

"Atia?"

"I can't put my finger on it," she said eventually. "I don't trust him."

"You need more than a vague idea, surely, for me to break off a betrothal with this potential?" asked Fabricius, looking irritated. "Remember how much money we owe!"

"I'm not saying that you should call off the arrangement," she said in a conciliatory tone.

"What then?"

"Just keep an eye on Flaccus when you're in Rome. You'll be spending plenty of time with him. That will give you a far better measure of the man than we could ever gain in one night." She caressed his arm. "That's not too much to ask, is it?"

"No," he murmured. A relenting smile twitched across his lips, and he bent to kiss her. "You do have a knack of sniffing out the rotten apple in the barrel. I'll trust you one more time."

"Stop teasing me," she cried. "I'm serious."

"I know you are, my love. And I'll do what you say." He tapped the side of his nose. "Flaccus won't have a clue, but I'll be watching his every move."

Atia's expression lightened. "Thank you."

Fabricius gave her backside an affectionate squeeze. "Now, why don't we say good-bye properly?"

Atia's look grew kittenish. "That sounds like an excellent idea." Taking his hand, she led him into the house.

An hour later, and a deathly quiet hung over the house. Promising a quick victory over the Carthaginians, Fabricius and Flaccus had departed for Rome. Feeling thoroughly depressed, Quintus sought out Hanno. There was little left to do in the way of household chores, and the Carthaginian could not refuse when Quintus asked him out into the courtyard.

An awkward silence fell the instant they were alone.

I'm not going to speak first, thought Hanno. He was still furious.

Quintus scuffed the toe of one sandal along the mosaic. "About last night," he began.

"Yes?" snapped Hanno. His voice, his manner was not that of a slave. At that moment, he didn't care.

Quintus bit back his reflex, angry response. "I'm sorry," he said sharply. "I was drunk, and I didn't mean what I said."

Hanno looked in Quintus' eyes and saw that, despite his tone, the apology was genuine. Immediately, he was on the defensive. This wasn't what he had expected, and he wasn't yet willing to back down himself. "I am a slave," he growled. "You can address me in whatever way you please."

Quintus' face grew pained. "First and foremost, you are my friend," he said. "And I shouldn't have spoken to you the way I did last night."

Hanno considered Quintus' words in silence. Before being enslaved, any foreigner with the presumption to call him "gugga" would have received a bloody nose, or worse. Here, he had to smile and accept it. Not for much longer, Hanno told himself furiously. Just keep up the pretense for now. He nodded in apparent acceptance. "Very well. I acknowledge your apology."

Quintus grinned. "Thank you."

Neither knew quite what to say next. Despite Quintus' attempt to make amends, a distance now yawned between them. As a patriotic

Roman citizen, Quintus would back his government's decision to enter into conflict with Carthage to the hilt. Hanno, while unable to join Hannibal's army, would do the same for his people. It drove a wedge deep into their friendship, and neither knew how to remove it.

Long moments dragged by, and still neither spoke. Quintus didn't want to mention the impending war because both had such strong feelings about it. He wanted to suggest some weapons practice, but that also seemed like a bad idea: for all that he now trusted Hanno, it seemed too much like the impending combat between Roman and Carthaginian. Irritated, he waited for Hanno to speak first. Angry yet, and fearful of giving away something of his escape plan, Hanno kept his lips firmly shut.

Both wished that Aurelia were present. She would have laughed and dissipated the tension in a heartbeat. There was no sign of her, however.

This is pointless, thought Hanno at last. He took a step toward the kitchen. "I'd best get back to work."

Irritated, Quintus moved out of his way. "Yes," he said stiffly.

As he walked away, Hanno was surprised to feel sadness rising in his chest. For all of his current resentment, he and Quintus shared a strong bond, forged by the incredible, random manner of his purchase, followed by the fight at the shepherd's hut. Another thought struck Hanno. It must have taken a lot for Quintus to come and apologize, particularly because of their difference in status. Yet here *he* was, haughtily walking off as if he were the master, and not the slave. Hanno turned, an apology rising to his lips, but it was too late.

Quintus was gone.

———

Several weeks passed, and the weather grew warm and sunny. Encouraged by the officers, widespread rumors of Hannibal's intentions had spread throughout the huge tented encampment outside the walls of New Carthage. It was all part of the general's plan. Because of the vastness of his host, it was impossible to inform every soldier directly about what was going to happen. This way, the message could be put across rapidly. By the time Hannibal called for a meeting of his commanders, everyone knew that they would be heading for Italy.

The entire army assembled in formations before a wooden platform not far from the gates. The soldiers covered an enormous area of ground. There were thousands of Libyans and Numidians, and even greater numbers of Iberians from dozens of tribes. Roughly dressed men from the Balearic Islands waited alongside rows of proud, imperious Celtiberians. Hundreds of Ligurians and Gauls were also present, men who had left their lands and homes weeks before so that they could join the general who would wage war on Rome. A small proportion of the soldiers would be able to see and hear whoever stood before them, but interpreters had been positioned at regular intervals to relay the news to the rest. There would only be a short delay before everyone present heard Hannibal's words.

Malchus, Sapho and Bostar stood proudly at the front of their Libyan spearmen, whose bronze helmets and shield bosses glittered in the morning sun. The trio knew exactly what was going to happen, but the same nervous excitement controlled them all. Since returning from their mission weeks before, Bostar and Sapho had put their differences aside to prepare for this moment. Now history was about to be made, in much the same fashion as when Alexander of Macedon had set forth on his extraordinary journey more than a hundred years previously. The greatest adventure of their lives was just beginning. With it, as their father said, came the chance of further revenge for Hanno. Although he didn't voice it, Malchus treasured a tiny, deeply buried hope that he might actually be alive. So too did Bostar, but Sapho had given up trying to feel anything similar. He was still glad that Hanno was gone. Malchus gave Sapho more attention and praise now than he could ever remember receiving before. And Hannibal knew his name!

The army did not have to wait long. Followed by his brothers Hasdrubal and Mago, the cavalry commander Maharbal, and the senior infantry officer Hanno, Hannibal approached the platform and climbed into view. A group of trumpeters came last, and filed around in front of the general's position, where they waited for their orders. Their leaders' appearance caused spontaneous cheering to break out among the assembled troops. Even the officers joined in. The men whistled and shouted, stamped their feet on the ground and clashed their weapons off their shields. As those who could not see joined in, the clamor swelled immeasurably. On and on it went, louder and louder, in a dozen tongues. And, as he had done on similar occasions, Hannibal did nothing to stop it. Raising both his arms, he let his soldiers' acclaim wash over him. This was his hour, which he had spent years preparing for, and moments like this boosted morale infinitely more than a host of minor victories.

Finally, Hannibal signaled to the musicians. Raising their instruments to their lips, the men blew a short set of notes. It was the call to arms, the same sound that alerted soldiers to the nearby presence of enemy forces. Immediately, the crescendo of sound died away, leaving in its place an expectant hush. Bostar excitedly nudged Sapho in the ribs, and received a similar dig in return. An admonitory look from Malchus had them both standing to attention as if on parade. This was no time for childish behavior.

"Soldiers of Carthage," Hannibal began. "We stand on the brink of a great adventure. But there are those in Rome who would stop us from the outset." He held up a hand to quell his men's angry response. "Would you hear the words of the latest Roman embassy to visit Carthage?"

A few moments went by as the interpreters did their work, and then an enormous cry of affirmation went up.

"'The heinous and unwarranted attack on Saguntum cannot go unanswered. Deliver to us, in chains, the man they call Hannibal Barca, and all of his senior officers, and Rome will consider the matter closed. If Carthage does not comply with this request, it should consider itself at war with the Republic.'" Hannibal paused, letting the translations sink in, and his soldiers' fury build. He gestured dramatically at those behind him on the platform. "Should these men and I hand ourselves in to the nearest Roman ally so that justice can be done?"

Again, a short delay. But the roar of "NO!" that followed exceeded the combined volume of all the cries that had gone before.

Hannibal smiled briefly. "I thank you for your loyalty," he said, sweeping his right arm from left to right, encompassing the entire host.

Another immense cheer shredded the air.

"Instead of accepting Rome's offer then, I would lead most of you to Italy. To carry the war to our enemies," Hannibal announced to more deafening acclaim. "Some must remain here, under the command of my brother Hasdrubal; your mission is to protect our Iberian territory. The rest will march with me. Because the Romans control the sea, we will travel overland and take them by surprise. You might imagine that we would be alone in Italy, and surrounded by hostile forces. But do not fear! Theirs is a fertile region, and ripe for the plunder. We will also have many allies. Rome controls less of the peninsula than you might think. The tribes in Cisalpine Gaul have promised to join us, and I have no doubt that the situation will be the same in the central and southern parts. It will not be an easy struggle, and I ask only those men who would freely accompany me to engage in this enterprise." Hannibal let his gaze wander from formation to formation, catching the eye of individual soldiers. "With all of your help," he continued, "the Republic will be torn asunder. Destroyed, so that it can no longer threaten Carthage!" Calmly, he waited for his message to spread.

It did not take long.

The noise of over a hundred thousand men expressing their agreement resembled a rumbling, threatening thunder. Malchus, Sapho and Bostar trembled to hear it.

Hannibal raised a clenched fist in the air. "Will you follow me to Italy?"

There was but one answer to his question. And, as every man in his army gave voice to the loudest cry of all, Hannibal Barca stood back and smiled.

In the weeks following their argument, Hanno and Quintus both made halfhearted attempts at reconciliation. None succeeded. Hurt by the other's attitude, and full of youthful self-importance, neither would give way. Soon they had virtually stopped talking to one another. It was a vicious circle from which there was no escape. Aurelia did her best to mediate, but her efforts were in vain. Yet for all of his resentment, Hanno had realized that he could not now run away. Despite his feud with Quintus, he owed him and Aurelia too much. And so, growing increasingly morose, he remained, wary always of Agesandros' menacing presence in the background. Quintus, meanwhile, threw himself into his cavalry training with the socii. He was often absent from the house for days at a time, which suited him fine. It meant that he didn't even have to see Hanno, let alone speak to him.

Spring was well underway when a note from Fabricius arrived. Followed by an eager Aurelia, Atia took it to the courtyard, which was filled with watery sunshine. Quintus, who was outside with Agesandros, would have to hear the news later.

Aurelia watched excitedly as her mother opened the missive and began to read. "What does it say?" she demanded after a moment.

Atia looked up. The disappointment on her face was clear. "It's a typical man's letter. Full of information about politics and what's going on in Rome. There's even a bit about some chariot race he went to the other day, but almost nothing about how he's feeling." She traced a finger down the page. "He asks after me, obviously, and you and Quintus. He hopes that there are no problems on the farm." At last Atia smiled. "Flaccus has asked him to send you his warmest regards, and says that although your marriage will have to be postponed because of the war, he cannot wait until the day it comes to pass. Your father has given him permission to write to you directly, so you may receive a letter from him soon."

Aurelia was pleased by news of the postponement, but the thought of her wedding day—and night—still made her turn scarlet. Catching sight of Hanno in the kitchen doorway, she went an even brighter shade of red. His being a slave did not stop her from thinking—yet again—that, despite his newly crooked nose, he was extremely good-looking. For an instant, Flaccus was replaced by Hanno in her mind's eye. Aurelia stifled a gasp and shoved the shocking image away. "That's nice. What else has Father to say?"

Hanno was oblivious to Aurelia's emotions. He was pleased because Julius had just told him to sweep the courtyard, which in turn allowed him to listen in on the conversation. With his ears pricked, he poked the broom into the crevices gaping between some of the tesserae on the mosaic floor, carefully hooking out as much dirt as possible.

Atia read on, sounding more interested. "The majority of what he writes about is the Republic's response to Hannibal. The Minucii and their allies are working tirelessly to help the preparations for war. Flaccus hopes to be made tribune of one of the new legions. Most importantly of all, Tiberius Sempronius Longus and Publius Cornelius Scipio, the two new consuls, have been granted the provinces of Sicily and Africa, and Iberia, respectively. The mission of the former is to attack Carthage while that of the latter is to confront, and defeat, Hannibal. Father is pleased that he and Flaccus will serve with Scipio."

"That's because all the glory will fall on the army that defeats Hannibal," mused Aurelia. Sometimes she wished she were a man, so that she too could go to war.

"Men are all the same. We women have to stay behind and worry," said her mother with a sigh. "Let's just ask the gods to bring both of them back safely."

Hanno didn't like what he had heard. Hated it, in fact. Stinking bloody Romans, he thought bitterly. There were no generals of any ability in Carthage, which meant that the Senate would recall Hannibal to defend the city, thus ending his plans to attack Italy. His departure would leave Iberia, Carthage's richest colony, at the mercy of an invading Roman army. Hanno's fingers clenched furiously on his broom handle. The war seemed over before it had begun.

Aurelia frowned. "Didn't an assault on Carthage come close to succeeding in the previous war?"

"Yes. And Father says that whatever Hannibal's qualities, Rome will be victorious. We have no reason to believe that the Carthaginians' resolve is any stronger than it was twenty years ago."

Hanno's black mood grew even worse. Fabricius was right. His city's record in the face of direct attacks was not exactly glorious. Of course Hannibal's return would make a huge difference, but would it be enough? His army wouldn't be with him: even without the Romans' control of the seas, the general simply didn't possess enough ships to transport tens of thousands of troops back to Africa.

It was then that Quintus arrived. Instantly, he took in Aurelia standing over his mother with the letter in her hand. "Is that from Father?"

"Yes," Atia replied.

"What news does he send?" he asked eagerly. "Has the Senate decided on a course of action?"

"To attack Carthage and Iberia at the same time," answered Aurelia.

"What a fantastic idea! They won't know what hit them," Quintus cried. "Where is Father to be sent?"

"Iberia. So too is Flaccus," said Atia.

"What else?"

Atia handed the parchment to Quintus. "Read it for yourself. Life goes on here, and I have to talk to Julius about the provisions that need buying in Capua." She brushed past Hanno without as much as a second glance.

Hanno's anger crystalized. Whatever debt he might owe, it was time to run away. Carthage would now need every sword she could get. Nothing and no one else mattered. What about Suni? asked his conscience. I have no idea where he is, thought Hanno desperately. What chance is there of finding him?

Quintus scanned the letter at top speed. "Father and Flaccus are going to Iberia," he muttered excitedly. "And I am nearly finished my training."

"What are you talking about?" Aurelia demanded.

He gave her a startled look. "Nothing, nothing."

Aurelia knew her brother well. "Don't go getting any crazy ideas," she warned. "Father said you were to remain here until called for."

"I know." Quintus scowled. "From the sound of it, though, the war *will* actually be over in a few months. I don't want to miss it." His gaze flickered across the courtyard and made contact with Hanno. Instantly, Quintus glanced away, but it was too late.

Hanno's fury overflowed at last. "Are you happy now?" he hissed.

"What do you mean?" Quintus replied defensively.

"The guggas will be defeated, again. Put in their rightful place. I expect you're delighted."

Quintus' face grew red. "No, that's not how it is."

"Isn't it?" Hanno shot back. Clearing his throat, he spat on the mosaic floor.

"How dare you?" Quintus roared, taking a step toward Hanno. "You're nothing but a—"

"Quintus!" cried Aurelia, aghast.

With great effort, her brother stopped himself from saying anymore.

Contempt twisted Hanno's face. "A slave. Or a gugga! Is that what you were going to say?"

Quintus' visage turned a deeper shade of crimson. Bunching his fists with anger, he turned away.

"I've had enough of this." Hanno grabbed his broom.

Aurelia could take no more. "Stop it, both of you! You're acting like children."

Her words made no difference. Quintus stormed out of the house, and Aurelia followed him. Hanno retreated to the kitchen, where misery settled over him as it never had before. The news he'd heard a few months before, of Hannibal's successful siege of Saguntum, and the challenge it had issued, had bolstered his flagging spirits. Given him a reason to go on. Fabricius' letter had destroyed this utterly. Rome's plan seemed unbeatable. Even if he reached Hannibal's army, what difference could he make?

———

Aurelia came looking for Hanno upon her return. She found him slumped on a stool in the kitchen. Ignoring the other slaves' curious stares, she dragged Hanno outside. "I've spoken to Quintus," she muttered the moment they were alone. "He didn't mean to offend you. It was just a spontaneous reaction to you spitting." She gave Hanno a reproachful look. "That was so rude."

Hanno flushed, but he didn't apologize. "He was gloating at me."

"I know it seemed like that," said Aurelia. "But I don't think that's what he was doing."

"Wasn't it?" Hanno shot back.

"No," she replied softly. "Quintus isn't like that."

"Why did he call me a gugga originally, then?"

"People say things that they don't mean when they're drunk. I suppose that you haven't called him any names in your head since?" Aurelia asked archly.

Stung, Hanno did not answer.

Aurelia glanced around carefully, before reaching out to touch his face.

Startled by the intimacy this created, Hanno felt his anger dissipate. He looked into her eyes.

Alarmed by her suddenly pounding heart, Aurelia lowered her hand. "On the surface, this argument looks quite simple," she began. "If it weren't for your misfortune, you would be a free man and, in all probability, enlisting in the Carthaginian army. Like Quintus will do in the legions. There would be nothing wrong with either of those actions. Yet Quintus is free to do as he chooses, while you are a slave."

That's it in a nutshell, thought Hanno angrily.

Aurelia wasn't finished. "The real reason, however, is that first you, and then Quintus, were hurt by what the other said. Both of you are too damn proud to make a sincere apology and put it behind you." She glared at him. "I'm sick of it."

Amazed by Aurelia's insight and sincerity, Hanno gave in. The quarrel had been going on long enough. "You're right," he said. "I'm sorry."

"It's not me you should be saying that to."

"I know." Hanno considered his next words with care. "I will apologize to him. But Quintus has to know that, whatever the law of this land, I am no slave. I never will be."

"Deep down, I'm sure he knows that. That's why he stopped himself from calling you one earlier," Aurelia replied. Her face grew sad. "Obviously, I don't think of you like that. But to everyone else, you *are* a slave."

Hanno was about to tell Aurelia of his plans, when, out of the corner of his eye, he sensed movement. Through the open doors of the tablinum, he could see into part of the atrium. Outside the square of floor illuminated by the hole in its roof, everything lay in shadow. There Hanno could discern a tall figure, watching them. Instinctively, he pulled away from Aurelia. When Agesandros walked into the light, Hanno's stomach constricted with fear. What had he seen or heard? What would he do?

Aurelia saw the Sicilian in the same moment. She drew herself up proudly, ready for any confrontation.

To their surprise, Agesandros came no nearer. A tiny smile flickered across his face, and then he disappeared whence he had come.

Hanno and Aurelia turned back to each other, but Elira and another domestic slave emerged from the kitchen. The brief moment of magic they had shared was gone. "I will talk to Quintus," said Aurelia reassuringly. "Whatever happens, you must hold on to your friendship. As we two will."

Keen to make things as they were before he left the farm forever, Hanno nodded. "Thank you."

Unfortunately, Aurelia was unable to remonstrate with her brother that day. As she told Hanno later, Quintus had taken off for Capua without a word to anyone but the bowlegged slave who worked in the stable. The afternoon passed and night fell, and it became apparent that he would not be returning. Hanno didn't know whether to feel angry or worried by this development. "Don't be concerned," Aurelia said before retiring. "Quintus does this sometimes, when he needs time to think. He stays at Gaius' house, and returns in a few days."

There was nothing Hanno could do. He lay back on his bedroll and dreamed of escape.

Sleep was a long time coming.

XI

THE QUEST FOR SAFE PASSAGE

After the fall of Saguntum, Bostar took to visiting his wounded men every morning, talking to those who were conscious and passing his hand over those who were still asleep, or who would never wake. There were more than thirty soldiers in the large tent, of whom half would probably never fight again. Despite the horror of his soldiers' injuries, Bostar had begun to feel grateful for his losses. All things considered, they had been slight. Far more Saguntines had died when Hannibal's troops had entered the city, howling like packs of rabid wolves. For an entire day, the predominant sound throughout Saguntum had been that of screams. Men's. Women's. Children's. Bostar squeezed his eyes shut and tried to forget, but he couldn't. Butchering unarmed civilians and engaging in widespread rape was not how he made war. While he hadn't tried to stop his men—had Hannibal not promised them a free rein?—Bostar had not taken part in the slaughter. Commanded by their general to guard the chests of gold and silver that had been found in the citadel, Malchus had not either. Bostar sighed. Inevitably, Sapho had.

A moment later, Malchus' touch on his shoulder made him jump. "It's good that you're up so early checking on them." Malchus indicated the injured men in their blankets.

"It's my job," Bostar replied modestly, knowing that his father would have already visited his own casualties.

"It is." Malchus fixed him with a solemn stare. "And I think Hannibal has another one for you. Us."

Bostar's heart thudded off his ribs. "Why?"

"We've all been summoned to the general's tent. I wasn't told why."

Excitement filled Bostar. "Does Sapho know?"

"No. I thought you could tell him."

"Really?" Bostar tried to keep his tone light. "If you wish."

Malchus gave him a knowing look. "Do you think I haven't noticed how you two have been with each other recently?"

"It's nothing serious," lied Bostar.

"Then why are you avoiding my gaze?" demanded Malchus. "It's about Hanno, isn't it?"

"That's how it started," Bostar replied. He began to explain, but his father forestalled him.

"There are only two of you now," said Malchus sadly. "Life is short. Resolve your differences, or one of you might find that it's too late."

"You're right," replied Bostar firmly. "I'll do my best."

"As you always do." Malchus' voice was proud.

A pang of sadness tore at Bostar's heart. *Did I do my best by letting Hanno go?* he wondered.

"I'll see you both outside the headquarters in half an hour." Malchus left him to it.

After telling his orderly to polish his armor, Bostar headed straight for Sapho's tent. There wasn't much time for getting ready, never mind a reconciliation. But their father had asked, so he would try.

Recognizing the tent lines of Sapho's phalanx by their standard, Bostar quickly located the largest tent, which, like his, was pitched on the unit's right. The main flap was closed, which meant that his brother was either still in bed, or busy with his duties. Given his brother's recent habits, Bostar suspected the former. "Sapho?" he called.

There was no answer.

Bostar tried again, louder.

Nothing.

Bostar took a step away. "He must be with his men," he said to himself in surprise.

"Who is it?" demanded an annoyed voice.

"Of course he's not," Bostar muttered, turning back. He untied the thong that kept the tent flap closed. "Sapho! It's me." A moment later, he threw wide the leather. Sunlight flooded inside, and Bostar lifted a hand to his nose. The reek of stale sweat and spilled wine was overpowering. Stepping over the threshold, he picked his way over discarded pieces of clothing and equipment. Bostar was shocked to see that every item was filthy. Sapho's shield, spear and sword were the only things that had been cleaned. They leaned against a wooden stand to the side. He came to a halt before Sapho's bed, a jumble of blankets and animal skins. His brother's bleary eyes regarded him from its depths. "Good morning," said Bostar, trying to ignore the smell. He hasn't even washed, he thought with disgust.

"To what do I owe the pleasure?" Sapho's voice was acid.

"We've been summoned to a meeting with Hannibal."

Sapho's lips thinned. "The general told you that over breakfast, did he?"

Bostar sighed. "Despite what you may think, I didn't save Hannibal's life to curry favor, or to make you jealous. You know I'm not like that." He was pleased when Sapho's eyes dropped away. He waited, but there was no further response. Bostar pressed on. "Father sent me. We need to be there in less than half an hour."

Finally, Sapho sat up. He winced. "Gods, my head hurts. And it tastes like something died in my mouth."

Bostar kicked the amphora at his feet. "Drank too much of this?"

Sapho gave him a rueful grin. "Not half! Some of my men broke into a wine merchant's when the city fell. We've kept it under guard since. You should see the place. There's vintage stuff from all over the Mediterranean!" His expression grew hawkish. "Shame his three daughters aren't still alive. We had some fun with them, I can tell you."

Bostar wanted to punch Sapho in the face, but instead he proffered a hand. "Get up. We don't want to be late. Father thinks Hannibal has a task for us."

Sapho looked at Bostar's outstretched arm for a moment before he accepted it. Swaying gently, he looked around at the chaos of his tent floor. "I suppose I'd better start cleaning my breastplate and helmet. Can't appear in front of Hannibal with filthy gear, can I?"

"Can't your orderly do it?"

Sapho made a face. "No. He's down with the flux."

Bostar frowned. Sapho was in no state to wash himself, prepare his uniform and present himself to their general in the time remaining. Part of him wanted to leave his brother to it. That's what he deserves, Bostar thought. The rest of him felt that their feud had been going on too long. He made a snap judgment. His own servant would have everything ready by now. It would only take him a few moments to get ready. "Go and stick your head in a barrel of water. I'll clean your armor and helmet."

Sapho's eyebrows rose. "That's kind of you," he muttered.

"Don't think I'm going to do it for you every day," Bostar warned. He gave Sapho a shove. "Get a move on. We don't want to be late. Hannibal must have something special lined up for us."

At this, Sapho's pace picked up. "True," he replied. He stopped by the tent's entrance.

Bostar, who was already following with Sapho's filthy breastplate, paused. "What?"

"Thank you," said Sapho.

Bostar nodded. "That's all right."

The air between them grew a shade lighter, and for the first time in months, they smiled at each other.

Bostar and Sapho found their father waiting for them near Hannibal's tent. Malchus eyed their gleaming armor and helmets and gave an approving nod.

"What's this about, Father?" asked Sapho.

"Let's go and find out," Malchus answered. He led the way to the entrance, where two dozen smartly turned-out scutarii stood. "The general is expecting us."

Recognizing Malchus, the lead scutarius saluted. "If you'll follow me, sir."

As they were led inside, Bostar winked at Sapho, who returned the gesture. Excitement gripped them both. Although they had met Hannibal before, this was the first time they'd been invited into his headquarters.

In the tent's main section, they found Hannibal, his brothers Hasdrubal and Mago, and two other senior officers grouped around a table upon which a large map was unrolled. The scutarius came to a halt and announced them.

Hannibal turned. "Malchus. Bostar and Sapho. Welcome!"

Father and sons saluted crisply.

"You will know my brother Hasdrubal," said Hannibal, nodding at the corpulent, brooding man with a florid complexion and full lips beside him. "And Mago." He indicated the tall, thin figure whose eager, hawk-like face and eyes threatened to fix one to the spot. "This is Maharbal, my cavalry commander, and Hanno, one of my top infantry officers." The first man had a mop of unruly black hair and a ready smile, and the other a stolid but dependable look.

The trio saluted again.

"For many years, Malchus acted as my eyes and ears in Carthage," Hannibal explained. "Yet when the time came for first his sons, and then he himself, to join me here in Iberia, no one was better pleased than I. They are good men all, and they proved their worth more than once during the siege, most recently when Bostar saved my life."

The officers murmured in loud appreciation.

Malchus inclined his head, while Bostar flushed at the attention. Beside him, he was aware of Sapho glowering. Bostar cursed inwardly, praying that the fragile peace between him and his brother had not just been broken.

Hannibal clapped his hands together. "To business! Come and join us."

They eagerly crossed to the table, where the others made room.

At once Bostar's eyes drank in the undulating coast of Africa, and

Carthage, their city. The island of Sicily, almost joining their homeland to its archenemy, Italy.

"Obviously, we are here, at Saguntum." Hannibal tapped his right forefinger halfway up the east coast of the Iberian peninsula. "And our destination is here." He thumped the boot-like shape of Italy. "How best to strike at it?"

Silence reigned. It was an affront to every Carthaginian's pride that Rome enjoyed supremacy over the western Mediterranean, an historical preserve of Carthage. Transporting the army by ship would be foolish in the extreme. Yet no one dared to suggest the only alternative.

Hannibal took the initiative. "There will be no assault by sea. Even if we took the short route to Genua, our entire enterprise could be undone in a single battle." He moved his finger northeast, across the River Iberus, to the narrow "waist" that joined Iberia to Gaul. "This is the route we shall take." Hannibal continued to the Alps, where he paused for a moment before moving into Cisalpine Gaul, and thence into northern Italy.

Bostar's heart quickened. Although Malchus had told him of Hannibal's plan, the general's daring still took his breath away. A glance at Sapho told him that his brother shared his feeling. Their father's face, however, remained expressionless. How much does he know? Bostar wondered. He himself had no idea how the immense task Hannibal had just mentioned would be achieved.

Hannibal saw Sapho straining forward eagerly. He raised an eyebrow.

"When do we march, sir?"

"In the spring. Until then, our Iberian allies have permission to return to their families, and the rest of the army can rest at New Carthage." He saw Sapho's disappointed look and chuckled. "Come now! Winter is no time to wage war, and things will be hard enough for us as it is."

"Of course, sir," Sapho muttered awkwardly.

"There are some things in our favor, however. Earlier in the year, my messengers journeyed to Cisalpine Gaul. They were received favorably by nearly all the tribes that they encountered," Hannibal said.

"In fact, the Boii and the Insubres promised immediate aid when we arrive."

Malchus and his two sons exchanged pleased glances. This was new information for all of them. Hannibal's companions did not react, however, instead studying the trio intently.

Hannibal held up a warning finger. "There are many hurdles to cross before we reach these possible allies. Traversing the Alps will be the greatest by far, but another will be the fierce natives north of the Iberus, who will undoubtedly give violent resistance. We already have plans in train for our journey through these regions. However, there is an area about which we know very little." Hannibal's forefinger returned to the mountains between Iberia and Gaul. He tapped the map meaningfully.

Bostar's mouth went dry.

Hannibal stared at Malchus. "I need someone to sound out the tribes' possible reactions to a massive army entering their land. To discover how many might fight us. I must have this information by the onset of spring. Can you do it?"

Malchus' eyes glittered. "Of course, sir."

"Good." Hannibal regarded Bostar and Sapho next. "The old lion might lead the pack, but he still needs young males to hunt successfully. Will you accompany your father?"

"Yes, sir!" the brothers cried in unison. "You show our family great honor by entrusting this mission to us, sir," Sapho added.

The general smiled. "I am sure that you will repay my trust amply."

Delighted by this recognition of Sapho, Bostar gave his brother a small, pleased look. He was rewarded with a fierce nod.

"What are your thoughts, Malchus?"

"We'll need to set out at once, sir. It's a long way to the Iberus."

"Nearly three thousand stades," agreed Hannibal. "As you know, it is generally peaceful as far as the river. After that, up to the border with Gaul, may be a different matter. The place is a jumble of mountains, valleys and passes, and the tribes there are rumored to be fiercely independent." He paused. "How many men will you require?"

"Winning our passage by force of arms is simply not an option. Nor is it our purpose. We are to be an embassy, not an army," said

Malchus. "What's important are the abilities to move fast and to see off possible attacks by bandits." He looked at his sons, who nodded in agreement. "Two dozen of my spearmen and the same number of scutarii should be sufficient, sir."

"You shall have the pick of any unit you wish. And now, a toast to your success!" Hannibal clicked his fingers and a slave appeared from the rear of the tent. "Wine!" As the man scurried off, the general looked solemnly at each of those around the table. "Let us ask Melqart and Baal Saphon, Tanit and Baal Hammon to guide and protect these valiant officers on their mission."

As the room filled with muttered agreement, Bostar added a request of his own. *Let Sapho and I put aside our differences once and for all.*

Braving frost, mud and bitter winter wind, the embassy slogged its way to the Iberus. Thereafter, the inhabitants inland could not be trusted, and so Malchus led them along the more secure coastal route, a densely inhabited area full of towns used to traders from overseas. The party passed by Adeba and Tarraco, before safely reaching the city of Barcino, which was located at the mouth of the River Ubricatus.

There were several routes through the mountains that led to Gaul, and Hannibal had advised that he would probably divide his army between them. This necessitated visiting the tribe that controlled each of the passes. A period of unseasonably calm, dry weather prompted Malchus to head north into the mountainous terrain first, rather than starting with the easiest way into Gaul, that which hugged the coastline via the towns of Gerunda and Emporiae. That could be left until last. Hiring locals as guides, the embassy spent many days on narrow paths that wound and twisted into the hills and valleys. Inevitably, the weather worsened, and a journey that might have taken several weeks stretched into two months. Pleasingly, their ordeals were not all in vain. The chieftains who received the Carthaginians seemed impressed with the tales of Hannibal's military victories throughout Iberia, and the descriptions of his enormous army. Most importantly, though, they welcomed the gifts Malchus offered: the bags of silver coinage, the finely made *kopides* and Celtiberian short swords.

Eventually, the only people left to contact were the Ausetani, who controlled the coastal route into Gaul. Having returned to the town of Emporiae to reshoe their horses and stock up on supplies, Malchus retired to the one inn which was large enough to quarter all of his men. He immediately demanded a meeting with their guides, three swarthy hunters. Soon after sunset, they convened around a table in his room. Small oval oil lamps cast a warm amber glow on to the grubby plaster on the wall. Malchus' sons sat opposite each other. Their relationship remained civil, even fairly cordial, but Bostar had stopped trying to be Sapho's friend. Each time he'd tried, his brother had remained indifferent to his advances. So be it, Bostar decided. It's better than fighting all the time. Such thoughts always brought Hanno, and his guilty wish that it had been Sapho who had been lost at sea, to mind. Disquieted, Bostar shoved away the idea.

Malchus himself served the guides with wine. "Tell me about this tribe," he commanded in rough Iberian.

The three glanced at one another. The oldest, a wiry man with a nut-brown, weather-beaten face, leaned forward on his chair. "Their main village is in the foothills above the town, sir. It's a straightforward journey."

"Not like the paths that we had to take before, then?"

"No, sir, nothing like that."

Bostar and Sapho were both relieved. Neither had enjoyed the days spent on winding, treacherous tracks, where a single slip meant a precipitous fall.

"How far?"

"It's not quite a day's ride, sir."

"Excellent! We'll set out at dawn," Malchus declared. He eyed his sons. "A night's rest upon our return, and we'll head south. Spring is around the corner, and we mustn't keep Hannibal waiting any longer."

The lead guide cleared his throat. "The thing is, sir, we were wondering if . . ." His nerve failed him and he stopped.

Keen to get in before Bostar, Sapho jumped in. "What?"

The man rallied his courage. "We wondered if you could pay us and make your own way there," he said falteringly. "We've spent so long away from our wives and families, you see?"

Malchus' brows lowered.

"The directions are simple. There's no way that you could get lost." He looked at his two companions, who shook their heads in vigorous agreement.

Malchus did not answer. Instead, he glanced at Bostar and Sapho. "What do you think?" he asked in Carthaginian.

Sapho bared his teeth. "He's lying," he snarled in Iberian. "I say we tie the double-crossing dog down on the table and see what he says after I've cut a few strips of skin off him." He calmly placed a dagger before him. "This will make the shitbag sing like a caged bird."

"Bostar?" asked Malchus.

Bostar studied the three guides, who seemed absolutely terrified. Then he looked at his brother, who was tapping his blade off the table's surface. He didn't want to upset Sapho, but nor was he prepared to see innocent individuals suffer for no reason. "I don't think there's any need for torture," Bostar said in Iberian, ignoring Sapho's scowl. "These men have been with us day and night for weeks. They've had no chance to commit treachery. I think they're probably scared of the Ausetani. But I see no reason why they shouldn't fulfill their oath, which was to guide us until we discharged them."

Malchus considered their answers in silence. At length, he turned to the lead guide. "Has my son the right of it? Are you frightened of the Ausetani?"

"Yes, sir. They're prone to banditry." There was a brief pause. "Or worse."

Alarm filled Bostar. Before he could react, Sapho butted in again. "When, precisely, were you going to tell us this?" he demanded.

He got no answer.

Sapho threw a triumphant look at Bostar. "Why don't we just get the directions, and then kill them?"

Perhaps his brother was correct, thought Bostar resentfully. He didn't want to admit that he'd made a bad judgment by trusting the guides.

His father's challenge surprised him. "And if they had warned us? What would we have done?"

A flush spread slowly up Sapho's face and neck. "Gone to the village anyway," he muttered.

"Precisely," replied Malchus evenly. He glared at the guides. "It's not that I wouldn't end your miserable lives for withholding vital information, but I see no point in killing you when we would have followed the same course of action anyway."

The three stammered their thanks. "We will be honored to guide you to the Ausetani settlement tomorrow, sir," said the lead guide.

"That's right. You will." Malchus' tone was silky soft, but there was no mistaking the threat in it. "Myrcan! Get in here."

A broad-chested spearman entered from the corridor. "Sir?"

"Take these men's weapons and escort them to their quarters. Set guards at the windows and door."

"Yes, sir." Myrcan held out a meaty hand and the guides meekly handed over their knives before following him from the room.

"It appears you both still have something to learn about judging men's characters," Malchus admonished. "Not everyone is as honorable as you, Bostar. Nor do they all require torturing, Sapho."

Both of his sons took a sudden interest in the tabletop before them.

"Get some rest," Malchus said in a more kindly voice. "Tomorrow will be a long day."

"Yes, Father." As one, the brothers shoved back their chairs and headed for the door.

Neither spoke on the way to their bedchambers.

⁓

The guide's estimate of the distance to the Ausetani village was accurate. After nearly a day's ride, the fortified settlement finally came into view at the end of a long, narrow valley. Perhaps half a mile away, it occupied a high, easily defensible point. Like many such in Iberia, it was ringed by a wooden palisade. The tiny figures of sentries could be seen patrolling the ramparts. Flocks of sheep and goats grazed the slopes to either side. It was a peaceful scene, but the guides looked most unhappy.

Malchus gave them a long, contemptuous stare. "Go!"

The three men goggled at him.

"You heard me," Malchus growled. "Unless you'd like to spend some time with Sapho here."

They needed no further encouragement and had the sense not to mention payment. Turning their mules' heads, the trio fled.

"It appears that we are about to enter a den of hungry wolves." Malchus regarded each of his sons in turn. "What's our best option?"

"Go straight in there and demand to see the headman," Sapho declared boldly. "As we did in every other village."

"We can't go back to Hannibal without some information," Bostar admitted. "But nor should we foolishly place our heads on the executioner's block."

Sapho's top lip curled. "Are you afraid even to enter that excuse for a settlement?"

"No," retorted Bostar hotly. "I'm just saying that we know nothing about these whoresons. If they're as untrustworthy as the guide said, charging in there like raging bulls will get their backs up from the very outset."

Sapho shot him a disbelieving look. "So what? We're emissaries of Hannibal Barca, not some pisspot Iberian chieftain."

They glared at each other.

"Peace," said Malchus after a moment. "As usual, both your opinions have some merit. If we had the time, I would perhaps advise waylaying one of their hunting parties. A few hostages would make a powerful bargaining tool before we made an entry. That might take days, however, and we must act now." He glanced at Sapho. "Not in quite the way you advised. We will take a more peaceable approach. Remember, the stroked cat is less likely to scratch or bite. Yet we must be confident or, like a cat, they will turn on us anyway."

Turning to their escorts, Malchus laid out the situation in Carthaginian and basic Iberian. There was little reaction. The Libyans and scutarii had been chosen for their loyalty and bravery. They would fight and, if necessary, die, for Hannibal. Wherever, and whenever, they were ordered to.

"Which of you two speaks the best Iberian?" Malchus asked his sons. While rusty, his command of the language sufficed most of the time. In a dangerous situation, however, it was best to minimize the chance of miscommunication.

"I do," replied Bostar at once. Although he and Sapho had spent roughly the same amount of time in Iberia, it was he who had shown more aptitude for the rapid-fire, musical tribal tongues.

Sapho concurred with a reluctant nod.

"You act as interpreter, then," Malchus directed.

Bostar didn't try to hide his smirk.

Without further ado, they set off. Malchus took the lead, with Bostar and a glowering Sapho following. Their escorts marched to their rear, first the spearmen, and last the scutarii. The party had not gone far when a horn blared out from the nearest hillside. It was quickly echoed by another nearer the village. Shouts rang out on the ramparts. When they were about four hundred paces from the settlement, the front gates creaked open, and a tide of warriors poured out. Forming up in an unruly mass that blocked the entrance, they waited for the Carthaginians to approach.

Bostar felt his stomach clench. He glanced sidelong at Sapho, who was half pulling his sword from its sheath before slamming it home again. He's worried too, thought Bostar. In front, the only sign of tension in their father was his rigid back. Bostar took heart from Malchus' self-assurance. Show no fear, he told himself. They will smell it the way a wolf scents its prey. Taking a deep breath, he fixed his features into a stony expression. Coming to the same realization, Sapho let go of his sword hilt. Their escorts marched solidly behind them, reassurance that if there was trouble, plenty of men would die before they did.

Malchus rode his horse straight up to the mob of Ausetani. Taken aback by his confidence and the size of his mount, some of the warriors retreated a little. The advantage did not last long. Prompted by their companions' angry mutters, the men stepped forward once more, raising their weapons threateningly. Shouted challenges rang out, but Malchus did not move a muscle.

Like most Iberian tribesmen, few of the Ausetani were dressed identically. Most were bareheaded. Those who wore headgear sported sinew, bronze bowl or triple-crested helmets. The majority carried a shield, although these also varied in size and shape: tall and straight-sided with rounded ends, oval, or round with a conical iron boss. All were brightly painted with swirling serpents, diamonds, or alternating thick bands of color. The Ausetani were also heavily armed. Every man carried at least one saunion, but many had two. In addition, each warrior had a dagger and either a *kopis* or a typical Celtiberian straight-edged sword.

Malchus turned his head. "Tell them who we are, and why we're here."

"We are Carthaginians," said Bostar loudly. "We come in peace." He ignored the sniggers that met this remark. "With a message for your chieftain, from our leader, Hannibal Barca."

"Never heard of the prick," bellowed a hulking figure with a black beard. Hoots of amusement from his comrades followed. Encouraged by this, the warrior shoved his way out of the throng. Long raven tresses spilled out from under his bronze helmet. His black quilted linen tunic could not conceal the massive muscles of his chest and upper arms, and his sinew greaves barely fitted around his trunk-like calves. He was so big that the shield and saunion clutched in his ham fists looked like child's toys. The warrior gave the Libyans and scutarii a contemptuous glance, before returning his cold gaze to Bostar. "Give me one good reason why we shouldn't just kill you all," he snarled.

Snarls of agreement followed his challenge, and the Ausetani moved forward a step.

Bostar tensed, but managed to keep his hands in his lap, on his reins. He watched Sapho sidelong and was relieved when his brother didn't reach for his sword either.

"The guide was telling the truth," Malchus remarked dryly under his breath. He raised his voice. "Tell him that we bring a message, and gifts, for his leader from our general. His chieftain will not be pleased if he does not hear these words for himself."

Carefully, Bostar repeated his father's words in Iberian. It was exactly the right thing to say. Confusion and anger mixed on the big man's face for a moment, but a moment later, he stood back. When one of his companions queried his action, the warrior simply shoved him aside with an irritated grunt. Relief flooded through Bostar. The first hurdle had been crossed. It was like watching a landslide beginning. First one man moved out of the way, then a second and a third, followed by several more, until the process took on a life of its own. Soon the group of Ausetani had split apart, leaving the track that led to the village's front gate clear apart from the warrior with the black beard. He trotted ahead to carry the news of their arrival.

Without looking to left or right, Malchus urged his horse up the slope.

The rest of the party followed, shadowed closely by the mass of warriors.

Inside, the settlement was like a hundred others Bostar had seen before. A central open area was ringed by dozens of single-story wooden and brick huts, the outermost of which had been built right up against the palisade. Plumes of smoke rose from the roofs of many. Small children and dogs played in the dirt, oblivious to the drama about to unfold. Hens and pigs scuffled about, searching for food. Women and old people stood in the doorways of their houses, watching impassively. The acrid smell of urine and feces, both animal and human, laced the air. At the far side of the open space stood a high-backed wooden chair, which was occupied by a man in late middle age, and flanked by ten warriors in mail shirts and crimson-crested helmets. The bearded hulk was there too, busily muttering to the chieftain.

Without hesitation, Malchus headed for this group. Reaching it, he dismounted, indicating that his sons should do the same. At once three Libyan spearmen darted forward to take the horses' reins. Malchus made a deep bow toward the chief. Bostar quickly copied him. It was prudent to treat the Ausetani leader with respect, he thought. The man was head of a tribe, after all. Yet he looked an untrustworthy ruffian. The chieftain's red linen tunic might be woven from quality fabric, and the sword and dagger on his belt well made, but the tresses of lank, greasy hair that dangled on to his pockmarked cheeks told a different story. So did his flat, dead eyes, which reminded Bostar of a lizard. Sapho was last of all to bend from the waist. His gesture was shallower than the others had been. His insolence did not go unnoticed; several of the nearby warriors snarled with anger. Bostar glared at his brother, but the harm had been done.

The trio of Carthaginians and the Ausetani leader stared at each other in silence for a moment, each trying to gauge the other. The chieftain spoke first. He aimed his words at Malchus, the embassy's obvious leader.

"He says that our message must indeed be important to keep his men from their sport," muttered Bostar.

"He's playing with us. Trying to put fear in our hearts," Malchus murmured contemptuously. "He's not about to kill us out of hand, or his warriors would have done so already. The news of our presence in the area must have reached him before now, and he wants to hear what we have to say for himself. Tell him what we told the other leaders. Lay it on thick about the size of our army."

Bostar did as he was told, politely explaining how Hannibal and his host would arrive in the next few months, seeking only safe passage to Gaul. There would be well-paid jobs for Ausetani warriors who wished to serve as guides. Any supplies required by the Carthaginians would be purchased. Looting and theft of the locals' property or livestock would be forbidden, on pain of death. As he spoke, Bostar studied the chief intently but was frustrated in his attempt to gauge what the man was thinking. All he could do was to continue in a confident, self-assured vein. Hope for the best.

Bostar began to wax lyrical about the different groups that made up Hannibal's immense force, describing the thousands of spearmen and scutarii like those who stood behind him; the slingers and skirmishers who softened up an enemy before the real fighting began; the peerless Numidian cavalry, whose stinging attacks no soldiers in the world could withstand; and the elephants, which were capable of smashing apart troop formations like so much firewood. Bostar was still in mid-flow when the chieftain peremptorily held up his hand, stopping him. "And you say this army is how big?" he demanded.

"A hundred thousand men. At the very least." The instant the words had left his lips, Bostar could see that the Ausetani leader did not believe him. His spirits fell. It was an enormous figure to take in, yet the other tribes visited by the embassy had done so. Perhaps, thought Bostar, it was because they were a lot smaller than the Ausetani. In those villages, the fifty Carthaginian soldiers had seemed altogether more intimidating than they did here. This tribe was a different proposition; reportedly, there were numerous other villages like this one. Combined, the Ausetani might be able to field a force of two or even three thousand warriors, which for Iberia was a considerable achievement. Imagining a host thirty to fifty times larger than that number called for a good imagination.

Sure enough, the chief and his bodyguards exchanged a series of disbelieving looks.

"Scum," Sapho whispered furiously in Carthaginian. "They'll shit themselves when they actually see the army."

Not knowing what else to do, Bostar plowed on. "Some evidence of our good faith." He clicked his fingers and a quartet of scutarii trotted forward, carrying heavy, clinking bags and armfuls of tightly rolled leather. Placing the items in front of the chieftain, they returned to their positions.

The gifts were opened and examined with unseemly speed. Avarice glittered in the faces of every Ausetani watching as mounds of silver coins showered on to the ground. There were loud mutters of appreciation too for the shining weaponry that emerged into view as the leather bundles were unrolled.

Malchus' attitude was still confident, or appeared to be so. "Ask the chief what answer he would have us take back to Hannibal," he directed Bostar.

Bostar obeyed.

The Ausetani leader's face grew thoughtful. For the space of twenty heartbeats, he sat regarding the riches laid out before him. Finally, he asked a short question.

"He wants to know how much more they can expect when Hannibal arrives," Bostar relayed unhappily.

"Greedy bastard," Sapho hissed.

Malchus' eyebrows drew together in disapproval, yet he did not look surprised. "I can promise him the same again, and the dog will probably let us go," he said. "But I have no idea if Hannibal will agree with my decision. We've already handed over a fortune." He glanced at his sons. "What do you think?"

"Hannibal will think we are fools, pure and simple," muttered Sapho, his nostrils flaring. "All the other tribes have accepted our gifts, yet this one got twice as much?"

"We can't offer him more or the son of a whore will think we're a walkover," Bostar conceded. He scowled. "Hannibal's goodwill should be more than enough for him!"

"But I don't think it will be," said Malchus grimly. "If that amount of silver and weaponry hasn't done it, then a vague promise certainly won't."

Bostar could see no way out that didn't involve major loss of face. Although he and his companions were few in number, *they* were the representatives of a major power, not these cutthroats around them. To accede to the chieftain's demand would show fear on their part, and by implication, weakness on the part of their general. His eyes narrowed as an idea struck. "You could promise him a private meeting with Hannibal," he suggested. "Suggest that an alliance between his people and Carthage would be beneficial to both parties."

"We don't have the authority to grant that," growled Sapho.

"Of course we don't," Bostar replied witheringly. "But it's not a climbdown either."

"I like it," breathed Malchus. He glanced at Sapho, who gave a sulky shrug. "I think it's our best shot. Tell him."

Calmly, Bostar delivered their answer.

A ferocious scowl spread across the chieftain's face straightaway, and he spat out an irate, lengthy response. It was delivered so fast that Malchus and Sapho struggled to understand much of it. Bostar did not bother translating before he replied. At once the leader's bodyguards and the huge warrior moved forward in unison. Simultaneously, the men who had followed the Carthaginians inside fanned out on either side of the party, surrounding it.

"What in the name of all the gods did he say?" Malchus demanded.

Bostar's lips thinned. "That the Ausetani have no need of an alliance with the louse-ridden son of a Phoenician whore."

Sapho clenched his fists. "How did you answer?"

"I told him that an immediate sincere apology *might* mean Hannibal's clemency when the army arrives. Otherwise, he and his entire tribe could expect to be annihilated."

Malchus clapped him on the arm. "Well said!"

Even Sapho gave Bostar a look of grudging admiration.

Malchus eyed the circle of warriors around them. "It appears that our road ends here then," he said in a hard voice. "We will never have the opportunity to avenge Hanno. Yet we can die well. Like men!" He turned toward their escorts, and repeated his words. He was pleased when, as one, they laid hands to their weapons.

"On your command, sir," muttered the officers in charge.

"Wait," interrupted Sapho. "I have an idea." Without asking for Malchus' approval, he drew his sword and moved to stand in front of the hulk who had laughed at them when they arrived. The warrior leered unpleasantly. "Can this freak actually fight?" Sapho demanded in reasonable Iberian.

The Ausetani leader couldn't believe his ears. Sapho barely reached up to the warrior's shoulder. "That's my eldest son. He's never been beaten in single combat."

"What's he doing?" Bostar whispered to Malchus.

For once, Malchus looked worried. "I don't know, but I hope the gods are smiling on him."

Sapho raised his voice. "If I defeat him, then you will apologize, accept Hannibal's gifts and allow us to leave unharmed. When our army arrives, you will offer it safe passage."

The chieftain laughed. So did everyone within earshot. "Of course. If you fail, though, he will take your head, and those of all your companions, as trophies."

"I would expect no less," Sapho replied disdainfully.

The chieftain gave a callous shrug. At his command, the mass of warriors formed a large, hollow circle. Malchus seized the initiative and used his soldiers to force a passage through so that they could form part of what was to be the combat area. He and Bostar stood at the very front. Many of the Ausetani did not like this move, and began pushing and shoving at the Carthaginian troops, until an angry shout from their leader stopped them. Surrounded by his bodyguards, the chief took up a position directly opposite Malchus.

Gripping his drawn sword, Sapho stalked through a narrow corridor of leering, unfriendly faces. A few paces behind him, the huge warrior received a rapturous welcome. When they were both in the center of the circle, the crowd of Ausetani closed ranks. From a distance of perhaps a dozen paces, the two faced each other. Sapho was armed with a sword and a dagger. In contemptuous concession, his opponent had laid aside his shield and saunion, leaving him with a long, straight, double-edged blade. It still looked like a totally uneven match.

Bostar's gorge rose. Sapho was a skilled swordsman, but he'd never faced a prospect like this. Judging by his father's clenched jaw and fixed expression, he was thinking similar thoughts. Whatever he had been thinking about Sapho recently, Bostar didn't want him to die losing to this giant. Closing his eyes, he prayed to Baal Saphon, the god of war, to help his brother. To help them all.

Sapho rolled his shoulders, loosening his muscles and wondering what was his best course of action. Why had he thrown down such a stupid challenge? The explanation was simple. Since Bostar had saved Hannibal's life, Sapho's jealousy had soared to new heights. There had always been a keen rivalry between them, but this was a step too far. In the months since they'd left Saguntum, Sapho had appeared to go along with Bostar's wish to lay the matter to rest, but the feeling gnawed constantly at his guts like a malignant growth. Perhaps now some of his wounded pride could be reclaimed. Sapho studied his opponent's bulging muscles and tried not to despair. What chance had he of succeeding? He had only one, Sapho realized with a thrill. His speed.

The chieftain raised his right arm, and a hushed silence fell. Glancing at both men to ensure they were ready, he made a downward chopping gesture.

With an almighty roar, the warrior launched himself forward, his sword raised high. For him, the contest was to be ended quickly. Brutally. Closing in on Sapho, he hammered down an immense blow. Instead of cleaving flesh, the blade whistled through the air to clash off the pebble-strewn ground, sending up a shower of sparks. Sapho was gone, dancing nimbly around to his opponent's rear. The warrior bellowed with rage and spun to face him. Again he swung at Sapho, to no avail. He didn't seem to care. With greater strength and reach, and a longer weapon, he had all the advantage.

Speed isn't enough, thought Sapho. Desperately, he twisted away from a thrust that would have driven through both his bronze breastplate and his rib cage had it connected. So far, the warrior's quilted linen tunic had turned away the glancing blows he had managed to land. Without getting dangerously close, it was impossible to do any more. Backing away from his sneering opponent, Sapho did not see one of the Ausetani stretch out his foot. An instant later, he tripped over it and fell backward on to the hard-packed dirt. Fortunately, he retained hold of his sword.

The warrior stepped closer and Sapho saw death looking him in the eyes. He waited until his enemy had begun to swing downward, and then, with all his might, he rolled away into the center of the circle. Behind him, Sapho heard his opponent's sword slam into the ground with a bone-jarring thump. Knowing that speed was of the essence, he turned over and over before trying to get up. Mocking laughs from the watching Ausetani filled the air, and the huge warrior raised his arms in anticipation of victory. Rage filled Sapho at their treachery. He knew too that this fight couldn't be won by ordinary means. It was time to cast the dice. Take his chance. He drew his dagger with his left hand, ignoring the jeers this provoked.

Breathing deeply, Sapho waited. What he needed the warrior to do was take a great sideways slash at him. The only way he could think of drawing the hulk in was to stay put—without defending himself. It was a complete gamble. If the other didn't take the bait and respond exactly as he wished, he'd be dead, but Sapho couldn't think of anything else to do. Weariness threatened to overcome him, and his shoulders slumped.

The huge warrior shuffled in, grinning.

With a thrill, Sapho realized that his opponent thought he'd given up. He didn't move a muscle.

"Prepare to die," the warrior growled. Lifting his right arm, he swung his sword around in a curving arc, aiming for the junction between Sapho's neck and shoulders. The blow was delivered with unstoppable force, at a target that was standing stock-still. To those watching, it looked as if the duel was over.

At the last moment, Sapho dropped to his knees, letting the other's blade split the air over his head. Throwing himself forward, he stretched out his arm and plunged his dagger into the warrior's left thigh. It wasn't a fatal wound, but nor was it meant to be. As he landed helplessly on his chest, Sapho heard a loud scream of pain. A grimace of satisfaction twisted his lips as he scrambled to his feet, still clutching his sword. A few steps away, the bleeding warrior was listing to one side like a ship in a storm. All his attention was focused on pulling the knife from his leg. Stabbing him in the back would be simple.

A quick glance at the snarling faces surrounding them helped

Sapho to make a snap decision. Mercy would be far more useful here than ruthlessness. Swiftly, he swept in and completed the task. Drawing his blade across the back of his enemy's left leg, he hamstrung him. As the bellowing warrior collapsed, Sapho stamped on his right hand, forcing him to drop his weapon. Touching the point of his blade to the other's chest, he growled, "Yield."

Moaning with pain, the warrior extended both his hands upward, palms extended.

Sapho lifted his gaze to the chieftain, whose face registered stunned disbelief. "Well?" he asked simply.

Eventually, the chief managed to compose himself. "I apologize for insulting Hannibal, your leader. The Ausetani accept these generous gifts, with thanks," he muttered with bad grace. "You and your companions are free to go."

"Excellent," replied Sapho with a broad smile. "Your son will be coming with us."

The chief jumped to his feet. "He needs medical attention."

"Which he will receive in plenty. We will leave him in the care of the best surgeon in Emporiae. You have my word on that." Sapho leaned on his sword slightly, eliciting a loud moan from the huge warrior. "Or I can end it right here. It's your choice."

The chieftain's lips peeled back with fury, but he was powerless in the face of Sapho's resolve. "Very well," he replied.

Only then did Sapho glance at his father and Bostar. Both gave him fierce nods of encouragement. Sapho found himself grinning like an idiot. Against all the odds, he had redeemed the situation, won his father's approval and his brother's admiration. Inside, though, he knew that the Ausetani would have to be defeated before this particular passage to Gaul was safe.

XII

PLANS

A boot in the ribs woke Hanno the next morning. Grunting in pain, he opened his eyes. Agesandros was standing over him, flanked by two of the largest slaves on the farm. Hanno knew them for dumb brutes who did whatever they were told. Sets of manacles hung from their ham-like fists. Confusion and dread filled Hanno. Quintus' and Fabricius' absence hit home like hammer blows. This had to be more than coincidence. "What was that for?" he croaked.

Instead of answering, the Sicilian kicked him again. Several times.

Protecting his head with his hands, Hanno rolled into the fetal position and prayed that Aurelia would hear.

At length, Agesandros ceased. He'd made no effort to remain quiet. "Gugga son of a whore," he snarled.

Through squinted eyes, Hanno looked up. He was alarmed to see the Sicilian clutching a dagger in one hand and a small purse in the other.

"I found these under your pathetic pile of possessions. So you would steal money and weapons from your owner?" Agesandros thundered.

"Probably cut all our throats in the middle of the night too, before running away to join your scumbag countrymen in their war against Rome."

"I've never seen those things before in my life," Hanno cried. Immediately, an image of Agesandros lurking in the atrium came to mind. That's what the Sicilian had been doing! "You bastard," Hanno muttered, trying to sit up. He received a kick in the face for his troubles. Sprawling back on his bedroll, waves of agony washed over him. Blood filled his mouth, and a moment later he spat out two teeth.

Agesandros laughed cruelly. "Fit him with manacles," he ordered. "Neck as well as ankles."

Dazed, Hanno watched as the slaves stepped forward and fastened the heavy iron rings around his flesh. Three loud clicks, and he was back to where he'd been in the slave market. As before, a long chain extended from the metal band around his neck. With a brutal tug, Hanno was jerked to his feet and toward the door.

"Stop!"

All eyes turned.

Still in her nightdress, Aurelia stood framed in the doorway to her room. "Just what do you think you are doing?" she screeched. "Hanno is a household slave, not one of the farm workers, to do with as you please."

The Sicilian bowed extravagantly. Mockingly. "Forgive me, my lady, for waking you so early. After hearing of the news in your father's letter, I became concerned about how this slave would react. I worried that he was planning to do you and your family harm, before escaping. Unfortunately, I was correct." He held up the evidence. "These clearly aren't his."

Horrified, Aurelia's gaze shot to Hanno. She flinched at the sight of his bloodied face.

"*Someone* planted them among my things," Hanno muttered, throwing Agesandros a poisonous look.

Understanding at once, Aurelia started forward. "You see?"

The Sicilian chuckled. "He would say that, wouldn't he? Every gugga's a liar, though." He jerked his head at the two hulks. "Come on. We have a long journey ahead of us."

"I forbid you," Aurelia shouted. "Do not move another step."

The slaves holding Hanno froze, and Agesandros turned. "Forgive me, my lady, but in this instance I am going to override your authority."

Atia's voice cut in like a whiplash. "What about mine?" she demanded. "In Fabricius' absence, I am in charge, not you."

Agesandros blinked. "Of course you are, mistress," he replied smoothly.

"Explain yourself."

Agesandros held up the knife and purse once more and repeated his allegations.

Atia looked suitably horrified.

"What would Fabricius say if he found out that I had left such a dangerous slave on the premises, mistress?" the Sicilian asked. "He would have me crucified, and rightly so."

You clever bastard, thought Hanno. Make your move when you only have two women to intimidate. Fabricius was far away, and who knew when Quintus would return?

Atia nodded in acceptance. "Where are you taking him?"

"To Capua, mistress. Clearly, the dog is too dangerous to sell as an ordinary slave, but I've heard of a local government official who died there recently. The funeral is in two days, and the man's son wants to honor his father's passing with a gladiator fight. A pair of prisoners are to fight each other to the death, and then the survivor is to be executed."

Atia's lips thinned. "I see. Will my husband be out of pocket?"

"No, mistress. For an event like this, I'll get far more than we paid for him."

Tears of impotent rage ran down Aurelia's cheeks. Frantically, she racked her brains. What could she do?

Atia crossed to give Aurelia a hug. "Don't fret. He's a slave, dear," she said. "A murderous one too."

"No," Aurelia whispered. "Hanno wouldn't do something like that."

Atia frowned. "You've seen the evidence for yourself. The only way we can confirm the Carthaginian's guilt is have him tortured and see what he says. Is that what you want?"

Defeated, Aurelia shook her head. "No."

"Fine. The matter's closed," her mother said firmly. "Now, I'm going for a bath. Why don't you join me?"

"I couldn't," whispered Aurelia.

"Suit yourself," said Atia. She turned to Agesandros. "Better get going, hadn't you? It's a long way to Capua."

The Sicilian flashed an oily smile. "Yes, mistress."

With a satisfied nod, Atia disappeared from sight.

Hanno, meanwhile, was in a daze. Agesandros must have been planning this ever since Quintus and Aurelia rescued me, he realized. Waiting for the right time.

His horror was only to grow.

"I forgot to say." Reveling in the moment, the Sicilian looked from Hanno to Aurelia and back. "The other fighter is also a gugga. A friend of this shitbag, I believe."

Hanno's stomach lurched. It seemed too much of a coincidence to be true. "Suniaton?"

Agesandros revealed his teeth. "That's his name, yes."

"No," cried Aurelia. "That is so cruel."

"Quite apt, I thought," said Agesandros.

Hanno's relief that Suni was alive vanished. Blinding fury consumed him, and he lunged forward, desperate to close with Agesandros. Within three steps, he was pulled up short. The slave holding the chain attached to his neck had simply tightened his grip. Hanno ground his teeth in rage. "You will pay for this," he growled. "I curse you forever. May the gods of the underworld act as my witness."

There were few who were not afraid of such powerful oaths, and Agesandros flinched. But he regained control quickly. "It's you who will be visiting Hades, along with your friend. Not me." Clicking his fingers at the slaves, he stalked to the front door.

Hanno could not bear to look at Aurelia as he was dragged away. It hurt too much. The last thing he heard was the patter of her feet on the mosaic, and her voice calling for Elira. Then he was outside, in bright spring sunshine. Walking to Capua, where he would fight Suniaton to the death. Hanno stared at Agesandros' broad back, begging all the gods for a lightning bolt to strike him down on the spot. Of course, nothing happened.

The last remnants of Hanno's hope disappeared.

It returned within a matter of moments. They had not even reached the end of the lane before shouts and cries rang out behind them. Agesandros spun around, and his eyes widened. Without even looking at Hanno, he sprinted back toward the farm buildings. In slow motion, Hanno turned to see what was happening. To his amazement, tendrils of smoke were rising from one of the granaries. Aurelia, he thought, exultantly. She must have started a fire.

There was no way under the sun that Agesandros could have done anything but return. Aurelia had bought him some time. How would that be enough? Hanno wondered, desperation tearing at his soul.

It was several hours before the blaze was brought under control. Roaring like a demon, Agesandros supervised as every slave on the farm ferried water to the grain stores. Even Hanno had his manacles unfastened for the task. Hurling the contents of their buckets on to the flames, the slaves ran to the well and back, over and over again. Aurelia and Atia watched from a distance. Horrified expressions adorned both their faces. There was no sign of Elira.

The Sicilian let no one rest until he was happy that the fire was dying down. Despite himself, Hanno felt a grudging admiration for Agesandros. Covered in soot from head to toe like everyone else, he looked exhausted. The granary's stone construction had helped, but the supreme effort the overseer had exacted from everyone was the main reason that the blaze had not spread to more of the farm buildings.

By the time the last of the flames had been extinguished, the afternoon was over. There was no question of walking to Capua that day. To Hanno's relief, the Sicilian didn't bother beating him further. His manacles were replaced, and he was locked into a small cell that adjoined Agesandros' quarters. In pitch darkness, Hanno slumped to the floor and closed his eyes. He was absolutely parched with thirst, and his belly was growling like a wild beast, but Hanno doubted that any food or drink would be forthcoming. He could only try to rest, and hope that Aurelia had another trick up her sleeve.

Hours passed. Hanno dozed fitfully, but the cold and his manacles prevented him from sleeping properly. Nonetheless, he dreamed of many things. The streets of Carthage. His two brothers, Sapho and

Bostar, training with swords. Hannibal's messenger visiting by night. Fishing with Suniaton. The storm. Slavery and his unlikely friendship with Quintus and Aurelia. Bloody war between Carthage and Rome. Two gladiators fighting before a baying crowd. The last images were horrifyingly violent. Covered in sweat, Hanno jerked upright.

Desolation swamped him. After all his requests to be reunited with Suniaton, this is what it would come to. They would die together to commemorate the death of a crusty Roman official. Frustration and rage filled Hanno by turns. Alone in the darkness, he prayed that Agesandros stayed to watch the fight. When he and Suniaton were handed their weapons, they could make a suicidal attack on the Sicilian. Gain some retribution before they died. His plan was implausible, but Hanno hung on to it for dear life.

Some time later, he was startled by the sound of a key entering the lock. Surely dawn had not come yet? Hanno backed fearfully away from the door, raising his hands against the arc of light that spread into the room. To his utter surprise, the person who entered was none other than Quintus, clad in a heavy cloak. He was clutching a bunch of keys in one hand and a small bronze lamp in the other. A sheathed gladius hung from a baldric over his right shoulder.

Hanno was stunned. "What are you doing here?"

"Helping a friend," replied Quintus simply. Placing the lamp on the floor, he tried a key on Hanno's fetters. It didn't work, but the second one did. A moment later, he had also unlocked the iron ring around his neck. Quintus grinned. "Let's go."

Hanno could scarcely contain his joy. "How did you know to come back?"

A wry smile tugged Quintus' lips upward. "You can thank Aurelia. The instant you had left, she sent Elira to find me. Next she set a fire in the granary."

Hanno was still confused. "But the keys," he said. "There was no time to make an impression of them."

"These are the originals," replied Quintus. He saw Hanno's bewilderment, and explained. "I commended Agesandros on his excellent work by giving him a jug of Father's best wine. The fool was delighted. What he didn't know was that I had laced it with enough papaverum to knock out an elephant. I simply waited until he had drunk it and fallen asleep. Then I took his keys."

"You're a genius. So is Aurelia." He grabbed Quintus' arm. "Thank you. I owe you both my life for the second time."

Quintus nodded. "I knew that Agesandros was lying about you planning to kill us. If you wanted me dead, you wouldn't have come back to save me at the hut. Besides, I know you would help me in a similar situation." He moved toward the door. "Now, come on. Dawn is not far off. Aurelia is at the pens, feeding the dogs scraps to keep them from barking, but she can't stay there forever. She said to say that you would be in her prayers." He didn't mention his sister's tears. What was the point? Hers was an impossible fantasy.

Sad that he would not see Aurelia, and unaware of Quintus' emotions, Hanno followed him outside. The farmyard was deserted, and the only audible sounds were Agesandros' loud snores. Within a hundred paces, they had left the buildings behind. Along the lane, the cypress trees stood tall and threatening, their branches creaking in the slight breeze. A crescent moon hung low in the sky, reminding Hanno of Tanit and home. And Suniaton. Suddenly, the immense relief he had felt at Quintus' appearance began to ebb away. He might be free, but his friend was not.

Quintus stopped when they reached the shadow of the trees. He lifted the baldric over his shoulder and handed the gladius to Hanno. "You'll need this." Next, he proffered his thick woolen cloak and a leather satchel.

Hanno muttered his thanks.

"The bag contains food for several days, and twenty-five didrachms. Make your way to the coast and take passage to Syracuse. You should be able to find a merchant ship there which can take you to Carthage."

"I'm going nowhere without Suniaton," said Hanno.

Quintus' face changed. "Have you gone mad?" he hissed. "You don't even know where he is being held."

"I'll find him," Hanno answered stolidly.

"And get yourself killed into the bargain."

"Would you leave Gaius behind if you were in my shoes?" Hanno demanded.

"Of course not," Quintus retorted.

"Well, then."

"Stubborn bloody Carthaginian. There's no telling you." Quintus scowled. "Going to Capua on your own is tantamount to committing suicide. I can't let you do that. Not after all the trouble I've gone to. Can you find the shepherd's hut where we fought the bandits?"

Hanno stared at Quintus, not understanding. "I think so, yes."

"Head up there and wait for me. I'll see about finding Suniaton later."

The immensity of Quintus' offer sank in. "You don't have to do this."

"I know." Quintus regarded him solemnly. "But you are my friend."

A lump rose in Hanno's throat. "Thank you. If I can ever repay this debt, I will. You have my word."

"Let us pray that I never have need to call on you." Quintus pushed him toward the hills. "Go."

With a lightness in his heart that he had not felt since leaving Carthage, Hanno ran off into the darkness.

Hanno made his way to the hut without difficulty, reaching it less than two hours after sunrise. He spent the climb marveling at how he'd escaped Agesandros' clutches for the second time. Of course it was solely thanks to Quintus and Aurelia. Yet again, Hanno was forced to admit that Romans were capable of great kindness. They were not all the deceitful monsters described by his father. His charitable feelings did not last long. Hanno only had to think of Flaccus and his tale to remember the incredibly harsh conditions imposed on Carthage at the end of the last war, and the arrogant manner with which Rome had treated her over Saguntum. Even the genial Martialis didn't like the Carthaginians. "Typical guggas," he'd said.

He calmed himself with thoughts of how a Roman—Quintus— was at this very moment trying to free Suniaton, a Carthaginian condemned to die. His ploy didn't last long. As the hours dragged by, Hanno found it ever harder not to head for Capua. His promise to Quintus was what made him stay. He busied himself by repairing the hut, which had been left damaged after the fight. First Hanno collected every piece of fallen wood he could find. Then, using some old but serviceable tools he found lying inside, he sawed and chopped the timber into suitable lengths. He was no carpenter, but the construction was straightforward. All he had to do was study the undamaged sides, and copy them. It was undemanding yet rewarding labor and, as the sun set, Hanno stood back and admired his handiwork.

Worry was niggling away at him, however. He could no longer ignore the fact that Quintus would not return that day. Did this mean that his attempt had failed? Hanno had no idea. He pondered his options for some time, concluding that it was too dangerous to return to the farm. Agesandros would be on the lookout for trouble. Nor was there any point in making for Capua. Hanno knew no one there, and if he didn't manage to find Quintus, he would have no idea what had transpired since the morning. His only choice was to stay put. Slightly more at ease, Hanno lit a fire in the hut's stone-ring fireplace, and wolfed down some of the olives, cheese and bread he found in the satchel.

Wrapped in Quintus' cloak, Hanno sat watching the yellow-orange flames and thinking of the people he held most dear in the world. His father. Sapho and Bostar. Suniaton. Hanno paused before adding two more individuals to the list. Quintus. Aurelia. How many of them would he ever see again? Sadness, his constant companion since the storm, washed over Hanno in great waves. In all likelihood, he would never be reunited with his family. They were probably with Hannibal's army in Iberia by now, with every chance of being killed. Although it was his greatest desire to find them, doing so in the midst of a war would be virtually impossible. Finding Suniaton was perhaps his best hope, Hanno realized. If, by some stroke of luck, this came to pass, he would leave, never to see Quintus or Aurelia again. That conclusion brought even more pain. All he could wish for was a reunion with his loved ones in the next world. This bleak insight was the last thing Hanno remembered as sleep drew him into its embrace.

Dawn found Hanno in a better frame of mind. There was much to be grateful for. Despite what he had been through, he was no longer a captive. Moreover, Quintus had a greater chance of freeing Suniaton than he did. If the attempt was successful, he and his friend had a reasonable chance of making it to the coast, and finding a ship bound for Carthage. Never give up hope, Hanno thought. Without it, life is pointless.

He spent the morning practicing with his gladius and scanning the slopes below for movement. It was nearly midday when Hanno spotted a lone figure on horseback. His heart leaped in his chest at the sight. There was no way of knowing who it was, so he withdrew into the cover granted by a clump of juniper trees some fifty paces from the hut. With bated breath, Hanno waited as the rider drew nearer. From its broad shoulders, he judged it to be male. There was no sign of any dogs, which pleased him. It increased the likelihood that this was not someone sent to track him down.

Finally, he recognized Quintus' features. Disappointment flooded Hanno that Suniaton was not with him. As the other drew close enough to speak, Hanno emerged from his hiding place.

Quintus raised a hand in apologetic salute.

"What happened? Did you discover anything about Suniaton?"

Quintus' lips twisted in a grimace. "He's still alive, but he was injured during training two days ago. The good news is that he won't be able to take part in the *munus*." He saw Hanno's alarm. "It's just a flesh wound. Apparently, he'll be fine in a month or so."

Hanno closed his eyes to relish the wave of relief. Suni wasn't dead! "The official's son wouldn't sell him, then?"

Quintus shook his head. "He didn't seem to care that you and Suniaton wouldn't be fighting each other," he said. "But he didn't want to sell Suni either. Stupidly, I let the mangy dog see how much I wanted to buy him. The prick told me to come back when Suniaton is fully recovered and I can see a demonstration of his full abilities. 'That will show you his true worth,' he said. I wouldn't hold your breath, though. The man fancies himself as a gladiator trainer. There must have been a dozen slaves with weapons training in his yard. I'm sorry."

Hanno felt the last of his reborn hope slipping away.

Quintus glanced uneasily down the slope. "You'd be wise to get moving."

Hanno gave him a questioning look.

"Agesandros was furious when he discovered that you were gone," Quintus said. "The arrogant bastard wouldn't take it from me that I had freed you. He said only my father had the power to do that. Naturally, my mother agreed with him. She's furious with me," he added glumly.

"But your father won't be back for months."

Quintus gave him a grim nod. "Precisely. Which makes you a runaway, and hunting *them* down is something Agesandros is rather good at. I told him that you headed toward Capua, and I think he believed me. He started looking in that direction." He winked. "Fortunately, Aurelia made Elira drag an old tunic of yours all the way to the river, and then swim downstream to a ford where her tracks would be mixed up with plenty of others. She left the garment in the water, which should trick the hounds."

"Your sister is incredible," said Hanno in amazement.

Quintus grinned briefly. "It would still be best to get a head start now. Skirt around the farm to arrive at Capua tomorrow morning. Agesandros should have returned home by that stage, and you can catch a boat downriver to the coast."

A knot formed in Hanno's stomach. "I can't desert Suniaton," he muttered. "He's so near."

"And so far," Quintus replied harshly. "He might as well be in Hades for all you can do."

"That's as may be," Hanno retorted. "But you said the official's son would talk again in a few weeks."

Unsurprised, Quintus sighed. "Stay, then," he said. "I'll bring you food every two or three days. I will try to keep an eye on Suniaton. We'll work out some way of getting him out."

Hanno could have cried with relief. "Thank you."

Quintus pulled around his horse's head. "Be vigilant. You never know when Agesandros might appear."

—···—

Bostar's phalanx was marching behind those of Sapho and his father, so the messenger reached him first. "Is there a Captain Bostar here?" he cried.

"Yes. What do you want?"

"Hannibal wants to talk to you, sir. Now," he said, matching the Libyans' pace easily.

Bostar stared at the strapping scutarius, who was one of the general's bodyguard. "Do you know what it's about?"

"No, sir."

"Did he want to see my father or brother?"

"Just you, sir," replied the Iberian stolidly. "What shall I say to the general? He's pulled out of the column about a mile back."

"Tell him I will be there at once." Bostar thought for a moment. "Wait! I'll come with you."

The scutarius looked pleased. "Very good, sir."

Bostar muttered instructions to his second-in-command, who was riding beside him, before turning his horse's head and directing it out of his soldiers' way. Few of the men looked up as he trotted by, but those who did grinned. Bostar nodded in acknowledgment, glad that his efforts in winning their trust had paid off. The Libyans' large round shields knocked off their backs as they walked, and their short spears looked skyward in a forest of points. A junior officer was situated every fifty paces, and beside each marched a standard-bearer. Their wooden poles were decorated with sun discs, lunar crescents and red decorative ribbons.

Bostar eyed the long, winding column approaching from the southwest. "Feast your eyes on that," he said to the scutarius, who was trotting alongside. "It's some spectacle."

"I suppose so, sir." The man cleared his throat and spat. "It would look a damn sight better with forty thousand more of my countrymen, though."

"Not all are as loyal as you and your comrades," replied Bostar. In his heart, he too was sorry that the host had shrunk by more than a third in little over three months. Much of the decrease could be accounted for by the casualties suffered thus far, and those who made up the garrisons along the route back to Iberia. In addition, plenty of men, perhaps ten thousand more, had been discharged by Hannibal before they could desert. To discuss the matter with an ordinary soldier was bad for morale, so Bostar kept his lips sealed. His spirits soon lifted, however. It was impossible not to be exhilarated by the sight of such a massive Carthaginian army, the first such to go on the offensive against Rome in more than a generation.

After the last of the spearmen had passed, there was a short delay until the next units reached them. These were massed ranks of fierce-looking, tattooed Libyan skirmishers in bare feet and red goatskin tunics. They were armed with small round shields and handfuls of javelins. Hundreds of Balearic slingers followed, wild half-dressed men from the Mediterranean islands, whose skill with their slings was legendary. Bostar wouldn't have trusted a single man among them, but they were a supreme asset to Hannibal's army.

After came the light Iberian infantry, the *caetrati*, with their round leather bucklers, javelins and falcata swords. Farther down the track, Bostar made out Hannibal and his officers, surrounded by the mounted part of his bodyguard, local cavalry in crested bronze helmets and red cloaks. Behind the general marched the heavy Celtiberian foot, the scutarii.

Bostar could not see the final units of the army, which trailed behind the baggage train, thousands of laden-down mules led by Iberian peasants. Protecting the rear were thirty-seven elephants, and more Celtiberians. Bostar thought that their uniform was probably the most striking in the entire force: black cloaks, bronze helmets with crimson crests and greaves made of sinew. Their shields were either round like those of the caetrati, or flat, elongated ovals, and they carried short straight swords and all-iron spears. Last of all, mobile and fast moving, were the many protective squadrons of Iberian and Numidian cavalry. These—the finest horsemen in the world—were Hannibal's secret weapon.

They reached the general's position not long after. The scutarius gave the password to the cavalryman who challenged them, which saw the protective cordon open up. Bostar dismounted quickly and threw his reins to the Iberian. As he approached, he felt Hannibal's eyes upon him. Bostar moved even faster. He snapped off a salute. "You wished to see me, sir?"

Hannibal smiled. "Yes. I wasn't expecting you so soon."

Bostar couldn't help but grin. "I wanted to find out what you had in mind for me, sir."

Hannibal glanced at the officers to either side. "Eager, this lion cub, isn't he?"

There was a ripple of laughter, and Bostar flushed, not least because the general and his brothers—the sons of Hamilcar Barca—were known as the "lion's brood."

Hannibal noticed at once. "Do not take offense, for I meant none. It's soldiers like you who are the backbone of this army. Not like the thousands of men I had to let go after our recent campaign. Faint hearts."

Bostar nodded gratefully. "Thank you, sir."

Hannibal turned his eyes to the southwest, whence they had come. "It's hard to believe that we only crossed into Gaul a few weeks ago, isn't it? Seems like we haven't fought a battle in an age."

"I won't forget the journey in a hurry, sir." After the hostile, sun-scorched lands north of the Iberus, Bostar appreciated the fertile land of southern Gaul, with its tilled fields, large villages and friendly natives.

Hannibal's nod was rueful. "Nor will I. Losing ten thousand men in under three months was most unfortunate. But it couldn't be helped. Speed was of the essence, and our tactics worked."

Mago shot his brother a disgruntled look. "Don't forget the same number of troops, plus cavalry, that you had to leave to keep the bastards pacified."

"Soldiers who will also protect the area against Roman invasion," retorted Hannibal. "After defeating the troublesome natives, they should be able to take on a legion or two." He scratched his beard and eyed Bostar. "The worst of the lot were that tribe you had trouble with. The whoresons who would have slaughtered you but for the duel your mad brother fought."

Bostar hid his amusement at Hannibal's description of Sapho. "The Ausetani, sir."

"The same ones who wouldn't allow the army to march through their lands unhindered. They were fools. But brave all the same," Hannibal acknowledged. "At the end, hardly any of them had wounds in their backs."

"They fought well, sir," agreed Bostar. "Especially the champion whom Sapho defeated. I counted ten of our soldiers lying around his corpse. His wound from the duel hadn't even healed either."

"Malchus pointed him out to me afterward," said Hannibal. "It's incredible that your brother managed to beat him in single combat. The man was as big as Herakles."

"He was, sir," agreed Bostar fervently. His memories of the fight were still vivid. "Sapho had the gods on his side that day."

"He did. For all his bravery, though, your brother has a tendency to be rash. To act first, and think later."

"If you say so, sir." While Bostar agreed with his general's assessment, it felt wrong to openly say so.

Hannibal gave him a shrewd look. "Your loyalty is commendable, but don't think I didn't hear about his refusal to pull back during that attack on Saguntum. If it hadn't been for you, hundreds of men would have lost their lives unnecessarily. Eh?"

Bostar met his general's gaze with reluctance. "Maybe so, sir."

"That's why you're here. Because you think before you take action." Hannibal waved at the rolling countryside, much of which was full of ripe wheat and barley. "Things are easy now. We can buy as much grain as we need from the locals, and live off the land the rest of the time. But the journey won't all be like this. The weather will get worse and, sooner or later, we'll come across someone who wants to fight us."

"Indeed, sir," said Bostar soberly.

"We can only pray that it's not the Romans at any stage before we reach Cisalpine Gaul. Hopefully, those bastards still have no idea of our plans. The good news is that my scouts, who have just returned from the River Rhodanus, saw no sign of them."

Mago's smile was like that of a wolf. "And the trail a legion leaves can't be missed, so we have one less thing to worry about. For now."

"Have you heard of the Rhodanus?" asked Hannibal.

"Vaguely, sir," said Bostar. "It's a big river quite near the Alps."

"That's right. By all accounts, most of the tribes in the area are well disposed toward us. Naturally, there's one that is not. The Volcae, they're called, and they live on both sides of the water."

"Will they try to deny us the passage, sir?"

"It would appear so," Hannibal answered grimly.

"That could be very costly, sir, especially when it comes to taking the horses and elephants across."

Hannibal scowled. "That's right. Which is why, while the army prepares to cross, you're going to lead a force upriver of the Volcae camp. You'll swim over at night, and find a hidden position nearby. Your dawn signal will tell me to order the boats launched." He smacked a fist into his palm. "We'll squash them like a man stamps on a beetle. How does that sound?"

Bostar's heart thumped in his chest. "It sounds good, sir."

"That's what I like to hear." Hannibal gripped his shoulder. "You'll get further instructions nearer the time. Now, you'll be wanting to get back to your men."

Bostar knew when he was being dismissed. "Yes, sir. Thank you, sir."

Hannibal called out when Bostar was ten steps away. "Not a word about this to anyone."

"Of course, sir," Bostar replied. The order was a relief, for it meant that Sapho would have no chance to be jealous because he had not been selected for the duty. Yet Bostar was already worrying how his brother would react when he did find out.

XIII

DEPARTURE

Hanno soon grew used to living in the hut, which had lain vacant since the shepherd's murder. According to Quintus, Fabricius' sheep were being grazed elsewhere and there was little likelihood of anyone passing by. Nonetheless, Hanno stayed alert. While Agesandros was his main concern, he had no wish to be seen at all. Hanno's luck held out; the only visitors he had were Quintus, and occasionally Aurelia.

There was little news of Suniaton. Quintus did not want to appear too eager by visiting the official's son earlier than had been arranged. Finally, though, Quintus reported that Suniaton had made an uneventful recovery. Hanno's spirits soared upon hearing this, but his hopes were immediately dashed. "The whoreson still won't sell. He says Suniaton is too promising a fighter. He wanted 250 didrachms for him." Quintus gave Hanno an apologetic look. "I haven't got that type of money. Father does, of course, but I'm not sure he'd give it to me, even if I managed to find him."

"We can't give up now. There must be another way," said Hanno fiercely.

"Unless we can bribe someone to let Suniaton escape . . . I just don't know who to approach." Quintus' frown disappeared. "I could ask Gaius." He held up a reassuring hand as Hanno jerked forward in alarm. "Gaius and I have been friends since we could walk. He doesn't necessarily approve of my helping you escape, but he won't tell a soul. Who knows? He might be prepared to help."

Hanno forced himself to sit down. Gaius' trustworthiness had already been proved by the fact that nobody had come looking for him at the shepherd's hut. It also seemed as if he was Suniaton's only hope. "Let us pray to the gods that he agrees, then."

"Leave it to me," said Quintus, hoping that his confidence in Gaius was not misplaced. In an effort to protect Hanno, he had concealed the fact that Suniaton was already fighting as a gladiator once more.

Time was not on their side.

———

When Quintus finally brought word that Gaius' efforts had come to fruition, Hanno's relief was overwhelming. Autumn had arrived, and the woods were a riot of color. The temperature had dropped noticeably too. Hanno was growing used to being woken by the cold at night. Quintus' direction to pack all his gear was most welcome. Hopefully, he'd be leaving the hut forever. "What are we going to do?" he asked as they headed toward Capua.

"Gaius didn't want me to say," Quintus replied, avoiding Hanno's gaze.

Worry clawed at Hanno's insides. "Why?"

Quintus shrugged. "I'm not sure. I think he wants to tell you himself." He saw Hanno's disappointment. "It's only a few hours longer."

"I know," Hanno replied, forcing a smile. "And I owe you both so much for what you've done."

"It's not about debts," said Quintus generously. "A man tries to help his friends if he can. Let's just hope that Gaius' idea works."

Hanno nodded grimly. If it didn't, there was a hard choice to be made. He couldn't hang around forever.

It was nearly dark by the time they reached Capua. Their journey had been uneventful, but Hanno still faltered as the massive walls loomed into view. Even though he was coming to help free Suniaton, entering the city now meant real danger. There would be guards at the gate who could ask awkward questions. Descriptions of him pinned to the walls of houses. Hanno knew how fugitive slaves were hunted in Carthage. It wouldn't be much different here. His feet dragged to a halt.

Quintus turned. "What is it?"

"I'm not just an escaped slave. What if someone recognizes me as a Carthaginian?"

Quintus' chuckle died away as he saw Hanno's real distress. "You don't have to worry," he said reassuringly. "There are plenty of dark-skinned slaves in Capua. Greeks, Libyans, Judaeans. No one knows the difference. And apart from Gaius, no one knows what you've done. Nor do they care. You're a slave, remember? Most people won't even notice you, let alone challenge you." He dismounted. "Follow me. Look miserable and don't catch anyone's eye."

"Very well," said Hanno, wishing that he had the comfort of a weapon to defend himself.

To his relief, things went smoothly. The sentries didn't even look up as he shuffled after Quintus. It was the same on the streets, which, thanks to the fast-approaching sunset, were emptying fast. People were more interested in getting home safely than studying a young noble and his slave. Housewives with baskets full of food muttered a few words with each other rather than having a full-blown gossip. Stallholders were boxing up their unsold produce and loading it on to mules. Many of the shops were already boarded up for the night.

Before long, they had reached Martialis' house. Quintus' loud knock was answered at once by Gaius himself, who grinned at his friend as he pulled open the gate. "I've been waiting for you." He gave Hanno a hard glance, but did not speak.

All of Hanno's doubts returned. He ducked his head awkwardly, telling himself that Gaius must be prepared to help. Why else were they here?

With several domestic slaves looking on, however, there was no chance of asking. One of them scurried past to take the horse's reins, and Gaius threw an arm around Quintus' shoulders. "Let's go inside. Father can't wait to see you. He ordered a piglet roasted in your honor."

Gaius eyed the stable boy. "Make sure my friend's slave gets fed. Find him a bed too."

"Yes, sir."

Hanno's unease abated a little when Quintus turned and gave him a wink. Hanno forced himself to relax as the gate shut, leaving him on the street. He followed the boy around the corner of the house to the stables, which were in a separate walled courtyard. The young slave proved to be as taciturn as he was ugly. They rubbed down, fed and watered Quintus' mount in complete silence, which suited Hanno down to the ground. Next they entered Martialis' kitchen through a door in the adjoining wall. Similar to Julius' jurisdiction, it was a hot, busy place, filled with the clatter of pans and shouted orders. The rich smell of cooking pork filled Hanno's nostrils and set his stomach rumbling. Keen to avoid attention, he found a quiet spot in the corridor that led to the pantry, where he sat down.

A few moments later, the stable boy appeared bearing two plates heaped high with bread, roast meat and vegetables. He shoved one at Hanno. "You're in luck tonight. The piglet could feed twenty people, so the master won't notice if his slaves also have a share."

"Thank you." Hanno seized the platter. This was a better feed than he'd had in months.

When they'd finished, the stable boy squinted at Hanno. "Do you play dice?"

Hanno did, but he felt as tense as the arm on a cocked catapult. So much was at stake tonight. "No."

Looking vaguely disappointed, the slave shuffled off. "Come on. I'll show you a place to sleep."

Hanno was taken back to the stables, and shown a quiet corner near the door. "No lights can be left in here. Too great a risk of fire." The stable boy indicated his small oil light. "I'll be taking this with me."

"Fine," replied Hanno.

With a shrug, the slave left him to it. As the flickering glow of the other's lamp receded, Hanno was left in complete darkness. He didn't mind about that. It was more the fact that, with Suniaton's escape so close, he was about to spend several hours alone. After a while, he began to look forward to the occasional stamp of a hoof or a gentle whinny.

The frequent noise of rats scurrying to and fro was less welcome, but it was a minor inconvenience compared to his reason for being there.

To Hanno's annoyance, the evening dragged by more slowly than an entire week. He spent an age praying to the gods, asking for their aid in ensuring that Gaius helped to free Suniaton. Growing frustrated with the overwhelming silence that met each of his requests, Hanno tried to sleep. He had no luck at all. His spirits rose when the stable boy and two other slaves entered the building. Despite his frustration, time *was* passing. Pretending to be asleep, Hanno heard them clamber up the rickety ladder to the hay store over the horses' stalls. Their incoherent mumbling led him to assume that they'd been drinking. Their oil light was extinguished almost immediately, and it wasn't long before a cadence of snores from above filled Hanno's ears. After what seemed an age, he felt his way over to the kitchen door, where Quintus had told him to wait.

When the door opened smoothly inward, it caught Hanno unawares. "Who is it?" he whispered nervously.

"Pluto himself, come to carry you away," Quintus muttered. "Who do you think?"

Hanno shivered. Even mentioning the Roman god of the underworld felt like bad luck. He offered up another prayer to Eshmoun, asking for his protection.

Quintus was followed by Gaius, who was carrying a small, shuttered lantern. Both were wearing dark cloaks.

Hanno could take it no more. "What are we going to do?"

"Outside." Gaius led them to the stable door, where he lifted the locking bar and gently laid it on the floor. A waft of cool air hit their faces as he tugged the door open. Gaius padded out and checked the street. "All clear!" he hissed an instant later.

Quintus shoved Hanno out first, and pulled the portal to behind them.

"Come on, Gaius. Are you finally going to tell us what you've planned?" asked Quintus.

Hanno's stomach clenched into a knot.

"I will," muttered Gaius, "but your slave should know something first."

"He's not a slave anymore," Quintus hissed. "I freed him."

"You and I know that that holds about as much water as a leaky bucket."

Quintus did not reply.

Hanno's breath caught in his chest. Gaius was clearly cut from different cloth to Quintus. He wanted to leave, but that would mean extinguishing whatever hope there was of freeing his friend. Gritting his teeth, he waited.

"I was stunned when you first told me what you'd done, Quintus," Gaius whispered. "I said nothing, of course. You're my oldest friend. But you took a step too far when you asked me to help free another slave. That I could not do."

"Gaius, I—" Quintus began. The poor light could not conceal the embarrassment in his voice.

"I changed my mind, however, when I found out who owned the slave you were interested in." Gaius paused. "The official who died was none other than the biggest persecutor of Oscan nobility that this city has ever seen. His shitbag of a son is little better. Stealing ... freeing ... one of his slaves is the least I would do to the bastard."

Hanno let out a long sigh.

"Thank you, Gaius," whispered Quintus. He wasn't going to question his friend's motives at a moment such as this.

At once Gaius brought them into a little huddle. "I started off by spending days hanging around in the street where the official's son lives. I found out little, but I did get to know the faces of everyone who lived in his house. Then my luck changed. About a week ago, I saw the majordomo coming out of a brothel in a different part of town."

"So what?" demanded Quintus. "That's hardly unusual."

Gaius' teeth flashed white in the darkness. "Except when I went inside and asked who he'd been fucking, the madam went all coy. I slipped her a few coins, and she soon changed her tune. It seems that the majordomo has a taste for young boys."

"Filthy bastard," muttered Quintus.

An image of Hostus popped into Hanno's mind. His father's enemy was known for a similar taste in flesh. "It's disgusting, but is it a crime?" he asked. "It's not in Carthage, unfortunately."

"The practice is frowned upon by many, but it isn't against the law for citizens, like us," Gaius replied. "Slaves are a different matter, however. I doubt that the official's son would be too pleased to find out about his majordomo's habits. The madam said that he tends to get overexcited. Violent. She's had to intervene a number of times to stop her boys from being badly injured."

"Fucking animal," said Quintus, looking revolted.

Hanno was just grateful that he and Suniaton hadn't been sold to a similar fate. "So you're blackmailing him?"

"Basically, yes," Gaius answered. "He's agreed to drug the slave who guards the door, which will give him a chance to let Suniaton out. Of course the poor bastard doorman will probably end up on a cross for letting another slave escape, but the majordomo doesn't care about that. He's only thinking of his own skin."

"And if he doesn't play along?" inquired Quintus. His words made Hanno's stomach clench.

"His owner will receive an anonymous letter detailing his sordid activities to the letter, and giving the brothel's address should he wish to corroborate the details."

"Excellent," murmured Quintus.

For a moment, Hanno's delight at Gaius' plan was soured by the knowledge that an innocent slave would suffer, or even die, so that Suni might be free. He quelled the thought without remorse. He would kill to save his friend. How was this any different? "It sounds foolproof," he said. "Thank you."

"I'm not doing it for you," Gaius replied curtly. "I'm doing it because it gives me an opportunity to get back at the official's son." He chuckled at the others' confusion. "By sunset tomorrow, everyone in the town will have heard the rumor that he likes to screw young boys. Not the best way to start a political career, is it?" He looked at Quintus, who gave a resigned shrug. "Best get moving now, though. Stay close."

Telling himself that it didn't matter what Gaius' reasons for helping were, Hanno followed the two Romans through the darkened streets. The only living thing that they encountered was a scrawny dog, which raised its hackles and growled at the interlopers to its territory. It darted, yelping, out of the way when Gaius aimed a hefty kick at it, and it wasn't long before they were crouched by the front door of a nondescript house, three shadows that could barely be seen. Apart from the chinks of light that escaped the wooden shutters of a flat on the opposite side of the lane, it was pitch black.

Checking the street yet again, Gaius rapped lightly on the door with his knuckles. There was no response from within, and Hanno began to panic. He glanced at the myriad of stars that lit the night sky. Eshmoun, he begged, do not forget Suniaton, your devoted follower, and son of your priest in Carthage. Great Tanit, have mercy.

His prayers were answered a moment later when, with a faint creak, the door opened inward. "Who is it?"

"Gaius."

A short man emerged cautiously on to the street. Seeing Quintus and Hanno, he stiffened. Gaius was quick to jump in with the reassurance that they were friends, and the figure relaxed a fraction. His receding hair, long nose, and darting eyes made him resemble a rat, thought Hanno distastefully. It was no surprise that he fucked little boys. Yet this was the majordomo of the house, who was also about to set Suniaton free.

"Well, where's the Carthaginian?" demanded Gaius.

"Just inside. I'll get him," the majordomo replied, bobbing his head. "And you'll say nothing to my master?"

"I give you my word," Gaius answered dryly.

The other nodded uneasily, knowing that this was all he'd get. "Very well."

He scuttled from view, and Hanno felt a tinge of suspicion at his speed. There was a short delay before he heard the sound of shuffling feet. Then Hanno saw a stooped figure framed in the doorway, and he leaped forward. "Suniaton?"

"Hanno?" croaked the other.

Throwing his arms around Suniaton, Hanno clung to his friend like a drowning man. He was dimly aware of the door shutting and a bolt sliding across to lock it. Hanno didn't care. Hot tears of joy scalded his cheeks; he felt moisture soak into his tunic as Suniaton wept too. For a moment, they just stood there, each reveling in the fact that the other was still alive. Abruptly, Suniaton's knees gave way beneath him.

Hanno had to stop him from falling. He studied Suniaton's face. Gone was the round-faced young man he was familiar with. In his place stood a gaunt-cheeked, unshaven wretch with long hair. "You're half starved," Hanno cried.

"It's not that," replied Suniaton. His eyes were deep pools of pain. "I'm hurt."

Suddenly, Hanno understood the reason for Suniaton's hunched posture. "How badly?"

"I'll live." Despite his brave words, Suniaton grimaced. "I got beaten in a fight two days ago. I've got several wounds, but the worst is a slash across the top of my right thigh."

Gaius thumped on the door. "Treacherous bastard! You said nothing about this."

To his surprise, the majordomo replied. "I was told only to bring him out at the appointed hour. No one said anything about whether he was well or not."

"You whoreson!" hissed Hanno. "I should cut your balls off." He leaned his shoulder against the timbers and heaved.

Quintus intervened. "It's not safe here." He moved to stand by Suniaton. "You take one arm, and I'll take the other," he said to Hanno.

Hanno nodded. There was no point wasting time. The majordomo could take his own chances now. Only the gods knew whether the drugging of the doorman would fool his master. It mattered not at all. They had to get Suniaton back to Gaius' house, where they could examine his wounds.

Fortunately, Suniaton was proved to be right about his injuries. Although he was in considerable pain, the clean sword cuts were not life-threatening. As far as Hanno could tell, they had been stitched reasonably well. Yet the worst wound concerned him greatly. The biggest muscle in Suniaton's right thigh had nearly been severed. There was nothing they could do about it, and so they prepared to leave. They had to get to safety before dawn. Bidding farewell to Gaius, the pair heaved Suniaton up on to Quintus' mount. Having bribed a sentry, they passed out of the town with relative ease. The horse's movement caused Suniaton so much pain, however, that he soon passed out. Hanno could do nothing but support his friend as he walked alongside. He would ask Quintus to get some papaverum from Elira later. For now, he thanked Tanit and Eshmoun, and asked for their continued blessing. Hopefully, Suniaton just needed time. Hanno was desperate to head for Iberia, but he would not leave his friend behind now.

The war would have to wait.

―――

Bostar eyed the figures on the other side of the Rhodanus. Although the deep, fast-flowing water was more than five hundred paces across at this point, the Volcae camp was easy to make out between the trees that dotted the far bank. There were scores of tents and lines of tethered horses, denoting the presence of hundreds of warriors. Sentries patrolled the waterline day and night. Given that the tribesmen normally lived on both sides of the river, their intent could not be more plain. They would pay dearly for their combative stance, thought Bostar. Hannibal had given him his orders not an hour since. Once he'd made an offering to the gods, it was time to go. His phalanx and the three hundred scutarii the general had insisted he also take were already assembled beyond the Libyans' tent lines. Their destination, an island at a narrow point in the river, was a day's march to the north.

Sapho's voice made him jump. "Why couldn't the stupid bastards be like the other tribes around here?"

"Sell us boats and supplies, you mean?" Bostar asked, trying to look pleased to see his brother. What was Sapho, who still had no idea of his mission, doing here at this early hour? Why did I mention it to Father? thought Bostar, panicking. He took a deep breath. Calm down. I asked him not to mention it to a soul. He won't have.

"Yes. Instead, they'll kill a tiny fraction of our troops before being annihilated themselves. Even simple savages such as they must know that our army can't be stopped from crossing the Rhodanus."

Bostar shrugged. "I suppose they're like the Ausetani. Defending their territory is a matter of pride. It doesn't matter how badly they're outnumbered. Death in battle is not something to be ashamed of."

"Sheep-shagging inbreds," said Sapho with a derisive snort. "Why can't they understand that all we want to do is cross this poxy river and be on our way?"

Bostar refrained from asking the obvious question: wasn't the response of the Volcae how Sapho, or he, might act in a similar situation? "Never mind. Hannibal gave them their chance. Now, what was it that you wanted? I was about to take my phalanx out on a march," he lied bluffly, unable to think of what else to say.

"Gods, your men must *love* you. Haven't we done enough of that recently? That explains why you're in full uniform at this hour." Sapho made a dismissive gesture. "It was nothing that can't wait. Just that I noticed plenty of game trails leading down to the water's edge. I thought I'd follow them beyond the camp. Would you like to come along?"

Bostar was completely taken aback by this. "What, and go looking for boar?" he faltered.

"Or deer." Sapho threw him a crooked, awkward grin. "Anything to vary our current diet."

"A bit of fresh meat wouldn't go amiss," Bostar admitted ruefully. He felt torn. The proposal was clearly a bridge-building effort on Sapho's part, but he couldn't disobey Hannibal's orders; nor could he reveal them. They were still top secret. What to say? "I'd love to, but not today," he managed eventually. "Who knows what time I'll get back?"

Sapho wasn't to be put off. "How about tomorrow?" he asked cheerfully.

Bostar's anguish grew. Great Melqart, he thought, what have I done to deserve this? He and his men would only be getting into position by the following evening. On the far bank. "I'm not sure . . ." he began.

Sapho's good humor fell away. "So you'd rather spend time with your men than your own brother?"

"It's not that," Bostar protested. "Going hunting with you sounds wonderful."

"What is it then?" Sapho snarled.

Bostar's mind was empty of ideas. "I can't say," he muttered.

Sapho's lip curled even further. "Admit it. I'm not good enough for you, am I? Never have been!"

"That's not true. How can you say such a thing?" Bostar cried, horrified.

"Bostar!" Their father's cheerful voice cut across the argument like a knife. Startled, both brothers glanced around. Malchus was approaching from the direction of his tent lines. "I thought you'd be gone by now," he said as he drew nearer.

"I was just leaving," replied Bostar uneasily. Let me get away without anymore problems, Baal Saphon, he prayed. "I'll see you later."

Bostar's plea was not answered; Malchus gave him a broad wink. "Good luck."

"Eh?" said Sapho with a puzzled frown. "Why would he need that on a training march?"

Malchus looked uncomfortable. "You never know, he might break an ankle. The trails around here are very uneven."

"That's a lie if I ever heard one. Besides, when have you ever wished us luck for so trivial a matter?" Sapho scoffed. He turned on Bostar. "Something else is going on, isn't it? That's why you won't come hunting!"

Bostar felt his face grow red. "I've got to go," he muttered, picking up his shield.

Furious, Sapho blocked his path. "Where are you going?"

"Get out of my way," said Bostar.

"Is that an order, *sir*?" Contempt dripped from the last word.

"Move, Sapho!" snapped Malchus. "Your brother's orders come from Hannibal himself."

"It's like that, is it?" Sapho stepped aside, his eyes filled with jealousy. "You could have said. Just a hint."

Bostar looked at him, and knew he'd made a mistake. "I'm sorry."

"No, you're not," Sapho hissed. He lowered his voice even further. "Lick-arse. Perfect fucking officer."

A towering fury took hold of Bostar. Somehow, he managed to keep it in check. "Actually, I said nothing because I didn't want you to feel that you'd been overlooked."

"You're so fucking kind," Sapho shouted, the veins in his neck bulging. "I hope you get killed wherever you're going."

Malchus' mouth opened in rebuke, but Bostar held his hand up. Oddly, his anger had been replaced by sorrow. "I trust that you wish the mission to be successful at least?"

Shame filled Sapho's face, but he had no chance to reply.

Bostar turned to Malchus. "Farewell, Father."

Malchus' eyes were dark pools of sorrow. "May the gods watch over you and your men."

Bostar nodded and walked away.

"Bostar!"

He ignored Sapho's cry.

It felt as if he'd just lost another brother.

~

Two days later, Bostar and his men were in position. Theirs had been a hard journey. After a long march on the first day, their guides had brought them to a fork in the Rhodanus. The island in the center of the river had made their crossing much easier. Not knowing if there were any Volcae on the opposite bank, they had waited until nightfall. Then, using rafts constructed from a combination of chopped-down trees and inflated animal skins, Bostar and ten handpicked men had swum to the other side. To their immense relief, the woods had been empty of all but owls and foxes. Soon after, the remaining soldiers had safely joined him. Bostar had not forgotten to give thanks to the gods for this good fortune. Hannibal and the entire army were relying on them. If they failed, hundreds, or even thousands, of men would die at the hands of the Volcae when the Carthaginian forces began to cross.

At sunrise, they had marched south, halting only when the enemy encampment had been identified. Leaving his party to rest in the dense thickets that occupied the high ground overlooking the river, Bostar and a few sentries had spent the night on their bellies, watching the Volcae sitting around their fires. The tribesmen seemed oblivious to any danger, which pleased him. Somehow that made his anguish over the argument with Sapho easier to bear. Bostar had no wish to be enemies with his brother. Let us both survive the struggle to come, he prayed, and make our peace afterward.

As dawn arrived, it became possible to make out the enormous Carthaginian camp on the far bank. With growing tension, Bostar waited until he could see troops near the water's edge, cavalrymen climbing into the larger craft, and infantry scrambling into the canoes. He even spied Hannibal in his burnished cuirass, directing operations. Still Bostar held on. Picking the right moment to charge was vital. Too soon, and he and his men risked being slaughtered; too late, and innumerable soldiers in the boats would die.

It wasn't long before the Volcae sentinels noticed the activity opposite their position and raised the alarm. Clutching their weapons, hundreds of warriors emerged from their tents and ran down to the bank. There they paced threateningly up and down, screaming abuse at the Carthaginians and bragging of their exploits. Bostar was thrilled. The enemy's camp had been abandoned, and every man's gaze was fixed on the flotilla of vessels opposite. It was time to move. "Light the fires!" he hissed. "Quickly!"

A trio of kneeling spearmen, who had been regarding him nervously, struck their flints together. *Clack, clack, clack,* went the stones. Sparks dropped on to the little mounds of dry tinder before each man. Bostar sighed with relief as a tiny flame licked first up the side of one pile, and then another. The third heap took flame a moment later. The soldiers encouraged the fires by blowing on them vigorously.

Fretfully chewing a fingernail, Bostar waited until each blaze was strong enough. "Add the green leaves," he ordered. He watched intently as thick eddies of smoke from the damp foliage curled up into the air and climbed above the tops of the trees. The instant it had, Bostar's gaze shot to the opposite bank. "Come on," he muttered. "You have to be able to see it now."

His prayers were answered as Hannibal and his soldiers sprang into action. Boat after boat was pushed out into the water. The larger craft, carrying the cavalrymen, who were each leading six or seven horses, stayed upstream. Their size and number helped to reduce the impact of the powerful current on the smaller vessels containing the infantry. The Volcae responded at once. Every man with a bow or spear pushed forward to the water's edge and waited for his chance.

"Come on," muttered Bostar to his three spearmen. "It's time to give those shitbags a surprise they'll never forget."

Moments later, he and most of his force were trotting down the slope toward the riverbank. The remainder, a hundred scutarii, were heading for the Volcae camp. They ran in silence, hard and fast. Rivulets of sweat ran from under Bostar's bronze helmet to coat his face. He did his best to ignore it, counting his steps instead. During the long wait, he had made repeated estimates of the distance from where they had lain hidden to the water's edge. Five hundred paces, Bostar told himself. To the enemy tents, it was only 350. It seemed an eternity, but the Volcae were so busy shouting at the approaching boats that they had soon covered a hundred paces without being challenged. Then it was 150; 175. Hannibal's boats had reached the midpoint of the river. As Bostar counted two hundred, he saw a figure turn to address one of his companions. An expression of stunned disbelief crossed the man's face as he took in the mass of soldiers running toward him. Bostar had covered another ten steps before the warrior's warning cry ripped through the air. It came far too late, he thought triumphantly.

Bostar threw back his head and roared, "Charge! For Hannibal and Carthage!"

There was an inarticulate roar of agreement from his men as they closed in on the bewildered Volcae, who were already wailing in fright at the prospect of being attacked from the front and rear. Suddenly, their enemies' distress grew even greater and Bostar glanced over his shoulder. To his delight, the Volcae tents were going up in flames. The scutarii were following their orders perfectly.

The warriors' disarray helped greatly to reduce the Carthaginian casualties. The tribesmen were far more concerned with protecting their own backs than aiming missiles at the helpless troops in their boats. However, their poor discipline and general panic meant that the Volcae had little success with Bostar's soldiers either. They loosed their spears and arrows in ragged, early volleys that had barely enough power to reach the spearmen's front ranks. Fewer than two dozen men had been downed before they had come within what Bostar considered proper range.

Calmly, he ordered his soldiers to throw their spears. This massed effort stood in stark comparison to the tribesmen's pathetic efforts. Hundreds of shafts curved up into the air, to fall in dense shoals among the unprepared Volcae, most of whom were not wearing armor. The volley caused heavy casualties. The screams of the injured and dying served to increase the warriors' fear and confusion. Bostar laughed at the magnificence of Hannibal's plan. One moment, the Volcae had been waiting for an easy slaughter, and the next, they were being attacked from behind while their tents went up in flames.

It was then that the lead Carthaginian boats pulled into the riverbank. Led by their general, scores of scutarii and caetrati threw themselves into the shallows. Their fierce battle cries were the final straw for the terrified Volcae, who could take no more. Faces twisted in fear, they broke and ran. "Draw swords!" Bostar shouted delightedly, leading his men to complete the rout. The crossing of the river was theirs, which proved that the gods were still smiling on Hannibal and his army.

Within a quarter of an hour, it was all over. Hundreds of Volcae lay dead or dying on the grass, while the broken survivors ran for their lives into the nearby woods. Squadrons of whooping Numidians were already in pursuit. Few of the fugitives would live to tell the tale of the ambush, thought Bostar. But some would, and the legend of Hannibal's passing would spread. Bloody lessons such as this were like the siege of Saguntum. They sent a clear message to the surrounding tribes that to resist the Carthaginian army resulted in just one thing. Total defeat. Bostar wished vainly that it proved to be this simple with the Romans.

His task completed, he stood his men down and went in search of Hannibal. By now, the bank was thronged with infantry, slingers and cavalrymen leading their horses away from the river. Officers shouted in frustration, trying to assemble their scattered units. The river was dotted with dozens of boats traveling in each direction. The mammoth task of ferrying tens of thousands of men and vast quantities of supplies over the Rhodanus was under way.

Bostar threaded his way through the soldiers, scanning the faces for his family. When he saw Malchus, his heart leaped with joy. Sapho was by his side. Bostar hesitated, before recognizing that he felt relief at the sight of his brother. He was grateful for this gut instinct. Whatever the circumstances of their parting, blood was thicker than water.

Telling himself that all would be well, Bostar raised a hand. "Father!" Sapho!" he shouted.

It rapidly became clear that Suniaton would take months to recover; that was, if his wounds ever healed fully. Hanno was not at all sure they would. Certainly, his friend would never be fit to fight again. There was little doubt now that Suniaton's heavy limp would be lifelong. But, as he repeatedly told Hanno, at least he was alive.

Hanno nodded and smiled, trying to ignore the resentment that clawed at his happiness over Suniaton's rescue. He failed, because his friend was not fit to journey on his own, and might never be. Hanno grew irritable and withdrawn, and took to spending his time outside the hut, away from Suniaton. This made him feel even worse, but when he returned, determined to make amends, and saw his friend hobbling about on his homemade crutch, Hanno's anger always returned.

On the fourth day, the pair had an unexpected visit from Quintus and Aurelia. "It's all right, there's been no news from Capua," Quintus said as he dismounted.

Hanno relaxed a fraction. "What brings you here then?"

"I thought you'd want to know. Father and Flaccus are about to leave. Finally, Publius Cornelius Scipio and his legions are ready."

Hanno's heart stopped for a moment. "Are they headed for Iberia?"

"Yes. The northeast coast. That's where they think that Hannibal is," replied Quintus in a neutral tone.

"I see," said Hanno, fighting to remain calm. Inside, his desire to leave had resurfaced. "And the army that's bound for Carthage?"

"It will be leaving soon too." Quintus looked awkward. "I'm sorry."

"There's nothing to be sorry for," Hanno muttered gruffly. "It's not your doing."

Quintus was still uncomfortable, because he moved off to check Suniaton's injured thigh without answering. Hanno thought guiltily, I should be doing that. For all the good it would do, his mind retorted. He'll never walk properly again.

Aurelia's voice cut into his reverie. "We won't see Father for months," she said sadly. "And Quintus never stops talking about going to join him. Before long, Mother and I may be left alone."

Hanno made a sympathetic gesture, but he wasn't concentrating; all he could think of was following Scipio's army to Iberia.

Aurelia mistook his silence for sorrow. "How could I be so thoughtless? Who knows when you will see your family?"

Hanno scowled, but not because of what she'd said. Hannibal and his host would shortly face a Roman consular army. Meanwhile, he was stuck here with Suniaton.

"Hanno? What is it?"

"Eh?" he answered. "Nothing."

Aurelia followed his gaze to Suniaton, who was gingerly following Quintus' instructions. The realization hit her at once. Like a cat, she pounced. "You want to go to war too," she whispered. "But you can't, because of your loyalty to Suni."

Stricken, Hanno stared at the ground.

Aurelia touched his arm. "There is no greater love you could show a friend than standing by him in his time of need. It requires true courage."

Hanno swallowed hard. "I should be happy to stay with him, though, not angry."

"You can't help it." Aurelia sighed. "You're a soldier, like my father and brother."

Almost on cue, Quintus came striding over. "What's that?"

Neither Aurelia nor Hanno answered.

Quintus grinned. "What's the big secret? Have you guessed that I'm going to go and find Father?"

Aurelia's mouth opened in horror. Hanno was similarly shocked, but before either could respond, Suniaton joined them, obviously intent on speaking. Surprised by the Carthaginian's interruption, Quintus deferred to him. Suni's words struck everyone dumb. "I know how hard it is for you, Hanno. Waiting for me to recover, when all you want to do is join Hannibal's army."

Hanno's guilt swelled immeasurably. "I will stay with you as long as necessary. That's all there is to it," he declared. Quickly, he turned to Quintus. "What made you decide to leave now?"

"I have to tell Father about the way Agesandros has been carrying on. Power has gone to his head."

Aurelia butted in angrily. "That's not your reason. It would be crazy to get rid of an experienced overseer at a time like this, and you know it. Besides, Agesandros hasn't done enough to warrant being replaced. We'll have to live with him."

Quintus set his jaw. "Well, I'm going anyway. My training is finished. The war could be over in a few months. I'll miss it if I just wait to be called up."

You underestimate Hannibal, thought Hanno darkly.

"You're crazy," accused Aurelia. "How will you find Father in the middle of a war?"

A flicker of fear flashed across Quintus' face. "I'll reach him before that," he declared, full of apparent bravado. "All I need to do is take passage to the Iberian port that Scipio made for. I'll buy a horse there, and follow the legions. By the time I find Father, it will be far too late to send me back." He glared, daring Hanno and his sister to challenge him.

"It's madness to talk about traveling so far on your own," Aurelia cried. "You've never been farther than Capua before."

"I'll manage," Quintus muttered, glowering.

"Really?" demanded Aurelia sarcastically. She was surprised by how angry she felt when she'd known this was going to happen sooner or later.

"Why wouldn't I?" Quintus shot back.

An awkward silence fell.

Suniaton cleared his throat. "Why don't you go with Quintus?" he asked, astonishing Hanno. "Two swords on the road will be better than one."

Suddenly, Aurelia's heart started pounding. Shocked by her emotions, she had to bite her lip not to protest aloud.

Hanno saw the flash of hope in Quintus' eyes. To his surprise and shame, he felt the same emotion in his heart. "I'm not leaving you, Suni," he protested.

"You've done more than enough for me, especially when it's my fault that we're here in the first place," insisted Suniaton. "You have been waiting your whole life for this war. I have not. You know that I'd rather be a priest than a soldier. So, with Quintus' and Aurelia's permission, I will remain here." Quintus nodded his acquiescence, and Suniaton continued, "When I'm fully recovered, I will travel to Carthage, alone."

"I don't know what to say," Hanno stuttered, his feelings fluctuating between sadness and excitement.

Suniaton held up a hand, stalling his protest. "I will have it no other way."

Hanno's protest died in his throat. "I'm still in your debt, Quintus," he said. "Accompanying you might repay part of that obligation. What do you say?"

"I'd be honored to have you as a companion," said Quintus, bowing his head to conceal his relief.

Now, Aurelia's grief knew no bounds. She was going to lose not only her brother, but also Hanno, and there was nothing she could do about it. A tiny sob escaped her lips. Quintus put an arm around her, and Aurelia managed to rally herself. "Come back safely."

"Of course I will," he murmured. "Father will also."

Nervously, Aurelia fixed her eyes on Hanno. "You too," she whispered.

Quintus' mouth opened as the two words hung in the air.

Hanno was stunned. Aurelia was promised to another, and a high-ranking Roman at that. Did she really mean what he thought? He studied her face for a moment.

"I will," he said finally. "One day."

XIV

CONFRONTATION

Fabricius stared at the Greek columns on the temples opposite the quay and smiled. "Very different to those at home," he said. "It feels good to be in a foreign land at last."

Five days before, the Roman fleet and its commander, the consul Publius Cornelius Scipio, had finally set sail. Fabricius and Flaccus had been on board one of the sixty quinqueremes that had left from Pisae, on the west coast of Italy. Hugging the Ligurian shoreline all the way to the Greek city of Massilia, a long-term Roman ally on the south coast of Gaul, the flotilla had arrived not two hours previously.

"Too many months were spent talking," Flaccus agreed. "It's time now to carry war to the Carthaginians, and settle the matter swiftly." He eyed Fabricius, who was nodding in vigorous agreement. "You don't like sitting on your hands, eh?"

"No." His recent spell in Rome had brought home to Fabricius the fact that he was no politician. He'd stayed in the capital because he was eager to fight. His desire for action, however, had vanished beneath a wave of debates in the Senate, just one of which could take more than a week. "I know that the politicians' original reasons for delaying were simple," he admitted. "With most of the army disbanded, it was logical to wait for the new consuls to be appointed before making any far-reaching decisions. But to take so long after that?"

"Don't forget the other matters of foreign policy which had to be discussed." Flaccus' tone was reproving. "Rome has many concerns other than what goes on in Iberia."

"Of course." Fabricius sighed. That had been one of the hardest lessons for him to learn.

"Philip V of Macedon has never been the greatest friend of Rome," said Flaccus. "But giving refuge to Demetrius of Pharos showed that he really wishes us ill."

"True." Demetrius, the deposed King of Illyricum, had himself been the cause of much recent trouble to the Republic. "Is a month of debates about the two of them really necessary, though?"

Flaccus' face took on a pompous expression. "Such is the Senate's way, as it has been for nearly three hundred years. Who are we to question such a hallowed process?"

Fabricius bit back his pithy response. In his mind, the Senate would work far more efficiently if only the debates were better controlled. He smiled diplomatically. "To be fair, it reacted fast when word came of the unrest among the Gaulish tribes."

Flaccus looked pleased. "And as soon as it became clear that the proposed new Latin colonies at Placentia and Cremona would not be enough, it requisitioned one of the legions from our expeditionary force. While I was stuck in Rome, raising and training the new units that were required, at least you got a taste of action!" He wagged a finger at Fabricius. "Three months of it."

Fabricius had grown used to the other's patronizing manner, but still found it irritating. "You weren't there. The Boii and Insubres are no pushover," he growled. "Don't you remember Telamon? We did well to end it so swiftly. Hundreds of our soldiers were slain, and many more were injured."

Flaccus flushed. "I apologize. I did not mean to belittle your efforts, or those of the men who died."

"Good," Fabricius replied, placated. "It doesn't take away from the fact that we should have been in Iberia three months ago!"

Flaccus made a conciliatory gesture. "At least we're in Massilia now. Soon the Saguntines will be avenged."

"A bit late, isn't it?" demanded Fabricius sourly. The Senate's refusal to act had meant leaving the Saguntines to their fate, which had not sat well with his conscience. It still didn't.

"Come now," entreated Flaccus. "We've just been through all that."

"I know," Fabricius replied heatedly. "But an ally of Rome should never be treated as Saguntum was."

Flaccus' voice grew soft. "You know that I agree with you. Did I not speak repeatedly in the Senate about the dishonor of abandoning the city?"

"You did." Yet you probably knew that your words would make little difference, thought Fabricius. It had sounded good, however, and showed a pleasingly combative side to his prospective son-in-law's character.

"Thank all the gods that we're serving under Scipio rather than Tiberius Sempronius Longus," said Flaccus. "We shall see action far sooner than they will. Last I heard, Longus' fleet wasn't going to be ready for another month."

"How frustrating."

"Whereas we can set sail the moment that the fleet's supplies of food and water have been renewed." Flaccus rattled the hilt of his ornamental sword.

"Let's not forget to hear what information the local intelligence has gathered," warned Fabricius. "Nothing has been heard of Hannibal for several months."

"That's because he's sitting on his hairy gugga arse in Iberia, drinking local wine and waiting for us to arrive!" Flaccus sneered.

"Maybe he is," said Fabricius with a smile, "but being forewarned is to be forearmed."

He had no idea that, within the next few hours, his words would be proven true.

Hannibal was no longer in Iberia.

According to the exhausted Massiliote messengers who rode in on lathered mounts, he was probably no more than a day's march away.

Flaccus and the other senior officers received an immediate summons to attend Scipio in his headquarters, a sprawling tent at the center of one of the legions' temporary forts. Fabricius was pleased and surprised to receive a similar order less than an hour later. As he arrived, Fabricius saw Flaccus standing outside with the other high-ranking officers, including Gnaeus, Scipio's elder brother, a former consul who was also his *legatus*, or second-in-command. Fabricius saluted, and nodded at Flaccus. To his surprise, his future son-in-law barely acknowledged the gesture. Indeed, his face wore such a thunderous expression that Fabricius wondered what had gone on in the moments prior. He had no time to find out. Recognizing Fabricius, the officer in charge of the sentries ushered him inside at once.

They found Scipio talking animatedly with a young Massiliote soldier over a table on which a crudely drawn map had been laid out. Both men were wearing Hellenistic bronze cuirasses, layered pteryges, which protected the groin and the tops of the thighs, and bronze greaves. Yet there was no question, even to the untrained eye, who was in charge. The Massiliote's armor was well made, but, with its magnificent depiction of Hercules' face, Scipio's positively exuded quality and wealth. The same could be said of his ornate plumed Attic helmet, which sat on a nearby stool. Although the Massiliote towered over the gray-haired consul, Scipio's confidence more than made up for the difference in height. Fabricius had come to know his commander a little, and liked him. Scipio's calm presence and direct manner were popular with everyone, from the rank and file to the military tribunes. Gnaeus, his brother, was no different.

Scipio looked up. "Ah, Fabricius! Thank you for coming."

Fabricius saluted. "How can I be of service, sir?"

"First meet the commander of the unit that brought us the dramatic news. Fabricius, this is Clearchus. Clearchus, meet Fabricius, of whom I have spoken."

The two exchanged courteous nods.

"Obviously, you have heard about Hannibal's whereabouts," Scipio inquired archly. "You'd have to be deaf not to."

Fabricius grinned. The news *had* been shouted from the rooftops. "They say that he and his army have crossed the Rhodanus, sir, and are camped on the eastern shore."

"Indeed." Scipio regarded the Massiliote. "Clearchus?"

"Since word came that Hannibal had crossed into Gaul, we have been patrolling deep inland, using small, highly mobile cavalry units. One such sighted the Carthaginians about two weeks ago, and shadowed them to the river's western bank. It's a long day's ride from here."

Fabricius' heart thumped in his chest. The rumor *was* true. "And their number?"

"Perhaps fifty thousand men all told. Not quite a quarter of that is made up of cavalry."

Fabricius' eyebrows rose. This was a larger army than he'd ever faced in Sicily.

Scipio saw his reaction. "I was surprised too. Hannibal means to attack Italy. Fortuna had been generous indeed to alert us to his purpose before he arrived. Go on, Clearchus."

"They camped by the river for several days, constructing rafts and boats, and no doubt planning their tactics against the Volcae, the hostile natives on the eastern side. The result was extraordinary, sir. Hannibal sent a strong force upriver, which crossed undetected and fell on the tribesmen's rear." Clearchus made a circle of his thumb and forefinger. "They crushed them with ease. Nearly the whole army has traversed safely since then. Only the elephants remain on the far bank."

"Imagine if we had landed a week earlier, and been there to contest the passage of the river. The war might already be over!" Scipio cried in frustration. His face turned cunning. "We still might have a chance, though, Clearchus?"

"That's right, sir. Getting the elephants across will take at least two to three days. Perhaps more. Several attempts have already failed."

"Excellent. Now, I need someone to take a look at the Carthaginian army. A Roman officer." Scipio glanced at Clearchus. "Not to belittle our Massiliote allies in any way."

"No insult taken, sir," said Clearchus, raising his hands.

"Naturally, others wanted this job, but I felt that the task was suited to a veteran. A man who knows how to keep his cool. I thought of you." Scipio fixed his eyes on Fabricius. "Well?"

Fabricius felt his breath quicken. Had Flaccus asked for the duty, and been turned down? That might explain his sour expression. "Of course I'll do it, sir."

Scipio gave a small smile of approval. "Speed is of the essence. If you leave at once, you could be back by tomorrow night. The next day, at the latest. I will want good estimates of their numbers, and a breakdown of the troop types."

Fabricius wasn't going to back down from a challenge like this. "I will do my best, sir."

"How many men have you?"

"About two hundred and fifty, sir."

"Take all of them. Clearchus will guide you." Scipio looked at the Massiliote. "How strong is your force?"

"Two hundred riders, sir, all experienced."

"It should be enough." Scipio turned back to Fabricius. "You're in charge. Avoid contact with the enemy unless it cannot be helped. Return quickly. I'll have the army ready to march the moment you return."

"Yes, sir." Fabricius saluted crisply; Clearchus did the same.

They left the consul poring over his map.

Fabricius wasted no time. Less than an hour later, he led the ten *turmae*—cavalry units—under his command out of the camp and toward Massilia's north gate. It was a pity that he hadn't had time to replace his losses from the recent campaign, thought Fabricius. Still, he was reasonably happy with the rest of his cavalrymen, who had fought well during the summer. As citizen cavalry, his men were equestrians, and most dressed in a Hellenistic style similar to his own. They wore Boeotian helmets and bleached white tunics, which had a purple stripe running from each shoulder to the hem. Sturdy leather boots that completely enclosed the feet were ubiquitous. All carried thrusting spears, and round cavalry shields, made of ox hide. Few carried swords. The heavy cavalry cloak, or *sagum*, owned by each man and used in bad weather, was tied up in a roll behind the saddlecloth.

They met Clearchus and his riders just outside the city walls. The Massiliote cavalry were irregulars, and no two were dressed alike. With their helmets, spears and small shields, however, they were similar in appearance to the Roman cavalrymen. Fabricius was reassured by Clearchus' calm manner, and the way his men responded to his orders. If it came to a fight, they'd probably do all right.

With the Massiliotes in the lead, they rode north, stopping only when it grew too dark to continue. Clearchus knew the countryside well, but, as he confided to Fabricius, it was possible that Carthaginian patrols could be operating in the area too. There was no point exposing themselves to unnecessary danger, and riding at night fell into that category. Fabricius did not argue. Clearchus' judiciousness made perfect sense. Ordering no fires to be lit, he had the men set up camp. Double the normal number of sentries were stationed around the perimeter. Long after the soldiers had retired, Fabricius walked from picket to picket, his ears pricked. This was a mission of the utmost importance. If that meant hardly any sleep, then so be it. Nothing could go wrong. Thankfully, he heard nothing other than the occasional screech of an owl.

He and Clearchus had their men up long before dawn. Tension among both sets of riders was immediately palpable. Contact with the enemy was likely before the day was out. After a brief chat with Clearchus, Fabricius sent ten Massiliote riders to scout the trail a mile in advance of the main party. One turma, under the command of his best decurion, accompanied them. Their orders were to return at the slightest hint of anything untoward.

Fabricius' hunch turned out to be the best decision he had ever made.

They had ridden for an hour or so when an outrider returned at the gallop. He dragged his horse to a stop beside Fabricius and Clearchus, who were riding together, and saluted.

Fabricius took a deep breath. "What news?"

"We've spotted a group of Numidians, sir. Perhaps two miles away."

Fabricius went very still. His memories of fighting against the lightly armed African horsemen were exclusively bad. "Did they see you?"

The cavalryman grinned. "No, sir. We were able to get behind a stand of trees."

Fabricius hissed in relief. Their mission had escaped discovery—for the moment. "How many of them were there?"

"Perhaps three hundred in total, sir."

"Anything else?"

"Yes, sir. The decurion said to tell you that there's a copse about a mile from here that would make a perfect place for an ambush. If you move fast, you could get in place before the Numidians reach it."

Fabricius' mouth went dry. Scipio had ordered him to avoid confrontation at all costs. How was that possible in this situation, however? To let the enemy cavalry pass while continuing with their own mission would leave his patrol at risk of attack from behind. Aware that everyone's eyes were on him, Fabricius closed his eyes. "Three hundred men, you say?" he demanded.

"Yes, sir."

Fabricius made up his mind. They were 450 strong. Easily enough. Opening his eyes, he laid a hand to his sword and was pleased by Clearchus' fierce nod of agreement. "Swiftly, then," he said. "Take us to the copse."

A short time later, Fabricius found himself in an excellent position overlooking the narrow track they had been following. Thanks to Clearchus' quick-witted suggestion, the entire patrol had ridden up and out of view well before the far entrance to the stand of trees. The trap would be sprung long before the Numidians saw their incriminating tracks—he hoped. Fabricius also wished that they could have concealed themselves better, and effected some method of preventing the Numidians from retreating. With time running out, that had not been possible. Instead, they had to place their trust in the gods. He glanced to either side, seeing the same tense expression on his riders' faces that he felt twisting his own.

The reasons were simple.

Soon, they would set eyes upon the first Carthaginian troops to act in aggression against Rome for more than twenty years. The enemy were not on Sicily either, their historical hunting grounds. The unthinkable had happened, and Fabricius still couldn't quite take it in. Hannibal was in Gaul, and heading for Italy! Calm down, he thought. Of more relevance right now was the fact that if he and his men weren't very lucky, the approaching Numidians would spot them and flee before the ambush began.

The following quarter of an hour felt like eternity to Fabricius. Focusing his gaze on the point where the track entered the copse, he ignored the faint jingle of harness around him, and bird song from the branches above. He couldn't block out all sound, however. A horse stamped a hoof as it grew restless. Someone coughed, drawing a muttered rebuke from the nearest officer. Fabricius glared at the rider responsible before returning his attention to the path. Spotting movement, he blinked. Then his arm shot out, pointing. "Pssst!" he hissed to the man on either side. A judder of anticipation rippled through the line of waiting cavalrymen.

Amazingly, the pair of enemy scouts who emerged into view were only a short distance in front of the main body of their countrymen. The Numidians appeared no different from the men Fabricius had fought in Sicily. Dark-skinned, lithe, athletic, they rode small horses without saddles, bridles or bits. Their loose tunics had large armholes and were pinned at the shoulder and belted at the waist. The Numidians carried javelins and light, round shields without bosses. Instead of looking around for danger, they were busy talking to each other. Given the empty countryside, thought Fabricius delightedly, it wasn't that surprising. He'd made similar mistakes himself before, and been lucky enough to get away with it.

In they rode, without so much as a glance up the gentle slopes where the Romans and Massiliotes lay hidden. Fabricius held his breath, counting the distance. Eighty, then fifty paces. The front ranks of Numidians entered the copse, and Fabricius' mind flashed back to the war in Sicily. They did not look like much, but these were some of the finest cavalry in the world. Sublime horsemen, they were best at skirmishing, and frustrating the enemy with their stinging attacks. He knew from personal experience that the Numidians' pursuit of a vanquished foe was even deadlier.

It was too soon to sound the charge. As many riders as possible had to come into the copse where the trees would ensnare them. With every passing moment, though, the risk of being discovered grew. Fabricius' stomach clenched painfully, but he did not stir. By the time two-thirds of the horsemen had ridden in, he saw that his men were on the verge of breaking ranks. He could no longer take the pressure either. "Charge!" he shouted, urging his horse down the slope. "For Rome!" Bellowing with excitement, 250 cavalry followed. An instant later, Clearchus and his Massiliotes emerged from the other side of the track, screaming at the top of their lungs.

Fabricius reveled in the look of stunned disbelief on the Numidians' faces. It was their job to ambush and fall on an unsuspecting enemy, not the other way around. Surprised, outnumbered and with the advantage of height against them, they instantly wheeled their mounts' heads and tried to flee. Within the space of a dozen heartbeats, total confusion reigned. Although some of those at the rear were already riding away, the vast majority were trapped by the trees. Horses reared in panic; men shouted contradictory orders at each other. Only an occasional rider prepared to fight. All the rest wanted to do was escape. Fabricius bared his teeth exultantly. They had ridden within thirty paces of the enemy without suffering a single casualty, and things were about to get even better. For all their horsemanship and skirmishing skill, the tribesmen were poor at close combat. "Ready spears," Fabricius yelled. "Kill as many as you can!"

With an inarticulate roar, his men obeyed.

⁓

Casting fearful looks over their shoulders, the surviving Numidians fled for their lives. Eyeing the bodies littering the ground, Fabricius estimated that more than a hundred of their number had been slain or injured in the initial ambush. The Roman and Massiliote casualties were perhaps half that number. Given the circumstances, this was more than satisfactory. Catching sight of Clearchus, Fabricius beckoned him urgently. "We've got to follow them," he said. "Stick tight to their tails, or there'll be no chance to assess Hannibal's forces."

Clearchus nodded. "The wounded, sir?"

"They can fend for themselves. We'll pick them up on the way back."

"Very good, sir." The Massiliote turned to relay the order.

"Clearchus?"

"Sir?"

"I want no further engagement with the enemy. A running battle could easily lead to disaster, especially if we encounter more Carthaginian forces. Our mission is more important now than killing a few more Numidians. Understood?"

Clearchus' teeth flashed in the sunshine. "Of course, sir. Scipio is waiting for us."

Soon all the able-bodied men had formed up and were ready to ride. Without a backward glance, Fabricius and Clearchus led them after the Numidians. This time, there was no advance party. They rode at top speed, four abreast, knowing that the chance of an attack from the panicked enemy riders was slim to none. It wasn't long before they glimpsed the last of the tribesmen, who screamed in dismay. At once Fabricius ordered his men to slow down. He was relieved when his command was obeyed without question. Poor discipline was too often the reason for battles being lost.

They followed the Numidians along the winding track for perhaps five miles. The flat terrain and the well-beaten track made the pursuit easy. Fabricius had no idea how far the Rhodanus was, but Clearchus reached him as they neared a low, stone-topped hill that stood alone, dominating the surrounding wooded area.

"The river is on the other side of that, sir."

Immediately, Fabricius held up his hand. "Halt!" As his order was obeyed, he fixed the Massiliote with his stare. "Let's go up. Just you and me."

Clearchus looked startled. "Are you sure, sir? There could be enemy pickets at its crest."

"They'll be running after the Numidians!" Fabricius replied confidently. "And when we come leathering back down here, I want everyone ready to ride, not bunched up on a narrow path."

Clearchus blinked; then a mischievous smile twitched across his lips. "I suppose two men against an entire host are as good as a few hundred."

With a fierce grin, Fabricius slapped his thigh. "That's the attitude." He turned to the nearest of his decurions. "Rest the men. We're going to take a look at what's on the other side of the hill. I want you ready to leave at a moment's notice."

"Yes, sir!"

Fabricius led the way up the path. He was surprised to find himself feeling more nervous than he had in years. He would never have expected to be the first Roman to set eyes on Hannibal's army. Yet here he was.

Nearing the crest, they found evidence of a sentry post: a stone fireplace full of smoking ash, and bedding rolls, which still bore the imprint of those who'd been sitting on them. They dismounted and tethered their horses before clambering to the peak. Instinctively, Fabricius went down on his belly. The first thing that caught his attention as he peered over the edge was the mob of yelling Numidians driving their horses down the slope. Behind them were a dozen or more running figures: the sentries from the abandoned picket. Fabricius' lips peeled up in a snarl of satisfaction, but as he took in the scene beyond, his mouth fell open in wonder.

In the middle distance glittered the wide band that was the River Rhodanus. Perhaps a hundred paces from the water's edge, the enemy tent lines began. They stretched as far as the eye could see. Fabricius was used to legionary camps that could hold 5,000 men, or even 10,000. What lay before him was much less organized, but far larger. It was more than twice as large as a consular army, which was made up of approximately 20,000 men. "You weren't exaggerating. This host is immense!" he muttered to Clearchus. "Scipio should have moved on your intelligence. We'd have caught the bastards napping."

The Massiliote looked pleased.

Fabricius scanned the encampment, mentally noting everything he saw. Hannibal had superior numbers of horsemen compared to an equivalent Roman force, which worried him. Few things were more important than the quantity of horse at one's disposal. There were the usual Carthaginian stalwarts: Libyan spearmen and skirmishers, Balearic slingers and Numidian and Iberian cavalry. Most plentiful of all were the infantry, the majority of which were scutarii and caetrati. And last but not least, there were the elephants: the battering rams that had so terrified Roman armies in the past. Perhaps twenty of the massive beasts were already on the near bank. "Gods," Fabricius whispered in amazement. "How in the name of Jupiter did they get them over the river?"

Clearchus touched his arm and pointed. "On those."

Fabricius peered at the two massive wooden rafts being pulled back to the far side by rowing boats. There, he could see a dozen or more elephants waiting to be ferried across. Before them, an enormous jetty formed by a double line of square platforms projected some sixty paces out into the fast-flowing water. Dozens of ropes and cables secured the makeshift affair to trees upriver from the pier. He shook his head at the scale of the engineering that had gone into the pier's construction. "I've heard that elephants are intelligent creatures. Surely they wouldn't just walk on to a floating square of wood?"

Clearchus squinted into the bright light. "I can see a layer of earth all along the walkway. Maybe it's meant to look like dry land?"

"Clever bastards. So they lead their charges to the end of the jetty, and on to the rafts. Then they cut them free and row across the river." Rapt, Fabricius watched as, encouraged by its mahout, an elephant was slowly led down the walkway. Even from a distance, it was clear that the creature was not happy. Bugles of distress blared out again and again. It had only walked a third of the jetty's length before it stopped dead in its tracks. In an effort to make the elephant continue, a group of men behind it began shouting and playing drums and cymbals. However, instead of continuing to the raft, which was now tethered to the end of the pier, the creature jumped into the water. There was a wail from its unfortunate mahout as he disappeared from sight, and Fabricius closed his eyes. What a way to die, he thought. When he looked up, the elephant was swimming strongly across the river. Fabricius was engrossed. He had never seen such an incredible sight before.

Suddenly, Clearchus tugged at his arm. "The Numidians have raised the alarm, sir."

At the edge of the camp, Fabricius could see the tribesmen milling around. Many were pointing at the hill and beyond. Faint shouts of anger carried through the air, and he smiled mirthlessly. "Time to go. Scipio will want to hear the news. Good, and bad."

—⁓—

Fabricius was delighted by Scipio's instantaneous response to his dramatic news. The consul was not afraid of confrontation. Ordering the heavy baggage to be loaded on to the quinqueremes for safety, Scipio led the army north as soon as was humanly possible. Nonetheless, it was three full days before the legions and their allies arrived at the point where the Carthaginians had crossed the river. It was a huge disappointment to find the vast encampment abandoned. As the Roman officers picked their way across the remnants of thousands of campfires, the only life to be seen were the skulking forms of jackals looking for scraps, and the countless birds of prey that hovered overhead for similar reasons.

Hannibal had gone. North, to avoid a battle.

Scipio had difficulty concealing his amazement. "Who would have thought it?" he muttered. "He is heading for the Alps, and thence to Cisalpine Gaul."

Fabricius was still astonished too. He knew no one who had even contemplated that Hannibal would pursue such a plan. Stunning in its simplicity, it had taken them all completely unawares. It was lucky chance that had them standing here today. Now Scipio faced a hard choice. What was the best thing to do?

The consul immediately convened a meeting of his senior officers on the riverbank. As well as Gnaeus, his legatus, there were twelve tribunes present, six for each regular legion. Following tradition, alternate legions had three senior tribunes, men who had served for more than ten years, while the others had two. The junior tribunes needed only to have seen five years' service. It was a mark of the times, and of the influence of the Minucii, that Flaccus, who had no military experience, should be accorded even the lower rank of junior tribune. As the patrol leader, Fabricius was also present. He felt distinctly nervous in the presence of so many senior officers.

"We are faced with four choices, all of them difficult," Scipio began. "To pursue Hannibal and force him to fight, or to withdraw to the coast and return with the whole army to Cisalpine Gaul. The third option would be merely to send word to the Senate of Hannibal's intentions, before continuing as charged to Iberia. Or . . . I could bring the news to Rome myself while Gnaeus takes the legions west." He scanned his officers' faces, waiting for a response.

Fabricius thought that either the second or fourth options were the best, but he certainly wasn't going to say anything before any of his superiors did. As the silence lengthened, it appeared that none of them were prepared to speak up either. Fabricius fumed. This was one of the most pivotal moments in Roman history, and no one wanted to say the wrong thing. That is, he realized, apart from one. Flaccus was shifting from foot to foot like a man possessed. Fabricius struggled to master his exasperation. Probably all that kept Flaccus' mouth shut was the desire not to breach military protocol by speaking out of turn, before the five senior tribunes.

Eventually, Scipio grew impatient. "Come now," he said. "Let us be frank. You may speak without fear of retribution. I want your honest opinions."

Gnaeus cleared his throat. "In theory, Hannibal should be confronted immediately. However, I wonder if it would be the right thing to do?"

"We know that his forces outnumber ours by at least two to one, sir," added a senior tribune quickly. "And if we suffered a setback, or even a defeat, what then? Massilia's defenses aren't up to withstanding a siege. All of the other legions are occupied on other duties, either in Cisalpine Gaul, or in Sicily with Consul Longus. We have no support to call on."

Sensible words, thought Fabricius. He was surprised to see Flaccus' face grow red with indignation.

Another senior tribune, an older man than the rest, stepped into view. "Is the enemy's strength so important, sir?" he demanded angrily. "Our legionaries are the finest soldiers in the world! They are used to winning victories against vastly superior numbers, and have done so against Carthaginian armies in the past. Why should they not do the same against this . . . *Hannibal*?" He filled the last word with contempt. "I say we follow him, and stamp on the gugga serpent before it slides into Cisalpine Gaul and prepares to bite us in the heel."

It was difficult to respond to the tribune's fierce words without seeming unpatriotic, and the first speakers sealed their lips. Even Gnaeus looked unsure. Naturally, Flaccus beamed and nodded in agreement, turning to his fellow junior tribunes for support. Cupping his chin with one hand, Scipio gazed at the nearby fast-flowing water. Everyone waited for his response.

Roman soldiers are indeed without equal, thought Fabricius, but the Carthaginian forces who had left this camp were led by a man who, in less than a year, had conquered large areas of Iberia, passed through the mountains into Gaul and, despite fierce opposition, successfully crossed an enormous river, elephants included. Chasing after Hannibal could prove disastrous.

Scipio held his counsel for an age. At length, he looked up. "It seems to me that pursuing a larger enemy force into unknown territory would be most unwise. As some have already said, we are alone here apart from our Massiliote allies, who do not number more than a few thousand. We must reconcile ourselves to the fact that the Carthaginians will enter Cisalpine Gaul within the next two months." Ignoring the shocked gasps this comment produced, Scipio continued, "Let us also not forget where Hannibal's main base is. If his access to that is cut off, his chance of supplies and reinforcements will be greatly reduced. With this in mind, I propose to hand the command of the consular army to my brother, and for him to lead it to Iberia." Scipio acknowledged Gnaeus' accepting bow. "I myself will return to Italy with all speed. I intend to be waiting for Hannibal when he makes his descent from the Alps. In this way both our problems will have been addressed, the gods willing."

Scipio's decisive manner was good enough for most of the tribunes, who muttered in agreement. Only the older man and Flaccus seemed unhappy. The former was experienced enough to know when to keep quiet, but the latter was not. Ignoring Fabricius' warning look, Flaccus started forward. "Think again, sir! Hannibal may win many allies among the discontented tribes in Cisalpine Gaul. The next time you meet his army, it could be far bigger."

Scipio's eyebrows rose at Flaccus' temerity. "Is that so?" he said icily.

Fabricius was impressed by his future son-in-law's insight, but it was time to shut up. Angering a consul was not an intelligent thing to do. Again, however, Flaccus ignored his pointed stare.

"It is, sir! For the honor of Rome, you must follow Hannibal and defeat him. Think of the shame of a foreign enemy, especially a Carthaginian one, setting his foot on Italian soil." Seeing his fellow officers' horrified expressions, Flaccus faltered. Then he looked for support. Finding none among his compatriots, his gaze finally fell on Fabricius. "You agree with me, don't you?"

Suddenly, Fabricius was the center of attention. He did not know what to say. Agreeing would make him party to Flaccus' insult to the consul. Refusing to agree would, in effect, renege on the newly founded alliance between his family and the Minucii. Both choices seemed as bad as the other.

To his intense relief, Scipio leaped in. "At first I thought you courageous for speaking your mind. Now I see that it was your arrogance. How dare you speak of Rome's honor when you have never drawn a sword in her defense? The only one here who has not, I might add." As Flaccus' cheeks flushed crimson, Scipio continued. "Just so you know, I too hate the idea of an enemy on Roman soil. Yet there is no shame in waiting to face an opponent on the best terms possible, and in Cisalpine Gaul we shall have the entire Republic's resources behind us."

"I'm sorry, sir," Flaccus muttered. "I spoke out of turn."

Scipio did not acknowledge the apology. "Next time you place your foot in your mouth, do not try to redeem yourself by asking a junior officer such as Fabricius to disagree with a consul. *That* is a shameful act." He stalked off with Gnaeus. The other tribunes fell to talking among themselves. They pointedly ignored Flaccus.

Fortunately, Flaccus' outrage was so great that he assumed Fabricius was of the same opinion as he. Complaining bitterly about the public humiliation he had just suffered, he accompanied Fabricius back to the legions. For his part, Fabricius was content to remain silent. He had dismissed Atia's concerns out of hand before, but Flaccus' rash action revealed monstrous arrogance, but also a worrying lack of awareness. What else was he capable of?

XV

THE ALPS

Hunching his shoulders against the early-morning chill, Bostar emerged from his tent. He gazed in awe at the towering mountains that reared up before him. The range stretched from north to south above the fertile plain, and occupied the entire eastern horizon. A dense network of pine trees covered the lower slopes, concealing any potential routes of ascent. The sky was clear, but the jagged peaks above were hidden yet by shrouds of gray cloud. Despite this, they were a magnificent sight.

"Lovely to look at, eh?"

Bostar jumped. Not many of the soldiers were stirring, but it was no surprise that his father was already up. "They are incredible, yes."

"And we've got to cross them." Malchus grimaced. "Our passage of the River Rhodanus seems trivial now, doesn't it?"

Bostar's laugh was a trifle hollow. If anyone had made such a statement a few weeks before, he wouldn't have believed it. Looking at the harsh slopes above, he knew that his father might well be correct. Expecting more than fifty thousand men, thousands of pack animals and thirty-seven elephants to climb into the realm of gods and demons bordered on genius—or madness. Feeling disloyal for even thinking the latter, Bostar glanced around. He was surprised to see Sapho approaching. After the Rhodanus, the brothers had ostensibly patched up their relationship, but the reconciliation had been little more than a façade for their father's benefit. The two avoided each other if at all possible. Bostar forced a smile. "Sapho." Try as he might, he could not help but feel hurt when his brother silently responded with a salute.

"That's not necessary, is it?" Malchus' tone was sharp.

"Sorry," said Sapho offhandedly. "I'm still half asleep."

"Yes, it's not exactly your time of day, is it?" retorted Bostar acidly. "That would be more like midday."

"Enough!" barked Malchus before Sapho could respond. "Why can't you at least be civil to each other? There's far more at stake here than your stupid feud."

As always, their father's outburst silenced the brothers. Unusually, it was Sapho who made the first effort. "What were you talking about?" he asked.

His attempt made Bostar feel obliged to reply. "Those." He pointed at the mountains.

Sapho's face soured. "Ill fortune awaits us up there. Countless men will be lost, I know it." He made the sign against evil.

"We've had such good fortune since the Rhodanus, though," protested Bostar. "The Romans didn't pursue us. Then the Cavares gave us gifts of food, shoes and warm clothing. Since we entered their territory, their warriors have kept the Allobroges at bay. Who's to say that the gods won't continue to smile on us?"

"The year's practically over. Winter will be here soon. It will be a superhuman task." An impossible task, thought Sapho dourly. Hell awaits us. He had never liked heights, and the prospect of ascending the Alps—especially in late autumn—filled him with a murmuring dread. Of course he could not admit to that, nor to his resentment of Hannibal for choosing such a difficult route, or for favoring Bostar above him. He jerked his head toward the south. "We should have traveled along the coast of Gaul."

"That would have meant a pitched battle with the forces our cavalry encountered near the Rhodanus, which was something Hannibal wanted to avoid." Despite his robust words, Bostar felt his spirits being dragged down. With the friendly Cavares returning to their homes, and nowhere to go other than up, there was no denying what they had let themselves in for. He was grateful when his father intervened.

"I want to hear no more talk like that. It's bad for morale," growled Malchus. He had similar concerns, but he wouldn't admit them to anyone. "We must keep faith with Hannibal, as he does with us. His spirits were high last night, weren't they?" He glared at his sons.

"Yes, Father," Sapho conceded.

"He doesn't *have* to wander around his men's campfires for half the night, sharing their poxy rations and listening to their miserable life stories," Malchus continued sternly. "He doesn't sleep alongside them, wrapped only in his cloak, for the good of his health! Hannibal does it because he loves his soldiers as if they were his children. The least we can do is to return that love with utmost fealty."

"Of course," Sapho muttered. "You know that my loyalty is beyond question."

"And mine," added Bostar fervently.

Malchus' scowl eased. "I'm glad to hear it. I know that the next few weeks will be our toughest test yet, but it's officers such as we who will have to give an example. To lead the men when they falter. We must show no weakness, just a steely resolve to reach the top of whichever pass Hannibal chooses. Don't forget that from there, we will fall upon Cisalpine Gaul, and after it, Italy, like ravening wolves."

Finally, the two brothers gave each other a pleased look. It lasted only an instant before they broke eye contact.

Malchus was already ten strides away. "Get a move on. Hannibal wants us all to see the sacrifice."

The brothers followed.

The flat, well-watered land where the Carthaginians were camped had provided respite to man and beast before the rigors that were to come. It also offered, Bostar realized, a place where Hannibal could address his troops, as he had at New Carthage before they'd left. Even though his forces were now considerably smaller, there were still far too many soldiers to be able to witness personally their general make an offering to the gods. That was why the commanders of every unit in the army had been ordered to bring a score or more of their men to the ceremony.

They made their way past rank-smelling Balearic slingers clad in animal skins and slender, dark-skinned Numidians with oiled ringlets in their hair. Burly scutarii and caetrati in sinew helmets and crimson-edged tunics stood with their arms folded. Alongside was Alete with twenty of his Libyan spearmen. Groups of bare-chested Gauls, their necks and arms decorated with torcs of gold, eyed the others present with supercilious stares.

Before the gathered soldiers stood a strongly built low wooden platform, and upon it a makeshift altar of stone slabs had been erected. In front stood fifty of Hannibal's bodyguards. A ramp led from the foot of the dais to the top, and beside it, a large black bull had been tethered. Six robed priests waited with the beast, which was snorting with unease. As Malchus led them to a position within a dozen steps of the soothsayers, Bostar shivered. In their gnarled hands—through the divination to come—lay the power to raise the army's morale, or to send it into the depths. Gazing at the nearby soldiers, Bostar saw the same concern twisting their faces that he was experiencing. There was little conversation; indeed an air of apprehension hung over the entire gathering. Bostar glanced at Sapho, whom he could read like a book. His brother was feeling the same way, or worse. Bostar sighed. Despite the ease of the last few days, the mountains' physical immensity had cast a shadow over men's hearts. There was only one person who could cast out that gloom, he thought. Hannibal.

The man himself bounded into view a moment later, ascending the ramp as if he were on the last lap of a foot race. A loud cheer met his arrival. Hannibal's bronze helmet and breastplate had been polished until they shone as if lit from within. In his right hand his falcata sword glinted dangerously; in his left, he carried a magnificent shield emblazoned with the image of a prowling male lion. Without a word, Hannibal strode to the edge of the platform and lifted his arm so everyone could see his blade. He let the troops focus on it before he pointed it to his rear.

"After so long, there they are! The Alps," Hannibal cried. "We have halted at our enemies' very gates to prepare for our ascent. I can see by your faces that you are worried. Scared. Even exhausted." The general's eyes moved from soldier to soldier, daring them to hold his gaze. None could. "Yet after the brutal campaign in Iberia, and the crossing of the Rhône, what are the Alps?" he challenged. "Can they be anything worse than high mountains?" He paused, glancing around questioningly as his words were translated. "Well?"

Bostar felt worried. Despite the truth in Hannibal's words, few men looked convinced.

"No, sir," Malchus answered loudly. "Great heaps of rock and ice is all they are."

Hannibal's lips tightened in satisfaction. "That's right! They can be climbed, by those with the strength and heart to do so. It's not as if we will be the first to cross them either. The Gauls who conquered Rome passed by this same way, did they not?"

Again the delay as the interpreters did their work. Finally, there was a mutter of accord.

"Yet you despair of even being able to get near that city? I tell you, the Gauls brought their women and children through these mountains! As soldiers carrying nothing but our weapons, can we not do the same?" Hannibal raised his sword again, threateningly this time. "Either confess that you have less courage than the Romans, who we have defeated on many occasions in the past, or steel your hearts and march forward with me, to the plain which stands between the River Tiber and Rome! There we will find greater riches than any of you can imagine. There will be slaves and booty and glory for all!"

Malchus waited as the general's words were translated into Gaulish, Iberian and Numidian, but as a rumble of agreement began to sweep through the assembled troops, he raised a fist into the air. "Hannibal!" he roared. "Hannibal!"

Quickly, Bostar joined in. He noted that Sapho was slow to do the same.

Shamed by their general's words, the soldiers bellowed a rippling wave of approval. The Gauls chanted in deep voices, the Libyans sang and the Numidians made shrill ululating sounds. The cacophony rose into the crisp air, bouncing off the imposing walls of rock before the gathering and thence up into the empty sky. The startled bull jerked futilely at the rope tethering its head. No one paid it any heed. Everyone's gaze was locked on Hannibal.

"Last night, I had a dream," he cried.

The cheering quickly died away, and was replaced by an expectant hush.

"I was in a foreign landscape, which was full of farms and large villages. I wandered for many hours, lost and without friends, until a ghost appeared." Hannibal nodded as his words spread and the superstitious soldiers glanced nervously at each other. "He was a young man, handsome, and clad in a simple Greek tunic, but there was an ethereal glow about him. When I asked who he was, he laughed and offered to guide me, as long as I did not look back. Although I was unsure, I accepted his proposal."

Hannibal had everyone's attention now, even that of the priests. Men were making the sign against evil, and rubbing their lucky amulets. Bostar's heart was thudding off his ribs.

"We walked for maybe a mile before I became aware of a loud crashing noise behind us," Hannibal went on. "I tried not to turn and see what was going on, but the sound grew so great that I could not help myself. I glanced around. What I saw made my throat close with fear. There was a snake of wondrous size following us, crushing every tree and bush in its path. Black thunderclouds sat in the sky above it, and lightning bolts flashed repeatedly through the air. I froze in terror." Hannibal paused.

"What happened next, sir?" cried one of Alete's Libyans. "Tell us!"

An inchoate roar of agreement followed. Bostar found himself shouting too. Visions like this—for surely that was what Hannibal had had—could portend a man's future, for good or ill. Dread filled Bostar that it was the latter.

Sapho could not dispel his unease about what lay before them. "He's making it up. So we'll follow him up into those damn mountains," he muttered.

Bostar gave him a disbelieving glance. "He wouldn't do that."

Sapho's jealousy of his brother grew. "Really? With so much at stake?" he retorted.

"Stop it! You'll anger the gods!" said Bostar.

Belatedly scared by what he'd said, Sapho looked away.

"Wait," hissed Malchus. "There's more."

"The young man took my arm, and ordered me not to be afraid," shouted Hannibal suddenly. "I asked him what the snake signified, and he told me. Do you want to hear what he said?"

There was a short pause.

"YES!" The bellow exceeded anything that had gone before.

"The devastation represents what will happen to Rome at the hands of my army!" the general said triumphantly. "The gods favor us!"

"Hurrah!" Bostar was so thrilled that he threw an arm around Sapho's shoulders and hugged him. His brother tensed, before stiffly returning the gesture. The exhilaration in the air was infectious. Even Malchus' normal solemnity had been replaced by a broad smile.

"HANN-I-BAL! HANN-I-BAL! HANN-I-BAL!" yelled the delighted soldiers.

While his troops cheered themselves hoarse, Hannibal made a gesture to the priests. With the aid of a dozen scutarii, the bellowing bull was hauled up the ramp until it stood in front of the altar. Hannibal stood to one side. At once the applause died away, and the worried looks returned to men's faces. Success was by no means guaranteed yet. The omens from the sacrifice also had to be good. Bostar found himself clenching his fists.

"O Great Melqart, accept this prize beast as a sacred offering, and as a gesture of our good faith," intoned the high priest, an old man with a gray beard and fleshy cheeks. His companions repeated his words. Raising the hood on his robe, the priest then accepted a long dagger. The bull's head was pulled forward, stretching its neck. Without further ado, the old man extended his arm and yanked it back, drawing the blade across the underside of the bull's throat with savage force. Blood gouted from the large wound, covering the priest's feet. The kicking beast collapsed to the platform, and the unneeded scutarii were waved back. Swiftly, the old man moved to kneel between the bull's front and back legs. With sure strokes, he slit open the skin and abdominal muscles. Steaming loops of bowel slithered into view.

The priest barely glanced at them as, still gripping the dagger, he shoved both his arms deep into the abdominal cavity.

"He's seen nothing bad so far. That's good," whispered Bostar.

It's probably all been arranged in advance, thought Sapho sourly, but he no longer dared speak his mind.

A moment later, the old man stood up to face Hannibal. His arms were bloodied to the shoulder, and the front of his saturated robe had turned crimson. In his hands, he held a purple, glistening lump of tissue. "The beast's liver, sir," he said gravely.

"What does it tell you?" There was the slightest trace of a quaver in Hannibal's voice.

"We shall see," replied the priest, studying the organ.

"Told you!" Bostar gave Sapho a hefty nudge. "Even Hannibal is unsure."

Sapho looked at Hannibal, whose face was now etched with worry. If their general was an actor, he was a damn good one. Fear suddenly clogged Sapho's throat. What was I thinking to call Hannibal's dream into question? Sapho couldn't think of a better way to call down the gods' wrath than to say what he just had. And there was Bostar, beside him, who was unable to put a foot wrong. Bitterness coursed through his veins.

"It is very clear," the priest announced loudly.

Every man present craned his neck forward, eager to hear.

"The passage of the mountains will be difficult, but not impossible. The army will descend upon Cisalpine Gaul, and there allies will flock to our cause. The legions that come to meet us will be swept away, as the mightiest of trees are by a winter storm. Victory awaits!"

"Victory! Victory! Victory!" chanted the soldiers.

Raising his hands for silence, Hannibal stepped forward. "I told you of my dream. You have heard the soothsayer make his pronouncement. Now, who will follow me across the Alps?"

The watching troops surged forward, shouting their acceptance.

Looking elated, Malchus and Bostar were among them. Sapho followed, telling himself that everything would be all right. The knot of fear and unease in his belly told another story, however.

———

Four days later, Sapho was beginning to wonder if his misgivings had been overblown. While the Carthaginians had encountered some resistance from the Allobroges, it had been swept aside by Hannibal's fierce response. Life in the mountains had settled into a reassuring routine, the same as they'd followed for months. Rise at dawn. Strike camp. Eat a cold breakfast. Assemble the men. Assume position at the head of the enormous column. Join the path eastward. March. Sapho was immensely proud that Hannibal had picked his unit to lead the army. Let Bostar suck on that, he thought. His brother's phalanx marched behind his. Malchus and his soldiers were with the rearguard, more than ten miles back down the stony track.

His duty carried with it huge responsibility. Sapho was on the lookout for danger at all times. For the thousandth time that morning, he eyed the heights around the flat-bottomed valley in which they currently found themselves. Nothing. Intimidated by Hannibal's seizure of their main settlement and, with it, all their supplies, the Allobroges had vanished into the bare rocks. "Good enough for the cowardly scumbags," muttered Sapho. He spat contemptuously.

"Sir!" cried one of the guides, a warrior of the Insubres tribe. "Look!"

To Sapho's surprise, the figures of men could be seen appearing on the track ahead. Where in the name of hell had they come from? He lifted his right arm. "Halt!" At once the order began passing back down the line. Sapho's jaw clenched nervously as he listened to it. He was stopping the progress of the entire army. It had to be done, however. Until proven otherwise, every person they encountered was an enemy.

"Should we advance to meet them, sir?" asked an officer.

"Not bloody likely. It could be a trap," Sapho replied. "The fuckers can come to us."

"What if they don't, sir?"

"Of course they will. Why else do you think they've slunk out of their rat holes?"

Sapho was right. Gradually, the newcomers approached: a group of perhaps twenty warriors. They were typical-looking Gauls, well built with long hair and mustaches. Although some wore tunics, many were bare-chested under their woolen cloaks. Baggy woven trousers were ubiquitous. Some wore helmets, but only a handful had mail shirts. All were armed with tall, oval shields and swords or spears. Interestingly, the men at the front were carrying willow branches.

"Are the dogs coming in peace?" asked Sapho.

"Yes, sir," answered the guide. "They're Vocontii, I think." He saw Sapho's blank look. "Neighbors—and enemies—of the Allobroges."

"Why doesn't that surprise me?" sneered Sapho. "Do any of you Gauls get on with each other?"

The guide grinned. "Not too often, sir. There's always something to fight over."

"I'm sure," Sapho said dryly. He glanced to either side. "Front rank, shields up! First and second ranks, ready spears!"

Wood clattered off wood as the spearmen obeyed his command. An instant later, the phalanx presented a solid wall of overlapping shields to its front. Over the shield rims, scores of spear tips poked forward like the spines on a forest of sea urchins.

Looking alarmed, the warriors stopped.

Sapho's lips peeled upward. "Tell them that if they come in peace, they have nothing to fear."

"Yes, sir." The guide bellowed a few words in Gaulish.

There was a brief pause, and then the Vocontii continued walking toward them. When they were twenty paces away, Sapho held up his hand. "That's close enough."

The guide translated his words, and the tribesmen dutifully halted.

"Ask them what they want," Sapho ordered. He fixed his attention on the one man who had answered all the guide's questions. A fine mail shirt covered the middle-aged warrior's barrel chest, and three gold torcs announced his wealth and status. What Sapho didn't like, or trust, was the man's walleye and permanent leer.

"They have heard of the size of our army and of our victories over the Allobroges, sir, and wish to assure us of their friendship," said the guide. "They want to guide us through their territory, to the easiest pass over the Alps."

"How charming," Sapho replied caustically. "And why in Melqart's name should we believe them?"

There was a shifty smile from the wall-eyed warrior as the guide interpreted. A wave of his hand saw several fat heifers herded into view.

"Apparently, they have a hundred of these to offer us, sir."

Sapho didn't let his pleasure show. That quantity of fresh meat would be very welcome. "The beasts don't count for much if the Vocontii steal them straight back. Hannibal needs far more assurance than that. What kind of guarantee of safe passage can the dirtbags offer?"

A moment later, fully half of the tribesmen took a step forward. Most obvious was the wide-faced young warrior with blond pigtails and finely made weapons. He looked decidedly disgruntled. An explanation from the deputation's leader followed.

"Apparently, the youngster is the chieftain's youngest son, sir. The rest are high-ranking warriors," said the guide. "They are to be our hostages."

"That's more like it," said Sapho. He turned to the nearest of his officers. "Go and find the general. Tell him what's happened. I think he'll want to hear their offer for himself." As the officer hurried off to do his bidding, Sapho resumed his study of the heights above. The fact that they were bare did not reassure him in any way. Gut feeling told him that the Vocontii were as trustworthy as a nest of snakes.

It wasn't long before Hannibal appeared. When he wasn't marching near the army's head, the general was to be found at its tail, and today it was the former. Sapho was flattered that Hannibal was not accompanied by any of his senior officers. He saluted crisply. "Sir!"

"Sapho." Hannibal reached his side. "So this is the deputation from the Vocontii, eh?"

"Yes, sir," Sapho replied. "The shifty-looking bastard over there is the leader."

"Tell me again what they've said," Hannibal ordered, scanning the warriors.

Sapho obeyed.

Hannibal rubbed his chin. "A hundred cattle and ten hostages. Plus the guides who will stay with us. It's not a bad offer, is it?"

"No, sir."

"You're not happy," said Hannibal with a shrewd look. "Why?"

"What's to stop them from simply rustling the beasts back from us, sir?" Sapho answered. "Who's to say that the hostages aren't peasants, whom the Vocontii chieftain wouldn't ever miss if they were executed?"

"Should I reject their offer?"

Sapho's stomach did a somersault. Give the wrong answer now, and Hannibal probably wouldn't ask him to lead the army again. Give the correct one, and he would rise in the general's estimation. Sapho was desperate for the latter. "There's no point, sir."

"Why not?" Hannibal demanded.

Sapho met his general's fierce gaze. "Because if you did, we'd have to fight our way through their territory, sir. If we play along instead, there's a reasonable chance of anticipating possible attacks while continuing the march without hindrance. If they prove to be trustworthy, so much the better. If not, then we at least gave it a try."

Hannibal did not reply immediately, and Sapho began to worry that he'd said the wrong thing. He was thinking of retracting his words when the general spoke.

"I like your thinking, Sapho, son of Malchus. It is easier to avoid treading on a serpent that is watched than to find it under any one of a thousand stones. It would be foolish not to take steps to prevent disaster, though. The baggage train and the cavalry must be moved to a position just behind the vanguard. They're the most vulnerable to being cut off."

At the front that could never happen, thought Sapho. "Yes, sir." He tried not to feel disappointed that Hannibal was taking charge. At least he'd led the army for a few days.

Hannibal surprised him. "We still need infantry to lead us. You've been doing an excellent job, so I want you to continue in your position."

Sapho grinned. "Thank you, sir!"

"I also want you to guard the hostages. At the slightest sign of treachery, you know what to do."

"I'll have them tortured and then crucified in full view of their compatriots, sir."

"Excellent. Do whatever you see fit." Hannibal clapped him on the arm. "I'll have the cavalry move up to your position at once. Start marching again as soon as they're in place."

"What about the mules, sir?"

"Getting them into position would be far too awkward now. We'll keep our fingers crossed for today and do it tomorrow."

"Yes, sir. Thank you, sir." Delighted, Sapho watched his general disappear back down the track. The passage of the mountains was proving to be far more rewarding than he could have anticipated.

———

For two days, the party of Vocontii led Sapho through their lands. The cavalry and baggage train followed slowly behind them, and after them came the rest of the army. Although there had been no attacks on the column, Sapho's distrust of the tribesmen who guided him remained. It grew stronger when, on the morning of the third day, the Vocontii chose a track that entered a valley much narrower than that in which they'd been marching. There was barely enough room for the ubiquitous pine trees to grow up its steep sides. Halting his soldiers, Sapho summoned the walleyed warrior. "Why aren't we staying on this path?" Sapho indicated the larger way to the right, which continued off into the distance. "It's wider, and the terrain looks to remain flatter."

The guide repeated his words in the local tongue.

The warrior launched into a long, rambling explanation, which involved much pointing and gesticulating.

"Apparently it ends in a sheer cliff face about five miles away, sir. We'd just have to turn around and come back here. This narrow one, on the other hand, leads gradually upward and will take us to the lowest pass in the area."

Sapho glared at the warrior, who simply shrugged. One of his eyes was looking at him, while the other was staring off into the sky. Sapho found it infuriating. It also made judging whether the warrior was lying exceptionally hard. He made up his mind. Sending a runner to ask Hannibal, who was with the rearguard, would entail a delay of three hours or more. "Fine," he growled. "We'll do as he says. Tell him, though, that if there's any trickery, he'll be the first to die." Sapho was pleased to see the warrior's throat work nervously when his threat was translated. He led the way confidently enough, however, allaying Sapho's concern a fraction.

His unease soon returned. It wasn't the stony and uneven track.

That was much the same as those they'd followed since entering the Alps. No, thought Sapho, it was the sheer rock faces that pressed in from both sides. They went on and on with no sign of widening out. It created a feeling of real claustrophobia. He didn't know exactly how high the cliffs were, but it was enough to reduce significantly the light on the valley floor. Sapho wasn't alone in disliking the situation. He could hear his men muttering uneasily to each other. Behind, there were indignant brays from the mules. Many of the cavalrymen were dismounting in order to lead their reluctant horses forward.

Sapho set his jaw. He had committed the army to this route. With a ten-mile column following, there was no turning back now. They just had to get on with it. Loosening his sword in his scabbard, Sapho ensured that he stayed close to the walleyed warrior. If anything happened, he *would* carry out his threat.

Pleasingly, they made slow but continuous progress for what remained of the morning. Men's spirits rose, and even the animals grew used to the confined space. Sapho remained on edge, constantly scanning the skyline above for any sign of movement. He tried to ignore the crick that was developing in his neck from always looking straight up in the air.

What attracted Sapho's attention first was not motion, but sound. One moment all that he could hear was the noises he'd heard daily since leaving New Carthage. Soldiers gossiping with each other. An occasional laugh, or curse. Officers barking orders. The creak of leather and jingle of harness. Hacking coughs from those with bad chests. The sound of men spitting. Brays from mules. Horses' whinnies. The next moment, Sapho's ears rang with a terrible, screeching resonance. He flinched instinctively. It was the noise of rock scraping off rock. With a terrible sense of dread, he looked up.

For a moment, Sapho saw nothing, but then the irregular edge of a block of stone appeared at the edge of the cliff far above. Frantically, Sapho raised a hand to his mouth. "We're under attack! Raise shields! Raise shields!" In the same instant, his head was turning, searching for the walleyed warrior. As the air filled with panicked shouts, Sapho saw the man had already elbowed past his comrades and was shouting at them to follow him. "You treacherous bastard!" Sapho shouted, drawing his sword. He was too late. Enraged, he watched as the Vocontii disappeared into a fissure in the rock not twenty paces away. Sapho cursed savagely. He had to stay where he was, and do what he could for his men. If he wasn't killed himself. One thing was certain: if any of the hostages, who were kept deep in the middle of his phalanx, survived, they would die the instant he could get to them.

The air filled with a rumbling thunder and Sapho glanced upward again. It was a terrifying sound, amplified a thousand times by the confining valley walls. Awestruck, he watched as several boulders, each the size of a horse, were pushed over the edge high above them. They picked up speed fast, and tumbled with ever-increasing speed down the vertiginous cliff face. Relief battled with horror as Sapho realized that none would strike him. Loud screams rose from the soldiers directly underneath the rocks, who could do nothing but watch their death hurtle toward them. Their cries revealed their awful, helpless terror. Aghast, Sapho could not take his eyes off the plummeting pieces of stone. A hot tide of acid flooded the back of his mouth as they struck their targets with deafening thumps, silencing their victims forever.

Their ordeal wasn't over, either. Farther down the cliff tops, in a position over the cavalry and the baggage train, Sapho could see more boulders being pushed toward the edge. He groaned. There was nothing he could do for those men and beasts either. Sapho took a deep breath. Best see to the injured, he thought. At least those can be helped.

The scream of battle cries filled their ears before they could do a thing. To Sapho's fury, files of Vocontii warriors came spilling from the fissure into which their guides had just vanished. More issued from another one alongside it. A red mist of rage replaced Sapho's dismay. He recognized the walleyed man and others of their guides among their number. Raising his spear, he roared, "Eyes front! Enemy attack!" His soldiers responded with alacrity. "Shields up! Ready spears!"

From the shouts behind them, Sapho could tell that the column had been attacked in other places too. "Rear five ranks, about turn!" he bellowed. "Advance to meet the enemy. Engage at will." That done, Sapho spun to face the Vocontii before them. The tribesmen were closing in fast, weapons held high. Sapho leveled his spear at the walleyed warrior. "You're dead meat, you stinking whoreson!"

His answer was an inarticulate snarl.

To Sapho's frustration, he did not get to close with the other. The phalanx's rigid structure meant that he could not move from his position, and the warrior was heading for a different part of the front rank. Sapho had to forget about him, as a tribesman with a dense red beard thrust his sword at his face. Rather than ducking below his shield rim, thereby losing sight of his enemy, Sapho jerked his head to one side. The blade whistled past his left ear, and Sapho thrust forward with his spear. There was a grating feeling as it slipped between two ribs, and then it ran deep into the other's unprotected chest. Sapho had no chance to pull free his weapon from the dying man's flesh. Releasing his grip on the shaft, he dragged free his sword. The warrior slumped to the ground, a disbelieving expression still twisting his features, and was immediately replaced.

Sapho's second foe was a bellowing bull of a man with a thick neck and hugely muscled arms. To Sapho's shock, the triangular point of his enemy's spear punched clean through the bronze and leather facing of his shield and smacked into his cuirass. A ball of agony exploded from Sapho's lower belly, and he reeled several steps backward, dropping his sword. Fortunately, the soldier behind was ready, and leaned forward, thereby preventing Sapho from falling over. Jammed in Sapho's shield, the tribesman's weapon was no longer usable. Quick as a flash, however, he ripped out a long dagger and reached over the top of Sapho's shield to lunge at his throat. Desperately, Sapho jerked his head backward. Slash after slash followed, and he knew that it would only be a moment before his throat was ripped open by the wickedly wielded blade.

It was with the utmost relief that Sapho saw a spear come in from the side to pierce the warrior's throat. It stabbed right through, emerging scarlet-tipped from the right side of his neck. A dreadful, choking sound left the Gaul's gaping mouth. It was followed by a tide of bright red blood, which spattered the front of Sapho's shield and, below, his feet. The spear was withdrawn, letting the dead warrior collapse on top of Sapho's first opponent.

"Gods above," Sapho muttered. He'd never been so close to death. He turned his head to regard his savior. "Thank you."

The spearman, a gap-toothed youth, grinned. "You're welcome, Captain. Are you all right?"

Sapho reached a hand under the bottom edge of his cuirass, which had a great dent in it. He probed upward, wincing at the pain this caused. When he pulled out his fingers, he was relieved to see that there was no blood on them. "I seem to be," he answered with relief. He stooped to pick up his sword. Returning his gaze to the fight, Sapho was gratified to see that the Vocontii charge had smashed apart against the phalanx's solid wall of shields. He wasn't surprised. While a few of his men might have been killed, it would take more than a charge by disorganized tribesmen to break them. It was time to lead a countercharge, thought Sapho. All reason left him, however, as he saw the walleyed warrior no more than twenty steps away, stooping to kill an injured Libyan even as he himself retreated. Dropping his useless shield, Sapho leaped forward. His desire to kill the deceitful tribesman gave him extra speed and he had covered maybe a third of the ground between them before the other even saw him. The warrior took one look and fled for his life. So did his comrades.

"Come back, you fucking coward!" Sapho screamed. He was oblivious to the fact that the phalanx's front-rankers had followed him. He increased his pace to a sprint, aware that if the other reached the gap in the rock, any chance of catching him would disappear. It was no good. The warrior seemed to have winged heels. But then fate intervened, and Sapho's enemy tripped on a protruding rock. He stumbled and fell to one knee. Sapho was on him like a dog cornering a rat. Instead of killing the tribesman, he smashed the hilt of his sword across the back of his head. Straightening, Sapho was able to slash another warrior's arm as he ran past. With a howl, the man blundered into the fissure and out of sight.

"Don't go in there!" Sapho shouted as the first of his spearmen arrived and made for the gap in the rock. "It's a death trap."

The soldiers reluctantly obeyed.

"I want twenty men stationed right here to make sure they don't try a counterattack." Sapho kicked the walleyed warrior, who groaned. "Someone, pick up this sack of shit. Find any of his compatriots who are alive, and tie them all up."

"What are you going to do with them, sir?" asked an officer.

"You'll see," Sapho replied with a wolfish smile. "First, though, we need to see what's going on behind us."

By the time they had reached the rear of the phalanx, the Vocontii who had been attacking there were gone. The corpses of fifteen or more warriors were sprawled on the ground, but that was of little satisfaction to Sapho. In this small section alone, at least fifty Carthaginian soldiers had been critically injured or crushed to death. Just beyond, so had the same number of mules and cavalry mounts. The ground was covered with blood, and the mangled bodies of men and beasts lay everywhere. The screaming of the injured, especially those who had been trapped when the boulders finally came to rest, was awful. Sapho closed his ears to their clamor, and concentrated on finding out what else had happened. Bostar was among the officers who reported to him.

Panicked by the falling rocks, an elephant had dashed three men to death with its trunk, before charging backward into the column, there to cause untold damage. Fortunately, its companions had been kept calm by their mahouts. The most frustrating discovery was that the Vocontii had stolen dozens of mules, leading them up the same precipitous paths that had served to launch their daring attack. They had even seized some captives. Despite this, Sapho knew that there was no point in pursuing the raiders. Moving on was more important than trying to save a few unfortunate soldiers. Once the dead and the blocks of stone had been rolled out of the way, the column would have to resume its advance.

Before that, however, there was something that Sapho had to do.

He made his way back to where the Vocontii prisoners were. With the ten hostages, they had twenty-two in total, sitting together and surrounded by a ring of spearmen. The only one who did not look fearful was the walleyed warrior, who spat at Sapho as he approached.

"Shall we execute them, sir?" asked an officer eagerly.

An angry mutter of agreement went up from the Libyans.

"No," Sapho replied. He ignored his men's shocked response. "Tell them that despite their brethren's treachery, they are not to be killed," he said to the interpreter. As his words were translated, Sapho was gratified to see traces of hope appear in some warriors' faces. He waited for a moment, enjoying his power.

"Please, sir, reconsider!" an officer enjoined. "They can't go unpunished. Think of our casualties."

Sapho's lips peeled into a snarl. "Did I say that they would go unpunished?"

The officer looked confused. "No, sir."

"We shall do to them what they did to us," Sapho pronounced. "Do not translate that," he snapped at the interpreter. "I want them to watch, and wonder."

"What do you want us to do, sir?"

"Tie the shitbags in a line. Next, get one of the elephants. Use it to shift a large rock. A rock so big that no men could ever move it."

A slow smile spread across the officer's face. "To dash out their brains, sir?"

"No," reproached Sapho. "We're not going to kill them, remember? I want the boulders dropped on their legs."

"And then, sir?"

Sapho shrugged cruelly. "We'll just leave them there."

The officer grinned. "It'll be dark before their scumbag companions can return. They'll be begging for death by that stage, sir."

"Precisely. They might think before attacking us a second time." Sapho clapped his hands. "See to it!"

He watched as the Vocontii prisoners were forced to lie down by a rocky outcrop. Sapho intervened to make sure that the walleyed warrior was last in the line. There was a short delay as an elephant was brought up from its position with the baggage train. Sapho waited with the interpreter by the first of the warriors, whose eyes were now bulging with fear.

Sapho looked up at the mahout. "Can you shift that boulder there?" He pointed.

"Yes, sir. Where?"

"On to these men's legs. But they mustn't be killed."

The mahout's eyes widened. "I think so, sir."

"Get on with it, then."

"Sir." Leaning forward, the mahout whispered in his huge mount's ear before tapping it behind the ear with his hooked staff. The elephant lumbered up to the stone that Sapho had indicated, and gripped the top of it with its trunk. There was a moment's silence before the slab began to move out of its resting place. The mahout muttered another command, and the elephant stepped up to rest the front of its head against the boulder, preventing it from picking up speed. Slowly, the beast reversed toward the prisoners, controlling its load's progress down the slight slope. Realizing at last what was about to happen, the Vocontii warriors began to wail in fear.

Sapho laughed. He scanned the heights above, and fancied he saw movement. "Yes, you fuckers," he screamed. "Look! We're about to give your friends a dose of their own medicine."

Several steps from the captives, the mahout made the elephant pause. He looked at Sapho questioningly.

"Do it."

A murmured word in its ear, and the elephant moved aside, letting the stone roll on to the first three warrior's legs. Strangled screams shredded the air. The sound was met by an immense cheer from the hundreds of watching Carthaginian soldiers. This, in their eyes, was vengeance for their dead comrades. Meanwhile, the tribesmen's companions struggled uselessly against their bonds, which had been pegged to the ground.

"Tell them that this is Hannibal's retribution for double-crossing us," Sapho thundered.

Pale-faced, the interpreter did as he was told. His words were met by a gabble of terrified voices. "Some are saying that they didn't know that we would be attacked," he muttered.

"Ha! They're liars, or fools, or both."

"They're asking just to be killed."

"Absolutely not." Sapho waved a hand at the mahout. "Do it again. Don't stop."

Rock after rock was lowered into place, smashing the legs of all but the last Vocontii warrior. When the elephant had maneuvered the final piece of stone into place, Sapho ordered the mahout to wait. Clicking his fingers to make sure that the interpreter followed him, he made his way to where the walleyed warrior lay. Purple-faced with rage, the tribesman spat a string of obscenities.

"Don't bother," said Sapho with a sneer as the interpreter began to speak. "I know what he's saying. Tell him that this is repayment for his deceit, and that a coward like him will never reach the warriors' paradise. Instead, his soul will rot for all eternity in hell." He eyed the mahout. "When he's finished, let the stone fall."

The elephant driver nodded.

"What in the name of all the gods is going on?" Somehow Bostar's voice penetrated the cacophony of screams echoing throughout the narrow gorge.

The interpreter stopped speaking. The mahout sat motionless atop his beast. Stiff-backed with fury, Sapho turned to find his brother regarding him with an outraged expression. He inclined his head mockingly. "I'm punishing these worthless whoresons. What does it look like?"

Bostar's face twisted. "Could you think of a crueler way to kill them?"

"Several ways, actually," Sapho replied amiably. "They all took too long, though. This method might be crude, but it's effective. It will also send a strong message to the rest of their pox-ridden, louse-infested tribe that to fuck with us carries a heavy price."

"You've already made your point!" Bostar indicated the line of screaming men. "Why not just stab this man in the throat and have done?"

"Because this one"—and Sapho kicked the walleyed warrior in the head—"is their leader. I've saved him until last, so he could watch his comrades suffer, and anticipate his own fate."

Bostar recoiled. "You're sick," he spat. "I command you to halt this outrage."

"You might outrank me still, *brother*, but Hannibal entrusted the vanguard to me, not you," Sapho said in a loud voice. "I'm sure that our general would love to hear why you countermanded his orders."

"Hannibal ordered you to kill any prisoners like this?" Bostar muttered in disbelief.

"He said I was to do as I saw fit," snarled Sapho. "Which I am doing. Now stand back!" He was delighted when, with slumped shoulders, Bostar obeyed. Sapho looked down for a final time at the walleyed warrior, who tried to spit at him again. Inspiration seized Sapho and he drew his dagger. Kneeling down, he shoved the tip into the man's right eye socket. With a savage wrench, he hooked out the eyeball. His victim's courage disappeared and a shriek of pure agony ripped free of his throat. Wiping his bloody hands on the warrior's tunic, Sapho stood. "I'm leaving him one eye so that he can watch the mightiest army in the world pass by," he said to the interpreter. "Tell him that." He glanced at Bostar. "Watch and learn, little brother. This is how enemies of Carthage should be treated." Without waiting for a response, Sapho jerked his head at the mahout. "Finish it."

Full of impotent anguish, Bostar walked away. He was unwilling to watch. Unfortunately, he couldn't block out the screams. What had his older brother become? he wondered. Why was Hanno the one who had been carried out to sea?

For the first time, Bostar allowed himself that thought without guilt.

XVI

JOURNEYS

Naturally, the Via Appia, the main road to Rome, led straight out of Capua. Not wishing to enter the town, Quintus first bypassed his father's farm and then took a smaller, cross-country track that meandered through a number of hamlets and past countless farms to join the larger way some miles to the north. Quintus rode his horse. As a supposed slave, Hanno sat on the back of an irritable mule, which was also laden down with equipment. They traveled in silence for the first hour. Both had much to think about.

Quintus now felt confident of finding his father. He was sad to have left Aurelia behind, but that was the way of the world. Their mother would look after her well. However, Quintus felt uneasy. Once their objective—that of finding his father—had been achieved, Hanno would depart to join the Carthaginian forces. Did that mean that they were *already* enemies? Thoroughly unsettled by this notion, Quintus tried not to think of it.

Hanno prayed that Suniaton would be all right and that they would find Fabricius swiftly. Then he would be free. He asked to be reunited with his father and brothers. If they were still alive, of course.

Hanno tried to be upbeat, and concentrated on imagining marching to war against the Romans. At once, however, another disquieting image popped up. Quintus and Fabricius would be serving in the legions. Unknowingly, Hanno had the same disturbing thought as Quintus, and buried it deeply in the recesses of his mind.

Not long after they had joined the Via Appia, they came upon a party of infantry marching south.

"Oscans," said Quintus, relieved to have something to talk about. "They're heading for the port."

Hanno knew that the River Volturnus ran in a southwesterly direction past Capua to terminate at the coast. "To be transported to Iberia?"

Ill at ease again, Quintus nodded.

Hanno ignored him, focusing instead on the approaching group. Apart from Fabricius' escort, he hadn't seen many soldiers in Italy. These were socii, not regular legionaries, but such men would constitute up to half of any army that faced Hannibal's. They were the enemy.

Some of the Oscans were bareheaded, but most wore bronze Attic helmets decorated in striking fashion with horsehair or feathers, which were dyed red, black, white or yellow. Their short wool tunics were also eye-catching, ranging from red to ochre to gray. Few wore shoes or sandals, but all had a broad leather belt covered in bronze sheeting, which was fastened with elaborate hooks. The soldiers were armed with light javelins and thrusting spears of different lengths; the rare men with swords carried the slashing kopis, a curved weapon originally used by the Greeks. The majority of their shields were similar to scuta, concave and ribbed, but smaller.

"It wasn't many generations ago that they were fighting Rome," Quintus revealed. "Capua has only been under Roman rule for just over a century. Many locals think it should reclaim its independence."

Hanno goggled. "Really?"

"Yes. It's a favorite argument between Martialis and my father, especially when they've been drinking." Quintus frowned, wondering if his mother felt similarly. She'd never said as much, but he knew that she was fiercely proud of her heritage.

Hanno was fascinated. His knowledge of the Republic's structure, and its relationship with the non-Roman cities and peoples of Italy, was patchy at best. It was interesting that natives of such a large and important city were unhappy being ruled by Rome. Could there be others who felt the same way? he wondered.

―――

As one of the junior tribunes of a legion, Flaccus should have accompanied his unit to Iberia. After his foolish outburst in front of Scipio, it would also have been wise for him to lay low for a time. As Fabricius rapidly discovered, that was not his way. Discovering that, in addition to Fabricius' cavalry, the consul was taking a single cohort back to Italy, Flaccus begged to be included. One tribune was needed to command the legionaries, he reasoned. Why should it not be he? To Fabricius' utter amazement, Scipio did not explode at the request. While clearly annoyed, the consul acceded. "By Jupiter, but you have a brass neck," he muttered. "Now get out of my tent."

Fabricius took a mental note of the incident, which revealed how far the power of the Minucii stretched. Although it mattered little which tribune accompanied Scipio, Flaccus' gall in asking would have been punished had he been anyone else. Rather than punishment, though, he had got his wish. As he said smugly to Fabricius later, the Minucii had a finger in every pie. "By the time we arrive in Italy, the clan will probably know about Hannibal's intentions." The only way that could happen, thought Fabricius, was if you had sent a message ahead of us. He couldn't believe that was the case. Had Atia been right about Flaccus? Wishing that his prospective son-in-law were less of a braggart, Fabricius consoled himself by imagining how his family would benefit from the Minucii's influence once Aurelia was married.

For his part, Fabricius was delighted to be heading for Italy. Although there would be plenty of action there, he wanted to be part of the army that faced the main threat. Naturally, this was Hannibal, not the commander he had left in Iberia.

―――

Sapho's brutal treatment of the prisoners did not stop the Vocontii from mounting further attacks. If anything, it increased their ferocity. More rocks were rolled down the slopes, causing heavy casualties among the soldiers and pack animals. During the late afternoon, the fighting grew so intense that the vanguard, including the cavalry and the baggage train, became separated from Hannibal and the bulk of the infantry. It remained so for the duration of the night. The following morning, to everyone's relief, the Vocontii had disappeared. Most supposed that their losses had eventually become heavy enough to make stealing supplies pointless. Yet the tribesmen had wreaked more than simple physical damage on the army. The terrifying ordeal helped morale to plummet among the less motivated units. Each night, hundreds of men vanished under cover of darkness. Hannibal had ordered that no one was to stop them. "Soldiers who are coerced into fighting make poor comrades," he said to Malchus.

The host marched on.

For eight days, the miserable, cold and footsore Carthaginians climbed. Their enemies were no longer the Vocontii or the Allobroges, but the elements and the terrain, which grew ever more treacherous. Wind chill, frostbite and exposure began to take their toll. From dawn until dusk, soldiers dropped to the ground like flies. At night they simply died in their sleep. They were weakened by hunger, exhaustion, insufficient clothing, or a combination of all three.

Hannibal's response to Sapho's robust defense of the vanguard had been to promote him. He had also left Sapho in charge of leading the column. Despite his joy at being equal to Bostar in rank, his responsibility was a double-edged sword. It was down to him and his men to act as trailbreakers, which was an utterly exhausting task. Boulders had to be moved. The track regularly needed repairing or strengthening. Casualties among Sapho's men soared. By the eighth night, he was on the point of physical and mental collapse. His dread of their passage of the mountains had been proved well founded. In his mind, they were all doomed. They would never find the promised pass that marked the high point of their journey. All that kept Sapho going was his pride. Asking Hannibal to relieve him of his command would be worse than jumping off a cliff. Yet Sapho didn't want to do that either. Incredibly, life was still better than death. Wrapped in five blankets, he huddled over a lukewarm brazier in his tent and tried to feel grateful. None of his men had the luxury of fuel to burn.

After a while, Sapho stirred. Although he didn't want to, it was time to check the sentries. It was also good for morale for him to be seen. He shed his blankets, pulled on a second cloak and wrapped a scarf around his head. As he unlaced the leather ties and opened the tent flap, a gust of bitingly cold wind entered. Sapho flinched, before forcing himself outside. Two sentries, Libyans, stood by the entrance. A pitch-soaked torch held upright by a small pile of stones cast a faint pool of light around them.

The pair stiffened to attention as they saw him. "Sir," they both mumbled through lips that were blue with cold.

"Anything to report?"

"No, sir."

"It's as cold as ever."

"Yes, sir," the nearest man replied. He doubled over as a paroxysm of coughing took him.

"Sorry, sir," said his companion nervously. "He can't help it."

"It's all right," Sapho replied irritably. He eyed the first soldier, who was wiping bloody sputum from his lips. A dead man walking, he thought. Sudden pity filled him. "Take the wretch inside to the brazier. Try and get him warm. You can stay there until I get back from my rounds."

Stunned, the second Libyan stammered his thanks. Sapho grabbed the torch and stalked off into the darkness. He would only be gone for a quarter of an hour, but it might provide the sick man with some relief. A sour smile traced his chapped lips. I'm getting soft, like Bostar. Sapho hadn't seen his brother since their argument over the Vocontii prisoners. As far as he was concerned, that was fine.

Taking great care on the icy ground, Sapho traced his way past his soldiers' tents. He glanced at the pair of elephants Hannibal had ordered to stay with the vanguard. The miserable beasts stood side by side, trying to maximize their warmth. Sapho even pitied them. Soon after, he reached the first sentries, who were stationed some two hundred steps from his tent. They were in a line across the path where the advance had stopped for the night. Exposed on three sides, it was the worst place to stand watch in the whole army. No fire could survive in the vicious, snow-laden wind that whistled down from the peaks. In order that the soldiers here didn't all die from exposure, Sapho had ordered their periods on duty shortened to just an hour at a time. Even so, he lost men every night.

"Seen anything?" he shouted at the officer in charge.

"No, sir! Even the demons are in bed tonight!"

"Very good. As you were." Pleased by the officer's attempt at humor, Sapho began to retrace his steps. He had only to check the sentries at the rear of the phalanx, and then he was done. Peering into the gloom, he was surprised to see a figure emerging around the corner of the outermost tent. Sapho frowned. The cliff might be twenty steps from the tent lines, but the wind was so powerful that a man could easily be carried over the edge. He had seen it happen several times already. Consequently, everyone walked between the tents, not around them. The man was carrying a torch, which meant that he was no enemy. Yet he'd just taken the most dangerous route past his phalanx. Why? What had he to hide?

"Hey!" Sapho shouted. "Stop right there!"

The figure straightened, and the hood of his cloak whipped back. "Sapho?"

"Bostar?" said Sapho incredulously.

"Yes," his brother replied. "Can we talk?"

Sapho staggered as a particularly savage gust of wind struck him. He watched, aghast, as it buffeted an unsuspecting Bostar sideways and on to one knee. As he struggled to stand up, another blast of air hit, carrying him backward and out into the blackness.

Sapho couldn't believe his eyes. He ran to the edge of the precipice, where he was astonished to find his brother clinging desperately to the protruding branch of a stunted bush several steps below him.

"Help me!" Bostar shouted.

Silently, Sapho stared down at him. Why should I? he asked himself. Of what benefit is it to me?

"What are you waiting for?" Bostar's voice cracked. "This damn branch will never hold!" Seeing the look in Sapho's eyes, he blanched. "You want me to die, don't you? Just as you were happy when Hanno was lost."

Sapho's tongue stuck to the roof of his mouth with guilt. How could Bostar know that? Still he didn't act.

The branch split.

"Fuck you to hell and gone!" screamed Bostar. Letting go with his left hand, he threw himself forward, searching for a fingerhold on the track. There would only be a moment before his body weight pulled him backward and into the abyss. Knowing this, Bostar scrabbled frantically to gain any kind of purchase in the rock-hard, ice-covered earth. He found none. With a despairing cry, he started to slide backward.

Sapho's gut instinct took over, and he leaned forward to grab his brother by the shoulders. With a great yank, he pulled him up and over the edge. A second effort saw them several paces away, on safer ground. They lay side by side for a few moments, their chests heaving. Bostar was the first to sit up. "Why did you save me?"

Sapho met his gaze with difficulty. "I'm not a murderer."

"No," Bostar snapped. "But you were glad when Hanno vanished, weren't you? With him out of the way, you had a chance to become Father's favorite."

Shame filled Sapho. "I—"

"It's strange," said Bostar, interrupting. "If I had died just now, you'd have Father all to yourself. Why didn't you let me slip into oblivion?"

"You're my brother," Sapho protested weakly.

"I might be, but you still stood there, looking at me when I first fell," Bostar retorted furiously. He regained control of himself. "Yet I have you to thank for saving my life. I am grateful, and I will repay my debt if I can." He carefully spat on the ground between them. "After that, you will be dead to me."

Sapho's mouth gaped. He watched as Bostar got up and walked away. "What will you tell Father?" he called out.

Bostar turned, a contemptuous expression twisting his face. "Don't worry. I'll say nothing." With that, he was gone.

Right on cue, a blast of icy wind hit Sapho, chilling him to the bone.

He had never felt more alone.

Quintus' and Hanno's departure left Aurelia feeling abandoned. Finding an excuse to head off to visit Suniaton was far from easy. She could not confide in her mother for obvious reasons, and she didn't like, or trust, her old Greek tutor. She was friendly with Elira, but the Illyrian had been in a bad mood recently, which made her poor company. Julius was the only other household slave Aurelia could be bothered with. After the excitement of her trips to the woods, however, discussion about what was on next week's menu was of little interest. Inevitably, she spent most of her time with her mother, who, since they'd been left alone, had thrown herself into household tasks with a vengeance. It was, Aurelia supposed, Atia's way of coping with Quintus' disappearance.

Foremost among their jobs was dealing with the vast amount of wool stockpiled in one of the sheds in the yard. It had been shorn from the sheep during the summer, and in the subsequent months, the women slaves had stripped the twigs and vegetation from the fleeces, before dyeing them a variety of colors: red, yellow, blue and black. Once dyed, the wool was ready for spinning, and then weaving. Although the majority of this work was done by slaves, Atia also contributed to the effort. She insisted Aurelia did so as well. Day after day, they sat in or walked around the courtyard, distaffs and spindles in hand, retreating to the atrium only if it rained.

"It's the job of a woman to keep the house and work in wool," said Atia one crisp morning. Deftly pulling a few unspun fibers from the bundle on her distaff, she attached them to her spindle and set it spinning. Her eyes lifted to Aurelia. "Are you listening, child?"

"Yes," Aurelia replied, grateful that Atia hadn't noticed her rolling eyes. "You've told me that a thousand times."

"That's because it's true," her mother replied primly. "It's the mark of a good wife to be proficient at spinning and weaving. You'd do well to remember that."

"Yes, Mother," said Aurelia dutifully. Inside, she imagined that she was practicing with a gladius.

"No doubt your father and Quintus will be grateful for any cloaks and tunics that we can send them too. I believe that the winters in Iberia can be harsh."

Guiltily, Aurelia applied herself to her task with more vigor. This was the only tangible way of helping her brother. She was shocked to find herself wishing that she could do the same for Hanno. He's one of the enemy now, she told herself. "Has there been any more news?"

"You know there hasn't." There was an unmistakable trace of irritation in Atia's voice. "Father will have no time to write to us. With the gods' blessing, however, he'll have reached Iberia by now."

"With luck, Quintus will find him soon," Aurelia responded.

Atia's composure cracked for an instant, revealing the sorrow beneath. "What was he thinking to go on his own?"

Aurelia's heart bled to see her mother so upset. Until now, she hadn't mentioned that Hanno had left with her brother. Saying nothing made things far simpler. Now, though, her resolve wavered.

A discreet cough prevented her from saying a word. Aurelia was annoyed to see Agesandros standing by the atrium doors.

In the blink of an eye, Atia's self-possession returned. "Agesandros."

"My lady," he said, bowing. "Aurelia."

Aurelia gave the Sicilian a withering look. Since his accusation of Hanno, she had avoided him like the plague. Now he had stopped her from consoling her mother.

"What is it?" asked Atia. "A problem with the olive harvest?"

"No, mistress." He hesitated. "I have come to make an apology. To Aurelia."

Atia's eyebrows rose. "What have you done?"

"Nothing that I shouldn't have, mistress," said Agesandros reassuringly. "But the whole business with the Carthaginian slave was most . . . unfortunate."

"Is that what you call it?" Aurelia interjected acidly.

Atia raised a hand, stalling her protest. "Continue."

———

Scipio was incensed, upon his arrival in Pisae nearly a week later, to be greeted by a messenger from the Senate. The consul's only thought was to travel north, to Cisalpine Gaul, and there take control of the legions presently commanded by a praetor, Lucius Manlius Vulso. Yet the note Scipio was handed suggested in no uncertain terms that it would be judicious to report to the Senate before taking further action against Hannibal. This was necessary because, as Scipio spat at Flaccus, he had "'exceeded his consular remit, by deciding not to proceed to Iberia with his army.'"

Flaccus innocently studied his fingernails.

"Someone must have sent word before we left Massilia," Scipio raged, staring pointedly at Flaccus. "Yet nowhere do I see any mention of the word *provocatio*. In other words, I could ignore this disrespectful note. I probably should. With every day that goes by, Hannibal and his army march closer to our northern borders. Sempronius has no chance of traveling from Sicily quicker than I can reach the north. Journeying to Rome will delay me by two weeks, or more. If Hannibal turns up during that time, the result could be catastrophic."

"That would scarcely be my fault," Flaccus replied smoothly.

Scipio's nostrils flared white with fury. "Is that so?"

Flaccus had the sense not to answer.

Reading the missive again, Scipio composed himself. "I will return to Rome as asked, but any responsibility for what happens because of the delay will fall on the heads of the Minucii, and on you particularly. Should Hannibal already be in the area when I eventually reach Cisalpine Gaul, I will make sure to position you in the front line every time we encounter the Carthaginians." Flaccus looked up in alarm, and Scipio snarled, "There you can win all the glory you desire. Posthumously, I expect." Ignoring Flaccus' shock, Scipio turned to Fabricius. "We shall take but a single turma to Rome. I want two spare horses for every rider. Your other men can buy new mounts, and then head north to join Vulso with the cohort of infantry. See to it. We ride out in an hour."

Flaccus followed Fabricius as he supervised the unloading of the mounts and equipment. The quayside at Pisae was a hive of activity. Freshly disembarked soldiers retrieved their equipment from piles on the dock and formed up in lines under their officers' eagle eyes. Fabricius' cavalrymen watched as specially constructed wooden frames lifted their horses out of the ships' bellies and on to dry land once more. Grooms stepped in, reassuring their unsettled charges, before leading them off to one side where they could be readied for the impending journey. As soon as the opportunity presented itself, Fabricius rounded on Flaccus. "What in the name of Hades is going on?"

Flaccus made a show of innocence. "What do you mean?"

"Any fool knows that the best thing is not for Scipio to go to Rome, but to Cisalpine Gaul, and with all haste. Yet you have conspired to make sure that he does the former."

Flaccus looked shocked. "Who's to say that I had anything to do with the news reaching Rome? Anyhow, I cannot answer for the actions of more senior members of my clan. They are men greater than you or I, men whose only interest is that of Rome. They also know Scipio for an arrogant individual whose main aim is to gain glory for himself; his recent actions prove this. He must be brought to book by his fellows and reminded of his position before it's too late.

"It's not as if we are without forces in the north," Flaccus went on persuasively. "Lucius Manlius Vulso is already in the area with a full-sized consular army. Vulso is an experienced commander, and I have no doubt that he is skilled enough to face, and beat, the rabble Hannibal will lead out of the mountains. Would you not agree?"

Fabricius felt his position waver. Scipio's confident decision to send his army on to Iberia while he himself returned to Italy had certainly been out of the ordinary. Initially, Fabricius had thought Scipio was showing genuine foresight, but Flaccus' words sowed doubt in his mind. It was hard to credit that a faction in Rome would endanger the Republic just to score points over a political rival. The Minucii must have their reasons for demanding to see Scipio, he reasoned. In theory, the legions in Cisalpine Gaul were fully capable of defending their northern border. Fabricius glanced at Flaccus, and saw nothing but genuine concern. "I suppose so," he muttered.

"Good. Let us travel to the capital without worrying about Hannibal, and see what our betters in the Senate would say to Scipio," said Flaccus earnestly. "The gugga can be dealt with immediately afterward, if Vulso has not already wiped him from the face of the earth. Are we agreed?" He stuck out his right arm in the soldier's fashion.

Fabricius felt uneasy. One moment Flaccus was talking as if those in Rome always acted unselfishly, and the next he was implying that Scipio's recall was a political tactic made with scant consideration of the danger posed by Hannibal. There was far more going on here than met the eye. In Fabricius' mind, the sole issue at hand was Hannibal, and how to deal with him. Those who sat in the Senate obviously did not appreciate that. Yet did it really matter, he wondered, if they went to Rome before Cisalpine Gaul? If Hannibal did succeed in crossing the Alps, his army would need a prolonged period of rest to recover from their ordeal. Forewarned, Vulso would be ready, and Scipio would not take long to travel from the capital. "We are agreed," he said, accepting Flaccus' grip.

"Excellent." Flaccus' eyes glittered with satisfaction. "By the way, don't take anything my brother says to heart. He is greatly looking forward to meeting you in private."

Feeling rather out of his depth, Fabricius nodded.

Hannibal's army reached the top of the pass the next day. Thrillingly, the watery sunshine revealed flat plains far below. The distant image could have been a mirage for all the use it was to them, thought Bostar bitterly. The slopes that led down toward Cisalpine Gaul were covered in frozen snow, which entirely concealed the path. Achieving a secure footing from now on would be more difficult than ever, and the price of failure was no less lethal than it had been since they'd entered the mountains.

To relieve his troops' suffering, Hannibal let them rest for two days at the summit. Of course there was more to his decision than simple kindness. Hundreds of stragglers, soldiers who would have died otherwise, managed to catch up with their comrades in this time, where they were greeted with relief but little sympathy. Even if they'd wanted to speak of their ordeal, few would have found an audience. Despair clawed constantly at men's hearts, rendering them insensible to the suffering of others.

Remarkably, hundreds of mules that had gone missing during the ascent also made their way into the camp. Although the majority had lost their baggage, they were still a welcome sight. In an effort to raise morale, Hannibal allowed the weakest beasts, numbering two hundred or more, to be slaughtered on the last evening before the descent. The fires needed to cook this meal consumed most of the army's remaining wood, but for the first time in weeks, his soldiers went to sleep with fresh meat in their bellies.

Bostar's deeply held hope that Hanno was still alive, and the presence of his father, were what sustained him through the agonies of the following day and night. He tried not to think of Sapho at all, instead concentrating on helping his soldiers. If Bostar had thought that the journey through the mountains up to that point had been difficult, then the descent was twice as bad. After more than a week above the snow line, the troops were chilled to the bone. Despite the Cavares' gifts of clothing and footwear, many were still not suitably attired for the freezing, hazardous conditions. Slowed by the cold, the Carthaginians stumbled over the slightest obstacles, walked into snowdrifts and collided with each other. This, when a simple trip meant death, instantly from the fall, or by slipping away into a sleep from which there was no wakening.

The soldiers died in other ways as well. Sections of the path cracked away under the weight of snow and men, sending hundreds into oblivion, and forcing those behind to repair the track in order to continue. The unfortunate mules were now prone to panic at the slightest thing, and their struggles were the cause of more casualties. Bostar found that the only way not to go mad in the face of so much death and destruction was to act as if nothing had happened. To keep putting one foot in front of the other. Step by grim step, he plodded on.

Just when he thought that things could get no worse, they did. Late the next morning, the vanguard arrived at a point where a landslide had carried away the track for a distance of one and a half stades. Sapho sent word back that neither man nor beast could proceed without losing their life. Here the drop was at least five hundred paces. Undeterred, Hannibal ordered his Numidians to begin constructing a new path across the obstacle. The rest of the army was ordered to rest as best it could. The news made many soldiers break down and weep. "Will our suffering never end?" wailed one of Bostar's men. Bostar was quick to issue a reprimand. Morale was painfully low, without being made worse by open despair.

All they had to go on were the garbled messages occasionally passed back from the vanguard. Bostar didn't know which to believe. The cavalry mounts were useful in pulling large boulders out of the way. Most of the work had to be done by bare hand. Hannibal had offered a hundred gold pieces to the first man over the obstacle. Ten men had fallen to their deaths when a section of the track had given way. It would take a week or more to clear the way for the elephants.

As darkness fell, Bostar's spirits were raised somewhat by a Numidian officer who was passing through Bostar's phalanx as he returned to his tent.

"Progress was good today. We've laid a new path over more than two-thirds of the landslide. If things proceed like this tomorrow, we should be able to continue."

Bostar breathed a huge sigh of relief. After nearly a month in the mountains, Cisalpine Gaul would be within reach at last.

His optimism vanished within an hour of work resuming the following morning when the cavalrymen exposed a huge boulder. It completely blocked the way forward. With a diameter greater than the height of two men, the rock was positioned such that only a few soldiers could approach at a time. Horses weren't strong enough to move it, and there was no space to lead an elephant in to try.

As time passed, Bostar could see the last vestiges of hope disappearing from men's eyes. He felt the same way himself. Although they weren't speaking, Sapho looked similarly deflated. It wasn't long before Hannibal came to survey the problem. Bostar's usual excitement at seeing his general did not materialize. How could anyone, even Hannibal, find a way to overcome this obstacle? As if the gods were laughing, more snow began to fall. Bostar's shoulders slumped.

A moment later, he was surprised to see his father hurrying to speak with Hannibal. When Malchus returned, he had a new air of calmness about him. Bostar squinted at the soldiers who were hurrying back along the column. He grabbed his father's arm. "What's going on?"

"All is not lost," Malchus replied with a small smile. "You will see."

Soon after, the soldiers returned, each man bent double under a pile of firewood. Load after load was carried past and set carefully around the base of the rock. When the timber had been piled high,

Malchus ordered it lit. Still Bostar did not understand, but his father would answer no questions. Leaving his sons to observe with increasing curiosity, he returned to Hannibal's side.

The soldiers who could see were also intrigued, but after the fire had been burning for more than an hour without any result, they grew bored. Grumbles about wasting the last of their wood began. For the first time since leaving New Carthage, Bostar did not immediately react. His own disillusionment was reaching critical levels. Whatever crackpot idea his father had had was not going to work. They might as well lie down and die now, because that was what would surely happen when night fell.

Bostar missed the construction of a wooden framework that allowed a man to stand over the top of the rock. It was only when the first amphorae were carried past that he looked up. Finally, his curiosity got the better of his despair. The clay vessels contained sour wine, the troops' staple drink. Bostar saw his father gesturing excitedly as Hannibal watched. Quickly, two strapping scutarii climbed the frame. To combat the extreme heat now radiating from the rock, they had both soaked their clothes in water. The instant they had reached the top, the pair lowered ropes to the ground. Men below tied amphorae to the cables, which were hauled up. Without further ado, the scutarii cracked open the wax seals and poured the vessels' contents all over the boulder. The liquid sizzled and spat, sending a powerful smell of hot wine into the faces of those watching. Realization of what they were trying to do struck Bostar like a hammer blow. He turned to tell Sapho before biting his lip and saying nothing.

The empty containers were discarded and replaced by full ones, and the process was repeated. There was more loud bubbling as the wine boiled on the superheated rock, but nothing else happened. The scutarii looked uncertainly at Malchus. "Keep going! As fast as you can!" he shouted. Hastily, they obeyed, upending two more amphorae. Then it was four. Still the rock sat there, immovable, immutable. Malchus roared at the soldiers who stood close by to add more fuel to the blaze. The flames licked up, threatening to consume the platform upon which the scutarii stood, but they were not allowed to climb down. Malchus moved to stand at the frame's base, and exhorted the soldiers to even greater efforts. Another two amphorae were emptied over the boulder, to no avail. Bostar's hopes began to ebb away.

A succession of explosive cracks suddenly drowned out all sound. Chunks of stone were hurled high into the air, and one of the scutarii collapsed as if poleaxed. His skull had been neatly staved in by a piece of rock no bigger than a hen's egg. His panicked companion jumped to safety, and the soldiers who had been tending the fire all retreated at speed. More cracking sounds followed, and then the rock broke into several large parts. Parts that could be moved by men, or smashed into pieces by hammers. The cheering that followed rose to the very clouds. As word spread down the column, the noise increased in volume until it seemed that the mountains themselves were rejoicing.

Elated, Bostar and Sapho rushed separately to their father's side. Joyfully, they embraced him one by one. They were joined by Hannibal, who greeted Malchus like a brother. "Our ordeal is nearly over," the general cried. "The path to Cisalpine Gaul lies open."

The two friends' first sight of the capital was formed by the immense Servian wall, which ringed the city and dwarfed Capua's defenses. "The fortifications are nearly two hundred years old," Quintus explained excitedly. "They were built after Rome was sacked by the Gauls."

May Hannibal be the next to do so, Hanno prayed.

"How does Carthage compare?"

"Eh?" said Hanno, coming back to reality. "Many of her defenses are much more recent." They're still far more spectacular, he thought.

"And its size?"

Hanno wasn't going to lie about that one. "Carthage is much bigger."

Quintus did his best not to look disgruntled, and failed.

Hanno was surprised that within the walls, Carthage's similarities with Rome grew. The streets were unpaved, and most were no more than ten paces across. After months of hot weather, their surfaces were little more than an iron-hard series of wheel ruts. "They'll be a muddy morass come the winter," he said, pointing. "That's what happens if it rains a lot at home."

"As in Capua," agreed Quintus. He wrinkled his nose as they passed an alleyway used as a dung heap. The acrid odor of human feces and urine hung heavy in the air. "Lucky it's autumn and not the height of summer. The smell then is apparently unbearable."

"Do many buildings have sewerage systems?"

"No."

"It's not much different to parts of Carthage," Hanno replied. It was strange to feel homesick because of the smell of shit.

The fuggy atmosphere was aided by the fact that the closely built structures were two, three and even four stories tall, creating a dimly lit, poorly ventilated environment on the street. Compared to the fresh air and open spaces of the Italian countryside, it was an alternative world. Most structures were open-fronted shops at ground level, with stairs at the side that snaked up to the flats above. Quintus was shocked by the filth of it all. "They're where the majority of people live," he explained.

"In Carthage, they're mostly constructed from mud bricks."

"That sounds a lot safer. The *cenaculae* are built of wood. They're disease-ridden, hard to heat and easy to destroy."

"Fire's a big problem, then," said Hanno, imagining how easy it would be to burn down the city if it fell to Hannibal's army.

Quintus grimaced. "Yes."

Along with its sights and smells, the capital provided plenty of noise. The air was filled with the clamor of shopkeepers competing for business, the shrieks of playing children and the chatter of neighbors gossiping on the street corners. Beggars of every hue abounded, adding their cries for alms to the din. The clang of iron being pounded on anvils carried from smithies, and the sound of carpenters hammering echoed off the tall buildings. In the distance, cattle bellowed from the Forum Boarium.

Of course Rome was not their main destination: that was the port of Pisae, from which Scipio and his army had set sail. Yet the temptation of visiting Rome had been too much for either of the friends to resist. They wandered through the streets for hours, drinking in the sights. When they were hungry, they filled their bellies with hot sausages and fresh bread bought from little stalls. Juicy plums and apples finished off their satisfying meal.

Inevitably, Quintus was drawn to the massive temple of Jupiter, high on the Capitoline Hill. He gaped at its roof of beaten gold, rows of columns the height of ten men and façade of brightly painted terracotta. He came to a halt by the immense statue of a bearded Jupiter, which stood in front of the complex, giving it a view over much of Rome.

Feeling resentful, Hanno also stopped.

"This must be bigger than any of the shrines in Carthage," said Quintus with a questioning look.

"There's one which is as big," Hanno replied proudly. "It's in honor of Eshmoun."

"What god is that?" asked Quintus curiously.

"He represents fertility, good health and well-being."

Quintus' eyebrows rose. "And is he the leading deity in Carthage?"

"No."

"Why has his temple the most prominent position then?"

Hanno gave an awkward shrug. "I don't know." He remembered his father saying that their people differed from the Romans by being traders first and foremost. This temple complex proved that Quintus' kind placed power and war before everything else. Thank all the gods that we have a real warrior in Hannibal Barca, he thought. If fools like Hostus were in charge, we would have no hope.

Quintus had come to his own conclusion. How could a race who gave pride of place to a fertility god's temple ever defeat Rome? And when the inevitable happens, what will happen to Hanno? his conscience suddenly screamed. Where will he be? Quintus didn't want to answer the question. "We'd better find a bed for the night," he suggested. "Before it gets dark."

"Good idea," replied Hanno, grateful for the change of subject.

Agesandros gave a tiny nod of thanks and turned to Aurelia. "I should have handled the matter far better. I wanted to apologize for it, and ask if we can make a new start."

"A new start?" Aurelia snapped. "But you're only a slave! What you think means nothing." She was pleased to see pain flare in his eyes.

"Enough!" Atia exclaimed. "Agesandros has served us loyally for more than twenty years. At the least, you should listen to what he has to say."

Aurelia flushed, mortified at being reprimanded in front of a slave. She was damned if she'd just give in to her mother's wishes. "Why would you bother apologizing now?" she muttered.

"It's simple. The master and Quintus may be gone for a long time. Who knows? It could be years. Perhaps you'll have more of a hand with the running of the farm." Encouraged by Atia's nod of acquiescence, he continued, "I want nothing more than to do my best for you and the mistress here." Agesandros made an almost plaintive gesture. "A good working relationship is essential if we are to succeed."

"He's right," said Atia.

"You owe me an explanation before I agree to anything," said Aurelia angrily.

The Sicilian sighed. "True. I did treat the gugga slave harshly."

"Harshly? Where do you get the gall?" Aurelia cried. "You were going to sell a man to someone who would make him fight his best friend to the death!"

"I have my reasons," Agesandros replied. A cloud passed across his face. "If I were to tell you that the Carthaginians tortured and murdered my entire family in Sicily, would you think differently of me?"

Aurelia's mouth opened in horror.

"They did what?" demanded her mother.

"I was away, fighting at the other end of the island, mistress. A surprise Carthaginian attack swept through the town, destroying all in its path." Agesandros swallowed. "They slaughtered everyone in the place: men, women, children. The old, the sick, even the dogs."

Aurelia could scarcely breathe. "Why?"

"It was punishment," the Sicilian replied. "Historically, we had sided with Carthage, but had switched to give our allegiance to Rome. Many settlements had done the same. Ours was the first to be captured. A message had to be delivered to the rest."

Aurelia knew that terrible things happened in war. Men died, or were injured terribly, often in their thousands. But the massacre of civilians?

"Go on," said Atia gently.

"I had a wife and two children. A girl and a boy." For the first time, Agesandros' voice cracked. "They were just babies. Three and two."

Aurelia was stunned to see tears in his eyes. She had not thought the vilicus capable of such emotion. Incredibly, she felt sorry for him.

"I found them some days later. They were dead. Butchered, in fact." Agesandros' face twitched. "Have you ever seen what a spear blade can do to a little child? Or what a woman looks like after a dozen soldiers have violated her?"

"Stop!" Atia cried in distaste. "That's quite enough."

He hung his head.

Aurelia was reeling with horror. Her mind was filled with a series of terrifying images. It was no wonder, she thought, that Agesandros had treated Hanno as he had.

"Finish your story," Atia commanded. "Quickly."

"I didn't really want to live after that," said Agesandros obediently, "but the gods did not see fit to grant my wish of dying in battle. Instead, I was taken prisoner, and sold into slavery. I was taken to Italy, where the master bought me." He shrugged. "Here I have been ever since. That pair were some of the first guggas I had seen for two decades."

"Hanno is innocent of any crime toward your family," Aurelia hissed. "The war in Sicily took place before he had even been born!"

"Let me deal with this," said her mother sharply. "Were you seeking revenge the first time that you attacked the Carthaginian?"

"Yes, mistress."

"I understand. While it doesn't excuse your actions, it explains them." Atia's expression hardened. "Did you lie about finding the knife and purse among the slave's belongings?"

"No, mistress! As the gods are my witness, I told the truth," said the Sicilian earnestly.

Liar, thought Aurelia furiously, but she dared say nothing. Her mother was nodding in approval. A moment later, her worries materialized.

"Agesandros is right," Atia declared. "Things will be hard enough in the months to come. Let us all make a new start." She stared expectantly at Aurelia. Agesandros' expression was milder, but mirrored hers.

"Very well," Aurelia whispered, feeling more isolated than ever.

XVII

DEBATE

Having found a cheap bed for the night, the two friends hit the nearest tavern. Drinking seemed the adult thing to do, but of course there was a darker reason behind it: their thoughts about the outcome of the war. Both felt more awkward than they had since falling out during Flaccus' visit. Aurelia was not there to mediate, so wine would have to do. Their tactic worked to some extent, and they chatted idly while eyeing the prostitutes who were working the room for customers.

It didn't take long before the wine began to affect them both. Neither were used to drinking much. Fortunately, they grew merry rather than morose, and the evening became quite enjoyable. Encouraged by a hooting Hanno, Quintus even relaxed enough to take one of the whores on to his lap and fondle her bare breasts. He might have gone further, but then something happened that took all their attention away from wine and women. Important news didn't take long to spread through cities and towns. People simply carried the word on foot, from shops to taverns, and market places to houses. Naturally, the accuracy of such gossip could not always be relied upon, but that did not mean there wasn't some truth to it.

"Hannibal is leading his army over the Alps!" cried a voice from outside the inn. "When he falls upon Italy, we shall be murdered in our beds!"

As all conversation ceased, the two friends stared at each other, wide eyed. "Did you know about this?" Quintus hissed.

"I had no idea," Hanno replied truthfully. "Why else would I have agreed to travel with you to Iberia?"

A moment later, a middle-aged man with a red face and double chin entered. His grubby tunic and calloused hands pointed toward him being a shopkeeper of some kind. He smiled self-importantly at the barrage of questions that greeted him. "I have seen Scipio the consul with my own eyes, not an hour since," he announced. "He has returned from Massilia with this terrible news."

"What else did you hear?" shouted a voice. "Tell us!"

A roar of agreement went up from the other patrons.

The shopkeeper licked his lips. "Running through the streets is thirsty work. A cup of wine would wet my throat nicely."

Hurriedly, the landlord filled a beaker to the brim. Scurrying over, he pressed it into the newcomer's hand.

He took a deep swallow and smacked his lips with satisfaction. "Tasty."

"Tell us!" Quintus cried.

The shopkeeper smiled again at his temporary power. "After landing at Massilia for supplies, Scipio heard word that Hannibal might be in the area. He sent out a patrol, which stumbled upon the entire Carthaginian army." He paused, letting the shocked cries of his audience fill the air, and draining his cup. The innkeeper refilled it at once. The man raised a hand. Instantly, silence fell. "When he heard, Scipio led his army north with all speed, his aim to force the enemy into battle. But when they arrived, Hannibal had gone. Vanished. His only intention can be to cross the mountains and enter Cisalpine Gaul. Before invading Italy."

Wails of terror met his final remark. The room descended into chaos as everyone screamed to be heard. Some customers even ran away, back to their houses. Quintus' face bore an expression of total shock, while Hanno struggled to control his exhilaration. Who else could be so daring, other than Hannibal? He wondered if his father had known about this tactically brilliant plan, and said nothing? At one stroke, his priorities had been changed utterly.

Quintus had realized the same thing. "I suppose you'll be leaving now," he said accusingly. "Why travel to Iberia now? Just head to Cisalpine Gaul."

Feeling guilty for even entertaining the idea, Hanno flushed. "This changes nothing," he replied. "We are going to Iberia to find your father."

Quintus looked Hanno in the eyes, and saw that he meant it. He hung his head. "I'm sorry for doubting your honor," he muttered. "It's shocking to hear news like this."

Their conversation was interrupted again. "Do you not want to know why the consul has returned?" bellowed the messenger, who was already on his fourth cup of wine. He waited as the room grew quiet once more. "Scipio has been recalled by the Senate because he sent his army on to Iberia rather than pursuing Hannibal. They say that the Minucii want him replaced with one of their own. Tomorrow, he will attend the Curia to explain his actions."

All thoughts of leaving Rome at dawn vanished from the pair's heads. What did it matter if they delayed their departure for a few hours to witness this drama unfold?

—————

Whatever Scipio's reception in the Senate might be, he was still one of the Republic's two consuls. At the walled gate that signaled the end of the Via Ostiensis, the road from Ostia, a fine litter borne by six strapping slaves awaited his arrival. He, Flaccus and Fabricius clambered aboard. A dozen lictores bearing fasces preceded the litter into the city. As soldiers under arms, Fabricius' thirty cavalrymen had to remain outside but this did not delay the party's progress. The lictores' mere presence, wearing their magnificent red campaign cloaks rather than just their usual togas, and with the addition of axes to their fasces, was enough to clear the streets. All citizens, apart from Vestal Virgins or married women, were obliged to stand aside, or face the consequences. Only the strongest and tallest men were picked to join the lictores, and they had been taught to use their fasces at the slightest opportunity. If ordered to do so, they could even act as executioners.

Fabricius had been to Rome several times, and always enjoyed the spectacle provided by the capital. The lictores' presence ensured that he gained the best possible impression of the city. People pushed inside the shops and into the alleyways to get out of the way. It was all a far cry from Capua, and even farther from Fabricius' farm, and yet it felt very similar. He tried to ignore the feeling of homesickness that followed. Their rapid progress to the Forum Romanum ensured that he had no time to wallow in the emotion.

As they entered the Forum, Fabricius' eyes were drawn to the Curia, the home of the Senate. Unremarkable apart from its great bronze doors, it was nonetheless the focal point of the Republic. He picked out the Graecostasis, the area just outside, where foreign embassies had to wait until they were called in. Today, accompanying one of the two most important men in the land, there was no such delay. The lictores swept up to the entrance, scattering the crowd of senators' sons who were hovering outside, listening to the debates within. Scipio alighted right before the portals; so too did Flaccus and Fabricius. All three were clad in their finest togas. Naturally, Scipio wore the grandest, a shining white woolen garment with a purple border.

Before leaving, Fabricius had secreted a dagger in the folds of his toga. After months on campaign, he felt naked without a weapon, and had scooped it up without even thinking. Yet it was a risky move: the lictores alone were allowed to bear arms within the Curia. Now, Fabricius cursed his impulsive decision. There was no way of getting rid of the dagger, though. He would have to carry it inside and hope for the best. His heart began to pound. Scipio had asked him to be present because he was the only Roman officer to have seen Hannibal's army. His testimony was vital for Scipio's defense. "I'm relying on you," the consul had said. "I know you won't let me down. Just tell them what you saw at the Carthaginian camp." Fabricius had promised to do so. He sneaked a glance at Flaccus, who looked rather pleased with himself. Confusion filled Fabricius. What role would he play in the drama to come?

The most senior lictor spoke with the guards before entering to announce Scipio's arrival. A hush fell inside. Upon the man's return, the twelve lictores re-formed in six columns of two. With a measured tread, they led the way into the Senate. Fabricius followed Scipio and Flaccus. He had to stop himself from staring like an excited boy. He'd never entered the seat of the Republic's democracy. Light flooded in through long, narrow windows set high in the walls. Running the length of the rectangular room, three low steps were lined by marble benches. Rank upon rank of standing toga-clad senators filled this space. To a man, their gaze was locked on Scipio and his companions. Struggling to control his awe, Fabricius kept his eyes averted from the senators. At the end of the chamber, he saw a dais upon which sat two finely carved rosewood chairs. These, the most important positions, were for the consuls.

The lictores reached the platform and fanned out to either side, leaving a space for Scipio to assume his seat. Flaccus and Fabricius remained at floor level. As Scipio sat down, the lictores smacked the butts of their fasces off the mosaic. The clashing sound echoed off the walls and died away.

There was a long pause.

Glancing sideways, Fabricius saw a tiny, satisfied smile flicker across the consul's lips. It was obviously up to Scipio to begin proceedings, and, in a pointed reminder of his rank, he was making the men who had recalled him to Rome wait. On and on the silence went. Soon Fabricius could see senators muttering angrily to one another. None dared to speak, however.

Finally, Scipio opened his mouth. "As I speak, the greatest threat to Rome since the barbarian Brennus approaches us through the Alps." He let his shocking words sink in. "Yet instead of letting me fulfill my duty, that of defending the Republic, you would have me return to explain my actions. Well, I am here." Scipio extended his arms, as if to welcome interrogation, and fell silent.

A deluge of questions followed. Practically half the senators present tried to speak at the same time. Many of their queries involved Brennus, the Gaulish chieftain who had led his fearsome warriors to the Capitoline Hill itself, and sacked Rome. In the process, he had left a weeping sore deep in the Roman psyche, a source of eternal shame. Fabricius did not know if Hannibal was truly that dangerous, but merely by mentioning Brennus, Scipio had scored the first points. Before the

Minucii could make a single accusation, the Senate's attention had been neatly diverted to something far more primeval.

Scipio wasn't finished. Lifting a hand, he waited for quiet. "I want to know why I was summoned here. Only then will I tell you anything of Hannibal and the enormous Carthaginian army which follows him."

Cries and protests filled the air, but Scipio simply folded his arms and sat back on his chair.

Second round to Scipio, thought Fabricius. His respect for the consul was growing by the moment.

Both young men were up late the next morning. A brief visit to the public baths helped to ease their pounding heads. Fortunately, both also had the wits to drink copious amounts of water. Relieving themselves was not an issue: all they had to do was dart up one of the many alleyways that contained dung heaps. Breakfasting on bread and cheese, they made their way to the Forum Romanum. Naturally enough, conversation was limited until they reached their destination.

Quintus soaked up the sight of the long, rectangular space. "It used to be a marsh, but now it's the largest open area within the city walls. This is the heart of the Republic," he said proudly. "The center of religious, ceremonial and commercial life. People come here to socialize, to watch court cases or gladiator fights, and to hear important public announcements."

"It has a lot in common with the Agora," said Hanno politely. Although it's not half as big, he thought.

Hundreds of shops lined the Forum's perimeter. They ranged from ordinary butchers, fishmongers and bakers to the grander premises of lawyers, scribes and moneylenders. Crowds of people thronged the whole area.

Quintus had been taught the Forum's layout. "There are the shrines of Castor and Pollux, and Saturn," he cried as they walked along. "And the circular temple of the Vestal Virgins."

"What's that?" asked Hanno, pointing at a grubby building along the northern side of the Forum.

"I think it's the *comitium*," Quintus replied. "It's a temple which was built during the foundation of Rome more than five hundred years before." His voice lowered. "Inside it is the *lapis niger*, a stubby pillar of black stone which marks the spot where Romulus, the founder of Rome, ascended to heaven. Beside is the rostra, the speaker's platform, which is decorated with the prows of captured ships." Quintus flushed and fell silent. The most recent additions were from Carthaginian triremes that had been captured in the last war.

Realizing, Hanno glowered.

The friends soon discovered that they had arrived just after Scipio had entered the Curia, but consoled themselves with the fact that they would be close at hand when he emerged. Huge crowds were already present. The news about Hannibal had spread all over the city by now. Everyone in Rome wanted to know what would happen next. Wild rumors swept from one end of the gathering to the other.

"Hannibal has a host of more than a hundred and fifty thousand men," cried a man with red-rimmed eyes.

"He has a hundred elephants, and twenty-five thousand Numidian cavalry," wailed another.

"They say that Philip of Macedon has mobilized his army and is about to attack us from the northeast," shot back the first man. "He's going to join with the Carthaginians."

"So is every tribe in Cisalpine Gaul," added a third voice.

Hanno's anger over the rostra was replaced by delight. If only a fraction of the gossip was true, Rome faced a catastrophe of enormous proportions. He glanced at Quintus, who was staring rigidly at the Curia, pretending to ignore what was being said.

An awkward silence fell.

⸻

A hush fell in the Senate as a stocky figure with wavy black hair and a ruddy complexion made his way into view. Bushy eyebrows sat over a pair of calculating blue eyes and a prominent nose. The senators around him moved deferentially out of the way. Flaccus gave the man a tiny nod, and Fabricius knew at once who it was. He was Marcus Minucius Rufus, a former consul, and Flaccus' brother. This was the preeminent member of the Minucii clan, and one of the most powerful men in Rome. No doubt he was the person responsible for the letter to Scipio.

"Consul," said Marcus, inclining his head in recognition. "We thank you for returning to Rome. It is an honor to see you once more." With the niceties over, his expression turned hawkish. "We were alarmed to hear that your brother was leading your legions to Iberia. This, so that you could return to Italy. We have asked you back to explain your extraordinary about turn, which goes completely against the Senate's decision made here not six months ago. You and Longus, your co-consul, have supreme command of the Republic's military forces. That is beyond doubt. Yet neither of you are immune to challenge, should that be necessary." Marcus half turned, smiling at the mutters of agreement that were becoming audible. "Clearly, I am not the only one to hold such an opinion."

One of Scipio's eyebrows arched. "And what opinion might that be?" he asked in a silky smooth tone.

Marcus' reply was urbane. "I speak of course, of the power of provocatio."

Some of the senators hissed with disapproval at this, but others shouted in agreement. Fabricius felt a nerve twitch in his face. He'd never before heard of one of the Republic's supreme magistrates being threatened with a criminal charge. He shot a glance at Flaccus, but could glean nothing from his face. Why were the Minucii seeking to depose Scipio during his consulship? Fabricius wondered. What purpose would it serve?

"Have you nothing to say?" Marcus asked, taking a smug look around the room. Like a tide that had just turned, the noise of those who supported him began to grow.

Fabricius glanced at Flaccus again. This time, he saw the same self-satisfied expression as the one adorning Marcus' face. Then it hit him. Flaccus had believed Scipio's account of the threat posed by Hannibal and, in his letter, told his brother of his concerns. Now Marcus, a previously successful general in his own right, wanted to become consul so that he could claim the glory of defeating the Carthaginians instead of leaving it to Scipio. This possibility, no, probability, Fabricius thought angrily, defied belief. All that mattered was defeating an enemy who posed a serious threat to the Republic. Yet to some of these politicians, it was more about making a name for themselves.

Bizarrely, Scipio laughed. "I find it remarkable," he said, "that I should be accused of exceeding my remit when in fact I have done more than my duty in fulfilling it. My army has been sent to Iberia as ordered; its commander, my brother Gnaeus, has a proven record in the field. Furthermore, upon realizing the implications of Hannibal's march across the Alps, and knowing that my colleague Longus would not have time to react, I returned to Italy with the intention of facing the Carthaginians myself. Immediately. Does that not prove my loyalty to Rome? And what should we think about those who would prevent me from doing my duty?"

In the uproar that followed, Scipio and Marcus stared at each other with clear dislike. But Marcus' response was swift. "I take it that you have seen Hannibal's 'enormous' army with your own eyes? Made a realistic estimate of the number of enemy troops?"

"I have done neither," replied Scipio in an icy tone.

"Are you a soothsayer, then?" Marcus asked, to gales of laughter from his supporters.

"Nothing like that." Scipio coolly indicated Fabricius. "I have with me the veteran cavalry officer who led the patrol that reconnoitred the Carthaginian camp's perimeter. He will be happy to answer any questions you may have."

Marcus regarded Fabricius with thinly disguised contempt. "Your name?"

Meeting Marcus' stare, Fabricius steeled his resolve. Whatever the other's rank, and however intimidating the scene, he would tell the truth. "Gaius Fabricius, sir. Equestrian and landowner near Capua."

Marcus made a dismissive gesture. "Have you much military experience?"

"I spent nearly ten years in Sicily, fighting the Carthaginians, sir," replied Fabricius proudly. He was delighted by the response of some of those watching. Many heads nodded in approval; other senators muttered in each other's ears.

Marcus pursed his lips. "Tell us what you saw, then. Let the Senate decide if it truly poses the threat that Scipio would have us believe."

Taking a deep breath, Fabricius began the tale of his patrol. He did not look at Marcus or anyone else. Instead he kept his gaze fixed on the bronze doors at the far end of the room. It was a good tactic, and he warmed to his topic as he continued. Fabricius spared no detail of the Carthaginian encampment, and was particularly careful to stress the number of enemy cavalry, the River Rhodanus' immense width and the Herculean effort of ferrying the elephants across it. Finishing, he looked to Scipio. The consul gave an approving nod. Flaccus' expression had soured. Had his prospective son-in-law thought that having to appear before the entire Senate would be too much for him? From the alarmed looks many senators were now giving each other, the opposite was true. Suddenly, Marcus seemed to be on the back foot.

Seizing the initiative, Scipio moved to the front of the dais. "Fabricius estimated the Carthaginian host to be greater in size than two consular armies. I'm talking about fifty thousand men, of whom at least a quarter are cavalry. Numidians, who bested our troops in Sicily on countless occasions. Do not forget the elephants either. Our combat record against *them* is less than valiant. We also have to consider the leader of this army. Hannibal Barca, a man who has recently conquered half of Iberia and taken an impregnable city, Saguntum, by storm. A general who is unafraid of leading his soldiers across the Alps in late autumn." Scipio nodded as many senators recoiled. "Many of you know the praetor Lucius Manlius Vulso, as I do. He is an honorable and able leader. But is he capable of beating a force twice the size of his, which also possesses superior numbers of horse, and elephants?" He looked around. "Is he?"

A brief, disbelieving silence cloaked the room. Then, sheer pandemonium broke out. Hundreds of worried voices competed with each other, but no individual would listen to what another was saying. Marcus tried to calm those around him, but his efforts were in vain. Fabricius couldn't believe it. Here were the men who ruled the Republic, squabbling and shouting like frightened children. He glanced at Scipio, who was watching the spectacle, waiting for an opportunity to intervene. Impulsively, Fabricius pulled out his dagger and handed it over. "It's yours, sir," he said passionately. "Like the sword of every citizen in Italy." Scipio's initial surprise was replaced by a wolfish smile. He accepted the blade before muttering an order to his lictores. The hammering of fasces on the floor drew everyone's attention.

Scipio raised the dagger high. "I have been handed this by Fabricius, who has broken the law by carrying it into the Curia. Yet he did it only because of his loyalty to the Republic. To show his willingness to shed his blood and, if necessary, to die in the struggle to overcome Hannibal. With determined soldiers like this, I promise you victory over the Carthaginian invaders! Victory!"

As a flock of birds seamlessly alters direction, the senators' mood changed. Their panic vanished, to be replaced by a frenzy of excitement. Spontaneous cheering broke out, and the atmosphere lightened at once. Scipio had won, thought Fabricius delightedly. Nobody but a fool would try and depose the consul now.

A moment later, Flaccus sidled over. "Happy?" he hissed.

Fabricius had had enough. "What was I supposed to do? Lie about what I saw?" he retorted. "Hannibal's army is huge. It's well armed, and led by a very determined man. We underestimate it at our peril."

Flaccus' expression grew softer. "Of course, you are right. You spoke well. Convincingly," he said. "And the danger must be addressed fast. Clearly, Scipio is still the man to do it. The resolve he has shown here today is admirable."

Looking at the displeasure twisting Marcus' face, Fabricius had difficulty in believing Flaccus' words. He shoved his disquiet away. Such things were no longer of importance.

All that mattered was defeating Hannibal.

Fabricius wasn't surprised when Scipio ordered him to proceed back to the city gate, there to ready his men. They would leave for Cisalpine Gaul within three hours. Flaccus would be with them too. Scipio rolled his eyes as he said it. "Some things cannot be changed," he muttered. Fabricius was relieved to be given his orders. He had seen enough of politics for a lifetime, and was uncertain what to think of Flaccus and his brother. Maybe Atia had been right? he wondered. Deciding to inform her of what had transpired by writing a quick letter before they set off, Fabricius exited the bronze doors and headed across the Forum.

XVIII

CISALPINE GAUL

There were only two occasions when the two friends heard something of what was going on inside. The first was when alarmed shouts rang out; the second, which followed directly after, was the sound of loud cheering. Almost at once, news spread through the assembled crowds that the Senate had given Scipio its resounding support. Now the consul was to head north with all speed, there to confront Hannibal. Before the pair had time to take the momentous information in, several figures hurried from the Curia. Suddenly, Quintus came to life. He gave Hanno a violent nudge. "Look," he hissed, taking a step forward. "It's Father!"

"So it is," Hanno muttered. He was even more shocked than Quintus. Why was Fabricius here? His next thought was far more worrying. How would Quintus explain his presence? A wave of terror struck him. What chance was there of Fabricius accepting Quintus' grant of freedom? Precious little. Hanno couldn't help thinking he should walk away into the crowd. He would be lost to sight in an instant. Free to make his own way north. Hanno wavered, but then his pride took over. *I am no coward who runs away and hides.*

Glancing around, Quintus sensed his unhappiness. Despite his excitement, he pulled himself up short. "It's all right," he said gently. "I'm not going anywhere."

"Eh? Why not?" Hanno cried. "This is a perfect opportunity for you."

"Maybe so, but it isn't for you."

Hanno colored. He didn't know what to say.

Quintus preempted him. "What possibility is there that Father will honor your manumission?"

"I don't know," Hanno muttered. "Not much, I suppose."

"Exactly," Quintus replied. "Which is the reason I'm staying right here. With you."

"Why would you do that?" asked Hanno, caught off guard.

"Have you forgotten last night already?" Quintus cuffed him on the side of the head. "You promised to accompany me to Iberia, even though you no longer had any need to go there. Plus you didn't make a run for it just now, which most people would have done. I have to repay your honor. Fair's fair."

"It's not that simple." Hanno indicated Fabricius, who was about to disappear from view. "Maybe he's not going with the consul."

"I'd say he is, but you're right. We should make sure." Quintus strode off. "Come on, let's follow him."

Hanno hurried to catch up. "What if he's going back to Iberia?"

"We'll talk about that afterward," Quintus answered. "In that eventuality, I suppose it would make sense to split up. Otherwise, I'm traveling with you to Cisalpine Gaul."

Hanno chuckled. "You're crazy!"

"Perhaps." Quintus gave him a lopsided smile. "But I still have to do the right thing."

"And once we get there?" Hanno asked uneasily.

"We'll part company. I'll find Father, and you"—there was an awkward pause—"can seek out Hannibal's army."

Hanno gripped Quintus' arm. "Thank you."

Quintus nodded. "It's the least I can do."

The army that straggled down into the green foothills of the Alps was a shadow of what it had been. All semblance of marching formation had long gone. Gaunt-faced, hollow-cheeked figures stumbled along, holding on to each other for support. The ribs on every surviving horse and mule stood out like the bare frame of a new-built ship. Although few had died, the elephants had suffered extraordinarily too. Bostar thought that they now looked like nothing more than giant skeletons covered by sagging folds of gray skin. The heaviest toll, however, was the number of men and beasts that had been lost during the passage of the mountains. The scale of it was hard to take in, but it was impossible to deny. Hannibal had insisted on a tally as his troops entered the flat plain where, exhausted beyond belief, they had first camped. Even when a margin of error was allowed for, the count revealed that perhaps 24,000 foot soldiers and more than 5,000 pack animals had deserted, run away or perished. Approximately 26,000 men remained, just a quarter of the number that had left New Carthage, and little more than one Roman consular army.

It was a sobering figure, thought Bostar worriedly, especially when there were peoples to fight other than the Romans. He was standing with other senior officers outside the fortified walls of Taurasia. It was the main stronghold of the Taurini, the hostile tribe into whose lands Hannibal's force had descended. To his left was Sapho's phalanx, and to his right, his father's. Alete was positioned beyond Malchus. Fully half of the Libyans were present: six thousand of Hannibal's best troops.

"Gentlemen."

At the sound of Hannibal's voice, Bostar turned. He scarcely recognized the shambling figure before him, clad in a ragged military cloak. Dank tresses of brown hair fell from under a simple bronze helmet, framing a gaunt face streaked with filth. The man sported a padded linen cuirass, which had clearly seen better days, a thrusting spear and an old, battered shield. He was the worst-dressed Libyan spearman Bostar had ever seen, and he stank to high heaven. Bostar glanced at the other officers, who appeared as stunned as he. "Is that you, sir?"

The belly laugh was definitely Hannibal's. "It is. Don't look at me as if I am mad."

Bostar flushed. "Sorry, sir. May I ask why are you dressed like that?"

"Two reasons. Firstly, as an ordinary soldier, I'm far less of a target to the enemy. Secondly, being anonymous allows me to mix with the troops and assess their mood. I've been doing that since we came down out of the mountains," Hannibal revealed. He turned to include all those present. "What do you think I've heard?"

Most of the officers, Bostar included, took a sudden interest in their fingernails, or a strap on their harness that needed tightening. Even Malchus cleared his throat awkwardly.

"Come now," said Hannibal in a bluff tone. "Did you really think that I wouldn't find out how low morale really is? Spirits are high among the cavalry, but that's because I looked after them so well in the mountains. Far fewer of them died. But they're unusual. Many of the men think we'll be annihilated the first time we encounter the Romans, don't they?"

"They'll fight anyway, sir!" Malchus cried. "They love you as no other."

Hannibal's smile was warm. "Worthy Malchus, I can always rely on you and your sons. I know that your soldiers will stay true, and so will the bulk of the army. But we require an immediate victory to raise the men's spirits. More importantly, we need food to put in their bellies. Our intelligence tells me that the stores behind those walls"—he indicated the fortress—"are full of grain. I would have bought it from the Taurini, but they rejected my overtures out of hand. Now they will learn the price of their foolishness."

"What shall we do, sir?" Sapho asked eagerly.

"Take the place by storm."

"Prisoners?"

"Leave none alive. Not a man, woman or child."

Sapho's eyes lit up. "Yes, sir!"

His words were echoed by a rumble of agreement from the others.

Hannibal stared at Bostar. "What is it? Are you unhappy with my command?"

"Must everyone die, sir?" Terrible images from the fall of Saguntum filled Bostar's mind.

Hannibal scowled. "Unfortunately, yes. Know that I order this for a particular reason. We are in a very fragile position. If a Roman army presented itself tomorrow, we would indeed struggle to defeat it. When they hear of our weakness, the Boii and Insubres will think twice before giving us the aid that they so eagerly promised last year. If that happens, we will have failed in our task before it has even begun. Is that what you want?"

"Of course not, sir," Bostar replied indignantly.

"Good," said Hannibal with a pleased look. "Slaughtering the inhabitants of Taurasia will send a clear message to the area's tribes. We are still a lethal fighting force, and they either stand with us, or against us. There is no ground in between."

Humbled, Bostar glanced down. "I'm sorry, sir. I didn't understand."

"Some of the others probably didn't either," answered Hannibal, "but they didn't have the courage to ask."

"I understood, sir," Sapho snarled.

"Which is the reason you're standing here today," said Hannibal grimly. "Monomachus too." He nodded at a squat man with a bald head. "The rest of you are present because I know that, as my finest officers, you will do exactly what I have ordered." He pointed his spear at the fortress walls. "I want the place reduced by nightfall. After that, your men can have the rest they so well deserve."

Bostar joined in the cheering with more enthusiasm this time. He caught a sneering Sapho trying to catch his eye, and ignored him. He would follow Hannibal's orders, but for a very different reason from his brother. Loyalty, rather than sheer bloodthirstiness.

—✦—

Despite Quintus' generosity in accompanying him north, Hanno found the journey grating. He still had to act like a slave. Quintus rode a horse, while he had to sit astride a cantankerous mule. He could not eat with Quintus, or share the same room. Instead, he had to take his meals with the domestic slaves and servants of the roadside inns they frequented, and to bed down in the stables with the animals. Oddly, Hanno's physical separation from Quintus began to restore the invisible differences between them.

In a bizarre way, both were relieved by this. What they'd seen and heard in Rome had hammered reality home as never before, shredding the camaraderie that had developed on the farm. They were traveling to a place where there could be no friendship between Carthaginian and Roman, only combat and death. Not speaking to each other obviated the need to think about what might happen in the future. Of course their silently adopted tactic did not work. Both felt great pain at their impending separation, which in all likelihood would be permanent.

The three hundred miles from Rome to Placentia dragged by, but the pair finally reached their destination having encountered few problems. All the empty ground outside the town was taken up with vast temporary encampments, full of legionaries, socii and cavalry. The tracks were jammed with units of marching men and ox carts laden with supplies. Stalls lined the margins of every way, hawking food, wine and equipment. Soothsayers offered their services alongside blacksmiths, butchers and whores. Musicians played drums and bone whistles, acrobats jumped and tumbled, tricksters promised a cure for every ailment under the sun. Snot-nosed children darted to and fro, playing with scrawny mongrels.

It was utter chaos, thought Hanno, but there was no denying that Hannibal had set himself a Herculean task. There were already tens of thousands of Roman troops in the area.

Quintus wasted no time. He hailed a passing centurion. "Has the consul arrived from Rome?"

"You're behind the times! He got here four days ago."

Quintus was unsurprised. Unlike them, Scipio and his party would have been changing their mounts every day. "Where are his headquarters?"

The centurion gave him an odd look, but did not ask why. While young, Quintus was clearly an equestrian. He pointed down the road. "That way. It's about a mile."

Quintus nodded his thanks. "What news of Hannibal?"

Hanno stiffened. This was the question he had been burning to ask.

The centurion's face darkened. "Well, believe it or not, the whoreson succeeded in crossing the Alps. Who'd have thought it?"

"Amazing." Quintus did not want to look at Hanno in case he was gloating. "What has he been up to since?"

"He attacked the Taurini stronghold of Taurasia, and massacred its inhabitants. Apparently, he's now on his way here, to Placentia. We're blocking his route to the scumbag Boii and Insubres, see?" The centurion half drew his gladius from its scabbard and slammed it home again. "There'll be one hell of a fight very soon."

"May Mars and Jupiter keep us in the palm of their hands," said Quintus.

"Aye. Now, I'd best be off, or my tribune will string me up by my balls." With a cordial nod, the centurion marched away.

Quintus and Hanno looked at each other. Neither spoke.

"You're taking up half the fucking road. Get out of the damn way!" shouted a man leading a train of mules.

They led their mounts to one side and into a gap between two stalls.

"This is it, then," said Quintus unhappily.

"Yes," Hanno muttered. He felt awful.

"What will you do?"

Hanno shrugged. "Travel west until I run into some of our forces."

Your forces, thought Quintus, not mine. "The gods grant you a safe passage."

"Thank you. May you find your father quickly."

"I don't think that will be a problem," Quintus replied, smiling.

"Even you would find it hard to get lost now," joked Hanno.

Quintus laughed.

"I wish that we could part under different circumstances," said Hanno.

"So do I," answered Quintus passionately.

"But we both have to do our duty by our people."

"Yes."

"Maybe we'll meet again one day. In peacetime." Hanno cringed inwardly. His words sounded false even to his own ears.

Quintus did not rebuke him, however. "I would like that too, but it will never happen," he said gently. "Go well. Stay safe. May your gods protect you."

"The same to you." At last, Hanno's eyes filled with tears. Clumsily, he reached out and embraced Quintus. "Thank you for saving me and Suniaton. I will never forget that," he whispered.

Quintus' emotions welled up. He awkwardly clapped Hanno on the back. "You saved my life too, remember?"

Hanno's nod was jerky.

"Come on," said Quintus, growing businesslike. "You need to get as far from here by nightfall as you can. No point having to try and explain yourself to one of our patrols, is there?"

Hanno drew back. "No."

"Help me up." Quintus lifted his left foot.

Grateful for the distraction, Hanno linked his hands together so that Quintus could step up and climb on to his horse's back. When it was done, he forced a smile. "Farewell."

"Farewell." Quickly, Quintus pulled his horse's head around and urged it on to the roadway.

Hanno watched as his friend was swallowed up by the mass of men jostling along on the muddy track. It was only when he could no longer see Quintus that Hanno realized he had forgotten to send a last farewell to Aurelia. Sadly, he clambered aboard his mule and headed in the opposite direction. Despite the inevitability of their parting, Hanno felt a void inside. Let us never meet again, he prayed. Unless it happens in peacetime.

A hundred paces away, Quintus felt the same way. Only now could he allow himself to grieve the loss of a friend. They had been through a great deal together. If Hanno were a Roman, Quintus thought, I would be proud to stand beside him in battle. Sadly, it was only the opposite that could ever come to pass. Jupiter, Greatest and Best, never let this happen, he prayed.

⁓

Not long after, Quintus found the consul's headquarters, a large pavilion surrounded by the cavalry tent lines. The *vexillum*, a red flag on a pole, made sure that every soldier could see Scipio's position. A few questions guided Quintus in the direction of his father, whom he found outside his tent, talking to a pair of decurions. To his relief, Fabricius did not immediately explode. Instead he quietly dismissed the junior officers. The moment that they were gone, however, he rounded on Quintus. "Look who it is!" Sarcasm dripped from his voice.

"Father." Feeling distinctly nervous, Quintus dismounted. "Are you well?"

"I'm fine," Fabricius replied. His eyebrows arched. "Surprised, though. Annoyed and disappointed too. You should be at home, looking after your mother and sister, not here."

Quintus shuffled his feet.

"Not going to answer that charge?" his father snapped. "Why are you not on a ship to Iberia? After all, that's where I should be."

"I traveled to Rome first," Quintus muttered. "I was there when Scipio spoke in the Curia. I caught a glimpse of you outside."

Fabricius frowned. "Why in Jupiter's name didn't you come up to me there?"

"The press was too great to reach you, Father. I didn't know where you were staying, or even that you were heading north with the consul," Quintus lied. "I found out later. It was easy enough to follow you."

"I see. Fortuna must have been guiding your path. The tribesmen around here aren't the friendliest," said Fabricius dourly. "It's a shame that you didn't make yourself known to me in Rome. You'd already be in Capua by now, or my name isn't Gaius Fabricius." His dark eyes regarded Quintus carefully. "And so you traveled up here alone?"

Quintus cursed inwardly. This was going even worse than he'd expected. He was such a poor liar when asked a direct question. "No, Father."

"Who was with you? Gaius, probably. He listens to Martialis as little as you do to me."

"No," Quintus mumbled.

"Who, then?"

Dreading his father's response, Quintus said nothing.

Fabricius' anger bubbled over. "Answer me!"

"Hanno."

"Who?"

"One of our . . . your . . . slaves."

Fabricius' face purpled. "That's not enough! Do you expect me to remember the name of every damn one?"

"No, Father," Quintus said quickly. "He's the Carthaginian that I bought after the bear hunt."

"Oh, him. Where is the dirtbag? Putting up your tent?"

"He's not here," replied Quintus, stalling for time.

Fabricius' eyes opened wide with disbelief. "Say that again."

"He's gone, Father," Quintus whispered.

"Louder! I can't hear you!"

A passing officer glanced over, and Quintus' mortification soared. "He's gone, Father," he said loudly.

"What a surprise!" Fabricius cried. "Of course he was going to run away. What else would the dog do with a host of his countrymen so near? I bet that he waited until the very last moment before disappearing too. Congratulations! Hannibal has just gained himself another soldier."

Quintus was stung by the truth in his father's words. "It's not like that," he said quietly.

"How so?" retorted Fabricius furiously.

"Hanno didn't run away."

"He's dead then?" Fabricius demanded in a mocking tone.

"No, Father. I set him free," Quintus blurted.

"*What?*"

With ebbing confidence, Quintus repeated himself.

Astonishment and disbelief mixed with the anger on Fabricius' face. "This goes from bad to worse. How dare you?" Stepping closer, he slapped Quintus hard across the face.

He reeled backward from the force of the blow. "I'm sorry."

"It's a little late for apologies, don't you think?"

"Yes, Father."

"It is not within your power to act in this manner," Fabricius ranted. "My slaves belong to me, not you!"

"I know, Father," Quintus muttered.

"So why did you do it? What in Hades were you thinking?"

"I owed him my life."

Fabricius frowned. "You're referring to what happened at Libo's hut?"

"Yes, Father. When he came back, Hanno could easily have turned on me. Joined the bandits. Instead, he saved my life."

"That's still no reason to free him on a whim. Without my permission," Fabricius growled.

"There's more to it than that."

"I should damn well hope so!" Fabricius looked at him inquiringly. "Well?"

Quintus snatched the brief respite from his father's tirade. "Agesandros. He had it in for Hanno from the first moment I bought him. Don't you remember what happened when the Gaul hurt his leg?"

"An overenthusiastic beating is no reason to free a slave," Fabricius snapped. "If it was, there would be no servile labor in the whole damn Republic."

"I know it isn't, Father," said Quintus humbly. "But after your letter arrived in the spring, Agesandros planted a purse and a dagger among Hanno's belongings. Then he accused him of stealing them, and planning to kill us all before he fled. He was going to sell Hanno to the same owner who had bought his friend. They were to be forced to fight each other as gladiators at a munus, he said. And it was all a complete lie!"

Fabricius thought for a moment. "What did your mother have to say?"

"She believed Agesandros," Quintus answered reluctantly.

"Which should have been good enough for you," Fabricius thundered.

"But he was lying, Father!"

Fabricius' brows lowered. "Why would Agesandros lie?"

"I don't know, Father. But I'm certain that Hanno is no murderer!"

"You can't *know* something like that," replied Fabricius dryly. Quintus took heart from the fact that some of the rage had gone from his voice. "Never trust a slave totally."

Quintus rallied his courage. "In that case, how can you depend on Agesandros' word?"

"He's served me well for more than twenty years," his father replied, a trifle defensively.

"So you'd trust him over me?"

"Watch your mouth!" Fabricius snapped. There was a short pause. "Start at the beginning. Leave nothing out."

Quintus realized that he had been granted a stay of execution. Taking a deep breath, he began. Remarkably, his father did not interrupt at all, even when Quintus related how Aurelia had set a fire in the granary, and how he and Gaius had freed Suniaton. When he fell silent, Fabricius stood, tapping his foot on the ground for several moments. "Why did you decide to help the other Carthaginian?"

"Because Hanno would not leave without him," Quintus answered. Then he added, passionately, "He is my friend. I couldn't betray him."

"Hold on!" interrupted Fabricius, ire creeping back into his voice. "We're not talking about Gaius here. Freeing a slave without the permission of his owner is a crime, and you have done it twice over! This is a very serious matter."

Quintus quailed before his father's fury. "Of course, Father. I'm sorry."

"Both of the slaves are long gone, if they have any sense," mused Fabricius. "Thanks to your impetuosity, I have been left more than a hundred didrachms out of pocket. So has the official's son in Capua."

Quintus wanted to say that Gaius had tried to buy Suniaton, but his father's temper was at fraying point. Buttoning his lip, he nodded miserably.

"As your father, I am entitled to punish you how I choose," Fabricius warned. "Even to strike you dead."

"I'm at your mercy, Father," said Quintus, closing his eyes. Whatever might happen next, he was still glad that he'd let Hanno go.

"Although you and your sister have behaved outrageously, I heard the truth in your words—or at least the belief that you were speaking the truth. In other words, you did what you thought was right."

Startled, Quintus opened his eyes. "Yes, Father. So did Aurelia."

"Which is why we'll say no more about it for the moment. The matter is far from settled, however." Fabricius pursed his lips. "And Agesandros will have some explaining to do when next I see him."

I hope I'm there to see that, thought Quintus, his own anger at the Sicilian resurfacing.

"You still haven't explained why you abandoned your mother and sister to make your way here." Fabricius pinned him with a hard stare.

"I thought the war might be over in a few months, like Flaccus said, Father. I didn't want to miss it," Quintus said lamely.

"And that's a good enough reason to disobey my orders, is it?"

"No," Quintus replied, flushing an ever deeper shade of red.

"Yet that's precisely what you did!" accused his father. He stared off into the distance. "It's not as if I haven't got enough on my plate at the moment."

"I'll get out of your way. Return home," Quintus whispered.

"You'll do no such thing! The situation is far too dangerous." Fabricius saw his surprise. "Scipio has decided to lead his forces over the river Padus, into hostile territory. A temporary bridge has already been thrown over to the far bank. Tomorrow morning, we march westward, toward Hannibal's army. No Roman forces are to be left behind, and the local Gauls can't be trusted. You'd have your throat cut within five miles of here."

"What shall I do, then?" asked Quintus despondently.

"You will have to come with us," his father replied, equally unhappily. "You'll be safe in our camp until an opportunity presents itself to send you back to Capua."

Quintus' spirits fell even further. The shame of it! To have reached Scipio's army only to be prevented from fighting. It wasn't that surprising, though. His actions had stretched his father's goodwill to the limit. At least Hanno had got away, Quintus thought, counting himself lucky that Fabricius hadn't given him a good hiding.

"Fabricius? Where are you?" cried a booming voice.

"Mars above, that's all I need," muttered Fabricius.

Astounded by his father's reaction, Quintus turned to see Flaccus emerge into view.

"There you are! Scipio wants another meeting about—" Flaccus stopped in astonishment. "Quintus? What a pleasant surprise!"

Quintus grinned guiltily. At least someone was pleased to see him.

"You sent for Quintus, I presume?" Flaccus didn't wait for Fabricius to answer. "What an excellent idea! His timing is impeccable too." He raised a clenched fist at Quintus. "Tomorrow, we're going to teach those bastard guggas a lesson they'll never forget."

"I didn't send for him," answered Fabricius stiffly. "He saw fit to leave his mother and sister on their own and turn up here without so much as a by-your-leave."

"The rashness of youth!" demurred Flaccus with a smile. "Nonetheless, you'll let him ride out with us in the morning?"

"I hadn't planned on it, no," said Fabricius curtly.

"What?" Flaccus threw him an incredulous look. "And deny your son a chance to blood himself? To take part in what could be one of our greatest cavalry victories ever? Scipio's boy is to come along, and he's no older than Quintus here."

"It's not that."

"What is it, then?"

"It's none of your concern," said Fabricius angrily.

Flaccus barely blinked at the rebuff. "Come now," he cajoled. "Unless the lad has committed murder, surely he should be allowed to be part of this golden opportunity? This could be the glowing start to his career—a career that will only blossom once your family is allied to the Minucii."

Furious, Fabricius considered his options. They were in this situation purely because of Flaccus' pushiness, yet it would look rude now for him to turn down Flaccus' proposal. It might also jeopardize Quintus' chances of advancement. Even when wedded to Aurelia, Flaccus would be under no legal obligation to help his brother-in-law. It was all down to goodwill. He made a show of looking pleased. "Very well. I'll ask the consul for his permission to let Quintus join my unit."

"Excellent!" cried Flaccus. "Scipio won't turn down a cavalryman of your son's quality."

Quintus couldn't believe the change in his fortunes. "Thank you," he said, grinning at both men. "I won't let you down, Father."

"Consider yourself lucky," Fabricius growled. He stabbed a finger into Quintus' chest. "You're not out of trouble yet either."

"The glory he'll win tomorrow will make you forget anything he's done," declared Flaccus, giving Quintus a broad wink. "Now, we'd best not keep Scipio waiting any longer."

"True," replied Fabricius. He pointed at a nearby tent. "There's an empty space in that one. Tell the men in it that I said you were to bunk in with them. We'll get you some equipment later."

"Yes, Father. Thank you."

Fabricius did not reply.

"Until tomorrow," said Flaccus. "We'll cover the field with gugga bodies!"

Instantly, an image of Hanno appeared in Quintus' mind's eye. Forcing a grin, he did his best to shove it away. Defeating the Carthaginians was all that mattered, he told himself.

XIX

REUNION

Hanno did not dare to try crossing the makeshift bridge over the Padus with his mount. He had tempted fate enough by riding out of the camp alone on his mule, a likely slave. There had to be at least two centuries of legionaries guarding the road that ran up to the crossing. No matter how dull their duty, Hanno doubted that they were stupid enough to let a dark-skinned man who spoke accented Latin pass by without question. He therefore rode west along the southern bank, searching for a suitable place to ford the river.

Winter gales had stripped the leaves from the trees, leaving the flat landscape stark and bare. It made it easy to spot movement of any kind. This suited Hanno down to the ground. Unarmed apart from a dagger, he had no desire to meet anyone until he crossed the river into the territory of the Insubres. They were mostly hostile toward the Romans. Even there, however, Hanno wanted to avoid human contact. In reality, he could trust no one but his own people, or the soldiers who fought for them. Although he was by no means safe yet, Hanno could not help feeling exhilarated. He could almost sense the presence of Hannibal's army nearby.

Hanno hardly dared to wonder if his own father and brothers were still alive, or with the Carthaginian forces. There was absolutely no way of telling. For all he knew, they could yet be in Iberia. Maybe they had been posted back to Carthage. What would he do if that were the case? Whom would he report to? At that moment, Hanno did not overly care. He had escaped, and, gods willing, would soon place himself under Hannibal's command: another soldier of Carthage.

For two days and nights, Hanno traveled west. He avoided settlements and farms, camping rough in dips and hollows where there was little chance of being discovered. Despite the severe cold, he forbore from lighting fires. His blankets were sufficient to prevent frostbite, but not to allow much sleep. It didn't matter. Staying alert now was critical. Despite Hanno's weariness, each new day of freedom felt better than the last.

His luck continued to hold. Early on the third day, Hanno reached a crossing point over the Padus. A collection of small huts huddled around the ford, but there was no one about. The days were short, and work on the land had ceased until spring. Like most peasants at this time of year, the inhabitants went to bed shortly after sunset and rose late. Nonetheless, Hanno felt very vulnerable as he stripped off by the water's edge. Placing his clothing in his pack, he rolled up the oiled leather tightly and tied it with thongs. Then, naked as the day he was born, he led the protesting mule into the river. The water was shockingly cold. Hanno knew that if they didn't cross it fast, his muscles would freeze up and he would drown. Winter rainfall ensured that its level was high, however, and for a time, his mount struggled against the current. Hanno, who was holding on to its reins and swimming as hard as he could, felt panic swelling in his chest. Thankfully, the mule possessed enough strength to carry them both into the shallows on the far side, and from there, on to the bank. The biting wind struck Hanno savagely, setting his teeth to chattering. Fortunately, only a small amount of water had entered his pack, meaning that his clothes were mostly dry. He dressed quickly. Then, wrapping his blanket around himself for extra warmth, he remounted and resumed his journey.

The day wore on and Hanno's excitement grew. He was deep in Insubres territory; Hannibal's army could not be far away. Since he'd been captured by the pirates, it had seemed impossible that he would ever be in such a position. Thanks to Quintus, it was now a reality. Hanno prayed that his friend would come through the impending war unharmed. Naturally enough, he quickly returned to thoughts of a reunion with his family. For the first time, Hanno's attention lapsed.

A short time later, he was brought back to reality with a jolt. Halfway down into a hollow, Hanno heard a blackbird sounding its alarm call, sharp and insistent. Scanning the trees on either side, he could see no reason for its distress. Yet birds did not react like that without cause. Acid-tipped claws of fear clutched at his belly. This was the perfect place for an ambush. For bandits to attack and murder a lone traveler.

Terror filled Hanno as, in the same instant, a pair of javelins scudded out of the bushes to his left and flew over his head. Praying that his attackers were on foot, he dug his heels into his mule's sides. It responded to his fear, and pounded gamely up out of the dip. Several more javelins hissed into the air behind them, but when Hanno glanced over his shoulder, his hopes vanished entirely. A group of mounted figures had emerged from the cover on each side. Six of them at least, and on horses. There was no chance of outriding his pursuers on a mule. Hanno cursed savagely. This was surely the cruelest turn of fate since he'd been washed out to sea. To have gone through all that he had, only to be murdered by a bunch of brigands a few miles from where Hannibal's forces lay.

He wasn't surprised when more horses and riders appeared on the road ahead, blocking it entirely. Gripping the dagger that was his solitary weapon, Hanno prepared to sell his life dearly. As the horsemen approached, however, his heart leaped. He had not seen any Numidian cavalry since leaving Carthage, but there could be no mistaking their identity. What other mounted troops scorned the use of saddles, bridles and bits? Or wore open-sided tunics even in winter?

Even as he opened his mouth to greet the Numidians, another flurry of javelins was hurled in his direction. This time, two barely missed him. Frantically, Hanno raised both his hands in the air, palms outward. "Stop! I am Carthaginian," he shouted in his native tongue. "I am Carthaginian!"

His cry made no difference. More spears were launched, and this time one struck his mule in the rump. Rearing in pain, it threw Hanno to the ground. The air shot from his lungs, winding him. He was vaguely aware of his mount trotting away, limping heavily. Within the blink of an eye, he had been surrounded by a ring of jeering Numidians. Three jumped down and approached, javelins at the ready. What a way to die, Hanno thought bitterly. Killed by my own side because they don't even speak my language.

From nowhere, inspiration hit him. He'd learned a few words of the sibilant Numidian tongue once. "Stop," Hanno mumbled. "I . . . friend."

Looking confused, the trio of Numidians paused. A barrage of questions in their tongue followed. Hanno barely understood one word in ten of what the warriors were saying. "I not Roman, I friend," he repeated, over and over.

His protests weren't enough. Drawing back his foot, one of the tribesmen kicked Hanno in the belly. Stars flashed across his vision, and he nearly passed out from the pain. More blows landed, and he tensed, expecting at any moment to feel a javelin slide into his flesh.

Instead, an angry voice intervened.

The beating stopped at once.

Warily, Hanno looked up to see a rider with tightly curled black hair standing before him. Unusually for a Numidian, he was wearing a sword. An officer, thought Hanno dully.

"Did I hear you speaking Carthaginian?" the man demanded.

"Yes." Relieved and surprised that someone present spoke his tongue, Hanno sat up. He winced in pain. "I'm from Carthage."

The other's eyebrows rose. "What in Melqart's name are you doing alone in the middle of this godforsaken, freezing land?"

"I was sold into slavery among the Romans some time ago," explained Hanno. "Hearing the news of Hannibal's invasion, I escaped to join him."

The Numidian didn't look convinced. "Who are you?"

"My name is Hanno," he said proudly. "I am a son of Malchus, who serves as a senior officer among our Libyan spearmen. If I reach Hannibal's army, I hope to be reunited with him, and my brothers."

There was a long silence, and Hanno felt his fear return. Do not desert me now, great Tanit, he prayed.

"An unlikely story. Who's to say that you are not a spy?" the officer mused out loud. Several of his more eager men lifted their javelins, and Hanno's heart sank. If they killed him now, no one would ever know.

"Hold!" snapped the officer. "If this man has really spent much time among the Romans, he may be useful to Hannibal." He grinned at Hanno. "And if you are telling the truth, I suspect that your father, whether he is with the army or no, would rather see you alive than dead."

Hanno's joy knew no bounds. "Thank you," he said.

The officer barked an order and the Numidians swarmed in, hauling Hanno to his feet. His wrists were bound with rope, but he was offered no further violence. As the warriors mounted up, Hanno was picked up and thrown roughly across the neck of a horse, in front of its rider. He didn't protest. With his mule injured, there was no other way of returning to the Carthaginian camp at speed. At least they weren't dragging him behind one of the mounts.

As the Numidians began to ride west, Hanno gave thanks to every god he could think of, but most importantly to Tanit, whom he'd forgotten to address before leaving his home in Carthage.

He wasn't out of the woods yet, but he felt that she was smiling on him once more.

—⁓—

Upon reaching Hannibal's camp, Hanno was lowered to the ground. He gazed around him in wonderment, absolutely exhilarated to see a Carthaginian host so near the Italian border. His heart throbbed with an unquenchable joy. He was back with his people! Yet Hanno was concerned by the army's size. It was far smaller than he'd expected. He was alarmed too by the soldiers' faces. Suffering was etched deep into every single one. Most had unkempt beards, and looked half starved. The pack animals, and particularly the elephants, looked even worse. Hanno shot a worried glance at the Numidian officer. "The crossing of the Alps must have been terrible," he said.

"You cannot even imagine it," the Numidian replied with a scowl. "Hostile natives. Landslides. Ice. Snow. Starvation. Between desertions and fatalities, we lost nearly twenty-five thousand men in a month. Practically half our army."

Hanno's mouth fell open in horror. Immediately, he thought of his father and brothers, who could easily be among the dead. He caught the Numidian watching him. "Why tell me this?" he stuttered.

"I can say what I like. The Romans will never find out," replied the other amiably. "It's not as if you could escape my men on foot."

Hanno swallowed. "No."

"Just as well you were telling the truth about who you were, eh?"

Hanno met the Numidian's gimlet stare. A sudden pang of terror struck him. What if no one could be found to vouch for his identity? "Yes, it is," he snapped, praying that the gods would not dash the cup of success from his lips at this late stage. "Take me to the Libyans' tent lines."

With a mocking bow, the Numidian led the way. He hailed the first spearman they met. "We are looking for an officer by the name of . . ." He looked questioningly at Hanno.

"Malchus."

To Hanno's utter joy, the man jerked a thumb behind him. "His tent is three ranks back. It's bigger than the rest."

"So far, so good," said the officer, dismounting gracefully. He indicated that Hanno should follow him. Three of his warriors took up the rear, their javelins at the ready. Carefully, they weaved their way between the closely packed tents.

"This looks like the one." The officer came to a halt outside a large leather pavilion. It was held up by multiple guy ropes staked into the ground. A pair of spearmen stood on guard outside.

A volcanic wave of emotion battered Hanno. Terror that his father would not be within. Joy that he might. Relief that, after all his ordeals, he was perhaps about to be reunited with his family. He turned to the officer. "Stay here."

"Eh? You're not in charge," the Numidian growled. "Until I hear otherwise, you're a damn prisoner."

"My hands are tied! Where am I going to go?" Hanno snapped back. "Stick a fucking spear in my back if I even try. But I'm walking over there on my own."

The Numidian saw the steel in Hanno's eyes. Suddenly, he realized that his captive might outrank him considerably. There was a gruff nod. "We'll wait here," he said.

Hanno made no acknowledgment. Stiff-backed, he walked toward the tent.

One of the spearmen started forward. "What's your business?" he demanded in a brusque tone.

"Are these Malchus' quarters?" asked Hanno politely.

"Who wants to know?" came the surly reply.

The last of Hanno's patience ran out. "Damn your insolence," he snarled. "Father? Are you there?"

The spearman, who had advanced a step, stopped in his tracks.

"Father?" called Hanno again.

Someone coughed inside the tent. "Bostar? Is that you?"

Hanno began to grin uncontrollably. Bostar had also survived!

An instant later, Malchus emerged, fully dressed for battle. He looked at his guards first, and frowned. "Who called my name?"

"It was I, Father," answered Hanno joyfully, stepping forward. "I have returned."

Malchus went as white as a sheet. "H-Hanno?" he stuttered.

With tears of happiness filling his eyes, Hanno nodded.

"Praise all the gods. This is a miracle!" cried Malchus. "But what are you doing, tied up like this?"

Hanno jerked his head at the Numidians, who were looking decidedly awkward. "They weren't sure whether to believe my story or not."

Drawing his dagger, Malchus sawed at the ropes that bound Hanno's wrists. The instant they had dropped away, he drew his son into his arms. Great shudders of emotion racked his frame, and for long moments, he clung to Hanno with a grip of iron. Hanno delightedly returned the embrace. Finally, Malchus stepped back to study him. "It is you," he breathed. A rare smile split his face. "How you've grown. You're a man!"

In contrast, Hanno could not get over how his father had aged. Deep lines now creased his forehead and cheeks. There were bags of exhaustion under his eyes, and his hair was more gray than black. But Malchus had a new lightness about him, an air Hanno had not seen since well before his mother's death. It was, he realized with a thrill, because of his return. "I heard you call out Bostar's name. Is Sapho here too?"

"Yes, yes, they both are. The pair of them should be back any moment," Malchus replied, filling Hanno with more joy. He glanced at the Numidians. "To whom do I owe my thanks?"

Saluting, the officer hurried forward. "Zamar, section leader, at your service, sir."

"Where did you find him?"

"About ten miles east of here, sir." Zamar shot an uneasy glance at Hanno. "I'm sorry for the rough treatment, sir."

"It's all right," Hanno replied. "Your men couldn't be expected to know that I was Carthaginian. At least you stopped them from killing me, and listened to my story."

Zamar dipped his head in gratitude.

"Wait here," ordered Malchus. Hurrying into the tent, he emerged with a large leather purse. "A token of my appreciation," he said, handing it over.

Zamar's eyes widened as he accepted the clinking gift, and his men exchanged excited looks. It didn't matter what was inside. The bag's obvious weight spoke volumes. "Thank you, sir. I am delighted to have been of service." Zamar made a deep bow, and withdrew.

"Come inside," Malchus muttered. Ushering Hanno within, he fussed over him as he hadn't done in years. "Are you hungry? Thirsty?"

Gratefully accepting a cup of wine, Hanno took a seat on a three-legged stool he remembered from their house in Carthage. Malchus sat opposite. Neither could take their eyes off the other, or stop smiling. "It's wonderful to see you," Hanno said.

"Likewise," Malchus murmured. "I had given you up for dead. To first of all survive a storm at sea ... well, Melqart must have laid his hand upon you and Suniaton." His brows lowered. "Is Suni dead?"

Hanno grinned. "No! He couldn't travel because he was injured, but he is being cared for by a friend. Soon he will be making his way to Carthage."

Malchus' frown cleared. "The gods be thanked. Now, you must tell me what happened."

Hanno laughed. "I could say the same thing, Father, seeing you here, on the wrong side of the Alps."

"That is a story worth hearing," Malchus agreed. "But I want to listen to yours first." He cocked his head. The sound of approaching voices carried inside, and he smiled. "I guess it will have to wait a while. You won't want to be telling it twice."

Hanno's face lit up. "Is that Sapho and Bostar?"

"Yes." His father winked. "Just sit there. Don't say a word until they see you."

Hanno watched excitedly as Malchus moved toward the front of the tent.

A moment later, two familiar figures entered. Hanno had to grip his stool to stop himself leaping up to greet them. "Good news, Father. Apparently, more than ten thousand Gaulish warriors are on their way to join us," Bostar announced.

"Excellent news," Malchus replied offhandedly.

"Aren't you pleased?" asked Sapho.

"We have an unexpected visitor."

Sapho snorted. "Who could be more interesting than that information?"

Silently, Malchus turned and indicated Hanno.

Sapho blanched. "Hanno?"

"No!" Bostar exclaimed. "It cannot be true!"

Hanno could not contain himself any longer. He leaped up and ran to greet his brothers. Laughing and crying at the same time, Bostar wrapped him in a huge bear hug. "We thought you were dead."

Laughing too, Hanno managed to extricate himself from Bostar's grip. "I should be, but the gods did not forget me." He reached out to Sapho, who awkwardly drew him into an embrace. Surely he can't still be angry about what happened in Carthage? Hanno wondered.

Sapho stepped back after only a moment. "How in hell did you get here?" he cried.

"Where is Suniaton?" Bostar demanded.

A stream of questions poured from their lips.

Malchus intervened. "Let him tell the whole story."

Hanno cleared his throat. All he could think of was the manner in which he'd left the family house on that fateful morning. He looked guiltily at Malchus. "I'm sorry, Father," he said. "I ought never to have run off like that. I should have stayed to do my duty."

"The meeting was of small consequence anyway. Like most of them," Malchus admitted with a sigh. "If I had been more understanding, you might have been less bored by such things. Put it behind you, and tell us how you survived that storm."

Taking a deep breath, Hanno began. His father and brothers hung off his every word. When he explained how he and Suniaton had been captured by the pirates, Sapho let out a grim chuckle. "They got their just desserts eventually."

"Eh?" Hanno gave his brother a confused look.

"I'll explain later," said Malchus. "Go on."

Quelling his curiosity, Hanno obeyed. His family's fury over the pirates was as nothing compared with their reaction to his purchase by Quintus.

"Roman bastard!" Sapho spat. "I'd love to have him here right now."

Hanno was surprised by the defensive feelings that flared up at once. "Not all Romans are bad. If it wasn't for him and his sister, I wouldn't be here."

Sapho scoffed. Even Bostar looked unconvinced. Malchus alone did not react.

"It's true," Hanno cried. "You haven't heard all of my story yet."

"True," admitted Bostar.

Sapho raised an eyebrow. "Surprise us," he said.

Amazed by the speed at which his customary anger toward his eldest brother had returned, Hanno continued with his story. He emphasized how Quintus had engineered not only his escape, but that of Suniaton, and how the young equestrian had accompanied him to Cisalpine Gaul rather than be reunited with his father in Rome.

"He sounds like a decent person. So does his sister, for all that she is a child. That in turn means that their father must be an honorable man," Malchus agreed. His jaw hardened. "It is a shame that the Roman Senate does not possess the same morals. You heard from the horse's mouth how the whoresons demanded Hannibal be handed over to receive Roman 'justice,' how they lied about us breaking the treaty which confined us to the area below the River Iberus. Their arrogance is without parallel! That's before dragging up Sicily, Sardinia and Corsica."

Sapho and Bostar growled in agreement.

Hanno felt a momentary sadness. Yet it was time to forget the kindness he had received. His father's words had made old resentment bubble up from the depths. He took a deep breath and exhaled slowly. Finally, I am where I longed to be, he thought. With my family. With Hannibal's army. And I am a soldier of Carthage. The Romans are our enemies. So be it. "You're right, Father. What is Hannibal's plan?"

Malchus gave him a wolfish smile. "To attack! We continue our march east tomorrow, in search of their legions."

"I know exactly where they are," Hanno replied, trying, and failing, not to think of Quintus.

"We'd best take you to Hannibal then," said Malchus, looking pleased.

"Really?"

"Of course. He'll want to hear everything you know."

Hanno turned to his brothers. "I'm to meet Hannibal!" he cried delightedly. Bostar grinned, but Hanno caught Sapho shooting him a sour glance. Old emotions flared up yet again. "What?" he demanded. "Are you not pleased?"

Sapho blinked. "Yes," he muttered.

"It doesn't look like it," said Hanno hotly.

"That's because he isn't," Bostar growled. "Our older brother gets jealous of anyone who might win favor from our general."

The veins in Sapho's neck bulged with fury. "Fuck you," he snapped.

"Sapho!" shouted Malchus. "Curb your tongue! You too, Bostar. Can we not forget our differences for once, on this most joyful of days?"

Shame-faced, Sapho and Bostar nodded.

Taking Hanno by the hand, Malchus led him away. "Come on," he ordered over his shoulder. Pointedly ignoring each other, Sapho and Bostar followed.

Hanno couldn't get over the level of animosity between his brothers.

What on earth had happened between them? He was amazed too at the ease with which Sapho still got his back up. Seeing Hannibal's tent in the distance, Hanno put his concerns from his mind. He was going to meet the finest Carthaginian general in history. The man who dared to attack Rome on its own territory.

With a ragtag, half-starved army, his cynical side added. Hanno could not let go of this worrying thought as his father led him and his brothers onward. How could they ever match the numbers of soldiers Rome could call upon?

Soon they had reached a large open area before their general's headquarters. The place was thronged. Hanno's eyes widened. Flanking the perimeter were hundreds of soldiers from all over the Mediterranean, men whom he'd heard much about, but never seen. Numidian and Iberian infantry mixed with Lusitanians. Spiky-haired, bare-chested Gauls stood shoulder to shoulder with Balearic slingers and Ligurian warriors. There were several nationalities of cavalrymen: Iberian, Gaulish and Numidian. Outside the main tent stood a large group of senior officers, resplendent in their polished muscled cuirasses, pteryges and crested helmets. Hannibal's purple cloak made him easy to pick out. A group of musicians was positioned nearby, their instruments at the ready: curved ceramic horns and *carnyxes*, vertical trumpets made of bronze, each topped by a depiction of a wild boar.

Hanno glanced at his father. "What's going on?"

Even Sapho and Bostar looked confused.

Frustratingly, Malchus did not answer. He walked on, up to the party of officers. A quick word in the ear of one of Hannibal's bodyguards saw them led straight to their leader's side. Recognizing Malchus, Hannibal smiled. Hanno felt as if he were in a dream come true.

Malchus saluted. "A word, if I may, sir?"

"Of course. Make it quick, though," Hannibal replied.

"Yes, sir. You know two of my sons, Sapho and Bostar," said Malchus. "But there is a third, Hanno."

Hannibal gave Hanno a curious look. "I seem to remember a tragedy at sea in which he'd been lost."

"You have a fine memory, sir. I discovered afterward, however, that by some miracle, Hanno had not been drowned. Instead, he and his friend were found adrift by some pirates. They sold both into slavery. In Italy."

Hannibal's eyebrows rose. "This couldn't be him?"

Malchus grinned. "It is, sir."

"Gods above!" Hannibal exclaimed. "Come here!"

Self-conscious in his ragged, filthy clothes, Hanno did as he was told.

Hannibal appraised him for several, breath-holding moments. "You have the look of Malchus all right."

Hanno didn't dare reply. His heart was thumping off his ribs like that of a wild bird.

"How did you escape?"

"My owner's son let me go, sir."

"Did he, by Melqart's beard? Why?"

"I saved his life once, sir."

"Intriguing." Hannibal stroked his chin. "Have you traveled far?"

"No, sir. He released me near Placentia."

"You are welcome. Your father and brothers are valuable officers. I hope that you will be too."

Hanno made an awkward half-bow. "I will do my best, sir."

Hannibal made a gesture of dismissal.

"Wait, sir," said Malchus eagerly. "Hanno's awe at meeting you has curdled his brains. He didn't say that Placentia is where Scipio and his army were camped."

Hannibal's face came alive with interest. "Scipio, you say? One of the Scipiones?"

"Yes, sir," Hanno replied, aware that every officer within earshot was now listening. "After missing you at the Rhodanus, he returned to Italy with all speed."

There was a general gasp of dismay.

"Has he brought his entire army with him?" asked Hannibal softly.

"No, sir. He sent it to Iberia, under the command of his brother."

"A shrewd general, then." Hannibal let out a slow breath. "Hasdrubal and Hanno will also have a fight on their hands. It is to be expected, I suppose." He fixed Hanno with his dark eyes again. "What of Scipio now?"

"He has thrown a bridge over the Padus, and was intending to march west on the day I fled."

Hannibal leaned forward. "When was that?"

"Three days ago, sir."

"So he cannot be far away. Excellent news!" Hannibal smacked a fist into his palm. "What of his forces?"

Hanno did his best to recount all that he had seen and heard since leaving Rome.

"Well done, young man," said Hannibal when he was done, making Hanno flush beetroot. "We shall face the first of our great tests soon. What we are about to observe now seems even more apt. Stay here with me and watch, if you will."

Stuttering his thanks, Hanno stood with Hannibal, Malchus and his brothers and watched as dozens of prisoners were led out into the open area before them.

"Who are they?" Hanno asked.

"Allobroges and Vocontii, prisoners taken during the passage of the Alps," replied his father.

Hanno's stomach clenched. The men looked terrified.

A fanfare from the musicians' horns and carnyxes prevented any further conversation. Hannibal stood forth when it finished. At once an expectant hush fell over the gathered troops. Everyone watched as a line of slaves carried out bronze trays, some of which were laden with glittering mail shirts. On others, helmets were piled high. There were gold arm rings and torcs, fine cloaks decorated with wolf fur and gilt-handled swords.

Hannibal let the prisoners feast their eyes on the treasure before he spoke. "You have been brought here to make a simple choice." He paused to allow his message to be relayed to the captives. "I will offer six men the chance to win their freedom. You will divide into pairs, and fight each other to the death. The three who survive will receive a good horse, their choice of everything on show and a guarantee that they will ride out of here unharmed. Those who do not volunteer will be sold as slaves." Again Hannibal waited.

A moment later, the warriors began shouting and raising their clenched fists in the air.

The lead interpreter turned to Hannibal. "They all want the honor, sir. Every last one."

Hannibal smiled broadly. "Announce that to my troops," he ordered.

A loud sigh of appreciation rose from the watching soldiers as the Allobroges' reply was translated.

Malchus bent to whisper in Hanno's ear. "Single combat to the death is much revered among the Gauls. This end is far superior to a life of slavery."

Hanno still didn't understand.

"I will not allow every man to do this," Hannibal proclaimed. "Form up in two lines." He waited as the prisoners were shoved into position. "Pick out every fourth man until you have six," he bellowed. His command was obeyed at once, and the remainder of the captives were shepherded to one side. The half-dozen warriors who had been chosen were each handed a sword and shield and, at a signal, were ordered to begin fighting. They went at each other like men possessed, and soon first blood had been spilled on the rock-hard ground.

"What's the point of this?" Sapho muttered after a few moments. "We should just kill them all and have done."

"Your damn response to everything," Bostar retorted angrily.

"Shhh!" hissed Malchus. "Hannibal does nothing by accident."

Again Hanno was surprised by the degree of acrimony between his brothers, but he was granted no chance to dwell on this troubling development.

The duels were short, and savage. Before long, three bloodied warriors stood over the bodies of their opponents, waiting for Hannibal's promise to be fulfilled. And it was. Each man was allowed his choice of the rich goods on the trays, before selecting a horse from those tethered nearby. Then, with the cheers of everyone present ringing in their ears, they were allowed to leave.

"Even more than this can be yours," shouted Hannibal to his men. "For you the prize of victory is not to possess horses and cloaks, but to be the most envied of mankind, masters of all the wealth of Rome."

The immense roar that followed his words rose high into the winter sky.

Impressed by Hannibal's tactic, Hanno glanced at Bostar.

"He will take us to the enemy's very gates," said his brother.

"That's right," declared Malchus.

"Where we'll slaughter every last one of the whoresons," Sapho snarled.

Hanno's spirits soared. Rome *would* be defeated. He felt sure of it.

XX

SETBACKS

S ome days later, Quintus was huddled around a campfire with a group of his new comrades. It was a dank, cold afternoon. A gusty wind set lowering clouds scudding over the camp, threatening snow and increasing the general misery.

"I still can't believe it," moaned Licinius, a garrulous Tarentine who was one of Quintus' tent mates. "To have lost our first battle against the guggas. It's shameful."

"It was only a skirmish," said Quintus morosely.

"Maybe so," agreed Calatinus, another of the men who shared their tent. Sturdily built, he was a year older than Quintus, but of similar outlook. "It was a damn big one, though. I bet you're all glad to be sitting here now, eh?" He nodded as his companions shook their heads in agreement. "Look at our casualties! Most of our cavalry and hundreds of *velites* killed. Six hundred legionaries taken prisoner, and Scipio gravely injured. Hardly a good start, was it?"

"Too true," said Cincius, their last tent mate, a huge, ruddy-faced man with a shock of red hair. "We've also retreated since. What must Hannibal think of us?"

"Why in Hades did we even pull back?" Licinius demanded. "After the bridge had been destroyed, the Carthaginians had no way of crossing the Ticinus to get at us."

Calatinus made sure no one else was in earshot. "I reckon the consul panicked. It's not surprising, really, with him being out of action and all."

"How would you know what Scipio thinks?" Quintus challenged irritably. "He's far from a fool."

"As if you'd know what the consul's like, new boy," Cincius snapped.

Quintus scowled, but had the wisdom not to reply. Cincius looked ready for a fight, and he was twice Quintus' size.

"Why didn't Scipio take his chance when Hannibal offered battle before our camp?" Cincius went on. "What an opportunity to miss, eh?"

There was a gloomy mutter of agreement.

"I say it's downright cowardly," said Cincius, warming to his theme.

Quintus' anger flared. "It's best to fight on the ground of one's choosing, at a time of one's choosing," he declared, remembering what his father had said. "You all know that! At the moment, we can do neither, and with Scipio injured, that position is unlikely to change in the near future. It made far more sense to remain in a position of security, here in the camp. Consider what might happen otherwise."

Cincius glared at Quintus, but, seeing the others subside into a grumpy silence, chose to say no more for the moment.

Quintus felt no happier. While Scipio's courage was in little doubt, that of Flaccus was a different matter. It had taken a sea change in his view of his prospective brother-in-law as a hero even to countenance such a thought, but the reality of what had happened at the Ticinus could not be denied. Flaccus had ridden out with the cavalry on the ill-fated reconnaissance mission at his own request. Still ecstatic about being allowed to accompany the patrol, Quintus had been there too. He and his father had seen Flaccus as the clash began, but not after that. He hadn't reappeared until afterward, when the battered remnants of the patrol retreated over the River Ticinus and reached the Roman camp. Apparently, he'd been swept out of harm's way by the tide of battle. Seeing that the Carthaginians had the upper hand, Flaccus had ridden for help. Naturally, the senior tribunes had declined to lead their legions, an infantry force, across a temporary bridge to face an enemy entirely made up of cavalry. What else could he have done? Flaccus had earnestly asked.

Of course there was no way of questioning Flaccus' account. Events were moving apace. They would just have to accept it. While Fabricius had not said as much to Quintus, he was clearly troubled by the possibility that Flaccus was a coward. Quintus felt the same way. Although he'd been terrified during the fight, at least he had stood his ground and fought the enemy. Aurelia must not marry a man, however well connected, who did not stick by his comrades in battle. Quintus poked a stick into the fire and tried not to think about it. He was annoyed to realize that the others had resumed their doleful conversation.

"My groom was drinking with some of the legionaries who guard Scipio's tent," said Licinius. "They said that a huge Carthaginian fleet has attacked Lilybaeum in Sicily."

"No!" exclaimed Cincius.

Licinius nodded mournfully. "There's no question of Sempronius Longus coming to our relief now."

"How can you be so sure?" demanded Quintus.

"The soldiers swore on their mothers' graves it was true."

Quintus gave him a dubious look. "Why haven't we heard it from anyone else, then?"

"It's supposed to be top secret," muttered Licinius.

"Well, *I* heard that the entire Boii tribe is marching north to join Hannibal," interjected Cincius. "If that's right, we'll be caught in a pincer attack between them and the guggas."

Quintus remembered what his father had told him. A monstrous calf, which was somehow turned inside out to expose all of its internal organs, had been cut out of a cow that could not give birth on a farm nearby. The damn thing had been alive too. An officer whom Fabricius knew had seen it while on patrol. Stop it, thought Quintus, setting his jaw. "Let's not get overexcited," he advised. "These stories are all too farfetched."

"Are they? What if the gods are angry with us?" retorted Licinius. "I went to the temple of Placentia to make an offering yesterday, and the priests said that the sacred chickens would not eat. What better evidence do you need?"

Quintus' anger overflowed. "Should we just surrender to Hannibal?"

Licinius flushed. "Of course not!"

Quintus rounded on Cincius, who shook his head. "Shut your damn mouths, then! Talk like that is terrible for morale. We're equestrians, remember? The ordinary soldiers look to us to set an example, not to put the fear of Hades in their hearts."

Shame-faced, the others took a sudden interest in their sandals.

"I've had enough of your whining," Quintus growled. He got up. "See you later." Without waiting for a response, he stalked off. His father would be able to shed a more positive light on what was going on. Quintus hoped so, because he was struggling with a real sense of despondency. He hid it well, but the savage clash with Hannibal's deadly Numidian horsemen had shaken him to the core. They were all lucky to have survived. No wonder his comrades were susceptible to the rumors sweeping the camp. Quintus had to work hard not to let his own fear become overwhelming.

His father was not in his tent. One of the sentries said that he'd gone to the consul's headquarters. The walk would do him good, Quintus decided. Blow out the cobwebs. His route took him past the tents of the Cenomani, local Gaulish tribesmen who fought for Rome. There were more than two thousand of the tribesmen, mostly infantry but with a scattering of cavalry. They were a clannish lot, and the language barrier compounded this difference. There was, however, a palpable air of comradeship between them and the Romans, which Quintus had come to enjoy. He hailed the first warrior he saw, a strapping brute who was sitting on a stool outside his tent. To his surprise, the man looked away, busying himself with the sword he was oiling. Quintus thought nothing of it, but a moment later, the same thing happened again. A bunch of warriors not ten steps from where he was walking gave him cold, stony stares, before turning their backs.

It's nothing, Quintus told himself. Scores of their men were killed the other day too. Half of them have probably lost a father or a brother.

"Aurelia! Aurelia!"

Atia's voice dragged Aurelia reluctantly from a pleasing dream, which had involved both Quintus and Hanno. Importantly, they'd still been friends. Despite the impossibility of this situation, and the urgency in her mother's tone, she was in a good mood. "What is it, Mother?"

"Get out here!"

Aurelia shot out of bed. Pulling open her door, she was surprised to see Gaius standing in the atrium with her mother. Both looked decidedly serious. Suddenly self-conscious, Aurelia darted back and threw a light tunic over her woolen nightdress. Then she hurried out of her bedroom. "Gaius," she cried. "How nice to see you."

He bobbed his head awkwardly. "And you, Aurelia."

His grave manner made Aurelia's stomach lurch. She glanced at her mother and was horrified to see that her eyes were bright with tears. "W-what is it?" Aurelia stammered.

"Word has come from Cisalpine Gaul," said Gaius. "It's not good."

"Has our army been defeated?" Aurelia asked in surprise.

"Not exactly," replied Gaius. "But there was a big skirmish near the River Ticinus several days ago. Hannibal's Numidians caused heavy casualties among our cavalry and velites."

Aurelia felt faint. "Is Father all right?"

"We don't know." Her mother's eyes were dark pools of sorrow.

"The situation is still very confused," muttered Gaius. "He's probably fine."

"Heavy casualties," repeated Aurelia slowly. "How heavy, exactly?"

There was no answer.

She stared at him in disbelief. "Gaius?"

"They say that out of three thousand riders, perhaps five hundred made it back to camp," he answered, avoiding her gaze.

"How in the name of Hades can you say that Father is alive, then?" Aurelia shouted. "It's far more likely that he's dead."

"Aurelia!" barked Atia. "Gaius is just trying to give us some hope."

Gaius flushed. "I'm sorry."

Atia reached out to take his hand. "There's nothing to apologize for. You have ridden out here at first light to bring us what information there is. We're very grateful."

"I'm not! How could I be grateful for such news?" Aurelia yelled. Sobbing wildly, she ran toward the front door. Ignoring the startled doorman, she pulled it open and plunged outside. She ignored the cries that followed her.

Aurelia's feet led her to the stables. They had long been her refuge when feeling upset. She went straight to the solitary horse of her father's that had been left behind. A sturdy gray, it had been lame at the time of his departure. Seeing her, it whinnied in greeting. At once Aurelia's sorrow burst its banks and she dissolved in floods of tears. For a long time, she stood sobbing, her mind filled with images of her father, whom she would never see again. It was only when she felt the horse nibbling at her hair that Aurelia managed to regain some control. "You want an apple, don't you?" she whispered, stroking its nose. "And I've stupidly come empty-handed. Wait a moment. I'll get you one."

Grateful for the interruption, Aurelia went to the food store at the end of the stables. Picking the largest apple she could find, she walked back. The horse's eagerly pricked ears and nickers of excitement made her sorrow surge back with a vengeance, however. Aurelia calmed herself with the only thing she could think of. "At least Quintus is safe in Iberia," she whispered. "May the gods watch over him."

Fabricius was closeted with Scipio, so Quintus didn't manage to meet with his father until later in the afternoon. When told about Quintus' comrades' scaremongering, Fabricius' reaction was typically robust. "Despite the rumors, Scipio is doing fine. He'll be up and about in a couple of months. The rumor about a Carthaginian fleet attacking Sempronius Longus I also know to be untrue. Scipio would have mentioned it to me. It'd be the same if he'd had any intelligence about the Boii rising up. As for these bad omens—has a single one of your companions actually witnessed one?" Fabricius laughed as Quintus shook his head. "Of course not. Apart from that calf, which was just a freak of nature, no one ever has. The chickens in Jupiter's temple might not be eating, but that's to be expected. Poultry are frail bloody creatures. They're forever falling sick, especially in weather like this." He pointed to his head, and then his heart, and last of all at his sword. "Trust in these before you worry about what other men say."

Quintus was heartened by Fabricius' attitude. He was also grateful that his father no longer mentioned sending him home. Nothing had been said since the defeat at the Ticinus. Whether it was because of the number of riders who had fallen, or because Fabricius had become reconciled to the idea of him serving in the cavalry, Quintus did not know—or care. His good humor was added to by the bellyful of wine and hearty stew that his father had provided, and he left in much better spirits than he'd arrived.

His good mood did not last long, however. The currents of air that whipped around Quintus as he struggled back toward his tent were even more vicious than earlier in the day. They cut clean through his cloak, chilling his flesh to the bone. It was so easy to imagine the gods sending the storm down as punishment. There was an awful inevitability about the snow that began falling a moment later. His worries, only recently allayed, returned with a vengeance.

What few soldiers were about rapidly vanished from sight. Quintus couldn't wait to climb beneath his blankets himself, where he could try to forget it all. He was amazed, therefore, to see the Cenomani tribesmen outside. They stood around blazing fires, their arms around each other's shoulders, singing low, sorrowful chants. The warriors were probably mourning their dead, thought Quintus, shivering. He left them to it.

Licinius was first to catch Quintus' eye when he entered the tent. "Sorry about earlier," he muttered from the depths of his blankets. "I should have kept my mouth shut."

"Don't worry about it. We were all feeling down," Quintus replied, shedding his damp cloak. He moved to his bedroll. It lay alongside that of Calatinus, who also gave him a sheepish look. "You might be interested to know that Scipio knows nothing of a Carthaginian fleet attacking Sicily."

An embarrassed grin creased Calatinus' face. "Well, if he hasn't heard of it, we have nothing to worry about."

"What about the Boii?" challenged Cincius aggressively.

Quintus grinned. "No. Good news, eh?"

Cincius' glower slowly faded away.

"Excellent," said Calatinus, sitting up. "So we just have to wait until Longus gets here."

"I think we should raise a toast to that day," Cincius announced. He nodded at Quintus as if to say that their disagreement had been forgotten. "Who's interested?"

There was a chorus of agreement, and Quintus groaned. "I can feel the hangover already."

"Who cares? There's no chance of any action!" Cincius leaped up and headed for the table where they kept their food and wine.

"True enough," Quintus muttered. "Why not, then?"

The four comrades were late getting to sleep. Despite his drunken state, Quintus was troubled by bad dreams. The most vivid involved squadrons of Numidian horsemen pursuing him across an open plain. Eventually, drenched in sweat, he sat up. It was pitch black in the tent, and freezing cold. Yet Quintus welcomed the chill air that moved across his face and arms, distracting him from the drumbeat pounding in his head. He squinted at the brazier, barely making out the last glowing embers. Yawning, he threw back the covers. If the fire was fed now, it might last until morning. As he stood, Quintus heard a faint noise outside. Surprised, he pricked his ears. It was the unmistakable crunching of snow beneath a man's feet, but rather than the measured tread of a sentry, this was being made by someone moving with great care. Someone who did not want to be heard.

Instinctively, Quintus picked up his sword. On either side and to the rear, the next tents were half a dozen paces away. In front, a narrow path increased that distance to perhaps ten. This was where the sound was coming from. Quintus padded forward in his bare feet. All his senses were on high alert. Next, he heard whispering. Adrenaline surged through him. This was not right. Groping his way back through the darkness, Quintus reached Calatinus and grabbed his shoulder. "Wake up," he hissed.

The only answer he got was an irritated groan.

At once the noise outside stopped.

Quintus' heart thumped with fear. He might have just attracted the attention of those on the other side of the tent leather. Letting go of Calatinus' tunic, he frantically pulled on his sandals. His fingers slipped on the awkward lacing, and he mouthed a savage curse. Finally, though, he was done.

As Quintus straightened, he heard a soft, choking sound. And another. There was more muttering, and a stifled cry, which was cut short. He rushed to Licinius' bedroll this time. Perhaps he wasn't so pissed. Placing a hand across the Tarentine's mouth, Quintus shook him violently. "Wake up!" he hissed. "We are under attack!" He made out the white of the other's shocked eyes as they opened. Licinius nodded in understanding, and Quintus took away his hand. "Listen," he whispered.

For a moment, they heard nothing. Then there was a strangled moan, which swiftly died away. It was followed by the familiar, meaty sound of a blade plunging in and out of flesh. Quintus and Licinius exchanged a horrified glance and they both leaped up. "To arms! To arms!" they screamed in unison.

At last Calatinus woke up. "What's going on?" he mumbled.

"Damn it, get up! Grab your sword," Quintus shouted. "You too, Cincius. Quickly!" He cursed himself for not raising the alarm sooner.

In response to their cries, someone pushed a blade through the front of the tent and sliced downward. Ripping the leather apart, he stepped inside. Quintus didn't hesitate. Running forward, he stabbed the figure in the belly. As the man folded over, bellowing in pain, a second intruder entered. Quintus hacked him down with a savage blow to the neck. Blood spattered everywhere as the intruder collapsed, screaming. Unfortunately, a third man was close behind. So was a fourth. Loud, guttural voices from outside revealed that they had plenty of back-up.

"They're fucking Gauls!" yelled Licinius.

Confusion filled Quintus. What was happening? Had the Carthaginians scaled the ramparts? Ducking underneath a swinging sword, he thrust forward with his gladius, and was satisfied by the loud cry this elicited. Licinius joined him. Side by side, they put up a desperate resistance against the tide of warriors trying to gain entry. It was soon obvious that they would fail. Their new enemies were carrying shields, while they were in only their underclothes.

More ripping sounds came from Quintus' left and he struggled not to panic. "The whoresons are cutting their way in. Calatinus! Cincius! Slash a hole in one of the back panels," he shouted over his shoulder. "We've got to get out." There was no response, and Quintus' stomach clenched. Were their comrades already dead?

"Come on!" Calatinus screeched a moment later.

Relief flooded through Quintus. "Ready?" he bellowed at Licinius. "Yes!"

"Let's go, then!" Quintus delivered a desperate flurry of blows in the direction of his nearest opponent before turning and sprinting for the rear of the tent. He sensed Licinius one step behind. Quintus reached the gaping hole in the leather in a few strides. He hurled himself bodily through it, landing with a crash at the feet of the others. As they hauled him up, he peered inside, and was horrified to see Licinius—almost within arm's reach—trip and fall to his knees. Quintus had no time to react. The baying Gauls were on his comrade like hounds that have cornered a boar. Swords, daggers and even an axe chopped downward. The poor light was not enough to prevent Quintus seeing the spurts of blood from each dreadful, mortal wound. Licinius collapsed on to the tent's floor without a word.

"You bastards," Quintus screamed. Desperate to avenge his friend, he lunged forward.

Strong arms pulled him back. "Don't be stupid. He's dead. We have to save ourselves," Cincius snarled. Quickly, he and Calatinus dragged him off into the darkness.

There was no pursuit.

"Let me go!" Quintus shouted.

"You won't go back?" insisted Calatinus.

"I swear it," Quintus muttered angrily.

They released him.

Quintus gazed around with horrified eyes. As far as he could see, pandemonium reigned. Some tents had been set on fire, vividly illuminating the scene. Groups of Gaulish warriors ran hither and thither, cutting down the confused Roman cavalrymen and legionaries who were emerging, half-clothed, into the cold night air. "It doesn't look like an all-out attack," he said after a moment. "There aren't enough of them."

"Some of the whoresons are already running away," swore Calatinus, pointing.

Quintus squinted into the glow cast by the burning tents. "What are they carrying?" His gorge rose as he realized. A great retch doubled Quintus over, and he puked up a bellyful of sour wine.

"The fucking dogs!" cried Cincius. "They're heads! They've beheaded the men they've killed!"

With watering eyes, Quintus looked up. All he could see were the trails of blood the Gauls had left in the dazzling white snow.

Cincius and Calatinus began to moan with fear.

With great effort, Quintus pulled himself together. "Quiet!" he hissed.

To his surprise, the pair obeyed. White-faced, they waited for him to speak.

Quintus ignored his instincts, which were screaming at him to search for his father. He had two men's lives in his hands. For the moment, they had to be the priority. "Let's head for the *intervallum*," he said. "That's where everyone will be headed. We can fight the whoresons on a much better footing there."

"But we're both barefoot," said Cincius plaintively.

Quintus bridled, but if he didn't let the others equip themselves with caligae from nearby corpses, frostbite beckoned. "Go on, then. Pick up a *scutum* each as well," he ordered. A shield was vital.

"What about a mail shirt?" Calatinus tugged at a dead legionary. "He's about my size."

"No, you fool! We can't afford the time. Swords and shields will have to do." Twitching with impatience, he waited until they were ready. "Follow me." Keeping an eye out for Gaulish warriors, Quintus set off at a loping run.

He led them straight to the intervallum, the strip of open ground that ran around the inside of the camp walls. Normally, it served for the legion to assemble before marching out on patrol or to do battle. Now, it allowed the bloodied survivors of the covert attack to regroup.

Many had had the same idea as Quintus. The area was packed with hundreds of milling, disorganized legionaries and cavalrymen. Not many were fully dressed, but most had had the wits to pick up a weapon as they fled their tents.

Fortunately, this was where the discipline of officers such as centurions came into play. Recognizable even without their characteristic helmets, there were calm, measured figures everywhere, shouting orders and forming the soldiers into regular lines. Quintus and his companions joined the nearest group. At that point, it didn't matter that they were not infantry. Before long, the centurions had marshaled a large force together. Every sixth soldier was issued with one of the few torches available. It wasn't much, but would do until the attack had been contained.

At once, they began sweeping the avenues and tent lines for Gauls. To everyone's frustration, they had little success. Their desire for revenge could not be sated. It appeared that as soon as the alarm had been raised, the majority of the tribesmen had made their getaway. Nonetheless, the search continued until the entire area had been covered.

The worst discoveries were the numerous headless bodies. It was common knowledge that the Gauls liked to gather such battle trophies, but Quintus had never witnessed it before. He had never seen so much blood in his life. Enormous splashes of red circled every corpse, and wide trails of it ran alongside the Gauls' footprints.

"Jupiter above, this will look like a slaughterhouse in daylight," said Calatinus in a hushed voice.

"Poor bastards," replied Cincius. "Most of them never had a chance."

An image of his father sleeping in his tent made Quintus retch again. There was nothing left to come up except bile.

Calatinus looked concerned. "Are you all right?"

"I'm fine," Quintus barked. Forcing down his nausea, he carefully scanned each body they came across. He begged the gods that he would not find his father. To his immense relief, he saw none who resembled Fabricius. Yet this did not mean a thing. They had covered but a small part of the camp. Only when daybreak came could he be sure.

The centurions kept every soldier on high alert for what remained of the night. The sole compromise they would make was to allow each makeshift century in turn to go to their tents and retrieve their clothing and armor. Fully prepared for battle, the legionaries and cavalrymen then had to wait until dawn, when it became clear that there would be no further attack. The men were finally allowed to stand down, and were ordered to return to their respective units. The cleaning-up operation would take all day. Disregarding this, Quintus went in search of his father. Miraculously, he found him in his tent. Tears came to his eyes as he entered. "You're alive!"

"There you are," Fabricius declared, waving at the table before him, which was laid out for breakfast. "Care for some bread?"

Quintus grinned. Despite his father's nonchalance, he had seen the flash of relief in his eyes. "Thank you. I'm famished. It's been a long night," he replied.

"Indeed it has," Fabricius replied. "And more than a hundred good men are gone thanks to those bastard Cenomani."

"You're certain that's who it was?"

"Who else could it have been? There was no sign of the gate being forced, and the sentries on the walls saw no one."

Realization struck Quintus. "That's why they were so surly yesterday!" Seeing his father's confusion, he explained.

"That clarifies a great deal. And now they've fled to the Carthaginian camp. No doubt their 'trophies' will serve as an offering to Hannibal," said Fabricius sourly. "Proof that they hate us."

Quintus tried not to think of Licinius' headless corpse, which he'd found in the wreckage of their tent. "What will Scipio do?"

Fabricius scowled. "Guess."

"We're to withdraw again?"

His father nodded.

"Why?" cried Quintus.

"He thinks it's too dangerous on this side of the Trebia. After last night, that's hard to argue with." Fabricius saw Quintus' anguish. "It's not just that. The high ground on the far bank is extremely uneven, which will stop any chance of attacks by the Carthaginian cavalry. We'll also be blocking the roads that lead south through Liguria to the lands of the Boii."

Quintus' protests subsided. Those reasons at least made sense. "When?"

"This afternoon, as it's getting dark."

Quintus sighed. The very manner of their retreat seemed cowardly, but it *was* prudent. "And then we sit tight?" he guessed. "Contain the Carthaginians?"

"Exactly. Sempronius Longus is traveling here with all speed. His forces will arrive inside a month." Fabricius' expression grew fierce. "Hannibal's forces will never stand up to two consular armies."

For the second time since the Cenomani attack, Quintus had a reason to smile.

"There you are. Your mother's been worried. She thought you'd be here."

At the sound of Elira's voice, Aurelia turned. The Illyrian was framed in the doorway to the stable. All at once, she felt very childish. "Is Gaius still here?"

"No, he's gone. Apparently, his unit is to be mobilized soon. He said that you would be in his thoughts and prayers."

Aurelia felt even worse.

Elira came closer. "I heard the news," she said softly. "Everyone did. We all feel for you."

"Thank you." Aurelia threw her a grateful look.

"Who's to know? Your father may well be alive."

"Don't," Aurelia snapped.

"I'm sorry," said Elira quickly.

Aurelia forced a smile. "At least Quintus is still alive."

"And Hanno."

Aurelia shoved away the pang of jealousy that followed Elira's words. Mention of Hanno inevitably made her think of Suniaton. She hadn't taken him any food for four days. He'd be running out of provisions. Aurelia made her mind up on the spot. Seeing Suni now would cheer her up. She squinted at Elira. "You liked Hanno, didn't you?"

Twin dimples formed in the Illyrian's cheeks. "Yes," she whispered.

"Would you help him again?"

"Of course," Elira answered, looking puzzled. "But he's gone, with Quintus."

Aurelia smiled. "Go to the kitchen and fill a bag with provisions. Bread, cheese, meat. If Julius asks, tell him that they're rations for our foraging trip. Fetch a basket too."

"What if the mistress wants to know where you are?"

"Say that we're going to look for nuts and mushrooms."

Elira's face grew even more confused. "How will that help Hanno?"

"You'll see." Aurelia clapped her hands. "Well, get on with it then. I'll meet you on the path that leads up to the hills."

With a curious glance, Elira hurried off.

—⁂—

Aurelia hadn't been waiting long before Elira came hurrying through the trees toward her. A small leather pack dangled from one hand, a cloak that matched her own from the other.

"Did anyone ask what you were doing?" Aurelia asked nervously.

"Julius did, but he just smiled when I told him what we were doing. He said to be careful."

"He's such an old woman!" declared Aurelia. She looked down and realized that she'd come out without her dagger or sling. It doesn't matter, she told herself. We won't be gone for long. "Come on," she said briskly.

"Where are we going?" asked Elira.

"Up there," replied Aurelia, waving vaguely at the slopes that loomed over the farm. Abruptly, she decided that there was no further need for subterfuge. "Did you know that Hanno had a friend who was captured with him?"

Elira nodded.

"Suniaton was sold to become a gladiator in Capua."

"Oh." Elira didn't dare to say more, but her muted tone spoke volumes.

"Quintus and Gaius helped him to escape."

The Illyrian was visibly shocked. "Why?"

"Because Hanno was Quintus' friend."

"I see." Elira frowned. "Has Suniaton got something to do with where we're going now?"

"Yes. He was injured when they rescued him, so the poor thing couldn't travel. He's much better now, thank the gods."

Elira looked intrigued. "Where is he?"

"At the shepherd's hut where Quintus and Hanno fought the bandits."

"You're full of surprises, aren't you?" said Elira with a giggle.

Aurelia's misery lifted a fraction and she grinned.

Talking animatedly, they walked to the border of Fabricius' land. The fields on either side were empty and bare, lying fallow until the spring. Jackdaws were their only company; flocks regularly flew overhead, their characteristic squawks piercing the chill air. Soon they had entered the woods that covered the surrounding hills. The bird cries immediately died away, and the trees pressed in from all sides with a claustrophobic air that Aurelia did not like.

When Agesandros stepped out on to the path, she screamed in fright. So did Elira.

"I didn't mean to scare you," he said apologetically.

Aurelia tried to calm her pounding heart. "What are you doing here?" she demanded.

He raised the bow in his hands. An arrow was already notched to its string. "Hunting deer. And you?"

Aurelia's mouth felt very dry. "Looking for nuts. And mushrooms."

"I see," he said. "I wouldn't stray too far from the farm on your search."

"Why not?" asked Aurelia, trying desperately to sound confident.

"You never know who might be about. Bandits. A bear. An escaped slave."

"There's little chance of that," Aurelia declared boldly.

"Maybe so. You're unarmed, though. I could come with you," the Sicilian offered.

"No!" Instantly, Aurelia regretted her vehemence. "Thank you, but we'll be fine."

"If you're certain," he said, stepping back.

"I am." Jerking her head at Elira, Aurelia walked past him.

"It's a bit late for mushrooms, isn't it?"

Aurelia's step faltered. "There are still a few, if you know where to look," she managed.

Agesandros nodded knowledgeably. "I'm sure."

Aurelia's skin was crawling as she walked away.

"Does he know?" whispered Elira.

"How could he?" Aurelia hissed back.

But it felt as if he did.

Many days passed by, and it became evident that there would be no battle. As Fabricius had said, no commander would choose to fight unless he could select the time and place. Scipio's refusal to move from the high ground and Hannibal's unwillingness to attack his enemy's position produced a stalemate. While the Carthaginians roamed at will across the plain west of the Trebia, the Romans stayed close to their camp. Hannibal's cavalry now severely outnumbered their horsemen. Patrols were so risky that they were rarely sent out. Despite this, Quintus found it hard to remain equable about their enforced inactivity. He was still suffering nightmares about what had happened to Licinius. He hoped that in battle he could purge himself of the disturbing images. "I'm going crazy," he told his father one night. "How much longer do we have to wait?"

"We'll do nothing until Longus arrives," Fabricius repeated patiently. "If we marched down to the flat ground today and offered battle, the dogs would cut us to pieces. Even without the difference in cavalry, Hannibal's army outnumbers us man for man. You know that."

"I suppose so," Quintus admitted reluctantly.

Fabricius leaned back in his chair, satisfied that his point had been made.

Quintus stared gloomily into the depths of the brazier. What was Hanno doing at this very moment? he wondered. It didn't seem real that they were now enemies. Quintus also thought of Aurelia. When would his recently composed letter reach her? If Fortuna smiled on them both, he might get a reply within the next few months. It was a long time to wait. At least in the meantime he was serving alongside his father. His sister, on the other hand, was not so lucky. Quintus' heart ached for her.

"Here you both are!" A familiar booming voice broke the silence.

Fabricius made a show of looking pleased. "Flaccus. Where else would we be?"

Quintus jumped up and saluted. What does he want? he wondered. Since the debacle at the Ticinus, they had hardly seen Aurelia's husband-to-be. The reason, all three knew, was Flaccus' conduct during that disaster. It was hard to dispel suspicion once it had taken root, thought Quintus. Yet he could not shake off his feeling. Nor, it appeared, could his father.

"Quite so, quite so. Who would be out tonight apart from the sentries and the deranged?" Chuckling at his own joke, Flaccus proffered a small amphora.

"How kind," Fabricius murmured, accepting the gift. "Will you try some?"

"Only if you will," Flaccus demurred.

Fabricius opened the amphora with a practiced movement of his wrist. "Quintus?"

"Yes, please, Father." Quickly, he fetched three glazed ceramic beakers.

With their cups filled, they eyed each other, wondering who would make the toast. At length, Fabricius spoke. "To the swift arrival of Sempronius Longus and his army."

"And to a rapid victory over the Carthaginians thereafter," Flaccus added.

Quintus thought of Licinius. "And vengeance for our dead comrades."

Nodding, Fabricius lifted his cup even higher.

Flaccus beamed. "That's fighting talk! Just what I wanted to hear." He gave them a conspiratorial wink. "I've had a word with Scipio."

Fabricius looked dubious. "About what?"

"Sending out a patrol."

"Eh?" asked Fabricius suspiciously.

"No one has been across the river in more than a week."

"That's because it's too damn dangerous," Fabricius replied. "The enemy controls the far bank in its entirety."

"Hear me out," said Flaccus in a placatory tone. "When Sempronius Longus arrives, he'll want fresh intelligence, and information on the terrain west of the Trebia. After all, that's where the battle will be."

"What's wrong with waiting until he gets here?" demanded Fabricius. "Some of his cavalry can do his donkey work."

"It needs to be now," urged Flaccus. "Presenting the consul with all the information he needs would allow him to act fast. Just think of the boost it would provide to the men's morale when we come back safely!"

"We?" said Fabricius slowly. "You would come too?"

"Of course."

Not for the first time, Fabricius wondered if it had been a good idea to betroth Aurelia to Flaccus. Yet how could he be a coward and offer to take part in such a madcap venture? "I don't know," he muttered. "It would be incredibly risky."

"Not necessarily," Flaccus protested. "I've been watching the Carthaginians from our side of the river. By *hora decima* every afternoon, their last patrol has vanished from sight. It's at least *hora quarta* the following morning before they return. If we crossed at night, and rode out before dawn, we'd have perhaps two hours to reconnoitre the area. We would be back across before the Numidians had finished scratching their lice."

Quintus laughed.

Fabricius scowled. "I don't think it's a very good idea."

"Scipio has already given his approval. I could think of no one better to lead the patrol, and he agreed," said Flaccus. "Come on, what do you say?"

Damn you, thought Fabricius. He felt completely outmaneuvered. Refusing Flaccus' offer could be seen as a snub to Scipio himself, and that was not a wise course of action. Furious, Fabricius changed his mind. "It could only be a small patrol. One turma at most," he said. "It would have to be under my sole command. You can come along—as an observer."

Flaccus did not protest. He turned to Quintus. "Your father is a shining example of a Roman officer. Brave, resourceful and eager to do his duty."

"I'm coming too," said Quintus.

"No, you're not," snapped his father. "It will be far too dangerous."

"It's not fair! You did things like this when you were my age—you've told me!" retorted Quintus furiously.

Flaccus stepped in before Fabricius could reply. "How can we deny Quintus such a chance to gain valuable experience? And think of the glory that will be heaped upon the men who brought Longus the information that helped him to defeat Hannibal!"

Fabricius looked at his son's eager face and sighed. "Very well."

"Thank you, Father," said Quintus with a broad smile.

Fabricius kept showing a brave face, but inside he was filled with fear. It will be like walking past a pride of hungry lions, hoping that none of them sees us, he thought. Yet there was no going back now.

He had given his word to lead the mission.

XXI

HANNIBAL'S PLAN

One morning, not long after the Carthaginians had driven the Romans back over the Trebia, Malchus was ordered to Hannibal's tent. While this happened regularly, he always felt a tremor of excitement when the summons arrived. After so many years of waiting for revenge on Rome, Malchus still thrilled to be in the presence of the man who had finally begun the war.

He found Hannibal in pensive mood. The general barely glanced up as Malchus entered. As ever, he was leaning over his campaign table, studying a map of the area. Maharbal, his cavalry commander, stood beside him, talking in a low voice. A thin man with long, curly black hair and an easy grin, Maharbal was popular with officers and ordinary troops alike.

Malchus came to a halt several steps from the table. He stiffened to attention. "Reporting for duty, sir."

Hannibal straightened. "Malchus, welcome."

"You asked to see me, sir?"

"I did." Still deep in thought, Hannibal rubbed a finger across his lips. "I have a question to ask you."

· 383 ·

"Anything, sir."

"Maharbal and I have come up with a plan. An ambush, to be precise."

"Sounds interesting, sir," said Malchus eagerly.

"We're hoping that the Romans might send a patrol across the river," Hannibal went on. "Maharbal here will organize the cavalry that will fall upon the enemy, but I want some infantry there too. They will lie in wait at the main ford, and prevent any stragglers from escaping."

Malchus grinned fiercely. "I'd be honored to take part, sir."

"I didn't have you in mind." Seeing Malchus' face fall, Hannibal explained, "I'm not losing one of my most experienced officers in a skirmish. I was thinking of your sons, Bostar and Sapho."

Malchus swallowed his disappointment. "They'd be well suited to a job like this, sir, and I'm sure delighted to be picked for it."

"I thought so." Hannibal paused for a moment. "And so to my question. What about your other son?"

Malchus blinked in surprise. "Hanno?"

"Is he battle-ready yet?"

"I put him into training straight after he returned, sir. Not being in Carthage, it was a little improvised, but he performed well." Malchus hesitated. "I'd say that he's ready to be commissioned as an officer."

"Good, good. Could he lead a phalanx?"

Malchus gaped. "Are you serious, sir?"

"I'm not in the habit of making jokes, Malchus. The crossing of the mountains left many units without officers to command them."

"Of course, sir, of course." Malchus gathered his thoughts. "Before Hanno was lost at sea, I would have had grave reservations."

"Why?" Hannibal's gaze was as fierce as a hawk's.

"He was a bit of a wastrel, sir. Only interested in fishing and girls."

"That's hardly a crime, is it?" Hannibal chuckled. "I thought he was too young to serve in the army back then?"

"He was, sir," Malchus admitted. "And, to be fair, he was excellent when it came to lessons in military tactics. He was skilled at hunting too."

"Good qualities. So, has your opinion changed since his return?"

"It has, sir," Malchus replied confidently. "He's changed. The things he experienced and had to live through would have broken many boys, but it didn't Hanno. He is a man now."

"You're sure?"

Malchus met his general's gaze squarely. "Yes, sir."

"Fine. I want you and your three sons back here in an hour. That'll be all." Hannibal turned back to Maharbal.

"Thank you, sir." Grinning with excitement, Malchus saluted and withdrew.

———

Confusion filled Hanno when his father told him the news.

"What does he want with a junior officer like me?"

"I couldn't say," Malchus replied neutrally.

Hanno's stomach twisted into a knot. "Are Sapho and Bostar also to be present?"

"They are."

That did little to reassure Hanno. Had he done something wrong?

"I'll leave you to it," said Malchus. "Make sure you're there in half an hour."

"Yes, Father." With a racing mind, Hanno set to polishing his new helmet and breastplate. He didn't stop until his arms burned. Then he rubbed his leather sandals with grease until they glistened. When he was done, Hanno hurried to his father's tent where there was a large bronze mirror. To his relief, Malchus wasn't there. He scowled at his reflection. "It'll have to do," he muttered.

As he walked to Hannibal's headquarters, Hanno was grateful that none of the soldiers hurrying to and fro gave him a second look. It wasn't until he reached the scutarii who stood guard outside the large pavilion that he became the focus of attention.

"State your name, rank and business!" barked the officer in charge of the sentries.

"Hanno, junior officer of a Libyan phalanx, sir. I'm here to see the general." Hanno blinked, half expecting to be told to get lost.

Instead, the officer nodded. "You're expected. Follow me."

A moment later, Hanno found himself in a large, sparsely furnished chamber. Apart from a desk and a few hide-backed chairs, it held only a weapons rack. Hannibal was there, surrounded by a circle of his commanders. Among them were his father and brothers.

"Sir! Announcing Hanno, junior officer of the Libyan spearmen!" the officer bellowed.

Hanno flushed to the roots of his hair.

Turning, Hannibal smiled. "Welcome."

"Thank you, sir."

"You all know about Malchus' prodigal son?" asked Hannibal. "Well, here he is."

Hanno's embarrassment grew even greater as the senior officers studied him. He could see Bostar grinning. Even his father had the trace of a smile on his lips. Sapho, on the other hand, looked as if he'd swallowed a wasp. Hanno felt a surge of annoyance. *Why is he like that?*

Hannibal looked at each of the brothers in turn. "You're probably wondering why I summoned you this morning?"

"Yes, sir," they answered.

"I'll come to my reason in a moment." Hannibal looked at Hanno. "You've heard no doubt of our severe casualties, suffered during the crossing of the Alps?"

"Of course, sir."

"Since then, we've been short of not just men, but officers."

"Yes, sir," Hanno replied. What was Hannibal getting at? Hanno wondered.

The general smiled at his confusion. "I'm appointing you to the command of a phalanx," he said.

"Sir?" Hanno managed.

"You heard me," replied Hannibal. "It's a huge leap, I know, but your father assures me that you've returned a man."

"I . . ." Hanno's gaze flickered to Malchus and back to Hannibal. "Thank you, sir."

"As you know, a phalanx should number four hundred men or so, but yours now barely musters two hundred. It's one of the weakest units, but the men are veterans, and they should serve you well. And, after your extraordinary ordeals, I have high expectations of you."

"Thank you, sir," said Hanno, acutely aware of the huge responsibility he'd just been handed. "I am deeply honored." Bostar winked at him, but he was irritated to see that Sapho's lips were pursed.

"Good!" Hannibal declared. "Now for the reason I called you all here today. As you probably know, there's been no action since we sent the Romans packing over the Trebia. Nor is there much chance of any in the near future. They know that our cavalry greatly outnumbers theirs, as does our infantry. From our point of view, it would be pointless to attack their camp. It's on such uneven ground that the advantage our horsemen grant us would be negated. The Romans know that too, so the mongrel bastards are happy just to block the road south and wait for reinforcements. We may have to wait until those forces arrive, but I'm not happy to sit about doing nothing." Hannibal turned. "Maharbal?"

"Thank you, sir," said the cavalry commander. "To try and encourage the enemy to send some men over the river, we've been giving the impression that our riders have become quite lax. Do you want to know how?" he asked.

"Yes, sir," the three brothers replied eagerly.

"We never appear on our side of the Trebia until late in the morning, and we always leave well before dark. Understand?"

"You want them to try a dawn patrol, sir?" asked Bostar.

Maharbal smiled. "Exactly."

Hanno felt his excitement grow. He didn't feel confident enough to ask a question, however.

Sapho did it for him. "What else, sir?"

Hannibal took over once more. "Maharbal has five hundred Numidians permanently stationed in the woods about a mile from the main ford over the river. If the Romans take the bait, and send out a patrol, they'll have to ride past our men. Not many of the dogs will escape when the Numidians fall on them from behind, but some might. Which is where you and your Libyans will come in."

Hanno shot a glance at Bostar and Sapho, who were grinning fiercely.

"I want a strong force of infantry to remain hidden near the crossing point. If any Romans do cross, they're not to be hindered, but when they return..." Hannibal clenched a fist. "I want them annihilated. Is that clear?"

Hanno glanced at his brothers, who gave him emphatic nods. "Yes, sir!" they cried in unison.

"Excellent," declared Hannibal. His gaze hardened. "Do *not* fail me."

———

Shortly after darkness had fallen the following evening, Hanno and his brothers led their units out of the Carthaginian camp. As well as their tents and sleeping rolls, the men carried enough rations for three days and nights. To Hanno's delight, the Numidians who were to guide them into position were led by no less than Zamar, the officer who'd found him near the Padus. Following the horsemen, the phalanxes quietly marched to the east, following little-used hunting tracks. As the sound of rushing water filled everyone's ears, Zamar directed them to a hidden dell which lay a couple of hundred paces from the area's main crossing point over the River Trebia. It was a perfect hiding place. Spacious enough to contain their entire force, but sufficiently close to the ford. "I'm leaving you six riders as messengers. Send them out the moment you see anything," Zamar muttered before he left. "And remember, when the Romans come, none are to be left alive."

"Say no more," Sapho snarled.

Although Bostar said nothing, Hanno saw a look of distaste flicker across his face. He waited until Zamar was out of sight before turning to his brothers. "What's going on?" he demanded.

"What do you mean?" asked Sapho defensively.

"You two are permanently like a pair of cats in a bag with each other. Why?"

Bostar and Sapho scowled at each other.

Hanno waited. The silence dragged on for a few moments.

"It's really none of your business," said Bostar at length.

Hanno flushed. He glanced at Sapho, whose face was a cold mask. Hanno gave up. "I'm going to check on my men," he muttered and stalked off.

They waited in vain through what remained of the night. By dawn, the Carthaginians were chilled through and miserable. To avoid any possibility of being spotted, no fires had been lit. While it hadn't rained, the winter damp was pervasive. Following strict orders, the soldiers remained in the clearing during daylight. The sole exceptions to this were a handful of sentries, who, with blackened faces, hid themselves among the trees lining the riverbank. Everyone else had to stay put, even when answering calls of nature. While some found the energy to play dice or knucklebones, most men stayed in their tents, chewing on cold rations or catching up on lost sleep. Still annoyed by his brothers' pettiness, Hanno spent his time talking to his spearmen, trying to get to know them. He knew by their muted reactions that his efforts would mean little until he'd led them into combat, but it felt better than doing nothing.

The day dragged past without event.

Night fell at last, and Hanno took charge of the sentries, who were stationed along the river's edge for several hundred paces either side of the ford. He spent his time wandering the bank, his eyes peeled for any enemy activity. There was little cloud cover. The myriad stars above provided enough light to see relatively well, yet hours went by without so much as a flicker of movement on the opposite side. By the time dawn was approaching, Hanno had grown bored and annoyed. "Where are the fuckers?" he muttered to himself.

"Still in their beds, probably."

Hanno jumped. Turning, he recognized Bostar's features in the dim light. "Tanit above, you scared me! What are you doing here?"

"I couldn't sleep."

"You should have stayed under your blankets anyway. It's a damn sight warmer than out here," Hanno replied.

Bostar crouched down beside Hanno with a sigh. "To be honest, I wanted to apologize about what happened yesterday with Sapho. Our argument shouldn't affect our dealings with you."

"That's all right. I shouldn't have poked my nose where it didn't belong."

A more comfortable air settled about them.

"We've actually been fighting for over a year," Bostar admitted a moment later.

Hanno was grateful for the darkness, which concealed his surprise. "What, the usual stuff with him being pompous and overbearing?"

Bostar's teeth glinted sadly in the starlight. "I wish it was just that."

"I don't understand."

"It started when you'd been lost at sea."

"Eh?"

"Sapho blamed me for letting you and Suniaton go."

"But you both agreed to do so!"

"That's not how he saw it. We hadn't patched things up by the time I was posted to Iberia, and it flared up again the instant he and Father arrived from Carthage months later."

"Why?"

"They'd had news of what had happened to you and Suni. Sapho was furious. He blamed me all over again."

"You mean the pirates?" Suddenly, Hanno remembered Sapho's comment the day he'd returned, and his father's promise to tell him what had happened. "I'd forgotten."

"There was so much going on," said Bostar. "All that mattered was that you had returned."

"We've got plenty of time now," retorted Hanno. "Tell me!"

"It was a few weeks after you'd disappeared. Thanks to one of his spies, Father got wind of some pirates in the port. Four of them were seized and taken in. Under torture, they admitted selling you and Suni into slavery in Italy."

Vivid images flashed through Hanno's mind. "Do you know any of their names?"

"No, sorry," said Bostar. "Apparently, the captain was an Egyptian."

"That's right!" said Hanno, shivering. "What happened to them?"

"They were castrated first. Then their limbs were smashed before they were crucified," Bostar replied in a flat tone.

Hanno imagined the terrible scene for a moment. "Not a good way to die," he admitted.

"No."

"But they deserved it," declared Hanno harshly. "Thanks to those whoresons, Suni and I should have died in the arena."

"I know," said Bostar with a heavy sigh. "Yet seeing what happened to the pirates changed Sapho in some way. Ever since, he's been much harder. Crueler. You saw how he reacted to what Zamar said. I know that we have to kill any Romans who might cross the river. Orders are orders. But Sapho seems to take pleasure in it."

"It's not nice, but it's not the end of the world, surely?" said Hanno, trying to make light of his brother's words.

"That's not all," muttered Bostar. "He thinks that I'll do anything to curry favor with Hannibal." Quickly, he related how he'd saved Hannibal's life at Saguntum. "You should have seen the expression on Sapho's face when Hannibal congratulated me. It was as if I'd done it to make him look bad."

"That's crazy!" Hanno whispered. "Are you sure that's what he thought?"

"Oh yes. 'The perfect fucking officer' he's taken to calling me."

Hanno was shocked into silence for a moment. "Surely, it hasn't been all him? There are always two sides to every argument."

"Yes, I've said some nasty things too." Bostar sighed. "But every time I try to sort it out, Sapho throws it back in my face. The last time I tried . . ." He hesitated for a heartbeat before shaking his head. "I've given up on him."

"Why? What happened?" asked Hanno.

"I'm not telling you," said Bostar. "I can't." He looked away, out over the murmuring river.

Troubled by what Bostar had said, Hanno did not press him further. He tried to be optimistic. Maybe he could act as a mediator? Imagining a world in which Carthage was at peace once more, Hanno pictured himself hunting with his brothers in the mountains south of their city.

Bostar nudged him in the ribs, hard. "Pssst! Do you hear that?"

Hanno came down to earth with a jolt. He leaned forward, listening with all his might. For a long time, he could make out nothing. Then, the jingle of harness. Hanno's senses went on to high alert. "That came from across the water," he muttered.

"It did," replied Bostar excitedly. "Hannibal was right: the Romans want information."

They watched the far bank like wolves waiting for their prey to emerge. An instant later, their patience was rewarded. The sounds of horses, and men, moving with great care.

A surge of adrenaline pulsed through Hanno's veins. "It has to be Romans!"

"Or some of their Gaulish allies," said Bostar.

It wasn't long before they could make out a line of soldiers and mounts, winding their way down the track that led to the ford.

"How many?" hissed Bostar.

Hanno squinted into the darkness. An accurate head count was impossible. "No more than fifty. Probably less. It's a reconnaissance patrol all right."

Stopping, the Roman riders gathered together in a huddle.

"They're getting their last orders," said Hanno.

A moment later, the first man quietly walked his horse into the ice-cold water. It gave a gentle, dissenting whinny, but some muttered reassurances in its ear worked wonders, and it continued without further protest. At once the others began to follow.

Bostar unwound his limbs and stood. "Time to move. Go and tell Sapho what's happening. The Numidians must be alerted immediately. Clear?"

"Yes. What are you going to do?"

"I'll go along the bank to the next sentry, and keep an eye on them until they're out of sight. We need to be sure that no more of the bastards are going to cross."

"Right. See you soon." Hanno backed away slowly until he was behind the cover of the trees. Treading lightly on the hard ground, he sped back to their secret camp. He found Sapho pacing the ground before his tent. Quickly, he filled his brother in.

"Excellent," said Sapho with a savage grin. "Before long, you will get to blood your men's spears, and perhaps your own. A special moment for you."

Hanno nodded nervously. Was he imagining Sapho's lasciviousness?

"Well, come on then! This is no time for standing around. Get your men up. I'll send out a few of the Numidians, and get my phalanx ready. Bostar will do the same no doubt, when he eventually gets here," said Sapho.

Hanno frowned. "No need for that," he said. "He'll be here any moment."

"Of course he will!" Sapho laughed. "Now get a move on. We'll need to move into position the instant the Romans have gone."

Hanno put his head down and obeyed. He didn't understand the feud between his brothers, but one thing was certain: Sapho still liked telling him what to do. Irritated, Hanno began rousing his men. When he heard a man grumbling, Hanno lambasted him from a height. His tactic seemed to work; it didn't take long for the soldiers to assemble alongside Sapho's phalanx.

Soon after, Bostar's shape emerged from the gloom that hung over the trees that lined the riverbank. "They've gone," he declared. He whistled at the last three Numidians. "Ride out at once. Trail the dogs from a distance. Return when the ambush has been sprung."

With a quick salute, the cavalrymen sprang on to their horses' backs. They headed off at the trot.

Bostar approached his brothers. "Our time here was not in vain," he said with a smile.

"Finally," drawled Sapho. "We've been waiting for you."

Why is he needling him like that? thought Hanno.

Bostar's jaw bunched, but he said nothing. Fortunately, his soldiers had heard their comrades getting up, and were doing the same. When he was done, the trio convened in front of their men.

"How are we going to work this?" asked Hanno.

"It's obvious," said Sapho self-importantly. "The phalanxes should form three sides of a square. The fourth side will be completed by the Numidians, who will drive the Romans into the trap. They'll have nowhere to go. All we have to decide is which phalanx holds each position."

There was a momentary pause. Each of them had reconnoitred the ground around the crossing point several times. The left flank was taken up by a dense patch of oak trees, while the right was a large swampy area. Neither constituted ground that horses would choose to ride over if given the choice. The best place to stand was on the track that led to the ford. That was where any action would take place.

As the youngest and most inexperienced, Hanno was content to take whichever of the flanks he was given.

"I'll take the central side," said Bostar abruptly.

"Typical," muttered Sapho. "I want it as well. And you don't outrank me anymore, remember?"

The two glowered at each other.

"This is ridiculous," said Hanno angrily. "It doesn't matter which one of you does it."

Neither of his brothers answered.

"Why don't you toss a coin?"

Still neither Bostar nor Sapho spoke.

"Melqart above!" exclaimed Hanno. "I'll do it, then."

"That's out of the question," snapped Sapho. "You've got no combat experience."

"Exactly," added Bostar.

"I've got to start somewhere. Why not here?" Hanno retorted. "Better this, surely, than in a massive battle?"

Bostar looked at Sapho. "We can't stand around arguing all morning," he said in a conciliatory tone.

Sapho gave a careless shrug. "It would be hard for Hanno to get it wrong, I suppose."

Feeling humiliated, Hanno looked down.

"That's unnecessary," barked Bostar. "Father has trained Hanno well. Hannibal himself picked him to lead a phalanx. His men are veterans. The chances of him fucking up are no greater than if I were in the center." He paused. "Or you were."

"What's that supposed to mean?" Sapho's eyes were mere slits.

"Stop it!" Hanno cried. "You should both be ashamed of yourselves. Hannibal gave us a job to do, remember? Let's just do it, please."

Like sulky children, his brothers broke eye contact. In silence, they stalked off to stand before their phalanxes. Hanno waited for a moment before realizing that it was up to him to lead the way. "Form up, six men wide," he ordered. "Follow me." He was pleased by his soldiers' rapid response. Many of them looked pleased by what had happened, which encouraged him further.

The three phalanxes deployed at the ford, in open order. Once they closed up, the spearmen would present a continuous front of overlapping shields. No horse would approach such an obstacle. The forest of spears protruding from it promised death by impalement to anyone foolish enough to try.

Hanno marched up and down, muttering encouraging words to his men. He was grateful that his father had advised him to recognize as many of his soldiers as possible. It was a simple ruse, yet not a man failed to grin when Hanno spoke to him by name. His efforts didn't take long, though, and soon time began to drag. Muscles that had been stirred into activity by their movement into position grew cold again. A damp breeze blew off the river, chilling the waiting soldiers to the bone. Allowing them to warm up was not an option, nor was singing, a common method of raising morale.

All they could do was wait.

Dawn came, but banks of lowering cloud concealed the sun. The sole sign of life was the occasional small bird fluttering among the trees' bare branches; the only sound the murmur of the river at their backs. Finally, Hanno's grumbling belly made him wonder if they should order an issue of rations. Before he could query this with his brothers, the sound of galloping hooves attracted everyone's attention. All eyes turned to the track leading west.

When two Numidians came thundering around the corner, there was a massed intake of breath.

"They're coming!" one shouted as he drew nearer.

"With five hundred of our comrades hot on their tails!" whooped the other.

Hanno scarcely heard. "Close order!" he screamed. "Ready spears!"

XXII

FACE-TO-FACE

Quintus had hoped that his unease would dissipate as they left the Trebia behind them. Far from it. Each step that his horse took farther into the empty landscape felt as final as if he had crossed the Styx to penetrate the depths of Hades itself. The eagerness he'd felt in his father's tent, with a belly full of wine, had totally vanished. Quintus said nothing, but a glance to either side confirmed that he was not alone in his feelings. The other riders' faces spoke volumes. Many were throwing filthy glances at Flaccus. Everyone knew that he was responsible for their misfortune.

At the front, Fabricius had no idea, or was choosing to ignore, what was going on. It was probably the latter, Quintus decided. These were some of the most experienced men in his command. Yet they were unhappy. Why had his father accepted the mission? Quintus cursed. The answer was startlingly simple. How would it look to Scipio if Fabricius had refused a duty like this? Terrible. Quintus eyed Flaccus sourly. If the fool hadn't put the idea in the consul's head, they'd all still be safe on the Roman side of the river. Guilt soon replaced Quintus' anger. By being so eager, he had probably helped push his father into accepting the suicide mission.

For, despite the fact that there was no sign of the enemy, that is what it felt like.

Quintus waited for only a short time before urging his horse forward to his father's position. Flaccus was riding alongside. He gave Quintus a broad wink. It wasn't entirely convincing.

He's frightened too, thought Quintus. That made up his mind.

Fabricius was intent on scanning the landscape. His rigid back told its own story. Quintus swallowed. "Maybe this patrol was a bad idea, Father." He ignored Flaccus' shocked reaction. "We're visible for miles."

Fabricius dragged his gaze around to Quintus. "I know. Why do you think I'm keeping such a keen eye out?"

"But there's no sign of anyone," protested Flaccus. "Not even a bird!"

"For Jupiter's sake, that doesn't matter!" Fabricius snapped. "All the Carthaginians need is one alert sentry. If there are any Numidians within five miles of here, they'll be after us within a dozen heartbeats of any alarm."

Flaccus flinched. "But we can't go back empty-handed."

"Not without looking like fools, or cowards," Fabricius agreed sourly.

They rode in silence for a few moments.

"There might be a way out," Flaccus muttered.

Quintus was ashamed to feel a flutter of hope.

Fabricius laughed harshly. "Not so keen now, are you?"

"Are you doubting my courage?" demanded Flaccus with an outraged look.

"Not your courage," Fabricius growled. "Your good judgment. Haven't you realized yet that Hannibal's cavalry are lethal? If we so much as see any, we're dead men."

"Surely it's not that bad?" protested Flaccus.

"I should have refused this mission, regardless of how it looked to Scipio. Let you lead it on your own. If anyone would follow you, that is."

Flaccus subsided into a sulky silence.

His father's outburst revealed the depths of his anger; Quintus was amazed.

Fabricius relented a fraction. "So what's your bright idea? You might as well tell me."

"We will report that the enemy cavalry was present in such numbers that we were unable to proceed far from the Trebia," said Flaccus with bad grace. "It's not cowardice to avoid annihilation. Who will gainsay us? Your men certainly won't talk about it, and no one else will be foolish enough to cross the river."

"Your capacity for guile never ceases to amaze me," snarled Fabricius.

"I . . ." Flaccus spluttered.

"But you're right. It's better to save the lives of thirty men in the way you suggest rather than throw them away through foolish pride. We will return at once." Fabricius reined in his mount, and turned to issue the order to halt.

Quintus sagged down on to his horse's back. His relief lasted no more than a heartbeat. From some distance away came the unmistakable sound of galloping hooves.

The eyes of every man in the turma turned to the west.

A quarter of a mile distant, a tide of riders was emerging from behind a copse of trees.

"Numidians!" Fabricius screamed. "About turn! Ride for your lives!"

His soldiers needed no urging.

Trying not to panic, Quintus did the same thing. The ambush might have been sprung early, but it remained to be seen if they could make it back to the Trebia before the enemy horsemen reached them.

It soon became clear that they would never reach the river in time. The Numidians were physically smaller than the Romans, and their mounts were faster. They were operating to a plan too. While some continued riding in direct pursuit from the south, others angled their path outward and to the west, effectively hemming the patrol against the Trebia. The Romans had to flee northward. Naturally, they made for the ford. There was no other option. It was the only one for miles in either direction.

"Get to the front," Fabricius shouted at Quintus and Flaccus. "Stay there. Stop for nothing."

Flaccus obeyed without question, but Quintus held back. "What about you?"

"I'm staying at the rear to prevent this becoming a complete rout," snapped Fabricius. "Now go!" His steely gaze brooked no argument.

Fighting back tears, Quintus urged his horse into a full gallop. It soon drew ahead of the other cavalrymen. Never had he been more glad of his father's insistence on taking the best mount available, or more ashamed that he could feel such relief. Quintus did not want to die like a rabbit chased down by a pack of dogs. With this dark thought fighting for supremacy, he leaned forward over his horse's neck and concentrated on one thing. Surviving. With luck, some of them would make it.

They had covered nearly a mile before the first Numidians had closed to within missile range. Riding bareback, half-clothed, the lithe, dark-skinned warriors did not look that threatening. Their javelins' accuracy proved otherwise. Every time Quintus looked around, another cavalryman had been struck, or fallen from his mount. Others had their horses injured, and were no longer able to keep up with their comrades. No one saw their swift and inevitable fate, yet their strangled cries followed in the survivors' wake, sending terror into their hearts. The Roman riders could not even respond. Their thrusting spears were not made to be thrown.

By the time Fabricius' men had covered another mile, the Numidians were attacking from three sides. Javelins were scudding in constantly, and Quintus could count only ten riders apart from himself, his father and Flaccus. At the bend in the track that led around and down to the ford, that number had been reduced to six. Desperately, Quintus urged his mount to even greater efforts. He didn't know why, but they seemed to have drawn slightly ahead of their pursuers. Perhaps they still had a chance? he wondered. With their horses' hooves throwing up showers of stones, they pounded around the corner and on to the straight stretch that led to the Trebia, a mere two hundred paces away.

All Quintus' hopes evaporated on the spot.

The tribesmen had held back in order to close the trap. Blocking the way ahead was a massed formation of spearmen. Their large, inter-locking shields formed three sides of a square, leaving the open side toward him. Quintus' eyes flickered around in panic. A dense network of trees lined the right-hand side of the road. There was no escape there. On the left was a large area of boggy ground. Only a fool would try to ride across that, he thought.

Yet one of the cavalrymen took this second option. He swiftly learned his lesson. Within twenty paces, his horse was belly deep in glutinous sludge. When the rider tried to dismount, the same hap-pened to him. Screaming with terror, he had soon sunk to his armpits. At last he stopped struggling, but it was too late. The best the man could hope for was an accurately thrown enemy javelin, thought Quin-tus bitterly. It was that, or drown in the mud.

Fabricius' voice snapped him back to the present. "Slow down! Form a line," he ordered in a stony voice. "Let us meet our death like men."

One of the five remaining cavalrymen began to make a low, keen-ing noise in his throat.

Suddenly, Quintus' fear became overwhelming.

"Shut your fucking mouth!" Fabricius shouted. "We are not cow-ards."

To Quintus' amazement, the rider stopped wailing.

"Form a line," Fabricius ordered again.

Moving together until their knees almost touched, the eight men rode forward. Wondering why he hadn't had a javelin in the back by now, Quintus turned. The Numidians had slowed to a walk. We're being herded to the slaughter like so many sheep, he thought in disgust.

"Keep your eyes to the front," Fabricius muttered. "Show the whore-sons that we are not afraid. We will look our fate in the eyes."

About 150 paces separated the Romans from the phalanxes. To Quintus, the distance felt like an eternity. Part of him wished that the travesty would just end, but he was also desperate not to die. Inexorably, the gap narrowed. A hundred paces, then eighty. Terrified now, Quintus glanced at his father. All he received in the way of reassurance was a tight nod. Quintus took a deep breath, forcing himself to be calm.

I am a boy no longer. How I face my death is my decision alone. I will make it as brave an end as possible.

"Ready spears," Fabricius ordered.

Quintus shot a look at Flaccus and was faintly pleased by his jutting chin. For all his arrogance, he was *not* a coward.

Sixty steps. They were nearing the distance of a long volley from the spearmen. As they crossed this invisible line, every one of the eight flinched. It was impossible not to. Yet nothing happened. Fabricius felt a new determination. They could ignore this torture if they wished. "Let's take some of the bastards with us! At the trot. Choose your targets!" he yelled, pointing his spear at a bearded Libyan.

Relieved that the movements of his horse concealed his shaking arm, Quintus took aim at a man with a notched helmet. Let it be over soon, he prayed. May the gods look after Mother and Aurelia. He heard the shout of orders as the Carthaginian officers prepared their soldiers for a final volley, saw hundreds of men's torsos twist as their right arms went back. Quintus closed his eyes. The darkness this granted was somehow comforting. He was aware of his pounding heart, and his mount between his knees. Bounded on each side by its companions, it would not stray from its course. All he had to do was hold on.

"Quintus?" bellowed a voice.

With a jerk, Quintus opened his eyelids. That shout had come from within the Carthaginian ranks. He glanced at his father. "Stop! You must stop!"

Something in Quintus' tone penetrated Fabricius' battle madness, and his fierce expression cleared. He raised his spear in the air. "Halt!"

Pulling hard on their reins, the Romans screeched to a halt ten paces from the forest of bristling spear tips. Unsettled, their horses tried to shy away. More than one Libyan shoved his weapon forward in an attempt to reach them. Quintus heard a familiar voice cry out in Carthaginian. Goose bumps rose on his arms. Ignoring his companions' confusion, he scanned the enemy ranks. He couldn't believe it when Hanno, clad in a Carthaginian officer's uniform, elbowed his way out of the phalanx a moment later. Quintus lowered his spear. "Hanno!"

"Quintus." Hanno's tone was flat. He spoke in Latin. "What are you doing here?"

"We were on a patrol," he replied. "A reconnaissance mission."

Hanno made a sweeping gesture with his right arm. "We control the whole plain. You must know that. What kind of fool would order an undertaking like that?"

"Our consul," Quintus muttered. He wasn't going to reveal Flaccus' involvement.

Hanno gave a derisory snort. "Enough said."

Quintus had the sense not to reply. He glanced at his father and saw that he too had recognized Hanno. Sensibly, Fabricius also said nothing. Flaccus and the cavalrymen looked baffled, and fearful. Quintus turned back to Hanno. He tried to ignore the fierce stares of the enemy soldiers.

"Hanno!" cried an angry voice. A torrent of Carthaginian followed as two more officers emerged, one from the phalanx on either side. The first was short and burly, with thick eyebrows, while the other was tall and athletic, with long black hair. Their features were too similar to Hanno's to be coincidence. They had to be his brothers, thought Quintus. "You found your family, then?"

"I did. And they want to know why you're still alive." Turning to his siblings, Hanno launched into a long explanation. With his stomach knotted in tension, Quintus watched. Their very lives depended on what was said. There was plenty of shouting and gesticulating, but eventually Hanno seemed satisfied. The shorter of his brothers looked most unhappy, however. He continued muttering loudly as the taller brother approached the Romans. His face was hard, but not without kindness, thought Quintus warily. He had to be Bostar.

"Hanno says that he owes his life to you twice over," Bostar said in accented Latin.

Quintus nodded. "That's true."

"For that reason, we have agreed not to slay you, or your father." At this, Sapho launched into another tirade, but Bostar ignored him. "Two lives for two debts."

"And the others?" asked Quintus, feeling sick.

"They must die."

"No," Quintus muttered. "Take them as prisoners. Please."

Bostar shook his head and turned away.

Cries of fear rose from the cavalrymen. Flaccus, however, sat up straight on his horse, gazing with contempt at the Libyans.

Quintus' gaze shot to Hanno, and found no pity there. "Show them some mercy."

"We have our orders," said Hanno in a harsh voice. "But you and your father are free to go." He snapped out a command, and the phalanx behind him split open, opening a passage to the ford.

An idea struck Quintus. "There is one other family member here."

Hanno turned. "Who?" he demanded suspiciously.

Quintus indicated Flaccus. "He is betrothed to Aurelia. Spare him also."

Hanno's nostrils flared in belated recognition. "If they are not married, he is not yet part of your family."

"You would not deprive Aurelia of her prospective husband, surely?" Quintus pleaded.

Hanno was shocked to feel resentful. "You ask for more than you know," he said from between gritted teeth.

"I ask it nonetheless," replied Quintus, meeting his gaze.

Hanno stalked closer to Flaccus. If the truth be known, he did not want to withdraw the hand of friendship so fast, but this *was* one of the enemy.

Incredibly, Flaccus spat a gob of phlegm at his feet.

Rage filled Hanno, and his hand fell to his sword. Before he could draw it, however, Sapho had stepped past. There was a spear gripped in his fists. Without saying a word, he shoved the blade deep into Flaccus' groin, below his armor, before ripping it out again. As his victim fell screaming to the ground, Sapho spun around. He aimed his bloody spear tip at Hanno. "We're not here to be friendly with these fucking whoresons," he snapped. "You and Bostar might have overridden me over releasing two of them, but you're not setting another one free!"

Hanno pointed grimly at the ford. "Go."

Quintus stared helplessly at Flaccus, who was clutching his wound while blood spurted from between his fingers. There was already a large pool beneath him. We can't just leave the poor bastard to die, Quintus thought. But what other choice have we?

Fabricius took the initiative. "May you meet each other in Elysium," he muttered to the cavalrymen. "Your family will be told that you died well," he said to Flaccus. Then, without so much as a backward glance, he rode toward the river. "Come on," he hissed at Quintus.

Trying to think of what to say, Quintus took a last look at Hanno. Rather than meet his gaze, the Carthaginian stared right through him. There was to be no farewell. Gritting his teeth, Quintus followed his father. At once his ears were filled with the cries of the five unfortunate cavalrymen, who were promptly surrounded and dispatched by the clamoring Libyans.

Father and son made their way unhindered to the ford, and into the water.

On the other side, it finally sank in that they had escaped.

A long, shuddering breath escaped Quintus' lips. Never let me meet Hanno again, he prayed. His former friend *would* try to kill him: there was no doubt about that. And Quintus realized that he would do the same. As cold misery gripped his heart, he stared back across the river. The Libyans were already marching away. They had left the crumpled forms of the Roman dead on the riverbank. The sight caused Quintus' shame to soar. Everyone deserved to be buried, or burned on a pyre. "Maybe we can retrieve the bodies tomorrow," he muttered.

"We'll have to try, or I'll never be able to look Aurelia in the eyes again," replied his father. *And the moment that the damn moneylenders hear that Flaccus is dead, they'll be all over me like a rash.* He glanced at Quintus. "It's all my damn fault. Flaccus and thirty good men are dead, because I agreed to lead the damn patrol. I should have refused."

"It's not up to you to make tactical decisions, Father," Quintus protested. "If you'd said no, Scipio could have demoted you to the ranks, or worse."

Fabricius shot Quintus a grateful look. "I'm only alive because of you. Helping the Carthaginian to escape and then manumitting him were good decisions. I'm grateful."

Quintus nodded sadly. His friendship with Hanno might have saved their lives, but this was not the way he'd have wanted it to end. There was nothing he could do to change things, however. Quintus hardened his heart. Hanno was one of the enemy now.

Fabricius rode straight back to the camp, and from there to the consul's command tent. Leaping from his horse, he threw his reins at one of the sentries and started toward the entrance. Quintus watched miserably from the back of his mount. Scipio would not want to speak to a low-ranking cavalryman such as he.

His father stopped by the tent flap. "Well?"

"You want me to come in?"

Fabricius laughed. "Of course. You are the sole reason we're still breathing. Scipio will want to hear why."

Reenergized, Quintus jumped down and joined his father. The sentries at the entrance, four sturdy *triarii*—veterans—wearing highly polished crested helmets and mail shirts, stood to attention as they passed. Quintus' chest swelled with pride. He was about to meet the consul! Until now, his only interactions with Scipio had been to salute and return a polite greeting.

They were ushered through various sections of the tent by a junior officer until they reached a comfortable area lined with carpets. The space was lit by large bronze lamps and contained a desk covered in parchments, ink pots and quills, various ironbound chests and several luxurious couches. Bolstered by cushions, Scipio was reclining on the biggest. His face was still an unhealthy gray color, and bulky dressings were visible on his injured leg. His son stood attentively behind him, reading from a half-unrolled manuscript. Scipio's eyes opened as they approached, and he acknowledged their salutes. "Well met, Fabricius," he murmured. "Is that your son?"

"Yes, sir."

"What's his name again?"

"Quintus, sir."

"Ah, yes. So, you have returned from your patrol. Did you meet with any success?"

"No, sir," Fabricius replied tersely. "In fact, the complete opposite. Before getting anywhere near the Carthaginian camp, we were ambushed by a hugely superior enemy force. They pursued us right to the riverbank, where a strong force of spearmen was waiting." He indicated Quintus. "We are the only survivors."

"I see." Scipio's fingers drummed on the arm of his couch. "How is it that you were not also killed?"

Fabricius met the consul's scrutiny with a solid gaze. "Because of Quintus here."

Scipio's brows lowered. "Explain."

Prompted by his father's nudge, Quintus told the story of how he had been recognized by a former slave of the family, whom he had befriended. He faltered when it came to explaining how Hanno had been freed, but encouraged by Scipio's nod, Quintus revealed everything.

"That is an incredible tale," Scipio acknowledged. "The gods were most merciful."

"Yes, sir," Quintus agreed fervently.

The consul looked up at his son. "You're not the only one able to rescue his father," he joked.

The younger Scipio blushed bright red.

Scipio's face turned serious. "So, a whole turma has been wiped out, and we know no more about Hannibal's disposition than yesterday."

"That's correct, sir," Fabricius admitted.

"I see little point in sending further patrols across the Trebia. They would meet the same fate, and we have few enough cavalry as it is," said Scipio. He pressed a finger against his lips, thinking. Then he shook his head. "Our main priority is to block the passage south, which we are already doing. The Carthaginians will not attack us here, because of the uneven terrain. Nothing has changed. We wait for Longus."

"Yes, sir," Fabricius concurred.

"Very good. You may go." Scipio waved a hand in dismissal.

Father and son made a discreet exit.

Quintus managed to contain his frustration until they were out of earshot. "Why doesn't Scipio *do* something?" he hissed.

"You want revenge for what happened at the ford, eh?" asked Fabricius with a wry smile. "I do too." He bent close to Quintus' ear. "I'm sure that Scipio would have moved against Hannibal again if he weren't . . . incapacitated. Of course he's not going to admit that to the likes of us. For the moment, we just have to live with it."

"Will Longus want to fight Hannibal?"

"I'd say so," replied his father with a grin. "A victory before the turn of the year would show the tribes that Hannibal is vulnerable. It would also reduce the number of warriors who plan on joining him. Defeating him soon would be far better than leaving it until the spring."

Quintus prayed that his father was correct. After all the setbacks they'd suffered, it was time for the tables to be turned. The quicker that was done, the better.

XXIII

BATTLE COMMENCES

Bostar waited until they'd got back to the Carthaginian camp before he launched his attack. The moment that their men had been stood down, he rounded on Hanno. "What the hell was that about?" he shouted. "Don't you remember our orders? We were supposed to kill them all!"

"I know," muttered Hanno. The sad image of Quintus and his father riding down to the Trebia was vivid in his mind's eye. "How, though, could I kill the person who had saved my life, not once, but twice?"

"So your sense of honor is more important than a direct order given by Hannibal?" Sapho sneered.

"Yes. No. I don't know," Hanno replied. "Leave me alone!"

"Sapho!" Bostar snapped.

Sapho raised his hands and stepped back. "Let's see what the general says when we report to him." He made a face. "I presume that you are going to tell him?"

Hanno felt a towering fury take hold. "Of course I am!" he cried.

"I've got nothing to hide. What, were you going to tell Hannibal if I didn't?" His mouth opened as Sapho flushed. "Sacred Tanit, you fucking were! Where did you get to be so poisonous? No wonder Bostar doesn't like you anymore." He saw Sapho's shock, and despite his anger, felt instant shame. "I shouldn't have said that. I'm sorry."

"It's a bit late," retorted Sapho. "Why should I be surprised that you've been talking about me behind my back? You little dirtbag!"

Hanno flushed and hung his head.

"I'll see you at the general's tent," said Sapho sourly. "We'll see what Hannibal thinks of what you've done then." Pulling his cloak tighter around himself, he walked away.

"Sapho! Come back!" Hanno shouted.

"Let him go," advised Bostar.

"Why is he being like that?"

"I don't know," said Bostar, looking away.

Now you're the one who's lying, thought Hanno, but he didn't have the heart to interrogate his older brother. Soon he would have to explain his actions to Hannibal. "Come on," he said anxiously. "We'd best get this over with."

⁓

Hanno was relieved to find that Sapho had not entered Hannibal's tent, but was waiting outside for them. Zamar, the Numidian officer, was there too. Announcing themselves to the guards, they were ushered inside.

Hanno slipped to Sapho's side. "Thank you."

Sapho gave him a startled look. "For what?"

"Not going in to tell your version of the story first."

"I might disagree with what you did, but I'm not a telltale," Sapho shot back in an angry whisper.

"I know," said Hanno. "Let's just see what Hannibal says, eh? After that, we can forget about it."

"No more talking about me behind my back," Sapho warned.

"It's not as if Bostar said much. He commented that after the pirates' capture, you had changed."

"Changed?"

"Grown tougher. Harder."

"Nothing else?" Sapho demanded.

"No." What in Tanit's name happened between you two? Hanno wondered. He wasn't sure he wanted to know.

Sapho was silent for a moment. "Very well. We'll put it behind us after we've reported to Hannibal. But understand this: If he asks me my opinion about the release of the two Romans, I'm not going to lie to him."

"That's fine," said Hanno heatedly. "I wouldn't want you to."

Their conversation came to an abrupt halt as they entered the main part of Hannibal's tent.

The general greeted them with a broad smile. "Word of your success has already reached me," he declared. He raised his glass. "Come, taste this wine. For a Roman vintage, it's quite palatable."

When they all had a glass in hand, Hannibal looked at them each in turn. "Well?" he inquired. "Who's going to tell me what happened?"

Hanno stepped forward. "I will, sir," he said, swallowing.

Hannibal's eyebrows rose, but he indicated that Hanno should continue.

Shoving away his nervousness, Hanno described their march to the Trebia, and the long wait in the hidden clearing. When he got to the point where the Roman patrol had crossed, he turned to Zamar. The Numidian related how his men had carried word to him of the enemy incursion, and of how the ambush had been sprung early by an over-eager section leader. "I've already stripped him to the ranks, sir," he said. "Thanks to him, the whole thing might have been a disaster."

"But it wasn't, thankfully," Hannibal replied. "Did any make it to the river?"

"Yes, sir," said Zamar. "Eight."

Hannibal winked. "That didn't leave much work for nine hundred spearmen!"

They all laughed.

"Did you find any documents on the Roman commander?"

Hanno didn't know how to answer. "No, sir," he muttered. From the corner of his eye, he could see Sapho glaring at him.

Hannibal didn't notice Hanno's reticence. "A shame. Still, never mind. It's unlikely that they would carry anything of importance on such a mission anyway."

Hanno coughed awkwardly. "I didn't manage to search him, sir."

"Why not?" asked Hannibal, frowning.

"Because I let him go, sir. Along with one other."

The general's eyes widened in disbelief. "You had best explain yourself, son of Malchus. *Fast.*"

Hannibal's intense stare was unnerving. "Yes, sir." Hanno hastily began. When he had finished, there was a pregnant silence. Hanno thought he was going to be sick.

Hannibal eyed Sapho and Bostar askance. "Presumably, he consulted with you two," he snapped.

"Yes, sir," they mumbled.

"What was your reaction, Bostar?"

"Although it was against your orders, sir, I respected his reason for wanting to let the two men go."

Hannibal looked at Sapho.

"I violently disagreed, sir, but I was overruled."

Hannibal regarded Zamar. "And you?"

"I had nothing to do with it, sir," the Numidian replied neutrally. "I was a hundred paces away with my men."

"Interesting," said Hannibal to Hanno. "One brother supported you, one did not."

"Yes, sir."

"Is this what I am to expect in future when I issue a command?" demanded Hannibal, his nostrils flaring.

"No, sir," protested Bostar and Hanno. "Of course not," Hanno added.

Hannibal didn't comment further. "Do I detect that there was quite an amount of disagreement?"

Hanno flushed. "You do, sir."

"Why was that?"

"Because we were given orders to let none survive, sir!" cried Sapho.

"Finally, we come back to the nub of the issue," said Hannibal. In the background, Sapho smiled triumphantly. "Under ordinary circumstances, this situation would be black and white. And if you'd disobeyed my orders as you have done, I would have had you cruci-fied."

His words hung in the air like a bad smell.

Fear twisted Sapho's face. "Sir, I . . ." he began.

"Did I ask you to speak?" Hannibal snapped.

"No, sir."

"Then keep your mouth shut!"

Humbled, Sapho obeyed.

Hanno wiped his brow, which was covered in sweat. I still did the right thing, he thought. I owed Quintus my life. Sure that, at the very least, a severe punishment was about to follow, he resigned him-self to his fate. Beside him, Bostar was clenching and unclenching his jaw.

"Yet what transpired happens but once in a host of lifetimes," said Hannibal.

Stunned, Hanno waited to hear what his general said next.

"A man can't go killing those who have helped him, even if they are Roman. I cannot think of a better way to anger the gods." Hannibal gave Hanno a grim nod. "You did the right thing."

"Thank you, sir," whispered Hanno. He'd never been so relieved in his life.

"I will let you off, Bostar, because of the unique nature of what happened."

Bostar stood rigidly to attention and saluted. "Thank you, sir!"

Hanno glanced at Sapho. His fear had been replaced by a poorly concealed expression of resentment. Did he want us to be punished? Hanno wondered uneasily.

"As well as satisfying your honor, your lenient gesture fulfilled an-other purpose," Hannibal continued. "Those two men will speak of little but the excellence of our troops. Some of their comrades will be demoralized by what they hear, which helps our cause. Despite your disobedience, you have achieved the result I wanted."

"Yes, sir."

"That's not all," said Hannibal lightly.

Hanno's fear returned with a vengeance. "Sir?"

"There can be no repeat of such behavior." Hannibal's voice had grown hard. "You have paid off your obligation to this *Quintus*. Should you see either him or his father again, you can act in only one way."

He's right, screamed Hanno's common sense. How can I remain friends with a Roman? Despite everything, his heart felt differently. "Yes, sir."

"Trust me, those men would bury a sword in your belly as soon as look at you. They are the enemy," growled Hannibal. "If you meet either again, you will kill them."

"Yes, sir," Hanno said, finally giving in. *But never let it happen.*

"Understand too that if any of you disobey my orders again, I will *not* be merciful. Instead, expect to end your miserable lives screaming on a cross. Understand?"

"Yes, sir," replied Hanno, shaking.

"You're dismissed," said Hannibal curtly. "All of you."

Muttering their thanks, Zamar and the three brothers withdrew.

Sapho sidled up to Hanno outside. "Still think you did the right thing?" he hissed.

"Eh?" Hanno gave his brother an incredulous look.

"We could all be dead now, thanks to you."

"But we're not! And it's not as if such a thing will ever happen again, is it?" demanded Hanno.

"I suppose not," Sapho admitted, taken aback by Hanno's fury.

"I'm as loyal as you or any man in the damn army," Hanno snarled. "Line me up some Romans, and I'll chop off all their fucking heads!"

"All right, all right," muttered Sapho. "You've made your point."

"So have you," retorted Hanno angrily. "Did you want us to be punished in there?"

Sapho made an apologetic gesture. "Look, I had no idea he might crucify you."

"Would you have said anything to Hannibal if you had?" challenged Bostar.

A guilty look stole across Sapho's face. "No."

"You're a fucking liar," said Bostar. Without another word, he walked off.

Hanno glared at Sapho. "Well?"

"Do you really think I'd want the two of you to die? Please!" Sapho protested. "Have some faith in me!"

Hanno sighed. "I do. I'm sorry."

"So am I," said Sapho, clapping him on the shoulder. "Let's forget about it, eh? Concentrate on fighting the Romans."

"Yes." Hanno glanced after Bostar, and his heart sank. His other brother looked angered by the friendly gesture Sapho had just made. Gods above, he thought in frustration, can I not get on with the two of them?

It appeared not.

Saturnalia was fast approaching. Despite Atia and Aurelia's melancholy, preparations for the midwinter festival were well under way. It was a way, Aurelia realized, of coping with the void both of them felt inside at her father's probable death, and the lack of word from Quintus. Life had to go on in some fashion, and losing themselves in mundane tasks had proved to be an effective method of maintaining normality. There was so much to be done that the short winter days flashed by in a blur. Atia's list of things to do seemed never-ending. Each evening, Aurelia was worn out, and grateful that her exhaustion meant deep slumber without any bad dreams.

One night, however, Aurelia did not fall asleep as usual. Her mind was racing. She and her mother were going to Capua in two days on a final shopping expedition. Dozens of candles were still required as gifts for their family friends and the guests. Not all of the food for their impending feasts had been ordered yet—there had been a mix-up with the baker over what was needed, and the butcher wanted far too much money for his meat. Atia also wanted to purchase pottery figurines; these were exchanged on the last day of the celebrations.

Despite her best efforts, Aurelia found herself thinking about Suniaton. After meeting Agesandros, she and Elira had made their way to the hut without any difficulty. Pleasingly, Suni's leg had healed enough for him to leave. He's long gone, thought Aurelia sadly. Suniaton had been her last link with Hanno, and in a strange way, Quintus and her father. It was entirely possible that she would never see any of them again. On the spur of the moment, she decided to visit the isolated dwelling one more time. What for, Aurelia wasn't sure. Perhaps the gods would offer her some kind of sign there. Something that would make her grief more bearable. Keeping this idea to the forefront of her mind, she managed to fall asleep.

Waking early the next morning, Aurelia dressed in her warmest clothes. She was relieved to find only a finger's depth of snow covering the statues and mosaic floor in the courtyard. Pausing to tell a sleepy Elira where she was going, and to raise the alarm if she was not back by nightfall, Aurelia went to the stables and readied her father's gray horse.

She had never ridden so far from the farm in the depths of winter before, and was stunned by the beauty of the silent countryside. It was such a contrast to the spring and summer, when everything was bursting with life. Most of the trees had lost their leaves, scattering them in thick layers upon the ground, layers that were now frozen beneath a light covering of snow. The only movement was the occasional flash of wildlife: a pair of crows tumbling through the air in pursuit of a falcon, the suggestion of a deer in the distance. Once, Aurelia thought she saw a jackal skulking off into the undergrowth. Gratifyingly, she heard no wolves, and saw no sign of their spoor. Although it was rare for the large predators to attack humans, it was not unheard of. The chances of seeing them grew as she climbed, however, and Aurelia was grateful that she had taken a bow as well as her sling.

Her anticipation grew as she neared the hut. Its peaceful atmosphere would assuage her worries about her loved ones. With a growing sense of excitement, Aurelia tied up her horse outside. She scattered a handful of oats on the ground to keep it happy, and stepped toward the door. A faint sound from inside stopped her dead. Terror paralyzed Aurelia's every muscle as she remembered the bandits whom Quintus and Hanno had fought. What had she been thinking to travel alone?

Turning on her heel, Aurelia tiptoed away from the hut. If she made it onto her saddle blanket, there was a good chance of escaping. Few men possessed the skill with a bow to bring down a rider on a galloping horse. She had almost reached her mount when it looked up from its oats, and gave her a pleased whinny. Frantically stroking its head to silence it, Aurelia listened. All she could hear was her heart pounding in her chest like that of a captured beast. Taking a good grip of the horse's mane, she prepared to scramble on to its back.

"Hello?"

Aurelia nearly jumped out of her skin with fright.

A moment passed. The door did not open.

Aurelia managed to calm herself. The voice had been weak and quavering, and certainly not that of a strong, healthy man. Gradually, her curiosity began to equal her fear. "Who's there? I'm not alone."

There was no response.

Aurelia began to wonder if it was a trap after all. She vacillated, torn between riding to safety and checking that whoever was inside did not need help. At length, she decided not to flee. If this was an ambush, it was the worst-laid one she could think of. Gripping her dagger to give her confidence, she padded toward the hut. There was no handle or latch, just a gap in the timbers to pull open the portal. With trembling fingers, Aurelia flipped the door toward her, placing her foot against the bottom edge to hold it ajar. She peered cautiously into the dim interior. Instead of the fire she might have expected, the round stone fireplace was full of ashes. Aurelia gagged as the acrid smell of human urine and feces wafted outside.

Finally, she made out a figure lying sprawled on the floor. She had taken it first for a bundle of rags. When it moved, she screamed. "S-Suni?"

His eyes opened wide. "Is that you, Aurelia?"

"Yes, it is." She darted inside and dropped to her knees by his side. "Oh, Suniaton!" She struggled not to weep.

"Have you any water?"

"Better than that: I have wine!" Aurelia ran outside, returning with her supplies. Gently, she helped him to sit up and drink a few mouthfuls.

"That's better," Suniaton declared. A tinge of color began to appear in his cheeks, and he cast greedy eyes at Aurelia's bag.

Delighted by his revival, she laid out some bread and cheese. "Eat a little at a time," she warned. "Your stomach won't be able to take anymore." She sat and watched him as he devoured the food. "Why didn't you leave after my last visit?"

He paused between mouthfuls. "I did, the next day. About half a mile down the track, I tripped over a jutting tree root and landed awkwardly. The fall tore the muscles that had just healed in my bad leg. I couldn't walk ten steps without screaming, never mind reach Capua or the coast. It was all I could do to crawl back to the hut. My food ran out more than a week ago, and my water two days after that." He pointed at the hole in the roof. "If it hadn't been for the snow that came through that, I would have died of thirst." He smiled. "They took their time, but the gods answered my prayers."

Aurelia squeezed his hand. "They did. Something told me to come up here. Obviously, you were the reason why."

"But I can't stay here," Suniaton said despairingly. "One heavy fall of snow and the roof will give way."

"Don't worry," Aurelia cried. "My horse can carry both of us."

His expression was bleak. "Where to, though? My leg will take months to heal, if it does at all."

"To the farm," she replied boldly. "I will tell Mother and Agesandros that I found you wandering in the woods. I couldn't just leave you to die."

"He might remember me," Suniaton protested.

She squeezed his hand. "He won't. You look terrible. Totally different from that day in Capua."

Suniaton scowled. "It's obvious that I am an escaped slave."

"But there won't be any way of proving who you are," Aurelia cried in triumph. "You can act mute."

"Will that work?" he asked with a dubious frown.

"Of course," Aurelia declared robustly. "And when you're better, you can leave."

A spark of hope lit in Suniaton's weary eyes. "If you're sure," he whispered.

"I am," Aurelia replied, patting his hand. Inside, however, she was terrified.

What other choice had they, though? her mind screamed.

More than two weeks later, Quintus was wandering through the camp with Calatinus and Cincius. The general mood had been improved dramatically seven days before by the arrival of Tiberius Sempronius Longus, the second consul. His army, which consisted of two legions and more than 10,000 socii, infantry and cavalry, had swelled the Roman forces to nearly 40,000 men.

Inevitably enough, the trio found their feet taking them in the direction of the camp headquarters. So far, there had been little news of what Longus, who had assumed control of all Republican forces, planned to do about Hannibal.

"He'll have been encouraged by what happened yesterday," declared Calatinus. "Our cavalry and velites gave the guggas a hiding that they won't forget in a hurry."

"Stupid bastards got what was coming to them," said Cincius. "The Gauls are supposed to be their allies. If they go pillaging local settlements, it's natural that the tribesmen will come looking for help."

"There were heavy enemy casualties," Quintus admitted, "but I'm not sure it was the total victory Longus is claiming."

Both of his friends looked at him in astonishment.

"Think about it," urged Quintus. It was what his father had said to him when he'd raved about the engagement. "We had the upper hand from the start, but things changed immediately once Hannibal came on the scene. The Carthaginians held their ground then, didn't they?"

"So what?" Cincius responded. "They lost three times more men than we did!"

"Aren't you pleased that we finally got the better of them?" demanded Calatinus.

"Of course I am," said Quintus. "We shouldn't underestimate Hannibal, that's all."

Cincius snorted derisively. "Longus is an experienced general. And in my book, any man who can march his army more than a thousand miles in less than six weeks shows considerable ability."

"You've seen Longus a few times since his arrival. The man positively exudes energy," added Calatinus. "He's keen for a fight too."

"You're right," said Quintus at last. "Our troops are better fed, and better armed than Hannibal's. We outnumber the Carthaginians too."

"We just need the right opportunity," declared Cincius.

"That will come," said Calatinus. "All the recent omens have been good."

Quintus grinned. It was impossible not to feel enthused by his friends' words, and the recent change in their fortunes. As always when Quintus thought of the enemy, an image of Hanno popped into his mind. He shoved it away.

There was a war on.

Friendship with a Carthaginian had no place in his heart any longer.

———

Several days passed, and the weather grew dramatically worse. The biting wind came incessantly from the north, bringing with it heavy showers of sleet and snow. Combined with the shortened daylight, it made for a miserable existence. Hanno saw little of either his father or brothers. The Carthaginian soldiers huddled in their tents, shivering and trying to stay warm. Even venturing outside to answer a call of nature meant getting soaked to the skin or chilled to the bone.

Hanno was stunned, therefore, by the news that Sapho brought one afternoon. "We've had word from Hannibal!" he hissed. "We move out tonight."

"In weather like this?" asked Hanno incredulously. "Are you mad?"

"Maybe." Sapho grinned. "If I am, though, so too is Hannibal. He has ordered Mago himself to lead us."

"You and Bostar?"

Sapho nodded grimly. "Plus five hundred skirmishers, and a thousand Numidian cavalry."

Hanno smiled to cover his disappointment at not also being picked. "Where are you going?"

"While we've been hiding in our tents, Hannibal has been scouting the whole area. He discovered a narrow river that runs across the plain," Sapho revealed. "It's bounded on both sides by steep, heavily overgrown banks. We have to lie in wait there until the opportunity comes—if it comes—to fall upon the Roman rear."

"What makes Hannibal think that they'll cross the river?"

Sapho's expression grew fierce. "He plans to irritate them into doing so."

"That means using the Numidians," guessed Hanno.

"You've got it. They're going to attack the enemy camp at dawn. Sting and withdraw, sting and withdraw. You know the way they do it."

"Will it drag the whole Roman army out of camp, though?"

"We'll see."

"I wish I'd been chosen too," said Hanno fervently.

Sapho chuckled. "Save your regrets. The whole damn enterprise might be a waste of time. While Bostar and I are freezing our balls off in a ditch, you and the rest of the army will be warmly wrapped up in your blankets. And if a battle does look likely, it's not as if you'll miss out, is it? We'll all have to fight!"

A grin slowly spread across Hanno's face. "True enough."

"We'll meet in the middle of the Roman line!" declared Sapho. "Just think of that moment."

Hanno nodded. It was an appealing image. "The gods watch over you both," he said. I must go and speak to Bostar, he thought. Say goodbye.

"And you, little brother." Sapho reached out and ruffled Hanno's hair, something he hadn't done for years.

———

Quintus was in the middle of a fantasy about Elira when he became aware of someone shaking him. He did his best to stay asleep, but the insistent tugging on his arm proved too much. Opening his eyes irritably, Quintus found not Elira, but Calatinus crouched over him. Before he could utter a word of rebuke, he heard the trumpets sounding the alarm over and over. He sat bolt upright. "What's going on?"

"Our outposts beyond the camp perimeter are under attack. Get up!"

The last of Quintus' drowsiness vanished. "Eh? What time is it?"

"Not long after dawn. The sentries started shouting when I was in the latrines." Calatinus scowled. "Didn't help my diarrhea, I can tell you."

Smiling at the image, Quintus threw off the covers and began scrambling into his clothes. "Have we had any orders yet?"

"Longus wants every man ready to leave a quarter of an hour ago," replied Calatinus, who was already fully dressed. "I've been shouting at you to no avail. The others are readying their mounts."

"Well, I'm here now," muttered Quintus, kneeling to strap on his sandals.

Before long, they had joined their comrades outside, by their tethered horses.

It was bitterly cold, and the north wind was whipping vicious little flurries of snow across the tent tops. The camp was in uproar as thousands of men scrambled to get ready. It wasn't just the cavalry who had been ordered to prepare themselves for battle. Large groups of velites were being addressed by their officers. Unhappy-looking *hastati* and *principes*—the men who stood in the legion's first two ranks—left their breakfasts to burn on their campfires as they ran to get their equipment. Messengers hurried to and fro, relaying information between different units. On the battlements, the trumpeters kept up their clarion call to arms. Quintus swallowed nervously. Was this the moment he had been waiting for? It certainly felt like it. Soon after, he was relieved to see his father's figure striding toward them from the direction of the camp's headquarters. Excited murmurs rippled through the surrounding cavalrymen. As one, they stiffened to attention.

"This is no parade. At ease," said Fabricius, waving a hand. "We ride out at once. Longus is deploying our entire cavalry force, as well as six thousand velites. He wants this attack thrown back across the Trebia without delay. We're taking no more nonsense from Hannibal."

"And the rest of the army, sir?" cried a voice. "What about them?"

Fabricius smiled tightly. "They will be ready to follow us very soon."

These words produced a rousing cheer. Quintus joined in. He wanted this victory as much as anyone else. The fact that his father hadn't mentioned Scipio must mean that the injured consul agreed with his colleague's decision, or had been overruled by him. Either way, they weren't going to sit by and do nothing.

Fabricius waited until the noise had died down. "Remember to do everything I've taught you. Check your horse's harness is tightly fastened. Take a leak before you mount up. There's nothing worse than pissing yourself in the middle of a fight." Hoots of nervous laughter met this comment, and Fabricius smiled. "Ensure that your spear tip is sharp. Tie the chinstrap on your helmet. Watch each other's backs." He scanned the faces around him with grave eyes. "May the gods be with you all."

"And with you, sir!" shouted Calatinus.

Fabricius inclined his head in recognition. Then, giving Quintus a reassuring look, he made toward his horse.

For the third time since dawn, Bostar scrambled up the muddy slope toward the sentry's position. More than anything, he wanted to warm up. Unfortunately, the climb wasn't long enough to shift the chill from his muscles. He glanced down at the steep-sided riverbank below him. It was filled with Mago's men: 1,000 Numidians and their horses, and 1,000 infantry, a mixture of Libyan skirmishers and spearmen. Despite the fact that the warmly dressed soldiers were packed as tightly as apples in a barrel, it seemed an eternity since they had arrived. In fact, it was barely five hours. Men are not supposed to spend a winter's night outdoors in this godforsaken land, thought Bostar bitterly. His bones ached at the idea of the warm sunshine that bathed Carthage daily.

Reaching the top of the bank, Bostar crouched down, using the scrubby bushes that regularly dotted the ground as cover. He peered into the distance, but saw nothing. There had been no movement since the Numidian cavalry had quietly passed by, heading for the Roman side of the river. Bostar sighed. It would be hours before anything of importance happened. Nonetheless, he had to keep his guard up. Hannibal had given them the most important task of any soldiers in his army. For what felt like the thousandth time, Bostar slowly turned in a circle, scanning the landscape with eagle eyes.

The watercourse that formed their hiding place was a small tributary of the Trebia, and ran north–south across the plain that lay before the Carthaginian camp. Following Hannibal's instructions, they had secreted themselves half a mile to the south of the area upon which he wished to fight. The general's reasons were simple. Behind them, the ground began to climb toward the low hills that filled the horizon. If the Romans took the bait, they were unlikely to march in this direction. It was a good place to hide, thought Bostar. He just hoped that Hannibal's plan worked, and that they weren't too far away from the fighting if, or when, the time came to move.

He found Mago lying alongside the sentry in a shallow dip, seemingly oblivious to the cold. Bostar liked the youngest Barca brother. Like Hannibal, Mago was charismatic and brave. He was also indomitably cheerful, which provided a counterweight to Hannibal's sometimes serious disposition. Smaller than Hannibal, Mago reminded Bostar of a hunting dog: lean, muscular and always eager to be slipped from the leash. "Seen anything, sir?" he whispered.

Mago turned his head. "Restless, aren't you?"

Bostar shrugged. "The same as everyone else, sir. It's difficult waiting down there without a clue what's going on."

Mago smiled. "Patience," he said. "The Romans will come."

"How can you be sure, sir?"

"Because Hannibal believes that they will, and I trust in him."

Bostar nodded. It was a good answer, he thought. "We'll be ready, sir."

"I know you will. That's why Hannibal picked you and your brother," Mago replied.

"We're very grateful for the opportunity, sir," said Bostar, thinking sour thoughts about Sapho. He and his older brother hadn't spoken since Hannibal's reprimand. Bostar felt regret that he'd only had the briefest of words with Hanno before they'd left the camp. He'd been angry that his younger brother seemed to be friendly with Sapho. Really, it was none of his business.

Mago got to his feet. "Have the men eaten yet?"

"No, sir."

"Well, if I'm famished, they must be too," Mago declared. "Let's break out the rations. It won't be a hot breakfast, like the lucky dogs back at camp will get, but anything's better than nothing. A man with a full belly sees the world with different eyes, eh?" He glanced at the sentry. "You won't miss out. I'll send someone up to relieve you soon."

The man grinned. "Thank you, sir."

"Lead on," Mago said.

Bostar obeyed. Mention of the encampment brought his father and Hanno to mind. If it came to a battle, they would be in the front line. Not quite in the center—that honor had been given to Hannibal's new recruits, the Gaulish tribesmen—but still in a dangerous position. The fighting everywhere would be intense. He sighed. The gods protect us all, he prayed. If it comes to it, let us die well.

———※———

Combining his riders with Scipio's depleted horsemen gave Sempronius Longus just over four thousand cavalry. The moment that the assembled turmae had heard their orders, they were sent out from behind the protection of the fortifications. Fabricius and his men were among the first to exit the camp.

Quintus blinked with surprise. Beyond the sentry posts lay open ground that rolled down to the river. It was normally empty of all but the figures of training soldiers or returning patrols. Now, it was occupied by thousands of Numidian tribesmen. Waves of yelling warriors were galloping into the Roman positions and loosing their javelins, before wheeling their horses in a tight circle and retreating. The unfortunate sentries, who only numbered four or five per outpost, received no respite. Scarcely had one set of Numidians disappeared before another arrived, whooping and screaming at the top of their lungs.

"Form a battle line!" Fabricius shouted. His call was already being echoed by other officers who were emerging from the camp.

With a pounding heart, Quintus obeyed. So did Calatinus, Cincius and his comrades, each turma fanning out six ranks wide and five riders deep. The instant they were ready, Fabricius shouted, "Charge!"

His men went from the trot into a canter. This was followed immediately by a gallop. For maximum impact, they had to hit the Numidians at full speed. That was if the enemy riders stayed to fight, thought Quintus suspiciously. His experience with the fierce tribesmen had taught him otherwise. Yet Longus was doing the right thing.

He could not just let his sentries be massacred within sight of his camp. Hannibal's men had to be driven off. With six thousand velites following hot on their heels, that would not be difficult.

The thunder of hundreds of hooves drowned out all sound except the occasional encouraging shout from Fabricius: "Forward!" As they closed in, each man let go of his reins and transferred the spear from his left hand, which also held his shield, to his right. From here on in, they would guide their horses with their knees. Now the months of careful instruction they had received would pay off. For all his comrades' skill, Quintus was still wary of the Numidians, who learned to ride almost before they could walk. He was heartened by the thought of the velites. Their help would make all the difference.

"Look! They've seen us!" shouted Calatinus, pointing at the beleaguered sentries, whose terrified expressions were being replaced by elation. "Hold on!"

"The poor bastards must have got the shock of their lives when the Numidians suddenly appeared," replied Quintus.

"We're coming none too soon," Calatinus added. "Many of the outposts have no defenders left."

They had closed to within fifty paces of the enemy.

"Time to even up the score," cried Quintus, picking out a slight Numidian with braided hair as his target.

Cincius' lip curled. "They'll turn and run any moment now, the way they always do."

Instead, to their amazement, the enemy riders turned and began driving their horses straight at the Roman cavalry.

"They're going to fight, not run." Quintus felt faintly nauseous, but he kept his eye on the Numidian who was riding straight at him. Oddly, it seemed the warrior had also chosen him.

"Pick your targets," Fabricius shouted, praying that the outcome of this clash proved different to the one at the Ticinus. "Make every spear count."

Seeing the Numidian loose a javelin in his direction, Quintus panicked. Fortunately, it missed, sailing between him and Calatinus. Quintus cursed savagely. The Numidian still had two javelins. Even as the thought went through his mind, the next one scudded his way. He bent low over his horse's neck, hearing it whistle overhead. Claws of desperation tore at him. How long would his luck hold out? He was fewer than twenty paces from his enemy. At that range and closing, the warrior could hardly miss.

The Numidian held on to his last javelin until he was practically on top of Quintus. His error meant that Quintus was able to catch the missile in his shield. He had to discard the useless thing, but he was also able to stab his spear deep into the Numidian's belly as he rode past. Side by side, Quintus and Calatinus struck the enemy formation. At once the world shrank to a small area in their immediate vicinity. Quintus' ears rang with the clash of arms and men's screams, a deafening cacophony that added hugely to the confusion. The press of opposing riders pushing against each other meant that he seldom fought the same opponent for more than a couple of strokes. Quintus' first opponent was a young Numidian who nearly took his eye out with a well-aimed javelin. He jabbed his spear unsuccessfully at the warrior before being swept twenty paces away, never to see him again.

In quick succession, Quintus fought two more Numidians, stabbing one in the arm and plunging his weapon into the other's chest. Next he went to the aid of a Roman cavalryman who was being attacked by three enemy riders. They fought desperately for what seemed an age, barely able to defend themselves against the Numidians' lightning-quick javelin thrusts. And then, like wraiths, the warriors were gone, galloping off into the distance. All across the battlefield, Quintus could see their companions doing the same. It was done with the ease of a shoal of fish changing direction. Unexpectedly, though, the Numidians reined in several hundred paces away. They began shouting insults at the Romans, who responded loudly and in kind.

"Mangy bastards!" shouted Cincius.

"Come back, you goat-fuckers!" roared Calatinus.

Quintus grinned. "We've driven them a good distance from the camp already."

"Yes," agreed Calatinus, whose face was drenched in sweat. "Time for a rest. I'm bloody exhausted."

"And me," added Cincius.

Fabricius and his fellow officers let the Roman cavalry catch their breath for a few moments. Clouds of condensation hung above the mass of horsemen, but were soon dispersed by the heavy sleet that began to fall.

"Time to move before you all freeze to death," bellowed Fabricius.

Quintus glanced at Calatinus and Cincius. "Ready for another bout?"

"Definitely," they snarled in unison.

Right on cue, Fabricius' voice bellowed the command. "Hold the line! Advance!" The call was repeated by all along the front rank. The Roman horsemen needed little encouragement, and urged their mounts forward. Once again, the ground shook as thousands of horses pounded across the soft ground. This time, the Numidians fought for only a short time before retreating. Yet the tribesmen did not go far. Instead, they turned to fight again. Without pause, the Roman cavalrymen charged at their enemies. Keeping up the momentum of an attack was vital.

Their confidence was boosted by the sight, to their rear, of six thousand velites pouring to their aid. The fact that they were on foot did not take away from the skirmishers' value. They would first consolidate and hold the area that had been taken back from the Numidians. If the enemy horsemen decided to stand their ground, the velites could support their comrades and tilt the balance in their favor. If, on the other hand, the Roman cavalrymen were driven back, then the velites would provide a protective screen for them to fall back through. It was a win-win situation, thought Quintus jubilantly.

At daybreak, the horns that normally signaled the Carthaginian troops to get up remained silent. Used to army routine, most men were already awake. Hanno smiled as he listened to the rumors filling the tents around him. The rank-and-file troops had no idea yet why they had not been ordered from their beds. The majority were happy not to inquire, but some of the more eager ones poked their heads outside. Their officers told them that nothing was wrong. Not wanting to pass up such a rare opportunity, the soldiers duly returned to the comfort of their blankets. For half an hour, an unusual calm fell over the encampment. To the Carthaginians, it was a small dose of heaven. Despite the inclement weather, they were dry, warm and safe.

Finally, the horns did sound. There was no alarm, just the normal notes that indicated it was time to rise. Hanno began moving from tent to tent, encouraging his men.

"What's going on, sir?" asked a short spearman with a bushy black beard.

Hanno grinned. "You want to know?"

"Yes, sir," came the eager reply.

Hanno was fully aware that every soldier within earshot was listening. "The Numidians are attacking the Roman camp even as we speak."

A rousing cheer went up, and Hanno raised his hands. "Even if the whoresons take the bait and follow our cavalry, it will take them an age to cross the Trebia. You have plenty of time to get ready."

Pleased mutters met this comment.

"I want you to prepare yourselves well. Stretch and oil your muscles. Check all your equipment. When you're ready, lay your arms aside and prepare a hot breakfast. Clear?"

"Yes, sir," his men shouted.

Hanno retired to his own tent in search of food. When that was done, he lay down on his bed and instantly fell asleep. For the first time since leaving Carthage, Hanno dreamed of his mother, Arishat. She did not seem concerned that Malchus and her three sons were in Hannibal's army. Hanno found this immensely reassuring. His mother's spirit was watching over them all.

Soon after, he was roused by the horns sounding the call that meant "Enemy in sight."

Hanno sat bolt upright in bed, his heart racing. The Romans *had* followed the Numidians! He and every man in the army were about to be given their first chance to punish Rome for what it had done to his people.

They would grasp it with both hands.

⸺

Little more than an hour later, eight thousand of Hannibal's skirmishers and spearmen, with Hanno among them, had been deployed about a mile and a half east of their camp. Behind this protective screen, the rest of the army was slowly assuming battle formation. Hearing that the entire enemy host was crossing the Trebia, the Carthaginian general had finally responded. Hanno was delighted by Hannibal's ingenuity. Unlike the Romans, who had not eaten and were even now fording chest deep, freezing water, Hannibal's soldiers had full bellies and came fresh from their fires. Even at this distance, the chill air was filled with their ribald marching songs. He could hear the elephants bugling too, protesting as they were taken from their hay and sent out to the flanks.

Hanno was positioned at the easternmost point of the defensive semicircle, nearest the River Trebia. It was where contact with the Romans would first be made. To facilitate the Numidians' withdrawal, gaps had been left between each unit. These could easily be closed if necessary. Five score paces in front of the Libyans' bristling spears, hundreds of Balearic slingers waited patiently, the leather straps of their weapons dangling from their fists. The tribesmen didn't look that impressive, thought Hanno, but he knew that the egg-sized stones hurled by their slings could travel long distances to crack a man's skull. The ragged-looking skirmishers' volleys could strike terror into an advancing enemy.

The wind had died down, allowing the gray-yellow clouds to release heavy showers of snow on the waiting troops. They would have to bear with it, Hanno decided grimly. Nothing would happen for a while. The Numidians were still retreating across the Trebia. When the Roman cavalry arrived, they probably wouldn't attack the protective screen. He was correct. Over the following half an hour, squadron after squadron of Numidians escaped between the phalanxes. Soon after, Hanno was pleased to recognize Zamar approaching. He raised a hand in greeting. "What news?"

Zamar slowed his horse to a walk. "Things go well. I wasn't sure if the Romans were up for a fight to start off with, but they poured out of their camp like a tide of ants."

"Just their cavalry?"

"No, thousands of skirmishers too." Zamar grinned. "Then the infantry followed."

Thank you, great Melqart, thought Hanno delightedly.

"We fought and withdrew repeatedly, and gradually led them down to the river. That was where we took most of our casualties. Had to make it look as if we were panicking, see?" said Zamar with a scowl. His face lifted quickly. "Anyway, it worked. The enemy foot soldiers followed their cavalry into the water and started wading across. To cap it all, that was when the snow really started falling. You could see the fuckers' faces turning blue!"

"Did they turn back?"

"No," replied Zamar with a grim pleasure. "They didn't. It might take the whoresons all day to get here, but they're coming. Their whole damn army."

"This really is it then," Hanno muttered. His stomach churned.

Zamar nodded solemnly. "May Baal Saphon protect you and your men."

"And the same to you," Hanno replied. He watched sadly as the Numidian led his riders to the rear. Would they ever see each other again? Probably not. Hanno didn't wallow in the emotion. It was far too late for regret. They were all in this together. He and his father. Sapho and Bostar. Zamar and every other soldier in the army. Yes, bloodshed was inevitable. So too were the deaths of thousands of men.

Even as he saw the first files of Roman legionaries filing into view, Hanno believed that Hannibal would not let them down.

XXIV

AT CLOSE QUARTERS

With the Numidians gone, Fabricius regrouped his riders on the near riverbank. The mass of horsemen crossed together and went pounding up the track, past the spot where their patrol had been annihilated by Hanno and his men. Trying not to think about what had happened, Quintus squinted up at the low-lying cloud. For the moment, the snow had stopped. He tried to feel grateful. "What time is it?" he wondered. "It has to be *hora quinta* at least."

"Who cares?" growled Calatinus. "All I know is that I'm parched with thirst, and bloody famished."

"Here." Quintus handed over his water bag.

Grinning his thanks, Calatinus took a few deep swallows. "Gods, that's cold," he complained.

"Be grateful you're not a legionary," advised Quintus. He pointed back toward the Trebia, where thousands of soldiers were already preparing to follow the cavalry across.

Calatinus scowled. "Aye. Fording that was unpleasant enough on a horse. I pity the poor bastard infantry. The damn river must be chest deep."

"It's the winter rain," said Quintus. "Even the parallel tributaries are waist high, so the poor bastards will have to immerse themselves repeatedly. It doesn't bear thinking about."

"A fight will soon warm them up," declared Cincius stoutly.

Quintus and his two comrades were among the first to emerge from the trees' protection. They reined in at once, cursing. Their chase was over.

A quarter of a mile away, stretching from left to right as far as the eye could see, stood the figures of thousands of waiting men. Carthaginian troops. "Halt!" bellowed Fabricius. "It's a protective screen. No point committing suicide." Cheated of the chance for further revenge on the Numidians, his men shouted insults after the retreating enemy riders.

Fabricius found Quintus a moment later. He smiled to see his son unharmed. "Quite a morning so far, eh?"

Quintus grinned. "Yes, Father. We've got them on the run, eh?"

"Hmmm." Fabricius was studying the brown-yellow clouds above. He frowned. "There's more snow coming, and we're going to have a long wait before the real fight begins. The legions and the socii will take hours to get in position. By that time, the men will be half dead with cold."

Quintus glanced around. "Some of them don't even have cloaks on."

"They were too keen to engage with the enemy," replied Fabricius grimly. "What's the betting that they didn't feed and water their horses?"

Quintus flushed. He hadn't remembered that most basic of duties either. "What should we do?"

"Do you see those trees?"

Quintus eyed the dense stand of beech a short distance to their left. "Yes."

"Let's take shelter there. Longus might not like it, but he's not here. We'll still be able to respond fast if there's any threat to the legionaries. Not that that's likely. Hannibal threw out this protective screen deliberately. He wants a proper battle today," Fabricius declared. "Until the fighting starts, or orders come to the contrary, we should try to keep warm."

Quintus nodded gratefully. There was more to war than simply defeating an enemy in combat, he realized. Initiative was also important.

And so, while the rest of the cavalry and the velites milled about uncertainly, watching the legionaries wading across the Trebia, Fabricius led his riders under cover.

By the time two hours had passed, Hanno was shivering constantly. His soldiers were in the same condition. It was absolute torture standing on an open plain in such bitter weather. Although the snow showers had died away, they had been succeeded by sleet, and the wind had recovered its viciousness. It whistled and whipped at Carthaginian and Roman alike with an unrelenting fury. The only opportunity Hanno's men had been given to warm up was when the instruction had come to withdraw toward their camp.

"Look at the whoresons!" cried Malchus, who had come over from his phalanx. "Will they never stop coming?"

Hanno eyed the ground opposite their position, which was being filled with a plodding inevitability. "It must be the entire Roman army."

"I'd say so," answered his father bleakly. Abruptly, he laughed. "However cold you think your men are, those fuckers are in a far worse state. In all likelihood, they've had no food, and now they're all drenched to the skin too."

Hanno shuddered. He could only imagine how cold the wind would feel on wet clothing and heavy mail, both of which carried heat away from the body anyway. Demoralizing. Energy-sapping.

"Meanwhile," his father went on, "we're ready and waiting for them."

Hanno glanced to either side. As soon as the Numidians had retreated safely, he and his men had pulled back to Hannibal's battle formation, which consisted of a single line of infantry in close order. The slingers and Numidian skirmishers were arrayed some three hundred paces in front of the main battle line. Their general had not placed his strongest infantry—the Libyans and Iberians—in the center. Instead, that space was filled by about eight thousand Gauls. "Surely we should be standing there?" he asked crossly. "Instead, it's our newest recruits."

Malchus gave him a calculating look. "Think about it. Listen to them."

Hanno cocked his head. The war cries and the carnyx blasts emanating from the Gauls' ranks were deafening. "They're delighted with the honor that Hannibal has granted them. It will increase their loyalty."

"That's right. To them, pride is everything," answered Malchus. "What could be better than being given the center of the line? But there's another reason. The heaviest fighting and the worst casualties will be there too. Hannibal is saving us and the Iberians from that fate."

Hanno gave his father a shocked glance. "Would he do such a thing?"

"Of course," replied Malchus casually. "The Gauls can easily be replaced. Our men, and the scutarii and caetrati, cannot. That's why we're on the wings."

Hanno's respect for Hannibal grew further. He eyed the seventeen elephants standing just in front of their position. The rest were arrayed on the other wing, before the Iberian foot soldiers. Further protection for the heavy infantry, he realized. Outside, on each flank, sat five thousand Numidians and Hannibal's Iberian and Gaulish horse. The Carthaginian superiority in this area would hopefully afford Hannibal a good chance of winning the cavalry battle. Meanwhile, the Gauls would have to resist the hammer blow delivered by the Roman legions to the center of the Carthaginian line. "Will the Gauls hold?" he asked anxiously.

"There's a decided chance that they will not," Malchus replied, clenching his jaw. "They might be brave, but they're poorly disciplined."

Hanno stared over at the tribesmen. Few of them wore armor. Even in this weather, most preferred to fight stripped to the waist. There was no denying that the legionaries' mail shirts and heavy scuta would provide them with a severe test. "If they don't break, however, and our cavalry are successful . . ."

Malchus' grin was wolflike. "Our troops on each side will have a god-given opportunity to attack the sides of the Roman formation."

"That's when Mago's force will appear."

"We must hope so," said his father. "For all of our fates will lie with them."

Hanno could hardly bear it. "So many small things have to succeed for us to win the day."

"That's right. And the Gauls will have the hardest task of any."

Hanno closed his eyes and prayed that everything went according to plan. *Great Melqart, you have helped Hannibal thus far. Please do the same again today.*

In the event, Fabricius spotted one of the consul's messengers well before Quintus and his comrades had warmed up. He rode to confer with him, and returned at the double.

"Longus wants all citizen cavalry positioned on the right flank, and the allied horse on the left. We've got to ride north, to the far end of the battle line."

"When?" asked Quintus irritably. His earlier excitement had been sapped by the mind-numbing cold.

"Now!" Fabricius called out to his decurions: "Have the men form up. We ride out at once."

As the cavalrymen emerged from the trees, Quintus could have sworn that the wind hit them with a new vigor, stripping away any of the warmth that they had briefly felt. That settled it, he thought grimly. The sooner the fighting began, the better. Anything rather than this torture.

Fabricius led them through the gaps in the three lines of soldiers to the front of the army. By the time they had reached open ground, Quintus had gained a good appreciation of the entire host. Longus had ordered the legions to deploy in traditional pattern, with a hundred paces between each line and the next. The veteran triarii were at the rear, in the middle were the principes, men in their late twenties and early thirties, and next came the ranks of the hastati, the youngest of the infantry. At the very front stood the exhausted velites, who, despite their recent travails, would be forced to engage the enemy first.

All three lines were composed of maniples. Those of hastati and principes comprised two centuries of between sixty and seventy soldiers. There were fewer triarii, however, and their maniples were made up of just two centuries of thirty men each. The units in each line did not yet form a continuous front. Instead, they were positioned one century in front of the other, leaving gaps equal to the maniple's frontage between each unit. The units of the second and third lines stood behind the spaces in front, forming a quincunx configuration like the "5" face on a gaming die. This positioning allowed a rapid transition to combat formation when the rear century in each maniple would simply run around to stand alongside the front one. It also permitted soldiers to retreat safely from the fighting, allowing their fresher comrades access to the enemy.

It was a long way to the edge of the right flank, so Quintus also had time to study the Carthaginian forces. These were arrayed about a quarter of a mile distant, sufficiently near to appreciate the enemy's superior numbers of cavalry, and the threatening outlines of at least two dozen elephants. The blare of horns and carnyxes carried through the air, an alien noise compared to the familiar Roman trumpets. It was clear that Hannibal retained fewer troops than Longus, but his host still made for a fearsome, if unusual, sight.

At length Quintus began to feel quite exposed. Fortunately, he didn't have to wait much longer. They passed the four regular legions, spotting Longus and his tribunes at the junction between these and the allied troops of the right wing. Finally, Fabricius' unit reached the Roman cavalry, which, with their arrival, numbered just under a thousand. There was more ribaldry as the assembled riders demanded to know where they had been.

"Screwing your mother!" shouted a wit among Fabricius' men. "And your sisters!"

Angry roars rose from the joke's victims, and the air filled with insults. A smile twitched across Fabricius' lips. He glanced at Quintus and registered his surprise. "Many of them are going to die soon," he explained. "This takes their minds off it."

The mention of heavy casualties made Quintus feel nauseous. Would he survive to see the next dawn? Would his father, Calatinus or Cincius? Quintus looked around at the familiar faces, the men he had come to know over the previous weeks. He didn't like all of them, but they were still his comrades. Who would end the day lying bloodied and motionless in the cold mud? Who would be maimed, or blinded? Quintus felt the first fingers of panic clutch at his belly.

His father took his arm. "Take a deep breath," he said quietly.

Quintus shot him a worried glance. "Why?"

"Do as I say."

He obeyed, relieved that Calatinus and Cincius were deep in conversation with each other.

"Hold it," Fabricius ordered. "Listen to your heart."

It wasn't hard to do that, thought Quintus. It was hammering off his ribs like that of a wild bird.

His father waited for a few moments. "Now let the air out through your lips. Nice and slowly. When you've finished, do the same again."

Quintus' eyes flickered around nervously, but nobody appeared to be watching. He did as he was told. By the third or fourth breath, the effect on his pulse was noticeable. It had slowed down, and he wasn't feeling as scared.

"Everyone is frightened before battle," said his father. "Even me. It's a terrifying thing to charge at another group of men whose job it is to kill you. The trick is to think of your comrades on your left and right. They are the only ones who matter from now on."

"I understand," Quintus muttered.

"You will be fine. I know it." Fabricius clapped him on the shoulder.

Steadier now, Quintus nodded. "Thank you, Father."

With his army in place, Longus had the trumpeters sound the advance. Stamping their numb feet on the semi-frozen ground, the infantry obeyed. Loud prayers to the gods rose from the ranks, and the standard-bearers lifted their arms so that everyone could see the talismanic gilded animal that sat atop the wooden poles they bore. Each legion had five standards, depicting respectively an eagle, Minotaur, horse, wolf and boar. They were objects of great reverence, and Quintus wished that his unit possessed them too. Even the allied infantry bore similar standards. For reasons unclear to him, the cavalry didn't.

Victory will be ours regardless, he thought. Urging his horse on with his knees, he rode toward the enemy.

———

It was imperative that their enemies marched beyond Mago's hidden position. Consequently, the entire Carthaginian army had to stay put as the Romans approached. It was a nerve-racking time, with little to do other than pray or make last, quick checks of equipment. Imitating his father, Hanno had given his men a short address. They were here, he'd told them, to show Rome that it could not trifle with Carthage. To right the wrongs it had done to all of their peoples. The spearmen had liked Hanno's words, but they cheered loudest when he reminded them that they were here to follow Hannibal's lead and, most importantly, to avenge their heroic comrades who had fallen since their departure from Saguntum more than six months before.

Their racket was as nothing compared to that of the Gauls, however. The combination of drumming weapons, war chants and wind instruments made an incredible din. Hanno had never heard anything like it. Musicians stood before the assembled warriors, playing curved ceramic horns and carnyxes at full volume. The tribesmen's frenzied response was to clatter their swords and spears rhythmically off their shields, all the while chanting in unison. Some individuals were so affected that they broke ranks, stripped naked and stood whirling their swords over their heads, screaming like men possessed.

"They say that at Telamon, the ground shook with their noise," his father shouted.

But they still lost, thought Hanno grimly.

The tension mounted steadily as the Roman battle line drew closer. It was immensely long, stretching off on both sides until it was lost to sight. The Carthaginian formation was considerably narrower, which threatened immediate flanking. Hanno's worries about this were forgotten as Hannibal ordered his skirmishers forward.

The Balearic slingers and Numidian javelin men bounded off, eager to start the battle proper. A vicious and prolonged missile encounter followed, from which the Carthaginians emerged clear victors. Unlike the wet, tired velites, who had been fighting for hours and had already thrown the majority of their javelins, Hannibal's men were fresh and keen. Stones and spears whistled and hummed through the air in their hundreds, scything down the velites like rows of wheat. Unable to respond in similar fashion, the Roman light troops were soon put to flight, retreating through the gaps in their front line. Hannibal immediately recalled his skirmishers, whose lack of armor made them vulnerable to the approaching hastati. As they trotted back through the spaces between the various Carthaginian units, they received a rousing cheer.

"A good start," Hanno yelled to his men. "First blood to us!"

A moment later, the Romans charged.

"Shields up!" Hanno yelled. From the corner of his eye, he was dimly aware of their Iberian and Gaulish cavalry, as well as the elephants, charging at the enemy's horsemen. He had literally an instant to pray that they succeeded.

Then the Roman *pila*, or javelins, began to arrive. Each hastatus carried two of the weapons, which gave their front line fearsome firepower. The missiles were thrown in such dense showers that the air between the two armies darkened as they flew. "Protect yourselves!" Hanno screamed, but it was only those in the front rank who could do as he said. The phalanx's formation packed men together so tightly that it prevented the rest from raising their large shields. As the javelins came hammering down, they gritted their teeth and hoped not to be hit.

Topped by a pyramidal point, the pila were fully capable of punching through a shield and piercing its bearer's flesh. And they did exactly that: killing, wounding, cutting tissue apart with ease. Hanno's ears rang with the choking cries of soldiers who could no longer talk thanks to the iron transfixing their throats. Screams rang out from those who had been struck elsewhere. Wails of fear rose from the unhurt as they saw their comrades slain before their eyes. Hanno risked a look to the front and cursed. While their first volley flew, the hastati had continued to advance. They were now less than forty paces away, and preparing to release again. He couldn't help admiring the legionaries' discipline. They actually slowed down or even stopped to throw their pila. As he already knew, it was well worth the effort to make an accurate shot. Lesser foes would have already broken and run beneath the rain of iron-tipped terror. Hanno was grateful that he was commanding veterans. While his men had suffered terribly, their lines remained steady. His father's phalanx looked rock solid too.

To his left, the Gauls were also suffering heavy casualties. Hanno could see some of them wavering, a worrying sign so early. But their chieftains were made of sterner stuff, shouting and exhorting their followers to stand fast. To Hanno's relief, the tactic worked. As the second shower of javelins was launched, the Gauls swiftly lifted their shields. While their response reduced the number of wounded and killed, it stripped many of the warriors of their main protection. Few things were more useless than a shield with a bent pilum protruding from it. Weirdly, this looked more to the Gauls' liking. Shouting fiercely, they prepared to meet the hastati head on.

Many of the men at the front of Hanno's phalanx were also now without shields. He cursed savagely. The gaps would provide the legionaries with opportunities too good to pass up, but there was nothing Hanno could do to remedy the problem. "Close order!" he shouted. As the command was repeated all along the line, he felt the shields of the men on either side slide against his to form a solid barrier. "Front two ranks, raise spears!" Scores of wooden shafts clattered off each other as those in the second row shoved their weapons over the shoulders of the soldiers in front. Hanno gritted his teeth. "This is it!" he roared. "Hold fast!"

He could pick out individuals now: there a stocky figure with a pockmarked face; beside him a young man wearing a pectoral breastplate who couldn't have been more than eighteen. His own age. He looked a bit like Gaius, Martialis' son. Unsettled, Hanno blinked. Naturally, he was mistaken: Gaius was a noble, and would serve in the cavalry. Who cares? he thought harshly. They are all the enemy. Kill them. "Steady," he roared. "Wait for my command!"

The hastati screamed as they closed in. Each man clutched a gladius in his right fist, and in the other he carried a heavy, elongated oval scutum with a metal boss. Like Hanno's men's shields, many Roman ones had designs painted on their hide covers. Bizarrely, Hanno found himself admiring the charging boars, leaping wolves and arrangements of circles and spirals. They contrasted strongly with the more ornate patterns favored by the Libyans.

Nervous, the man beside him shoved his spear forward too soon, and Hanno's attention snapped back to the present. "Hold!" he ordered. "Your first thrust has to kill a man!"

One heartbeat. Two heartbeats.

"Now!" Hanno roared at the top of his voice. In the same moment, he thrust forward with his weapon, aiming it at the face of the nearest hastatus. On either side, hundreds of Libyans did the same. Hanno's speed caught the legionary off guard, and his spear tip skidded over the top of the other's scutum to take him through the left eye. Aqueous fluid spattered everywhere and an agonizing scream ripped free of the hastatus' throat. Hanno's instinct was to shove his spear even deeper, making the blow mortal, but he stopped himself. The man would probably die of his injury. More importantly, he would not take any further part in the battle. With a powerful twist, Hanno pulled the blade free. Iron grated off bone as he did so and the bellowing hastatus collapsed.

Hanno barely had time to breathe before another legionary came trampling over his first opponent and deliberately barged straight into him. If it hadn't been for the fact that his shield was locked with that of the man on either side, Hanno would have fallen over. As it was, he was knocked off balance and struggled to regain his footing. This was precisely what the hastatus had intended. Bending his right elbow, he stabbed his gladius over the top of Hanno's shield. Frantically, Hanno twisted his head to one side, and the blade gouged a deep line across the cheekpiece of his bronze helmet before skimming through the hair on the side of his head. The hastatus snarled with anger and pulled back his weapon to deliver another blow. Hanno struggled to use his spear, but his opponent was too close to reach him easily. Panic bubbled in the back of his throat. The battle had hardly started, and already he was a dead man.

Then, out of the blue, a spear took the hastatus through the throat, making his eyes bulge in shock. He made a choking gasp as the blade slid out of his flesh, and dropped like a stone, sending gouts of blood all over Hanno's shield and lower legs. "My thanks!" Hanno shouted at the soldier behind him. He couldn't turn around to express his gratitude, because another hastatus was already trying to kill him. This time, Hanno managed to fend off his attacker with his spear. Cursing loudly, they traded blows back and forth, but neither could gain an advantage over the other. Things were taken out of both their hands a moment later when a man a few steps to Hanno's right, who had discarded his pilum-riddled shield, was killed. Two hastati forced their way into the space at once, shouting at their comrades to follow them. Hanno's opponent knew that this was too good a chance to pass up. In the blink of an eye, he had shoved his way after his fellows. To Hanno's relief, he was granted a brief respite.

Panting heavily, he glanced to either side. Claws of worry raked at his insides. The phalanxes were holding their own, but only just. To his left, the Gauls were struggling to contain the same intense assault. Worryingly, the hastati there had already been joined by the principes. The Gauls had even less prospect of holding back these legionaries, thought Hanno sourly. Most of the principes wore mail shirts, making them much harder to kill. Thus far, however, the tribesmen were not retreating. Despite their lack of armor, they persisted in fighting to the death. Already the ground beneath their feet was a churned-up morass of corpses, discarded weapons, mud and blood.

Desperately, Hanno cast his eyes to the Roman left flank. His heart lifted. Thanks to the Iberians and Gauls, it had been shorn of its cavalry protection. There was no sign of Hannibal's heavy cavalry, however, which meant it was still pursuing the Roman horse. Hanno's worry increased tenfold. If that battle hadn't been won, they might as well all give up now. Then his attention was drawn by hundreds of figures who were swarming toward the enemy's left flank. To his delight, he saw that they were hurling javelins and firing sling stones. It was the Carthaginian skirmishers!

A yelling hastatus jumped into the attack, preventing Hanno from any further thought. He fought back with renewed determination, using the greater length of his spear to stab at the Roman's face. The fight wasn't over by any means. There was hope yet.

As they rode toward the Carthaginians, Quintus forgot his father's reassuring words. He felt sick to the stomach. How could a thousand men prevail against what looked like more than five times that number? It simply wasn't possible.

Calatinus also looked unhappy. "Longus should have split our horsemen equally," he muttered. "There are nearly three thousand allied riders on the other flank."

"It's not fair," moaned Cincius.

"The figures still don't equate," Quintus replied wearily.

"I suppose. It's not even as if the bastards coming toward us will be scared. They've already tasted victory over us." Calatinus cursed the consul heartily.

"Come on! We should be able to stall the enemy attack," encouraged Quintus. "Hold the line, and stop the enemy from having free rein over the battlefield."

Calatinus' grunt conveyed all types of disbelief. Cincius didn't seem convinced either.

"Listen to our infantry," cried Quintus. The noise of their tread was deafening. "There are more than thirty-five thousand of them. How can Hannibal with his little army, made up of a hodgepodge of different nationalities, prevail against that type of might? He can't!"

His comrades looked a trifle more confident.

Wishing that he felt as certain as he sounded, Quintus again fixed his gaze to the front.

The first of the enemy riders were now very close. Quintus recognized them as Gauls by their mail shirts, round shields and long spears. He squinted at the small, bouncing objects tied to their horses' harnesses. To his horror, he realized they were severed human heads. These warriors could be some of their so-called allies, and the heads those of his former comrades. Of Licinius, perhaps.

Calatinus had seen the same thing. "The fucking dogs!" he screamed.

"Yellow-livered sons of whores!" Cincius bellowed.

A towering rage also filled Quintus. He wasn't going to flee from cowards like these. Men who would kill others as they slept. *I would* rather die, he thought. Quintus raised his spear and chose a target, a warrior on a sturdy gray horse. The magnificent gold torc visible over the top of the Gaul's mail shirt revealed him to be an important individual. So did the three human heads bouncing off his mount's chest. He would be a good start, Quintus decided.

However, the tide of battle swept Quintus away from the Gaul he'd aimed for. In hindsight, it was a good thing. The tribesman was immensely skilled. Quintus watched in horror as a Roman rider fewer than twenty paces away was skewered through the chest by the Gaul's weapon. The force of the impact punched the man off his saddle blanket, dropping him dead to the dirt below. The horse behind stumbled over the corpse, unbalancing its rider, and rendering him easy prey for the Gaul, who was now swinging a long sword. He took off the cavalryman's head with a great sideways lop. Quintus had never seen blood spray so high in the air. Gouts of it went everywhere as the panicked horse galloped off. It was perhaps a dozen steps before its dead rider toppled off.

At once the Gaul sawed on his mount's reins and jumped down. Quintus' amazement turned to disgust. The warrior was after another head. He would have given anything just then to be able to reach the Gaul, but it was not to be. He nearly lost his own head to a swinging sword, managing to dodge it only because its bearer uttered a loud war cry as his killing stroke came down. As it was, Quintus nearly fell off his horse. With a speed born of utter desperation, he managed to regain his seat in time to parry his opponent's next powerful blow.

Fortuna was smiling on him in that instant, for the warrior was even younger than he, and, as Quintus realized, far less skilled. A more experienced man would have already despatched him. The Gaul was not lacking in bravery, however, and they hammered fiercely at each other for a few moments before Quintus found an opportunity to strike. The other's wild swings left his right armpit exposed. Taking a gamble that he could react faster than his enemy, Quintus did not defend against the next strike. Instead, bending low over his horse's neck, he listened to it whistle overhead. While the Gaul was still coming to the end of his swing, Quintus came up like a striking snake. He buried his spear in the other's side, sliding it neatly into the armhole of his mail shirt. With nothing but a tunic to stop its progress, the blade slid between the man's ribs, through one lung and into his heart. It was as clean a stroke as Quintus had ever made, killing instantaneously. He would always remember it not for that, however, but for the brief burst of shock and pain in the Gaul's eyes before they went dark forever.

When Quintus looked up, he quailed. Most of the nearby Roman riders had been cut down. The others were fleeing. There was no sign of Calatinus, Cincius or his father. Quintus' vision was filled with Gauls. Behind them came hundreds of Iberians. He would be dead long before those riders arrived, however. Three Gaulish warriors were heading straight for him. Despairing, Quintus picked the man he thought would reach him first. It would make little difference, but he didn't care. His father was dead, and the cavalry battle half lost. What did it matter if he also fell? Raising his spear, Quintus screamed a final cry of defiance. "Come on, then, you bastards!"

The trio of warriors roared an inarticulate response.

A horrifying image of his own head as a trophy filled his mind. He banished the image. Just let the end be quick, Quintus prayed.

XXV

UNEXPECTED TACTICS

Bostar had barely been able to contain himself since the sentry's report that the enemy was crossing the river. He and Sapho had clambered up the bank to lie beside Mago, who was trembling with excitement. With every nerve stretched taut, they'd watched as the Roman cavalry and velites were gradually followed by the allied infantry and the regular legionaries. Only then did it sink in.

"The Roman commander has no interest in nibbling at the bait," muttered Mago excitedly. "He's swallowed it in one great bite. That's his whole fucking army!"

They exchanged nervous grins.

"The fighting will start soon," said Sapho eagerly.

"It's not time to move yet," interjected Bostar at once.

"That's right. We have to wait until the perfect moment to fall upon the Romans' rear," warned Mago. "Moving too early could cost us the battle."

Knowing that Mago was correct, the brothers reluctantly stayed put. The wait that followed was the longest of Bostar's life. Mago's incessant twitching and the savagery with which Sapho bit his nails told him that they felt the same way. It was no more than three to four hours, but at the time it seemed like an eternity. Naturally, the news that the Romans were on the move had spread through their two thousand soldiers like wildfire. Soon it became difficult to keep them silent. It was understandable, thought Bostar. There was only so long that one could take pleasure in being out of harm's way rather than facing mortal danger—especially when one's comrades were about to fight for their lives.

Even when the clash of arms became audible, Mago did not move. Bostar forced himself to remain calm. The rival forces of skirmishers would meet first, and then pull back. Sure enough, the screams and cries soon abated. They were replaced by the unmistakable sound of thousands of feet tramping the ground in unison.

"The Roman infantry are advancing," said Mago in an undertone. "Melqart, watch over our men."

A knot of tension formed in Bostar's belly. Facing so many of the enemy would be terrifying.

Beside him, Sapho shifted uneasily. "The gods protect Father and Hanno," he whispered. Their enmity momentarily forgotten, Bostar muttered the same prayer.

The crashing sound that reached their ears a moment later was as deafening as thunder. Yet there were no threatening storm clouds above, no flashes of lightning to sear their eyeballs. It was something altogether more lethal. More terrifying. Bostar trembled to hear it. He had witnessed terrible things since the war started: the immense block of stone that had nearly killed Hannibal; the scenes at the fall of Saguntum; avalanches sweeping away scores of screaming men in the Alps. But he had never heard the sound of tens of thousands of soldiers striking each other for the first time. It promised death in any number of appalling ways, and Hanno and his father were caught up in it. Somehow Bostar kept still, trying his best to block out the screams that were now discernible amid the crescendo of sound. His tactic didn't work for long. He looked at Mago, who gave him a tiny encouraging nod.

"Is it time yet, sir?" Bostar asked.

Mago's eyes glittered eagerly. "Soon. Prepare your men to move out. Tell the same to the officer commanding the Numidians. At my signal, bring them up."

"Yes, sir!" Bostar and Sapho grinned at each other as they hadn't done in an age, and hurried to obey.

From then on, time moved in a blur, a continuum that Bostar could only remember afterward in a series of fractured images. The frisson of excitement that shivered through the waiting soldiers when they heard their orders. Mago's head silhouetted as he peered over the riverbank, and his beckoning arm. Reaching the top, and being awestruck by the colossal struggle going on over to their left. Who was winning? Was Hanno still alive? Mago shaking his arm and telling him to keep focused. Telling the men to unsling their shields from their backs and ready their weapons. Assembling their phalanxes in open order. Watching the thousand Numidians split, placing half their number on each side of the infantry. Mago's raised sword pointing at the enemy and his cry, "For Hannibal and for Carthage!"

And the run. Bostar would never forget the run.

They did not sprint. It was more than half a mile to the battlefield. Exhausting themselves would give away all the advantage they had been granted. Instead they moved at a fast trot, leaving plumes of exhaled breath in their wake. The cold air was filled with the low, repetitive thuds of horses' hooves and men's boots and sandals on the hard ground. No one spoke. No one wanted to. Everyone's eyes were locked on what was unfolding before them. Amid the confusion, one thing was clear. There was no sign of the enemy's cavalry, which meant that the Iberian and Gaulish horsemen must have driven them off. On the Roman flanks, the allied infantry were struggling against the Carthaginian elephants, skirmishers and Numidian horsemen. In itself, these were major achievements, and Bostar wanted to cheer. But he did not utter a word. The battle's outcome still hung in the balance. As they drew closer, he saw that the fighting in the center was incredibly fierce. The legionaries there had actually moved in front of their wings, which meant that they had pushed the Gauls who formed the central part of Hannibal's line backward.

They had come not an instant too soon, thought Bostar.

Mago came to the realization at the same time. "Charge!" he screamed. "Charge!"

With a wordless roar, Bostar, Sapho and their soldiers obeyed, increasing their speed to a dangerous, breakneck pace. Any man who tripped now risked breaking an ankle or a leg. But no one cared. All they wanted to do was to start shedding their opponents' blood. To bury their weapons in Roman flesh.

The last moments of their run were surreal. Exhilarating. Thanks to the deafening sounds of battle, there was no need to worry about how much noise they made. The triarii in the enemy's third rank—their targets—were not looking behind them. Unsurprisingly, the veterans were engrossed by the bitter struggle going on to their front, and were preparing to join in. They had no idea that two thousand Carthaginian soldiers were about to strike their rear at a full charge. Bostar would always remember the first faces that turned, casually, for whatever reason, to look around. The sheer disbelief and terror that twisted those faces to find a group of the enemy fewer than thirty paces away. The hoarse screams as the small number of triarii who were aware tried to warn their comrades of their deadly peril. And the satisfaction as they smashed into the Roman ranks, drawing their weapons down on the backs of men who did not even know they were about to die.

For the first time in his life, Bostar was overcome by battle rage. In the red mist surrounding him, it was easy to lose count of the number of men he killed. It was like stabbing fish in a rock pool off the coast of Carthage. Thrust forward. Run the blade in as deep as possible. Withdraw. Select another target. When eventually his blunted spear stuck in a triarius' backbone, Bostar simply discarded it and pulled out his sword. He was vaguely aware that his arm was bloody to the elbow, but he didn't care. *I'm coming, little brother. Stay alive, Father.*

Eventually, the veteran legionaries managed to turn and face their attackers. The fight became harder, but the advantage was still with Mago's men, who could now see that the enemy's flanks had broken. Bostar exulted. The combined wave of Carthaginian troops and cavalry on the allied infantry's undefended side had proved too much. Prevented from wheeling to face the threat, they had been mercilessly hacked to pieces.

Now, dropping their weapons, the survivors turned and ran for the Trebia. Bostar threw back his head and let free an animal howl of triumph. To the rear, he glimpsed thousands of their cavalrymen waiting for just such an eventuality. The allied troops would not go far. Suddenly, a veteran with a notched sword blade drove at him and Bostar was reminded that their own task was not over. Although the triarii were suffering heavy casualties, the rest of the legionaries were still moving forward into, and through, the lines of Gauls. Like a battering ram, they could only be resisted for so long. Bostar's elation died away as he realized that some of the Libyan phalanxes had also given way. They quickly crumbled before the legionaries' relentless assault. Catching Sapho's attention, Bostar pointed. His brother's face twisted in rage. With renewed energy, they both threw themselves at the triarii.

"Hanno! Father!" Bostar shouted. "We're coming!"

Too late, his heart screamed back.

When Aurelia entered the bedroom, her mother barely stirred. Elira, who was sitting by the bed, turned.

"How is she?" Aurelia whispered.

"Better," the Illyrian replied. "Her fever has broken."

Some of the tension went from Aurelia's shoulders. "Thank the gods. Thank *you*."

"Hush," murmured Elira reassuringly. "She was never that ill. It's a bad winter chill, that's all. She'll be up and about by Saturnalia."

Aurelia nodded gratefully. "I don't know what I'd do without you. It's not just caring for Mother these past few days. You made all the difference in Suni's—" She looked over her shoulder guiltily. To her relief, there was no one in the atrium. "I mean Lysander's recovery."

Elira waved a hand in dismissal. "He's young, and strong. All he needed was some food and warmth."

"Well, I'm thankful to you nonetheless," said Aurelia. "So is he."

Elira bobbed her head, embarrassed.

Things had moved on since she had returned to the farm with a half-conscious Suniaton two weeks previously, thought Aurelia, looking down at her sleeping mother. Fortunately, Atia had not questioned her story of finding him in the woods. In a real stroke of luck, a heavy snowstorm later that night had concealed the evidence of her tracks up to the hut. Unsurprisingly, everyone had taken Suniaton for a runaway slave. As agreed, he had pretended to be mute. He also put on a good show of appearing simple. Agesandros had been suspicious, of course, but there had been no trace of recognition in his eyes at any stage.

Aurelia had given the Sicilian no chance to have anything to do with Suniaton. Any master who wanted his property back could come looking for the boy, she had said to her mother. Until then, she was going to keep him. "Lysander, I'll call him, because he looks Greek."

Atia had smiled in acceptance. "Very well. If he even survives," she'd joked.

Well, he had, thought Aurelia triumphantly. Suni's leg had recovered enough for him to limp about the kitchen under Julius' instruction. For the moment, he was safe.

What frustrated Aurelia most was the fact that she could rarely talk to him. The best they could manage was an occasional snatched conversation in the evenings, when the other kitchen slaves had gone to bed. Aurelia used these moments to ask Suni about Hanno. She now knew much about his childhood and family, his interests, and where he had lived. Aurelia's reason for wanting to know about Hanno was quite simple. It was a way of not thinking about her betrothal. Even if Flaccus had been killed with her father, her mother would soon find her another husband. If Flaccus had survived, they would be wed within the year. One way or another, she would have an arranged marriage.

"Aurelia."

Her mother's voice jerked Aurelia back to the present. "You're awake! How do you feel?"

"Weak as a newborn," Atia murmured. "But better than I did yesterday."

"Praise all the gods." Tears leaped unbidden to Aurelia's eyes.

Finally, things were looking up.

———

Her mother's improvement lifted Aurelia's mood considerably. For the first time in days, she went for a walk. The chill weather meant that the snow that had fallen over the previous few days had not melted. Aurelia didn't want to go far from her mother or Suni. Just venturing a short distance along the track toward Capua felt wonderful, however. She relished the crunch of the frozen snow beneath her sandals. Even the way her cheeks rapidly went numb felt refreshing after all the time she'd spent indoors. Feeling more cheerful than she had in a while, Aurelia let herself picture a scenario in which her father had not been killed. She imagined the joy of seeing him walk through the front doors.

With this optimistic thought uppermost in her mind, she returned to the house.

As Aurelia crossed the courtyard, she saw Suniaton. He had his back to her, and was carrying a basket of vegetables into the kitchen. Her spirits lifted even higher. If he was able to do that, his leg must have improved further. She hurried after him. Reaching the door, Aurelia saw Suniaton lifting his load on to the work surface. All the other slaves were busy in other parts of the room. "Suni!" she hissed.

He didn't react.

"Pssst! Suni!" Aurelia stepped inside the kitchen.

Still he did not respond. It was then that Aurelia noticed his stiff-backed stance. Claws of fear raked her belly. "Sunny, it's so sunny outside," she said loudly.

"I could have sworn you said S-u-n-i," Agesandros purred, stepping from the shadows beside the kitchen door.

Aurelia blanched. "No. I said it was sunny. Can't you see? The weather's changed." She gestured outside at the blue sky above the courtyard.

She might as well have been speaking to a statue. "Suni— Suniaton—is a gugga name," said the Sicilian coldly.

"What's that got to do with anything?" Aurelia retorted desperately. Her gaze shot to Julius and the other slaves, but they were carefully pretending not to notice what was going on. Despair filled her. She wasn't the only one who was scared of the vilicus. And her mother was still sick in bed.

"Is this miserable wretch Carthaginian?"

"No. I told you, he's Greek. His name's Lysander."

From nowhere, a dagger appeared in Agesandros' hand. He pricked it to Suniaton's throat. "Are you a gugga?" There was no response, and the vilicus moved his blade to Suni's groin. "Do you want your balls cut off?"

Petrified, Suniaton shook his head vehemently.

"Speak, then!" Agesandros shouted, returning the dagger to Suni's neck. "Are you from Carthage?"

Suniaton's shoulders sagged. "Yes."

"You *can* talk!" crowed the Sicilian. He rounded on Aurelia. "So you lied to me."

"What if I have?" Aurelia cried, genuinely angry now. "I know what you think of Carthaginians."

Agesandros' eyes narrowed. "It was odd when this scumbag arrived, half-dead. With a recently healed sword injury. I bet he's the runaway gladiator." Like a hawk, he pounced on Suniaton's reactive flinch. "I *knew* it!"

Think! Aurelia told herself. Quickly, she drew herself up to her full height. "Surely not?" she snapped haughtily. "That creature would have fled long ago."

"He might have fooled you, but there's no drawing the wool over my eyes." Agesandros leaned on his blade. "You're no simpleton, are you?"

"No," Suniaton mumbled wearily.

"Where's your friend?" the Sicilian demanded.

Don't say anything, thought Aurelia pleadingly. He's still not sure.

To her horror, Suniaton's courage flared one last time. "Hanno? He's long gone. With any luck, he'll be in Hannibal's army by now."

"Shame," murmured Agesandros. "You're of no further use, then." Smoothly, he brought down his dagger and slipped it between Suniaton's ribs, guiding it into his heart.

Suniaton's eyes bulged in shock, and he let out a shuddering gasp of pain. His limbs went rigid before relaxing slowly. With an odd tenderness, Agesandros let him down. A rapid flow of blood soaked the front of Suni's tunic and spread on to the tile floor. He did not move again.

"No! You monster!" Aurelia shrieked.

Agesandros straightened. He studied his bloodied blade carefully.

Panicking, Aurelia took a step backward, into the kitchen. "No," she cried. "Julius! Help me!"

At last, the portly slave came hurrying to her side. "What have you done, Agesandros?" he muttered in horror.

The Sicilian didn't move. "I have done the master and mistress a service."

Aurelia couldn't believe her ears. "W-what?"

"How do you think he'd feel to discover that a dangerous fugitive—a gladiator—had contrived to join the household, placing his wife and his only daughter in danger of their lives?" asked Agesandros righteously. He kicked Suniaton. "Death is too good for scum like this."

Aurelia felt herself grow faint. Suniaton was dead, and it was all her fault. She could do nothing about it either. She felt like a murderess. In her mother's eyes, the Sicilian's actions would be completely justifiable. A sob escaped her lips.

"Why don't you attend to the mistress?" There was iron below Agesandros' apparent solicitousness.

Aurelia rallied herself. "He's to have a decent burial," she ordered.

The Sicilian's lips quirked. "Very well."

Aurelia stalked from the kitchen. She needed privacy. To wail. To weep. She might as well be dead, like Suniaton—and her father. All she had to look forward to from now on was her marriage to Flaccus.

Suddenly, an outrageous image popped into Aurelia's mind. It was of her, standing on the deck of a ship as it sailed out from the Italian coast. Toward Carthage.

I could run away, she thought. Find Hanno. He—

Leave everything you've ever known behind to find one of the enemy? Aurelia's heart shouted. That's madness.

It was only the bones of an idea, but her spirits were lifted by its mere existence.

It would give her the strength to carry on.

※

Quintus didn't notice Fabricius appearing by his side. The first thing he knew was when his reins were grabbed from his hands and his horse's head was yanked around to face to the rear. Using his knees to control his own mount, Fabricius headed east. Quintus' steed was happy enough to follow. Although it had been trained for cavalry service, the middle of a battle was still a most unnatural place to be. Quintus' initial joy at seeing his father alive exceeded his desire to fight for a moment, but then the balance reversed. "What are you doing?"

"Saving your life," his father shot back. "Are you not glad?"

Quintus glanced over his shoulder. There wasn't a living Roman cavalryman in sight, just a swarming mass of enemy horsemen and riderless mounts. Thankfully, the Gauls who'd been heading for him had already given up the chase. Like their compatriots, they had dismounted to hunt for trophies. A huge sense of relief filled Quintus. Despite his decision to stand his ground, he *was* glad to be alive. Unlike poor Calatinus, Cincius and his other comrades, who were probably dead. Shame followed swiftly on the heels of this emotion. He grabbed back his reins and concentrated on the ride. On either side, scores of other cavalrymen were also fleeing for their lives.

Their common destination seemed to be the Trebia.

Off to one side, both sets of opposing infantry were now locked together in a bitter struggle, the outcome of which was totally unclear. On the fringes of the conflict, Quintus could see the shapes of the enemy's elephants battering the allied foot soldiers. The massive beasts were supported by horsemen, and he guessed it had to be the Numidians. It could only be a matter of time before the Roman flanks folded. Then Hannibal's soldiers would be free to swing around and attack their rear. That was even before the rest of the Carthaginian cavalry returned to the conflict. Quintus blinked away tears of frustration and rage. How could this have happened? Just two hours before, they had been pursuing an enemy in disarray over the Trebia.

Hoarse shouting dragged Quintus' attention back to his own surroundings. To his horror, the Gauls to their rear had resumed the chase. With their gory trophies taken, the tribesmen were eager for more blood. His stomach churned. In their present state, the nearest cavalrymen were in no state to turn, stand and fight. Nor was he, he realized with shame. Quintus wondered if it was the same on the other flank, where the allied horse had been positioned. Had they too broken and fled?

Fabricius had also seen their new pursuers. "Let's head that way." Surprisingly, he pointed north. He saw Quintus' questioning look. "There'll be too many trying to ford the river where we crossed before. It will be a slaughter."

Quintus remembered the narrow approach to the main crossing point and shuddered. "Where should we aim for?"

"Placentia," his father replied ominously. "No point returning to the camp. Hannibal could take that with little difficulty. We need the protection of stone walls."

Quintus nodded in miserable acceptance.

Doing their best to bring along as many others as they could, they turned their horses' heads. Toward Placentia, where they might find refuge.

It was ironic, thought Hanno, that his life had been saved by Roman efficiency. It wasn't because he and his men had been victorious. Far from it. The Libyans' position adjoining the Gauls meant that many of them had shared the tribesmen's fate. When the Gauls had finally crumbled before the mass of heavily armed legionaries, some of the phalanxes had been dragged in. The spearmen in question were slaughtered to a man. Sheer luck had determined that Malchus and Hanno's units had not been affected. Battered and bloodied, they had fought on, even as they were pushed to one side by the massive block of Roman soldiers.

Somehow, Hanno utilized the natural breaks in the fighting to regain better control of his phalanx. He ordered the spearmen to the rear to pass their shields forward. The same was done with spears, allowing his unit to resume, at the front at least, a more normal appearance. Malchus emulated Hanno. With their defensive shield walls restored, the two phalanxes were a much harder proposition to overcome. Without their pila, the Romans had to rely on their gladii, which were shorter than the Libyans' spears. It did not take the legionaries facing Hanno's unit long to realize this. Seeing the hastati and principes to their right advancing without difficulty through the remnants of the Gauls, they broke away to follow their comrades.

Hanno's exhausted men watched with a sense of stunned relief.

Then, quite suddenly, the Romans were gone. Oddly, they didn't wheel around to attack the rear of the Carthaginian line. Hanno couldn't believe it. There were still isolated pockets of fighting, small groups of legionaries who had been cut off from their comrades, but the vast majority of the enemy infantry had broken through Hannibal's center. They showed no interest, however, in doing anything except beating a path to the north. As far as Hanno was concerned, they could go. His men weren't capable of mounting a meaningful pursuit. Nor were his father's. No command issued from the musicians stationed by Hannibal's side, proving that their general was of the same mind. Having arrayed his foot soldiers in a single line, he had no reserve to send after the retreating legionaries.

Chest heaving, Hanno studied the scene. There was no sign of the allied infantry. The combination of elephants, Numidians and skirmishers must have routed them from the field. Off to his right, which had been the phalanx's front until the Romans had pushed them sideways, the battleground was now almost devoid of life. Suddenly, Hanno was overcome with a heady combination of exhilaration and fear. They had won, but at what price? He looked up at the leaden sky and offered up a heartfelt prayer: Thank you, great Melqart, all-seeing Tanit and mighty Baal Saphon, for your help in achieving this victory. You have been merciful in letting both me and my father survive. I humbly beseech that you have also seen fit to spare my brothers.

He took a deep breath. *If not, let all their wounds be at the front.*

Soon there was an emotional reunion with his father. Bloodspattered and steely-eyed, Malchus said nothing when they drew close. Instead he pulled Hanno into a tight hug that spoke volumes. When he finally let go, Hanno was touched to see the moisture in his own eyes mirrored in his father's. Malchus had shown more emotion in the last few weeks than at any time since his mother's death.

"That was a hard fight. You held your phalanx together well," Malchus muttered. "Hannibal will hear of it."

Hanno thought he would burst with pride. His father's approval meant ten times that of their general.

Malchus' businesslike manner returned fast. "There's still plenty of work to be done. Spread your men out. Advance. Tell them to kill any Romans that they find alive."

"Yes, Father."

"Do the same for those of our men who are badly injured," Malchus added.

Hanno blinked.

Malchus' face softened for a moment. "They'll die in far worse ways otherwise. Of cold, a wolf bite, or exposure. A swift end from a comrade is better than that, surely?"

Sighing, Hanno nodded. "What about you?"

"Those who are lightly wounded might survive if we can carry them from the field. It will be dark within the hour, though. I must act fast." He gave Hanno a shove. "Go on. Look for Sapho and Bostar as well."

Did his father mean alive or dead? Hanno wondered nervously as he walked away.

His men responded with enthusiasm to the idea of killing more Romans. Unsurprisingly, they reacted less well to doing the same to their comrades. Few objected, however, when Hanno explained the alternatives to them. Who wanted to die the lingering death that awaited when night fell?

In a long line, they began advancing across the battlefield. Beneath the struggle of so many men, the ground had been churned into a sludge of reddened mud that stuck to Hanno's sandals. Only the tiniest areas of snow remained untouched, startling patches of brilliant white amid the scarlet and brown coating everything else. Hanno was stunned by the scale of the horror. This was but a tiny part of the battlefield, yet it contained thousands of dead, injured and dying soldiers.

Pitifully small figures now, they lay alone, heaped over one another and in irregular piles, Gauls entwined with hastati, Libyans beneath principes, their enmity forgotten in the cold embrace of death. While some still clutched their weapons, others had discarded them to clutch at their wounds before they died. Spears dotted the bodies of many Romans, while countless pila were buried in the Carthaginian corpses. So many severed limbs were lying around that Hanno was soon sick. Wiping his mouth, he forced himself to continue searching. Again and again he saw Sapho and Bostar's faces among the slack-jawed dead, only to find that he was wrong. Inevitably, Hanno felt his hopes of finding his brothers alive wither and die.

It was especially hard to look at the soldiers who had lost their extremities. The lucky ones were already dead, but the rest were screaming for their mothers while what blood was left in them spurted and dribbled out on to the semi-frozen earth. It was a mercy to kill them.

Yet for every gruesome sight that Hanno beheld, there was another one to exceed it. It was the suffering of those of his own side that tore at his heart the most. He had to force himself to examine these unfortunates. It was his job to judge the severity of their injuries and make a snap decision if they should live or die.

It was usually the latter.

Gritting his teeth, Hanno killed men who were shuddering their way into oblivion, holding their intestines, the rank smell of their own shit filling their nostrils. Those who lay moaning and coughing up the pink froth that signified a lung wound also had to be slain. More fortunate were the men who wailed and thrashed about, clutching at the arm that had been sliced open to the bone, or the leg that had been hamstrung. Their reaction to Hanno and his soldiers, the lone uninjured figures among them, was uniform. It did not matter whether they were Libyan, Gaulish or Roman. They reached out with bloodied hands, beseeching him for help. Muttering reassurances to the Carthaginian troops, Hanno offered the enemy wounded nothing but silence and a flashing blade. It was far worse than the savagery of close-quarters combat, and soon Hanno was utterly sick of it. All he wanted to do was find his brothers' bodies and return to the camp.

When first the familiar voice of Sapho, and then Bostar, called out his name, Hanno didn't react. As their shouts grew more urgent, he was thunderstruck. There they were, not fifty paces away, in the midst of Mago's men. It was a miracle, Hanno thought dazedly. It had to be, for all four of them to survive this industrial-scale butchery.

"Hanno? Is that you?" Sapho demanded, unable to keep the disbelief—and joy—from his voice.

Hanno blinked away his tears. "It is."

"Father?" Bostar's tone was strangled.

"He's unhurt," Hanno yelled back, not knowing whether to laugh or cry. In the event, he did both. So did Bostar. An instant later, even Sapho had tears in his eyes as the three came together in a fierce embrace. Each stank of sweat, blood, mud and other smells too foul to imagine, but none of them cared.

Their arguments had been forgotten for the moment.

The only thing that mattered was that they were still alive.

At last, grinning like fools, the brothers pulled apart. Not quite believing their own eyes, they held on to one another's arms or shoulders for a long time afterward. Inevitably, though, their gaze was drawn to the devastation all around. Instead of the din of battle, their ears rang with the sound of screams. The voices of the countless injured and maimed, men who were desperate to be found before darkness fell and a certain fate claimed them forever.

"We won," said Hanno in a wondering tone. "The legionaries might have escaped, but the rest of them broke and ran."

"Or died where they stood," Sapho snarled, his customary hardness already creeping back. "After what they've done to us, the whoresons had it coming!"

Bostar winced as Sapho gestured at the piles of dead, but he nodded in agreement. "Don't think that the war has been won," he warned. "This is just the start."

Hanno thought of Quintus and his dogged determination. "I know," he replied heavily.

"Rome must pay even more for all the wrongs it has done to Carthage," intoned Bostar, raising his reddened right fist.

"In blood," Sapho added. He reached up to clasp Bostar's hand with his own.

Both looked expectantly at Hanno.

An image of Aurelia, smiling, popped into Hanno's head, filling him with confusion. It took but an instant, however, before he savagely buried the picture in the recesses of his mind. What was he thinking? Aurelia was one of the enemy. Like her brother and father. Hanno could not truly bring himself to wish any of the three ill, but nor could they be friends. How could that ever be possible after what had gone on here today? On the spot, Hanno decided never to think of them again. It was the only way he could deal with it.

"In blood," he growled, lifting his hand to enclose those of his brothers.

They exchanged a fierce, wolfish smile.

That is what we are, thought Hanno proudly. Carthaginian wolves come to harry and tear at the fat Roman sheep in their fields. Let the farmers of Italy tremble in their beds, for we shall leave no corner of their land untouched.

Quintus' abiding memory of their ride to Placentia was the extreme cold. The wind continued to blow from the north, powerful gusts that threatened to dislodge an unwary rider from his seat. While it didn't succeed in doing that, the chill air penetrated every layer of Quintus' clothing. Initially, he had been kept warm by the effort and thrill of the chase, and latterly by the fear that kept his heart hammering off his ribs. Now, his sweat-soaked clothes felt as if they were about to freeze solid. Everyone was in the same position, of course, so he gritted his chattering teeth and rode on. After what they'd all been through, silence was best.

Lost in their own private worlds of misery, the twenty cavalrymen brought together by Fabricius simply followed where they were led. Hunched over their horses' backs, helmetless and with their sodden cloaks pulled tightly around them, they were a pathetic sight. It was as if each one knew that Hannibal's army had prevailed. Yet in reality, they didn't, thought Quintus. The battle had still been raging when they'd fled. It was hard to see how, though, with their flanks exposed, Longus' legions could have seized victory.

Quintus felt like a coward, but his fear had abated enough for him to consider fighting again. He'd ridden to the front of their little column a number of times, intent on remonstrating with his father.

Fabricius had been in no mood for conversation. "Shut your mouth," he snarled when Quintus had suggested turning back. "What do you know of tactics?" A short while later, Quintus tried again. On this occasion, Fabricius let him have it. "Once cavalry break, it's unheard of for them to rally and return to the fight. You were there! You saw the way they ran, the way I struggled to get this many men to follow me *away* from the battle. Do you think that in this weather, with night coming, they would turn and face the Gauls and Iberians again?" He glared at Quintus, who shook his head. "In that case, what would you have us both do? Commit suicide by charging at the enemy alone? Where's the damn point in that? And don't give me the 'death with honor' line. There's no honor in dying like a fool!"

Shaken by his father's anger, Quintus hung his head. Now he felt like a total failure as well as a coward.

They rode without speaking for a long time after that.

Fortuna finally lent the weary cavalrymen a hand, guiding them to a spot where the Trebia was fordable. By the time they'd reached the eastern bank, it was nearly dark. As miserable as he'd ever been in his life, Quintus looked back over the fast-flowing water into the gathering gloom. More snow was falling, millions of little white motes that clouded his vision even further. The scene was so peaceful and quiet. It was as if the battlefield had never existed. "Quintus." Fabricius' tone was gentler than before. "Come. Placentia is still a long ride away."

Quintus turned his back on the River Trebia. In a way, he realized, he was doing the same on Hanno and his friendship. Feeling hollow inside, he followed his father.

⁓

They reached Placentia about an hour later. Quintus had never been so glad to see the walls of a town, and to hear the challenge of a sentinel. The lines of frightened faces on the ramparts above soon distracted him from thoughts of sitting by a fire, however. Word of the battle had arrived before them. Despite the sentries' fear, Fabricius' status saw the gate opened quickly. A few barked questions at the officer of the guard revealed that a handful of cavalrymen had made it to the town ahead of them. Their garbled account appeared to have the entire army wiped out. There had been no sign of Longus or the infantry yet, which had only fueled the fears of the soldiers who were manning the defenses. Fabricius was incensed by the harm that the unsubstantiated reports would have already caused and demanded to see the most senior officer in the town.

Not long after, both men were wrapped in blankets and drinking warm soup in the company of no less than Praxus, the garrison commander. The rest of their party had been taken off to be quartered elsewhere. A stout individual with a florid complexion, Praxus barely fitted into his dirty linen cuirass, which had seen better days. He paced up and down nervously while father and son thawed out by a glowing cast-iron brazier. At length, he could hold in his concerns no longer. "Should we expect Hannibal by morning?" he demanded.

Fabricius sighed. "I doubt it very much. His soldiers will be in need of rest as much as we are. You shouldn't give up on Longus just yet either," he advised. "Last I saw, the legionaries were holding their own."

Praxus winced. His Adam's apple bobbed up and down. "Where are they then?"

"I don't know," Fabricius replied curtly. "But Longus is an able man. He will not give up easily."

Praxus resumed his pacing and Fabricius left him to it. "Worrying about it won't do any good. This fool won't be able to stop the rumors either. He probably started half of them," he muttered to Quintus before closing his eyes. "Wake me up if there's any news."

Quintus did his best to stay alert, but it wasn't long before he too grew deliciously drowsy. If Praxus wanted his fireside chairs back, he could bloody well wake them up, Quintus thought as sleep claimed him.

Sometime later, they were woken by a sentry clattering in, shouting that the consul had arrived at the gates. It seemed a miracle, but as many as ten thousand legionaries were with him. Quintus found himself grinning at his father, who winked back. "Told you," said Fabricius. Praxus' miserable demeanor also vanished, and he capered about like a child. His sense of self-importance returned with a vengeance. "Longus will have need of my quarters," he declared loftily. "You'd best leave at once. One of my officers can find you rooms." He didn't give a name.

Fabricius' top lip lifted at the sudden return of the other's courage, and his bad manners, but he got up from his chair without protest. Quintus did likewise. Praxus barely bothered to say good-bye. Fortunately, the officer who'd initially brought them from the gate was still outside, and upon hearing their story, agreed to let them share his quarters.

The three hadn't gone far before the heavy tramp of men marching in unison came echoing down the narrow street toward them. Torchlight flickered off the darkened buildings on either side. A surge of adrenaline shot through Quintus' tired veins. He glanced at his father, who looked similarly interested. Quintus' lips framed the word "Longus?" His father nodded. "Stop," he requested. The officer complied, as eager as they to see who it was. Within a few moments, they could make out a large party of legionaries—*triarii*—approaching. The soldier at the outside edge of each rank carried a flaming torch, illuminating the rest quite well.

"Make way for the consul!" shouted an officer at the front.

Quintus sighed with relief. Sempronius Longus had survived. Rome had not lost all its pride.

The triarii scarcely broke step as they passed by. One of the two most important men in the Republic did not wait while a pair of filthy soldiers gaped at him. Especially on a night like this.

Quintus couldn't stop himself. "What happened?" he cried.

His unanswered question was carried away by the wind.

They gave each other a grim look and resumed their journey. Soon after, they happened upon a group of principes. Desperate to know how the battle had ended, Quintus caught the eye of a squat man carrying a shield emblazoned with two snarling wolves. "Did you win?" he asked.

The princeps scowled. "Depends what you mean by that," he muttered. "Hannibal won't forget the legionaries who fought at the Trebia in a hurry."

Quintus and Fabricius exchanged a shocked, pleased glance. "Did you turn and fall on the Carthaginian rear?" asked Fabricius excitedly. "Did the allied infantry throw back the elephants and the skirmishers?"

The soldier looked down. "Not exactly, sir, no."

They stared at him, not understanding. "What then?" demanded Fabricius.

The princeps cleared his throat. "After breaking through the enemy line, Longus ordered us to quit the field." A shadow passed across his face. "Our wings had already broken, sir. I suppose he wasn't certain that we could turn the situation around."

"The allied troops?" Quintus whispered.

The silence that followed spoke a thousand words.

"Sweet Jupiter above," swore Fabricius. "They're dead?"

"Some may have escaped back to our camp, sir," the princeps admitted. "Only time will tell."

Quintus' head spun. Their casualties could number in the tens of thousands.

His father was more focused. "In that case, I think it's we who will be remembering Hannibal rather than the other way around," he observed acidly. "Don't you?"

"Yes, sir," the princeps muttered. He threw a longing glance at his comrades, who were disappearing around the nearest corner.

Fabricius jerked his head. "Go."

In a daze, Quintus watched the soldier scuttle off. "Maybe Praxus was right," he muttered. "Hannibal could be at the gates by dawn."

"Enough talk like that," his father snapped. His lips peeled back into a feral snarl. "Rome does not give up after one defeat. Not with foreign invaders on her soil!"

Quintus' courage rallied a fraction. "What of Hannibal?"

"He'll leave us to it now," Fabricius declared. "He will be content to gather support from the Gaulish tribes over the winter."

Quintus was relieved by his father's certainty. "And us?"

"We will use the time to regroup, and to form new legions and cavalry units. One thing Rome and her allies are not short of is manpower. By the spring, the soldiers lost today will all have been replaced." *And I'll have won a promotion which will keep the moneylenders at bay.* Fabricius grinned fiercely. "You'll see!"

At last Quintus took heart. He nodded eagerly. They would fight the Carthaginians again soon. On equal or better terms. There would be a chance to regain the honor that, in his mind, they had left behind on the battlefield.

Rome would rise again, and wrench victory from Hannibal.

Author's Note

I t is an immense privilege to be accorded the opportunity to write a set of novels about the Second Punic War (218–201 BC). I have been fascinated by the time period since I was a boy, and I, like many, regard this as one of history's most hallowed episodes. The word "epic" is completely overused today, but I feel that it is justified to use it with reference to this seventeen-year struggle, the balance of which was uncertain on so many occasions. If it had tipped but a fraction in the opposite direction during a number of those situations, life in Europe would be a very different affair today. The Carthaginians were quite unlike the Romans, and not in all the bad ways history would have us believe. They were intrepid explorers and inveterate traders, shrewd businessmen and brave soldiers. Where Rome's interests so often lay in conquest by war, theirs lay more in assuming power through controlling commerce and natural resources. It may be a small point, but my use of the word "Carthaginian" rather than the Latin-derived "Punic" when referring to their language is quite deliberate. The Carthaginians would not have used the term.

Many readers will know the broad brush strokes of Hannibal's war with Rome; others will know less; a very few will be voracious readers of the ancient authors Livy and Polybius, the main sources for this period. For the record, I have done my best to stick to the historical details that have survived. In places, however, I have either changed events slightly to fit in with the story's development, or invented things. Such is the novelist's remit, as well as his/her bane. If I have made any errors, I apologize for them.

The novel starts with a description of Carthage in all its magnificence. In the late third century BC, it was an infinitely grander city than Rome. I have taken the liberty of describing the fortifications present at the time of the Third Punic War (149–146 BC). I did this because we do not know what defenses were in place in Hannibal's time. Because the incredible and impressive structures that held off the Romans in the final conflict were built sometime in the fifty years after Hannibal's defeat, I did not feel that using them was a major digression from fact.

Describing Carthaginian soldiers, both native and nonnative, is a whole minefield of its own. We have little historical information about the uniforms that Carthaginian citizens and the host of nationalities who fought for them wore, or the type of equipment and weapons that they carried. Without several textbooks and articles, which I'll name later, I would have been lost. Another difficult area was Carthaginian names. In short, there aren't very many, or at least not many that have come down to us, more than 2,200 years later. Most of the ones that have survived are unpronounceable, or sound awful. Some are both! Hillesbaal and Ithobaal don't exactly roll off the tongue. Hence the main Carthaginian protagonist is called Hanno. There were important historical characters with this name, but I desperately needed a good one for my hero, and they were in very short supply.

The siege of Saguntum happened much as I've described. Anyone who visits Spain's eastern coast could do worse than climb the huge rocky outcrop near modern-day Valencia. It's such an impressive place that it's not hard to imagine Hannibal's soldiers besieging it. The formidable size of his army is attested by the ancient sources, as are the ways it was reduced by deaths, desertions and release from service.

Whether any troops were left as garrisons in Gaul, we do not know. There has been much argument over which route the Carthaginian army followed after the Pyrenees, and where it crossed the River Rhône. The Volcae were surprised from the rear by a party of Carthaginians who had crossed upriver; their commander was one Hanno, not Bostar, however. The elephants were ferried over the river in the manner I've described.

The dramatic confrontation between the Roman embassy and the Carthaginian Council of Elders apparently took place as I've portrayed it. So too did the chance encounter between a unit of Roman cavalry and one of Numidians in the countryside above Massilia. I altered events, however, to take Scipio back to Rome before he traveled to Cisalpine Gaul to face the invaders. Minucius Flaccus is a fictitious character, but Minucius Rufus, his brother, is not.

Most controversy over Hannibal's journey concerns which pass his host took through the Alps. Having no wish to enter into such debates, I merely used the descriptions which Polybius and Livy gave us to set the scene. I truly hope that I managed to convey some of the terror and elation that would have filled the hearts of those hardy souls who followed Hannibal up and over the Alps' lofty peaks. The speech he gave to his troops before they started climbing was very similar to the one I described. Although not every source mentions the scene with the boiling wine and the boulder, I felt that I had to include it.

The term "Italy" was in use in the third century BC as a geographical expression; it encompassed the entire peninsula south of Liguria and Cisalpine Gaul. The term did not become a political one until Polybius' time (mid–second century BC). I decided to use it anyway. It simplified matters, and avoided constant reference to the different parts of the Republic: Rome, Campania, Latium, Lucania, etc.

My description of the calf born with its internal organs on the outside is not a figment of my imagination—I have performed two cesarean sections on cows to deliver the so-called *schistosomus reflexus*. They were without doubt the most revolting things I've ever set eyes upon. On one occasion, the unfortunate calf was still alive. Although this happened only fifteen years ago, the farmer's superstition was obvious and he became extremely agitated until I had euthanized it. We can only imagine what kind of reaction such a creature might have provoked in ancient times.

The duels between the Carthaginian prisoners, and the rewards on offer to those who survived, are described in the ancient texts. So too is the fate of Taurasia. When it came to making a point, Hannibal was as ruthless as the next general. The Roman losses in the Ticinus skirmish were severe and the savage night attack by some of their so-called Gaulish allies only served as another knock to Scipio's confidence. I invented the Carthaginian ambush at the River Trebia, but the details of the remarkable battle that unfolded afterward are as exact as I could make them. Hannibal's victory on that bitter winter's day proved beyond doubt that his crossing of the Alps was no fluke. As the Romans would repeatedly discover in the months that followed, he was a real force to be reckoned with.

A bibliography of the textbooks I used while writing *Enemy of Rome* would run to several pages, so I will mention only the most important, in alphabetical order by author: *The Punic Wars* by Nigel Bagnall, *The Punic Wars* by Brian Caven, *Greece and Rome at War* by Peter Connolly, *Hannibal* by Theodore A. Dodge, *The Fall of Carthage* by Adrian Goldsworthy, *Armies of the Macedonian and Punic Wars* by Duncan Head, *Hannibal's War* by J. F. Lazenby, *Carthage Must Be Destroyed* by Richard Miles, *The Life and Death of Carthage* by G. C. & C. Picard, *Daily Life in Carthage (at the Time of Hannibal)* by G. C. Picard, *Roman Politics 220–150 BC* by H. H. Scullard, *Carthage and the Carthaginians* by Reginald B. Smith and *Warfare in the Classical World* by John Warry. I'm grateful to Osprey Publishing for numerous excellent volumes, to Oxford University Press for the outstanding *Oxford Classical Dictionary*, and to Alberto Perez and Paul McDonnell-Staff for their superb article in volume III, issue 4 of *Ancient Warfare* magazine. Thanks, as always, to the members of www.romanarmy.com, whose rapid answers to my odd questions are so often of great use. I also have to mention, and thank, the three Australian brothers Wood: Danny, Ben and Sam. Their excellent mini travel series, *On Hannibal's Trail*, couldn't have screened on BBC4 at a better time than it did, and was a great help to me when writing the chapter on crossing the Alps.

I owe gratitude too to a legion of people at my wonderful publishers, Random House. There's Rosie de Courcy, my indefatigable and endlessly encouraging editor; Nicola Taplin, my tremendous managing editor; Kate Elton, who was generous enough to welcome me into the big, brave world of Arrow Books; Rob Waddington, who ensures that my novels reach every possible outlet in the land; Adam Humphrey, who organizes fiendishly clever and successful marketing; Richard Ogle, who, with the illustrator Steve Stone, designs my amazing new jackets; Ruth Waldram, who secures me all kinds of great publicity; Monique Corless, who persuades so many foreign editors to buy my books; David Parrish, who makes sure that bookshops abroad do so too. Thank you all so much. Your hard work on my behalf is very much appreciated.

So many other people must be named: Charlie Viney, my agent, deserves a big mention. Without him, I'd still be working as a vet, and plugging away at my first Roman novel. Thanks, Charlie! I'm very grateful to Richenda Todd, my copy editor, who provides highly incisive input on my manuscripts; Claire Wheller, my outstanding physio, who stops my body from falling to bits after spending too long at my PC; Arthur O'Connor, the most argumentative man in Offaly (if not Ireland), who also supplies excellent criticism and improvements to my stories. Last, but most definitely not least, Sair, my wife, and Ferdia and Pippa, my children, ground me and provide me with so much love and joy. Thank you. My life is so much richer for having you three in it.

GLOSSARY

acetum: vinegar, the most common disinfectant used by the Romans. Vinegar is excellent at killing bacteria, and its widespread use in Western medicine continued until late in the nineteenth century.

Aesculapius: son of Apollo, the god of health and the protector of doctors. Revered by the Carthaginians as well as the Romans.

Agora: we have no idea what Carthaginians called the central meeting area in their city. I have used the Greek term to differentiate it from the main Forum in Rome. Without doubt, the Agora would have been the most important meeting place in Carthage.

Alps: In Latin, these mountains are called *Alpes*. Not used in the novel (unlike the Latin names for other geographical features) as it looks "strange" to modern eyes.

Assembly of the People: the public debating group to which all Carthaginian male citizens belonged. Its main power was that of electing the suffetes once a year.

Astarte: a Carthaginian goddess whose origins lie in the East. She may have represented marriage, and was perhaps seen as the protector of cities and different social groups.

atrium: the large chamber immediately beyond the entrance hall in a Roman house. Frequently built on a grand scale, this was the social and devotional center of the home.

Baal Hammon: the preeminent god at the time of the founding of Carthage. He was the protector of the city, the fertilizing sun, the provider of wealth and the guarantor of success and happiness. The Tophet, or the sacred area where Baal Hammon was worshipped, is the site where the bones of children and babies have been found, giving rise to the controversial topic of child sacrifice. For those who are interested, there is an excellent discussion on the issue in Richard Miles' book, *Carthage Must Be Destroyed*. The term "Baal" means "Master" or "Lord," and was used before the name of various gods.

Baal Saphon: the Carthaginian god of war.

bireme: an ancient warship, which was perhaps invented by the Phoenicians. It had a square sail, two sets of oars on each side, and was used extensively by the Greeks and Romans.

caetrati (sing. *caetratus*): light Iberian infantry. They wore short-sleeved white tunics with a crimson border at the neck, hem and sleeves. Their only protection was a helmet of sinew or bronze, and a round buckler of leather and wicker, or wood, called a *caetra*. They were armed with *falcata* swords and daggers. Some may have carried javelins.

caligae: heavy leather sandals worn by the Roman soldier. Sturdily constructed in three layers—a sole, insole and upper—*caligae* resembled an open-toed boot. The straps could be tightened to make them fit more closely. Dozens of metal studs on the sole gave the sandals good grip; these could also be replaced when necessary.

carnyx (pl. *carnyxes*): a bronze trumpet, which was held vertically and topped by a bell shaped in the form of an animal, usually a boar. Used by many Celtic peoples, it was ubiquitous in Gaul, and provided a fearsome sound alone or in unison with other instruments. It was often depicted on Roman coins, to denote victories over various tribes.

Carthage: modern-day Tunis. It was reputedly founded in 814 BC, although the earliest archaeological finds date from about sixty years later.

cenaculae (sing. *cenacula*): the miserable multistory flats in which Roman plebeians lived. Cramped, poorly lit, heated only by braziers, and often dangerously constructed, the *cenaculae* had no running water or sanitation. Access to the flats was via staircases built on the outside of the building.

Choma: the man-made quadrilateral area which lay to the south/southeast of the main harbors in Carthage. It was probably constructed to serve as a place to unload ships, to store goods, and to act as a pier head protecting passing vessels from the worst of the wind.

Cisalpine Gaul: the northern area of modern-day Italy, comprising the Po plain and its mountain borders from the Alps to the Apennines. In the third century BC, it was not part of the Republic.

consul: one of two annually elected chief magistrates, appointed by the people and ratified by the Senate. Effective rulers of Rome for twelve months, they were in charge of civil and military matters and led the Republic's armies into war. Each could countermand the other and both were supposed to heed the wishes of the Senate. No man was supposed to serve as consul more than once.

Council of Elders: Carthaginian politics, with its numerous ruling bodies, is very confusing. The Council of Elders was one of the most important, however. Its members were some of the most prominent men in Carthage, and its areas of remit included the treasury and foreign affairs. Another ruling body was the Tribunal of One Hundred and Four. Composed of members of the elite aristocracy, it supervised the conduct of government officials and military leaders; it also acted as a type of higher constitutional court.

crucifixion: contrary to popular belief, the Romans did not invent this awful form of execution; in fact, the Carthaginians may well have done so. The practice is first recorded during the Punic Wars.

decurion: the cavalry officer in charge of ten men. In later times, the decurion commanded a *turma*, a unit of about thirty men.

didrachm: a silver coin, worth two drachmas, which was one of the main coins in third century BC Italy. Strangely, the Romans did not make coins of their own design until later on. The *denarius*, which was to become the main coin of the Republic, was not introduced until around 211 BC.

Eshmoun: the Carthaginian god of health and well-being, whose temple was the largest in Carthage.

falaricae (sing. *falarica*): a spear with a pine shaft and a long iron head, at the base of which a ball of pitch and tow was often tied. This created a lethal incendiary weapon, used to great effect by the Saguntines.

falcata sword: a lethal, slightly curved weapon with a sharp point used by light Iberian infantry. It was single-edged for the first half to two-thirds of its blade, but the remainder was double-edged. The hilt curved protectively around the hand and back toward the blade; it was often made in the shape of a horse's head. Apparently, the *caetrati* who used *falcata* swords were well able to fight legionaries.

fasces: a bundle of rods bound together around an axe. The symbol of justice, it was carried by a lictor, a group of whom walked in front of all senior magistrates. The fasces symbolized the right of the authorities to punish and execute lawbreakers.

fides: essentially, good faith. It was regarded as a major quality in Rome.

fugitivarius (pl. *fugitivarii*): slave-catchers, men who made a living from tracking down and capturing runaways. The punishment branding the letter "F" (for *fugitivus*) on the forehead is documented; so is the wearing of permanent neck chains, which had directions on how to return the slave to their owner.

Genua: modern-day Genoa.

gladius (pl. *gladii*): little information remains about the "Spanish" sword of the Republican army, the *gladius hispaniensis*, with its waisted blade. It is not clear when it was adopted by the Romans, but it was probably after encountering the weapon during the First Punic War, when it was used by Celtiberian troops. The shaped hilt was made of bone and protected by a pommel and guard of wood. The *gladius* was worn on the right, except by centurions and other senior officers, who wore it on the left. It was actually quite easy to draw with the right hand, and was probably positioned like this to avoid entanglement with the *scutum* while being unsheathed.

gugga: in Plautus' comedy, *Poenulus*, one of the Roman characters refers to a Carthaginian trader as a "gugga." This insult can be translated as "little rat."

hastati (sing. *hastatus*): experienced young soldiers who formed the first ranks in the Roman battle line in the third century BC. They were armed with mail or bronze breast and back plates, crested helmets, and *scuta*. They carried two *pila*, one light and one heavy, and a *gladius hispaniensis*.

hora secunda, the second hour; *hora quarta*, the fourth hour; *hora undecima*, the eleventh hour: Roman time was divided into two periods, that of daylight (twelve hours) and of nighttime (eight watches). The first hour of the day, *hora prima*, started at sunrise.

Iberia: the modern-day Iberian Peninsula, encompassing Spain and Portugal.

Iberus: the River Ebro.

Illyricum (or Illyria): the Roman name for the lands that lay across the Adriatic Sea from Italy: including parts of modern-day Slovenia, Serbia, Croatia, Bosnia and Montenegro.

intervallum: the wide, flat area inside the walls of a Roman camp or fort. As well as serving to protect the barrack buildings from enemy missiles, it could when necessary allow the massing of troops before battle.

kopis (pl. *kopides*): a Greek sword with a forward curving blade, not dissimilar to the *falcata* sword. It was normally carried in a leather-covered sheath and suspended from a baldric. Many ancient peoples used the *kopis*, from the Etruscans to the Oscans and Persians.

lictor (pl. *lictores*): a magistrates' enforcer. Only strongly built citizens could apply for this job. Essentially, *lictores* were the bodyguards for the consuls, praetors and other senior Roman magistrates. Such officials were accompanied at all times in public by set numbers of *lictores* (the number depended on their rank). Each *lictor* carried a fasces. Other duties included the arresting and punishment of wrongdoers.

Ligurians: natives of the coastal area that was bounded to the west by the River Rhône and to the east by the River Arno.

Lusitanians: tribesmen from the area of modern-day Portugal.

Massilia: the city of Marseille in modern-day France.

Melqart: a Carthaginian god associated with the sea, and with Hercules. He was also the god most favored by the Barca family. Hannibal notably made a pilgrimage to Melqart's shrine in southern Iberia before beginning his war on Rome.

mulsum: a drink made by mixing four parts wine and one part honey. It was commonly drunk before meals and during the lighter courses.

munus (pl. *munera*): a gladiatorial combat, staged originally during celebrations honoring someone's death.

Padus: the River Po.

papaverum: the drug morphine. Made from the flowers of the opium poppy, its use has been documented from at least 1000 BC.

peristyle: a colonnaded garden that lay to the rear of a Roman house. Often of great size, it was bordered by open-fronted seating areas, reception rooms and banqueting halls.

pilum (pl. *pila*): the Roman javelin. It consisted of a wooden shaft approximately 1.2 m (4 ft.) long, joined to a thin iron shank approximately 0.6 m (2 ft.) long, and was topped by a small pyramidal point. The javelin was heavy and, when launched, all of its weight was concentrated behind the head, giving it tremendous penetrative force. It could strike through a shield to injure the man carrying it, or lodge in the shield, making it impossible for the man to continue using it. The range of the *pilum* was about 30 m (100 ft.), although the effective range was probably about half this distance.

Pisae: modern-day Pisa.

Placentia: modern-day Piacenza.

praetor: one of four senior magistrates (in the years 228–198 BC approximately) who administered justice in Rome, or in its overseas possessions such as Sardinia and Sicily. He could also hold military commands and initiate legislation. The main understudies to the consuls, the praetors convened the Senate in their absence.

principes (sing. *princeps*): these soldiers—described as family men in their prime—formed the second rank of the Roman battle line in the third century BC. They were similar to the *hastati*, and as such were armed and dressed in much the same manner.

provocatio: an appeal on behalf of the Roman people, made against the order of a magistrate.

pteryges: also spelled *pteruges*. This was a twin layer of stiffened linen strips that protected the waist and groin of the wearer. It either came attached to a cuirass of the same material, or as a detachable piece of equipment to be used below a bronze breastplate. Although *pteryges* were designed by the Greeks, many nations used them, including the Romans and Carthaginians.

quinquereme: the principal Carthaginian fighting vessel in the third century BC. They were of similar size to triremes, but possessed many more rowers. Controversy over the exact number of oarsmen in these ships, and the positions they occupied, has gone on for decades. It is fairly well accepted nowadays, however, that the quinquereme had three sets of oars on each side. The vessel was rowed from three levels with two men on each oar of the upper banks, and one man per oar of the lower bank.

Rhodanus: the River Rhône.

Saguntum: modern-day Sagunto.

Saturnalia: a festival that began on 17 December. During the week-long celebrations, ordinary rules were relaxed and slaves could dine before their masters; at this time, they could also treat them with less deference. The festival was an excuse for eating, drinking and playing games. Gifts of candles and pottery figures were also exchanged.

saunion: also called the *soliferreum*. This was a characteristic Iberian weapon, a slim, all-iron javelin with a small, leaf-shaped head.

scutarii (sing. *scutarius*): heavy Iberian infantry, Celtiberians who carried round shields, or ones very similar to those of the Roman legionaries. Richer individuals may have had mail shirts; others may have worn small breastplates. Many *scutarii* wore greaves. Their bronze helmets were very similar to the Gallic Montefortino style. They were armed with straight-edged swords that were slightly shorter than the Gaulish equivalent, and known for their excellent quality.

scutum (pl. *scuta*): an elongated oval Roman army shield, about 1.2 m (4 ft.) tall and 0.75 m (2 ft. 6 in.) wide. It was made from two layers of wood, the pieces laid at right angles to each other; it was then covered with linen or canvas, and leather. The *scutum* was heavy, weighing between 6 and 10 kg (13–22 lbs.). A large metal boss decorated its center, with the horizontal grip placed behind this. Decorative designs were often painted on the front, and a leather cover was used to protect the shield when not in use, e.g. while marching. Some of the Iberian and Gaulish warriors used very similar shields.

Scylla: a mythical monster with twelve feet and six heads that dwelt in a cave opposite the whirlpool Charybdis, in the modern Straits of Messina.

socii: allies of Rome. By the time of the Punic Wars, all the non-Roman peoples of Italy had been forced into military alliances with Rome. In theory, these peoples were still independent, but in practice they were subjects, who were obliged to send quotas of troops to fight for the Republic whenever it was demanded.

stade: from the Greek word *stadion*. It was the distance of the original foot race in the ancient Olympic games of 776 BC, and was approximately 192 m (630 ft) in length. The word "stadium" derives from it.

strigil: a small, curved iron tool used to clean the skin after bathing. First perfumed oil was rubbed in, and then the *strigil* was used to scrape off the combination of sweat, dirt and oil.

suffete: one of two men who headed the Carthaginian state. Elected yearly, they dealt with a range of affairs of state from the political and military to judicial and religious issues. It is extremely unclear whether they had as much power as Roman consuls, but it seems likely that by the third century BC they did not.

tablinum: the office or reception area beyond the *atrium*. The *tablinum* usually opened on to an enclosed colonnaded garden, the peristyle.

Tanit: along with Baal Hammon, the preeminent deity in Carthage. She was regarded as a mother goddess, and as the patroness and protector of the city.

Taurasia: modern-day Turin.

tesserae: pieces of stone or marble that were cut into roughly cubic shape and fitted closely on to a bed of mortar to form a mosaic. This practice was introduced in the third century BC.

Ticinus: the River Ticino.

Trebia: the River Trebbia.

tribune: senior staff officer within a legion; also one of ten political positions in Rome, where they served as "tribunes of the people," defending the rights of the plebeians. The tribunes could also veto measures taken by the Senate or consuls, except in times of war. To assault a tribune was a crime of the highest order.

trireme: the classic ancient warship, which was powered by a single sail and three banks of oars. Each oar was rowed by one man, who on Roman ships was freeborn, not a slave. Exceptionally maneuverable, and capable of up to eight knots under sail or for short bursts when rowed, the trireme also had a bronze ram at the prow. This was used to damage or even sink enemy ships. Small catapults were also mounted on the deck. Each trireme was crewed by up to thirty men and had around two hundred rowers; it could carry up to sixty infantry, giving it a very large crew in proportion to its size. This limited the triremes' range, so they were mainly used as troop transports and to protect coastlines.

triarii (sing. *triarius*): the oldest, most experienced soldiers in a legion of the third century BC. These men were often held back until the most desperate of situations in a battle. The fantastic Roman expression "Matters have come down to the *triarii*" makes this clear. They wore bronze crested helmets, mail shirts and a greave on their leading (left) legs. They each carried a *scutum*, and were armed with a *gladius hispaniensis* and a long, thrusting spear.

tunny: tuna fish.

turmae (sing. *turma*): a cavalry unit of thirty men.

velites (sing. *veles*): light skirmishers of the third century BC who were recruited from the poorest social class. They were young men whose only protection was a small, round shield, and in some cases, a simple bronze helmet. They carried a sword, but their primary weapons were 1.2 m (4 ft.) javelins. They also wore bear- or wolf-skin headdresses.

Vespera: the first watch of the night.

vilicus: slave foreman or farm manager. Commonly a slave, the *vilicus* was sometimes a paid worker, whose job it was to make sure that the returns on a farm were as large as possible. This was most commonly done by treating the slaves brutally.

Vinalia Rustica: a Roman wine festival held on 19 August.

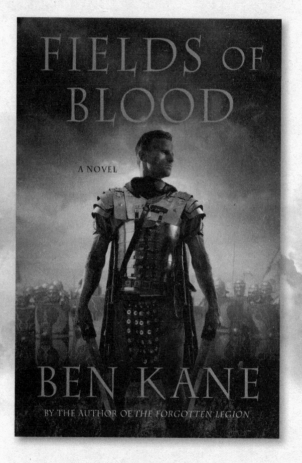